BAYONETS, BALLOONS & IRONCLADS

BAYONETS, BALLOONS & IRONCLADS

BRITAIN AND FRANCE TAKE SIDES WITH THE SOUTH

Volume III of The Britannia's Fist Trilogy

Peter G. Tsouras

An Alternate History

SKYHORSE PUBLISHING

Skyhorse Publishing books may be purchased in bulk at special discounts for sales promotion, corporate gifts, fund-raising, or educational purposes. Special editions can also be created to specifications. For details, contact the Special Sales Department, Skyhorse Publishing, 307 West 36th Street, 11th Floor, New York, NY 10018 or info@skyhorsepublishing.com.

Skyhorse® and Skyhorse Publishing® are registered trademarks of Skyhorse Publishing, Inc.®, a Delaware corporation.

Visit our website at www.skyhorsepublishing.com.

10 9 8 7 6 5 4 3 2 1

Library of Congress Cataloging-in-Publication Data is available on file.

Cover design by Owen Corrigan
Cover photo: *The Monitor and Merrimac: The First Fight Between* Ironclads by Louis Prang & Co.

Print ISBN: 978-1-62914-462-7
Ebook ISBN: 978-1-62914-867-0

Printed in the United States of America

This book is dedicated to the English-speaking Fighting Man, American, Briton, Irishman, Canadian, Australian, and New Zealander, Liberator and Breaker of Tyrants.

CONTENTS

INTRODUCTION

The eruption of war in September 1863 between the British Empire and the United States struggling in its own Civil War should have spelled the collapse of that Union. With ten times the industrial capacity of the Northern states, a larger population, and a world-dominating fleet, a British victory should have been inevitable. If that were not enough, Louis Napoleon brought France immediately into the war against the Union. At the same time British and French logistics and financial support of the Confederacy revitalized its armed forces, doubling their combat potential. The Union's cup of misery ran over when a major revolt in the Midwest by antiwar Democrats, the Copperheads, broke out in deadly earnest as British troops burnt the Hudson Valley and threatened New York City.

Victory should have been inevitable — famous last words. The Union found itself in the condition described by Samuel Johnson, in which the prospect of being hanged concentrates the mind wonderfully. That concentration and a lot of hard fighting gaffed off disaster in the opening months of the war as told in the first two volumes of this trilogy, *Britannia's Fist* and *A Rainbow of Blood*. It was the considered opinion of the neutral great powers that the weight of British, French, and Confederate power would undoubtedly shift the balance in the next year and grind the Union down.

This final volume relates the history of the continuation of that struggle to its end. The Americans were able to bring four combat multipliers to their aid that gave them a fighting chance against the weight of their enemies' power. The first was the establishment at Lincoln's direction of a national intelligence organization, the Central Information Bureau (CIB), to bring under one hand all the localized and uncoordinated efforts that had arisen. This was the creation of Maj. Gen. George H. Sharpe, who had created from a standing start the first

all-source intelligence organization in history upon his appointment by
Maj. Gen. Joseph Hooker in February 1863 as the Army of the Potomac's
chief of the new Bureau of Military Information (BMI). Sharpe's efforts
were decisive in the Union victory at Gettysburg and came to the
attention of President Lincoln, who had become intensely dissatisfied
with the haphazard and unproductive use of military intelligence. It
became quickly known that Sharpe had the full backing of the President
as well as a secret and bottomless purse.

Sharpe quickly built an effective national organization and replicated
the BMI for every field army. Information flowed in all directions so that
no command lacked for current intelligence. The motto of the CBI was
"Share Information," with all commands of the Army and Navy and
with any of the civilian agencies that had a need for such information,
such as the State Department and Treasury.

Sharpe also, at Lincoln's direction, resurrected the Army Balloon
Corps, which had been allowed to fall into disuse, and incorporated it
into the CBI, giving it an aerial reconnaissance capability. Companies of
the Balloon Corps were assigned to the BMI of every field army. The use
of telegraphers in the balloons gave commanders real time intelligence.

The core of the CBI was its analysis department headed by the
talented young officer, Lt. Col. Michael D. Wilmoth, who repeatedly
demonstrated that the organized collection and evaluation of
information, much of it from open sources, would precisely inform
the sword where to strike and the shield where to block. Additionally,
Sharpe created a cipher and telegraph department. Cipher clerks from
the CBI accompanied every commander of a field army. Another
department controlled agent networks not only in the Confederacy
but in Canada and Europe as well. Still another capability was special
operations, largely the realm of the 3rd Indiana Cavalry Regiment that
had been assigned to the BMI. These operations were run by the Army
of the Potomac's former chief of scouts, the redoubtable red-haired
Maj. Milton Cline.

The totality of the CBI's efforts was a great combat multiplier for the
Union, allowing its government and armed forces to focus its resources
and efforts where they would do the most good. Sharpe excelled in this
role. He was one of the best-educated men in the country, had served
overseas as U.S. counsul in Vienna and Rome, spoke fluent French, and
had a very cosmopolitan outlook. His training as a lawyer organized his
mind and gave him the skills of a master interrogator who never had to
employ harsh methods, proving in that business that honey does catch
more flies than vinegar. Lincoln came to rely on Sharpe more and more,
not just for advice on intelligence matters, but on larger issues of policy

as well. They hit it off personally as well. Sharpe was almost as good a storyteller as Lincoln.

The second combat multiplier for the Union was the array of new weapons and ordnance technologies that had emerged in the war but had been poorly exploited if not outright sabotaged up to time of war with Britain. For the Army these included repeating small arms and the first of what would later be called machine guns. Lincoln had been a great friend of technology and personally ordered the creation of the Army Balloon Corps and on his own authority had bought the first machine guns, which he christened the coffee mill gun, for its ammunition hopper that so resembled a coffee mill. About sixty such guns were eventually bought. The even more effective gun created by Richard Gatling had been twice tested by army boards, which enthusiastically called for their purchase, but the arch-conservative chief of the army's Ordnance Bureau, Brig. Gen. James Ripley (called Ripley van Winkle by his staff) was so opposed to what he called "newfangled gimcracks" that he did everything in his power to ensure that such weapons were not acquired. This included repeating small arms of which a number of excellent models, such as the Sharps, had been developed by Americans and were available. Ripley was not replaced until shortly before the outbreak of the war with Britain.

The removal of Ripley and the crisis of the war now allowed if not demanded the full rationalization of the production and employment of such weapons. Ripley had argued that the ammunition expenditure of such weapons was not sustainable, failing to comprehend that the seven-to-one firepower advantage of repeating small arms would be crushing on the battlefield. You would not have to fight many battles with that sort of advantage. The decision was made to standardize the small arms of the army with the new Spencer rifle, considered the best, as well as the Sharps, which was already in production and was an excellent weapon. The Colt Small Arms Company subcontracted to produce the Spencer in its huge factory. The coffee mill gun and the Gatlings were also ordered in large numbers and organized into batteries for the field armies. Interestingly, none of these types of weapons were being produced or even developed in Great Britain at the outbreak of the war. At that time the British were contracting with an American inventor to use his copyrighted conversion kit to turn their Enfield rifle into a single-shot breechloader.

The Navy had been more technology friendly as befitted the nature of its service. Rear Admiral John Dahlgren in his long service with naval ordnance had developed the most effective muzzle-loading smooth bore gun in the world at that time. The Dahlgren gun, the first to be developed on scientific principles, threw a 440-pound shot or 400-pound shell, the largest projectiles in the world. No Dahlgren gun ever burst, and their striking power was such that the Royal Navy had attempted to buy them before war. The contest then between the U.S. and Royal Navies would consistently find the Americans with the heavier, more destructive guns. The Royal Navy, on the other hand, had a huge advantage in number of ships and with the seizure of Martha's Vineyard off Massachusetts was able to support a major blockade of the Northern coast, though not without great difficulty, and cut the United States off from world trade as well as hunt American shipping from the high seas.

The Navy's advantage in new technology lay in the development and production of the new monitor-type ironclads. The *Passaic*-class monitors followed the victory of the USS *Monitor* over the CSS *Virginia* broadside ironclads at the battle of Hampton Roads in 1862. It was these monitors that were decisive in defeating the Royal Navy's attempt to break the Union blockade of Charleston. A follow-on class, however, ran into crippling production problems that made the vast expense in financial and industrial resources a complete failure. A good part of that failure was the cutthroat competition among producers for scarce resources and skilled labor as well as insufficient government funding. The federal government at the outbreak of the Civil War was a very small organization whose peacetime responsibilities had been small; it simply had not been organized for world war and its economic demands.

The third combat multiplier addressed just this problem. The industrial base of the United States was essentially self-sufficient, but the production of the means of war was not a coordinated effort, resulting in great waste and lost opportunities. The President appointed the young Andrew Carnegie to head the new War Production Board (WPB) to bring order to this chaos. Carnegie's great talent was in seeing emerging technologies and ideas and propelling them forward by hiring the best people and giving them great initiative. He was responsible for persuading Colt to produce the Spencer rifle. Spencer had the superior weapon, and Colt had the factory to produce it. His genius was to put the two together in a happy marriage. Under his leadership the WPB coordinated the allocation of war materials, labor, and funds to ensure the efficient and maximum production of the nation's needs for war.

The fourth combat multiplier was the alliance with Russia. Nothing filled the British elite with more apprehension than Russian ambitions in the Balkans and Middle East which would take them over the corpse of the Ottoman Empire to Egypt itself. That would allow them to put a boot on British communications with India, the richest source of Imperial wealth. The British prime minister, Benjamin Disraeli, was particularly sensitive of this threat.

He should have been. Russia wanted revenge. The British and French had humiliated Russia in the Crimean War, and the Russians believed the greatest threat they faced in the future was British world hegemony. They also saw the growing power of the United States as the only possible counterweight and so did everything they could with diplomatic advice and support to help the Union survive, especially against British and French efforts to force a mediation that would surely have resulted in Southern independence. A British attack on the United States while it was locked in its Civil War was sufficient cause for the Russians to form an alliance. They would never have a better chance to clip Britain's wings. That opportunity also fed their national ambition to champion the Orthodox Christian populations of the Balkans and the Middle East under the Turkish yoke and especially to plant the cross once again on the dome of the Orthodox Cathedral of the Hagia Sophia (Holy Wisdom) in Constantinople after its four-hundred-year profanation as a mosque.

Against these desperate American efforts to even the score, the British Empire had immense resources to draw upon. Great Britain's industrial base was ten times that of the Northern states and produced four times as much iron. The British merchant fleet dominated the seas until just before the war when the American merchant marine narrowly edged it out in the carrying trade of the world. Whereas the American government lived hand-to-mouth financially, the British economy was the major source of capital in the world. Additionally, the Empire itself generated immense wealth. Truly, the British had the three most important things necessary to make war: money, money, and more money.

All that money paid for the Royal Navy with its unbroken traditions of victory and its unparalleled professionalism and skill, as well as new ironclads being built in every shipyard. It also paid for an army whose infantry battalions, the thin red line, were world famous for their adamantine stubbornness and ferocity in battle. Great commanders such as Lt. Gen. James Hope Grant, the best of Victoria's generals had been sent to command the British forces in North America and within a day of his landing had crushed the American VI Corps at the battle of Kennebunk. The rising star of the British Army, Brevet Brig. Gen. Garnet Wolseley, had saved the British army defeated at Clavarack that same month and organized an intelligence operation that dueled with Sharpe's along the American-Canadian border. That first clash of Empire and Republic welded the peoples of the Canadian provinces into a nation more than a hundred years of peaceful development would have done; their militia battalions fought alongside the British Imperial battalions with great resolve and courage.

The French Empire also had immense financial and military resources to throw into the scales. In itself it would have been a major threat to the United States. Louis Napoleon had promptly signed an alliance with the Confederacy, which the British had been more hesitant to do because of the intense domestic antipathy to slavery, preferring the status of co-belligerent rather than formal ally, to the intense bitterness of Jefferson Davis. Whatever the diplomatic nicety described the relationship between Britain and France and the Confederacy, their loans filled the Confederate treasury and their war material flooded into Southern ports.

The first phase of the war had ended in a state of tense expectation. The Union had survived, barely survived, the first onslaught of the might of Britain and France in league with the Confederacy. The British had overrun Maine and besieged the vital port of Portland, the terminus of the Grand Trunk Railway that ran through upper New England to Quebec and the rest of Canada. It was the lifeline of British North America, and the British would hold Maine and the railway at all costs. A coup de main against Portland, a vital link in that railway, nearly succeeded and turned into a hard siege. The British defeated the relief of Portland in the battle of Kennebunk.

The British also had struck down from Montreal to seize Albany and terrorize the Hudson Valley, hoping to paralyze the most important industrial state of the North. Almost simultaneously with their defeat at Kennebunk the Americans defeated the British army in New York at the battle of Claverack and drove it back into Canada. The battle had turned on not just hard fighting and leadership but on the coffee mill gun.

The Royal Navy's attempt to break the blockade at Charleston resulted in the first fleet engagement in which ironclads were the chief combatants. In that battle, the American monitors proved superior to the British broadside ironclads, and the Royal Navy suffered its most catastrophic defeat at sea in three hundred years.

A French fleet destroyed the U.S. Navy's two light Gulf blockading squadrons. Out of occupied Mexico marched a reinforced veteran army commanded by the able Maj. Gen. Achille Bazaine, who promptly defeated the American army under Maj. Gen. Nathaniel Banks at the battle of Vermillionville in western Louisiana in conjunction with Confederate forces. New Orleans fell to the new allies as their combined armies marched up the Mississippi to besiege Port Hudson. The fall of New Orleans once again severed the Mississippi's outlet to the sea for the Union.

On the same day as Clavarack the Army of Robert E. Lee attacked Washington in conjunction with the Royal Navy's attack up the Potomac. The attack was defeated only by the narrowest of margins, and those were due to the employment of the Balloon Corps and the coffee mill gun. Nevertheless, the attack left Alexandria and much of Washington in ruins, including the Washington Arsenal and the Washington Navy Yard, the largest of either kind in the country. It was a severe blow to the country's war effort. Yet all through the winter, the factories, mills, and shipyards of the North worked through the day and night producing the new means of war. Women flooded into the workforce to replace the men who had volunteered for the Army and Navy. Across the Atlantic, the factories, mills, and shipyard of Great Britain also worked unceasingly. Britons too felt the power of patriotism, and their army and navy did not want for volunteers either as the country's new reserve forces, the Rifle Volunteer Corps (RVC), also swelled in number and drilled with a new sense of purpose.

The early severe winter in North America mercifully shut a snowy curtain down on the fighting. Thus the situation stood as the winter waned in early 1864 to let men once again spill their blood on land and sea and in the air.

POINT OF DEPARTURE

I have made every effort to portray weapons as they actually functioned. For example, the U.S. Navy's Dahlgren smoothbore guns were more powerful and reliable than any contemporary gun in the Royal Navy. Technological innovations were all within the capabilities of the period. Their hurried development can be attributed to the motivation found in Samuel Johnson's comment.

Throughout this trilogy, I have attempted to illustrate the growing power of technology and especially what could have been achieved had that technology been more rationally exploited instead of being suppressed, bungled, or even sabotaged, as in the case of repeating weapons such as the Spencer rifle, the coffee mill and Gatling guns, balloons, and submersibles. The development of a national intelligence organization also would have been a logical extension of an already existing and successful organization, the Army of the Potomac's BMI.

As it was, in reality the Union prevailed without these advantages but only barely. Union morale was nearly exhausted by the election of 1864, so much so that Lincoln fully expected to be defeated. Only the fall of Atlanta to Sherman and Mobile to Farragut revived that morale, albeit temporarily. The Copperhead conspiracy to sabotage the war had widespread support and had a draining effect on the war effort by undermining morale both in the camp and at home. Even as late as early 1865, Grant and his staff were anxious to end the war because of waning support. Major General Sharpe was paying intense interest in the Confederate attempt to arm slaves to fight for the Confederacy in the last months of the war just because of its potential to prolong the conflict beyond the patience of the North. The quality of replacements had also fallen dangerously. The yeoman American was no longer volunteering. Instead, replacements were now bounty men, drafted men, and immigrants right off the boat. Of the latter, only the Irish showed any fight.

It has been said that the North fought the Civil War with one arm tied behind its back. At no time did the North mobilize for total war, as understood in the twentieth century, and fully exploit its industrial and manpower potential. War with Great Britain and France then would be the trigger in this trilogy for total war mobilization. It was only under these conditions and the constraints under which both the British and French had to operate that the United States had any hope of surviving, much less being victorious. Thus this trilogy's grand point of departure is the collision that provokes total war and changes the paradigm under which these societies made war.

Almost all the figures in this story are historical, acting according to character and past performance. A few fictitious characters have been added to further the plot, such as Lt. Col. Michael Wilmoth, whom I modeled on a superb young intelligence analyst with whom I have worked. Such fictitious characters have been noted with an asterisk in the Dramatis Personae section.

As always my deepest appreciation goes to my wife, Patty, for her unwavering an cheerful support of my pursuit of Clio. I want to thank special friends who patiently and most intelligently acted as sounding boards in the creation of this trilogy, particularly William (Bill) F. Johnson, Dr. Steven Badsey, and Thomas Bilbao. A thousand thanks for your criticism, advice, and good judgment. My mapmaker, Jay Karamales (Olorin Press), has again done a splendid job to match his work in the first two volumes of this trilogy. My heartfelt thanks goes also to my agent, Fritz Heinzen, whose knowledge of the publishing world continues to astound and inform me, and to the good people at Skyhorse Publications, especially its editorial director, Jay Cassell, and Jon Arlan, who work so hard to turn my poor manuscript into that wonder of wonders — a book.

Peter G. Tsouras
Lt. Col., USAR (ret.)
Alexandria, Virginia

MAPS

DRAMATIS PERSONAE

Abel, Frederick. Chief chemist of the Chemical Establishment of the Royal Arsenal at Woolwich.

Adams, Charles Francis. Former U.S. Ambassador to the Court of St. James, son of President John Quincy Adams, and grandson of President John Adams.

Adams, Charles Francis, Jr. Lt. Col., 1st Massachusetts Cavalry, and son of Ambassador Charles Francis Adams.

Adams, Henry. Son of Charles Francis Adams and first ambassador to the Republic of Ireland.

Babcock, John C. Civilian order-of-battle analyst and Director, Bureau of Information (BMI), Headquarters, Army of the Potomac.

Baker, Lafayette. Director of the Secret Service of the War Department.

Barton, Clara. Volunteer nurse with the Union Army in the defenses of Washington.

Bazaine, François Achille. Marshal of France, French Imperial Army Commander, French Forces in North America, and the Armée de la Louisiane in support of the Confederacy.

Bazalgette, George, VC. Lieutenant Colonel, Royal Marines and commander of daring special operations for the British Fleet in American waters.

Beauregard, Pierre Gustave Toutant de. General, CS Army, commander of the coastal defenses of South Carolina and Georgia.

Booth, Edwin. Greatest tragic actor of the American stage of the nineteenth century and loyal to the Union.

Booth, John Wilkes. Fiery dramatic actor, brother of the more famous tragedian, Edwin Booth, and a rabid Southern sympathizer.

Bright, John. Radical member of Parliament, one of the great reformers of the age, and advocate of the cause of the Union, derisively referred to as the "Member for America."

Brunnow, Baron Phillip de. Imperial Russian ambassador to the Court of St. James.

Butler, Benjamin Franklin. Major General, U.S. Volunteers; Commander, Army of the James.

Candy, Charles. Brigadier General, U.S. Volunteers, commander, First Brigade, Second Division, XII Corps, Army of the Hudson.

Carnegie, Andrew. Railroad executive, entrepreneur, chosen by Lincoln to rationalize American war industry as chairman of the War Production Board (WPB).

Carney, Anson. Scout, Bureau of Military Information (BMI), Army of the Potomac.

Chamberlain, Joshua Lawrence. Major General, U.S. Volunteers; commander of Fortress Portland.

Chebyshev, Piotr Afansievich. Captain, HIMS *Bogatyr*, of the Russian Pacific Squadron.

Clemmons, Samuel. American writer and comedian known by his pen name of Mark Twain.

Cline, Milton. Major, 3rd Indiana Cavalry, and senior reconnaissance and special operations officer of the U.S. Central Information Bureau (CIB).

Cobham, George A. Jr. Brigadier General, U.S. Volunteers; commander, Second Brigade, First Division, XII Corps, Army of the Hudson.

Coles, Cowper Phipps. Captain, RN, innovator and inventor of an armored turret, and commander of the HMS *Prince Albert*.

Cullen, Paul. Roman Catholic Archbishop of Dublin and head of the church in Ireland.

Cushing, William "Will" Alonzo. Captain, U.S. Navy, noted for his daring special operations, and first commander of the Naval Aeronautic Service (NAS).

Custer, George Armstrong. Brigadier General, U.S. Volunteers; commander, Cavalry Division, Army of the Hudson.

Dahlgren, Ulric. Colonel, U.S. Volunteers, hero of Gettysburg, son of Adm. John Dahlgren, and leader of the "Dahlgren Raid" on England.

Dana, Charles. U.S. Assistant Secretary of War and former editor, *New York Tribune*.

Davis, Jefferson. President, Confederate States of America.

Denison, George. Colonel, Canadian Militia; commander of the Royal Guides.

Disraeli, Benjamin. Prime Minister and leader of the Tory or Conservative Party in Great Britain.

Dixon, Manly. Colonel, Royal Engineers, and superintendent of the Royal Small Arms Factory Enfield (RSAF).

Douay, Félix Charles. Major General, French Imperial Army; second in command, Armée de Louisiane.

Douglass, Frederick. Leading African American abolitionist and supporter of Lincoln in the war for the Union.

Doyle, Sir Hastings. Major General, British Army; commander, Portland Field Force.

Dulaine, Clio. New Orleans *libre*, mistress of Marshal Bazaine, and agent of the U.S. Central Information Bureau (CIB).

Dunn, Robert. Lieutenant Colonel, British Army, Acting Commander, 11th Hussars.

Ford, John T. Owner of Ford's Theater in Washington and a friend of Edwin Booth.

Fox, Augustus "Gus." U.S. Assistant Secretary of the Navy, essentially in modern terms, Chief of Naval Operations.

Franklin, William B. Major General, U.S. Volunteers; commander, XIX Corps, Army of the Gulf.

Geary, John W. Major General, U.S. Volunteers; commander, 2nd Division, XII Corps, Army of the Hudson.

George William Frederick Charles, Prince and 2nd Duke of Cambridge. Cousin of Queen Victoria and Commander-in-Chief of the British Army.

Gorchakov, Aleksandr Mikhalovich. Prince and Russian Foreign Minister.

Grant, James Hope. Lieutenant General, British Army; considered the best general in the Empire, commander of Her Majesty's military forces in British North America.

Grant, Ulysses S. Lieutenant General, U.S. Army; general-in-chief of the Armies of the United States.

Gregg, David M. Brigadier General, U.S. Volunteers; commander, 2nd Cavalry Division, Cavalry Corps, Army of the Potomac.

Grierson, Benjamin. Major General, U.S. Volunteers, commander of the cavalry division of the Army of the Mississippi.

Hamilton, James, 1st Duke of Abercorn. Lord Lieutenant of Ireland.

Hampton, Wade. Major General, C.S. Army; commander of Wade Hampton's Division, Cavalry of the Army of Northern Virginia.

Hancock, Winfield Scott. Major General, U.S. Volunteers; commander, Army of the Rappahannock.

Hogan, Martin. Private, U.S. Volunteers; young Irish immigrant and scout for the Bureau of Information (BMI), Army of the Hudson.

Hooker, Joseph. Major General, U.S. Army; commander, Army of the Hudson.

Hope, Sir James. Admiral, Royal Navy; commander of the Iron Fleet.

Ireland, David. Colonel, U.S. Volunteers; commander, Third Brigade, Second Division, XII Corps, Army of the Hudson.

Kelly, Patrick. Brigadier General, U.S. Volunteers; commander of the Irish Brigade in the expedition to liberate Ireland.

Knight, Judson. Sergeant, Union Army; Chief of Scouts, Army of the Hudson.

Lamson, Roswell Hawk. Captain, U.S. Navy; captain of the USS *Kearsarge*.

Layard, Austin David. Member of Parliament, Undersecretary to Lord Russell at the Foreign Office, and envoy to Jefferson Davis.

Lee, Fitzhugh. Major General, C.S. Army; commander of Fitzhugh Lee's Cavalry Division, Cavalry of the Army of Northern Virginia.

Lee, Robert E. General, C.S. Army; commander, Army of Northern Virginia.

Lew, Elizabeth Van. Ardent Unionist, agent of the U.S. Central Information Bureau (CIB), and head of the its Richmond spy network.

Lewis, Pryce. British expatriate and agent of the U.S. Central Information Bureau (CIB).

Lincoln, Abraham. 16th President of the United States and Commander-in-Chief, in the epic struggle for the survival of the Union.

Lisovsky, Stefan S. Rear Admiral, Russian Imperial Navy; commander of the Baltic Squadron. supporting the Union.

Long, E.T., Sir. Rear Admiral, Royal Navy; commander of the Australian Squadron.

Longstreet, James. Lieutenant General, C.S. Army; commander, First Corps, Army of Northern Virginia.

Lowe, Thaddeus. Scientist, Colonel, U.S. Volunteers; founder and commander , U.S. Army Balloon Corps.

Lynn, John. Stationmaster of Gorham, New Hampshire, and leader of the Coos County militia.

Lyons, Lord. Former British ambassador to the United States before the declaration of war.

McBean, William. Colonel, British Army; commander of the 78th (Highland) Foot at the battle of Chazy, and commander, 12th Brigade at the battle of Saco.

McCarter, Michael William. Former sergeant of the Irish Brigade discharged for wounds after Chancellorsville and recalled by Hooker.

McCullough, Richard G. Agent of the Confederate State Department Secret Service.

McEntee, John. Captain, U.S. Volunteers; Chief, Bureau of Military Information (BMI), Army of the Hudson.

McPhail, James L. Deputy Chief, U.S. Central Information Bureau (CIB).

Meade, George Gordon. Major General, U.S. Volunteers; commander, Army of the Potomac.

Meagher, Thomas Francis. Major General, U.S. Volunteers; commander of the expedition to liberate Ireland.

Merritt, Wesley. Brigadier General, U.S. Volunteers; commander, Reserve Brigade, Cavalry Corps, Army of the Potomac.

Milne, Sir Alexander. Vice Admiral, Royal Navy; commander of the North American and West Indies Station.

Montgomery, James. Colonel, U.S. Volunteers, commanding a brigade of colored troops transferred to XVIII Corps.

Muravyov-Karsky, Nikolay Nikolayevich. General, Russian Imperial Army; military governor of the Caucasus.

Napier, Sir Robert. Major General, Indian Army; commander of the Dublin Field Force.

Nickolay, John. One of President Lincoln's two private secretaries.

Norie, Henry Hay. Captain, commander, 9th Company, Ayrshire Rifle Volunteer Corps.

Palmer, George. Lieutenant Colonel; commander, West Essex Yeomanry.

Popov, Andrei Alexandrovich. Rear Admiral, Russian Imperial Navy; commander of the Russian Pacific Squadron.

Porter, David Dixon. Rear Admiral, U.S. Navy; commander of the Mississippi Squadron.

Rimsky-Korsakov, Nikolai. Lieutenant, Imperial Russian Navy; Russian representative on the Dahlgren Raid.

Rowan, Stephen Clegg. Captain, U.S. Navy; commander, USS *Ironsides*, and acting commander, South Atlantic Blockading Squadron.

Ruger, Thomas H. Brigadier General, U.S. Volunteers; acting commander, First Division, XII Corps, Army of the Hudson.

Sanders, George Nicholas. Kentucky planter and agent of the Confederate State Department Secret Service.

Scarlet, Sir James Yorke. Lieutenant General, British Army; Adjutant to the Forces, and commander at the battle of Tallaght.

Schurz, Carl. Major General, U.S. Volunteers; commander, Third Division, XI Corps, Army of the Hudson.

Seward, William H. U.S. Secretary of State and close friend of President Lincoln.

Sharpe, George H. Major General, U.S. Volunteers; Director of the Central Information Bureau, and commander of the 120th Regiment, NY Volunteers.

Sheridan, Phillip H. Major General, U.S. Volunteers; commander, Cavalry Corps of the Army of the Potomac.

Sherman, William Tecumseh. Major General, U.S. Volunteers; commander, Army of the Hudson.

Smith, William Farrar "Baldy." Major General, U.S. Volunteers; commander, Army of the James.

Spencer, Christopher. Mechanical genius and inventor of the Spencer repeating rifle.

Stanton, Edwin M. Implacable, able, and vengeful U.S. Secretary of War.

Steinwehr, Adolph von. Brigadier General, U.S. Volunteers; commander, Second Division, XI Corps, Army of the Hudson.

Stevenson, Thomas G. Colonel, U.S. Volunteers; commander of a brigade transferred to XVIII Corps.

Stimers, Albert Crocker. General Inspector of Ironclads, U.S. Navy.

Stoekel, Baron Eduourd de. Russian ambassador to the United States.

Stuart, James E. B. (JEB). Major General, C.S. Army; commander, Cavalry, Army of Northern Virginia.

Taylor, Richard. Lieutenant General, C.S. Army; son of President Zachary Taylor, and commander, Western Louisiana District.

Thomas, George. Major General, U.S. Volunteers, "the Rock of Chickamauga," who succeeded Rosecrans as Commander, Army of the Cumberland.

Turnour, E.W. Captain HMS *Charybdis*; commander of the Royal Navy squadron at Victoria Island, British Columbia.

Victoria. Alexandrina Victoria, Queen of the United Kingdom of Great Britain and Ireland, ascended her throne on 20 June 1837.

*Vivian, Paul H. Colonel, U.S. Volunteers; commander, Third Brigade (succeeding Col. David Ireland), Second Division, XII Corps, Army of the Hudson.

Weitzel, Godfrey. Maj. Gen., U.S. Volunteers; commander, XVIII Corps, Army of the James.

Welles, Gideon. War Democrat and flinty U.S. Secretary of the Navy.

Wells, William. Colonel, U.S. Volunteers; commander, 1st Vermont Cavalry, 3rd Brigade, Cavalry Division, Army of the Hudson.

Wetherall, E.R. Colonel, British Army, and commander, Guards Brigade, British Imperial forces in British North America.

Whitman, Walt. Nurse to wounded Union soldiers, poet, and sometime clerk for the United States Government in Washington, D.C.

*Wilkes, Ashely. Major, C.S. Army, Cobb's Legion (9th Georgia Cavalry Regiment), Wade Hampton's Cavalry Division, Cavalry of the Army of Northern Virginia.

*Wilmoth, Michael D. Lieutenant Colonel, U.S. Volunteers; Director of Analysis (DA), Central Information Bureau (CIB), and protégé of George H. Sharpe.

Wilson, James H. Brigadier General, U.S. Volunteers; and commander, 3rd Cavalry Division, Cavalry Corps, Army of the Potomac.

Wilson, Sir Robert, VC. Retired captain of the 9th Lancers living in Waltham Abby.

Wolseley, Garnet J. Brigadier General, British Army, Imperial forces in British North America.

Wright, Horatio G. Major General, U.S. Volunteers; commander, VI Corps, Army of the Rappahannock.

Wright, Michael. Sergeant Major and aide to Maj. Gen. Thomas Francis Meagher.

Zeppelin, Count Ferdinand von. Captain, Prussian Army, official observer of the American Civil War.

Zipperer, Christian Edward 2nd Lieutenant, 7th Georgia Cavalry Regiment, Cavalry Corps, Army of Northern Virginia.

1

"I've Been Turned into a Complete American Now"

The Captain of USS *Catskill*[1] in his little armored pilot house atop the ship's great turret screamed through the speaking tube, "Hard to larboard, hard to larboard!" He could not take his eyes off the British ship steaming straight for him amidships. It had come out of the smoke, its engines straining to churn its paddlewheels at maximum speed of twelve knots. The monitor could manage at most six knots, but it could barely begin to move by the time HMS *Buzzard*[2] smashed into it. The British sloop screamed as its copper bottom rode up over the Catskill's low freeboard deck forward of the turret. The monitor's bow dipped below water as the weight of the sloop pulled the ironclad down by its starboard side. Inside men were thrown against machinery or bulkheads. The turret spun uncontrollably down to starboard on its great spindle.

Maj. George Bazalgette, VC, Royal Marines Light Infantry (RMLI), was the first to leap over the *Buzzard*'s rail and onto the deck of the monitor now three inches underwater. Twenty Royal Marines and a dozen armed tars followed. One team ran to the turret. They would have thrown grenades through the gun apertures, but they were pointing directly down toward the water. Another group found a deck hatch that led to the interior of the ship. They were about to blow it with a special explosive charge, but it flew open of its own as a man threw himself up the ladder. He was pulled out by the first Marine, as were three more who tried to escape the same way. Then the Marines plunged down the ladder and into the bowels of the ship.

Bazalgette climbed a metal ladder to the top of the turret. The hatch to the armored pilot house clanged open, and an American naval officer stumbled out and right up against Bazalgette's sword. "Strike, damn you, strike!" The captain looked to the bow. His eyes widened at the sight of *Buzzard*'s bow pointing into the air as it rested on his deck and his crew climbing out of the hatch their hands in the air. He glanced to the stern to see a British sailor haul down the Stars and Stripes. He pulled himself together. "It seems, sir, my ship is already yours."

HAMPTON ROADS, 10:20 A.M., MONDAY, MARCH 14, 1864

An hour before Bazalgette leapt over the side, the admiral commanding the British flotilla in Hampton Roads murmured quietly to himself, "Yes." It was not an emphatic, triumphant yes, for that level of emotion simply wouldn't do. It was just a calm statement of fact. The American ironclads were steaming out of Norfolk Navy Yard.[3] They had taken the bait. And it was very attractive bait. More than forty Royal Navy vessels were crowding Hampton Roads to attack Fortress Monroe, the key to the entire Chesapeake.

The Chesapeake was the largest estuary in the United States, surrounded by Maryland and Virginia and constituted the drainage of the District of Columbia and six states from more than 150 rivers and streams. It ran two hundred miles from the Susquehanna River in the north to the Atlantic Ocean in the south.[4] Just south of the Potomac it reached its widest point at thirty miles. Its average depth was forty-six feet and deepest at 208 feet, though sandbars and shallows made for narrow channels. Directly west of its entrance to the Atlantic was the James Peninsula through which Maj. Gen. George McClellan had two years ago attempted to steal a march on Richmond. The peninsula was bound on the north by the York River and the south by the James, which led to Richmond. The entrance to the James was the wide stretch of water known as Hampton Roads, and across this body was the Norfolk Navy Yard to which the North and South Atlantic Blockading Squadrons had withdrawn after the Third Battle of Charleston.[5] At the head of the Peninsula was Fortress Monroe. That fortification and the U.S. Navy forces at Norfolk effectively closed Richmond itself from communication by sea and made it difficult for ships to proceed up the Potomac and further up the bay to Baltimore. It was the key to the Chesapeake.

The British warships were wreathed in smoke as they pounded away at the fort, but the greatest firepower came from the ships and craft of "The Great Armament," a collection of cast-iron armored floating batteries that had been built in the Crimean War specifically to smash the defenses of Russia's capital of St. Petersburg, the great Russian naval base at Kronstadt. The Great Armament was paraded for the Queen after that war ended in a dramatic exercise at Spithead, an obvious warning not only to St. Petersburg but to Paris and Washington too. Supporting the batteries of the Great Armament were almost thirty gunboats, small ships armed with one to six guns and designed to attack coastal targets and operate in shallow and confining estuaries.[6]

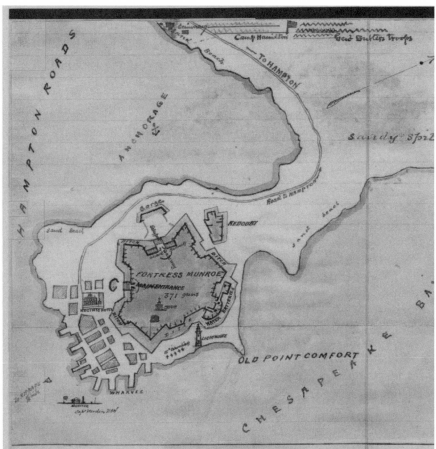

Absent from the operations in the bay were British ships-of-the-line, the battleships of yore. Their easy destruction at Charleston with such terrible loss of life had caused the British to keep them out of possible engagements with monitors. Their armament largely of old 68-pounder guns had proven utterly inadequate. A few were used in the blockade. Instead, a strong force of frigates and corvettes armed with more powerful 8- and 10-inch guns were assembled as the backbone of the British presence in the bay.

After the Royal Navy's humiliating defeat the previous November at Charleston, it had concentrated its efforts to make sure the Americans would be eternally sorry for ever having started this war.[7] Nothing sparked the adamantine resolve of the island race than a sound defeat. But the Royal Navy was presented with an immense strategic problem, the prospect of having to blockade the wild Atlantic coast of the Northern states. The blockade of France in her earlier wars was child's play compared to this. Then the Royal Navy had its own bases, right across the Channel. In this war, its only bases were Halifax and Bermuda, far too distant to support the distant blockade. Of course, Confederate ports were useful but only to a small degree. The U.S. Navy when it was blockading the Confederacy's southern Atlantic Ports needed forward operating bases on that coast itself. To whittle the problem down, Milne seized Martha's Vineyard in late November. Just off the coast of Massachusetts, it would serve to support the ships stopping up Boston and the other major New England ports.

The Royal Navy was supporting its operations in the Chesapeake from its forward operating base at Wilmington, North Carolina, eagerly provided by the Confederates who were desperate to earn an open alliance with the British. The blockade of such a long coast put a premium on the use of the smaller sloops and the gunboats that could dart in and attack American coastal targets. Unfortunately, the British had transferred most of these gunboats and many of the sloops from West Africa where they had been used to suppress the slave trade. Their absence led to a spike in the slaving for the Brazilian and Confederate markets, the latter having been restarted since the 1808 abolition on the importation of slaves in the Constitution was now a dead letter.[8] For a nation that so detested slavery, Britain blithely had stripped its naval forces from suppressing the slave trade to fighting as an ally of a slave state. The irony was not lost on the growing opposition to the war led by John Bright in the House of Commons.[9]

With the fall of Fortress Monroe and the Norfolk Navy Yard, the Royal Navy would have a perfect forwarding operating bases from which to cover the Middle Atlantic States. The Royal Navy's analysis for the British

1861 war plan against the United States concluded that most of the major American ports such as Baltimore, Philadelphia, and New York were not vulnerable to an attack by sea because they were located up great fort-guarded rivers rather than being coastal cities. Milne's near success when a flotilla of his smaller ships had slipped up the Potomac to come within an eyelash of taking Washington in conjunction with an attack by Lee's army last November raised doubt in that conclusion. That near success, however, had only been possible because of the cooperation of the Robert E. Lee's Army of Northern Virginia. The Royal Navy would not have such assistance in attacks against those major northern cities so that was option was never seriously considered.

BAY OF BENGAL, 9:12 A.M., MONDAY, MARCH 14, 1864

She was a fat merchantman thirty-six hours out of Calcutta, heavy with a load of cotton for England's hungry mills. Her lookout spotted a plume of smoke over the horizon, and then another. In another four hours a sleek screw ship bore down on them from the direction of the smoke. She flew the Royal Navy ensign, her guns were run out, and she signaled for the merchantman to stop and prepare for inspection.

Her captain ordered immediate compliance, and as soon as her engines came to full stop, the Royal Navy ensign came fluttering and the Stars and Stripes flew up in its place. It was a stunned captain who watched as American Marines boarded his ship followed by a naval officer.

The captain's presence returned in a rush. "What is this outrage, sir? You have no right to board this ship under such threat."

A bemused smile crossed the American's face. "I am Lieutenant Wilson of the USS *Wyoming*, sir. I presume you are the ship's master? If so, you will provide me with your papers and cargo manifest— immediately."[10]

The captain continued to bluster and complain all the way to his cabin. Finally, the American had had enough. "Are you unaware, Captain, that our two countries are at war? And, therefore, your ship is a lawful prize of war? Now be so good as to provide those documents."

The American took a few minutes to review them. "It is your misfortune, Captain, to master a British ship carrying a cargo consigned to British merchants. If your cargo had been the property of a neutral, it might have saved your ship. Gather your personal belongings and order your crew to do the same."

Now aboard the *Wyoming*, the British captain cried out in grief and rage as the fires began to lick up the rigging of his ship and then gushed out of the holds. The cotton would make a bonfire visible for miles before she went under.

SHIRAKAVAN, ARMENIA, 8:10 P.M., TUESDAY, MARCH 15, 1864

General Nikolai Nikolayevich Muravyov-Karsky felt the cold in his bones as he sat on his horse on a small hill overlooking the Russian-Ottoman border. Below him the Cossack raiding party galloped into the night.

Their objective was a nameless Armenian village in the Ottoman province of Kars a dozen versts from where Muravyov-Karsky waited. They found it asleep and shabby, and their stay did not improve it. The Armenians, as fellow Christians, they merely robbed, moderately. The Turks, they killed. All but one. He was thrown at the feet of the Cossack commander's horse. Three men kicked him to his feet. Blood poured from his torn scalp down his long white robe. It was all he could do to keep his feet. The screams of his raped women penetrated even the fog of his pain. Hatred of the Turk burned deep in the Cossacks, the descendants of runaway serfs who had formed a warrior society to guard the Russian marches against the constant raids that fed Islam's insatiable desire for slaves. Until the reign of Catherine the Great those raids had been so destructive as to negate the vigorous increase of the Russians. So many Russians had filled the rowing benches of the Sultan's galleys, that the Turks had joked that there must be no men left in Russia. Now the whip was in the other hand.

The Armenian interpreter puffed himself up as the Cossack commander gestured toward the Turk with his whip. He said, "Your Honor, this is the local Turkish landowner."

The Cossack looked down on him. Behind him the Turk's house was beginning to burn, its light glinting off the silver accoutrement's of the officer's long coat. "Dog, we have spared you to carry a message to your masters. We know the way to Kars very well. Muravyov-Karsky commands again."

A few hours later the officer was reporting to Muravyov-Karsky, who nodded. The general was an old man at sixty-nine, full of battle honors and memories. He had seen war first against Napoleon, chased Polish rebels, and hammered the Turks again and again. For his last great feat the nation had acclaimed him "Karsky" for having taken the great Turkish fortress of Kars after an epic siege in 1855. His acclamation was more thunderous for it was Russia's only victory in the Crimean War.

Muravyov-Karsky had been asked by the tsar himself to go back to his old command in the Caucasus to ostentatiously give the Turks cause to fear again for their great fortress that secured Ottoman Armenia. The eyes of the Sublime Porte must be drawn to the east and fixed there. And what could do that better than the reputation of the man who had taken the fortress once before. That and Cossack frightfulness, but then it was in the language the Turks understood.

As the old general guided his horse back to his headquarters and its warm bed, his thoughts went back to the siege. He had given the Turks the honors of war, for they had fought hard and valiantly even as they starved, but had it not been for the Englishman who commanded them, the gallant William Fenwick Williams, he would have made short work of them. Then again his opponent's skill and valor had only added to his own glory when the fortress finally capitulated. He had also had the honor to escort the captured Englishman to St. Petersburg and personally present him to Tsar Alexander II.

He had heard that Fenwick Williams had been made commander in British North America as a reward for his defense of Kars. Canada — an exotic place, he thought. He wondered how his old enemy was doing now that Canada was the cockpit of this new war between the British and the Americans.

THE WHITE HOUSE, WASHINGTON, DC, 7:30 P.M., MONDAY, MARCH 14, 1864

Pryce Lewis was nervous to meet the President. He was born a Welshman but called himself English, by which he meant a Briton. He was a spy. Not as one might think, a British spy. He had spent nineteenth months in the infamous Confederate prison, Castle Thunder, in Richmond for spying for the Union as one of Alan Pinkerton's agents. He had seen a companion hanged, but only the hand of Providence had saved him from that same noose. He found himself recounting to Lincoln how he had been taken from his cell in early September of last year to the exchange boat on the James River.

"There it was, hanging limply from the flag-of-truce boat, Mr. President. The American flag. I turned to my friend, Scully, and I said, 'If before this I had any English feeling left, I've been turned into a complete American now.'"[11] He looked up at Sharpe who had hired him for the CIB after his return to Washington.

There were several million Britons living in the United States, mostly in the North, part of the great wave of immigration that had brought the Germans and Irish, as well as Scandinavians, Dutch, and French, to find a new life. But the ties of blood and affection were the most durable of all. Yet, they had come to make a new life, and most had found it, grew roots, and bore children in the new land. For many the war brought as indescribable a grief as Americans north and south had felt when the Republic sundered across the affections of countless families. For many, the choice was clear. They had come to America to escape a hopeless future that soured them on the land of their birth. Such was Andrew Carnegie, who despised the British class system, hierarchies of church and society, and above all, the Royals. Now his genius was multiplying the strength of American industry.

Lewis recalled to Lincoln the story of another Briton, John Richardson, who had taken part in the Charge of the Light Brigade, where he had charged past the Russian guns and received two wounds from Cossack lances. Richardson had written, "I was in Hulme Barracks. I was absent for six days, and the adjutant (John Yates) called me a scamp when I returned. I replied, 'I am not like you—a coward. I saw you run from a mounted Cossack; and further you never went down in the charge.' After this I was up to my neck in trouble and eventually I was tried and got fifty lashes and ordered to be imprisoned. My bad back took ways and festered and I was in hospital for twenty-eight days. During that time a letter was sent out of the hospital to an editor, was published, describing how they flogged me in the riding school, like a dog. The Colonel employed lawyers and endeavored to get the writer's name, but the editor would not give way. My father being an educated man, wrote to the Duke of Cambridge, and he ordered me to be liberated and discharged at once. I sailed for America and enlisted in the New Jersey Volunteers, and fought in the Battle of Pittsburg."[12] He had also said that the future for a worn-out soldier was only the workhouse. Here he had a future.

There were many more native-born Britons in Union Blue, and many had fought at Portland, Kennebunk, and Clavarack. How it must have caught in their throats to see across the field the lines of red coats and above them Union flag of the United Kingdom, the superimposed flags of England and Scotland, the crosses of St. George and St. Andrew, and to hear the skirl of bagpipes. For most, in the end, it was the ties to the land of their children rather than that of their fathers that mattered. Still, for many the choice had been an agony.

To a man and a woman they had detested slavery, and Britain's unofficial alliance with the slave power had set aside any lingering loyalties. Sharpe underlined this by saying, "In fact, sir, Britons living in the South have been reliably Union men." So it was the attachment to their new homes and abhorrence of slavery had steeled them to the choice.

Lewis was clearly one for whom the conflict of divided loyalty had been a painful nettle to grasp. His new attachment to the American flag had been followed almost immediately by the war with Britain. He had candidly told Sharpe after he had returned to Washington, "I've served this government well and taken the Secret Service oath of loyalty over and over again. But when it comes to swearing that I'll take arms against my own sovereign, I'll seem them damned."[13] If ever there was a conflicted man it was Pryce. Yet it was human nature to hold conflicting beliefs, such as the theories of Darwin and of the Bible's creation.

The lawyer in Sharpe, not the litigator but the artful fashioner of solutions, saw an opportunity rather than a stone wall in Lewis's outburst.

"Lewis, my man, this is not an obstacle. This country owes you much for what you have done, risked, and endured for its sake."

Lewis looked puzzled, but Sharpe went on, "We still have need of good agents against the Rebellion. And the Rebellion has friends who do not speak English." He leaned back in his chair and tapped the ash off his cigar. "You know how events have turned against us in Louisiana due to the French." The words "the French" immediately stiffened Lewis's back. Yes, an appeal to a Briton's opinion of his traditional enemy was always sure to get a rise. "I could use a good man in Louisiana to help us against the Rebels and the French."

Lewis snatched at the offer.

So it was that the meeting in the White House took place. Lewis had just returned from a few months in New Orleans. Sharpe thought his report important enough for Lincoln to hear it himself. "I passed myself off as a British cotton buyer, which earned me a lot of trouble with the French who are crawling all over the city. It is clear they consider New Orleans and Louisiana to belong to them already. More than one of them told me that. The changing of the French honor guard at the Cathedral of St. Louis is quite a spectacle that attracts a large crowd every day."

"What do the locals think, then?" Lincoln asked.

"Well, sir, the whites of French or Spanish descent would look very favorably on a permanent French presence. Most of the English-speaking people are Rebels to the bone. Those who were Unionists were hunted down after the city fell."

"I want to know what happened to the freedmen," Lincoln said.

"Many fled. The rest were rounded up by the slave hunters and returned to their masters. But the free coloreds, the *libres,* as they're called, were left alone. The city would come to a halt if they were oppressed."

Sharpe added, "This is the kernel of the issue."

Pryce-Lewis went on. "The French are spreading a lot of gold around New Orleans; it's buying a lot of friends. And they are spreading it among the *libres* even more liberally. Bazaine's mistress, Clio Dulaine, is a *libre* and my chief contact."

Lincoln looked thoughtful. "And the Rebels cannot be deaf, dumb, and blind to all this."

Sharpe said, "No, sir. But what can they do? My agents in Richmond tell me Jeff Davis is seething over this, but the Confederate Government has taken huge French loans. Unlike the British, the French have signed a formal treaty with Confederacy, and they owe the recapture of New Orleans to them. They had to acknowledge French hegemony over Mexico, a bitter pill for them. They were auditioning for that same role."

Lincoln seemed to enjoy his counterpart's dilemma. "Yes, take money from someone, and you put yourself in an inferior position."

"Bazaine is clearly acting on orders."

"Yes, of course. It is bad enough that the French aid the Rebellion, but that they want to then claim Louisiana and Texas for the French Empire is a new level of perfidy."

"A national trait, I'm afraid, sir." Sharpe had lived a year in Paris after law school perfecting his French.

"And do they think that Davis will ultimately take that as a price for continued alliance?"

"That would be naïve of the French to think so, and that is not a national trait. Our job then is to help the Rebels and the French along with the falling out that is sure to come. Where there is chaos, there is profit."

JERSEY CITY, NEW JERSEY, 7:25 P.M., MONDAY, MARCH 14, 1864
John T. Ford was delighted to share the train ride to Philadelphia with Edwin Booth. He was hoping to persuade the great tragedian to play Hamlet in Washington at his theater. It was cold on the platform, and he paused to pull up his coat collar when he saw a tall young man on the platform edge pushed by the shoving crowd against the car. The train began to move, and the young man lost his balance and began to slip down between the wheels of the train and the platform. The train whistle blew, signaling its departure. Ford looked on in horror at the young man's inevitable death.

Booth saw the same thing, dropped his valises, stuck his ticket in his teeth and pushed through the crowd. Before the young man slipped all the way down and under the wheels, a powerful hand reached down, grabbed his coat, and hauled him up. The young man instantly recognized Booth and blurted out, "That was a narrow escape, Mr. Booth! Thank you so much, sir. You saved my life." He reached out to shake Booth's hand and introduced himself. "Lincoln, Robert Lincoln.[14]

Booth replied, "Anyone would have done the same." It was time to board; they quickly shook hands and boarded separately. It had not occurred to Booth or Ford that the young man was the oldest son of Abraham Lincoln, who was traveling from Harvard to Washington to visit his parents. Young Lincoln had not wanted to call attention to his father's position.

OFFICE OF THE STATE DEPARTMENT SECRET SERVICE, RICHMOND, VIRGINIA, 7:30 P.M., MONDAY, MARCH 14, 1864
Richard G. McCullough was in what some might call the poison and dagger service of the Confederacy. He had been summoned to a meeting at the State Department's Secret Service office for his expertise in sabotage

devices. There he met a few men he already knew, as well as a George Nicholas Sanders, a planter from Kentucky. Saunders would be in charge of a new operation, one that had the interest of the highest levels of the government.

The fifty-two-year-old Saunders was an intense man with a passion for destroying tyrants, of whom in his mind Abraham Lincoln was chief. From an early age he had been intoxicated by revolution, and as U.S. counsul-designate in London in the early 1850s had ostentatiously hosted men like Lajos Kossuth of Hungary, Giuseppe Mazzini and Giuseppe Garibaldi of Italy, Alexandre Auguste Ledru-Rollin of France, and Alexander Herzen of Russia. So blatant had been his association with these famous revolutionaries that it caused the U.S. government considerable embarrassment as their seeming sponsor. He went so far as to write an open letter to the French people encouraging them to overthrow the Emperor Napoleon III, a gross breach of propriety by an official of a friendly government. His true intention was assassination, a political action from which he did not shrink. His actions led to the Senate's refusal to confirm him.[15]

Someone had suggested to him now that there was a young actor in Washington who would be quite useful for his new mission if handled properly. He had worked for the Confederacy before.

2

"I Can Hang You"

Muravyov-Karsky was behind in his news. Fenwick Williams had been replaced in October of the last year. Another commanded in British North America now, and there was not a Briton or Canadian in uniform who did not feel confident of the fact. Pvt. Timothy Dunn leaned his Enfield against a tree, pulled his greatcoat collar up, and stuck his hands in his pockets. It was cold in the shadows of the trees even in the early afternoon—cold and silent as only a windless winter day in a forest could be. His thoughts went back to the rough passage from Ireland late last year. The commanding general himself accompanied the 29th Foot on the voyage, had earned their respect by his interest in their care, and, wonder of wonders, serenaded the men as part of an officer string quartet. Dunn replayed in his mind the sweet, lilting hymn, "Abide With Me," that officers had played, and it did not seem as cold.

Lost in his thoughts, Dunn did not detect the two men slipping through the trees nearby heading south. His battalion's picket line was too widely spread, and the two American scouts flitted like shadows among in the shade of the dark trees. Sgt. Judson Knight was a big man with the talent becoming invisible. Bold he was, like so many redheads, and by turns clever and cool, which may explain why he was Chief of Scouts, Army of the Hudson. With him was Cpl. Martin Hogan, not two years from the crossing from Ireland, lithe and quick, and like Knight, cable of the most shameless daring.

On cat's paws they moved, silent and seeking the shadows. They bore a precious gift for Hooker. Locked in their minds were the sight of endless columns of great-coated British troops and Canadian militia moving south, tramping along country roads half mud and half ice. Just as precious and even more dangerous was the folded note in cipher hidden in Knight's left boot. It was the payoff to satchels of American gold spread carefully in Canada by agents of the American Central Information Bureau (CIB), Lincoln's new national intelligence organization and its master, Brig. Gen. George H. Sharpe. Knight had no idea what the cipher contained; that wasn't his business. His contact in St. John just south of Montreal had passed it to him and fled.

After hours, it seemed, Knight and Hogan had passed the British picket line and could breathe a bit freer and move even faster. That was their mistake and bad luck too. Coming in the other direction was another group of men on the same mission. Three men of the Royal Guides, who had just slipped back across the Canadian border from a scouting mission of the American positions around Plattsburg. They had just mounted their waiting horses when Knight and Hogan walked into the same small clearing. Now Knight had a rule that to be a good scout, you should avoid a fight unless it was life or death. This was life and death. The Canadians had just looked up to see them. Knight drew his pistol and shot the first man and ran forward so fast that he pulled the shot man off his saddle and mounted it himself. The second Guide had reached for his carbine when Hogan shot him too. The third man was quicker and cooler. His shot dropped Hogan. Knight spurred his horse into the third man and rode him down. He pulled around and jumped to the ground to find Hogan holding his shoulder.

His hands brought Hogan up to a sitting position as he looked him over. "Luck of the Irish, it's through and through, my boy." He grinned at the young man, who did not feel all that lucky. "Come on, let me help you up onto one Her Majesty's fine mounts." Shouts jerked their heads around. The picket guard was rushing forward to the sound of the gunfire. He helped Hogan to a horse to put one foot in the stirrup when the guard burst into the clearing. They stopped only long enough to fire. Hogan's horse went down screaming, and Hogan fell with another wound. "Go!" he shouted. "Leave me!" It took only a split second for Knight to throw himself into another saddle and gallop away, his body bent over the side of the horse away from the enemy, an old Comanche trick the Army had learned painfully on the Plains and taught him by Maj. Gen. Phil Kearny, who had fallen at Second Bull Run.

More shots sang past him as he disappeared weaving through the trees as fast as his horse dared to go.[1]

HEADQUARTERS, THE ROYAL GUIDES, ST. BERNARD-DE-LACOLLE, 4:05 P.M., TUESDAY, MARCH 15, 1864

Col. George Denison was not a happy man. The Royal Guides, as his militia cavalry troop had been called, was a family inheritance, raised by his grandfather and commanded as well by his father. Denison had trained them into superlative scouts, and their desperate charge at

Claverack into an American cavalry division had won him imperishable glory. And captivity. It had not tempered his hatred of Americans. Upon his exchange in January he had rebuilt the Guides, and under the direction of his friend Wolseley had sent them across the border to fill their ears and eyes with the enemy's activities.[2]

Denison did not command from afar. He hovered over the border, keeping a close hand on his scouts. It gnawed at him that officers did not go on scouting missions, not a gentlemanly activity for either army. So he personally sent them off and welcomed them back to eagerly debrief them. Denison took any harm done to one of his lads as a personal injury. Now two of his boys were dead, one in hospital, and with only one prisoner to show for it.

They had just brought the man from the surgeon's patching to Denison's forward headquarters nearby. If it had been up to Denison, he would have used medical care as a reward for a forthcoming man, but the new commanding officer's orders had made it clear that the rules of civilized warfare would be strictly followed.

"I can hang you for any number of reasons."

"Well, saar, it's lucky I am to have a choice when most get none on how to die."

"I assure you they all end the same way, badly."

"Oh, saar, it's ashamed you should be to so threaten an innocent man."

Denison's fist made the table bounce. "Innocent man! The cheek! I know exactly who you are." He went to the door and shouted out, "Sergeant Dumfries! You may fashion the noose now. And be quick about it."

He walked around behind his prisoner. "Hogan, is it?"

"Yes, saar."

"Hogan, ever seen a man hanged?"

"Yes, saar. Courtesy of Her Majesty's government in Ireland. Some poor starving man was such a danger to the Crown that they hanged him good and proper for stealing a loaf during the Hunger. Yes, saar, I've seen a man hanged."

"So you admit to being a British subject."

"A misfortune of birth, saar."

Denison purred, "Ahhh."

"A misfortune I have corrected by becoming an American citizen as soon as I shook off the evil of the crossing."

"Alas, Hogan, you have no proof. I find you in arms against Her Majesty's soldiers on the territory of Her Majesty, with the very brogue of your tongue proclaiming you a subject of the Crown. We hang traitors."

"Oh, saar, and it was George Washington himself who spoke with a British accent, no doubt, who ran your Tory grandfather out of the States and up here."

Denison reddened. No Anglo-Canadian liked to be reminded that most of them were descended from loyal Americans who could not abide the new Republic after the Revolution or were "encouraged" to leave. He tried something else, "Well, Hogan, you must be referring to my grandfather's great good judgment. But we are wasting what little time you have left on this earth talking about MY grandfather.

"Let's just say I believe you are an American. Now I can hang you for being a spy. If I wasn't in such a hurry to hang you, I could spend the day finding even more reasons.

"Saar, it's a soldier of the United States Volunteers I am, and I claim the protection of my uniform."

"Uniform, Hogan? I know that no matter what the Americans wear as a uniform, they will never look more than buffoons, but you are not wearing any uniform at all. Your rag-pickers clothes are most hangable."

"Well, saar, you accidentally got a mite of the truth in that sentence, all bent and inside out it was."

"I'm sure it's enough to hang you, were it as small as the widow's mite."

"I was wearing a Union cap when your men attacked us for no reason at all." Under the laws of war, that was sufficient uniform to give him the protection of the laws of war among civilized nations.

"Cap, I see no cap."

"Well, saar, it was lost in the scuffle as those blackguards of the 29th who beat me black and blue. And me just taking a walk through the woods for me health."[3]

ST. BERNARD-DE-LACOLLE, 5:22 P.M., TUESDAY, MARCH 15

Lt. Gen. Sir James Hope Grant commanded Her Majesty's forces in British America. He had swept in like a whirlwind to crush the American relief of Portland at the battle of Kennebunk, Maine, in October but was too late to avert the catastrophe that befell the main British army at Claverack in upstate New York. Widely acknowledged as the best of Victoria's generals, it had not been his skill that had saved the Province of Quebec from Hooker's invasion, but the white curtain of a sudden early winter.

The snow was still on the ground when he began moving his Imperial (British) and Canadian battalions out of their winter quarters into field camps to the south of St. John, which the Quebecois insisted on calling Saint-Jean. He seldom saw his own headquarters as he moved from one camp to another down the still icy roads through the intermittent French farms and their enveloping forests of maple and oak, still black and leafless against the snow.

He met Brig. Gen. Garnet Wolseley at a country inn at Lacolle within rifle shot of the New York border. The one-eyed hero of Claverack had rallied the survivors in a running fight with Hooker's cavalry led by that wild yellow-haired brigadier. It was a brilliant retreat that already London was ranking with Sir John Moore's escape after Corunna. Jumped from lieutenant colonel to brigadier, he had become Grant's right-hand man.

Before long they were joined by Denison, who briefed them immediately. "A damned Irishman. An American scout, of course. Trying to get back to his lines, it seems. There were two; they stumbled upon my Guides coming back from the American side. Vile coincidence. There was a shootout, and two of my men were killed. Both Americans would have got away, but the picket guard came up too fast."

Wolseley's one eye focused. "God knows how long they had been behind our lines and what information they were bringing back. Did you get anything out of the Irishman?"

"No, damn his eyes. A cool one and impertinent." He recounted the interrogation, to his advantage, of course. His imitation of Hogan's brogue was quite good. At that Grant and Wolseley burst out laughing. Wolseley had a great contempt for the Irish. He had been born in Ireland, but made it clear at every opportunity to state he was not Irish but Anglo-Irish, a world of difference. He would have been only too happy to hang Hogan, but his reason had a sure break on his prejudices. "Well, let him think on the hangman's noose for a while, while we 'look' for this mysterious Union cap. It may curdle his Gaelic effrontery. Dead he's just another Irishman who won't be missed. Alive, he still may be of use to us."

He went on, "The lower class of Irishmen are the great danger. They have gone in such number to fill the ranks of the Northern Army, expressing the most decided hatred of the British government, forfeiting all allegiance to their mother country and vowing vengeance to all connected with it. The real born Americans might be treated as prisoners of war, as might the Germans and other foreigners, for thy owe our government no allegiance, whereas the Irish who may invade Canada are all traitors, having been born British subjects, they have no right to wage war against their real sovereign, and every Irishman found in Canada with arms in his hands ought to be strung up to the first tree they come to as traitors to their lawful king and country.

"Besides these who may be taken in the ranks of the enemy are many of the same class who have gone to Canada and having the same feeling as the others will be more likely to assist than oppose their countrymen. These characters are to be found about all the towns in great numbers and will not be easy to deal with. They know the country and can point out the places most worthy of notice and eligible for plunder."[4]

Wolseley had warmed Denison to the subject of loyalty. "I can answer for Her Majesty's Canadian subjects. The descendants of those who removed here from America are loyal to the core. They have been reinforced by generations of officers and soldiers who have settled here and were followed by immigrants of the better class from the old country. In all fairness there have been many Americans who have settled here, and their children are good and loyal subjects."

"But our French inhabitants are not of a very warlike habit, I must admit. If the Americans get across the border here, they will find themselves in French territory. At the same time they dislike the Yankees, and would not willingly submit to their rule. They are fonder of their own laws that they still possess and are more attached to them and their religion than they be to any rule Brother Jonathan might wish to introduce. They are quite under the control of their priests and will be guided by them. So it is not likely any Americans would be tolerated." He grew thoughtful for a moment. "What they might be, were the Americans to win, is another consideration."

Grant had not said much. He was not a big talker, and what he did say was laconic to the point of obscurity. Whatever he said, though, was likely to be accompanied by a lot of praying. And now his mind was on the escaped scout. He had to assume the scout would report what he had surely seen. Grant struck his fist into the palm of his other had. He said, "We move now."

HEADQUARTERS, ARMY OF NORTHERN VIRGINIA, GORDONSVILLE, VIRGINIA, 1:25 P.M., THURSDAY, MARCH 17, 1864

It was a worried Lt. Gen. James Longstreet who rode the last leg of his journey from Tennessee by train. His staff had never seen him so withdrawn and tactfully left him to his thoughts. He hardly noticed the fact that the train made the best time that line had seen since the war started was pulled by a new English engine of great power.

His thoughts were with the two divisions of his once mighty First Corps of the Army of Northern Virginia that he had led to Tennessee just in time to cinch the great victory at Chickamauga. They were in the long line of trains that would be arriving over the next few days. Only half the men he had led West were still with the colors. The rest were dead, filling the hospitals of Atlanta, or prisoners of war.

Failure like shrieking furies gave him no piece. He had replaced Lt. Gen. Braxton Bragg, who had let slip a complete victory at Chickamauga and bungled the siege of the Chattanooga where the rest of the Union Army of the Cumberland had fled. Then, folly upon folly, Bragg had tried to relieve his chief of cavalry, the terrifying Nathan Bedford Forrest. He especially terrified Bragg as much as he did the Yankees. He tried to take Forrest's cavalry away from him with an order sent by messenger so he would be as far away as possible when the volcano flew. Distance did not allow Forrest to cool. He tracked Bragg down to the other end of the Confederate lines, called him out, and shot him in the foot. Had he thought Bragg was any sort of a man, he would have shot him dead. Both armies were intent on the upcoming court-martial of the famous Forrest.

The command of the Army of Tennessee had fallen into Longstreet's lap almost by acclamation of the army; President Davis's orders were a simple ratification. Now in command, Longstreet acted with all the determination and daring of the man Lee called "My Old Warhorse." He threw his First Corps at Brown's Ferry, the open jugular of the trapped Army of the Cumberland in Chattanooga. The Ferry was hardly defended, and he approached in the cloak of dusk. They had charged into hell. It was Malvern Hill and Pickett's Charge all over again.

He could still hear the high-pitched whine of what he later learned were Mr. Gatling's repeating guns. All he could see in the gloom was the muzzles sparking orange as they fired and fired with that devil's own high-pitched whine. He saved what he could that night.

By late November, Grant had maneuvered and fought him out of his stranglehold on Chattanooga. Then it was a fighting retreat back into Northern Georgia, relieved only by the brilliant defensive operations of Maj. Gen. Patrick Cleburne, whom Davis would call "The Stonewall of the West." Lee insisted that Longstreet and his corps return to the Army of Northern Virginia. It was painful to turn over the army to another and more painful still to know that Davis had not appointed the man he had strongly recommended — Cleburne's sin had been to write a manifesto in January recommending that freedom be offered to any slave (and his family) who was willing to fight for the Confederacy. He had concluded that even with the French and English as allies, the Southern manpower well had run dry and that slavery should be sacrificed for independence. Davis had been outraged and ordered the manifesto suppressed. He also blighted the advancement of the finest officer outside of Lee's army.[5] With his new allies, he believed victory was certain and required no concessions on the South's peculiar institution.

Lee and an honor guard were waiting for Longstreet at the Gordonville station. He quickly noticed that the guard and the band were in completely new gray regulation uniforms of good cut. Lee came forward as Longstreet dismounted the train and saluted his old commander. The furies seemed to recede out of respect for Lee. For a moment as he looked into Lee's warm brown eyes, he felt like he was home again. Lee said simply, "Welcome back, General. The army is whole again with its First Corps come home. Let us ride to headquarters."

That ride was a revelation. Everything in the camp was new. There were acres of new white tents and row after row of fine new English artillery. As on the station, every man was in a new, well-cut regulation uniform, and the men no longer had that constantly hungry look. It was more than a shock; it did not look like the same army where there was no such thing as uniformity, a hungry army living from hand to mouth. There had been a certain virtue and fortitude in such storied want. This new plenty would take getting used to.

There was more than that to widen his eyes. He saw dozens of men in British scarlet and French dark-blue tunics and red trousers, more of the latter, though. Lee could see his surprise and said, "Our liaisons, General. There must be several hundred with us, about two-thirds French, I would stay. President Davis is much put out that the English have not agreed to a formal alliance as have the French. The English say that a co-belligerence is sufficient to both our purposes."

Longstreet said, "We hardly saw a single Frog in Tennessee."

Lee went on. "More importantly, English and French weapons and supplies are coming in to our ports faster than we can unload them. Iron rails by the tens of thousands are allowing us to rebuild our railroad system. You know how often our subsistence hung by thread because the railroads were falling apart. There is no little satisfaction that these rails before England entered war were going to the North."[6]

Longstreet noticed that Lee was his old self again, not the man who had offered after Gettysburg to relinquish command the army that had become indelibly associated with the name Lee. Longstreet, though, rather than being reassured became suddenly apprehensive. He could hear the screeching of the furies and the high-pitch whine from hell.[7]

HEADQUARTERS, FORTRESS PORTLAND, MAINE, 1:38 P.M., THURSDAY, MARCH 17, 1864

"Balloons! Balloons!" Every head turned to the south where the soldier pointed. A few men scrambled to the top of the piles of snow-crusted broken brick and timber that had once been the stout homes and businesses of Portland.

"Hurrah!" rent the air as hats flew and men stomped the ground in glee. Maj. Gen. Joshua Lawrence Chamberlain choked back the overpowering urge to burst into tears of relief. His brother slapped him on the back, "Lawrence, Lawrence, we're saved. Hallelujah! God be praised!" Other men were weeping as Chamberlain composed himself.

"Tom, get a hold of yourself. Run to the square and see that the crews are ready to secure the ropes." The younger man was off in a sprint. Chamberlain sat on a stump of a wall to think now that hope had come alive again. Sharpe had come through. In the six months of grim siege, Chamberlain had clung to the order from the President that Sharpe had slipped through the lines. "Hold on, Gallant Portland. Help is on the way." With the messenger, one of the fabled scouts of George H. Sharpe, were a pair of the most beautiful major general's shoulder straps he had ever seen. His defense of his state's capital had jumped him from colonel to major general in one leap. He laughed to himself when he thought that it had been his opponent, Lt. Gen. Sir Hastings Doyle, who had chivalrously informed him of his promotion, so cut off had the garrison been in the early stage of the siege.

More of Sharpe's messengers had slipped through in the succeeding months to keep Chamberlain apprised of events in the country and the efforts being made to come to the relief of Portland. Chamberlain could hardly believe what the men related. A great fleet of balloons was building, bigger than anything dreamed of before, able to carry the ammunition that was running low. As a harbinger of that promise, every few weeks a balloon or two of the size Chamberlain had seen with the Army of the Potomac drifted across the sky to settle among the ruins to unload a few hundred pounds of medical supplies and valuable small weight supplies and carry off a half–dozen wounded and sick.

Somehow the word had got out of the fleet of giant balloons that would be the salvation of Portland, and now the entire garrison had come alive cheering and waving flags as the squadron neared. The word had got out to the British as well. Their camp had also come alive but with planned purpose.

From four thousand feet and a dozen miles away, Col. Thaddeus Lowe scanned with his long brass glass the siege-shattered city, the enemy lines, and the Royal Navy ships that stopped up Portland Harbor. This was his hour, Commander of the United States Balloon Corps. He had been recalled from failure by Sharpe, who rescued him from the Army's mismanagement and placed him under his own Central Information Bureau (CIB), with a purse that had no bottom. Plans that had been only dreams in the minds of America's foremost aeronaut suddenly had been turned into reality as the workshops, factories, and foundries of the Union had bent to the will of war. Sometime in the winter the name was changed from balloon to airship.

Lowe rode his flagship, the airship *George Washington*, the first of its class of fifty of the U.S. Army's great ships of the air, followed by the *Nathaniel Greene*, the second of the great airships. Lowe looked about him at the Leviathan of the Air, as he called it, at the huge cigar-shaped balloon encased in its frame of the thinnest lathe. The lift given by the great hydrogen balloon was immense by any standard, five full tons of cargo. But even more amazing was the freeing of the balloon from the whims of the air's currents. In a special frame was a small steam engine, adapted from the Navy's steam launch engine, that powered a propeller that gave the balloon thrust. It had been reengineered to half its size and its body comprised of the thinnest possible steel, instead of iron, and galvanized with tin or plated with copper to prevent any accidental ignition. The new War Industries Board (WIB), under the steady hand of that "Scotch devil," Andrew Carnegie, had assigned this project the highest priority to bring together the best engineers, machine-shops, and materials. But ten men had died until the exhaust filters had been devised to capture the smallest spark from the long exhaust tube that trailed behind the balloon.

The British had seen the air armada as well. Hastings Doyle rushed out of his tent at the alarm. An aide ran up and handed him his glass. "Wolseley's intelligence was spot on," he said to himself, lost in wonder at the approaching armada of the air. The camp was all action now as the entire besieging force put the "balloon" plan, as it was dubbed, into operation. That plan was the result of analysis by the Montreal Ring as the group of talented men Wolseley had gathered around him was called. They had culled every bit of information from the Royal Navy's experience in the Battle of Washington and that of their Confederate allies.

The British government had been loath to enter into a full alliance with the Confederacy. It was a diplomatic high-wire act of sorts. To most of the British public, the Confederacy represented slavery, a thoroughly odious practice the Empire had outlawed in 1833. You could not find a Briton to support it though you looked high and low. So the war had to be dressed up in patriotic ribbons as an outraged response to the unprovoked American destruction of a Royal Navy frigate in British waters. That the American warship had been hunting down a British-built Confederate commerce raider that British connivance had allowed to escape Liverpool harbor, was something that was known in too many quarters. So diplomatic distance had to be kept between Her Majesty's government and Mr. Davis's. It was easier said than done, as a forest of masts of British ships loaded with the materials of war crowded the major Southern harbors no longer shut by the Union blockade, as the hospitals of Charleston were still filled with wounded British sailors from the Third Battle of Charleston, as the Southern navy yards serviced the Royal Navy before their own ships, and as the flow of intelligence from the Confederacy on their common enemy flowed unstinted.

And now the fruit of that relationship was about to be tested. Crews rushed to the new anti-balloon gun battery. These were Armstrong guns that had been remounted on the strangest contraptions, more like huge lazy susans that could easily pivot in any direction. The guns were fitted into elevated carriages mounted on rails that would absorb the recoil.

The airships were heading for the center of Portland when the battery opened fire. One shot passed directly over Lowe's head and between the struts that held the balloon to the basket. He scanned the enemy camp with his glass and found the strange battery. He said, "Helmsman, take us over that battery. Signal the *Greene* to follow us."

The closer they got to the battery, the more accurate the guns became, sending shot after shot through the balloon gasbags. Unfortunately, simply penetrating the gasbags did nothing more than let out hydrogen. There was no ignition of the escaping hydrogen, which, lighter than air, drifted upward and away from the engines. Lowe was about to compensate for the loss of lift by getting rid of some weight.

When they were directly overhead, the bombs went over the side, specially redesigned 72-pound 9-inch shells. As they fell earthward, a British shell found the *Greene*'s basket. It disintegrated in a shower of debris, its engine falling like a huge stone to crash and careen through a line of tents as a spark ignited the hydrogen-laced air in a thunderous pulse of blue-orange fire. The *Washington*'s bombs laced across the battery as the *Greene* died in flames and floated earthward. They fell over the battery, smashing the gun carriages on their pivots and wiping out their crews.

Lowe was not satisfied and pointed to the helmsman a position behind the British lines. "Take me there." The airship sailed over the British camp, alive with running men, many of them firing upward. There below them appeared the British ammunition dump upon which Lowe dropped the last of his bombs. The force from the exploding dump physically pushed the airship away even as it was turning back to Portland.[8]

A SPECIAL RAILROAD CAR TRAVELING NORTH BETWEEN ALBANY AND PLATTSBURG, NEW YORK, 10:00 A.M., FRIDAY, MARCH 18, 1864

Ulysses S. Grant looked out at the endless dense forests broken only by the occasional small town as his special train chugged north from the ruins of Albany. The view enforced a concentration which was just what he needed. He was on his way to inspect the Army of the Hudson and interview its commander. The three stars of a lieutenant general glittered on his shoulder straps. It was a rank only once held before and that by George Washington and no one since. Until now.

Grant was not immune to ambition, but he controlled it better than the man he was going to see. He let his deeds carry his ambition.

He caused Lincoln few headaches and just got things done, to the enormous relief of the commander-in-chief. So when Lincoln came to make the choice for a single all-powerful general-in-chief, he found it easy. Grant had never boasted that the country needed a dictator, as had Hooker before Chancellorsville. Grant had never created cabal after cabal to undermine his predecessors as had Hooker. Grant had just laid victories before Lincoln and asked for little.

Hooker's ego had been riding as high as one of Lincoln's balloons after saving New York at the battle of Claverack in New York, the same day of the Royal Navy-Confederate attack on Washington. He had become the darling of the press, which he took great efforts to seduce. Hooker's supporters had pointed out that Hooker had laid the glorious laurels of Claverack at the nation's feet. Yes, but Grant had given the country Forts Donelson and Henry, Shiloh, Vicksburg, and latest of all, Chattanooga. He had come to the rescue of the trapped and dying Army of the Cumberland, saved it, and defeated his old friend Longstreet.

But it was Hooker who was much on Grant's mind. He was not a subordinate man. Meade, on the other hand was exactly that. Grant had just come from his headquarters at the Army of the Potomac fully having intended to replace him with one of his own family of generals from the West. But Meade beat him to the point and graciously offered to step down so that Grant could have full confidence in the commander of the Army of the Potomac. Of course, Grant had declined to replace Meade after that act of selflessness.[9]

It was vital that all his army commanders pull together as a team. He would trust Sherman with his life, Thomas was sound as a rock, and Meade was selfless and reliable. That left Hooker. He turned to Sharpe, the only other man to share his cabin. Lincoln trusted him implicitly and seemed to rely on him in countless ways. Only William Seward, the Secretary of State, shared such confidence. Grant was about to find what sort of man this nondescript man in his early thirties was: middle height, short dark hair on a round head, and drooping mustache. Not much to look at, but Grant, of all men, was not concerned about looks. What could the man do was the question he always asked. Grant had not batted an eye in dismissing old friends who were not up to the job. Weeks ago he had already answered his own question when Sharpe presented his first weekly intelligence summary to him in December after Chattanooga when Lincoln summoned him to Washington. Grant had never had such a comprehensive look at the enemy before. He had been happy in the past just to find the enemy and then hang on to the death. That had served as an army commander, but to lead a nation in war needed more, far more. And Sharpe spilled his treasures out every week for Grant.[10]

One of the choicest gems had not cost the Treasury a penny but had been found right out in the open, fished out of the Library of Congress. The British very conveniently published with great regularity the *United Service Magazine and Naval and Army Journal*. Sharpe had brought in his order-of-battle office chief. In an army of young men, Grant was startled by how young this lieutenant colonel was. The only thing that marred his youthful appearance was the red gash of a scar across his forehead. Sharpe said, "General, may I present Lt. Col. Mike Wilmoth. He keeps track of the enemy for me."

Grant nodded and said, "Colonel, how old are you? And where are you from?"

"Twenty-four, sir. Indiana."

Sharpe added, "Colonel Dahlgren is not even twenty-one, General. And like Dahlgren, his appointment is directly from the President for both valor and ability. I will tell you about that later, sir. Go on, Mike."

Wilmoth unrolled a large map of the British Isles. "General, the British print every few months a complete list of the stations of the British Army around the world. Our latest issue states the list is corrected to the twenty-seventh of August last [Appendix A]. It tells us where every battalion, battery, and engineer company was located at that time. The dots on the map represent infantry battalions. Most of their regiments consist of a single battalion numbering about a thousand men, a few have two battalions, and only a handful three or four. Cavalry regiments have only one battalion. So it's easier just to show the battalions. Each dot indicates how many battalions are at each location. We count thirty-one cavalry regiments and one hundred fifty-two infantry battalions. Their distribution around the world tells us what they likely are able to send to North America."

He unfolded another chart. "In Great Britain and Ireland they had forty infantry battalions and thirteen cavalry regiments. The Mediterranean garrisons had thirteen infantry battalions, the West Indies six, Australia and New Zealand seven, Africa five, China three, and Mauritius two. In India and Ceylon there are fifty-two infantry battalions and twelve cavalry regiments. The establishments of these units appear to be smaller than those in Britain. But we assess that the British Army has two hundred twenty thousand regulars of which about one hundred thousand are in the British Isles."

Sharpe interrupted here. "What is important here, sir, is that almost half of the British Army is unavailable for use in North America. They won't touch as much as drummer boy in their Indian garrison, not after having the bejezus scared out of them by the Great Mutiny just seven years ago. And just to make sure, our Russian friends are making mischief out there from their conquests in Central Asia. If there's an ember of the Great Mutiny left in the subcontinent, the Russians will find it and blow gold dust on it. India is the famous jewel in the crown, the source of most of their imperial wealth, the lodestone of empire. They dare not risk it. Another large force is tied down with a very serious native revolt in New Zealand." He nodded to Wilmoth to continue.

"Before the war they had reinforced their forces in Canada to fourteen battalions, of which four were destroyed outright at Clavarack. Just before the battle, they landed another twenty thousand men through the captured ports of Maine, marched them around Portland to the Grand Trunk Railroad. That force consisted of thirteen battalions, two cavalry regiments, and two artillery brigades. The entire force was from the British Isles." For the first time, Wilmoth glanced at his notes. "Yes, one of them is another battalion, the 2nd, of the Grenadier Guards."

Sharpe added, "Oh, yes, they took the loss of the 1st Battalion very, very badly. So the 2nd will have to go and wade through a river of Yankee blood to set the world right again."

Grant was soaking up every word as he calmly puffed on his ever-present cigar. He asked, "Well, where else can they find troops to send over here?"

Wilmoth said, "Their Mediterranean garrisons can supply another half-dozen battalions since the main threat had been the French, and they are now allied with the British. Perhaps two from the West Indies, one from China, and one or two from Africa. Perhaps ten in all."

"Are they tapped out in the British Isles? Can they send more than what they already have?"

"Yes, General, I believe they can. Late in the fifties there was another French invasion scare, and they created Rifle Volunteer Corps battalions. The public response was very enthusiastic. Even though each man had to supply his own uniform and rifle, they raised over two hundred thousand men in these units. They already had a hundred fifteen thousand or so in the Yeomanry, cavalry organized mostly around the tenants on the great estates, and the militia.[11] Parliament recently passed a law allowing these RVC battalions to be deployed overseas in wartime." He looked at Grant as if he were enjoying a private joke. "People think that only stolen secrets are valuable, but it is amazing what you can find right out there in the open in the Library of Congress."[12]

Sharpe laughed. "Didn't have to pay a penny for that information, either."

Grant puffed an artful ring of smoke. "So the enemy is patriotic too. How unfortunate for us." He smiled. "So, let me see if I read the implications here. They still have another twenty-seven battalions in the British Isles. Theoretically, they could send over the entire force and backfill it with these rifle corps. Right?"

"Theoretically, yes, General. But they would never send all the royal guard regiments over."

Sharpe said, "Yes, they parade too well to actually get dirty. You'd have to scare them near to death, and that would take a Napoleon on the loose from Elba.

"That brings me to the main purpose of our meeting, General. The President wants to scare them, yes, but in such a way that they keep everybody at home, regular and volunteer."

Grant put out his cigar and leaned forward.

PLATTSURGH RAILROAD STATION, 12:10 P.M., FRIDAY, MARCH 18, 1864
"Damn." Grant's jaw set as his train rode into the station. He had informed Hooker that he most emphatically did not want any special military show for his visit. And there it was — an entire brigade drawn up as an honor guard and massed regimental bands thundering away. It was lost on him; he liked to say he could recognize only two tunes — one was "Yankee Doodle", and the other wasn't. More to the point, he hated to think how long the men had been there in the chill.

He glanced at Sharpe, who just shrugged knowingly. Grant had asked Sharpe blunt questions about Hooker. It was Hooker as the new commander of the Army of the Potomac in February 1863 who had appointed to Sharpe to create something entirely new in the world of war, a professional organization devoted to the collection and analysis of intelligence, the Bureau of Military Information (BMI). It was Sharpe who handed Bobby Lee's head on a silver platter to Hooker. Within two months of taking the job, Sharpe and his small staff had identified the location of almost every regiment in the Army of Northern Virginia, calculated its strength to within a handful of men, and put his finger on the miserable state of their logistics and communications. This was the genesis of the Chancellorsville campaign.[13]

All Hooker had to do was execute his own plan boldly, but he hesitated while that man wild Jackson's Second Corps had fallen upon his flank like the hounds of hell. Still he might have pulled it off. He rode bravely in front of his battle line on his white horse to rally the men. Yet the odds had lengthened when a cannon ball shattered the porch post next to him throwing half the bean to strike him along the length of his body, badly concussing him. He wandered in a daze into defeat.

Again it had been Sharpe who had been first off the mark in discovering Lee's movement to invade the North in June 1863. On Sharpe's word, Hooker moved the Army of the Potomac so fast that it crossed the Potomac River ahead of the Army of Northern Virginia. But in the weeks that followed, Hooker's confidence frayed, and he lashed out at everyone, saying things to Sharpe that all around them considered something no gentleman should endure.[14] Hooker's growing hysteria had alarmed Lincoln so much that when the general threatened to resign once too often, the President promptly accepted.

This was the man who had left his command drenched in failure, drinking the dregs of humiliation both for his soldier's pride and his overweening ambition. The irony was that he was a brave man and a good fighting general. When the British invaded upstate New York that September shortly after the war started, seized Albany, scorched the Hudson Valley, and threatened New York City itself, Hooker was in the city on leave. Two corps of Meade's Army had just entrained to go to the relief of the Army of the Cumberland shut up in Chattanooga when they were diverted to New York and ennobled with the new name of the Army of the Hudson.

The only man in New York with experience in commanding an Army was Hooker. Lincoln overcame his misgivings and his secretary of war's opposition by shrewdly observing that Hooker of all men had something to prove, a mighty motivator. Indeed he did, promptly marched north to glory and victory near a tiny hamlet called Claverack. Only the sudden onset of an early blizzard had stalled his pursuit just south of the Canadian border.

He spent the winter warmed with the glow of vindication, keeping court of sorts in Plattsburg for the throng of supporters who rushed there to feed his ambition. The hero of the Union, the savior and darling of New York, was thus shocked in February to read that Lincoln had appointed U.S. Grant as general-in-chief of the armies. His nose went noisily out of joint. Grant would have been deaf not to hear of it. More than a few men had pointed out that Hooker had formed just such a cabal to undermine his superior, Major General Burnside, after the battle of Fredericksburg.

Now Grant was stepping off the train straight into the sort of military spectacle that he disliked and put on by the man who coveted his job. On the platform was Hooker standing ostentatiously by himself with his entire staff and all his senior commanders behind him as a silent Greek chorus in a sea of flags and bunting.

Just then the honor guard shouted the first of three deafening huzzahs. Grant inwardly cringed but outwardly just hardened his face. Hooker and his entourage saluted. Grant returned the salute, and Hooker stepped forward to offer his hand. Grant took it and squeezed. Hooker returned the squeeze. The onlookers assumed the long handshake was sign of cordiality. They did not see the expressions on the two men as they kept on squeezing.

"I thought I made it clear there was to be no ceremony, General Hooker."

That, and the blood loss to his hand, made it clear to Hooker that his gracious insubordination had been noted. He suddenly let go and smiled. "It is a great honor to have you here. Allow me to introduce my officers."

Sharpe had remained on the shadowed step of the railway car. His eyes scanned the crowd until he found Lt. Col. John McEntee, Hooker's intelligence officer and Sharpe's old friend. The two were Ulster men from the Kingston-Roundout area of New York fifty miles up the Hudson from the city. When Sharpe started up the BMI, he had asked for McEntee and made him his deputy, and an able one he had been, shrewd and active.[15] When Lincoln brought Sharpe to Washington in July of the last year to create the NIB, McEntee had succeeded to his position with the Army of the Potomac. But Sharpe had pulled him out with a few order-of-battle clerks and a handful of good scouts to set up a BMI for the new Army of the Hudson. Because of McEntee and his team, Hooker had been able to fight Claverack with his eyes wide open. He owed no little thanks to them for the victory.

McEntee waited on the platform until the bigwigs moved off. He walked right over to Sharpe, who reached down to shake his hand. "Come on in, John. We need to talk." A big red-haired man had followed a few paces behind McEntee. Sharpe called out, "Sergeant Knight! Good to see you. Give the colonel and me a few minutes, then I want to talk to you." Knight nodded.

"Well, sit down, John." McEntee was a sharp-faced, wiry man, the kind who came to the point. "George, something is up. And I don't like it because I don't know what for sure. The enemy might as well have thrown up the Great Wall of China across the border. It has been well nigh impossible to get my scouts through to take a look. Jeb Stuart could take lessons from the security they have up there."

Sharpe knew it had to be Wosleley, his shadowy counterpart. Before this war, they had met at the Ebbit's Grill for dinner quite by accident and stared across the table, both pretending not to know who the other was. Wolseley had been playing the part of a British civilian visitor. By now Wilmoth had quite a dossier on him, savior of the beaten British Army at Clavarack and right-hand man to their new commanding general. He would have been disappointed if Wolseley did not have a thick file on him as well. Yes, it had to be Wolseley.

He said so. McEntee replied, "Well, Wolseley may be pulling strings up in Montreal, and the one who's closed the border, but it's that bastard Denison who is giving me fits. His Royal Guides are constantly probing our lines, and I know they are getting through. We've killed a few who got careless, which is something they don't often do. Knight can tell you about his run-in with them. But that's not why I brought him along. He just got back in late last night." He motioned through the window for Knight to come in. He looked at Sharpe. "There was a shootout, and they got young Hogan." Sharpe sighed. Hogan was one of the best scouts the army had for all his only twenty-two years, and a cheery young man, the kind that lights up a room.

Knight laid out a map. "We picked up the cipher from your agent outside Montreal."

McEntee pulled the cipher out of his coat pocket and gave it to Sharpe. "Hope you brought your cipher clerk? As you know, we don't have the cipher for this level code.

Sharpe looked around to the back of the car where a young corporal was sitting quietly. "Mason, time to do your magic." The young man disappeared with the ciphered message.

Knight went on, "It's only thirty miles or so to Montreal from the border." He smiled."I wish Richmond had been as close to the Army of the Potomac. Most of the area on both sides of the border is thick forest, maple and oak. It opens out a lot with French farms and villages the closer you get to Montreal. But we stuck to the woods even though we were wearing civilian clothes.

"General, for the last week, the Brits and Canadians have been moving south out of the Montreal area–horse, foot, and artillery. St. John is their headquarters, but they just kept moving south. There seemed to be a solid wall of pickets south of Lacolle and a lot of troops in the town too. Cavalry too, with lances. Never seen such fancy uniforms.

The locals all speak French. And since we don't, it made it kinda hard to fool information out of them in their own language like we used to do in Virginia. Then again, it was easy to pass ourselves off as English-speaking Canadians. The Frenchies, those who spoke some English, confirmed that troops were moving everywhere south. Farm horses and corn and hay commandeered for Crown promissory notes. They weren't too happy about that. A lot of them think those notes won't be worth much soon."

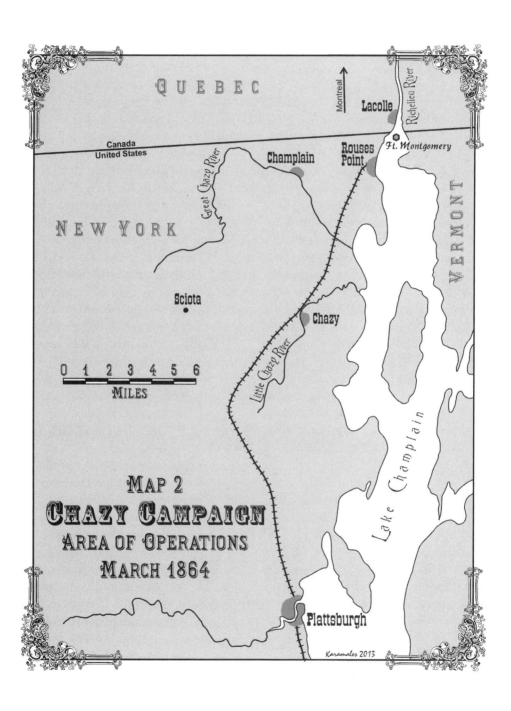

MAP 2
CHAZY CAMPAIGN
AREA OF OPERATIONS
MARCH 1864

Sharpe commented, "Yes, Jim McPhail's network up there is reporting that there are a lot of hands eager for American gold, such as the agent you met. Still, the reporting is also worrisome. The peace element up there, especially the English-speaking part has shut up. And the French haven't been too vocal either. Clavarack did something up there. It was like Fort Sumter for us. Fixed our resolve and put us in a fighting mood. You know, most of the English-speaking population is descended from Tories who fled after the Revolution. They may sound like us, but their attachment to the Crown is an inheritance they cherish."

McEntee laughed. "A lot of good it will do them. Come what may we will have Canada. The inhabited part doesn't go on and on like the Confederacy. The people peter out fifty miles north of the U.S. border. You know, people say that even if we don't subdue the South, we will have Canada as compensation."

Sharpe grew serious. "John, the people who have come to our country came because they wanted to be here, to be part of us. We've expanded across an almost empty continent that way, only a few Mexicans and Indians in the way. We've never attempted to conquer and incorporate three million people who never were and don't want to be part of the United States. Yes, we can conquer Canada, but keeping it will be more trouble than it's worth. We will be as popular as the English in Ireland. In any case, John, let's not count our chickens before they're hatched."

The cipher clerk returned to hand Sharpe the message. He read it and jumped out of his seat. "We need to find Grant and Hooker immediately."

THE NEW YORK–CANADIAN BORDER, TWO MILES NORTH OF ROUSE'S POINT, 1:20 P.M., FRIDAY, MARCH 18, 1864

Hope Grant sat his horse in a copse of trees out of sight of the American pickets a mile away. His greatcoat was buttoned tight against the early morning cold. His woolen scarf, a gift from some Canadian girl, "a war of red and white in her cheeks," wrapped his neck. "Damn," he muttered. He wondered if he might actually campaign in decent weather somewhere. India was, well, India, the proverbial sweatbox crawling with flies and doubling you over with Dehli belly. And Canada was an icebox that could turn fingers and toes black if you weren't careful. Nothing in between. Of course, there had been the north China plain in summer when he had led the expedition that sacked the Imperial Summer Palace and humbled All Under Heaven. Who would have thought China could be so hot?

He forgot the cold as the 9th (The Queen's Royal) Lancers trotted by with a troop of the Royal Guides riding ahead and a battery of Armstrong guns behind. At that very moment south of Rouse's Point, a handful of disguised Guides were cutting the telegraph wires to Plattsburgh. The 9th had been his own regiment in India, and under his command Victoria Crosses had rained down on its men for their deeds in the crushing of the Great Mutiny. They had earned from their enemies the epithet of "The Dehli Spearmen" and had been described by an ally as "the beau ideal of all that British Cavalry ought to be in Oriental countries." They wore a distinctive Uhlan type helmet with a brass badge of two crossed lances with a Crown resting above and "9th Lancers" below. Their dark-blue winter coats hid their blue and scarlet uniforms. Red and white pennons flew on their lances.

Following the lancers was the 1st Montreal Brigade, which had fought at Claverack, its Imperial and Canadian battalions brought back to strength by drafts from England and local recruiting. The First Battalion, the Rifles, uniformed in forest green and black, were out for revenge. The sting of defeat at Clavarack was still sharp. That had been the first field from which the Rifles had been driven since fighting the French in Spain, an intolerable shame that could only be wiped out in blood. Grant had kept them brigaded with the three Canadian battalions they had fought with, the oldest in the Canadian militia: 1st Battalion the Prince of Wales Regiment that had torn the hole through the Yankee ranks, that had almost collapsed their army; the 2nd Battalion Queen Victoria's Rifles; and the 3rd Battalion, Victoria Volunteers Rifles of Montreal (Appendix B). English-speaking Canada had been stunned by the defeat and such loss of life. But defeat presents a fork in the road, one to the emotional relief of surrender, the other to resolve. Canada had chosen the latter and was in this war to the knife.

Right after the Rifles came two full batteries of Armstrong guns. A lot of thought went into this unorthodox use of the guns. That use was meant to counter something the Americans had used to turn the tide at Clavarack.

Behind them came the 12th Brigade. First in column was the 78th (Highland) Regiment of Foot, the Ross-shire Buffs, their scarlet coats and buff facings, also hidden by their dark-blue greatcoats. Their shakos bore the elephant badge with the word "Assaye" to commemorate the future Duke of Wellington's great victory in India in 1803 and their fifty-four years service in the subcontinent (1803–57). Their motto was "Cuidich 'n Rhi" (Help to the King), as legend has it from the cry of Lord Kintail, ancestor of the MacKenzies of Seaforth, as he saved the Scottish king Alexander III from a charging stag. This war had found them at garrisoned at Dover from where they took ship in the great reinforcement that had brought Grant himself to Canada.[16]

Grant recognized its acting commander, Lt. Col. William McBean, VC. Home on leave from his own regiment, the 93rd Highlanders, the command of the 78th had fallen to him when its commander dropped dead of a heart attack. McBean had been in London at the War Office paying his respects when the word of the vacancy arrived by telegram. Timing was everything.

McBean was a man after Grant's own heart. He had risen from private to lieutenant colonel all in the 93rd and had won his Victoria Cross in the main breach of the Begum Bagh at Lucknow in 1858. A flood of mutineers were trying to escape when then Lieutenant McBean threw himself into their path, and with his heavy cavalry saber cut down ten in single combat. As a havlidar (officer) of the mutineers came at him, the Highlanders made ready to shoot him, but McBean called them not to interfere. So like heroes on the plains of Troy they fought it out with their swords, until McBean feinted a cut but then drove his point through the enemy's chest. As the rush of Highlanders passed him, he paused to pull out of his thigh the sword left by another mutineer. When the general pinned the VC on him and remarked that it was good day's work, McBean replied, "Tuts, tuts, it dina tak me aboune twenty meenits."

Behind the Highlanders marched the 26th Foot, which had been stationed in Gosport, Hampshire, and embarked at the same time. "More old friends," thought Grant. The 26th had been with him in China and now wore a dragon badge on their shakos in memory of that campaign. They had embarked along with the 73rd (Perthshire) Foot, which had marched down from Aldershot. This regiment had originally been the 2nd Battalion of the famed Black Watch (42nd Foot) and befitting its origin with the senior Highland regiment of the army, it had combat record of great distinction. Its self-sacrifice had become legend. In 1851 off Cape Town their transport sank. The women and children had been put into the boats when their officers told the men that the only way they could save themselves was to swim for the boats, but that might endanger the women and children. Not a man stirred from the ranks, and of the 357 men who drowned that day, fifty-six were from the 73rd, the most of any regiment on board. In 1862 the regiment had had the honor of Perthshire added to their designation in honor of their Highland origins.

Bringing up the tail of the column were several battalions of Canadian militia, for a brigade strength of over four thousand men and twelve guns. Behind them came another brigade. Grant had concentrated a full British division of four brigades, over seventeen thousand men. Another division was concentrated at St. John, ready to move.

Grant's mind was no longer with the marching columns, but casting deep across the border. Thanks to the Royal Guides and Wolseley's agents in the United States, he had a clear picture of the Army of the Hudson. Geography was the key to Hooker's fate. New York south of the border was sparsely inhabited. The thick forests of the Adirondack Mountains still hemmed men in to a narrow ribbon of partially cleared land of fields and orchards paralleling Lake Champlain, which still was too ice-choked to be anything but another barrier. Emptying into the lake were numerous creeks, most flanked by marshes. Most of the few towns were trumped-up villages hugging the lakeshore. The railroad was the only easy communication running along the lake.

Hooker's pursuit of the beaten British after Claverack had taken him as far as the border when an unseasonable blizzard had closed operations until spring. The harsh winter made it impossible to maintain his army in camps. He had to string out his regiments in the small towns running as far back as fifty miles from the border. Rouse's Point, just inside the border and next to where the Richelieu River emptied into the lake, was his forward position, which he garrisoned with a single brigade. Opposite Rouse's Point across a bridge was a small island on which the Union had built the three tier limestone Fort Montgomery now manned by artillery troops. Two miles to the west in the town of Champlain was another brigade. Six miles south was the third brigade in small town of Chazy (pronounced shai-ZEE).[17] These were the three brigades of the 2nd Division of Maj. Gen. John W. Geary's XII Corps.

The rush of volunteers and of discharged men returning to the colors after the joint blows of the British invasion and the Copperhead rising had filled out Geary's shrunken regiments, which required a major reorganization, as it did in the rest of the field armies of the Union.[18] For example, Col. Charles Candy's 1st Brigade (2nd Div, XII Corps) had marched to Clavarack with six regiments. The entire division consisted of 4,100 men in fourteen regiments. With the regiments now near full strength, only three were required to make a brigade. He now had eight thousand in nine regiments. Hooker formed the extra regiments into two more brigades, repeating the process throughout the rest of the Army of the Hudson. The extra brigades allowed him to create enough new formations so that both corps were at full establishment of three divisions of three brigades each, over fifty thousand men. Similarly his cavalry division, commanded by the boy wonder, the newly promoted Maj. Gen. George Armstrong Custer, had been raised to three brigades at five thousand men. With artillery and other arms, Hooker commanded over sixty thousand, a far cry from the twenty thousand he had led onto the field at Claverack.

On the other hand, Hope Grant had barely thirty thousand men south of Montreal, an equation that Hooker was looking forward to solving in the Spring. The Spring. It was a month away at least this far north. Even in Virginia Hooker had to wait until the end of April for the road to be dry enough and the forage beginning to sprout before beginning the Chancellorsville Campaign. He calculated he had another

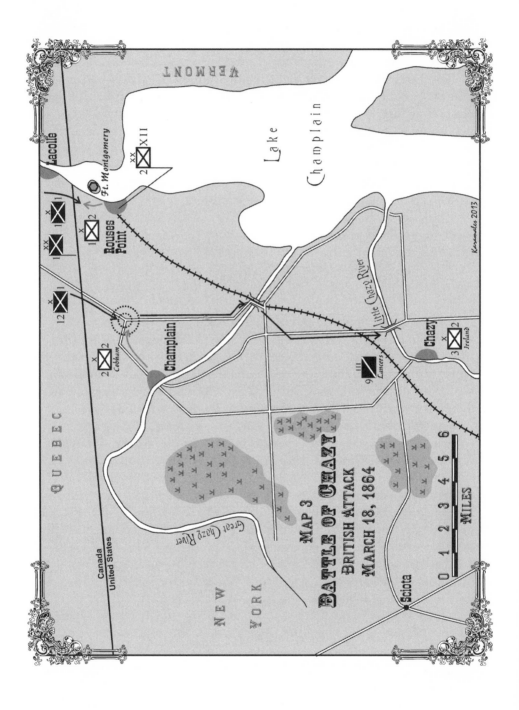

MAP 3
BATTLE OF CHAZY
BRITISH ATTACK
MARCH 18, 1864

month before it was feasible to attack, and he would be across the border on the first good day and plant the Stars and Stripes on old Montreal's citadel. He had been given to commenting, "Third time's lucky," to his staff, a reference to the American failures in the War of 1776 and 1812 to conquer Canada. He was too clever by half, and word of it had traveled to Washington and back up to Canada by way of Wosleley's organization in the North. He had leaked it to the press, which screamed it from every front page in British North America. You could hear the resolve tightening from Halifax to the Great Lakes.[19]

The story had also stopped off at the White House by way of Secretary of War Stanton, who had never been overly enamored of Hooker. Lincoln just shook his head. "Stanton, I tell you, if there is a man for counting his chickens before they are hatched, it is Hooker. Do you remember how before Chancellorsville, he had said, 'May God have mercy on General Lee for I shall have none'? To my mind, blaspheming is not a tactful way to start a campaign when you need everyone you can get on your side. Now, Hooker at least this time has not goaded the Almighty. I suppose there is that to be grateful about."

Stanton felt this was time to insert a knife. "I would not be surprised if he has started to talk again about how the country needs a dictator."

Of that Hooker was entirely innocent. He had taken that lesson to heart. Besides, he thought, the election was in November. Why talk about dictatorship when the presidency was guaranteed once he sat as conqueror in Montreal? For that reason, no man was more impatient for the daffodils to appear than Joseph Hooker. Yes, daffodils and Montreal. They made an appealing vision but one that was at least six weeks away. Right now his problem was entertaining U.S. Grant. After his victory, he would have Grant's job, and then after the election, he would have Lincoln's. He laughed to himself when it occurred to him that there were two Generals Grant standing in his way, briefly standing in his way, he thought.

HEADQUARTERS, ARMY OF THE HUDSON, PLATTSBURGH, NEW YORK, 1:20 P.M., FRIDAY, MARCH 18, 1864

U.S. Grant was puffing hard on his cigar as Hooker used the map to show the location of all his divisions. "I don't like it, Hooker, you're spread out too far. Geary's hung up there on the border all by himself. Your next division is here in Plattsburgh, all of twenty miles from Geary. That's a day's hard march."

"General, I can have this division there in a few hours by train."

"That's a mighty big assumption. Do you remember, Hooker, what the sergeants at West Point used to call the definition of the assumption?

The Mother of All Fuck Ups. I found that out at Pittsburg Landing two years ago. It is not an edifying experience, I can tell you."

He got up and stabbed at the map with his cigar. "I want you to concentrate the XII corps in the area of this triangle of Champlain and Rouse's Point and Chazy. Then I want you to have your next corps within supporting distance."

"But, General, the weather is still . . ."

"Hang the weather. I tell you, you should never toy with a man named Grant," he said. Grant hoped Hooker was clever enough to catch the double entendre. "Sharpe has filled me in on him. The man is the best they have. He moves like lightning and strikes like a sledgehammer. Much like someone we used to know in the Old Army, a certain Thomas Jackson. You remember Cadet Jackson, don't you?"

The mention of Stonewall Jackson, the author of Hooker's humiliation, only served to get Hooker's back up. He took a step forward when he heard loud voices in the outer room. Then the double doors swung open, Sharpe and McEntee followed by Knight stormed in followed by a clucking chief of staff and aides.

Sharpe spoke. "Gentlemen, I must speak to you alone. It is of the greatest urgency." Hooker signaled, the gaggle of onlookers fled, and the doors closed.

"The cipher that our man in Montreal passed to Sergeant Knight warns us that the enemy plans to attack us by the twenty-first. The British commanding general has ordered the concentration of thirty-five thousand men just south of St. John."

Hooker snorted, "Impossible. The weather works for him as little as it does for us. We are equally bound."

Grant said, "If I recall Prof. Mahan's class. That's what the Romans thought of Hannibal and the French of Suvorov."[20]

THE CANADIAN–AMERICAN BORDER BETWEEN LACOLLE AND ROUSE'S POINT, 2:07 P.M., FRIDAY, MARCH 18, 1864

The Rifles fanned out in open order with the Prince of Wales Regiment to their right and the other two Canadian battalions following to the rear. Both batteries rode behind the last battalions. They came out of the woods to cross a strip of fallow fields. On the other side was another woods hiding the American picket line. The pickets had been alert and were firing. A courier was galloping to summon their supports. The Rifles and Canadians made good time across the still frozen ground and burst into the woods driving the pickets back in a rush and out across the fields on the other side. Just as the Rifles and Canadians began to follow, a stream of fire laced along their front dropping a dozen men. As if on signal the rest fell back into the woods and took to the ground.

The next woodline was thickening with men in blue, the 29th Ohio Volunteer Infantry, but the source of that concentrated fire was a battery of what looked at that distance like small artillery pieces. These were the rapid-firing repeating coffee mill guns that had turned the tide at Claverack and cut down the Grenadier Guards like grass before the scythe just as the guardsmen were about to seal the British victory. American factories had worked around-the-clock shifts to send battery after battery to the field armies. Some were even getting the new repeating gun built by Mr. Gatling in Cincinnati. But Hooker had had priority for the coffee mills guns and had almost one battery of six guns per brigade.

For the attacking brigade to continue across that beaten zone would have been suicide. Just such a moment had been planned for. The Imperial batteries rode up into the woods; the guns were dragged through the trees and carefully positioned just inside the wood line. Spotters climbed up the trees and pinpointed the coffee mill battery. The steel breeches of the Armstrongs flew open to take their shells. They shone with polish, not a speck of rust. Too many had failed at Claverack because of lack of such elementary care. That had been taken care of through intensive retraining of the artillery, especially the NCOs, till it was a greater sin to find a speck of dirt on the inside of the breech than an unpolished button. These were the most accurate guns in the world and the first all-steel breech-loaders. There had been much conservative resistance to a gun that loaded from the wrong end, but defeat had been the most effective reformer.

It took only a few shells for adjustment and soon they were converging on the coffee mill battery in a hail of splinters that swept away the crews then began to fall among the trees shattering limbs to send swarms of deadly wooden splinters into the American infantry. Then the Rifles and Canadians rose to their feet, glad to be off the cold ground, and swept out of their woods. Their guns continued to fire over them driving the Americans deeper into woods. The infantry was able to close without much loss and drive the disconcerted Americans back from tree to tree.

The commander of the 9th Lancers waited with his men along the road to the rear watching the smoke from the infantry fight, impatient for his part. Then a rocket shot out of the woods, and he gave the command forward at the trot down the road. They passed through the woods just in time to see the Americans racing to the rear from the same woods over more farmland interspersed with orchards. They would have been easy to ride down, but he had other orders and continued along the road. They had not gone five hundred yards when they ran right into an American 3-inch battery galloping to the sound of the guns. Lances leveled the British cavalry rode right in among the guns and caissons, spearing man after man off horse and vehicle. In ten minutes the battery was a shambles, its 150 men dead, captured, or fled. The prisoners were let go to run away as the commander resumed the ride down the road. He had not time or men to waste on escorting prisoners to the rear.

After that taste of blood, the 9th was in high fettle. Cavalry hated the guns. Instead of more guns, they came across only an occasional rider or supply wagon and let them go minus their transport; nothing was to slow them down until they reached their objective, the railroad bridge over the Great Chazy River four miles south of the border. With the bridge taken, Geary's railroad communication with the rest of the Army of the Hudson would be cut and Hope Grant would have a sizable water barrier as an excellent defensive line.

Rouse's Point was alive with moving men. By sheer coincidence, the American division commander was inspecting the garrison brigade when the courier galloped into the town just as rumble of guns and rifle fire became audible. Maj. Gen. John W. Geary was not a man to sit idly by in an emergency. He ordered the garrison brigade forward with its two remaining regiments to the stem the British advance and completely missed the fact that the Lancers were now miles south of him. He had sent a rider to the brigade in Champlain three miles to the west to summon help, but the man had been snatched up by the Lancers. He was just riding out with the brigade as the military telegrapher ran out to tell him the wires were down. His alert to Hooker and his order for his third brigade at Chazy to march could not be sent. He would have to fight it out with what he had. He waved his hat to the two regiments, "Give 'em hell, Buckeyes!"

The men of the 5th and 7th Ohio Regiments needed no urging; the core of them were hard-bitten veterans who had rushed to the colors within weeks of the attack on Fort Sumter in April 1861. They knew their business. The enemy had driven the 29th Ohio out of the woods and were following close on their heels. The retreating Buckeyes passed through the intervals of the advancing two regiments. Their line of battle emerged from the crowd of retreating men and hit the Rifles and Canadians hard. A thick cloud of black powder smoke enveloped both firing lines. Geary decided to leave the brigade commander to do his job as he spurred off to personally bring up the brigade at Chazy.

Even though no messenger had got through to the brigade at Chazy, the sound of guns carried so well that even a deaf man could have heard. Yet its commander, Brig. Gen. George Cobham, waited for orders that never came. His regimental commanders implored him, but he waited and the men, all in marching order, grumbled. Forty minutes later, he ordered them forward. The relief of tension was such that the first regiment almost broke into a run to get started. In minutes the brigade of Pennsylvania regiments was rushing to the fight only a few miles away.

The country through which they advanced was rolling farmland and woods. Ahead of them was Prospect Hill, over which their road ran. It was the point to which Geary had headed with a few aides and a signal team, but the oncoming Lancers had forced them to hide in an orchard. For Geary it would be a long day. At that moment, Cobham rode ahead with an aide and reached the crest at the same moment as a dozen Highlanders, advance guard of the 78th Foot. Cobham promptly surrendered as a Highlander ran back to tell McBean of what they had seen coming up the road.

The British brigade commander was struck with the same indecision that had earlier afflicted Cobham. McBean, who had seen more active campaigning as a private in India than the lord commanding the brigade, drew his sword in an act of decision, and said loudly, "Send in the Tartan, man!"[21]

Shocked out his stupor, the man nodded. "Yes, of course. Off with you, McBean."

The Scotsman stood in his stirrups and shouted down the length of his column, "Cuidich 'n Rhi!" The men thundered back, "Cuidich 'n Rhi!" The 78th stepped off at the double quick, its companies moving from column to line lapping over both sides of the road as it climbed to the crest of the hill. Behind him a Royal Artillery battery lashed their horses forward to the top of the hill.[22]

The first the Pennsylvanians knew that the enemy was close was when the tide of Scots poured over the hill straight for them. McBean riding at their head ordered the charge, and now the Americans heard for the first time, the wail of "Cuidich 'n Rhi!" and the skirl of bagpipes. The lead regiment, the 109th Pennsylvania, tried to deploy into line, but the Highland tide with its leveled bayonets swept into them. They had hardly got off a shot before the impact. Then they were fighting for their lives against the best bayonet men in the world. They broke and fled to the rear pushing through the ranks of the next regiment trying to form, masking the pursuing Scots.

"On, laddies, on!" shouted McBean as he rode with the tide of his regiment. He did not see the battery of coffee mill guns unlimbering ahead of him. The retreating enemy masked them as well. The last of the fugitives had pushed themselves through the ranks of that part of the 29th Pennsylvania just ahead of him. The coffee mills now had a clear field of fire. Their *click-bang* staccato screamed as the Highlanders began to fall.[23]

3

"Press on, McBean, Press on!"

Fifteen ships rode at anchor in the bay. The six warships of the Russian squadron were by far the most powerful.[1] Most of the rest were fast screw transports. The only American warship was the USS *Kearsarge*. The Brooklyn Navy Yard had repaired the damage she had taken in the battle of the Upper Bay where the Royal Navy had pursued her. The British had taken it amiss that the *Kearsarge* had sunk a British warship that attempted to snatch back the British-built commerce raider it had just seized off the Welsh coast, the spark that had ignited this war.

Her captain, Roswell Hawk Lamson, had become a national hero for bearding the lion in his den and been jumped to the exalted rank of full captain, almost unheard of for a twenty-five-year-old. He had commanded the USS *Gettysburg* and sent off to intercept the Confederate commerce raider as it left Liverpool.[2] He did indeed seize it, but a British frigate thought otherwise. *Gettysburg* was getting the worst of it when *Kearsarge* appeared and put a lucky shot in the frigate's magazine. Aboard the *Kearsarge*, Lamson took command when her captain fell in the battle of the Upper Bay of New York. A grateful President had confirmed him in that command.[3]

Lamson was thin and dark haired with a vandyke beard he grew to make himself look older than he was. His youth made no difference to the Russian Naval Infantry who saluted him as he came over the side of the *Aleksandr Nevsky*, the squadron flagship. He was greeted by Admiral Lisovky's flag captain who was to escort him to the meeting of ship's captains. He had not taken two steps when an American colonel stumped through the crowed of officers, calling out, "Roswell, Roswell!"

A handsome blond young man, even younger than Lamson, came up and stuck out his hand. It was Ulrich Dahlgren, a colonel at twenty-one for his deeds at Gettysburg. The son of Rear Adm. John Dahlgren, he had lost a leg in the pursuit of Lee's army after Gettysburg and now dragged along a cork leg. He had been the best dancer in Washington, but a cork leg took the fun out of that. As it turned out, he was not the only beau to sit out the dances. All the girls flocked over to him and left the rest of the young men without partners. Losing the leg had interfered with his dancing, but he forced himself to learn to ride again and became again a fine horseman.

That leg had not stopped him from shimmying over a fallen mast to board HMS *Black Prince* at the battle of Charleston and accepting the surrender of its captain. He had been recuperating from the loss of his leg and visited his father commanding the South Atlantic Blockading Squadron off Charleston and had volunteered to help man a Marine gun crew on USS *New Ironsides*, his father's flagship. The U.S. Navy had been overjoyed to capture one of the two largest warships in the world, but it grated that it was an Army officer who had had the honor of its capitulation.[4]

Dahlgren and Lamson had met while the *Gettysburg* was under conversion to a warship the previous August. Lincoln had taken an interest in the ship and given it its name and dragged young Lamson off to meet Dahlgren as he was recuperating at his father's house near the Washington Navy Yard. They had hit it off immediately. Lincoln had commented that he liked his young stallions to run in the same pasture; each made the other run faster. Now they were in that proverbial pasture.

The object of their meeting today had been set in motion months ago. They had been called to Washington by Lincoln's direct order, all very mysterious, and met at the Willard Hotel in early December. As per their instructions they left the hotel at ten in the morning to find an enclosed carriage waiting for them. A lieutenant introduced himself and asked them to wait in the carriage. He said they were waiting for one other officer.

Sgt. Maj. William McCarter finally found him in Kelly's Saloon three blocks from the Willard. Maj. Gen. Thomas Francis Meagher was holding court to an admiring crowed of Irishmen. One of them was proudly reciting Meagher's grand speech to the English judge that had condemned him for his part in the Young Ireland rising of 1849.

"Pronounce then, my lord, the sentence which the laws direct, and I will be prepared to hear it. I trust I shall be prepared to meet its execution. I hope to be able, with a pure heart and perfect composure, to appear before a higher tribunal, a tribunal where a judge of infinite goodness will preside and where, my lord, many of the judgments of this world will be reversed."

Hearty applause and cheers filled the saloon as Meagher raised his glass to the crowd. His face was flushed, and McCarter had seen this before in his chief before. Then Colonel Meagher had resigned in despair at the hard use of his old Irish Brigade. Now he was the glory of both America and Ireland, the man who had saved the day at Clavarack commanding the once reviled XI Corps.

McCarter pushed through the crowd to gently take Meagher by the arm and whisper to him. "They are waiting for you, General. You must not be late."

Then to McCarter's distress, Meagher spoke expansively to the crowd waving his glass. "Men of Ireland, it will be but a few short months until Canada falls to the grand Army of the Hudson in which ten thousand of our countrymen serve. If you could only be with us when an Irishman hauls down England's flag from the fortress at Montreal!" The crowd went wild with a roar that shook the windows.

"And I tell you that when that day comes, England will have to free Ireland to get Canada back!" This time the crowd surged to Meagher and lifted him on their shoulders carrying him in vivid procession around the saloon. It was all McCarter could do to finally pull Meagher away and out the door. His walk back to the Willard was none too steady.

McCarter had to help him into the carriage. Meagher grinned. "Well, Col. Dahlgren, what a surprise. The last time we met was before Gettysburg, you were still a captain and one of my aides, and now if the newspapers are only half correct, by rights you should be a general." Dahlgren introduced him to Lamson. "Ah, another hero!" He heartily shook Lamson's hand. He leaned back and said, "We heroes three! Yes, there must be some desperate business about for the three of us to be in the same carriage on confidential orders."

Meagher glowed with an easy charm that attracted other men to him. Above all he was what the Irish called a proper gentleman: a faultless education, a gracious manner, and a poetry about him of ancient Irish heroes and their bards.[5] He had recruited the Irish Brigade and led it sword in hand to bloody glory on field after field. His men had called him Meagher of the Sword, an epithet he treasured more than any other. A superb battlefield commander, he was always where danger was the thickest, some said. Others said that his nerve had failed at Fredericksburg, where he lingered in the town while his men marched into slaughter.

He had come to America in probably the most dramatic fashion possible. His sentence to death was commuted to life exile to the western fastness of Australia. An American ship, the *Elizabeth Thompson*, chartered by his Young Ireland friends in America, had swooped down at a prearranged time and snatched him from the shore of Van Dieman's

Land. In America his cause remained the freedom of Ireland, and when Civil War came, he recruited the famed Irish Brigade to lead it through a hail of lead to earn a reputation for high-flying bravery second to none. One familiar observer noted, "Other men go into fights finely, sternly, or indifferently, but the only man that really loves it, after all, is the green immortal Irishman. So there the brave lads from the old sod, with the chosen Meagher at their head, laughed and fought, and joked as if were the finest fun in the world."[6]

Suffering an emotional breakdown at the sight of some much blood and carnage after Fredericksburg, Meagher resigned his commission.[7] That had been a mistake, and he came to abase himself in the corridors of power to be returned to the colors, but no one had time for this washed-up Irishman. That is, until the British attacked up through the Upper Bay of New York and fought a battle for all the city to see. He had recruited fifteen thousand Irish in two days and received in thanks a major general of volunteers commission. Hooker chose him to command the XI Corps, which he led gallantly at Clavarack.

Now he was in the closed carriage with two of the most famous young men in America. As the carriage clattered up Vermont Avenue, Meagher said to the escort, "And let me ask the obvious question, Lieutenant. Where is it we are going?"

"Sir, we are going to the President's cottage at the Old Soldiers Home."

"And now that you are in a talking mood, young man, could you be telling us *why* we are going to the President's cottage at the Old Soldiers Home?"

"I am not at liberty to say, General."

Meagher just smiled as Dahlgren and Lamson looked at each other in expectation of an adventure in the making. The carriage turned onto Rhode Island Avenue and in a few minutes onto 7th Street. In a few more minutes, they had left the city behind them and were driving through the country. There was not much traffic on the road. They passed a small broken-down one-pony cart on the side of the road and around a bend two men walking on the road gingerly trying to avoid the mud holes. One was a bearded civilian, the other was a soldier on crutches. Dahlgren stuck his head out of the window and ordered the driver to stop. The lieutenant looked flustered and said, "Gentlemen, my orders were that we were to stop for nothing."

But Dahlgren was already stepping down from the carriage, stepping awkwardly with his cork leg. The two men had stopped and were looking at them. The soldier saluted, and the civilian said, "Good day, sir." Dahlgren noticed that the civilian's blue eyes shone with a sympathy he had seen in few men.

Dahlgren asked, "Was that your cart back there?" The bearded man said yes. "And where are you going?"

The bearded man replied, "I was taking this soldier back to the Harewood Hospital nearby when the cart broke down. It looks to rain, and I thought we could not wait for a ride that might never show." He went on to say that he was a volunteer helper at the military hospitals in Washington. The young soldier had been lost in the shuffle of being transferred up by rail from the Army of the Potomac.

"Well, then we are your ride," Dahlgren said. The escort started to insist on not being diverted, but Dahlgren put him his place. An officer took care of his men, and they took care of him. More than that, a soldier was in a profound sense responsible for every other soldier.

It took only a few minutes to find the hospital to drop off the two men. The civilian extended his hand to Dahlgren. "Thank you kindly, Colonel."

Dahlgren replied, "It has been our pleasure. It is good work you do for the men, Mr...."

"Whitman," the man said. "Walt Whitman."

HEADQUARTERS, ARMY OF THE HUDSON, PLATTSBURGH, NEW YORK, 2:15 P.M., FRIDAY, MARCH 18, 1864

Hooker's military telegraph noted the break in the wire the same time as Geary's. They did not think it ominous. The severe winter had brought wires down before, and everyone knew active campaigning was at least a month away. The first Hooker and U.S. Grant heard of the downed wires was when an aide rushed back to tell them that the order to alert Geary could not be sent because of a break in the wire somewhere between them. By then, though, the orders had already been rushed to Brig. Gen. Thomas Ruger to move his first division by train to reinforce Geary.[8] Bugles were echoing through the town just as the men were lining up to eat.

Hooker was on the first train, and to his surprise and annoyance, so was the General-in-Chief of the Armies of the United States. Grant had intended to accompany one of his major field armies in the upcoming campaign season, and now was as good a time as any. Sharpe and his small staff also climbed aboard. It was already dark when the train pulled out with its command car and a full brigade loaded in the cars behind. Hooker ordered the engineer to open the throttle wide. It would take less than an hour to get to Fort Montgomery at this speed.

But for the mischief of the Royal Guides it could have done just that. Six miles north of Plattsburgh, a heap of brush and deadwood gathered under a railroad bridge was fired. The flames shot up to curl around the sides of the bridge and lick up through the open ties.

PROSPECT HILL, CLINTON COUNTY, NEW YORK, 2:35 P.M., FRIDAY, MARCH 18, 1864

As soon as the last Union soldier from the regiment shattered by the Highlanders had run past, the coffee mill guns opened up on their pursuers. The front ranks of the Scots went down as if they had been tripped by a wire. That was the moment as well when the commander of the Royal Artillery battery on Prospect Hill could direct his guns accurately. The press of the retreating enemy had masked the coffee mill guns. Now that they were clear, the flash of their muzzles in the growing dusk picked them out. The British gunners had despaired that the enfolding gloom would make them useless, but now they had just enough light left. The captain shouted, "Fire!" Projectiles from the six steel breech-loading guns spat down the hill and right into the enemy battery. The Armstrong guns were the most accurate in the world, and the British gunners were unequaled. Now that they had learned that the delicate pieces demanded constant attention to keep the breeches clean in order to seal properly, they were like Jupiter hurling thunder bolts.

The American regiment recoiled as the coffee mills guns in their center were shattered or blown into the air. They were only able to get off a ragged volley at the charging 78th before the Highlanders were among them with the bayonet. At that moment the 73rd and 26th Foot flooded around the American flanks. The American regiment collapsed and fled into the dark.

McBean was organizing his men for a pursuit when Hope Grant rode up to him and said, "Let them go." He turned to the brigade commander who had made an appearance at last. "Your Canadian battalions can pursue. Put the rest on the road. *Now*, sir!"

HEADQUARTERS, IRELAND'S BRIGADE, CHAZY, NEW YORK, 4:30 P.M., FRIDAY, MARCH 18, 1864

To the north, Col. David Ireland's brigade at Chazy was completely unaware of the commotion in either direction. The first they knew was the firing from the bridge guards when the 9th Lancers rode them down and clattered over the bridge in the dark to raid into the village where the men in blue were also lining up for dinner at dozens of company messes, their weapons stacked in front this barn or that church where they had been billeted to shelter the Upstate winter. Without their weapons at hand, they were speared by the score as the Lancers rode through the small town streets and the camps chasing the Americans from tent to wagon. It would give birth to a new regimental motto, "The Dinner Guests."

Ireland had burst out of his own headquarters in the local hotel to see the Lancers race past him down the street spearing a crowed of unarmed men fleeing ahead of them. One of them spurred his horse onto the wooden sidewalk and drove his lance into Ireland's aide. The general leaped up and grabbed the man by the collar off his horse before he could pull his lance from the dead man. A headquarters guard bayoneted him and then fell as a Lancer officer shot him with his revolver as he rode by. Another Lancer charged onto the sidewalk and drove his lance clear through the colonel's body. He too was too was dragged off his horse by a half-dozen men and his head bashed in by rifle butts.

More and more men rallied to this half dozen. Many had found their way back to their own and other quarters to snatch rifles and cartridge belts and formed into fragments of their units. By instinct they gathered in larger groups until enough armed men were organized into a skirmish line to drive the Lancers from the camp. Infantry well in hand were more than a match for cavalry that did not have a good field to charge over. The bugles sounded recall to the Lancers who fell back to the bridge. Now all they could do was hold until relieved. They barricaded the bridge and dismounted to hold it with their carbines. They looked into the gloom to see the flames from buildings in Chazy that had caught fire.

CHAZY, NEW YORK, 6:32 P.M., FRIDAY, MARCH 18, 1864

The senior regimental commander in Ireland's Brigade pulled the shattered command together in the light of Chazy's burning buildings. Fire crackled from the area around the bridge where he had sent several companies to prevent the enemy from crossing again.

Col. Paul H. Vivian was in a bloody-minded mood as he took the report of the other regimental commanders. This graduate of Union College in Schenectady, New York, was a good soldier and had marched off with his militia regiment when Lincoln had first called for volunteers after Fort Sumter. He had risen from captain to colonel in the three bloody years since. He loved his regiment in that way that only soldiers know, men from all over the state, the 78th New York, self-styled the Cameron Highlanders. He had risen by astute leadership and a good-hearted concern for his men that won their respect and admiration. He had been especially solicitous of the hundred or so young men, volunteers from Union College who had signed up after the British attack last September and been assigned to his regiment as replacements. They had seen the elephant for the first time that night, and some lay scattered around bearing those gaping lance woods, others pulled into the brigade hospital, and dozens missing. Vivian felt a special responsibility for them.[9]

Union College had been a center for abolitionism in the North before the South seceded, and no institution had been more dedicated to the end of slavery. So it was no wonder that graduates like Vivian, who had become prosperous in middle age, had joined the colors. He did not have the time to reflect on the irony that a nation that abhorred slavery and been the first to abolish it in the Western world had been so adept at riding down and spearing his poor boys in whom antislavery ardor had burned so bright.

The men of the brigade, New Yorkers all, were also in a bloody-minded mood. They did not like the idea of having been chased through the streets by enemy cavalry spearing them as if on the hunt. They were veterans, and it had scalded their pride. They would get even. Vivian's job was to direct that bloody-mindedness like the tip of a spear. He surveyed the scene around the bridge and ordered up two guns to make sure any Lancers who tried to cross the bridge again would do so only through a hail of canister.

Then he assembled his shrunken brigade. He intended to take the brigade and drive off the enemy cavalry, but charging across a defended bridge in the dark was not his idea of sound tactics, especially since canister could go both ways across the bridge. He just could not risk that there was artillery on the enemy side hidden among the trees and buildings.

In the light of his headquarters he examined Ireland's map of the area. He turned to the acting commander of the 60th New York and said, "Bring up H Company." As he waited, he said, "Gentlemen, the enemy is holding the bridge, but nature has already given us a continuous bridge over the river—the ice." The winter had been hard and had frozen the water deep, but a warm spell had melted enough of the ice to form pools of water; then another cold snap had covered the surface again with ice.

The men of H Company trotted up, and Vivian said, "Gather round, boys." When they had crowded around him in a tight semicircle, he said, "Boys, I know this is your home county. Some of you even are from Chazy, and so you know this ground. Put your heads together and find me a way across the river so we can take the British in the rear at the bridge."

The cold was also on the mind of McBean as he marched the 78th south. He had shuddered to think how the 93rd would have fared if they had been brought from the heat of India to the cold of North America as quickly as the Highlanders of the 78th. He mentioned this to Hope Grant, who rode at his side, but got only a grunt of agreement in reply. After a few miles, they were met by a patrol of Lancers. The young subaltern in command informed Grant of the raid on the enemy's camp at Chazy and that the Lancers were holding the bridge. Grant turned to McBean and only said, "Press on, McBean. Press on," as he spurred his horse down the road followed by the Lancers.

RAILROAD BRIDGE OVER GUAY CREEK, NEW YORK, 6:43 P.M., FRIDAY, MARCH 18, 1864

The train engineer saw the unmistakable glow of a fire down the track and slowed his engine until it was clear one of the bridges was ablaze. He pulled to a stop. Hooker bounded out of his car demanding of the engineer the reason for their halt. The man spat a wad of tobacco and pointed up ahead. Hooker asked, "How far to the bridge over the Little Chazy?"

"Oh, about four miles or so," the engineer answered. "Mighty cold for a walk; gonna get worse as the night wears on."

Hooker was already sending aides down the length of the train to order the men to detrain and form up. U.S. Grant had climbed down to hear all this and stood there chewing on a cigar. He had to admit that Hooker, when he was roused, was a man of action, clear-headed action.

Hooker looked around and found McEntee at hand. "Scouts out, now."

"Knight and the others are already out, General." McEntee held open a map as a private held a lamp over it. "Chazy's only four miles away. The road crosses the river near the town. That is the fastest route to the border."

By this time Brig. Gen. Ruger and his brigade was ready to march. "Get on the road immediately and force march your men to Chazy. Secure the bridge and wait for further orders. I will ride ahead with my staff and escort to see what is up." He turned to Grant. "With respect, General, I suggest you return to Plattsburgh when this train departs."

"I never go back, General." Grant's stance told Hooker that it was useless to argue with a man who would ride over the roughest ground simply to avoid backtracking. Hooker's staff and hundred man cavalry escort were ready. Hooker charged his escort commander to remember that the general-in-chief of the armies was riding with them and to put his protection first and foremost in his mind. Then he spurred forward into the dark.

UPSTREAM, LITTLE CHAZY RIVER, 7:32 P.M., FRIDAY, MARCH 18, 1864

The H Company boys had been quick to find just the crossing point that Vivian had in mind, two miles upstream. It was a natural ford, shallow and frozen to the bottom, a place where in the fine Upstate summers they had fished and swum as little boys. Now they strung themselves out through the night with lanterns to guide the rest of the brigade. Vivian pulled his men out of their warms barns and other buildings where their cooks had fed them from what food they could salvage from their overrun kitchens. The colonel wanted them warm until the moment they had to march. He was not a one for having men just stand around, and in this weather he felt no one needed to practice to be miserable. As soon as the last man joined the ranks, he gave the command. Two thousand men did a left face with a hard snap. They were eager to go.

The men crossing points had only one fault. No horse or wheel would be able to get up the far bank's winding foot paths. Without a thought Vivian ordered the 3-inch battery back to help defend the bridge. The coffee mill battery sent their horses and limbers back as well, but the pieces were light enough for the crews to carry and manhandle up the bank. Then they would drag them along. Some of the infantry was detailed to carry extra ammunition.

At that moment, Hope Grant and his escort rode up to the bridge. Grant took the report from the commander. A shell crashed over the bridge from the American side, shot at random to keep the British down. Grant grumbled, "Have to do something about that." In half an hour the hard-marching 78th Highlanders arrived, having outdistanced the rest of its brigade. With them came a battery of Armstrongs, which were immediately sited to defend the bridge. For artillery the best defense was essentially offensive—firing its guns was the same in the attack or defense. Soon British shells were shrieking through the night to keep the Americans down.

One of those shells landed amidst Hooker's party as he rode into town guided by the firing at the bridge. Before exploding it decapitated a horse and split its rider in two. Its burst killed four more men and several horses. More were wounded, and there was nothing so hysterical or heart-rending as the panicked pain of a dumb beast. The rest of the men dismounted and got off the road. Twenty of the cavalry dismounted and moved forward on foot in a skirmish line. The burning buildings in the town offered just enough light at this distance so they would not fall into any holes.

Soon they were met by guards who directed them to the bridge. Hooker found a captain who laid out what had happened to the brigade. Ireland was dead, Vivian had taken the brigade off into the night, and there were only four hundred men to hold the south side of the bridge against God knows what on the other side. It would be an hour before the brigade behind them caught up and morning at least before other brigades would arrive from Plattsburgh. All he could do was wait. Wait for the scouts to come back. Wait for the brigade to arrive. Wait to hear what that damned fool Vivian had done. He was not a happy man.

McEntee asked the officer, "Did you take any prisoners?"

"I think we took some wounded prisoners. A handful maybe, but they're back in town." He then proudly produced a Lancer's helmet.

McEntee took it and held it up to the light. "Well, Wilmoth's order-of-battle was spot on. He told us the 9th Lancers were south of Montreal." He handed it to Hooker.

"Just what I need, another souvenir." Then he brightened, thinking of the nickel-plated Royal Guides helmet McEntee had given him just as Clavarack was about to kick off. "Well, McEntee, maybe this will bring good luck, like last time." He tossed it to his orderly. The captain's face fell as his prized souvenir disappeared.

Vivian was a pretty thick-skinned sort and would not have cared even if he had heard Hooker. Right now he was intent on picking his brigade down frozen roads and fields. His Chazy boys were in the lead, so they wasted no time in the dark. In fact the moon had climbed into the sky on this clear starry night. Its ambient light was just enough to cast pale shadows over the way.

It was not moonlight that alerted them, though. It was the tramp of boots. Vivian was up with the Chazy boys when he heard the tread of hundreds of men and horses and the creek and crunch of artillery pieces, caissons, and limbers over the frozen road. They crept closer to hide behind a field stone wall and watched the almost ghostly procession in heavy greatcoats, its frozen breath floating above as the moonlight washed the color from the faces of men only intent on putting one foot before the other. For ten minutes he watched as the endless column marched on. He did not know that these were the last three Imperial regiments of the brigade that had fought at Prospect Hill or that behind it was a third brigade of another four thousand men and a half-dozen more batteries.[10] It was clear, though, that there were enough to force the bridge and scatter the few companies he had left to guard the south side of the river. He would have to give them something else to think about.

He hurried back to the head of his column, which was perpendicular to the road the enemy was marching on. It would take time to maneuver two thousand men into line and more so in the dark. But then the column might have passed. One of the Chazy boys had thought the thing through himself. He touched Vivian on the shoulder. "Sir, you know, the road loops around to the right not too far from where we are. That means our men are parallel to that road."

Vivian could have kissed him. Now all he had to do was order a right face and his brigade would be on line facing the road. His regimental commanders were waiting where he had left them at the head of the column. A few hurried orders and they were racing to their units to gather their company commanders. Vivian could hear the click of bayonets recede down the dark column. Twenty minutes later his two thousand men were crossing the hard furrows of a wheat field and through a small apple orchard. The brigade's coffee mill battery was carried by its crews. Quiet was the word. No shouted commands. Now was when discipline and habit kept a unit together in the moon-dappled dark.

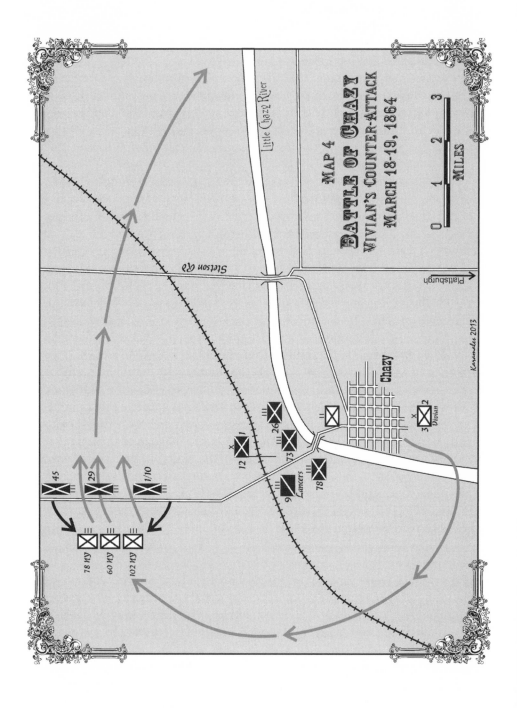

MAP 4
BATTLE OF CHAZY
VIVIAN'S COUNTER-ATTACK
MARCH 18-19, 1864

At last a moving dusky beast appeared flowing along to the accompaniment of the rattles and creaks of a moving column, here and there a glint from the moonlight off a shiny piece of metal. Otherwise they were quiet, also the sign of a discipline of long-service men conserving their strength, but the tramp of their boots on the hard ground muffled the noise of the approaching enemy. The Americans halted in fits and starts as the command was whispered along the ranks. The command to prepare to fire followed in a hush with the plea to "for God's sake, fire low." Vivian had told his commanders to attack as soon as they came within undetected range. That meant close range.

But the enemy in some sense would need to cooperate with those plans. Up to now they had been. A British courier had left the crowded road to cut across the field over which the Americans were marching and trotted right into them. Quick-witted, he turned his horse and spurred it to the wall, shouting an alarm. Heads in the British column turned.

The commander of the 102nd New York bellowed through the dark, "Fire!"[11]

THE BRIDGE AT CHAZY, NEW YORK, 7:35 P.M., FRIDAY, MARCH 18, 1864

Until his follow-on brigade arrived, Hooker decided that the best thing he could do was to keep the enemy occupied. He had the four companies Vivian had left behind to deliver a hot fire across the bridge and along the banks. When the battery of 3-inch guns arrived, he put them right into the fight to send shell and case shot into the dark. It was not dark too long, for the guns had set several buildings on fire, illuminating the night. Hooker roamed the firing positions of his few hundred men to encourage them with the presence of their army commander. Besides, he was enjoying the hell out it even as another aide was killed at his side.

McEntee was in town interrogating the least seriously wounded of the dozen Lancers in the brigade hospital. It was a more innocent age, and most were willing matter-of-factly to tell him what he wanted to know. None would have knowingly betrayed their mates, but it never occurred that army gossip could hurt anything. So he pieced together a reasonable enemy order-of-battle. Sharpe, with nothing to do, had helped and, if anything, had extracted more information. George H. Sharpe was every inch the gentleman, the scion of Hudson River gentry, cosmopolitan from his years in Europe. The effect on the British prisoners made them even more forthcoming.

The two compared notes and then compared them to the order-of-battle that Wilmoth had pieced together from agent network the CIB had set up in Canada. When they were satisfied, they sought out Hooker. They found him in a small house behind some trees that sheltered them from the bridge. He was giving orders to a gaggle of captains. U.S. Grant sat quietly in a chair by the fireplace smoking another in his inexhaustible supply of cigars.

Hooker saw them come in and dismissed the captains with, "To your posts." He looked expectantly at McEntee.

"General, we have information from the prisoners. It appears that the enemy general Grant has at least a full British division against us. That is four brigades plus artillery and this one regiment of cavalry. With auxiliary Canadian battalions, he should have at least fifteen thousand men across the border by now."

"What's across the bridge now?"

"These men only knew about their own regiment being here but expected to be relieved by infantry and artillery."

Just then, a solid shot shattered a tree in the grove outside, shattering a window with splinters. "I would say they have artillery by now," Hooker laughed. "But it's the infantry I'm worried about. And I don't think they have any yet. The only small arms fire we are getting are from cavalry carbines."

McEntee added, "I sent Knight and his scouts across the river downstream to see what else he could find."

Then outside a voice said, "I must find General Hooker!" Then a man came through the door. It was Brigadier General Ruger, commanding the XII Corps' First Division. "General, my lead brigade has arrived. The next two should be here by morning."

Hooker made his decision. "I can't wait for the scouts. Ruger, take that bridge immediately. They've only got dismounted infantry and few guns. Once the enemy infantry arrive, we will never get across it." U.S. Grant just watched.

Ruger was a good soldier, but he recognized a forlorn hope. He left quietly to organize the attack. Hooker followed to observe when Grant called him back.

"General, I must caution you to wait for reinforcements or the enemy will beat you in detail. With one brigade, you are only striking with an open hand. Wait for the rest of the corps and you can strike with a closed fist."

Hooker was not about to be thwarted. "I must not give them time to reinforce the bridge, General."

To Sharpe's surprise, Grant merely said, "As you wish, General. I will not interfere with your immediate conduct of this battle." Hooker stormed off. It occurred to Sharpe that Grant had just given Hooker the rope to hang himself with.

NORTH OF THE CHAZY, 8:45 P.M., FRIDAY, MARCH 18, 1864

Fire! The volley from the 102nd New York flared in a searing flash, and the column on the road opposite flew apart. Then Vivian's old 78th New York stopped and fired. The 60th New York had only just come through the apple orchard when it stopped and fired as well. Then they charged the road. They had struck half of the 29th Foot and part of the 1/10th Foot. The road was filled with dead and dying, but the survivors moving by instinct of long, hard service automatically formed a firing line, often only one man deep, and fired in the direction of the volley flash. But the Americans were upon them as their ramrods shot down the barrels of their rifles as they tried to reload. Bayonet to bayonet now it was. And the thin red line buckled and lurched back and then disappeared in the dark-blue tide, though there was not a soldier of the Queen who did not sell himself dearly. They died, but they died hard.

Vivian found the coffee mill battery lurching behind the attack over the hard-rutted field. "Off to the right, boys! Set up so they can't come back down the road on us." He clapped their captain on the shoulder and pointed in the direction he wanted them to go. The moon was high and speckled the ground with shadows, just enough light to see a few dozen yards. They rushed off and had not even set up when they saw coming out the dark a line of bayonets.

"Oh my God!" shouted one of the gunners and fled into the night. The rest of the men were frozen in surprise for only a moment until the voice of their senior sergeant bellowed through the night. "To your guns!" They flew to their pieces, unlimbered, and swung them around.

Too late, too late. A volley from the dark cut down half the men. Then there was a shout as the British charged. But unlike an artillery piece, a coffee mill gun needed only one man to turn the crank to fire it. And two men sprang over the bodies of the dead and wounded to do just that. *Click-bang, click-bang...* they sputtered to life, then rose to that steam hammer staccato as waves of bullets raked back and forth across the charging British front. The men in front tumbled down, but those behind came on jumping over the fallen right into the bullet stream until they were among the guns stabbing the gunners. The battery was gone, but almost fifty British soldiers had been killed or wounded in that short charge.

On the road Vivian was trying to put his regiments in some order. He heard the coffee mills come to life and then stop suddenly. The enemy was firing back down the road at both ends of their severed column. Then from the northern end a gun barked and a shell came straight down the road bowling over twenty-three men. Case shot followed. "Off the road, boys, off the road!" Vivian shouted, the command relayed down the line. His brigade ran into the field on the other side of the road.

The British had reacted with practiced instinct to the blow out of the dark and counterattacked against both ends of where they thought the Americans had come. So it was that the surviving companies of the 29th had wrapped around the American right flank and straight into the coffee mills. To the south the 1/10th did the same, followed by most of the 45th Foot. They barely avoided shooting into each other when they met.

The dark made the simplest maneuver excruciatingly slow and multiplied the already awful terrors of the battlefield. Vivian was having the same problem on the other side of the road as men got lost or wandered away into the night. At least they could watch the sputtering fuses of the British shells streaking down the empty road thankful that they were no longer in the way. Vivian was thinking to himself, "How the hell did I get myself into this mess?" His counterpart on the other side of the road was in a similar quandary. They had found no Americans. "Where in bloody hell are they?" They called it the fog of war.[12]

CHAZY RIVER BRIDGE, NEW YORK, 9:30 P.M., FRIDAY, MARCH 18, 1864
If Ruger was going to send his brigade over that bridge and into the mouth of hell, he wanted to throw some hell of his own. He added a battery of six bronze Napoleons to the 3-inch battery that Vivian had sent to send a sheet of shell and case shot over the bridge. That was all he could do. The rest of it was up to the brigade commander. But this was Ruger's old brigade, the 2nd Brigade, 1st Division, XII Corps. Now he could only watch as they went across that awful hundred feet of death. The men lay or knelt in the road to avoid the shells crashing through the darkness. The 107th New York would lead; he walked over to them and saw that many had their names and next of kin written on pieces of paper and pinned to their backs. The Catholics were saying their rosaries. He could hear snatches of "Our Father," but most were silent. He was heartsick.

Tearing himself away Ruger crept up to the wrecked house across from the bridge to find the brigade commander and his staff making final preparations in the shelter of a stone root cellar. He found Grant and Sharpe outside and was struck at how calm Grant was as the cannon barked and jerked in the very yard. A yellow lantern glow came out of the cellar entrance. He stepped inside to find Hooker giving the brigade commander minute orders on the organization of the attack. "General," he said, "Col. Hamilton knows his brigade well. It were best he worked out these details himself."

Hooker gave Ruger a hard look and turned to the other officer."Colonel, you have your orders." Hamilton and his staff left quickly, not wanting to be around when generals locked horns.

Even in the lantern light, Hooker's face was flushed. "Ruger, don't get in my way. No one will say I was drunk in this battle." He pushed Ruger aside and left the cellar. Ruger paused a moment to calm himself when a shell burst outside, blowing the cellar door off its hinges. He rushed out. The shell had burst right over Hooker, and the jagged steel had torn his left arm off. Ruger pulled out his field tourniquet and tightened it around the stump.

Then he looked up. The same shell had also killed Hooker's orderly and aide and struck down Grant. Sharpe was kneeling next to him as he sat on the ground holding his head in both hands as blood poured through his fingers. Ruger ran over. Sharpe looked up, and said, "You are senior officer on the field, Ruger. I suggest you cancel that attack." A medical orderly ran up and took one look at Grant. Kneeling down, he gently pried off Grant's fingers. Sharpe looked at Ruger again. "Man, save your men." Ruger ran off in the direction of the brigade.

The orderly said, "Thank God, just a scalp wound. They bleed like hell and look worse than they are." He pressed a lint bandage to Grant's forehead, then unwound another bandage to tie it on. "Don't worry, General. You'll be fine, up and about in a few days."

Grant threw his arm up. "Let me up, Damnit!"

"General, you should stay still till we can get you to the hospital."

"Soldier, I thank you, but I have work to do." He struggled to his feet steadied by Sharpe and the orderly. He swayed a bit and said, "Where is my cigar?" He took two steps and fainted.[13]

It was only then that Sharpe realized that he himself and not Ruger was the senior officer on the field.[14]

The other Gen. Grant would have been infinitely relieved to know the effect of that British shell on the American side of the bridge. The sudden increase in artillery fire had signaled only one thing—the Americans were going to rush bridge, and all he had was one battery and a few hundred dismounted Lancers with poor carbines. The artillery slackened unexpectedly. What on earth was going on? McBean arrived just then with his Highlanders and more artillery. Grant sketched the situation to him. The Scotsman said, "Aye, sir, sounds a bit strange, but I would be more wurri'd aboot the battle goin' on behind us."

NORTH OF THE CHAZY RIVER, 9:52 P.M., FRIDAY, MARCH 18, 1864

That battle had turned into a temporary standoff separated by a road filled with dead and wounded. The British and American brigades stood to in the cold and dark, their freezing breath hanging like a mist over them as every man wondered what was next. Both commanders sent out skirmish lines to feel for the enemy. They found each other at the road coming out the gloom like wraiths, no one knowing for sure until up close who was who, made more difficult by the fact that each side wore dark-blue greatcoats. Their voices were more likely to betray them, flat American a's against the burr of Scotland, or the swallowed final syllables of Essex, or "friend" against "mate." Fists and bayonets were used as often as firearms. The commanders heard the crackle and flash of gunfire between them.

That was enough for the British brigadier. He bawled out, "The brigade will advance."

Vivian heard the faint echo of the command and the rustle as several thousand men started to advance. His own skirmishers were running back to rejoin their regiments. He noticed a knot of prisoners behind herded to the rear. A voice next to him said, "And General Sharpe will be mighty pleased of that present." Vivian turned to see a large man in civilian clothes and a pair of revolvers stuck in his belt. He recognized the Chief of Scouts of the Army of the Hudson. "I bet you had a grand time getting here, Colonel, but I don't think you want to stay much longer. The country between here and the river is crawling with the English. Hooker sent me to scout out places to cross the river on the ice, and I thought he would appreciate it if I looked deeper into things."

Vivian's relief was immense. Knight filled him in on what he knew until he had gone scouting, which to Vivian was more than enough — Hooker was concentrating the Army of the Hudson and was in person at Chazy. But what to do? It was after midnight. If Sergeant Knight's observations of the enemy in the area were correct, and they always were, then the sunrise would put paid to his command. "Sergeant Knight, I have some local boys who know this area like the backs of their hands. If you need them, they are yours, but get us to one of those crossings."

The tail of Vivian's command had just disappeared through the line of trees between two fields, when the British skirmishing line swept over the spot where they had waited only minutes before. They moved on and caught up with the American rearguard in a sharp firefight, but the Americans pulled out and disappeared into the dark. The brigadier rode up and called them back. It was bad enough to fight a battle in the dark with an enemy that stayed in one place. It was entirely foolhardy to go hunt him in the dark in strange country.

The Americans trudged on through the night. On the way they picked up Geary and his party trying to make their way to Chazy. Geary did not know how close he came to being shot in the dark by very nervous men. He was elated to have found one of his own brigades and listened intently to Vivian's account of his nighttime adventures. "I have you to thank for rescuing some part of the day. You are all that is left of the division. I've had a bad day, Colonel, a bad day. I had to stand by, no hide, while Cobham's Brigade was surprised and routed. I don't know what had happened to Candy's. The last I saw they were attacking the enemy."

4

An Arithmetic Problem

THE WHITE HOUSE, WASHINGTON, DC, FRIDAY, MARCH 18, 1864
Lincoln had been spending all day between the War Department and Central Information Bureau waiting for every telegram that trickled in over the wires of the unfolding British attack. The chief telegrapher at the War Department watched the look of shock spread over the President's face as he read the telegram relating Hooker and Grant's wounding. One shell had taken out the Union's two most victorious generals. Lincoln fell into the big stuffed chair that was normally reserved for him. He leaned his head into one hand. Stanton read it next. His face set like stone. He scribbled out a message on a telegram blank. "Send it now," he ordered. The message crackled over the lines to Sherman.

An hour later Lincoln crossed the street back to the White House, the weight of the world ready to break his back. An hour later James McPhail, Gus Fox, and Andrew Carnegie, the members of the War Production Board (WIB), sat silently as Lincoln read their joint report. McPhail was Sharpe's deputy and represented the CIB while his boss was on the border with Grant. McPhail had been the Provost Marshal of Maryland before Sharpe asked him to help found the CIB. As the Romans used to say of a man, "You can trust him in the dark."[1] It was just the quality that Sharpe needed in the man who ran his agent lines in Canada and the Confederacy.

Gustavus Fox was there representing the interests of the Navy since so much of the work of the WIB concentrated on organizing the resources to build the monitors. He was Mr. Navy, officially the Assistant Secretary of the Navy, and in effect, its chief of naval operations in modern terms. No man was more receptive to new technologies, opportunities, and talent. Much of the Navy's success in the war was due to his foresight and energy.

Carnegie was there as board chairman. Lincoln had commissioned the WIB shortly after the war began. Carnegie's task was one that had never been set before another American — to organize the factories, foundries, workshops, shipyards, and mines of the country to withstand the enormous struggle with the greatest industrial power the world had known. Carnegie at age twenty-eight had already made his mark. In the opening days of the Rebellion when Washington was defenseless, he pushed the trains to bring the first troops to the capital, and then at First Bull Run had organized the hospital trains that saved so many lives. He was a man who could get things done by the uncanny welding of the ability to see the essence of a problem or opportunity and then finding the talented men to turn that vision into reality. Born in Scotland into a family of poor weavers, the man was as true an American patriot as any whose ancestors came over on the *Mayflower*. He had left poverty in Scotland, despising the British establishment and particularly the royals. Like so many millions of other Britons and Irish, he had found an opportunity here that was simply nonexistent in the lands of their birth.[2]

Lincoln sat at his desk, his glasses low on his nose as he read their report. Every few minutes he would stop and write a note on as slip of paper. Finally, he put the report down and said, "Let me see if I can summarize the problem, boys." He got up to pace the room in his slippers. "We have gone to war with the greatest industrial power in the world in the midst of a major expansion of that industry."

Carnegie nodded. "Aye, sir."

"And they are completely self-sufficient in the needs of their industry. Food and raw materials, like cotton, make up ninety-five percent of imports."

Carnegie nodded again. He had heard how Lincoln studied a problem until he knew it inside and out.

"They are building almost three hundred steamships a year, and British ships carry a quarter of the world's trade."

Another nod.

"And the Library of Congress tells me that the British census of 1860 counted 27.8 million people." He rummaged through the papers in the alcoves above his desk and pulled out a paper. "Yes, England has 18.8 million, Scotland three million, and Wales one million. And, of course, Ireland has five million. There used to be over three million more Irish.[3] And there are three million Canadians We must not, of course, forget the French. Their 1861 census counted 37.4 million Frenchmen.[4] And the Secretary of the Interior has informed me that our own 1860 census counted 20.5 million free persons in the loyal states.

"Now, boys," he said, as he stood over them, "We already had our hands full with our wayward Southern friends. It seems to me that we have a serious arithmetic problem. If my ciphering is right, the British, French, and Confederates have about eighty million people against our twenty million. But our Rooshan friends, who are taking their sweet time to declare war, have about seventy-four million people.[5] That may sound like a big deal, boys, but I have my doubts. Most of those people are ignorant peasants; how useful are they going to be? The British and French thumped them pretty good in their own backyard ten years ago. The difference is that our army reads. Every other man in the British Army is illiterate and about ninety percent of the Rooshans. This is the first time in history where almost the entire army knows how to read and write. Free, literate men fight hard because they know what they're fighting for."

Lincoln scratched his thatch of unruly hair and sat down. "Literacy aside, the numbers still don't add up. What I need from you boys is how we are going to solve this arithmetic problem."

Fox was first off the mark. It was a Navy issue, and no one would speak but him. Carnegie's great talent was recognizing talent and harnessing it to his object. Fox was all talent, and his devotion to the Navy and innovation fit perfectly within that plan. They moved in tandem.

"Mr. President, we've got 'em beat!" Lincoln rocked back in his chair as Fox stood up to emphasize what he had just said. "The Royal Navy used to be the greatest Navy on the seas, but the Admiralty will now pay for its refusal to jump out of the rut of tradition.

"When the Royal Navy decided to build ironclads they did so with as little imagination as possible. They kept to the broadside design that had stood their wooden fleet well for centuries. Except for the all-iron *Warrior* and *Resistance* classes, they simply have cut down wooden ships-of-the-line and added iron plates. They did not have the crisis of our war and the imminent threat of the Confederate ironclad *Virginia* to sharpen our wits.

"We were at that point, as Mr. Johnson put it, where the prospect of being hanged concentrates the mind wonderfully. It was then that Mr. Ericsson's genius and the crisis met to create our all-iron monitor fleet with its revolutionary turret and low freeboard hull design.

"The British had no such spur, only the challenge of the French broadside ironclad *Gloire* class. They did not go beyond that concept except in superior detail. They are building ships like the *Black Prince* and *Resistance* that we sank at Charleston. They are stuffed with much smaller guns than our monitors which are invulnerable to them. Our eleven and fifteen-inch Dahlgren guns, on the other hand, tear the guts out of British ships. The only innovation we are aware of, thanks to General Sharpe, is that the British have remounted some of their smaller-caliber Armstrong breech-loading rifles to shoot at balloons.

"They have built what they themselves call 'iron towers,' ships much bigger than ours but less capable. Their crews number often as high as six hundred, five to six times the crews of our monitors. They need that many men to work such a large ship and to work all those guns that do us little harm. Their ships are sinkholes of men for little value. They have fifteen of these old designs under construction [Appendix C]. Perish the British Empire rather than suffer British officialism to be urged beyond its wonted pace!

"Look at the tables, sir. We are going to reap the benefit of the monitor-building programs already underway. You will see that we will have twenty new monitors joining the fleet this year, with five at the end of this month and two more in April, seven more in June and July, four in August and September, and the last two in December [Appendix D]. As you, know we are also laying down the hulls for ten more of Mr. Ericsson's *Dictator* class. He has also thrown himself into developing the new, larger *Washington* class as well."

Carnegie took up the argument. "We have achieved remarkable results in just the four months the War Production Board has been operating. The most important improvement we have made was the bill you pushed through Congress to put the various Army and Navy ordnance and supply bureaus under our supervision." His bright-blue eyes twinkled as he went on. He was a world-class charmer. "The Bureau system, I must say, was an ingenious device for giving to incapacity, indifference, and stupidity the solemn sanction of official utterance; for reducing the pace of the swiftest to that of the lowest; the zeal, intelligence, and energy of the ablest to the capacity of the most sluggish in comprehension and the most inert in action."

Lincoln nodded. "Ah, yes, the Stevens-Sumner Contracting Reform Act was another one of those helpful measure we were able to slide through Congress. It seems they only do the sensible thing when they are scarred witless. It was just after the attack on Washington last November when I recalled Congress. The sight of the half-burned city was enough to grease a lot of reform."[6]

Fox leaned forward to summarize, "It's going to be a fine Navy day, Mr. President, a fine Navy day. I have no doubt that this year we will see the blockade off. We will even be able to cross the ocean and see how England likes to be blockaded."

McPhail's clear, calm voice cut right through the optimism. "The Central Information Bureau disagrees."

Fox whipped around, his face flushed. McPhail locked eyes with him and did not blink. Carnegie had feared just such a scene. The CIB and the Navy profoundly disagreed over the downstream ramifications of this information. It had taken all of the little Scotchman's charm to keep Fox and Sharpe from going to war over this issue. It did not help that Sharpe was an Army officer. Fox was naturally pugnacious and protective of the Navy's interest and resented Sharpe's meddling in what he insisted was solely a naval issue. He had once said, "I feel my duty is twofold, first to beat our Southern friends, second to beat the Army."[7]

Their eyes remained locked until Lincoln said, "Tell me why."

"The Navy's figures are one hundred percent correct, sir. But they are not the only figures that matter. They must be compared to the Royal Navy's building program. I do not think Mr. Fox realizes the extent to which the shock of Charleston has shaken the foundations of the Admiralty.

"Disraeli has used their defeat to shake things up and clean house, much as we have done. The British press has announced wholesale retirements and resignations. Our sources in Britain also inform us that a new class of monitor-like ships, the *Revenge* class, of at least twenty ships, designed by Capt. Cowper Coles, the inventor of the British turret system, is being laid down as we speak. He has the favor of the Queen because the late Prince Consort Albert had been his patron. More importantly, he has the support of Disraeli and the Cabinet.

"What worries Gen. Sharpe, sir, is the fact that British industry is many times ours. We know that the Britain produced 3,827,000 tons of iron in 1860. Last year's estimate is 4,510,000 tons.[8] That compares to the 920,000 tons we produced in 1860. Most of our production, however, is from out-of-date processes, from small bloomeries and furnaces only a half dozen of which employed more than 1,500 men. Only in the past decade have we begun to exploit the immense coal deposits that lie between Pittsburgh and Chicago. Even by 1860 fully seventy percent of our iron production was fueled by charcoal. And we have not been able to meet domestic requirements from our own production. Fully half of our yearly requirement for rails in 1860 was produced in Britain. We produced 205,000 tons of rails in 1860 and over 300,000 last year; this year we expect to reach 400,000 tons and will be self-sufficient.[9]

"We believe that almost forty percent of British iron was shipped to the United States in 1860.[10] The British will not miss the loss of our market. Our sources tell us an almost endless numbers of rails are being shipped to the South to replace their worn out or destroyed systems. And Britain's shipbuilding and other armament industries will soak up the rest. We assess that those twenty monitors of the *Revenge* class will be at sea in eighteen months at most, surely with more classes following right after."

Lincoln asked, "You're sure about this eighteen months?"

McPhail replied, "Sir, General Sharpe believes this a conservative estimate. The British yards are working in three shifts."

Lincoln turned to Carnegie and said, "How are we doing in finding a substitute for niter, Carnegie?" Niter was the one ingredient for gunpowder that the United States had to import. And Britain had a monopoly based on its sources in India. Chile's deposits had recently opened up, but the blockade made that irrelevant. Lincoln was so concerned about the country's niter supply that he had personally engaged a chemist to find an alternative ingredient for gunpowder, but that had failed. His concern, however, had ensured that by the time the war with Britain had begun, four thousand tons of niter had been stockpiled. Still, it would not last in a long war, a year at most. Then the United States would be reduced to turning over dung heaps and raking cave floors for the niter crystals that formed naturally. The Confederates had been forced to these measures and could barely produce enough to keep their end of the war going.[11]

Carnegie frowned. It was one of the priorities Lincoln had given him last November, and it had not yielded even to his charms. "Dupont tells me that his experiments with niter substitutes have gone nowhere. Guncotton is a possibility, but it has proved too volatile so far."

Lincoln slumped a bit in his chair.

Carnegie thought it best to get other bad news out of the way at this time. "Luckily, we are self-sufficient in almost everything else. With two exceptions—we face a shortage of rubber, sir, and whale oil. Rubber has so many uses these days in industry, I don't know where to begin. With the loss of our whale oil reserves when the British burned Hudson last year,[12] we should have already started to run out. The oil wells in Pennsylvania have come to our rescue. The Standard Oil Company has been able to begin distilling kerosene on a large scale as a substitute to light the country's lamps."

A smile crossed Lincoln's face. "That reminds me of a comment someone made the other day about how cooperative the State of Pennsylvania has been with Standard Oil. Yes, it's because Standard Oil has done everything with the Pennsylvania state legislature but refine it."

When the snickers had died down, Lincoln got back to business and said, "Carnegie, all well and good. But what I need are big numbers to solve this arithmetic problem. What about the repeaters?" It was Lincoln who had introduced the inventive genius, Chris Spencer, to Carnegie and recommended that he figure out some way to get the young man's superb repeating rifle into large scale production. The result had been that the Colt Firearm Company had subcontracted to produce the Spencer at its huge factory in Connecticut and discontinue its own Colt repeater, a less capable weapon. Colt would profit enormously by this because it acquired 50 percent of the Spencer patent in the deal.

Good news now. "It took Colt a few months to retool his factory to make Chris Spencer's repeater, but I can report, sir, that they are coming out at three thousand a week now, and we expect that to go up to five thousand by next month and ten thousand by June. Springfield Arsenal is also retooling to produce the Spencer and should be ready within six weeks to begin production. By the end of the year, we expect to be producing fifty thousand Spencers a month."

One of the first decisions of the WPB, at the canny suggestion of Colt's general manager, was to designate the Spencer the new standard infantry rifle. Production of all other types was to halt as soon as Spencer production came on line. Springfield Arsenal and other producers of the standard Springfield muzzle-loading musket were also converting that weapon into a single-shot breechloader based upon a simple design that the former chief of the Army's Ordnance Bureau had suppressed. The Sharps Rifle Company (no relation to Maj. Gen. George H. Sharpe) people took this decision to standardize the Spencer badly since they too produced an excellent repeater, but a common sense exception was made for them since they were already in production and able immediately to produce ten thousand weapons a month. The Board felt that this bridge production was vital to cover the period when Colt and Springfield as well as other manufacturers had halted production to retool.

PORT HUDSON, LOUISIANA, FRIDAY, MARCH 18, 1864

Just as Lincoln adjourned the meeting, a French shell blew through the top foot of a parapet at Fort Hudson, spraying clods of red clay in every direction and then bouncing down inside the bastion. It spun as its fuse threw off sparks. Every man within a dozen yards threw himself to the ground just as the shell exploded. It had been like this for days, an endless shelling by the big French siege guns arrayed around the Union fort at Port Hudson. After New Orleans had fallen to the Union in April 1862, the Confederates had built this great fortress to control the Mississippi only a hundred miles upstream from the Crescent City. It was twin to Vicksburg further up the river, and for over a year the two fortresses had closed off the vital waterway to the Union. But Vicksburg had fallen on the Glorious Fourth of July 1863 and starving Port Hudson four days later.

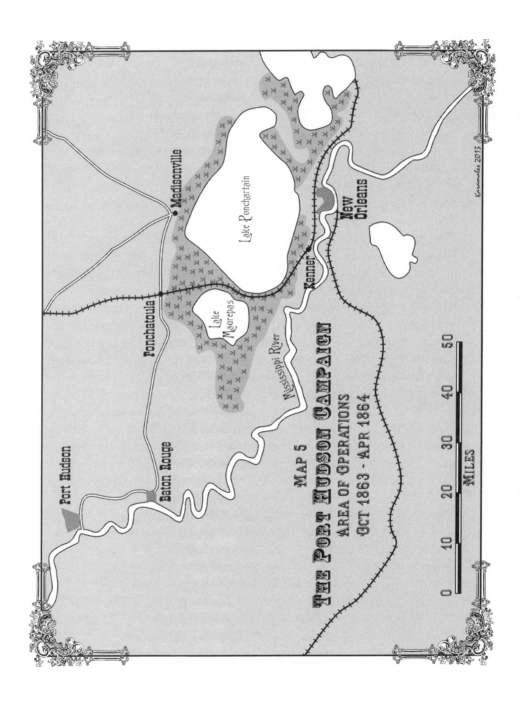

Port Hudson

Baton Rouge

Ponchatoula

Madisonville

Lake Ponchartain

Lake Maurepas

Mississippi River

Kenner

New Orleans

Kassandra 2013

MAP 5
THE PORT HUDSON CAMPAIGN
AREA OF OPERATIONS
OCT 1863 - APR 1864

0   10   20   30   40   50
MILES

Now it was the Union that held Port Hudson and manned its miles of expertly laid out earth works that artfully followed the deep gullies and ravines around it. The Confederates had built well, and into this refuge the remnants of the Union army destroyed at Vermillionville the previous October had staggered after an epic retreat through swamp and bayou. Their commander, Maj. Gen. William Franklin, now senior officer in Louisiana, quickly drew the remaining Union forces in the fortress, burning the vast depots at Baton Rouge just ahead of Lt. Gen. Richard Taylor's Confederates.

The echoing of a dozen French bugles drew the men of the 1st Corps d' Afrique to their feet. They were Uhlman's Brigade of the 6th through 10th Regiments, Corps d'Afrique. Their origin was in the Confederate Louisiana Home Guards, a militia regiment of free blacks and black officers. After New Orleans fell to the Union in early 1862, one tenth of the regiment volunteered to serve the Union. By the next year the Corps d'Afrique was formed on a regular basis made up of, at first, free Louisiana blacks. So many runaway slaves were eager to join that regiment after regiment was formed. The 1st Regiment, which had retained its black line officers, distinguished itself in the unsuccessful May assault on Port Hudson. All other regiments were allowed only white officers. Their chaplains were their own black ministers.

Now they dusted the red clay powder off themselves and stood to their positions, every ear drawn to signal for an attack. A chaplain walked behind the firing line, his back straight as he passed the crouching men, his deep voice reciting the warrior verses of the Old Testament

> "Thou shalt not be afraid for the terror by night; nor for the arrow that flieth by day. Nor for the pestilence that walketh in the darkness; nor for the destruction that wasteth by noonday."

A voice began in a cross between a hum and a hymn, a living rhythm. It spread down the parapet till the entire corps was filling the stillness before the assault with this fervent accompaniment to the chaplain.

> "A thousand shall fall at thy side, and ten thousand by the right hand; but it shall not come nigh thee. Only with thine eyes shalt thou behold and see the reward of the wicked."[13]

The French had driven parallel trenches within a few dozen yards of the forward bastion. They were now packed with men ready to attack, black and white men, Sudanese infantry and French officers, in the forward trenches. They heard the singing and the words of the chaplain as it flowed over the wall and down into their trenches. Every eye instinctively turned upward, every ear compelled to hear even what they could not understand.

> "It is God that girdeth me with strength, and maketh my way perfect. He teacheth my hands to war, so that a bow of steel is broken by mine arms. Thou hast also given me the shield of salvation. "

The men in the trenches had seen the red hand of war all too often no to be disconcerted by the power above them. These men would take much killing.

> "I have pursued mine enemies, and overtaken them: neither did I turn again till they were consumed. I have wounded them that they were not able to rise. For Thou has girded me with strength unto battle; Thou hast subdued under me those that rose up against me. Thou hast also given me necks of mine enemies that I might destroy them that hate me. They cried but there were none to save them: even unto the Lord, but He answered them not. Then did I beat them small as the dust before the wind: I did cast them out as the dirt in the streets."[14]

The chaplain threw his arms upward in supplication, and shouted:

> "The Lord is my rock, and my fortress, and my deliverer; my God, my strength in whom I will trust; my buckler, and the horn of my salvation, and my high tower."[15]

The corps responded with a thunderous amen that turned the heads of the French and Confederate senior officers hundreds of yards away. As if it had been choreographed, a French rocket shot up over beaten ground.

Suddenly the trenches erupted with hundreds of men in red trousers and blue coats rushing forward, the tricolor waving here and there above them. Shouts of *"En avant! En avant!"* rose above the din. The French artillery redoubled its efforts sending shell after shell into the bastion over the heads of their assault parties.

Although the French and Confederate armies had closed on Port Hudson in October, it had taken since then for the French artillery siege train to cross the Atlantic. That was the easy part. Just above New Orleans, Union gunboats still controlled the Mississippi blocking the water route for the heavy guns. They had to be taken by a combination of rail and road to the siege works around Port Hudson. And this is where the problems of the Franco-Confederate forces began to multiply.

Supplies and reinforcements flowed into Port Hudson thanks to the U.S. Navy's control of the river. By the late winter, Franklin commanded an army barely smaller than his enemy. He used cavalry aggressively to raid the Franco-Confederate supply columns and continuously threatened them with infantry sallies through the vast piney woods that surrounded Port Hudson, all of which drained men from the siege works. But with each month more and more French troops arrived until Marshal of France Françoise Achille Bazaine counted sixty-five thousand men under his command in Louisiana, more than double the Confederate troops in the entire District of the Gulf. Confederate Lt. Gen. Richard Taylor found the French day by day more overbearing. Bazaine continued to purr about Napoleon III's benign intentions, but he took greater liberties with each week. The latest was to place a French guard of honor at St. Louis Cathedral in New Orleans, the prerogative of a sovereign monarch. It had not gone unnoticed. Worse were the rumors of French confidential discussions with influential Creole leaders in the city on the possibility of a return to French sovereignty for Louisiana. Hints of titles and offices and gold francs were scattered about — delicately, of course. The fact that these discussion were carried out in French with a Francophone New Orleans elite only added weight to their intent and worry in Richmond.

There was no head of state more jealous of the sovereignty of his government than Jefferson Davis. General Taylor, his son-in-law, kept him well-informed of Bazaine's activities, but Davis was on the horns of a dilemma. The French alliance, which was formalized in the previous December with the Treaty of Richmond, was vital to the survival of the Confederacy. Bazaine's army was the only reason the Union had been driven out of New Orleans and back up the river. Bazaine had crushed the Union army under Nathaniel Banks at Vermillionville the previous October, for which he had received a marshal's baton, but not the title he had craved. And it was French loans (and British) that had relieved so many of the difficulties of the Confederacy. Not the least of which was the want of luxuries; now every woman of quality seemed to be displaying the latest Paris fashions. Three years of stored cotton bought a lot of French quality in all of the finer things of life.

Davis could push back only so hard with the French; he realized that when you took someone's money, you were no longer a completely free agent. Yet push back he did wherever possible only to find he was pushing against a French pillow. The French never confronted, resisted, or insisted, but they did suggest, delicately, of course. Their suggestions for all their exquisite manners had the same sort of power of a reminder that the Confederates were in no position to argue the point.

THE WHITE HOUSE, WASHINGTON, DC, FRIDAY, MARCH 18, 1864

After his meeting with the War Production Board, Lincoln had need of advice of a different kind later that same day. Secretary of State William Seward and former ambassador to the Court of St. James, Charles Francis Adams had arrived together

Adams had been a perfect choice to represent the United States in London. The appointment of the son and grandson of presidents who had both also served as ambassadors there was meant as a mark of respect to the British. His breeding was impeccable by British standards and his integrity never questioned. What he missed in the subtleties of diplomatic indirection he made up in a relentless advocacy of American interests that earned the respect of the British. Among his friends were the great reformers, the independent Radicals, John Bright and Richard Cobden. He had a wealth of knowledge of who was who in British politics, a resource Lincoln was eager to tap.

"Tell me, Adams, about Disraeli's cabinet. Has he had as easy a time with his as I have had with mine?" Seward burst out laughing. He knew the political genius that was required of Lincoln to hold together a cabinet most of whose members had thought they could all do a better job than the simple rail splitter form Illinois, first of whom had been at one time Seward himself.

Adams leaned forward on his cane. "Mr. President, the British cabinet system is quite different from ours. The prime minister is only head of government; the Queen is the head of state. You as president hold both offices. The prime minister is, in effect a member of the cabinet, which represents the interest of his party. The cabinet is the collective leadership of that party. You, like the centurion in the Bible, can say, 'I tell a man to come and he cometh; I tell a man to go and he goeth.' But the most important decisions of a British government are collective ones of the entire cabinet."

Lincoln smiled. "The centurion never had my cabinet."

Adams went on. "Ministers act with more independence than in an American cabinet, yet all important issues are arrived at by a consensus in cabinet. It is a rare PM who acts against the judgment of his cabinet.

"Disraeli has retained the men that Lord Derby had selected as a shadow cabinet before the Palmerston government fell. They are men of ability and experience. The British parliamentary system ensures that prospective cabinet officers progress through a series of lesser appointments that season and prepare them for high office, much like Roman officialdom.

"For example, Lord Stanley, the Foreign Secretary, who was Lord Derby's son, has extensively toured the empire and was appointed undersecretary for foreign affairs in his father's first government in 1852. In his father's second government, he held the office of Secretary of State for the Colonies in 1858 and then President of the Board of Control while at the same time exercised a leadership role in pushing important legislation through Parliament. He followed that by becoming Secretary of State for India where he left an excellent record as an administrator."

Seward added, "The Stanleys are the richest land-owing family in England and of such prominence that after the Greeks tossed out their Bavarian king, they had their heart set on Victoria's second son, Prince Alfred. When he declined they sought a great and wealthy English noble. A testament to Lord Stanley's good sense was that he avoided that 'bed of thorns.'"

Adams resumed. "I have it on authority that he has stated that the normal attitude of a British foreign secretary was like that of a man floating down a river and gaffing off whatever obstacles threatened his vessel."[16]

Lincoln nodded. "He seems a man of practical good sense. Any man who has sat in my chair knows that events control him far more than he controls events. Heaven help us from the man who thinks events are like an orchestra to be conducted. That reminds me of something General Grant told me. He said that leading an army is just like conducting an orchestra until some sonofabitch climbs out of the orchestra pit and starts chasing you around the stage with a bayonet."

Adams paused. "I could go on, but it is more of the same; the Disraeli cabinet is able and experienced. They stepped into office able to devise and execute policy."

At that moment the door opened, and two men were shown into Lincoln's office.

"Sumner, good of you to come," Lincoln said as he extended his big hand. Senator Charles Sumner was a big bear of a man, not nearly as tall as Lincoln's six foot four inches, but he made it up in bulk. A shock of brown hair framed a face that men were remarking more and more resembled that of Edmund Burke, great Conservative member of Parliament and friend of America during the Revolution. Perhaps the comparison was prompted by the fact that Sumner had been as great a friend of Great Britain as Burke had been of America.

The Republican from Massachusetts, chairman of the Senate foreign relations committee, was more than an Anglophile. As a young man he had traveled to Great Britain and by his modest good manners, charm, and the good sense to immediately seek out a fine English tailor, was ushered into the highest society. This innocent from Boston had been shocked to find out the British actually played cards for money. Before the Civil War the British had considered only Edward Everett, the great American orator, a more perfect model of a British statesmen than Sumner. His friendship for the British had taken a difficult turn with the start of the Civil War. Britain's barely disguised support of the Confederacy had collided with Sumner's profound antislavery convictions. Those very convictions had so enraged a South Carolinian member of the House of Representatives before the war that this Southern gentleman had marched into the Senate chamber and so brutally caned Sumner over the head that it was feared he would never recover.

But recover he did. Massachusetts refused to replace him, letting his empty desk in the Senate chamber as a reproach to the slave power until he could resume his duties, his antislavery convictions now haloed with the blood of martyrdom. He had few friends in the Senate, but his influence in the North was immense. And for that reason, Lincoln found his council useful, not only on the issue of the black man, but for his shrewd observations of the British, and more.

As for the black man himself, Lincoln then turned to Douglass as a great smile lit his face. "Douglass, I have great need of you. Please, sit, both of you." He motioned to the two winged-back chairs that framed the fireplace. He took a moment to stir the fire with a poker, then pulled up a chair.

For a moment he considered the two men before him. Sumner he had come to know well since assuming the presidency. Douglass he had only met last year when Lincoln became the first president to receive a black man in the White House. But in a profound way, he had consulted Douglass far more than Sumner. Son of slaves, Douglass, like Lincoln was the quintessential American self-made man. He possessed a world-class intellect married to kingly bearing, presence, and an eloquence devoted to the freedom of his race that announced themselves with the éclat of Jovian thunderbolts. His speeches had reached audiences that totaled in the many hundreds of thousands and done more to stir the abolitionist feelings of Northern white men to boil than any other man. Like Cromwell he was the living embodiment of the idea that it was not enough to strike when the iron is hot but to strike to *make* the iron hot.

For the first two years of the war, he had despaired of Lincoln, thinking that he would compromise with the Slave Power. It was only after the Emancipation Proclamation that he realized what Lincoln had so subtlety had understood. The war against the Confederacy was itself the furnace of revolution, a revolution in the minds of men. Only when the furnace glowed white hot would it burn away the illusion that the nation had shattered for any reason but slavery. It was slavery that was the enemy of the Union and of free men everywhere. For this the nation would fight.

The obdurate heart of this resolve was represented by the three Massachusetts men in the room. Only Douglass was not born and bred to the Cromwellian Puritanism of the Old Bay State. But in his likeness to an Old Testament prophet, he was as much of Massachusetts as its granite.

Seward was the first to speak. Lincoln had no more loyal cabinet officer and friend than Seward, ever since the Secretary of State realized that Lincoln, the unknown prairie politician, was not about to be only a figurehead. They were one of the great collaborations in history. But Seward exercised a very un-New England use of profanity and hyperbole. As the Civil War was erupting he had openly stated that a good war with Great Britain would bring the country back together. He opened the meeting by briefly reviewing the few scrapes of news of fighting on the New York border. "We will see this damned thing through. Victory or death is the watchword throughout the country, I say," whacking the table with his fist for emphasis.

It was almost a cue. Lincoln said, "That reminds me of the story of the soldier whose two sisters had embroidered a belt for him that read, 'Victory or Death!'

"'No, no,'" the soldier says. "Don't put it quite that strong. Put it 'Victory or get hurt pretty bad.'"[17] Even the deadly serious Adams surprised himself by laughing, but quickly brought himself under control.

Today Lincoln was again in a playful mood. "Sumner, do you have any friends left in England?"

Sumner winced. Lincoln was referring to Sumner's speech of September 10 of last year. With the beginning of the Civil War, Sumner's correspondence to his friends in the highest circles of British society assumed a new importance as he pressed the position of the Union. To his old friend John Bright, he had also poured out his frustrations with the course of the war, asking once, after Burnside's fiasco at Fredericksburg, if it might be possible to "send us an Englishman who will handle . . . two hundred thousand men." He had also been unrelenting in equating British actions with blatant support of the Slave Power. Like a constant drip of water on stone, they were slowly but surely having an effect on British opinion at the highest levels. But by the summer of 1863 he had feared that the growing crisis over the Laird Rams affair would lead to war and prepared a manifesto laying out American grievances against Great Britain. Edward Everett had warned him that the speech "would be appropriate as a manifesto or a declaration of war."[18] Unknown to him,

Everett's fears proved prescient and the speech appropriate. Four days before he had delivered the speech, the battle of Moelfra Bay, sparked by the attempted escape of one of the Laird Rams from Liverpool, had occurred. Britain's declaration of war was skimming across the Atlantic as he spoke in Boston.[19]

Lincoln already knew the answer to his question. Sumner's correspondence had continued, though more circumspectly. As General Sharpe was the first to admit, the Canadian border leaked like a sieve in both directions. Letters went back and forth, and Lincoln had been keen to read everything Sumner forwarded. It was as important to keep his fingers on the pulse of British as well as American public opinion, and for this Sumner's letters were priceless. The insight they gave him into the British leadership was more than priceless.

"Tell me, Sumner, did you ever meet Disraeli?"

Sumner sighed. "Yes, back in '40. I thought he was one of the most vulgar fops I ever saw."

"Oh my, I hope you didn't tell him that to his face."

"No, but I made a point of snubbing him."

For the first time Douglass spoke. "That was a mistake, Senator. I saw him speak in the House during the debate on the repeal of the Corn Laws almost twenty years ago." Douglass had toured England with as much social success as Sumner a half decade later. "He spoke against Sir Robert Peel, and his philippics were among the most scathing and tortured of anything in their line to which I have listened. His invectives were all the more burning because delivered with the utmost coolness and studied deliberation." He had Lincoln and Sumner's full attention. "Mr. President, Disraeli is a most dangerous man."[20]

Adams added, "During my time in England, despite the fact that Disraeli as leader of the Tories in Parliament led his strong minority in sharp attacks on the policy of the Palmerston government, he never once did so on what they called the 'American question,' despite repeated urging by the friends of the South."[21]

Lincoln asked, "Why?"

"I believe he has no natural animus against the United States, a feeling that was rife among the Tories. He also broke with Lord Derby, the leader of the Tory Party before the latter's incapacitation last year, in defending the United States during the Trent Affair, saying that he thought America had been placed in a very difficult position in which she had acted honorably. After Palmerston's government declared war, he turned those very talents Douglass here has referred to against Lord Russell, the Foreign Secretary, during inquiries in the House of Commons. Made Russell sweat, and the man can't afford to lose another ounce. I have no doubt Disraeli knows exactly what ignited the war."

Sumner added, "Bright informs me that there are two things that drive Disraeli. He is drunk on fame. And he will maintain the empire at all costs, at all costs."

"So he won't take it kindly if we decide to keep Canada?"

"Mr. President, Disraeli will spend the treasure of a hundred years of empire to ensure the survival of that empire."

Douglass spoke again. "If I learned anything of the British in my stay there, it is that they are implacable, especially if they have been humiliated. They are Romans in that."

"So we shouldn't beat them too much, is that it, gentlemen?" It was not a question that they could answer, nor one Lincoln expected them to. "Well, our Irish project should put that to the test, I think." His eyes twinkled with another story. "You know, Paddy is always up for a fight. We just have to point that pugnacious disposition to something useful. This reminds me of an emigrant form Ireland. Pat arrived in New York on election day, and was, perhaps, as eager to vote early and late and often. So, upon his landing at Castle Garden, he hastened to the nearest voting place, and as he approached, the judge, who received the ballots, inquired, 'Who do you want to vote for? On which side are you?' Poor Pat was embarrassed; he did not know who were the candidates. He stopped, scratched his head, then, with the readiness of his countrymen, he said: 'I am fornent the government, anyhow. Tell me, if your Honor plases, which is the rebellion side, and I'll tell you how I want to vote. In Ould Ireland, I was always on the rebellion side, and by Saint Patrick, I'll stick to the same in America.'"[22]

He got up, suddenly serious, and stood before the fire grate. "You know, I did my best to avoid this war. 'One war at a time,' I said to everyone. 'One war at a time.' And we would have got through it too, except for the Laird Rams. The British just could not leave well enough alone. And now we both are in a war that neither of us wanted." He shook his head. "I thought I had a knotty problem with war production, but that is just a ball of string compared to this Gordian Knot. Anyone seen Alexander's sword?"

PORT HUDSON, LOUISIANA, FRIDAY, MARCH 18, 1864

The French gunners were superb. Shot after shot tore away chunks of the parapet manned by the men of the Corps d'Afrique. The French assault regiments had dashed from its forward trenches toward the point on the bastion where the shells were concentrated.

The tip of the assault was not French, though. It was Sudanese in sky-blue uniforms. Napoleon III had pressured the ruler of Egypt to loan him a regiment of African Muslim slave soldiers better able to survive the yellow-fever Vera Cruz coast. They had come north with the French army out of Mexico with a reputation for savagery and had fought at Vermillionville where their massacre of surrendered Union soldiers had soiled the honor of the victory. Bazaine had waited until this moment for an opportunity he could punish them in a useful way. Their white officers led from the front, mindful of the disgrace they must expiate. Behind them the horde ran ululating, *"Allah u akbar!"*

Behind the parapets the Union black soldiers and their white officers crouched as the French shells pounded the earthen ramparts of the bastion flinging bodies through the air. The crew of the brigade's single coffee mill gun had thrown a blanket over their piece to keep the flying dirt from the disintegrating parapet off the mechanism. Through the deafening artillery *"Allah u akbar!"* keened to a howl closer and closer. Then the shout went up within the bastion, "Up, boys, up!" Men threw themselves forward in firing position. *"Allah u akbar!"*

"Fire!" The front of the Sudanese wave collapsed, but those behind surged over the fallen. *"Allah u akbar!"* The wave of sky blue flowed forward dropping bodies by the score, but still they came. *"Allah u akbar!"* Most of their white officers were down by now, but still they came. They crossed the last open space and impaled themselves on the abattis, bunching up as those in front tried to climb over the stake-studded logs. Here the canister caught them, sweeping away dozens with each discharge. The French artillery had ceased; their men were too close to the bastion walls. Now the coffee mill gun's *click-bang* sounded as the gunner began turning the crank, and the faster he turned it, the faster the staccato steam hammer sound became. The Sudanese were melting away, their wild charge hung up on the abattis. *"Allah u akbar,"* died away, replaced by a wail of fear. Suddenly they broke to the rear and through the ranks of the follow on French line regiment, which would do no better.

The boys of the Corps d'Afrique waved their caps and cheered as their chaplain raised his hands to heaven and shouted, "God be praised!"

THE LONDON GUILDHALL, FRIDAY, MARCH 18, 1864

At the moment Lincoln was making his wry comment on not beating the English too much, their Prime Minister was bringing the attendees at the Lord Mayor's dinner to their feet in thunderous applause. Again and again he had put his finger on the country's "inexhaustible" resources available in a righteous war. Now Benjamin Disraeli ended, saying, "She is not a country that when she enters into a campaign has to ask herself whether she can support second or third campaigns. She enters into a campaign which she will not terminate till right is done."

Lord Derby's (son of the late party leader and pronounced "Darby," as God intended it) applause was, however, pro forma. Described as the most isolationist Foreign Secretary Great Britain had known, he was privately aghast as the fact that his country was in an open-ended war, with not some alien, despotic regime, but flesh of its flesh and bone of its bone. His tentative attempts to haul Disraeli down from his war to the death position had got him nowhere.

Strangely to Derby and to Lord Salisbury, Secretary for India, Disraeli was obsessed with the Russian threat to the Ottoman Empire, a throwback, they thought, to the Crimean War of the previous decade. Salisbury recalled Disraeli's impassioned argument to the Cabinet:

> If the Russian had Constantinople, they could at any time march their Army through Syria to the mouth of the Nile, and then what would be the use of our holding Egypt? Not even the command of the sea could help us under such circumstances . . . Our strength is on the sea. Constantinople is the Key to India and not Egypt and the canal the French are building.[23]

His Cabinet colleagues were at a loss at Disraeli's constantly looking over his shoulder at Russia while engaged in a deadly struggle with the United States. The British public was inflamed to avenge the unparalleled naval and military defeats of British arms at Charleston and in upstate New York the previous October. To be sure, Disraeli was first of the pack baying for revenge. With a longer view, a twenty-first-century historian would write that "Disraeli had always been brilliant at seizing political advantages from a situation—improvising opinions and positions, and then, in the aftermath of triumph, consolidating his position and making something of it which was truly statesmanlike."[24] Had he not as the Conservative Party leader in the House of Commons brought down the Russell administration by loyally supporting the war but at the same time undermining those in power who had allowed it be brought on? Providentially, Lord Derby's late father, the head of the Conservative Party had retired for ill health at this time, allowing Disraeli to ride the Conservative tide right into Number 10 Downing Street. But now the war was his.

And who was this man wielding the might of the greatest empire of modern times? Lord Salisbury said of him that "one burning desire dominated his actions—zeal for the greatness of England was the passion of his life."[25] Nothing could place him at a greater distance from Lincoln, who had described glory as "that attractive rainbow, that rises in showers of blood—that serpent's eye that charms to destroy."[26] Yet each was determined to make his mark on history. Disraeli put it, "We are here for fame." Lincoln was the more subtle when he spoke of the desire to make life worthy of remembrance. Outwardly, Disraeli, who had been the byword for foppish elegance, could not have been more different from Lincoln, who was simply oblivious to fashion. Disraeli's lavender kid gloves were a universe away from Lincoln's ill-fitting and rumpled plain black suits.

Both were also known for a lack of malice and a refusal to exact personal or political revenge on their opponents and detractors and both aroused the love of those around them for the same reason—they were men of "patience, gentleness, unswerving and unselfish loyalty." Both were superb politicians with a shrewd judge of human nature. They also had that indefinable something that made men listen. When Disraeli stood in the House to speak, the anterooms and lobbies emptied out as members rushed to take their green leather seats. He had a clear, rich voice that grew more beautiful as he extended it to the furthest benches. And he always had something worth hearing. Lincoln's oratory had moved history. His 1860 Cooper Union speech in New York had rumbled like a political earthquake through the North that landed him in the White House. But his speech at Gettysburg, so short that the cameramen had not time to take a picture, had left the vast crowd awestruck and speechless.

Yet neither man was typical of his country's elite. Disraeli was the converted Jew, who for all his sincere devotion to the Church of England, provoked a seamy prejudice in certain circles that the genius of the English people was able to rise above. He succeeded by sheer ability and became the indispensable man to the Conservative Party, which he had been actively transforming to a party that appealed across class lines. Lincoln was the ultimate outsider. For his origins to be more humble, his father would have to have been a slave. His Western accent grated on sophisticated Eastern ears, and his ungainly appearance, utterly unmodified by any sense of sartorial style, provoked the cruelest derision. As Disraeli was making over his party into a new national force, Lincoln had leaped aboard the new Republican Party and rode it to its first victory and sunk its foundations deep into the country, north of the Mason–Dixon Line, at least.

Disraeli's leadership of the nation in war was being likened to that of the Elder Pitt, the savior who had lead Britain to triumph in the Seven Years War over a hundred years before. Disraeli rallied the nation and marshaled its might for the struggle against the upstart republic. If the Liberator, Simon Bolivar, had once remarked that the army was a sack with no bottom, he obviously had not had the staggering wealth of the British Empire at his call. Another factor was Disraeli's ability to give voice to the mind of the British people. Their pride had been wounded by their defeats and had awakened an iron determination to be avenged. So the House voted tax rates that had not been seen since the wars of Napoleon, and Britain paid.

The flood of Southern cotton had put millions of idled mill workers and others back to work. The loss of the immense Northern market for British iron had been partially replaced by the South's pent-up demand for rails, bridging, and other iron products. Much of the rest had been soaked up by the vast shipbuilding programs that had filled every capable shipyard in the United Kingdom with the keels, ribs, and armor of the new ironclad classes that had been rushed into design. Vulcan's forge glowed as his hammer beat from one end of the island kingdom to another.

Still, Disraeli looked east over his shoulder more and more.

His colleagues had repeatedly argued that the tsar's determined efforts to avoid war with Britain after the battle of the Upper Bay of New York was proof that he did not intend war. Alexander II had to publicly eat his pride to apologize officially to the Court of St. James and to the Queen personally for the participation of Russian warships in the battle. He had pleaded that they had been drawn unintentionally into the battle in defense of a friendly port. It was all intensely regrettable that Admiral Lisovsky had acted without orders. The tsar went so far as to sack the admiral, publicly, that is. Intent on extracting revenge from the Americans and gratified by the tsar's humiliating acknowledgment of Britain's power, the Cabinet had been glad to back off a second war with Russia. The thrashing Russia had received in the Crimean War continued to pay dividends.

Thus it came as a shock to the Cabinet to be presented with a copy of the secret Russo-American treaty of alliance sold by a file clerk at the American State Department. Gen. Sharpe may have created a robust and talented American national intelligence system, but the British had centuries of successful espionage experience that allowed them to artfully cultivate traitors. The source of this document was not the only agent they were running either.

The evidence now seemed to tumble into their arms. Three American-designed monitors were discovered to be fitting out at the huge Russian naval base at Kronstadt that guarded the approaches to St. Petersburg. With the Great Armament sent to American waters, the Russians were now doubly sure of defending their capital from the Royal Navy.[27]

ST. PETESBURG, RUSSIA, MARCH 19, 1864

The English, for all their empire, were more than a little tone deaf when it came to understanding other peoples. They had seriously misread Russia in the lead up to the Crimean War just as they were doing now. What they simply did not comprehend was the enormous motive force of the piety of the Russian people. A warning had been sounded the year before in the first volume of Alexander Kinglake's masterful series on the Crimean War:

When the Emperor of Russia sought to gain or to keep for his Church the holy shrines of Palestine, he spoke on behalf of fifty millions of brave, pious, devoted subjects, of whom thousands for the sake of the cause would joyfully risk their lives. From the serf in his hut, even up to the great Tsar himself, the faith professed was the faith really glowing in his heart, and violently swaying his will.[28]

It should have come as no surprise then when news of the victory of American and Russian ships in the battle of the Upper Bay of New York had reached Alexander II, he had fallen on his knees, crossed himself, and exclaimed, "Glory to God!" The young Tsar-Liberator at that moment embodied the dream of every Russian to plant the Cross of Christ once more on the dome of the Cathedral of the Holy Wisdom (Hagia Sophia) in Constantinople. The fate of the greatest church in Christendom, until the building of St. Peters in Rome, epitomized the fate of the Orthodox world. The Ottoman tide had finally washed over the battered walls of Theodosius to flood into the vast marble and mosaic-glittering interior of the cathedral on that evil Tuesday in May 1453.[29] Mehmet II the Conqueror himself rode his white horse inside to order it converted into a mosque. His armies and those of successors swept over the last of the Orthodox kingdoms in the Balkans. The only Orthodox monarch to survive this tide was the Grand Prince of Moscow. And that throne was sorely beleaguered. The sultan's Tatar vassals slaved and raided into Russia for centuries, filling their galleys and harems with Russian and Ukrainian slaves.

And to the court of Ivan III fled the niece of Constantine XI, the Emperor of the Romans, who had thrown away his life in the defense of Constantinople, a heroic end for the last of the Caesars. Ivan took the princess to wife, and from that moment was transformed from prince to Caesar (tsar in Russian) for the dower of the princess was nothing less than the legitimacy of Rome itself, that had passed with Constantine the Great to Constantinople. Moscow was proclaimed the Third Rome with the codicil that there would be no other. And slowly Russia grew in strength, first crushing the Tatar kingdoms that had tormented it, then moving like a glacier inexorably east and south against the borders of the Ottoman Empire. Russia had become the Champion of Orthodoxy, and every victory shone with the glory of Holy Crusade.

The Crimean War had been sparked by the Russian desire to protect the Orthodox subjects of the Sublime Porte from the outrages of their Muslim rulers. Four hundred years these peoples had suffered; only the Greeks had broken away in the early part of the century, but the southern Slavs still writhed under the Ottoman yoke as did countless other Greeks, Armenians, and Arab Christians in the Middle East.[30]

For the Russians that war had been a holy crusade to free the fettered Orthodox peoples, but the British had chosen to see it only in its great power context. A Russia triumphant over the corpse of the Ottoman Empire was a threat to Egypt and more importantly to India, the jewel in the crown, and largest source of imperial revenue. So there was seen the spectacle of Christian Britain and France going to war with Christian Russia to prevent the liberation of millions of Christians oppressed by Muslim Turks. It became fashionable to preach from Church of England and French Catholic pulpits of the barbarous and superstitious-ridden Orthodox Church and ennoble the Turk who had ridden into the Hagia Sophia with his warhorse red to the fetlocks with Christian blood.

Alexander II had only come to the throne in the last year of that war and had to admit it was lost. For the first time he drank the cup of humiliation pressed to lips by Britain. He vowed he would never do it again. His almost servile attempts to stay out of war with Britain the previous fall had only been a deception, a word for which the Russians set much store. The treaty with the Americans would become operative at the optimum time for Russia and that would be spring when the new grass would feed the chargers and artillery horses of Russia, when the roads would dry for marching armies.

The American alliance to the casual observer was an odd one. Yet for the Russians it was a matter of deep strategic interest. Ever since the American Revolution, Russia had been a benign if not friendly power. At either ends of the planet form each other, they simply had no strategic conflicts. Instead, trade and lessons learned in taming vast virgin continents were freely exchanged. For example, the ships of the Russian squadron in New York were American designed and their guns American cast. Americans were building Russia's railroads as well. But it was not these matters drove the alliance. It was fear. Russia's defeat in the Crimean War had convinced Alexander II and his people that the greatest threat they faced was British world hegemony. And the only counterweight they saw was the rise of the American republic. Now that republic was in danger of self-destruction, the rebellion armed and equipped by Britain. In the first years of the American Civil War, Russia had maneuvered skillfully to prevent an Anglo-French-forced mediation on the Americans that would have resulted in Southern independence. Its mature diplomatic advice had saved the Lincoln administration from more than one pitfall. Russia's primary foreign policy objective had become preservation of the American Union. With the British attack on the United States, that policy required more than diplomatic support. It demanded that Russia throw her sword on the scales of war.

5

Breaking Out

As much as Dahlgren liked the sea, standing on the bridge with Captain Lamson during a late-winter Atlantic gale put too high a premium on steady footing. He had sense enough to realize a cork leg was a liability and excused himself to go below, leaving Lamson in his element. The young captain was actually enjoying himself as the rain streamed down his slicker.

Growing up the son of the most famous admiral in the Navy had long since cured Dahlgren of seasickness. He found his cabin and threw himself into a chair. The heaving of the ship ensured he would have no guests, except perhaps that Russian naval ensign, Nikolai Rimsky-Korsakov, sent along as His Imperial Majesty's representative on this expedition. His American staff were soldiers and landlubbers, all a shade of pale green and immobile in their quarters, each surely cursing his decision to volunteer for this mission. It gave Dahlgren time to think.

He picked up the thread, remembering back to when Meagher, Lamson, and he had arrived at the President's cottage at the Old Soldiers Home outside of Washington the previous December. They were ushered to the library, where the fireplace glow seemed to bring out the red richness of the wood paneling. Seated at a long, green felt-covered table in the middle of the room were Gus Fox, Edwin Stanton, James McPhail, and a Russian admiral, surely Rear Admiral Lisovsky. Lamson recognized and exchanged smiles with Henry Adams. A few junior officers of both services were setting up maps on boards. Their eyes gathered this in with a glance, but the man standing in front of the three-sided bay window instantly drew their attention. Lincoln's long presence was illuminated by the cool winter's light from the windows. He turned and smiled as all three officers came to attention. "Our heroes three," he said then came over to shake their hands.

"General Meagher, fortune's child, there's no man I'd rather have here today." Meagher glowed at the compliment.

Then he put his hand on Dahlgren's shoulder in the proud but gentle way of a father. "My boy," he said. Dalghren's father was Rear Adm. John Dahlgren. The admiral, then a captain, commanded the Washington Navy Yard, had quickly become an indispensable source of technical information on ordnance and sound military common sense. They had become fast friends, and when the then Capt. Dahlgren had returned broken from Gettysburg, hovering near death from the loss of a leg, Lincoln had sat at his bedside holding his hand. His own little boy, Willie, had died eighteen months before, and his soul-rending grief found solace in helping this young man hold onto life. For his heroism at Gettysburg, Lincoln jumped him from captain to well-deserved colonel before his twenty-first birthday.[1]

Then he turned to Lamson. "So, Roswell, there's been a lot of water under the bridge since that day we met in Washington while you were fitting out *Gettysburg*. Victory hangs on that name."[2]

Introductions were made, and Lincoln retreated to stand with his back to the warmth of the fireplace. "I tell you outright that the war is not going well, despite the victories that you have won. The British have us in the slow squeeze of a python. That is the way they have always won. Over time, their wealth and industrial strength will simply overwhelm us. We need a way to make the python let us go long enough for us to be able to turn out enough of Chris Spencer's repeaters, Mr. Gatling's guns, Col. Lowe's balloons, and some of Mr. Fox's surprises to throw onto the scales. That's where you three come in." You can give us time by setting big fires in the enemy's backyard, big enough that they dare not send another man or ship to our shores." He nodded to McPhail, who summarized the British advantages in industry, manpower, etc.

Fox picked up the narrative. "We propose to make two simultaneous raids on the British Isles." An ensign pulled the cloth cover off a map of the United Kingdom. Fox's pointer stabbed at Dublin first. "General Meagher, we prose to slip the Irish Brigade under your command into Dublin and take it by coup de main. Admiral Lisovsky's squadron will escort the brigade's transports and then raid the Irish Sea, dash south, and out into the open ocean again to prey upon the enemy's shipping."

Young Adams added, "And declare the Irish Republic which, I, as the representative of the President of the United States on your expedition, will recognize as an independent nation."

Meagher leaped to his feet, drew his sword, and threw it on the table. "Unto death!" Tears coursed down his face. "God bless the United States and the Republic of Ireland." He stood there and wept unashamedly. The goal of his life, a free Ireland, was suddenly real for this great-hearted Gael. All were moved by the response of the man called Meagher of the Sword.

Fox's pointer moved east across the Irish Sea, Wales, and the breadth of England to its east coast. "The objective of the second raid is the Royal Small Arms Factory, Enfield in Essex, and the Royal Power Mills as Waltham Abbey nearby. Captain Lamson will escort the transports with a cavalry regiment. Colonel Dahlgren will command the raid." He paused to let it sink in. Then he went on. "Enfield is barely twenty-five miles north of London. No enemy has penetrated England so close to London by land since William the Conqueror."[3]

Lincoln observed the sudden body language ripple in both men and the glow that sparkled their eyes. They had volunteered without a word.

Now months later with the waves pounding the *Kearsarge*, Dahlgren's enthusiasm was submerged in thoughtful appraisal of the plan whose details he had helped work out with Lt. Col. Charles Francis Adams, Jr., the commander of the 1st Massachusetts Volunteer Cavalry Regiment, which comprised the raiding force aboard the huge SS *Vanderbilt* plowing through the waves behind the *Kearsarge*.[4] The *Vanderbilt* was one of the tycoon's gift to the United States and one of the fastest and largest commercial ships in the world.[5] They would be flying false British colors all the way as a precaution, though the seas would be relatively empty in the hard winter weather, especially as Lamson was taking them out of the normal shipping lanes. Things would get riskier as they entered the North Sea and approached the Essex coastline, and riskier still as they entered the mouth of the Thames, then madness itself as they galloped the twenty-five miles to Enfield, and impossible as they galloped back to escape under Lamson's wing. Even locked in cold contemplation, Dahlgren was game. The bold glory of it was more than worth the throw to him. He suspected, though, that Lincoln's object would be satisfied if they simply raised hell, regardless of whether a man got home.

In another part of the North Atlantic, Meagher was contemplating just the same thought through the amber hue of a bottle of fine Irish whiskey. He had not noticed the disappearance of Lisovsky's smallest and fastest ship, HIMS *Almaz*. He sailed on the SS *Northern Star*, another of Vanderbilt's ships. Five other ships, including another Vanderbilt vessel, SS *Ariel*, carried the rest of his brigade shepherded by Lisovsky's squadron. For Meagher and the other Irish, there was no consideration of going home. For them, Ireland was home, the Old Sod, live or die. There would be no escape back to the New Sod as many of the Irish had come to call the United States. Unlike Dahlgren and his Massachusetts men, almost every one of the men in the Irish Brigade had been born a British subject. The British would be loathe to accept their new allegiance to the United States, especially since by declaring the Irish Republic, they would be renouncing their new allegiance and falling back within the jurisdiction of the Crown as rebels.

Henry Adams had tried to finesse the point during the voyage. Meagher went over the young man's arguments and found them too clever by half. The English were second to none as sticklers after points of international law, but when it came right down to a threat to their power, they could be world-class hangmen. The spirit of Judge Jeffreys came right out.[6] Meagher himself had come within an ace of such a fate.

Now, he thought, what would a well-brought-up man like young Adams know of such things. Adams had served as a private secretary to his father, Charles Francis Adams, the ambassador to the Court of St. James, and by all accounts aped the studied uselessness of British society. His father had hoped to force some character into him and sent him off with Lamson back in September to be a political advisor should he need one while ensuring the Laird Rams did not escape from their yard at Birkenhead. In the fighting that followed he had surprised everyone by his astute political advice and even more by an act of gallantry in saving Lamson's life. He had come back from the expedition something of a hero, and his elegantly written and argued articles in the American press had been used to justify the American actions to the civilized world in the chain of actions that had led to this war. The British Foreign Office had been to great pains attempting rather unsuccessfully to refute them. Seward had shrewdly picked him to be ambassador designate to the yet to be born Irish Republic. If the scheme failed, he would serve the useful purpose of the noble martyr.

He had explained to Meagher that "throughout this expedition, General, the Irish Brigade will remain under the jurisdiction of the United States. Even after the proclamation of the Irish Republic, you will remain under that jurisdiction. You will assist and support those elements of the Irish population, your Fenian friends, that will 'officially' declare the republic, only in the capacity of an ally. Thus you retain protection under the laws of war. After Britain recognizes the Irish Republic, well then, that is something that will have to be worked out then."

Meagher could only think of Judge Jeffreys.

ROYAL NAVY BASE, HALIFAX, NOVA SCOTIA, 4:45 P.M., TUESDAY, MARCH 22, 1864

The lieutenant was still obviously shaken from his ordeal. Tossing about the sea in this weather for three days in a crowded ship's boat would try anyone's nerves. Rear Adm. Sir Alexander Milne, commanding the Royal Navy's forces in this theater, interviewed the man himself.

The lieutenant was still shivering, and Milne pressed a cup of tea into his hands. "We saw them at dawn. Dozens of ships heading out to sea. *Nile* signaled to engage. I was with Captain von Donop on the bridge of *Jason*. We beat to quarters." He held the teacup with both hands to soak up the warmth. His eyes closed for a moment; then he gulped the tea down.

Milne was a patient man, but he had just learned of the loss of two of his blockade ships. HMS *Nile* was a ship-of-the-line, his own flagship, and *Jason* a corvette patrolling the waters off New York City.[7]

The lieutenant looked up. The tea had done him good, and he put down the empty cup. "We never had a chance, sir. This huge monitor led the other ships, Russians, six of them. Then there was the balloon flying over them."

"Go on, Lieutenant."

"*Nile* gave her a broadside, the monitor, but she just plowed through the shot. When she fired, my God! Two of the biggest muzzles I've ever seen were in that turret. She gutted *Nile* like a fish. I can still see those shells, as big as boulders, striking *Nile*. The balloon circled us, *circled* us, sir, *circled* us, moved as if it were steered. I thought balloons went with wind, but this thing just flew around and over us. And it wasn't round but cigar-shaped. Then it was dropping bombs on *Nile*. I saw them fall from the balloon. By then she had started to burn." His eyes told Milne that he was back there then.

"The Russians by then were all around us, two frigates and three corvettes and a sloop. Captain von Donop wouldn't strike, and we went down. I saw him last on the bridge shaking his fist at the Russians. The last I saw of the *Nile* was her burning"

"You said that there were dozens of enemy ships."

"Yes, sir, the rest were all merchantmen and transports."

"Did none of them stop to pick up survivors?"

"Aye, sir, one did, but the weather picked up and our boat got carried off. It was only God's mercy that your dispatch boat found us."

The balloon the lieutenant had observed was the U.S. Navy's *Steven Decatur* of the Washington class, sister to the Army's *George Washington* that had just resupplied Portland. The Navy's new Naval Aeronautical Service (NAS) had been given the second balloon of the class, not without a knock-down, drag-out Army-Navy fight that had to be settled by Lincoln himself. A dozen more were building at the Washington Navy Yard. Lincoln's Solomon-like solution was to have every second airship of the *Washington* Class go to the Navy. A smaller and lighter class, the *Nathan Hales*, were also under construction but in Connecticut. Their mission would be reconnaissance.[8]

On the way back to their Long Island base, Capt. Will Cushing and crew broke open a bottle of champagne to toast the destruction of the first warships at sea by airship. His feat in the defense of the Navy Yard in the battle for Washington—sinking British ships in the East River by dropping bombs with Col. Thaddeus Lowe from his tethered balloon— had transformed the twenty-one-year-old lieutenant into a captain overnight and commander of the new Naval Aeronautical Service (NAS). His reputation even before that battle had been awe-inspiring for its daring ever charmed with success. The old admirals looked upon him as the personification of the intrepid ideal of a naval officer. He had excelled in the small boat operations on Virginia's rivers where he led special operations under no one's eye but his own. To a man, every crew he commanded wanted to follow him to his next command.

More bottles were also opened and a generous rum ration issued to the crew aboard the USS *Dictator* as it headed back to the Brooklyn Navy Yard. This action too was its maiden voyage, rushed to completion after the start of the war and exercised in the Upper Bay of New York and Long Island Sound. John Ericsson's pet project was the leviathan of monitors at 4,438 tons and 312 by 50 feet. Her two 15-inch Dahlgren guns in a single turret and 174-man crew had outfought the smaller sixty-eight guns of the *Nile* and its crew of six hundred. Her captain walked the deck after the toasts and leaned against the metal railing to watch the bonfires that had been British ships slowing disappearing in his wake.[9]

For Milne this news was unnerving. Two more of the Royal Navy's ships destroyed so easily. And worse a large enemy force has broken into the Atlantic, six Russians and an enormous American monitor and a dozen merchantmen and transports. He did not know that the lieutenant had not seen the monitor return to the American coast.

He immediately dictated a dispatch to the Admiralty detailing this information and its implications, the most important of which was that the Russians had committed an open act of war. That dispatch would go with the one he had written that very morning of the news of the battle at Hampton Roads, happier news, indeed—two monitors taken or sunk and Fortress Monroe being steady reduced to rubble by the Great Armament.[10] Unofficial coordination with the Confederates would also be yielding dividends. Lee would send a strong force to attack the Norfolk Navy Yard from the land. With the Royal Navy controlling Hampton Roads, the great American navy yard with all its facilities would fall. The remainder of the monitor force that had defeated the Royal Navy would then be sunk or captured. The navy yard itself would be an enormous asset as a forward operating base almost on the doorstep of the American capital. And there was not a thing the Americans could do about it. Monitor construction was concentrated north of Baltimore. No city located on the waterways that fed Chesapeake Bay could build a monitor to send south to challenge Milne's ships which could then eventually range north up the bay and into the Potomac and Patapsco Rivers to threaten Washington and Baltimore. With the eventual fall of Fortress Monroe, the James River would then be open to ocean-going ships destined for Richmond. That, in turn, would facilitate the support of the Army of Northern Virginia, now dependent on supplies coming through Wilmington, North Carolina.

This news was the sort of slowly gathering strategic advantage that won wars by wearing down an enemy. Ask the French. Yet, on the heels of this news that would ring the bells of every church in the United Kingdom, came that of the escape of this Russo-American squadron with all its implications, especially that Russia was now in the war. The peal of the bells would then wring with foreboding.

COOPERSVILLE, NEW YORK, 5:05 P.M., TUESDAY, MARCH 22, 1864

Hope Grant recognized the culminating point of his spoiling attack into New York had passed.[11] He had wrecked one American division on the eighteenth, taken almost three thousand prisoners, and unbeknownst to him wounded both Hooker and Grant. He had concentrated twenty-five thousand men for this effort, but realized that their continued presence in the area north of the Little Chazy River simply made them a stationary target for the rapidly concentrating Army of the Hudson which outnumbered him two to one. He strung out his brigades on the north bank of the Little Chazy with the 12th opposite the town of Chazy covering the bridge, the Dublin Brigade to the east covering the Stetson Road Bridge, and the 1st Montreal Brigade filling out the line to Lake Champlain. The 9th Lancers were his personal reserve on the river line. The Hamilton Brigade he strung out five miles to the west to the village of Sciota as an anchor to guard his flank against the inevitable flanking maneuver. His second division was already on the move south and should cross the border in two days. He wanted that reserve close at hand for a very good reason. (map)

The enemy's new commander had shown surprising skill and aggressiveness over the last three days. He was surprised when Wolseley informed him the commander was George H. Sharpe, the American spy chief. Grant rolled his eyes. "Setting a fashion. You started it, Joe. Spy chiefs commanding armies. What next, female generals?" He coughed up a very good "harumph!'

Spy chief or no, Grant realized Sharpe needed watching. The man was not confining himself to the narrow strip of farmland paralleling Lake Champlain, barely three miles wide. Grant had that fingertip feel for the danger. Denison's scouts were reporting movement of large cavalry and infantry forces through the woods to the west. At the same time Sharpe's artillery was pounding the British severely from south of the Little Chazy River. The British simply did not have the ammunition for such an extended gunner's slugging match. What he had was coming down the railway to a supply dump just over the Great Chazy River near Coopersville.

He poured over the map. "See here, Joe," he said to Wolseley. "Pull back to this river line." He pointed to the Great Chazy River, which emptied into Lake Champlain three miles north of the Little Chazy River, their current defensive line. From the lake the river angled sharply northwest for eleven miles almost reaching the Canadian border before dipping south.

"Yes, I see. We refuse our right by angling it up with river, and Sharpe's outflanking move to the west will not catch anything. The weather is still too bad for them to stay in the field much longer."

"Give them a real twist too." He meant that they would remain in possession of a sliver of New York, sure to gall the Americans. Then he added, "Get them moving at dusk."

At that moment, Custer was leading a cavalry charge into the small village of Sciota eight miles to the west.

SHORELINE OF LAKE CHAMPLAIN, NEW YORK, 7:12 P.M., TUESDAY, MARCH 22, 1864

The night with all its stars had just settled over the lake shoreline when two Union brigades in very open order, their companies on line, marched onto the ice of the lake. Sharpe had had parties out the night before cutting holes in the ice to measure its depth. It was still frozen deep, deep enough for thousands of men to cross with their coffee mill and artillery batteries. Even as he shivered in his greatcoat, Sharpe thanked God for the hard upstate winters. Now he stood on the ice, encouraging the men as they stepped onto the surface. Every man's shoes were wrapped in cut-up blankets to protect against the cold and provide some traction. The frosty breath of thousands of men rose in wisps as they picked their down the bank onto the ice. [12]

The XI Corps commander, Maj. Gen. Adolph von Steinwehr, a former soldier in the German Brunswick Army, joined him to wish his boys well.[13] This normally "cool, collected and judicious" officer was still apprehensive about this damned foolhardy maneuver he had called it to Sharpe's face the night before when it had been proposed. Sharpe had just smiled. He raised his left arm and waved his hand. Then when the von Steinwehr was looking at the hand, he brought his right around in a sudden punch that stopped within an inch of his nose. The German instinctively stepped back, but it would have been too late had Sharpe intended to connect his fist with the man's nose. "You see, Adolph, the simplest deceptions work. Our artillery has kept them focused on the river in front of them, and Custer's encirclement to the west will draw them that way as well. They will be looking in every direction but the lake."

He paused then said, "Remember what the late great Stonewall said, Adolph? 'Always mystify, mislead, and surprise the enemy.' You and I were both at Chancellorsville, and it was on your flank that he fell, did he not?" Steinwehr could only nod, his mind flinching as it brought up the sheer terror and chaos as waves of shrieking Johnnies coming out of nowhere had shattered his command. "Well, then, hat's off to a great teacher. Our enemies will find we have been diligent students."

NORTH BANK OF THE GREAT CHAZY RIVER NEAR CHAZY, 11:30 P.M., TUESDAY, MARCH 22, 1864

Wolseley found McBean in the steeple of a church. The Scot pointed south across the river into the night. Large fires dotted the hidden landscape for miles. "Dunna ken aboune you, but we're in fer it come daylight."

"Hope Grant's timing, it seems, was perfect, McBean. They will be on us in the morning." They had been hearing the movement of artillery all night as well. McBean had already been informed by dispatch rider to get ready to pull out as the staff worked out the march order and route of the brigade.

Sharpe was indeed massing most of the rest of his two corps south of the Little Chazy. He wanted to fix Grant's attention on the south bank. The fires drew attention as nothing else would. They also served to keep the men warm as temperatures plummeted at night. A soldier from Russia had come forward with his experience in the tsar's army on how to stay warm. So the men huddled around big bonfires or when sleep was necessary lined up in groups of a hundred each man holding part of a long rope in his hands, and then the group coiled up. A hundred men could sleep on their feet that way and stay surprisingly warm with all that massed body heat. Every hour or so, the huddle would uncoil and recoil the opposite way so the men on the outside could be on the inside.

The British and Canadians were just happy to be on the move to generate some body heat. Despite their excellent cold-weather clothing, being out in this weather for days on end was starting to wear. There was a bustle all along the Little Chazy as they made preparations to move, all under the eye of Knight and his scouts. The British picket line had been too effective for them to slip across the frozen river, but there had been no pickets along the frozen lakeshore. It was Knight who had blazed a trail across the lake at night and sneaked in among the British from that unguarded direction. He had personally briefed

Sharpe. "If a few men can get behind that way, a whole brigade could do it too."

And now five thousand men in two brigades were doing just that. Their way was lit by oil lamps sitting in barrels sawn in half up and down with their backs to the further lakeshore. The insides had been painted white to reflect the light. They were strung out in rows five hundred yards apart. As Knight was signaling with colored lights that the enemy was preparing to move, von Steinwehr's brigades were following the barrel lights across the lake.

Col. Wladimir Krzysanowski walked at the head of his brigade, his feet crunching on the ice. Like so many other men in XI Corps he had rushed to the colors to defend his adopted land when the war broke out. He had raised the 58th New York, known as the Polish Legion, in New York City, and recruited into its ranks not just Poles but Russians, Danes, Frenchmen, Germans, and Italians. The regiment was trudging right behind him now, this little foreign legion, as were the other two New York regiments of the brigade. Krzysanowski went over in his mind his objective on the map that Sharpe had shown him — the bridge over the Great Chazy at Coopersville, barely four miles from the spot where Wolesely and McBean were conferring. Just across the river, the British had set up their base of supply at a railroad siding that allowed trains to come down directly from Montreal. Hope Grant's route of withdrawal was directly up the Stetson Road to the bridge at Coopersville.

"Damn! I've been too clever by half," Sharpe said to himself when he read Knight's message. He laughed. "Grant's humbugged me. The British are on the move. I had hoped to fix them not scare them away. Now it will be a race for the Coopersville Bridge." Von Steinwehr was too polite to comment on what happened to damn fool schemes. The wind picked up just then, and he pulled the collar of his greatcoat tighter around his neck. He looked up at the clouds racing east past the moon.

ON THE ICE OF LAKE CHAMPLAIN, 1:20 A.M., WEDNESDAY, MARCH 23, 1864
The thunder of an explosion of artillery fire to the southwest jerked every head in the two brigades on the ice in that direction. They could see the fiery arcs of the shells raining down on where the British had been. Krzysanowski was suddenly worried; the artillery bombardment had not been part of the plan he had been briefed. Instead of hesitating, he passed the order to quicken the pace.

Sharpe had decided to toss the humbug back into Grant's hands. It was one thing to withdraw quietly in the night out of contact with the enemy. It was quite another to retreat while still engaged with an aggressive enemy. Sharpe calculated that Grant might find it preferable to stay put and fight it out.

Hope Grant was just then riding down the Stetson Road to hurry up the withdrawal when the American guns opened up a quarter mile north of Chazy. The trains had already been put on the road, and now they panicked. The American artillery had set range tables for just this critical road in the days before. Their shells burst up and down its length, smashing wagons and butchering teams with jagged metal. Grant now found himself in the face of a stampede of terrified drivers and teams as they raced up the road. He and his lancer escort barely bounded into field to escape the panic. They took off across the field in the direction of the Little Chazy now illuminated by a burning farmhouse.

RUINS OF SCIOTA, NEW YORK, 1:30 A.M., WEDNESDAY, MARCH 23, 1864
Custer had retreated out of Sciota faster than he had charged into it. His scouts had assured him that there were only a few Canadian companies guarding this little hub of rural roads. He needed it if he were to fall on the enemy's flank and rear near the border. Instead of a few companies he found a full battalion of their volunteer infantry who seemed to have learned a thing or two at Clavarack, and three companies of British troops of the 1/47th Foot who had forgotten more than the Canadians had learned.

Custer liked to take things at the bounce, at the charge, but he had found a stoutly defended cluster of houses and barns. So he sent a cavalry brigade to cut all the roads leading into Sciota and waited with a studied lack of patience for the first infantry brigade of the following division to arrive and reduce the place. It had taken several hours of repeated assaults under heavy artillery support. Everything that could go wrong in a night battle did go wrong. Only as the houses and barns began to burn was there sufficient illumination to keep regiments from firing into each other.

Barely fifteen minutes before he had taken the surrender of the remaining enemy and congratulated the wounded Canadian captain who surrendered the heap of ashes and corpses that had once been a happy village (the British had not single officer left). He rode off into the night hoping to catch up with his cavalry brigade that he had ordered ahead and hurry them on. The infantry would have to trudge on behind. He was already behind schedule, an intolerable state that he would move heaven and earth to correct. For him the dark, cold, and snow on the ground were no excuses.

SOUTH BANK OF THE LITTLE CHAZY RIVER, NEW YORK, 1:45 A.M., WEDNESDAY, MARCH 23, 1864
Along a three-mile stretch of the river the bugles sounded the advance; their noise, magnified by the darkness, shrieked like banshees across the frozen water. Regiment after regiment pounded the air with hurrahs.

The sudden artillery bombardment had caught the British in the middle of their preparation to withdraw. Casualties had been relatively light given it was mostly unaimed fire, but horses had bolted and men run to cover. More dangerous were the coffee mill guns spraying bullets across the river, but it was the American gunners that had served their purpose in disrupting the enemy's departure. Into this chaos rode Hope Grant. He knew that if he did not extricate his men quickly, two American corps would be surging over the frozen river.

He sent couriers racing up and down the river to order an immediate withdrawal across open fields to the Coopertown bridge. Riding along the north bank of the river, he ran into Wolseley riding toward him. Grant leaned over to him. "Damned clever chap over there, Joe. Get everyone out now. Can't wait. I want . . ." then he lurched in the saddle as a coffee mill bullet stream sought out the gleam of his escort's lance heads and stitched through the mounted group on the road. Wolseley caught him in his arms as he fell from his horse. His own horse, badly wounded, fell to its knees. With strength he did not know he had, he threw himself and Grant from the slashing hooves and into the bushes.

Grant was bleeding from leg and shoulder, but no arteries were spurting, good sign. A lancer stumbled into the bushes and collapsed next them. Grant roused himself to one elbow. "Help him, Joe," he grunted and then fell back. Wolseley looked the man over, but he was dead. He bent over Grant, and heaved him up over his shoulder, and thanked God the general had been thin as a rail. The coffee mill gun had gone silent, and now his surviving escort was stumbling over the road looking for Grant. He cried out, "Here, here, the general." They rushed to him. Field bandages came out and wrapped his wounds. Lances were lashed to saddle blankets to form a litter and four men heaved him to their shoulders. One sergeant leaned over the general and held his hand. "We was with ye in India, sir. Not to worry."

LAKESHORE, ONE MILE EAST OF THE COOPERSVILLE CROSSING, 1:30 A.M., WEDNESDAY, MARCH 23, 1864

Will Mason held up his lamp and swung it back and forth as he looked out onto the blackness of the shoreline. "Do you see anything yet?" His partner was also swinging a lamp and answered, "No, nothing, but do you hear that?" The two scouts left there by Sergeant Knight listened intently to the dark, and gradually a shuffling noise, then the clink of accoutrements, became inescapable. The scouts now began to shout as they waved their lamps. In moments an officer came scrambling up the shore, saying a heartfelt if heavily accented, "Thank God!" Seconds later a wave of infantry came out of the darkness and crunched onto the beach sand, followed by one after another.

Leaving his staff to organize the rest of the command, Colonel Krzysanowski put the 58th New York on the road paralleling the Great Chazy on its south bank, the road to the Cooperville bridge, barely a mile away. The sound of artillery and bugles flew through the night air from the south. "Hurry, boys, hurry," he said as he set the hard pace.

THE BRIDGE AT CHAZY, NEW YORK, 1:47 A.M., WEDNESDAY, MARCH 23, 1864

Wolseley had no problem finding the bridge; American artillery was pouring over it from a dozen batteries. He could see the fire from their muzzles and the arc of their shells with their glowing fuses. It was a wonder and a relief to find McBean still alive. He was in a ditch with several hundred of his men. The Scotsman saw Wolseley in the glare of a burning shed, picking his way over the debris and shouted, "Get over here, ye damned fool." Wolseley threw himself into the ditch as a shell cut down the last two members of his staff following him.

McBean just grinned. "Must admit it now; these Jonathans shoot better than the Sepoys. I think their infantry will be over the bridge soon." The question of what next to do hung in the air. He went grim as Wolseley told him about Grant. "Worst luck, and Grant the best there ever was."

"McBean, you must hold the bridge for an hour while we get the rest of the army away."

"Aye, the tartan will hold."

"Godspeed, Scotland!" And Wolseley was off into the dark.

Not a moment too soon. The guns stopped suddenly. He knew it was time. He climbed out of the ditch. "Fix bayonets!" A clatter of bayonet sockets fixed onto rifles echoed down the ranks. "The 78th will advance!"

A man shouted, "Scotland forever!" and the regiment took up the cry. From across the bridge a voice replied, "Ireland for longer!" They could hear the laughter roll from the Americans massed there.

Then the drums started to beat the charge and a shout of "Hurrah!" came from the American side. The 78th stepped forward. A man suddenly darted back out of the ranks. McBean strode forward sword in hand to run the coward through, then saw the man snatch up a bayonet from the ground and fix it to his rifle. He looked up. "I wasna' runnin' awa,' sir." He rushed back to take his place.

On the American side of the bridge, as the men of Ruger's brigade gave their hurrah, Sharpe shook hands with Colonel Ruger, who then drew his sword. He drove the sword through his cap and walked to the head of the assault column; the artillery resumed sending solid shot, shells, and case shot streamed over the river to converge into the barricades at the other end of the bridge. The 9th Lancers had torn the field stone field walls apart nearby to build this stout defense. Now splinters of rock and large stones flew from each impact. The first two Highland companies threw themselves behind the pile as it shuddered and heaved with each strike. The others knelt behind them as the American ordnance flew overhead. The few foolish men to poke their heads up lost them.

Ruger bounded down the plank bridge at a run, his men following eight across, a solid mass of dark blue, the new moon dappling their blued bayonets held at port arms across their chests. The bridge sang as their feet flew across it. McBean scrambled to the top of the barricade just in time to see Ruger running ahead of his men.

"Up, laddies," he shouted, and two dozen men heaved themselves to the top as more men fanned out to the sides of the bridge. "Fire!"

The first ranks tumbled onto the bridge, but the press behind them simply flowed over the bodies. Ruger miraculously was untouched as he flew at the barricade and reached the top. The Highlander who had dropped his bayonet knocked aside Ruger's sword and rammed his blade through his chest and with a practiced twist, pulled it out. The dead man tumbled down onto the planks. He fell just as the tide swarmed over him and up the pile with a snarl. They had seen their colonel fall in those last few seconds, and the killing madness was upon them. The Scots held the top of the barricade until rifle fire thinned their number, then the Americans were over the top. McBean shot the first man and then another whose body fell on him; his sword and pistol fell from his hands as the weight of that big, dead man held him down. The fight swept past him as the Americans poured over the barricade. It was then that he heard, "Cuidich 'n Rhi!" like the sound wave of a large gun. "Cuidich 'n Rhi!"

The rest of the regiment had been kneeling behind the barricade; there had been no room for all of them at its top. Now they rushed forward, their pipers keening their way, to save their colonel. The surge of men in blue stopped and then began to back up as the bayonet drill of the Highlanders stabbed and thrust them back, leaving a trail of bodies. The rear ranks fired over them to cut down the enemy on the top of the barricade. In minutes they cleared the last American from the barricade and then fired down into the packed ranks on the bridge. Again the American guns came to life; case shot swept the Scots off the top of the barricade. Helping hands threw the dead man off McBean and pulled him to his feet. "Tuts, tuts, laddies. Just find me ma' sword." As soon as he was handed it, a dozen men dragged boxes behind the barricade and began to pass out grenades, light their fuses, and throw them into the crowded ranks on the bridge. Each blast brought screams from the Yanks. McBean crawled to the top and peered over to see that the Americans had pulled back across the body-carpeted bridge.

THE COOPERSVILLE BRIDGE, 2:02 A.M., WEDNESDAY, MARCH 23, 1864

Colonel Krzysanowski huddled with the scouts who had rejoined the column three hundred yards from the bridge. Will Mason was grinning in the lamplight hidden under a greatcoat as he pointed at something on the colonel's map. "Wagons are almost stampeding over the bridge, sir. Something's scared the bejezus out of them."

The Polish colonel almost licked his lips at the prospect of getting among the enemy's trains. "But what of the bridge guards?"

"Maybe a company of Canadians. Frenchies. We got close enough to hear them talk. Maybe twenty are guarding the bridge; the rest are probably asleep in their camp on the other side of the river."

Krzysanowski whispered to a sergeant, "Bring me Jean Pierre." When the Frenchman arrived, the colonel explained that he wanted him and several of the other French immigrants in the 58th to wander up to the bridge as if they were fellow Canadians speaking French to get them to lower their guard. "*Mon colonel,*" he replied, "these Quebecois speak French, of course, but it is a very old-fashioned Norman country French. They would know instantly that I am not one of them." The colonel looked disappointed, but the Jean Pierre suggested, "Why not send Valois? He is Quebecois."

"But do we trust him? To deceive his own people?"

"Ah, *mon colonel*, if he had wanted to desert, it would have been easy to do it by now. He bears no great love for Canada or the Queen. The poor man married a Protestant girl. The Church excommunicated him, and her brothers beat him half to death. The Queen's court would not hear the case. So he came south and vowed never to return. Yes, I think we can trust him."

So it was that Louis Michel Valois, sergeant of the Union Army, sauntered down the road with three other French speakers, and engaged the guards in a friendly conversation, pulling out a bottle of wine to make it even friendlier as they all leaned against the bridge railing to let the wagons rush by. Valois passed himself off as part of the advance party of a battalion coming up from the lake road. So the guards were not surprised when the 58th came marching out of the dark; their dark-blue greatcoats in the moonlight were indistinguishable from British ones.

The officer of the guard sent a squad to stop the wagons to let the infantry cross; they were smiling when the first rank marched onto the bridge and suddenly rushed them. Not a shot was fired as they were disarmed. The rest of the column rushed over the bridge to capture the other guards and then overrun their camp. The wagon drivers had no idea what was going on, only that their desperate desire to get over the bridge had been thwarted. Their panic had not been wrung out of them in the two miles they had come from the Little Chazy. Krzysanowski played into their fears by ordering them over the bridge and into the wagon park with the rest of the trains that had come from the Little Chazy. Near the wagon park he found a locomotive and fifty cars on a siding fully loaded with supplies, an unsuspected bonus. The night was yielding much success.

The rest of his brigade and the Hecker's follow-on brigade were arriving. Krzysanowski knew he could hold the bridge and river line against anything that might come his way.

THE STETSON ROAD BRIDGE OVER THE LITTLE CHAZY RIVER, 2:15 A.M., WEDNESDAY, MARCH 23, 1864

Wolseley's orders to the Dublin Brigade to hold the next bridge over the river did not arrive in time. The brigade responded to Grant's original withdrawal command, and despite the losses from enemy artillery had put themselves on the Stetson Road to march north to Coopersville. Steeled to take heavy casualties, the Americans stormed over the bridge without losing a man. The British were gone. Further down the Little Chazy, the 1st Montreal Brigade, had also pulled out up the Lakeshore road paralleling the lake. Each column had about three miles to cover to reach Coopersville, about an hour or more at a good marching pace, but those wraith children of the night, confusion and caution, would slow them down.

The 12th Brigade was also on the march north, leaving the valiant Scots to cover their departure. They had five miles to go and on a road through woods so thick that they blotted out the moonlight. They would be the last over the Coopersville bridge.

Those valiant Scots were about to be swamped. Two more assaults over the bridge had been beaten back while the Americans were crossing the ice up and down stream by brigades. Their infantry could cross easily enough now that now no one would be contesting their way, but the bridge was vital to get horses and guns across. Still the Scots hung on as their flanks were pressed in.

Sharpe was about to cross the river on foot with his staff, when an aide found him. "Sir, General Sherman has arrived at the railhead and will be here as soon as they unload his horse."

"My compliments to General Sherman, Captain. You can show him the spot where I crossed." He could not afford to delay operations at this moment by trying to pass command in the middle of the most difficult of all military operations, a night battle.

On the other bank, he stood to listen to the fighting around the bridge as an endless column of men marched passed him and into the night. To the east he could see only the fiery arcs of his own artillery landing where the British had been.

He quickly found that despite the local guides and a good supply of oil lanterns, torches, and the pale glow of a dimming moon, the night acted like a lead weight on every action. Feeling one's way in the dark was a deep phobia of the human race, and it was compounded infinitely when tens of thousands of men were trying to do it at the same time and half of them wanted to kill you.

McBean was too good an old soldier to not know how to take advantage of that very fear. He had barely five hundred men left on their feet now. He had given Wolseley his hour or as close to it as he dared. First the companies at the bridge slipped away hidden by the stone barricade. Then he pulled back the flanking companies. One by one they broke contact and hurried into the dark. It was now that the value of a long service army organized into brotherhoods that were formally called regiments showed its value. They held together despite the dark, dragging their wounded with them. The Americans kept firing into the ghostly shadows long after the last Scot disappeared.

"We Cannot Lose a Fleet"

FIVE MILES NORTH OF SCIOTA, NEW YORK, 4:03 A.M., WEDNESDAY, MARCH 23, 1864

Custer had pushed and bullied his command along a single, poor country lane hemmed in by forest and swamp. And when that gave out, it was through those thick woods that his cavalry picked its way. Men were constantly getting lost in the dark. Then crossing the frozen tributary of the Great Chazy and Bear Creek slowed them down even more. The horses had to be walked carefully over the ice. He had lost touch with the infantry brigades, and the guns had already been left behind. He called another halt. His aide lifted a lantern over the map. "If this is Bear Creek that we have just crossed, then all we have to do now is follow it as it feeds into the Great Chazy. Then it's only a three miles to Champlain." Champlain was his objective, the cork in the bottle that would trap the enemy. That's if he arrived with any troops.

He paused a moment before giving the command to resume the march. "By then it should be daylight." Even in thick gloves his hands were cold. "God, I have come to hate the night."

COOPERSVILLE ROAD, NEW YORK, 4:10 A.M., WEDNESDAY, MARCH 23, 1864

That was a sentiment shared by just about everyone on both sides. As soon as the battle became mobile, the dark had broken down command and control. Lost men were wandering all over the area between the Little and Great Chazy Rivers. Most of the soldiers in both armies were now going into twenty-four hours with no sleep, and everyone could have used a hot meal to ward off the energy-draining cold. The countryside was full of stragglers from both armies who had slipped away to find shelter from the cold around makeshift fires or broke into the farmhouses, barns, and sheds scattered about.

Sharpe's plan had been brilliant, but he had not counted on a boatload of friction that a night winter operation would bring on. As long as the plan was on a static river line, it was relatively easy to control, but now that most of his two corps had marched off into the night, things that could go wrong suddenly all seemed to wrong at the same time. At least he was encouraged by the sound of a serious fight to the north. He could only hope his subordinate commanders were pressing forward.

For Wolseley his problem was immediate and only a few hundred yards away. He galloped forward and ran into a courier who couldn't wait to blurt out what he had seen. The enemy was at strength in front of the Coopersville bridge. They had engaged the withdrawing column. The man had no idea of what was going on with all the firing to the east.

That fight had started when the advance guard of the 1st Montreal Brigade pitched into the rear guard of Colonel Hecker's brigade. Both units were traveling along the road to Coopersville, but the British brigade had picked up a few American stragglers which gave them warning that an American brigade was not too far ahead.

Col. Pitt Rivers was just the man for that moment. A Grenadier Guardsman, he had found himself in command of the 1st Rifles after their commander had been killed at Clavarack. That certainly would not have gone down well with the Rifles had not Rivers been well-known for his talent for organization and improvement of the rifle in the British Army. After the fight at Rouse's Point, he replaced the fallen brigadier and had handled the brigade well. With the brigade's right on the river, he wheeled the Rifles and the Canadian Queens Own Rifles out into the fields on the left with orders to swing right as soon as they heard firing from the advance guard, the Victoria Volunteer Rifles of Montreal. The Prince of Wales Regiment he held in reserve. He passed the word down the column that the Americans ahead stood between them and a hot meal across the river.

The Canadians in the advance guard picked up their pace to close with the tail of Hecker's brigade, a few companies of the 82nd Illinois. Fortune, then having given Rivers the advantage of picking up stragglers now threw its favor to the Americans. The Canadians did not see the straggler sitting by the road, emptying the pebble from his shoe. Pvt. Daniel Spindler at first thought it was another American regiment, but a few British accents convinced him otherwise. In the darkness both sides looked much alike in their dark-blue greatcoats and headgear. Spindler could only think of his friends up ahead. He realized what was going to happen. The patriotism of this eighteen-year-old recent immigrant from the Rhineland burned with a bright-blue flame like so many other Germans. His company, Company C, was the rearguard. They were almost all Jewish immigrants, from Chicago, as was their able regimental commander, Col. Edward Saloman. Spindler had been recruited with his entire *Deutsches Sport Verein* (German Sport Club). He was a champion runner, lithe and quick.

He simply stepped onto the road between companies. The Canadians were intent on what lay ahead, not what was marching with them. No one cared if they noticed how Spindler trotted up ahead passed the ranks on the road. If they did notice, he was probably a messenger. Then he simply disappeared into the field on the left. He sprinted forward and almost immediately caught his foot on a stone and fell face forward onto the frozen ground. His nose bloody and the wind knocked out of him, he lay still for a moment, only to hear the rustle and crunch of a large body of men behind him. He barely got up on one elbow before a boot stepped on his back, then another kicked him in the head as it went by. His body nearly tripped one man who swore, "Bloody hell," but moved on. Spindler pulled himself up with great effort; the blood from his nose was freezing on his wispy blond beard. His hands had been scrapped in the fall, and his knees ached from their impact on the hard ground.

He was completely disoriented as he got to his feet, peering around into the night washed only by the palest of moonlight. The sound of the enemy unit that had walked over him receded in the dark. He realized that his weapon was missing. No use to look for it now. He stood still for the barest moment and then remembered that the moon had been on his right. Maybe two minutes had passed. He headed off back to where he thought the road was.

He found it, rather, he heard it by the thudding shuffle of a unit on the march. The moonlight glinted off their bayonets and brass. For what he had to do, Spindler could not join the column again. He would risk the parallel field again. Now he began to run, risking the furrows, and he flew past the column on the road. The cold air burned his lungs, but he quickly found his pace, all fluid grace, that took him past company after company. If any head turned in the column, he was gone before they could think about it. One, two, three companies he passed, then a break and more marching troops, and again he passed them like a ghost, one company after another. Then the road was empty and quiet. He veered onto it and ran for all he was worth. All he could hear was the smooth workings of his lungs and the blood rushing through his heart. Then again the clink of accoutrements and the glint of metal.

"*Kameraden!*" he screamed as he kept running. "*Kameraden, Alarm! Alarm! Die Englander!*"

First Lieutenant William Loeb stopped suddenly as the shout reached him. He was at the tail of Company D and commanded the rear guard of the 82nd Illinois. A Rhinelander, like Spindler, Loeb was a good soldier whose quick wits had earned him a commission from the ranks. Even before Spindler reached him he gave the order to halt and turned his rearguard around to block the road.

Spindler flew out of the dark almost into Loeb's arms. Between deep gulps of air, he got out what he had seen. Excited he spoke in German, *"Die Englander, Herr Oberleutnant, die kommen."* As soon as Spindler was able to explain that not only were the enemy approaching up the road but had swung out into the field in a great arcing movement, Chancellorsville and Gettysburg flamed through Loeb's mind. On both those fields, the Germans had had the great bad luck to be struck in the flank. It is a rare army that does not buckle and break under such an attack, yet the Germans had been blamed for both disasters, and earned by it the derisive epithet of the "Damned Dutch."

Loeb said out loud, *"Nie wieder!"* (Never again!) and sent his fastest runners up the column to warn its regiments of the impending blow out of the night. As they got the word, company after company halted and formed line of battle to their left. They had only minutes to spare as the swinging door of the British flanking movement began to close with the Americans just as the Queen's Own Rifles ran into the fire of the American rearguard.

The Rifles had been the base of the arc and were the first. Out of the darkness they emerged into the weak moonlight and right into the volleys of 82nd. At that range it was like a hammer. The Rifles staggered as their ranks thinned suddenly. Then their superb training took over as they returned fire. Pitt-Rivers's horse had gone down in the volley, and he leapt off the dying beast and landed on his feet. "Forward the Rifles! Give them the bayonet!" He raced through the ranks to lead them and felt a red hot poker slam through his left ear. He put his hand to the ear and felt the hot blood and mangled flesh, and he just kept on running forward.

STETSON ROAD NEAR COOPERSVILLE, NEW YORK, 4:20 A.M., WEDNESDAY, MARCH 23, 1864

Wolseley had had little time to enjoy the irony of having succeeded to effective command of an army a second time in this war. Clavarack had been bad enough, but at least that had been in daylight. Three hours now, and it would be light enough to see, and Coopersville was less than a quarter mile away. He had found the Dublin Brigade and marched north with it.

He worrying about what had happened to the couriers he had sent to the officer commanding the depot north of the Coopersville bridge. That officer had been ordered to make preparations to receive the army, resupply and feed it.

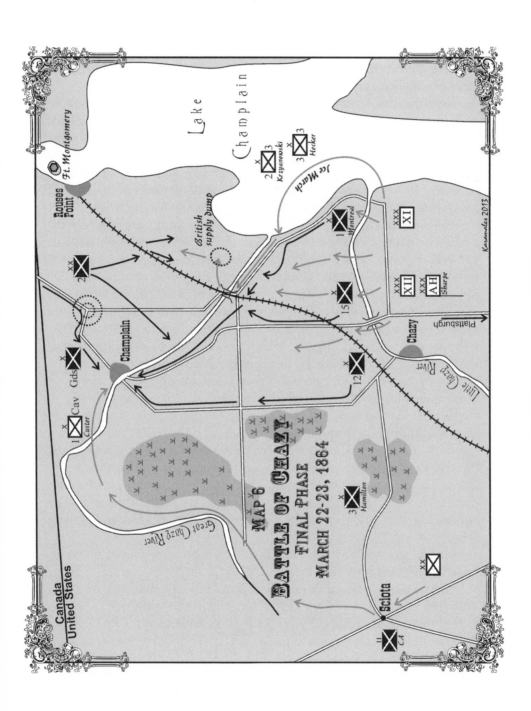

Lake Champlain

Ft. Montgomery

Rouses Point

British supply dump

Champlain

1 Cav Gds
Custer

2

Canada
United States

Great Chazy River

MAP 6
BATTLE OF CHAZY
FINAL PHASE
MARCH 22-23, 1864

Hamilton

Sciota

C.A

2
Krzyzanowski

3
Hecker

Ice March

Montreal

15

XI

XII   AH
Sharpe

Chazy

Plattsburgh

Little Chazy River

12

Karsmides 2013

His worry was answered by a burst of gunfire ahead. Minutes later another burst of gunfire came from the northeast followed by sustained firing. Then artillery joined in.

He looked at the Dublin Brigade's commander, who was looking off into the dark in that direction. "The Americans cannot have beat us to Coopersville," he said.

Rear guards would turn on their pursuers again and again to engage the enemy and force them to deploy, which took time. Then before becoming decisively engaged, they would slip away to repeat the process. So who was firing at Coopersville? It was more than ominous to hear the noise of the delaying actions in their rear and what was starting to sound like a good knock-down-drag-out battle in their front. And over ten thousand British and Canadian troops were in between.

He paused to consider what the hell was going on. He had the Dublin Brigade in column behind him. From the silence to his left rear 12th Brigade must have disengaged successfully and be on the way north on a parallel road with the Dublin Brigade. Thank God for McBean. He hoped he had got some of his Scotties out of that forlorn hope. The Hamilton Brigade—the 1/47 and its Canadian battalions? He had no ideas if his couriers had reached them with the orders to withdraw. That left only the Montreal Brigade, which would have been pulling out to the east, and that's where all the firing was coming from. If so, who were they fighting, and where did they come from? He'd have to tuck those questions away for later. In any case, there was a major fight in the direction of the bridge the Dublin Brigade had to cross. The question then was should he throw Dublin Brigade into the fight in order to get across the bridge or sidestep west, avoid the fight altogether, and march directly to Champlain where he hoped the advance elements of the 2nd British Division would be arriving. That would require him to abandon the Montreal Brigade to its fate. There was no time to dawdle. The Americans were pressing on their rear. He muttered to himself, "Damn this confusion."

Had he known how confused the Americans were at that moment, he would have wept with relief.

Sharpe too had heard the sudden sound of battle that had mystified Wolseley, but he had a better idea of what it meant. He struck the open-gloved palm of his left hand with his right in exclamation. "By God, the Pole has done it!" He turned to his staff. "Now all we have to do is keep pushing the enemy up against our men on the Great Chazy, and we've got 'em trapped." T'wer easier said than done, though. Control was needed to do just that, and control was what had broken down in the darkness. He sent couriers, aides, and staff officers off into the night, but they had to pick their way slowly over unfamiliar ground abounding in moving units and stragglers, all of whom reacted with fear and violence to any unexpected approaching horse and man. Two of his couriers had actually been fired upon, and one wounded, by nervous troops. Hardly any of Sharpe's couriers and aides had returned. Worse yet, the British rearguards had done their work of delay all too well. Sharpe's divisions were moving at a snail's pace, and every time they were forced to deploy, they shed men lost in the night. The pursuit had broken down. The fact that he had very little staff left was proof that his need for information was not being met.

It was then that firing started from the regiment trailing him. Then cries of "Cease fire! Cease fire!" came out of the dark. "General Sherman! General Sherman!" The firing rippled to an end, as an officer rode up to the lantern light around Sharpe. "My God, sir, you've nearly killed General Sherman!" Then a party of a dozen emerged onto the road drawn by the light. At the head was a very angry William Tecumseh Sherman.

"Where's Sharpe?" he barked. His unkempt red beard seemed to bristle as the light picked out its color. He didn't wait for an answer but rode right up to Sharpe. "Well, General, aside from nearly killing your new commanding general, you have plainly lost control of this battle. Shot at three times as we tried to find you."

Before Sharpe could answer, Sherman leaned over and clapped him on the shoulder. "We rarely fight at night, and never on this scale, General, for just this reason." But the anger had drained away, as he began to gather the threads of command into his hand. "But, I tell you, Sharpe, you popped the enemy out of his position like a pine knot in a fire." He was without question in command. "Now, Sharpe, it will be daylight in a few hours. Tell me what you have set in motion, and let's see what we can do."

At that moment Wolseley decided that abandoning the 1st Montreal Brigade was unthinkable. The British Army would never live down such a thing. The Dublin Brigade, less one battalion as rear guard, deployed across the Stetson Road and advanced in the direction of the battle.

Wolseley was fortunate not to know that Custer's lead cavalry regiment, the 6th Michagan, was riding into Champlain, the key crossing point over the Big Chazy River, on the British main supply route, that very moment. Sharpe's trap had been sprung.

In fifteen minutes firing erupted along the entire front of Dublin Brigade as they encountered the makeshift barricades that Krzysanowski had thrown up in front of the bridge over the Great Chazy. Just when speed of flight was most necessary, Wolseley had committed himself to a time-consuming, bloody pounding.

TWO MILES NORTH OF CHAZY, 5:10 A.M., WEDNESDAY, MARCH 23, 1964
McBean's Higlanders kept their pursuers at bay, turning again and
again with a deadly snarl on the narrow country road through the
woods. Their rearguard actions allowed the rest of 12th Brigade to move
as quickly north as the narrow, rutted road and the darkness of the trees
hemming the road and blocking the wan moonlight.

The brigade commander's withdrawal orders had stated he was to
take a position north of the Great Chazy at Champlain, but the sound of
the guns to his right overrode those orders. As soon as the road left the
woods, he marched them across country to the sound of the guns.

At Champlain Custer was congratulating himself as the hero of the
battle, despite the fact that he had only his old 6th Michigan Cavalry
with him as the rest of his cavalry brigade was dibbling in. The infantry
division following his cavalry was still laboriously crossing the creeks
and woods. He gave little thought to them, though it had been the
infantry that had stormed Sciota when his cavalry had been repulsed. As
it was, his own men were so exhausted that few pickets were set and then
haphazardly. Exhaustion had set in; these early morning hours were the
most seductive of sleep, and the men were further lulled by a breeze from
the west that blew deliciously warm. So it was that they did not detect
the approach of the British 2nd Division, well-warned of the American
presence by Denison's scouts.

The command sped down the column of the 11th Hussars (Prince
Albert's Own) to prepare for action. The "Cherry Pickers" had received
their regimental motto from having been attacked in Spain by the French
while raiding a cherry orchard. Their cherry-colored trousers, unique
in the British Army, though, were adopted from the colors of the late
Prince of Wales House of Saxe-Coburg und Gotha when he became
the regiment's colonel. Victoria had personally provided each man of the
regiment on their departure with small box of chocolates with Albert's
picture as a sign of royal favor. She would be intent on their performance,
wishing them to add luster to their glory won in the Charge of the Light
Brigade in the Crimea.

The only officer to win the Victoria Cross in that charge and the first
Canadian to win it was now sitting his six-foot-three-inch frame on a
very large horse at the head of the column. His long sword wielded by
a long arm had emptied many Russian saddles to save the lives of two
Hussars on that day in the Crimea. Now he drew it deliberately from
its scabbard to let the rasp sound like a plucked harp string. Lt. Col.
Alexander Robert Dunn was acting commander of the Cherry Pickers that
day; his colonel was down with fever in Montreal. For York-born Dunn

(present-day Toronto), the transfer of the Hussars to North America was more than defending the Empire, it was defending his home. He vowed never to let an American cross the border as long as a Hussar was alive.

When Denison's men said they had identified Custer himself, Dunn said a quiet prayer in thank-you. Custer's boasting that he would carry the Stars and Stripes into Montreal had made him a public villain in Canada. Dunn told himself that he would do his best to make sure that Custer did, indeed, see Montreal but only as a guest of Her Majesty's Government.

The Cherry Pickers snatched the one sleepy patrol that had wandered lazily over the Great Chazy as they trotted down Prospect Hill Road to the bridge to Champlain. Barely a quarter mile from the bridge, two of Denison's scouts reported to Dunn that the bridge was lightly guarded. From where they stood, Dunn could see the lanterns hanging from the bridge and glow of light from the windows of the town. He was hoping the Americans were sleeping well.

They were. Even Custer, who normally had the metabolism of a four-year-old, was nodding off when the Cherry Pickers took the bridge at the charge, running down the few guards who were still awake. Custer was instantly up and dashed out of the house he had commandeered as his headquarters without his shirt or weapons. A Hussar squad rode up; an officer pointed his sword at him and demanded the location of Custer. George instantly pointed in the opposite direction. "He took off that way." The Hussars spurred away in hot pursuit.

Custer's aide and orderly dragged him inside, where they armed themselves as the Hussars swarmed through Champlain cutting down anyone in the street. The Michiganders of the 6th may have been caught unawares, but they were still good soldiers now goaded out sleep by a rush of energy. And they all had Chris Spencer's wondrous repeaters. Every house became a blockhouse that spat fire, emptying saddle after saddle. A few men were able to get to the barns where their horses had been stabled, saddled them, and burst out firing.

Another one of Custer's regiments, the 1st Michigan, was just on the outskirts of the town when the Hussars charged. Bone weary, many sleeping in their saddles, they were instantly awake at the sound of the fight nearby. Now they charged, the first two companies, into town in fours to crash into milling Hussars. Saber against saber and man to man in a style a thousand years old, they fought. The remaining companies dismounted and advanced as dismounted infantry.

Amid the swirling and hacking sabers rode Dunn, his blade dripping blood as he shouted encouragement to the Cherry Pickers. Then he saw him. The man was unmistakable. His long blond hair and red bandana had made Custer famous. With a shout, Dunn bulled his way through the press of horseman. His big horse simply rode one American down. Another tried to block his way, and Dunn's saber cleaved him from neck to collar bone. Custer saw Dunn at the same instant as the Hussar wrenched his blade from the dead man who slipped off his horse. And before Custer knew it he was parrying a bone-numbing blow from the enemy's saber that nearly unhorsed him. Custer's horse was more agile and responded to his lightest pressure with his knees, carrying him away from those scythe-like swings of Dunn's blade. And Custer used that control to turn and attack with the quickness of a serpent's tongue that nicked Dunn's sword arm. The saber would have fallen to the ground hand it not been tied by a lanyard around his wrist. But when he had it in hand again, the fight had carried Custer away from him.

The American was rallying his troopers for another charge down the street when among the Hussar's a flood of men in blue greatcoats pushed. The 55th Foot had pounded over the bridge after the Hussars, and behind them were three more British and Canadian battalions of the Portsmouth Brigade. The action in the streets of Champlain quickly was becoming an infantry fight, and the amount of lead in the air made it too dangerous for horses. The Michiganders took cover with their repeaters as the first sliver of dawn peered over the horizon, and the wind blew warm.

HEADQUARTERS IN THE FIELD, ARMY OF THE HUDSON, 6:20 A.M., WEDNESDAY, MARCH 23, 1864

Sharpe had taken it well when Sherman arrived. More ambitious than most, Sharpe stifled resentment at the glory of the impending victory falling to Sherman. He dutifully slipped into second-in-command and took some comfort at Sherman's praise. But now he had his hands full riding up and down the firing line of the dawn battle flaring south of the Great Chazy, encouraging the men and reporting back to Sherman the ebb and flow of the fighting.

Hanging Billy[1] had picked up the threads of the situation with the speed of a man blessed with *coup de oui* (stroke of the eye), that ability to take in a situation at a glance that marked the great captain. He realized that what must be the bulk of the British had been banging away at the Americans holding the Coopersville bridge. He had thrown his divisions at them as they came up. The British had turned half their force back to face them. The dawn was now revealing the masses of men engaged, the din of their guns, marked by the black powder cloud that would have blanketed them had not the wind blown it quickly away. Krzysanowski and Hecker's brigades had been pressed back to an arc around the bridge. Only their coffee mill guns kept the bayonet-charging British at bay.

Wolseley rode into just such a bullet. His own horse took a burst into its chest and fell screaming to its knees. He barely leaped off in time to miss its flailing hooves. All around him were the thinning ranks of the Rifles who stood their ground, firing with deliberate aim to bring down the coffee mill gunners in Hecker's Brigade. Wisps of black powder smoke blew past him as he staggered to his feet. A Rifleman caught him before he fell. "There ye go, sir. Steady now."

Pitt-Rivers found him and offered him his brandy flask. He seemed to be enjoying himself despite the ruin of one ear. "Great fun! See how my Rifles shoot, man!" He didn't flinch as bullets sang over and around him, dropping men at his elbow. Wolseley fixed him with his single baleful blue eye. "Break contact. Sidestep to the east and cross the river ice and come up on the other side of the bridge." He then staggered off to find his other commanders. He did not notice the first warm raindrops that sprinkled the ground.

Wolseley found both brigadiers from the Dublin and 12th Brigades were down, their places taken by senior regimental commanders, those that were left. By then he had found another horse and giving the orders to retreat to the northwest toward Champlain. He had no idea of the fight raging there so consumed was he to get out of the enfolding trap, for as he looked south in the light of early dawn the countryside and roads were dense with dark-blue American columns.

If he had looked toward Champlain, he would have seen the black powder smoke and that from burning houses drifting east. The fighting there had become a race of reinforcements. Custer's remaining Michigan cavalry regiments from his old 2nd Brigade fed into the battle as soon as they arrived. The small 3rd Brigade of cavalry should have been right behind them. Only then did he give a thought to the infantry division snaking its way through the swamp and forest. As it was he had fought the British infantry brigade to a standstill. Their repeaters had made all the difference. Yet even that was a waning asset. His ammunition wagons were nowhere in sight. He could not hold them off much longer without more ammunition.

With the dawn, the British added artillery to the pot, and it was very good artillery. Three batteries of Armstrong guns were lacing his positions with accurate fire. He could see more troops flowing across the bridge. He glanced down the road leading west. "Come on. Damn it. Come on!" Then something caught his ear, something between the guns and din of rifle fire. He listened again. It was a high-pitched squeal that came clearer and clearer, until his aide muttered, "Bagpipes."

It was the 1st Battalion, the Scots Fusilier Guards, who had earned much glory on the stricken field of Clavarack October last. With the pipes now could be heard the deeper rumble of the drums of the 2nd Battalion, the Grenadier Guards, intent on revenge for the slaughter of their first battalion on that same field. The Brigade of Guards swept forward straight into the American repeater fire, the Fusiliers on the right and the Grenadiers to their left. Their ranks thinned as they swept around burning buildings, trampled over garden fences and bodies, but still they came. Their ammunition running low, the Americans fell back or were overrun by the stabbing bayonets of the big guardsmen. Custer fed his last arriving regiments into the fight, but they only slowed the tide of the guards and all those guns. Within a half hour Custer and what was left of his cavalry stumbled west out of what was left of Champlain. On the outskirts of the town, the Guards were halted and raised a cheer as the last of Custer's men faded back down the road and into the woods. No one had noticed how the sky had turned black with roiling clouds. To accompany their cheers, from the clouds a crack of thunder accompanied a jagged lighting bolt. Then the clouds released their deluge. Nature herself had flung down its curtain on the battle of Chazy.

THE COOPERSVILLE BRIDGE, 9:38 A.M., WEDNESDAY, MARCH 23, 1864
The men of Krzysanowski's brigade would have cheered Sherman if they had not been so wet. The warm rain fell in a flood of big, heavy, warm drops that were already softening the ground into mud. The men were soaked to the bone in their sodden greatcoats. Sherman knew instinctively that the sudden and dramatic break in the weather from extreme cold to spring would explode the sick lists. Still, he did not stint his praise of the brigade, and they appreciated it even if they did not cheer. They appreciated even more the end of the battle and the rain that soaked them also was the rain that made fighting impossible. Not only were the roads beginning to ooze mud, but the very act of loading a muzzle-loading rifle by first tearing open a cartridge would be impossible, for the rain would soak the powder. Most of his men did not have repeaters yet.

The British had disengaged and marched away, sloshing through pools of slush turning every so often to present a hedge of bayonets to the gingerly pursuing Americans whose hearts did not seem in it either. The four miles to Champlain took eight hours until the last regiment closed on the town as the columns limped along, every man sagging under exhaustion and a sodden greatcoat. That last shrunken regiment announced itself with the skirling tune of "Scotland Forever," a bit out of tune given that their bagpipes were as soaked as they were. McBean and the 78th Highlanders were the last regiment off the field.

TELEGRAPH OFFICE OF THE WAR DEPARTMENT, WASHINGTON, DC, 5:35 P.M., WEDNESDAY, MARCH 23, 1864

Lincoln had been there all night waiting for news of the battle. Nothing had come in despite repeated inquiries. The last news they had was from Sherman at Plattsburg at midnight on his way to take command of the Army of the Hudson. Now the telegraph began to spit out and endless stream of dots and dashes. Lincoln had almost leapt out of the big easy chair reserved for him to hover over the telegrapher and read each word as the man's hand flew over the pad:

> I present to you a signal victory, the harbinger of victories to come. I assumed command in the midst of the night battle launched by Gen. Sharpe. The army had already driven the British from its positions along the Little Chazy River and was driving the enemy back towards the Great Chazy River when Gen. Sharpe graciously relinquished command. The enemy retreated but fought a stubborn rearguard battle. They were heavily reinforced by a second division at Champlain at which time torrential rains put a halt to further operations. The British army is now entrenching from Champlain to Rouses's Point on Lake Champlain, a distance of four miles. Enemy losses have been heavy, and we are in possession of several thousand prisoners.[2]

As Lincoln read Sherman's telegram, another report on the battle was carried by special courier onto a fast British warship at Halifax to speed the news to London.

> To the Secretary of State for War:

> I have the honor to report the success of our arms in a series of engagements lasting from March 18th to the 23rd instant along the Canadian-American border in upper New York State.
> Lt. Gen. Sir James Grant struck in a spoiling attack at the American Army of the Hudson on March 18th, with one division of the Montreal Field Force, immediately destroying the enemy's forward division. The First Division came to a halt along the line of the Little Chazy River. The enemy subsequently assembled the entire Army of the Hudson for a major assault employing strong flanking forces to the west and to the east across the ice

of Lake Champlain on the night of March 22nd. As it was not General Grant's intention to become decisively engaged, he ordered a withdrawal back to the line of the Great Chazy River. It was at this time that General Grant was severely wounded. I assumed command. The enemy's attempts at encirclement were both defeated by the hard fighting of the First Division and the timely reinforcement of the Second Division. The Field Force then established itself securely on the line of the Big Chazy River when operations were brought to halt by torrential rains.

Almost two thousand prisoners were taken and overall enemy losses cannot be less than ten thousand men. Our own losses number fewer than five thousand.

I wish to bring to your Lordship's attention, the gallant conduct Brigade of Guards whose charge at Champlain defeated the enemy's attempt at encirclement form the west and of the 78th Foot which held the bridge over the Little Chazy River against the most determined assaults allowing 12th Brigade to withdraw in safety.

I have the honor to be your obedient servant,
Wolseley

SAMUDA BROTHERS SHIPYARD, PORTSMOUTH, ENGLAND, 7:40 P.M., THURSDAY, MARCH 24, 864

Oil lamps were strung from one end of HMS *Prince Albert* to another as the workmen and mechanics of Samuda Brothers Shipyard worked into the night to make the repairs made necessary by the ironclad's shakedown cruise. Capt. Cowper Phipps Cole prowled the ship, supervising every aspect of the repairs, especially to the ship's powerful engines and the ammunition hoists to the twin turrets. This thin, intense officer with the elegant, long blond beard was not a man to accept slack work or second best. *Prince Albert* was the Royal Navy's first all iron, armored and turreted warship, Cole's own design. There had been other iron, armored ironclads, but *Prince Albert* boasted the first turrets, and she had four, more than any American monitor. He had set the date of one week from today to get the ship back to sea again. He desperately hoped that with the repairs completed, he could prove to the Admiralty that she should be sent to North America. He lived for the chance to throw *Prince Albert* into a pounding match with American monitors.

He had powerful patrons in both the queen and Disraeli, the queen because the ship was named after her late husband whom in death had assumed the aura of a saint to her, and Disraeli because it cemented his close relationship with the queen whom he genuinely admired, though it did not hinder him from using that relationship to his political advantage. Her sponsorship of the ship ensured its construction the highest priority and its inventor and captain carte blanche in his demands to the Admiralty. Unknown to him, his orders to join the fleet in North American waters had already been approved by the Prime Minister himself in a very unusually direct involvement in the details of a ministry.[3]

Even by the standards of the latest American monitors, *Prince Albert* was an impressive ship. The turrets could turn 360 degrees smoothly in a minute on a highly efficient system of rollers. Originally, they had been rotated by an eighteen man crew, but Coles had followed John Ericsson's example and replaced them with an engine when he found that in actual sea trials it took close to fifteen minutes to rotate the turret. He had also insisted that each turret be armed with the new sixteen-ton, 9-inch rifled muzzle-loading guns designed by Lynall Thomas that would come closer to the American 15-inch Dahlgren muzzle-loading smoothbores in striking power than any other British gun but also would have the immense advantage of being rifled which would allow it to strike targets accurately at almost double the effective range of the Dahlgrens.[4] [5]

Disraeli could think of no better gift to the queen than that the ship bearing her husband's name be covered with glory. It was not mere flattery though that caused him to guide the ship to its destiny. He faced enormous opposition from the naval establishment, despite a purge of the most ossified elements of the Admiralty. They were happy to build more but improved versions of the broadside that had been lost at Charleston. The recent victory at Hampton Roads had given them comfort that turreted warships had a special vulnerability that broadside ironclads did not. He was convinced, though, that it was a unique situation based upon the element surprise that was not likely to be repeated. For Disraeli then, it was his relationship with the queen that gave him an edge to push Coles' design to the fore which in turn further deepened Victoria's faith and reliance in him. It was a very useful relationship.

WASHINGTON NAVY YARD, 2:44 P.M., THURSDAY, MARCH 24, 1864

Lincoln's carriage rumbled through the gates of the Navy Yard with his cavalry escort, sabers drawn. He was fascinated by the frenzy of construction and activity in the Navy's foremost center of technical skill and construction. The brick yards in the area and in the rest of the country were baking brick around the clock to feed the war's insatiable appetite for industrial construction. Huge sheds were going up where there had been open ground last year, but Lincoln had not come to see men lay brick. What he came to see was hidden by a ten-foot-high new brick wall that enclosed a large area backing onto the river. A whole company of Marines guarded the enclosure night and day.

Its gates opened quickly for him as the Marines snapped to present arms. Inside he was met by Gus Fox and said, "Well, Gus, I'm always glad to come to the Navy Yard for another one of the Navy's happy surprises. I was impressed with the *Alligator* when I saw it tested in the river here a year ago. You tickled my curiosity something fierce."

"Well, Mr. President, let me just say that this will go some way to helping you with your arithmetic problem."

Fox then introduced a little Frenchman whose naturalization papers Lincoln had signed himself only a few days ago. The Frenchman bowed deeply as Lincoln climbed out of the carriage, "*Monsieur le President*, it is *un grande honeur* to welcome you."

Lincoln just extended his hand. "So this is the prophet without honor in his own country, or, I must correct myself, his old country." Brutus de Villerois just beamed. The French Navy's rejection of his boat had sent him to the United States in time to build a salvage version in Philadelphia just as the war broke out. The police had promptly arrested him as his boat surfaced on the river, but the Navy had immediately seen its potential and gave him a contract to build a naval version. Thus was born the USS *Alligator*, the first successful submersible warship in the world. It had more than proved itself at the battle of Charleston when it sank a British frigate with a spar torpedo. Now the Navy could not build enough of them.

Fox knew that Lincoln was like a child in a toy store when it came to the mechanical inventions of war, and no man was a greater booster of the advantages that came with such skill. He led Lincoln to a large brick shed past more Marine guards. The interior was one vast assembly hall. A row of de Villeroi's children lay in various stages of construction. Lincoln counted them though he had already known there were five with another class planned. While the original *Alligator* had taken refuge at the Norfolk Navy Yard, its captain had been summoned to Washington to share his experience and observations. That had resulted in a major modification to the design, important enough to be designated a new class, the *Sharks*.

The *Alligator* had been built originally to clear Confederate harbor and river obstructions, but its success in battle opened new opportunities as a ship killer. The most important change was to marry an element of Confederate-designed semi-submersible, CSS *Indian Chief*, whose plans had been brought out of Charleston by two deserting Confederate sailors. The U.S. Navy referred to this type of boat as a David.[7] That feature was the addition of an engine to allow rapid propulsion. The boat would have almost no profile except a small smokestack and air pipe that at night were practically invisible. When it was not feasible to sail in this manner, the smoke stack and pipe could be lowered and sealed while a team of eight oarsmen, as they were quaintly called, turned the cranks that in turn powered the propeller as the boat became a true submersible.[8]

Lincoln wandered slowly through the warren of cables, stacked hull plates, barrels of rivets, and machines to reach the boat that seemed the most completed. Its thirty-five tons lay forty-seven feet long in its wooden braces, its iron hull painted a new dark green. A man was leaning over the deck stenciling USS *Shark* on its bow and beneath it an attacking shark, its jaws agape. Lincoln ran his hand over the hull and said, "Paint her good, young man." The painter had just noticed the President and dropped his brush. Lincoln's hand darted out and caught it by the handle.

"Oh, Mr. President, I'm so sorry."

"Been painting long?"

"I just started, sir." Then Lincoln noticed he was missing a foot. He was one of the military invalids who were given priority in hiring. When critical war production work was declared off limits to the draft, there had been a flood of applications. America's factories did not want for willing hands after that, but Lincoln had insisted that the war-wounded be given first crack.

"Well, son, everybody's got to start somewhere." He reached up and handed the brush to the young man, who leaned over the side to take it.

"Thank you, sir!"

"Sir," Fox interrupted, "you'll find this interesting." He waved his hand at the wooden stairs that led to a platform and the boat's hatch. De Villeroi disappeared down the hatch first. Lincoln peered down into the boat and was surprised to see that the interior was painted a flat white. He lowered his gangly frame inside and instantly had to bend over. Though the boat had six feet from keel to hull, his six feet four inches made him hunch over. Parallel rows of glass ports studding the upper bulkhead that would allow for some illumination through shallow water.

De Villeroi was standing in front of a large metal box, of which he seemed obviously proud. Lincoln was happy to give him a cue by asking, "And what is this, professor?" He sat down on one of the oarsmen's benches to get the kink out of his neck.

The Frenchman explained that it was the air purifier and renewer. One man in the crew would continue to pump the interior air as it grew stale through this device, and it would come fresh out the other side. "With this, *Monsieur le President*, the crew can stay underwater for long periods."

"Well, how does it work?"

"Most simple! The air is pumped through a solution of lime water. It freshens the air by removing the impurities that would otherwise cause men to die of asphyxiation."[9]

Lincoln shook his head. "And you thought of this yourself?"

De Villeroi simply bowed in response.

"Well, Louis Napoleon's loss is our gain."

"If the boat is near enough to the surface, air can also to be supplied from the surface by two tubes with floats, connected to an air pump inside, as you see here."

Lincoln's eyes darted around the bright interior. That was a cue that de Villeroi used to begin showing him one innovation after another. He ignored the fact that it was Navy engineers who had redesigned the hand crank system to power the propellers and replace the side-mounted paddles he had designed. The Navy also added the engine after the David design. The final item was a demonstration of the diver lock out chamber. A Navy diver was fitted into his diving suit. His air hose was passed through a hole in the chamber door and fixed to his suit. Then another crewman shut the door. "At this point, sir, the chamber is flooded. When that is done, the diver opens the outer door and drops to affix a torpedo to an enemy vessel. The captain then detonates the topedoes by connecting an insulated copper wire from the torpedoes to a battery in the vessel. The diver can also replace the torpedo on the spar attached to the bow." Lincoln was so impressed he asked to go with the diver through the hatch and exit outside the boat and then return the same way.

Thanking de Villeroi, Lincoln drew Fox out of the shed along the slipway leading to the river. When they were alone, he said, "Now, tell me, Fox, when will they be ready? Rations are getting low out at Fort Monroe and Norfolk." He was referring to the difficulty of getting bulk supplies needed by the fort and particularly the fleet bottled up at the Norfolk Navy Yard. Heavy and bulk stores such as coal and ammunition in particular needed to go by ship, but the Royal Navy had plugged up the mouth of the Chesapeake. Something was needed to encourage them to leave.

"The *Shark* drops into the water next week. The next two boats in three weeks, and the last by the end of April. Add two weeks trial and training to each boat."[10]

"Keep to it, Fox, keep to it. We cannot lose a fleet."

HEADQUARTERS, ARMY OF NORTHERN VIRGINIA, GORDONSVILLE, VIRGINIA, 5:33 P.M., FRIDAY, MARCH 25, 1864

Longstreet and Lee watched the train to Richmond disappear down the track as the presidential honor guard and band marched back to camp. Lee said, "Ride with me," and led them out of town and onto a country road. It was a beautiful, bright, late-March day with the sky an intoxicating bright blue. Already the daffodils were sending up their leaves, and the crocus sparkled yellow and blue. Lee's color bearer and escort kept a tactful distance in the rear.

The train had carried President Davis and a British military and naval delegation back to Richmond. They had been closeted with Lee for an entire day. Lee had asked for Longstreet to accompany him to see the President off. Davis had been quite cordial to Lee's commander of the mighty First Corps. Longstreet was now all ears.

"General, I have a task for you that requires the detachment of your corps." That corps that had been so badly thinned at Chickamauga and then the retreat from Chattanooga was at full strength again, as were all of Lee's regiments. With the British and French in the war, thousands of deserters had returned to the colors and many thousands more had been freed from garrison duty on the Atlantic and Gulf coasts.

"Our British friends require Norfolk Navy Yard to sustain their fleet in its operations against the North. President Davis has pledged to do everything in our power to assist them."

Longstreet thought he knew what was coming next, but he was surprised when Lee said, "You will attack the enemy in the Virginia Peninsula and put Fort Monroe under siege."

"General Lee, for a moment I thought you wanted me to return to attack Suffolk, which defends the Navy Yard, as I did last summer."

Lee stopped and petted Traveler. "We will do by indirection what last summer did not yield to direct action."

Longstreet waited for Lee to expand on this thought.

"The key to Norfolk is not the fortifications at Suffolk, but the Virginia Peninsula. The enemy must supply those forces south of Suffolk by a laborious route across three peninsulas and three rivers." By this he meant the Northern Neck, the Rappahanock River, the Virginia Peninsula, the York River, the James Peninsula, and then across the James River to Suffolk. "The British have made sure that nothing comes by way of the Chesapeake."

Longstreet nodded his head. "We cut off their supply line by taking the Virginia Peninsula. Then they wither on the vine and must surrender."

"With God's help."

THE FARM OF DR. SAMUEL MUDD, CARROL COUNTY, MARYLAND, 6:15 P.M., FRIDAY, MARCH 24, 1864

The handsome young man with the black hair and mustache dismounted and knocked on the door. He was welcomed inside. "Mr. Booth, I am Dr. Mudd. My wife and I have seen you perform and are your deepest admirers." John Wilkes Booth looked for Mrs. Mudd, but she was nowhere to be seen, nor were there any of Mudd's slaves present, only a man in his early fifties. Mudd quickly introduced him as George Sanders. He had arrived by the ratline that ran from Richmond in Virginia across the Potomac into southern Maryland and then into Washington, courtesy of the 9th Virginia Cavalry. The pleasantries were exchanged.

Booth was what would later be called a sleeper. He was a Confederate asset reserved for special missions. The last one had been an attempt to kidnap Lincoln, which failed through no fault of Booth. It was due to the last-minute escort this General Sharpe had sent scurrying after Lincoln after he had left his headquarters and was walking across Lafayette Square to the White House. The snatch was going to be there, and Booth had been waiting on a park bench to do his part to hustle Lincoln into a passing wagon. The sight of the escort had killed the operation just as the wagon started to rumble forward.[11]

Saunders had read over the report from their chief agent, James Smoke, who was later killed in his attempt to kill Lincoln in the chaos of the attack on Washington last October. Booth had not been present and did exactly what a sleeper should after a botched operation. He went back to sleep ready to be roused when the Confederacy would again need him.

That time had come. Saunders studied the dapper young man who simply radiated a dynamic presence and confidence. The arrogance came across too. The reports on him spoke of a fiery nature and intense vanity, useful traits to manipulate a man by. Saunders complimented his acting, discussing several of the plays he claimed to have seen. As he went on, he could not help but notice how Booth was preening over every word especially when Sanders said, "The talk of Richmond is that you will be the South's unquestioned champion of the stage after the war, surpassing even the great talent of your famous father." He paused for the effect. Not every actor trod the boards. "And certainly your brother."

Oh, what a nerve he hit with that one. Booth was positively glowing. So the theater gossip of Booth's jealousy of his older brother, Edwin, was true, thought Sanders. Well, he had seen them both, and he could see why the younger Booth was jealous. Edwin *was* the better actor. His tragic performances were sublime. John Wilkes's weak acting was overshadowed by his violent physicality on the stage and the smoldering looks that seemed to make so many women daft. Sanders appreciated that, and he could only wistfully imagine how many bedroom doors that opened. There was something more to the gossip, though, something about the brothers' politics. Edwin was by all accounts loyal to the Union. John Wilkes' intemperate support for the Confederacy had strained their relationship.

All this ran through Sanders's mind as he saw the moment right to drop the line that mattered most. "The Confederacy has need of a man of your talents and patriotism, Mr. Booth. I assure you, sir, I am not betraying confidences by repeating what has been said at the highest levels of the government in Richmond."

UNION HALL, SAN FRANCISCO, CALIFORNIA, 9:12 P.M., FRIDAY, MARCH 25, 1864

The young man on the stage paused for the laughter to die down, then said, "An old lady friend of mine had gotten ill, and no manner of cures could help her. I said, 'I can cure you in a week.' I told her she must give up swearing, drinking, and gambling. She said she couldn't give up swearing, drinking, and gambling, that she had never done any of those things."

He waited, tickling the audience's expectation (his sense of timing was perfect), flicked an ash off his cigar, and deadpanned, "Well there you have it. She was like a sinking ship, with no freight to throw overboard. Why, just one little vice would have saved her."

The laughter came in waves as the audience tasted the joke over and over again and each time found it funnier. The speaker had achieved some note as a humorist in Virginia City across the Sierras in Nevada and had just moved to San Francisco. He had been an inspired choice to entertain the elite of the city and their Russian guests in Union Hall, one of the largest and most magnificent buildings in the United States built with the endless sparkling gold dust washed out of California's mountains and rivers.

Tonight it hosted Rear Adm. Andrei Alexandrovich Popov and his officers of the Russian Pacific Squadron. The Russians had arrived the previous October at the same time as the Baltic Squadron had arrived in New York. The Russians, though still neutral, had effectively guarded the port by their presence against any sudden British descent.

The speaker's words were not lost on the English-speaking Russians whom, the Americans were delighted to note, had a wonderful sense of humor themselves.[12] They applauded enthusiastically as his routine wandered into current events: "England's coat of arms should be a lion's head and shoulders welded onto a cur's hindquarters." Then he brought the house down: "I perceive now that the English are mentioned in the Bible: 'Blessed are the meek, for they shall inherit the earth.'" English arrogance was a byword in both Russia and America, and the room roared.

Now the speaker said it was not fair to concentrate only on the English. He had a word or two for their friends. "France," he said, was a strange country that "has neither winter nor summer nor morals — apart from these drawbacks, it is a fine country." He let each point sink in, banked the laughter, and went on, savoring the little dramatic pauses.

"M. de Lamester's new French dictionary just issued in Paris defines virtue as 'A woman who has only one lover and doesn't steal.'

"The French" he said, flicking another ash, "are polite, but it is often mere ceremonial politeness. A Russian imbues his polite things with a heartiness, both of phrase and expression that compels belief in his sincerity." With this compliment to their guests, the Americans rose to their feet and applauded for five minutes.

Then unexpectedly, he seemed to wander onto the subject of Turkey, a word he said with an obvious bad taste in his mouth. For fifteen minutes he regaled the audience with the backwardness of the Turks, then slowing draining the humor as he painted their bestial cruelties. The Russians leaned forward. "I wish Europe would let Russia annihilate Turkey a little," another pause, "not much, but enough to make it difficult to find the place again without a divining rod or a diving-bell."

As Sam Clemmons took his seat to lively applause, he congratulated himself that he had had the wit to buy a few Russian officers drinks, find out what was really on their minds, and fashion his routine accordingly.

7

Philosopher Generals

The stitches in Grant's scalp itched enough to drive any other man to distraction, but he just ignored it through his ability to focus on what was important. Now that focus was on Lincoln. Grant thought the President had seemed preoccupied through lunch. Stanton had carried much of the conversation.[1] When the table had been cleared, Lincoln said with his eyes off in the distance, "Do you know I think General Fremont is a philosopher." Maj. Gen. John C. Fremont had finally resigned. A popular figure who had run for president twice, he rejoined the Army when the war broke out and caused nothing but trouble for Lincoln, who finally sent him off without a command. There the man had languished. Even the entreaties of his wife, Jesse, had failed to move the President. Finally Fremont had simply resigned.

Lincoln went on, "He is really a great man. This war has not produced another such man. He has grappled with that greatest of ancient and wise admonitions 'know thyself,' and certainly he is intimately acquainted with himself, knows for what he is fitted as well as for what he is unfitted as any man living, for much to my relief and greatly to the interest of the service to which has resigned his position in the army. I am in hopes some other dress parade commander will study over this advisory self-examination of 'know thyself' and follow his example. If they will only do so, I would be greatly relieved. They will have done their duty, and the country will be benefited."[2] He sighed.

Grant could see how Lincoln's shoulders sagged with the burdens of the war. A heavier burden than most was the deals with the devil that Lincoln had had to make to sustain the war against the Confederacy in the first two years since Secession. The support of the abolitionists and hard war Republicans was vital, and they could only be placated by the appointment of politically sound generals of their own background. So Lincoln had appointed Nathaniel Banks, former governor of Massachusetts and Speaker of the House to command in Louisiana where his political talent was bent to organizing a Union state government. Unfortunately, his military talents were lacking, and he been crushed at the battle of Vermillionville by the consummate Marshal Bazaine. They had lost almost all of Louisiana and control of the mouth of the Mississippi.[3]

Another such thorn was Maj. Gen. Benjamin Franklin Butler, who commanded the Army of the James, which included X and XVIII Corps, over thirty thousand men, which garrisoned Fort Monroe and the James Peninsula as well as across Hampton Roads south of Suffolk, an area that also contained the Norfolk Navy Yard.[4] Another Massachusetts politician, Butler was always eager to assume authority in the absence of official instructions. Early in the war this had been a godsend when he had effectively suppressed Baltimore's secessionist mobs to ensure the arrival of troops to garrison Washington and then had detained the state legislature to prevent it to vote secession. As commander of Fortress Monroe early in the war he had refused to return runaway slaves on the grounds that they would be used to support military operations as laborers, describing them as contraband of war, the first form of freedom slaves had been given. Lincoln supported this measure, which would be of immense future value in undermining slavery.

He had been Banks's predecessor in New Orleans and put his political talents to immediate use by effectively suppressing open support for the Confederacy. When the ladies of New Orleans took to insulting Union soldiers, Butler threatened to treat them as women of the town, earning the epithet of Beast Butler. An enterprising merchant had had Butler's portrait painted on the bottom of a shipment of chamber pots and sold out in an hour.

As useful as those political talents had been, it was ultimately his military talents that were vital, and of these, he had pitifully few. Louisiana and the James Peninsula had been military backwaters. Now they were critical, active theaters of war. The British desperately wanted Norfolk Navy Yard as a forward operating base for their blockade. Wilmington in North Carolina was the closest important Southern port. The Royal Navy did not have another base between it and Martha's Vineyard, which they had seized earlier off the coast of Massachusetts.

"I have no confidence in Butler either, Mr. President."

"Then in whom do you have confidence for such a post?"

"Maj. General William Smith."

Lincoln glanced at Stanton, who nodded approval, but he had already made up his mind. He no longer needed to curry support with the abolitionist crowd. The war with Britain had brought unanimity of support.

William Farrar "Baldy" Smith had opened the "cracker line" over steep mountains to keep the Army of the Cumberland fed and fit as it prepared to break out of siege at Chattanooga. Grant had been enormously impressed with Baldy's determination, innovation, and drive, which burnished his reputation as a brilliant engineer. He was just the man to hold a desperate post. In fact, Smith had been Grant's choice to replace Meade in command of the Army of the Potomac, but he had been moved by the latter's selflessness in the service of his country and retained him in command. Still, he had insisted on Smith's promotion to major general, which Congress had approved on March 9.

It had required his insistence. Smith had left a bad taste in a lot of mouths in Washington. After the bloodbath at Fredericksburg in December 1862, Smith had moved with Maj. Gen. Franklin, now commanding at Port Hudson, to remove the commander of the Army of the Potomac, Maj. Gen. Ambrose Burnside, who, of course, needed removing. The man was honest, loyal, and just out of his element as the commander of large formations, and bad luck stuck to him like tar. Still, for Smith and Franklin, it was professional ruin. Burnside was relieved, but so were they. The Army instinctively recoils from officers who conspire to remove their commander. Now fate, luck, good timing, what have you, had restored both officers to critical commands, commands of great peril.

Lincoln said, "Stanton, you will take care of this."

HORSEGUARDS BARRACKS, LONDON, 7:15 P.M., SATURDAY, MARCH 25, 1864

Prince George, 2nd Duke of Cambridge and general commander-in-chief of the British Army, had been a very busy man since the war had started. Few men of his rank had such an encyclopedic knowledge of the army as he did, which was of great value in marshalling the forces of the empire. Unfortunately, a goodly part of that knowledge concerned the social standing of the officers, which he much preferred to brains. Disraeli had let out a long sigh when he was told of the duke's retort to one of his more intelligent subordinates. "Brains? I don't believe in brains! You haven't any, I know, sir!"

Even the prime minister would find it beyond his powers to remove him. He was a cousin of Victoria's, a grandson of George III. Neither was he an outright amateur; he had been a soldier all his life and had ably commanded the 1st Division, made up of the Guards and Highland Brigades, in the Crimean War, and had fought well at the Alma, Inkerman,

Balaklava, and Sevastopol and he had only been invalided home when his health broke. To his credit, he had an intense interest in the welfare of the soldier and technological innovation in artillery and small arms. He was also oblivious to the intellectual and doctrinal changes those innovations would require. At that time, 75 percent of military literature came from Germany, 24 percent from France, and only 1 percent from Britain. Unintentionally, he explained the intellectual stagnation in British military thinking when he said famously, "There is a time for everything, and the time for change is when you can no longer help it."[5]

At the age of forty-five he was in his prime—experienced, energetic, and devoted to the army. The loss of the 1st Battalion, the Grenadier Guards, at the battle of Clavarack, had sent him into a frenzy of activity to avenge that loss by sending the strongest possible force to North America. When he had wanted to strip the Mediterranean garrisons, Disraeli had asked him, "And what proximate reserve, my Lord, would we have should the Russian bear lunge southward again?"

"Prime Minister, I do not doubt that the drubbing they received ten years ago still is all too fresh in their minds, treaty or no treaty with the Americans."

Disraeli sighed again.

FORTRESS PORTLAND, 2:22 P.M., SATURDAY, MARCH 25, 1864

Chamberlain sat in his bombproof listening to the exploding British shells and feeling the vibrations ripple through the ground. Every shell seemed to sprinkle dust from the heavy beams in the ceiling. He looked up at the ornate carving of the beams and reflected that once they had graced some fine mansion.

The British siege artillery and the guns of the Royal Navy's ships in the harbor kept up an almost constant shelling that kept the garrison under cover. Things had only gotten worse in the last month, despite the occasional arrival of one of Professor Lowe's marvelous new balloons to carry out the wounded. It was their only link to the outside world and news of the war elsewhere. The garrison had been buoyed by the news of the victory at Clavarack in late October and lately of Port Hudson's survival of the latest French attacks, and the fighting at Chazy, of which they did not know the outcome. But there had been little else of hope except the constant admonition to hold on.

That was becoming harder and harder. The winter had been brutal. Casualties had grown, and now the sick list was growing alarmingly as food was running low. The same sudden warm weather that had halted the fighting in New York had washed over Portland's ruins as well turning everything to mud. The sudden change of weather had also added to the sick list. Despite the bombardment, Chamberlain faithfully toured the fighting positions to keep up the spirits of his men, but today the shells rained much too heavily even to think of leaving the bombproof.

Adding to his problems was the tightening British security. His scouts now found it impossible to slip out of the city and observe the enemy.

AT SEA IN THE NORTH ATLANTIC, 2:27 P.M., SATURDAY, MARCH 26, 1864
The Russian squadron and its transports had taken a more indirect route than the Dahlgren expedition after their breakout through the blockade. The latter had a longer distance to go to reach the coast of Essex. Both groups sailed out of normal shipping lanes, under false colors (British), to avoid even the sparse winter traffic that might betray them to watchful eyes. Even that tactic was not enough to avoid other ships. Admiral Lisovsky took no chances on the three occasions when sails were sighted. His squadron pounced on them. Two were British and one was Dutch. The enemy ships he sank, and the Dutchmen he put a crew aboard to accompany them home slowly.

To all of this Meagher was an interested observer, drawing special pleasure in seeing the British merchant colors slip under the water. But he was drawn back to the final review of the plans of his expedition by his staff.

Dublin was the prize. She was the golden key to Ireland. Ironically she was built by King John to be the first fetter of the island. With one blow that fetter would be struck off in the same place by the sons of Ireland returned in Union blue. The New Sod would come in liberation of the Old Sod. More than a few of the men in the Irish Brigade had been born in America.

But high talking and low planning had been the bane of every Irish patriotic rising in the last five hundred years. Grant had picked Meagher's staff, not all of them Irish, but hardheaded Yankees, who knew a thing or two about the details of getting things done. And Sharpe had emptied his cornucopia of intelligence to aid them. Col. Patrick Kelly, commander of the 88th New York, had been promoted to brigadier and given command of the brigade itself. Kelly was an immigrant from County Galway and had fought with the brigade in every one of its engagements. He had led the brigade's six hundred survivors into the attack at the Wheat Field at Gettysburg after the famous benediction and absolution by Father Corby, the brigade chaplain. Acknowledged as a superb leader, Kelly, as one officer noted, "was not lavish with praise. When he did bestow it, the few words went a long way. . . . 'Well done, my brave byes,' to the little remnant of the (Irish) Brigade at the battle of Bristoe when they went through the manual (of arms) under fire at Coffee Hill . . .' was worth as much as five hundred."[6]

Meagher and many of his men had an intimate knowledge of Dublin, but that was not enough. All he had to do was look at the detailed map of the city prepared by Wilmoth and his staff. Every barrack and its garrison marked out—Royal, Richmond, Marlborough, Islandbridge, and Beggar's Bush. And not least of all the military posts was the Magazine Fort. Meagher laughed to himself as a remembered a few lines from Jonathan Swift.

"Now's here's a proof of Irish sense
Here Irish wit is seen
When nothing's left that's worth defence,
We build a Magazine."[7]

Wilmoth's order-of-battle also revealed that two of the four infantry battalions garrisoning the city had already departed for Canada, as did most of the artillery brigade One cavalry regiment and two infantry regiments remained at the great training ground of the British Army in Ireland, the Curragh Plain, north of Dublin, after a like force had also been sent to Canada. The only other British troops in Ireland were two cavalry regiments at Cahir in south Tipperary and Dundalk to the north in County Louth. Other than these, there were nine battalion depots in Ireland, essentially recruiting and training centers for deployed regiments.

If the barracks and magazine the keys to military power, then Dublin Castle, a vast pile in the middle of the city, was the seat of British rule of Ireland. Take that seat and any British immediate reaction would be paralyzed. With luck they would snatch the Lord Lieutenant of Ireland, James Hamilton, 1st Duke of Abercorn, there. It was his official residence, usually occupied during the social season from January until St. Patrick's Day. With any luck they would still find him there.[8] If not, he would likely be found not far away in the Viceregal Lodge in Phoenix Park, its ten-mile (sixteen-kilometer) perimeter wall enclosing 1,750 acres (707 hectares) of grass, tree-lined avenues, and monuments.[9]

His thoughts turned to the men in the transports. Leaning against his cabin bulkhead was the old battle-stained color of the 69th New York, the core of the brigade, given him when he had resigned. He had wept when saw after Gettysburg how few remained with the colors, and those of the 63rd and 83rd New York and 28th Massachusetts, and 116th Pennsylvania. Ah, but that clever rascal Sharpe had come up with a solution. Volunteers of Irish descent were called for from the entire Union Army for an undisclosed but hazardous mission. Now there was no better way to attract the Irish than to mix a bit of mystery with danger.

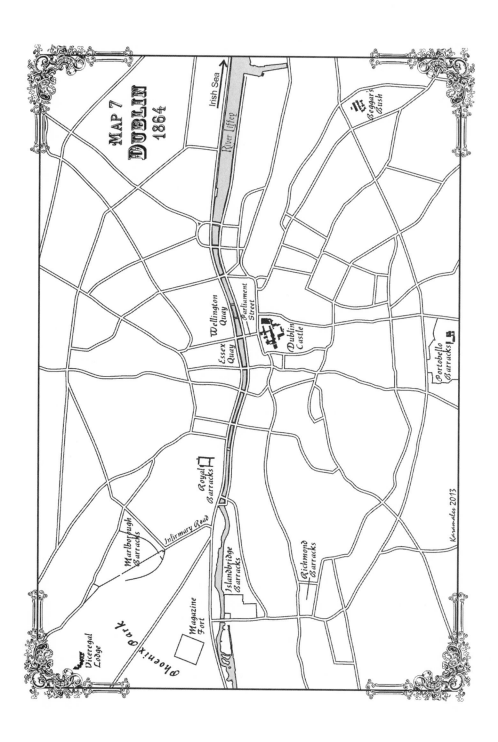

MAP 7
DUBLIN
1864

Irish Sea

River Liffey

Beggar's Bush

Wellington Quay

Parliament Street

Essex Quay

Dublin Castle

Portobello Barracks

Royal Barracks

Infirmary Road

Marlborough Barracks

Islandbridge Barracks

Richmond Barracks

Magazine Fort

Phoenix Park

Viceregal Lodge

Kavanagha 2013

Sharpe had gone that one better and let it be put about that they would be formed into a special corps that would lead the way for the conquest of Canada. And Canada would be traded to England for the liberty of Ireland. And by the thousands they volunteered until he could have filled up an entire corps not just a brigade.

Every man had been vetted both by Sharpe and the Free Ireland movement, and none were told the mission as they disappeared into the armed camp of instruction on Long Island, New York. There Meagher and his officers had trained them hard all through the winter with promises to explain all when the time came. There was no leave granted at all. No one but Meagher and a few officers were allowed out of the camp, which was patrolled by a cavalry and two other infantry regiments. Security was as tight as men could make it. But it needed one thing more—example. Meagher formed the brigade in a horseshoe one frozen January day and shot three men who had deserted. A week before their departure, a new unit arrived to join the brigade—a company of Colonel Lowe's Balloon Corps.

The day they embarked, Meagher had addressed them all in a grand formation with all the eloquence of a fabled king of old in the telling of the bards. They cheered until the very angels wept. Then Father James Corey stepped forward, and the entire brigade knelt as he made over them the sign of the cross and exclaimed, "*Te absolvo!*"

Meagher in the remembering of that divine moment was swept away with what lay ahead. With any luck, Meagher thought, with any luck . . .

AT SEA IN THE NORTH SEA, 2:45 P.M., SATURDAY, MARCH 26, 1864

While Meagher was lost in his reverie, a thousand miles away, USS *Kearsarge* and SS *Vanderbilt* plowed through the heavy late-March seas to pass the Orkneys into the North Sea. *Kearsarge's* engines had to strain to keep up with the huge liner.

When she was built in 1855, she was the fastest, largest steamship in the world, a world record-breaker. *Vanderbilt* was chosen for the Dahlgren expedition because of that very speed. Dahlgren's expedition had farther to go than Meagher's, and if both groups were to strike the same day, then Dahlgren's ships had to be veritable greyhounds of the sea.

Vanderbilt was far more than speed. When built she was described in awestruck terms as a leviathan, the largest ship ever built. When most large steamships had three decks, she had five. At an enormous length of 335 feet with a cargo capacity of five thousand tons, she was indeed a monster of the sea. Her twin sidewheels measured forty-two feet in diameter. Sixty tons of bolts and ninety-four of wrought iron straps reinforced her enormous wooden beams. Her twin engines each generated 2,500 horsepower, and her four boilers weight sixty-two tons apiece. Those engines gave her the power to race at sustained high speeds. To keep pace, *Kearsarg*'s engines had been replaced with the latest high horsepower cross beam models from Cornelius Vanderbilt's own shipyard.[10]

Vanderbilt had already gone to war two years before when, in the crisis of the CSS *Virginia's* revolutionary threat, Cornelius Vanderbilt, the great tycoon, had patriotically offered her to the nation. He said to Lincoln that he "was determined that I would not allow myself to do anything by which I could be ranked with the herd of thieves and vampires who were fattening off the government by means of army contracts." He rushed to New York, saw to the strengthening of the ship's prow with a ram and iron plating, and then sailed her directly to Hampton Roads. His plan was simply to ram and swamp the Merrimac with the vast bulk of his ship. The captain of the *Virginia* took the threat so seriously that he refused to venture out into waters deep enough for the *Vanderbilt* to fight, but the new USS *Monitor* arrived to pursue it into shallow waters for their epic duel.[11]

She now carried the one thousand men of Dahlgren's expedition – six hundred men of the 1st Massachusetts Cavalry, three hundred Marines, and a battery of Mr. Gatling's guns. Every cavalryman and Marine was armed with the new Spencer rifle. And there was only a single horse for a raid whose final dash would require six hundred of them. A two-week sea voyage in winter weather does much to debilitate horses, the worst of which is brine rot, the sores of stressed confinement at sea. Men can stay fit through exercise about a large ship, but cavalry horses need daily exercise impossible onboard, and even if they had been walked healthy down the gangplanks, they would not be fit for sudden exertion. But there was an exception in the fine black reserved for Dahlgren. A large cargo area had been left empty for her exercise, and she was sleek and eager to kick back her heels. A natural and graceful horseman, even after the loss of his leg from his Gettysburg wound, Ulrich spent hours every day with the black, riding her slowly around the cargo bay and seeing to her care.

Though bold of action, his was a precise mind. Again and again he went over his plan with Adams. It was a mission to make the hair stand on end. So every detail had to be checked and gone over until the entire operation became almost a motor reflex.

The maps of Essex and Middlesex lay on the table in their cabin held down against the heaving power of late March seas by books on eastern England, railway timetables, and horse farms. Circled in red were Royal Small Arms Factory Enfield and the Royal Gunpowder Mills at nearby Waltham Abby. Dahlgren threw down a pencil and leaned back in his chair, a twinkle in his eye. "Charlie, Meagher's got the easier mission by far. He intends to stay where he is. We have to get out when we're done. You know how harebrained this scheme is. I know why Alexi volunteered."

Ensign Rimsky-Korsakov, the representative of His Imperial Majesty's
Navy, was tinkling away on a tiny piano he had brought aboard. "He
volunteered because Admiral Lisovsky had ordered him to, and Tsar
Alexander II had ordered Lisovsky to be helpful. But, Charlie, why on
earth did you volunteer?"

A thin, bearded man, Adams was one of those rare New Englanders
you would naturally warm up to. "Well, I'll tell you. You see, representing
the United States in England has been the family business for eighty years
now. It's a legacy of sorts." Dahlgren laughed. Adams father, Charles
Francis Adams, Sr., had been ambassador to the Court of St. James, as
had his great grandfather and grandfather, Presidents John Adams and
John Quincy Adams. "It's expected. Why, even my little brother Henry
has joined the family business though he's going to help Meagher set up
a new branch in Ireland."

"Fair enough, though I didn't follow my father into the Navy and
they don't get much more Navy than he is."

"Well, why on earth, Ullie, with your father an admiral, did you end
up in the Army?"

Dahlgren laughed again. "The highest bid won. Gus Fox offered to
appoint me as a ship's master, but Stanton gave me an army captain's
commission on the spot. It helps to know the right people." Or have
the right father. Through Rear Adm. Dahlgren, Lincoln and had come to
know Ulrich as did other senior members of the government. The young
man had impressed them as a volunteer when he led naval gun crews
to the defense of Harper's Ferry and fell over themselves to give him
a commission when expressed an interest in becoming an officer. As a
nineteen-year-old captain he became an aide first to Major General Sigel
then to Meade himself. He found himself in war, volunteering for every
desperate mission. He led a cavalry raid into Fredericksburg. At Brandy
Station he led a regiment after its commander was lost to cut its way
through Stuart's cavalry. Danger drew Dahlgren like a magnet attracted
iron filings. Others might say like a moth to a flame.

Adams had been struck by the young man's intensity and concentration.
Although Adams himself was only twenty-nine, Dahlgren was still only
twenty-one (b. April 3, 1864), a hero twice over, and a full colonel. The
confinement of the voyage had worn on him, but he filled the time as they
were doing now with going over the operation again and again.

He pointed to the town of Colchester on the map. "We're in great luck
that the only garrison in Essex is Colchester, and then it has only two depot
battalions, caretaking and training of recruits. They're not likely to field
anything serious in time to bother us." Adams mused out loud, "Colchester,
you know, was ancient Camulodunum and became the Roman capital of
the province of Britain until Boudicca's revolt. It was rebuilt as *Colonia*

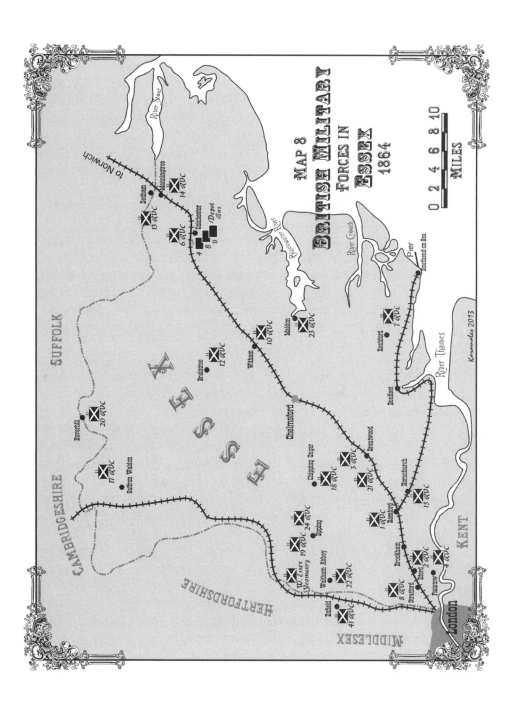

Victricensis. They say Camulodunum is Arthur's Camelot." Dahlgren gave him a "what does that have to do with anything" look. He said, "Well, my brother used to write me of what he saw in Britain when he served as my father's private secretary."

Then Adams remembered Wilmoth's briefing on British strength. What bothered him was the number of Volunteer Rifle Corps and Yeomanry Cavalry squadrons that could suddenly come to life and throw their plans awry. He said as much to Dahlgren. Wilmoth's order-of-battle for Essex had identified the location of twenty RVCs and three squadrons and two batteries of the West Essex Yoemanry Regiment.[12]

"We'll create so much chaos that they will run into each other rather than us."

"I'm not so sure. Even the smallest thing can knock this expedition into a cocked hat."

Dahlgren grew serious and thoughtful. "Yes, I know, Charlie, but we shall be at our objective before they even begin to realize we are there. Then we shall be back aboard ship while they are still hunting us where we are not." He grinned again. "Remember, Charlie, in chaos there is profit. I remember George Sharpe using that expression at Gettysburg."

Adams gazed across the map. From the sea to Enfield and Waltham Abby and back looked an awfully long way.

EPPING FOREST, ESSEX, ENGLAND, 2:30 P.M., SUNDAY, MARCH 27, 1864
The seven hundred or so men of the 41st Middlesex (Enfield Locke) Rifle Volunteer Corps took its Sunday after church drills seriously. Most of them were employees of the Royal Small Arms Factory Enfield (RSAF) and had paid for their own green uniforms with red facings as well the fine Enfield Rifles they all carried. They took an extra pride in their weapons for they themselves had fashioned them. They were especially smart on parade that day. Col. Manly Dixon, Royal Engineers, and Superintendent of the RSAF was trooping the line along with the local military notable, Lt. Col. George Palmer, commander of the West Essex Yeomanry.[13]

Palmer had ridden the five miles from his estate at Nazeing, a splendid example of Georgian architecture with its graceful Ionic columns. He was inordinately proud of his militia cavalry, having personally founded the unit; many of the men were his tenants or young gentlemen of the neighboring area. It was a very small regiment, but it had come to assume a larger and larger part of his life. With the war he had exercised the regiment regularly and secretly hoped for foreign service; there were rumors that yeomanry would be called. At the age of sixty-three his seat was still as perfect as any gentleman's in England.

Watching the parade among the other guests was a man who walked with a limp from a Russian ball at the battle of the Alma in the Crimea, and his left hand was missing two fingers from a Sepoy sword during the Great Mutiny. Sir Robert Wilson, VC, late captain of the 9th Lancers, had retired after the Mutiny and bought a fine house at Waltham Abbey. There were rumors that he had done quite well in the sack of Dehli and stories of rubies the size of pigeon eggs.[14]

Monday early the men of the 41st would join the rest of the almost two thousand men that produced the 1853 pattern Enfield Rifle at the RSAF, just over the county border in Middlesex, in an endless stream that not only kept the British Army and the Rifle Volunteer Corps well-armed but had equipped much of the Confederate States Army as well.

The factory had become the industrial showcase of Victorian England. The fact that it had been born in chaos was overlooked. The 1853 pattern Enfield had been introduced just as the Crimean War created a huge demand for small arms. Private contractors upon which the British Army relied for its weapons failed badly to meet this demand. The decision was made to rebuild the small government Royal Ordnance Manufactory at Enfield Locke in Middlesex as a major arms producer. The issue of meeting demand, however, would run into the same antiquated and time-consuming production methods that afflicted private contractors and in which the rifle parts were not interchangeable. A government factory would also have the advantage of labor peace. The workers at private contractors often used the opportunity of a new contract to go on strike for higher wages.

In desperation the British sent a delegation to the United States to examine the American method of mass production and interchangeable parts. The U.S. government threw open the red carpet for them, and they toured not only Springfield and Harper's Ferry Arsenals but private manufacturers such as Colt as well as non-weapons producers. They were profoundly impressed not only with level of American technological ingenuity in the creation of labor-saving machinery but the greater care American industry took of its workforce and wrote that "the Americans displayed a degree of ingenuity which English industrialists would do well to imitate." Given carte blanche they bought American machinery to equip the rebuilt factory which went into operation just as the Crimean War ended. Royal Small Arms Factory Enfield (RSAF) was given its new name on July 21, 1855, amid the massive construction of its new facilities costing the immense sum of a quarter million pounds. Almost the entire workforce was replaced by new workers trained in mass production. By 1859 RSAF was producing five times as many small arms as all other sources combined, which forced private manufacturers also to switch to mass production methods. By 1860 the factory was turning out 1,774 rifles a week or over ninety thousand a year. Between 1859 and early 1864, RSAF produced almost a half a million small arms.[15]

The heart of the factory was the large room (Machine Shop 1), measuring 500 by 180 feet, lit by saw tooth overhead windows, and packed with machinery for every stage of mass production—machines for rough boring and others of rifling barrels, copying lathes for fashioning gunlocks, shaping (or milling) machines, and dozens more filled the room between iron columns and a web of pulleys and belts and the steam pipes that warmed the building. Power was provided by two 40-horsepower steam engines. The nearby barrel mill was powered by a 70-horsepower steam engine supplemented by water wheels. A smithy and a foundry were in separate buildings.[16]

Ironically, the plant manager was an American named James McKee, a Southerner by birth. He had been hired away by the British commission from Springfield Arsenal at the time of their visit. He had succeeded the original American manager, James Burton, a Virginian and former chief engineer at Springfield Arsenal and later manager of the Richmond Armory for the Confederacy. Other Americans had come with him to work in management. Those of Northern sentiment had quit when the war broke out, but McKee had stayed on delighted to be serving both the Confederacy and his old employer at the same time.

Those who stayed included Oramel Clark, who expertly managed the stocking department. His services had been critical to the entire production of the factory. His shop used twenty-three machines employing sixteen separate functions to produce two hundred stocks a day.[17] The single greatest bottleneck in production had been the curing of the famed British black walnut stocks, which could take up to three years. In a separate building a special dessicating room twenty-four by fourteen feet and twelve feet high utilizing hot air had already been built at great cost, which reduced the drying time to four to five weeks.[18] A third building stored completed stocks.

No railroad ran to the RSAF, but bulk supplies came up the River Lee that flowed almost completely around the factory. About a mile further down the river was the Royal Gunpowder Mills at Waltham Abby.[19] It too had been rebuilt in the crisis of the Crimean War with steam-powered mills and now supplied both the army and navy with all their propellants and explosives as well as much of the domestic market for explosives. It too was supplied by barge from the River Lee, but in 1859 a special railroad system on 18-inch tracks had been built to move supplies and ammunition components within the grounds of the mills.

Gunpowder had been produced at Waltham Abby since 1666; the mills were acquired by the Crown in 1787 and came to occupy 170 acres with buildings widely separated for safety reasons. Those housing the more hazardous processes were surrounded by brick or earth embankments called traverses.[20] In a similarly protected building special research was being conducted on the use of gun cotton as a propellant by Frederick Abel, one of the leading British authorities on explosives and a member of the Royal Society who worked for Chemical Establishment of the Royal Arsenal at Woolwich. He split his time between Woolwich and Waltham Abby. If he were to be found at the powder mills, his capture was a high priority that Lincoln himself had designated after Wilmoth's research showed how critical he was to the development of this new propellant.[21]

PORT HUDSON, LOUISIANA, 2:37 P.M., MONDAY, MARCH 28, 1864

For two days barges unloaded regiment after regiment of Union cavalry at the Port Hudson docks. An entire division of six thousand men and their animals filled out the immense space within the lines of the fort as they set up camp.

"I don't intend for them to get too comfortable." Major General Franklin had been an eager observer of the arrival of such an addition to his command. "I tell you, Grierson, people will forget your Newton Station raid after your boys get their teeth into what I have planned for them." Maj. Gen. Benjamin Grierson was not a man to be frightened by such an announcement. In an age of beards, he had a particularly formidable one. He stroked it in satisfaction. He had been jumped to division command for that very raid Franklin had mentioned, a raid of such daring that it made him a national hero.

While Grant had struggled to drop his army below Vicksburg in 1863, he had sent Grierson with his brigade on a diversion down into the heart of Mississippi to raise hell in the enemy rear. That he did in spades, leaving a trail of Sherman's hairpins,[22] burned rail yards and depots, and terrified civilians. He riveted the attention of the Confederate Command on himself and not on Grant, who successfully landed his army south of Vicksburg. Grierson brilliantly evaded every pursuer and finally led his exhausted command into Baton Rouge to the delighted surprise of the garrison. Now he was back in Louisiana with an entire division.

Franklin introduced Grierson to Rear Adm. David Porter, who commanded the Navy's Mississippi squadrons and then unfolded his map on a camp table. Port Hudson huddled against the Mississippi's eastern shore. To the south were the camps of the besieging Franco-Confederate army. Technically it was not really a siege, because the fort was not surrounded. The Union Navy still controlled the Mississippi above Baton Rouge and its transports kept the garrison well-fed and supplied. To the east and north of the fort stretched an endless and almost roadless pine forest. Settlement had followed the river, the mightiest, easiest, and cheapest road to travel of all. The one road that mattered was the one from the railroad station at Ponchetoula forty-two miles due east from Baton Rouge. It was the Franco-Confederate main supply route.

"This is the key, Grierson. The damned key to turning these Frogs and their Rebel lickspittles out of Louisiana. Because there is no direct railroad or even road from New Orleans to here, they must bring their supplies by rail to Ponchetoula and then by wagon to Baton Rouge, and from there to their camps here, another twenty-odd miles. Right below Ponchetoula the railroad crosses this endless swamp. Smash the station and tear up the track a mile into the swamp, and they'll never get another croissant up from New Orleans. Think what fun you can have with that."

Grierson, of all people, realized what cavalry operations on the ground were like, despite neat map solutions. He was already weighing it. "I want to scout it out thoroughly first, of course. Tell me, how are they are defending their supply route?"

"I'd say they have almost as many cavalry on that line as you have here and blockhouses every mile." He smiled. "I've only had two cavalry regiments, but they've raised holy hell with them. So Bazaine has decided to give his cavalry and Taylor's something to do. They patrol the line constantly. He is a formidable opponent; he understands logistics."

Porter had not said anything more than a few pleasantries but now grinned like a wolf. "I can give you all the diversion you want along the river."

THEATRE DE ORLEANS, BOURBON STREET, NEW ORLEANS, 9:42 P.M., THURSDAY, MARCH 31, 1864

Bazaine was surprised. The music and the musicians were excellent and the audience refined. Of course, he thought, it was the French influence. His acceptance of an invitation had run through white New Orleans like the news of a breached levee. The author of the piece, *The Quasimodo Symphony* (Edmond Dédé), its conductor (Samuel Snaer, Jr.), the musicians, and the audience were what was called *gens de couleur libre* (free people of color) or colloquially, *libres*, the descendants of white fathers and black mothers over a hundred years. They were a distinct class between privileged whites and black slaves, a unique phenomenon in the South, especially in its prosperity.[23]

In 1850 an overwhelming majority of the free Negro men in New Orleans worked as carpenters, masons, cigar makers, shoemakers, clerks, mechanics, coopers, barbers, draymen, painters, blacksmiths, butchers, cabinetmakers, cooks, stewards, and upholsters. . . .

The 1,792 free Negro males listed in the 1850 census were engaged in fifty-four different occupations; only 9.9 percent of them were unskilled laborers. Some of them even held jobs as architects, bookbinders, brokers, engineers, doctors, jewelers, merchants, and musicians. [24]

New Orleans's paternalistic and socially less rigid French and Spanish past had encouraged this community even to the creation of *libre* militia regiments. Benjamin Bulter had transformed those regiments into the first black units incorporated into the Union Army, known as the Corps du Afrique, which also recruited among freed slaves. The First Regiment had even retained its black officers. These were the men who had flung themselves at Port Hudson during the Union siege and earned the respect of the Army. The story of their repulse of the Sudanese earlier this month had excited their community, for many a son, brother, or husband was with them.

Bazaine and other French agents were making discreet but determined efforts to woo the *libres*. Again and again, he emphasized their French connection. For their part, they were startled and amused when he appealed to the French blood in their veins, a statement of family they never thought to hear from a white man. He spoke of the composer, Dédé, and how his talents had only been allowed to bear fruit in France, and he was only one of many such examples. To this he added many more names, such as Norbert Rillieux, who had also been educated and taught in France, a brilliant chemist whose discoveries revolutionized the distillation of sugar. Judah Benjamin, the future Confederate Secretary of War, had been an enthusiastic supporter. French incessantly repeated that slavery had been outlawed in the French Empire.

French gold francs had also been spread among the *libres* as they had among elements of the white population of New Orleans, among gentle hints at the opportunities that beckoned if the Crescent City were once again French. Freedom and opportunity lay not only with a Union victory. His *libre placée*, the stunning beauty, Clio Dulaine, was both an advisor of uncommon political instincts and connections among her own people. She was the perfect mistress for a Frenchman — voluptuous, shrewd, and intelligent. She sat in his box, an open statement.

It would have been immeasurably distressed Bazaine to know that she also worked for George Sharpe. She also took gold sovereigns from the British who wanted to stay informed of their French ally's plotting, but with Sharpe she shared everything and for nothing.

For Lt. Gen. Richard Taylor, commander of the District of Louisiana, and son-in-law to President Jefferson Davis, Bazaine could have a hundred *placées* as far as he cared and parade them as well. It was the New Orleans style. Bazaine's wooing of the *libres* had not gone unnoticed, though, nor had the sudden appearance of a large amount of French gold coin, not all of which could be accounted for by French military purchases in the city. And then there were the increasing number of symbolic displays that only a sovereign power could display, such as a guard of honor at St. Louis Cathedral. Their meetings had become increasingly tense, though Bazaine purred that these were simply marks of French affection for the city that was so French. That had not assured Taylor, who reported in detail to Davis. And that put Davis on the horns of a dilemma. No chief of state was more jealous of his country's sovereignty than Jefferson Davis. At the same time, he recognized that British and French aid was vital to the establishment of the sovereignty of a free and independent Confederate States of America. He could therefore, remonstrate, insist, and deplore but he could not alienate the French. The great victory at Vermillionville and the recapture of New Orleans they owed to the French but that came with a price. There were now more French troops in Louisiana than Confederates.

ROMFORD RAILWAY STATION, ESSEX, 10:22 A.M., FRIDAY, APRIL 1, 1864
The station master was more than usually attentive to his watch. Other station masters throughout Britain were similarly preoccupied. The main lines of the railway system were giving priority to troop trains as the second wave of reinforcement for British Forces in North America was in motion.

It was not just red coats on the trains but large numbers of men in Rifle Green, scores of the Rifle Volunteer Corps that had been called to active service. For the first time, such volunteers would see service in a war theater outside the home islands. Many of the RVCs would go to man the garrisons left empty by the regulars in Britain and Ireland gone to Canada. Even the Guards regiments would be sending more of their battalions across the Atlantic.

There was strong opposition in the Cabinet to so depleting the regular garrisons. The intelligence that the Russians and Americans had signed a secret treaty of alliance against Great Britain and France had unnerved more than a few of them, particularly, the Foreign Secretary Lord Derby. He argued that the battalions strung across the empire should be called upon more. Of course, no one included India in that suggestion. The embers of the Great Mutiny still glowed here and there, at least in the traumatized imagination of the British. Battalions in South Africa, the Caribbean, New Zealand, and China were ordered to war. But Disraeli stood firm against touching any of the thirteen battalions garrisoning Gibraltar and the islands, Malta, Corfu, and Cephelonia, much to the relief of the latter's garrison considered with Canada to be the best peacetime posting in the Empire. That was the imperial reserve should Russia actually enter the war. He had insisted that they actually be reinforced by a dozen of the RVCs.

So it was that the Romford station master heard with relief the engine of the train coming south from Colchester. Right on time. He looked with apprehension to the platform where the 18th Essex RVC from nearby Chipping Onger stood in formation waiting to load the train. One of the two RVC from neighboring Brentwood had left three days ago. His own son was already gone with Romford's own 1st Essex to embark for Canada at one of the great ports in Hampshire on the Channel. He had paid for the boy's uniform, rifle, and kit with great pride, now tempered with a father's very real dread that hung in the back of his mind.

As the train slowed to a halt, women of the Romford Aid Society rushed to the track to hand food packets and tobacco to the red-coated soldiers in the car, replacements from the three depot battalions at Colchester on their way to replace losses or bring battalions up to strength. They had already taken care of the local boys in green. Tomorrow he expected a train with RVCs from Suffolk and Norfolk to the north. He saw his own wife with the other women waving good-bye to the boys on the train as it departed fifteen minutes later. He took her by the hand as she looked up to him. "I think somewhere someone is helping our William. And our John."

The station master caught himself. Like many British families, they had another son in America. They had waited each letter with desperate hope. John had been five years in America and the last two in Union blue. He had fought at a place called Gettysburg. "There, there, woman. Remember, our William's a man and must do his part," he said, despite the fear that welled up in him. "Let us ask God to hold both our sons in His hands."

That night after dinner and prayers he sat down and wrote the member of Parliament for West Essex a letter asking why his country was engaged in a war of brother against brother.

NUMBER 10, DOWNING STREET, LONDON, 5:05 P.M., FRIDAY, APRIL 1, 1864

Disreali cleared his calendar every time one of Senator Sumner's letters was passed to him. It was clear that Lincoln was speaking through Sumner. He had no doubt of it. But before he could trust the words, he had to understand Lincoln. Today the French journalist, Ernest Duvergier de Hauranne, was being ushered into his library. The Frenchman bowed low. The unexpected offer of an interview from the British Prime Minister was a great honor.

After the usual courtesies, Disraeli said, "Monsieur de Hauranne, you have met Lincoln. I would appreciate your confidential impressions of the man."

De Hauranne warmed to the subject immediately. He recounted his meeting with Lincoln when he had been introduced by Senator Sumner. "His voice is far from musical; his language is not flowery; he speaks more or less like an ordinary person from the West, and slang comes easily to his tongue.

"Beyond this, he is simple, serious, and full of good sense. He made some comments on Mr. Everett and on the unrealistic hopes the Democratic party entertained four years ago that it could impose its policies on the victorious Republicans. The remarks may have been lacking in sparkle, but the thought behind them was subtle and witty. I took away from my ten-minute interview an impression of a man who is doubtless not very brilliant, not very polished, but worthy, honest, capable, and hard-working. I think the Europeans who have spoken or written about him have been predisposed to consider it amusing to exaggerate this odds ways. What a stupid and egregious error."[25]

After de Hauranne left, Disraeli leaned back in his chair to ponder his growing picture of his great adversary. His thoughts recalled the comments of the British journalist, Edward Dicey, who had also shared his thoughts with Disraeli. He had described Lincoln's off-putting and ungainly appearance and then said, "And then add to all this an air of strength, physical as well as moral, and a strange look of dignity coupled with all this grotesqueness, and you will the impression left upon me by Abraham Lincoln. You would never say he was a gentleman; you would still less say he was not one. Still there is about him a complete absence of pretension, and an evident desire to be courteous to everybody, which is the essence, if not the outward form, of high breeding."

Then Dicey suddenly became animated. "There is a softness, too, about his smile, and a sparkle of dry humor about his eye which redeem the expression of his face and reminded me more of the late Dr. Arnold, as a child's recollection calls him to me, more than any other face I can call to memory."

Disreali had also been struck by another of Dicey's observations. "It struck me that the tone in which he spoke of England was, for an American, was unusually fair and candid." [26]

RUSSIAN EMBASSY, LONDON, 6:15 P.M., FRIDAY, APRIL 1, 1864

The captain of the HIMS *Variag* bowed low before Baron Phillip de Brunnow, His Imperial Majesty's ambassador to the Court of St. James and handed him a dispatch.

This was the trigger Brunnow had been dreading. His instructions from the tsar had been clear. Upon notice that Lisovsky's squadron was at sea, he was to deliver Russia's declaration of war. Upon him, however, was the delicate timing of the deed. He was to estimate when the squadron was within a day of the British coast before delivering the declaration. That estimate would depend upon the advice of this captain. He had not been fully informed of the circuitous route by which Sharpe had coordinated these plans now in motion with St. Petersburg, but he was aware that they existed and his role in them. The captain of the *Variag* assured the ambassador that the same information was on its way to St. Petersburg aboard the screw clipper, HIMS *Almaz*, which had taken a more direct route to the Baltic.

The ambassador looked up from reading the dispatch. "When does Lisovsky estimate he will strike, Captain?"

"Two days, Excellenz, the third of April."

The dispatch now felt like lead in his hands. Two days. Then he must make that fate-laden ride to the Foreign Office to see Lord Derby and deliver what he knew would be a death sentence to countless men. He remembered all too well, the endless death lists from the Crimean War, his own oldest son among them. Now his youngest boy was an ensign in the Preobrazhensky Guard, the regiment that had pride of place among all the regiments of the Russian Army, founded by Peter then Great himself. Surely, the tsar would not wish that regiment, bearing the name of the Holy Transfiguration, to be absent from the redemption of Constantinople.

THE FOREIGN OFFICE, LONDON, 6:30 P.M., SATURDAY, APRIL 2, 1864
Ambassador Brunnow moved slowly as befitted his old age, but his white hair was more a badge of his sagacity than his infirmities. Slowness was now a friend. He knew Lord Derby would not be at his office when he called without notice. It would take time to find him, if he were in London at all and not gone to his estate. The upper reaches of official London disappeared from London over weekends, even in wartime.

The only official at the ministry was little more than a clerk whose chore it was to accept correspondence. He was equally flustered and scandalized to find himself before the dean of the diplomatic community who demanded immediate audience with the Foreign Minister. When messengers did indeed confirm that Derby had left for his estate, Brunnow handed a sealed envelope to the clerk. "Please, ensure that this document is delivered to Lord Derby at once. It is a communication of the utmost importance from His Imperial Majesty." He then left. The clerk decided to forward it by messenger to Derby the next morning and then went back to his desk to attack a stack of correspondence from various British embassies in South America requesting increases in their tropical post allowances.

8

Vae Victis

It was just such a night that Gen. Sir Hastings Doyle had been waiting for. It had been raining hard and steady for two days. He had chosen those hours when a man is most lulled into the arms of Orpheus, and he had judged correctly. Exhausted and increasingly hungry, too many of the guards along the edge of the bay-ringed city slept.

The boats crept on muffled oars toward the city's splintered docks and the broken sea wall. Royal Marines crowded them, huddled in their dark-blue greatcoats gripping their rifles with bayonets fixed. The rain made it a night for the bayonet. Pouring a powder charge down a rifle barrel in a heavy rain would only spoil the charge. The naval ratings pulled on the muffled oars with a smooth glide that caused nary a splash.

It had been a long and costly siege, and Doyle had been issued an ultimatum by Hope Grant to clean this up before the roads dried enough for the Americans to make another lunge north to relieve the beleaguered city. There was no more time. The city had stood siege since September of last year and had proved a particularly tough nut. Portland was essentially a peninsula stuck into the bay; its landward defenses ran across a narrow neck of land which limited the area that could be directly attacked by Doyle's troops. That had not stopped his artillery and the guns of the Royal Navy in the bay from reducing the Portland to a heap of broken brick and splintered wood.

The Confederates had relayed the intelligence that the U.S. VI Corps was to be reinforced with the IX Corps. Even the reinforcements Doyle had received would not be enough to both maintain the siege and turn and defeat the enemy coming north. Doyle's force had been able to do just that last October when it had met and defeated VI Corps at Kennebunk in southern Maine. It still rankled that Hope Grant had arrived in time to take control of the battle from him and win its laurels. Not a few laurels awaited in Portland.

The first boat glided smoothly to the dock, and the Jollies quietly climbed out to disappear toward the first row of shattered buildings. Other boats found the rubble incline spilled from the gun-shattered sea wall and snaked up it also to be swallowed by the night. Drousy sentries fell one by one as the Jollies slipped deeper and deeper into the town. Behind them more boats arrived with the men of the Slashers of the 63rd Foot. Then the signal of three green rockets went up into the rain-washed sky, and three guns in rapid succession boomed across the bay.

With a crash the massed British artillery fired at the landward defenses of the city giving every impression that the infantry attack was to follow. Most of the garrison was already in those landward defenses. Chamberlain had leapt from his bed in the cellar when the rumble of the artillery had shaken the house. He was barely dressed when he heard firing and shouts above him. Pistol drawn he rushed up the stairs to see a man with bayonet leveled coming down. He shot first, and the body tumbled down. He barely hugged the wall as the man fell past him. Then up again to find his headquarters a shambles of bodies. He stepped over them in the hallway and crept toward the door, the sound of guns and screaming men filtering in through the rain. One dash and he would be outside.

Then behind him he heard the clear click of the hammer of a pistol being cocked. "Drop the pistol," an English voice said.

SOUTHEND-ON-SEA, ESSEX, ENGLAND, 7:00 A.M., SUNDAY, APRIL 3, 1864
From the deck of *Vanderbilt*, Dahlgren watched in amazement as the ship approached the famous Southend Pier. The great wooden structure seemed to go on and on, as it jutted seven thousand feet into the sea. Southend Pier was the longest in the world and served the resort community of Southend-on-Sea on the east coast of Essex north of the Thames estuary mouth. Mudflats extended so far from the shore that large boats, much less ships of any size, could not put in near the beach and nothing could approach at low tide. Even at high tide the depth was never more than eighteen feet. Building the pier and running the London, Tilbury, and Southend Railway line to Southend had created one of the favorite of all British sea resorts.

Vanderbilt and *Kearsarge* had hidden in the dense flow of ships heading up the Thames for London. No one thought to question *Kearsarge's* impersonation of a Royal Navy ship, and *Vanderbilt* hugging close fell under that protection.

As she nosed up to the pier, lines were thrown down. Her engines reversed to bring her to a halt, then stopped. Sailors swarmed onto the empty pier securing the ship. Dahlgren had not waited for the ship to stop pierside but had gone to the cargo hold for the black. He mounted with his good leg, and an aide strapped down the cork and wooden one. The gangways came down and first off the ship were the Marines with Dahlgren at their head riding his black, which pranced down the ramp and shook its head in delight to see the sun and breath the open air. He let the animal ride up and down the pier getting is land legs as the Marines formed up.

With the Marines had come Lt. Rimsky-Korsakov, looking splendid in his Russian naval dress uniform. Two Russian naval infantrymen, the hulking Feodor and Sergei, assigned as servants and bodyguards, stood behind him, rough men who had both fought in the defense of Sevastopol in the Crimean War when the ensign was still a little boy. Sergei held the flag of the Russian Emperor, on a yellow field the black double-headed eagle surmounted by the imperial crown with an icon of St. George slaying the dragon on a shield on the raptor's chest. The words of Admiral Lisovsky came back to the lieutenant as he stood in the salt breeze looking at the flag. The admiral had his bad moments, but this was not one of them. He looked at Rimsky-Korsakov with all the authority of the Russian Imperial Navy as he gave his orders. "Nikolai Andreyevich," he said, using his name and patronymic, a mark of closeness that surprised the young man," and then, stopped and gave him the look that a father would give a son, and resumed now addressing him in the diminutive, "Kolya, my boy, I entrust the banner of His Imperial Majesty to you to carry into the heart of England. Carry it with honor, and no matter what else happens all Russia will rejoice at your deeds. And because the honor of Russia is in your hands, I promote you to the rank of lieutenant, my own flag lieutenant."

Dahlgren smiled at him and then nodded to the Marine major, "Unfurl the colors." The case came off the flag, and the Stars and Stripes caught the sea breeze and rippled above them with a snap. "Quick time, march!" and they were off.

The customs officer of Southend-on-Sea was halfway down the pier in his light, open buggy. The ships had been seen from shore, but it was so early in the season for anyone to dock, that he decided to personally see to them. He was surprised to see the column marching to him. Soldiers? At Southend? And in dark blue? A Rifle Volunteer Corps, not doubt, he thought, but didn't they wear dark green? The sky was overcast, so he could not tell for sure. Then the closer he got, the flag declared itself as the breeze billowed it out.

Americans? Can't be. He was too dumbstruck to do anything but come to a halt as the column reached him.

The mounted officer rode up to him, a lithe, young blond man with a wisp of a beard on his chin. There were gold eagles on his shoulder straps. "And who might you be, sir?" the young man said.

"H-H-Her Majesty's customs officer of Southend-on-Sea."

Dahlgren touched the brim of his cap, "I thank you for the official welcome to England, sir. Unfortunately, I must poorly repay your courtesy. You, sir, are my prisoner. Now, please, be a good gentleman and go quietly with the sergeant."

HIMS *ALEKSANDR NEVSKY*, LIFFEY RIVER MOUTH OFF DUBLIN, 7:26 A.M., SUNDAY, APRIL 3, 1864

Stefan Lisovsky crossed himself and said a prayer to the Virgin. His chaplain had been praying almost every waking hour since the squadron had slipped out of New York. Hundreds of wax candles had puddle before his icons of the Virgin and St. Andrew, who first brought Christianity to Russia. It was St. Andrew's cross, a light-blue diagonal cross or saltire on a white field that was the Andreyevsky ensign or Russian naval ensign, and Lisovsky now ordered it raised and the British naval ensign lowered. He would not sail into the heart of Dublin under false colors.[1]

Meagher had been pacing the deck all morning as the green coast of Ireland had appeared. His staff had busied themselves with the last of their preparations for landing, but now clustered along the railing to drink in the smell of the Old Sod as it blew off the land.

Leaving three of his ships to guard the river mouth channel, Lisovsky escorted the gaggle of transports with the Irish Brigade aboard up the river on the morning tide. A customs boat hailed them but was ignored. The captain of the vessel wondered why Royal Navy warships would fly the Scottish flag. Dublin began to spread out on both sides of the river, one of the great cities of the British Empire, its skyline a field of church spires. Sunday morning it was, and this city rested, as God intended, as the land had begun to bud and flower in the embrace of an Irish spring. Most officials would be at home, their offices shut. The gates of the garrisons would be open for the one free day of the week. Those soldiers not still lounging the barracks were out and about.

The decks of the transports were packed with men in full kit and bayonets fixed staring in wonder as the city flowed by. Home. Many had been born and raised here. For many others it had been the port of emigration to America. Five thousand men seemed to hold their breath in expectation.

The *Nevsky,* the 1,800-ton SS *Northern Light,* and 2,300-ton *Ariel* the pulled up to Essex and Wellington Quays on the south side of the river.[2] The other ships pulled past to continue upriver into the city. Their targets were farther away. Meagher was the first man down the gangway as soon as it thudded onto the stone quay. A dozen gangways on the *Northern Light* were emptying men of his old 69th New York with the same speed that had been practiced again and again on Long Island. The color guard of the regiment formed in front, the Green Flag of Ireland hanging next to the American flag. Beyond them, the 28th Massachusetts had flowed out the *Ariel* just as quickly.

Meagher did not look back as Russian Naval Infantry secured the quay.[3] He plunged down Parliament Street with the 69th at his heels at double time aimed straight for the main gate to Dublin Castle, their bayonets at port arms creating a swaying blued-bayonet hedge on the formation's left as their feet thudded in time on the cobbles.

Within minutes they were at the gates of Dublin Castle to the astonishment of the two guards in their sentry boxes. They wore RVC green. If they had been British regulars, their reaction would have been swift—bayonets leveled and shoulder to shoulder as they died in place. But RVC lads were as green as their uniforms. Their rifles were snatched from dumbfounded hands as they were pulled from their boxes and pushed up against the wall.

The column broke in two and flowed through the Gates of Fortitude and Justice flanking the Bedford Tower and into the great Upper Yard. Companies peeled off, each with its special mission, but Meagher continued across the yard with Companies A, B, and C straight for the official apartments of the lord lieutenant of Ireland.

Down the Liffey, the other ships were sending their streams into Dublin's streets on both sides of the river. From Wolfestone Quay on the north side, the 63rd New York split, one half for Royal Barracks and the other for Marlborough Barracks a little farther away. The gunners pulled their Gatlings and 3-inch guns behind them. On the south side of the river, 83rd New York and 116th Pennsylvania struck out for Islandbridge and Richmond Barracks. The 28th Massachusetts, despite landing near Dublin Castle, had the farthest to go of any regiment, splitting itself in two to take Beggar's Bush and Portobello Barracks deeper south in the city.

Dubliners stood in bewildered silence as the columns flowed past them, their powers of observation dampened by the seeming impossible. Troops, not in any uniform they recognized, were in the heart of Dublin. This had come out of the blue, no forewarning, made all the more shocking by shattering the calm of a Sunday morning. Then the eye went upward to the flags at the head of every column. For many of the Catholics, sight of the long-forbidden Green Flag of Ireland with its golden harp of memory and next to it the American banner meant hope for the many kin that made the crossing. For the Anglo-Irish, and the English, Scots, and the loyal Catholic Irish, recognition ignited a far different reaction—absolute shock, then an inchoate rage that caused them to rush about in an uproar while the bolder among their Catholic neighbors cheered. But most people were filled with a natural dread and rushed home to bar their doors and await events. Somewhere church bells began to ring again and not for mass, church, or chapel.

For the two captains in scarlet riding south down Infirmary Road bordering Phoenix Park, the appearance of the column in blue marching toward Marlborough Barracks was announced by that sudden, discordant pealing. Then the gunfire from the storming of the nearby Royal Barracks added its "harsh sharps and discords." They spurred toward the column to ask the RVC what on earth was going. They had that unarticulated unease that something was amiss; RVCs wore mostly green and not dark blue. The Royal Artillery wore dark blue but not as plain as this, and the gunners would not be caught dead marching like the infantry.

They pulled up just as the breeze unfurled the colors. This time the recognition was immediate and direct. Perhaps it was the leveled rifles of the first two ranks. An officer stepped forward, and in a clear Irish voice announced, "You gentlemen have the honor to be my first prisoners of the day. Please, dismount. It is not fitting that I should walk while prisoners ride."

The bolder of the two replied, "The hell you say!" The officer shot him. He jerked the rains as he clutched at the hole in his chest. His horse pulled right and reared toward the head of the column, which instinctively drew back. The other officer spurred his horse to the right and took the wall into the park in clean jump.

HEADQUARTERS, ARMY OF THE POTOMAC, BRANDY STATION, VIRGINIA, 5:30 A.M., SUNDAY, APRIL 3, 1864

George Meade's sharp tongue did not faze John C. Babcock, his dapper chief intelligence officer. The commander of the Army of the Potomac, unaffectionately known as the "Snapping Turtle," was notorious for his intemperate outbursts to his staff. He had alienated Sharpe, to whom he had owed so much for his victory at Gettysburg. Only Lincoln's transfer of Sharpe to form the National Intelligence Bureau had prevented an open break.

Babcock traveled in less exalted circles and had only accepted a commission at Sharpe's urging. He had been the most famous enlisted scout in the Army of the Potomac when George McClellan commanded. Tardy George was so impressed that he had as a favor to Babcock released him from military service and had Pinkerton hire him as a civilian employee. After Lincoln relieved McClellan, Pinkerton departed, and between the two of them they took all of the intelligence files of the army. The new commander, Maj. Gen. Ambrose Burnside, retained Babcock as the only element of Pinkerton's intelligence operation that remained. He painstakingly recreated the Confederate order-of-battle from file copies of reports received by the War Department.

When George Sharpe was ordered to create the Bureau of Military Information in March 1863 by Hooker, Burnside's successor, he found in Babcock a master of order-of-battle, that art of intelligence that determines the enemy's organization and strength, not only from captured documents, enemy newspapers, but also from interrogations of Confederate prisoners, for which he had an extraordinarily fine touch. Within six weeks Babcock's analysis had pegged the strength of the Army of Northern Virginia's to within 1,500 men, a breathtaking level of precision. At Gettysburg his analysis was crucial on the second day to inform Meade that they had identified every regiment in Lee's army except those in Pickett's Division, thus identifying his only reserve, information that steeled Meade to fight it out.[4]

Meade's outburst could not last forever. Babcock just waited for the man to stop and catch his breath. At last the moment came. "General, I thought you would like to know that Lee is detaching Longstreet again."

"Damnation! Where is he going this time?" Whenever Lee needed to send a corps on an independent mission, it was his "Old Warhorse" Longstreet that he chose. Last year had sent him on a campaign to overrun Union forces at Suffolk across the James River from Fortress Monroe. Only the Navy's gallant defense of the river line frustrated his attempt. His second mission was more attended by success. He took two divisions to reinforce Bragg's Army of Tennessee and arrived in time to crush the Union flank and win the blood-soaked battle of Chickamauga.

"The James Peninsula."

"You're sure?" Meade was a commander who liked to go over the sources of intelligence himself.

"We've had a dozen deserters in the last five days who have told some version of the same story.

"Well, you know Lee has sent deserters to us with misleading information before."

"But he's never sent us slaves to do that. He has no idea they are some of our best informants. And we have two officer body slaves, both from Longstreet's First Corps, who have told us the same thing as well as word from one of our best agents in the enemy's rear."

"General Sharpe has also authorized me to inform you of a new source of information from within Richmond itself, for your ears only. A certain lady in the enemy's capital has contacted us with a desire to provide information for the sake of the Union"

"A woman?"

"Our Rose Greenhow, but much better, according to Sharpe."[5] Babcock replied. "She's already proven her bona fides by arranging the escape of so many of our officers in Libby Prison. Col. Paul Revere, you will remember, was one of them."

It had been an enormous black eye for the Confederates that more than fifty Union officers had escaped. Meade thought back to his conversation with Revere and the man's undying devotion to this "ministering angle" who had not only seen to their escape from the pesthole of Libby Prison but had smuggled them from one safe house to another and then out of Richmond and down to Fort Monroe. She was already well-known to the prisoners for her visits to provide them with food, clothing, and medicine. He revealed her name only in the strictest confidence: Elizabeth Van Lew, a blue-blooded member of Richmond society and an ardent Union patriot.

He said, "Oh, the Van Lew woman."

Babcock was surprised. "Sir, I must emphasize that her name is not be repeated to anyone. She is at great risk, and Lee has spies in our camp as we have in his."

"Of course, of course." He thought for a moment. "Lee is gambling that Longstreet can reach Monroe before we are able to begin our campaign. He thinks we will wait for the new grass to feed our horses and for the roads to dry enough in late April. He's taking the risk of detaching one-third, and I would say the best third, of his army. If there was one Confederate I would like to be gone from Lee's army, it is Longstreet." Meade's interpersonal skills may have been lacking, but he was one Union general whom Robert E. Lee respected. He had said of Meade just before Gettysburg when he learned of his appointment to command the Army of the Potomac that Meade would make no mistake of which Lee could take advantage but would be sure to take advantage of any mistake Lee made.

THE VAN LEW TRUCK FARM OUTSIDE RICHMOND, VIRGINIA, 6:12 A.M., SUNDAY, APRIL 3, 1864

Van Lew watched the Confederate cavalryman ride slowly up the road toward her farm with the sun rising at his back. He was nondescript save for the red hair and beard, and in his greeting his accent was pure Virginia. Yet, Van Lew knew immediately from the password he dropped in his greeting that he was the Union contact she had expected.

He identified himself as Maj. Milton Cline. Sharpe could think of no one more able to make contact with Van Lew. Cline had been the Chief of Scouts of the Army of the Potomac and worked directly for Sharpe. The man was a phenomenal scout, able to blend in among the Confederates with a butter-wouldn't-melt-in-his-mouth coolness and a great actor's skill of living his part. Before Chancellorsville he had passed himself off as a Confederate soldier to an officer touring all the brigades of Lee's army, adding vital information to Babcock's order-of-battle. At Gettysburg he acquired the information, again by impersonating a Southern cavalryman, that vital dispatches from Richmond were expected at a certain time and place. That led to Sharpe's plan for a snatch-and-grab raid led by Ulrich Dahlgren and Cline that delivered the dispatches to Meade and further hardened his resolve to stand and fight at Gettysburg.[6]

Although Cline could go Southern with ease, he was New York born and raised and had moved to Indiana where he joined the 3rd Indiana Cavalry at the start of the war. Hooker had used these Hoosiers for special operations and after they captured a Confederate ship on the Potomac had earned the name of Hooker's Horse Marines. Sharpe had acquired his services for the CIB, found an Indiana state volunteer commission for him, and sent him there with the Horse Marines to ferret out the rising Copperhead conspiracy, which he had done with great success. That had shown that Cline could operate not just as a lone scout but also with the most delicate of situations. So when Sharpe considered who best to send to make contact with Van Lew, only Cline, the human chameleon, would do.

Van Lew showed him to the little parlor in the farmhouse. She did not usually live there but in Richmond where she owned a distinguished home, columned Greek front and all, in the heart of the city. She waved to him to sit. "May I offer you coffee or tea, sir?" Her thin face with sharp features did not make her a pretty woman, but she was what they called handsome, the special accolade for a woman of presence and character. Before he could answer, she said, "Now that the English are filling Southern harbors, nothing is in short supply." Cline chose coffee and remarked that in the North it was now in short supply also due to the English.

As the coffee was served, Van Lew said that he could speak freely around her people. Cline said, "I don't worry, Miss Van Lew. In my experience no slave has ever betrayed a Union soldier behind the lines.

"I'm sure that is true, Major, but my people are not slaves. I freed them all as soon as my father died. They work for an honest wage. Most of our soldiers who have escaped from Libby Prison could only have done so with the aid of my people. They are in this war as much as any soldier."

"Indeed, ma'am, indeed." He leaned over to emphasize that it was time to do business.

"General Sharpe wishes me to thank you in the fullest terms for the information you sent through General Butler. We have confirmed it through other sources as well, but as he said, it is better to drink directly from the well. He asks me to inquire of your sources."

This was obviously something she did not want to do. "I must protect those sources, Major. Surely, you understand that the more people who know, the more risk they suffer."

"I must be frank, madam. Our knowledge of your sources allows us to gauge their credibility and your usefulness. I assure you, though, that that knowledge is shared with only the most trusted officers of General Sharpe's organization." He paused, and then added, "And General Grant and the President."

She seemed to brighten up at that. "We have had difficulty acquiring a trusted agent in Richmond, madam, and General Sharpe believes you fill that bill. Your own *bona fides*, in your gallant help to our prisoners, have more than established that." He did not mention that Grant had almost immediately from his appointment as General-in-Chief had told Sharpe to "get me inside Richmond." It was almost a God-sent miracle that shortly thereafter General Butler had forwarded Van Lew's information, which she had had smuggled through the lines to Fort Monroe.

"You must understand, Major, that despite all the bravado here about loyalty to the Rebellion, there are many in Richmond who have remained loyal to the flag. Virginia did not go easily into secession. It has been my honor to hold this loyal community together, though they are hunted and oppressed. Let me just say that loyal men work in the Army and Navy Departments who risk their lives for their true country. Then there are others, such as Samuel Routh who runs the Richmond, Fredericksburg, and Potomac Railroad (RF&P) and who directly supplies Lee. His information is of the utmost accuracy. He can also, shall I say, prove incompetent, when necessary.

"Richmond leaks like a sieve. The loyal community just laps it up and brings it to me, and I am determined to pass it on to our government."

"I must ask, though, how you can do so when you have so clearly stated your loyal opinions in public and have become such an open relief to our prisoners?"

Van Lew smiled. "I have cultivated a certain eccentricity to the point where I am dismissed simply as Crazy Bet. I put on a pretty good show of it too, I must say." As a member of Richmond society, she also profited from a degree of elite tolerance. "But I don't want you to think that I rely solely on that. I have taken on a border whose presence is proof of my harmlessness as well as my loyalty." She sipped her coffee, and her eyes twinkled over the cup. "I offered free room and board to General Wyndham, the Provost Marshal General of the Confederacy as my patriotic duty to the cause, and he accepted, the greedy, little man. Who then would question the lady who boards the chief jailer and spy-catcher in the Confederacy?"

SOUTHEND-ON-SEA, ESSEX, ENGLAND, 11:15 A.M., SUNDAY, APRIL 3, 1864
The small resort community had been locked down tight. The Marines quickly seized the telegraph office and the railway station, while other squads blocked all then roads leading out of the resort. The half-dozen unarmed constables were locked up in their own jail while the mayor was found and brought in state of jabbering hysteria to the station where Dahlgren had set up his headquarters. There he joined the station master, a tower of stone-faced British reserve. One look silenced the mayor into only an odd whimper.

They faced Dahlgren, who had found a chair in the station master's office. He was reading the train schedule and then looked up. The station master immediately fixed on the sky-blue eyes. They were the reflection of a blue gas flame. He sensed without even forming the conscious thought that this was a dangerous man as a man senses the snarling power of a sleek hunter. When he did speak, his voice was clipped and to the point. "My name is Colonel Dahlgren. Your town is now under the military jurisdiction of the United States Army. Any attempt at resistance by the civilian population will result in the full application of the laws of war, meaning, gentlemen, anyone bearing arms or assisting those who bear arms will be summarily shot. Do I make myself clear?"

The mayor fell over himself in blubbering agreement. The station master just folded his arms and looked daggers at Dahlgren. The younger man paused to consider the station master's emphatic body language, then said, "Station master, is this railway schedule correct?" The plan hinged on whether the one excursion train from London was on time.

"That is for you to find out, sir."

"I'm sure I will. Sergeant, take the mayor outside and shoot him." The man cried out in terror as the Marine dragged him outside. "Now station master, it would be easier all around if you would answer my question."

"You may shoot me as well, but I will be damned if I help an invader."

"Then, sir, you should be able to understand the sentiments of my countrymen." They could hear the mayor outside begging for mercy. Then a shot, and he was silent. The station master looked at Dahlgren and despised him for smiling. His fists balled as he took a step forward to growl, "Do your worst."

Dahlgen pulled himself to his feet. "I assure you, sir, you would not enjoy that at all." He looked at the station master, a hint of admiration in his face. A distant train whistle turned his head in its direction. He took out his pocket watch and flipped open the cover. "Well, station master, it seems your schedule is correct after all. You could have saved the mayor an ordeal." He touched his fingers to the brim of his cap and walked out. He passed the sergeant, who was holding a bound and gagged mayor. "Take him back in, Sergeant, and let him clean himself."

The train slid to a stop at the station, the doors flew open, and light crowd on early holiday descended upon the platform to be herded together by the Marines. Dahlgren heaved himself onto a box and shouted for order. "Listen to me, all of you. Essex is now under the military occupation of the United States army of invasion. You will be confined to this town until the army of Gen. Ulysses S. Grant completes the conquest of this kingdom. As I speak that army is landing all over England." He paused for a moment to point to Rimsky-Korsakov and the imperial banner. "And also the forces of the Russian tsar."

Dahlgren rather enjoyed that. See how the hell the English liked that, even if it only a rumor to scare the bejuzus out of them. Then he added, "Our monitors have defeated the Royal Navy in a great battle. You are now defenseless." This island race had become far too used to carrying war to someone else's country. The stunned look of "the world turned upside down" on their faces told him how sharp would be the arrow that flew on the wings of that rumor.

Confirmation came marching up in the column of the 1st Massachusetts, their saddles and bridles over their shoulders marching up to the platform. Adams rode a horse onto the platform and saluted Dahlgren. "You like her, Ulrich? Found her in the riding stables and a dozen more. Better yet, the transit corrals were filled, just like Wilmoth said." Essex was a horse-raising county with a number of large horse-farms that bred and trained horses to the saddle. Most were destined for the British army cavalry remount school at Maidenstone in Kent and were collected from the horse-farms in this part of Essex because the London-Tilbury-Southend line was one of the few railway spurs off the main line that ran from London northeast through Colchester and on to Norwich in Suffolk.

"No time to waste, Charlie. Get your people going." If either of them were believers in luck, they did not seem to question how long their surfeit would last. As for Dahlgren, he had come to believe that he rode the lightning.

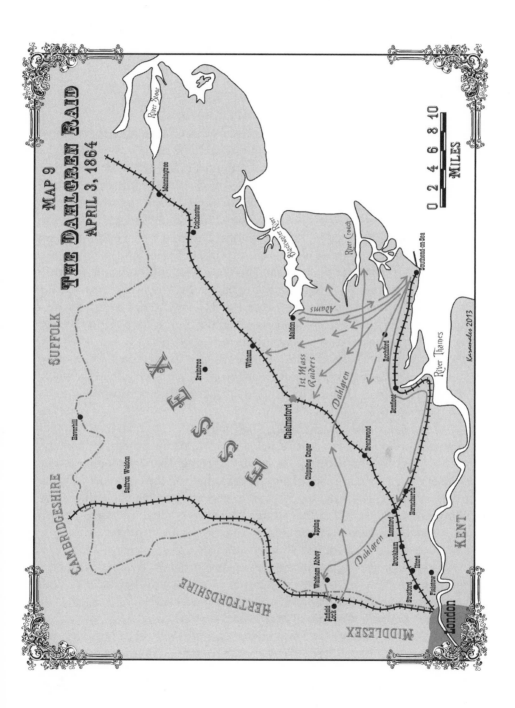

MAP 9
THE DAHLGREN RAID
APRIL 3, 1864

Aboard the *Kearsarge*, Lamson nervously paced his quarterdeck while at the same time envying Dahlgren and Adams their adventure. They would be consumed by action while his ship and *Vanderbilt* sat alongside Southend Pier watching the commerce of the world sail in and out of the Thames estuary as they waited the raiders' return. "Hurry up, Uly, for God's sake hurry."

DUBLIN CASTLE, 2:49 P.M., SUNDAY, APRIL 3, 1864

The great coat of arms that hung over the entrance to the state apartments, the Lion and Unicorn of the United Kingdom, came crashing to the pavement below. It was Meagher's first official act after declaring the Irish Republic to the Fenian crowd that had thronged to Dublin Castle as word spread through the city that the Americans and Meagher had arrived. They had cheered themselves to a state of near intoxication as the Union flag (of the United Kingdom) fluttered down and the green flag raced up the flagpole to snap triumphantly in the Spring breeze.

No one was more elated that Meagher. The city had fallen within eight hours of their landing. The dream had come true. All of the barracks had fallen with their garrisons surrendered. They did not have a chance. Aside from a duty officer, the regimental officers of each regiment had been at home or in church. Ammunition had been safely locked away, and the men had been sleeping late on their only free day. Even those inclined to resist found themselves confronted with American bayonets with Irish brogues rushing into their barracks with cannon and Gatlings to back them up.

In his elation, Meagher shrugged off the failure to seize the Viceroy of Ireland at his lodge in Phoenix Park. He could thank the British captain who had spurred his horse to take the park wall rather than surrender. People were already crowding the balcony of the lodge and the entrance, pointing to then smoke rising from the Royal Barracks as they listened to the sound of gunfire rising from the other nearby barracks. When the captain rode up all eyes fixed on him as he shouted, "Where is the Viceroy?"

A man on the balcony replied, "I am he, Captain. What news?"

"American troops are in the city, Your Lordship. I barely escaped a column marching up Infirmary Road to Marlborough Barracks." There was a sharp gasp from the group around the viceroy.

"Are you sure, Captain? I find it . . . ."

"They shot Captain Butler, who was riding at my side. I only escaped by jumping the wall. They were Irish men in American uniforms, my Lord."

"Then ride to the Curragh and tell the garrison I order them to Dublin at once." He turned to a servant. "My horse immediately. We are leaving." Meagher's detachment reached the lodge just as the viceroy and the captain galloped off to the northwest.

Meagher shrugged it off. He had what for him was a more pressing problem. He was on his own; Lisovsky had departed immediately with the afternoon tide. Barely two hundred of native-born Catholic soldiers who had taken the Fenian oath came forward when called to declare themselves from among the British prisoners. There would have been more, but half the normal garrison had already taken ship for Canada and been replaced with English and Scottish RVCs. Still, there should have been more for over one-third of the garrison of Ireland before the war had taken the oath to a free Ireland.[7] The oath was heady thing to give when its fulfillment remained only a dream. Now it was here, a real and hard thing, more than a line to cross but an abyss to stare down into and make the soul shiver. Others found on their shoulders the hand of the spirit of their regiments, the honor of countless men who had shared the hard comradeship of these living families of men. Those who had lived by the unspoken iron code that they could never let the regiment down, dreaded to face not only their mates but on judgment day the ghosts of the regiment, and found their feet fixed to the ground.

To these few hundred a thousand more volunteers from the civilian population had already come forward. Meagher formed the veterans and the volunteers into the 1st (Brian Boru) and 2nd (Daniel O'Connell) Regiments of the Army of Ireland. There were more than enough captured Enfields to arm them, and when the Magazine Fort fell, more than enough ammunition. Their regimental colors were at hand, sewn in America by Irish seamstresses. Green they were with the Golden Harp in one corner and the regimental number in red in the center on a white shield. Yet there were two dozen such flags meant for many more volunteers.

Meagher remained confident that he would quickly issue those flags, but for the moment the two were just enough to take posts of honor on either side of the throne in the white and gold presentation room of the castle. The room had been converted to a symbol of royal authority for a visit of the late King William IV. Victoria herself had sat there when she had visited Ireland during the Famine to receive the well-fed Anglo-Irish elite. Now the room was filled with the Fenian leadership of Dublin, their voices rising in waves of growing elation.

Meagher stepped to the platform upon which the throne stood. Out flashed the sword he had carried on the Peninsula, in the awful and glorious charge at Antietam, and in the carnage of Fredericksburg. The blade glittered in the light that poured through the windows as he held it high. Then he turned, held it in both hands, kissed it, and laid it over the arms of the throne. The shout of approval rolled out through the window and turned every head in the yard below. It was the grandest such gesture with a sword since Brennus, the Celtic chieftain who sacked Rome, threw his own blade onto the tribute scales in the spirit of *vae victis*—woe to the vanquished. Come what may, at that instant Meagher of the Sword had become legend.[8]

SOUTHEND-ON-SEA, ESSEX, 2:55 P.M., SUNDAY, APRIL 3, 1864

The five remaining companies of the 1st Massachusetts Cavalry cheered as the train bearing the other five companies left the station yard. Adams turned to his assembled company commanders and said, "You know what to do."[9] They returned to their units, and in minutes the companies trotted out of Southend on the roads that would take them throughout southeastern Essex.

Dahlgren put them out of his mind to concentrate on what lay ahead for him and the rest of the 1st Mass. He knew Adams would raise enough hell to thoroughly confuse the British while he slipped through. He rode in the locomotive with a few of the Massachusetts troopers, who had been railroad men in civilian life, to watch with guns drawn over the British crew. That crew had refused to cooperate until they saw the mayor taken out behind the station house followed by that shot. Time would work for Dahlgren; it was only thirty-five miles from Southend-on-Sea to Romford, and coincidentally the train's normal speed was thirty-five miles an hour. So one hour to Romford, bypassing the usual stops along the way with another half hour for stops between stations for his men to jump out and cut the telegraph wires that paralleled the track. They rattled through the small towns along the route stations—Benfleet, Stanford-le-Hope, Hornchurch—noting the puzzled looks of the few passengers on the platforms. Dahlgren flipped open his watch. Yes, he said to himself, on schedule.

Adams was also on a schedule, but his was not one driven by railway timetables. His five companies had broken up into twenty detachments, each with an American flag, each and every one to proclaim in every village and town that they were the vanguard of General Grant's army of invasion, declare the inhabitants now under the military authority of the United States Army, and put every municipality under contribution. To emphasize the point, they burnt Crown property of military value, such as it was in quiet rural Essex. Before too long trails of smoke climbed into the sky following the north and westward ride of the raiders. The British would later make much of the destruction of the occasional bridge, railway station, and post office, likening it, with a very un-British exaggeration, to the swath of wanton ruin left by William the Conqueror through southern England after the battle of Hastings in 1066.

Ultimately, the Massachusetts men would reach the railway line between Colchester and Romford, twenty miles away, where they would tear up the tracks here and there. Adams with the largest detachment headed fourteen miles due north to the port of Maldon. A major railway spur connected the port with the main railway. It would provide another focus of alarm for the British, a burned port and severed railway, hopefully enough confusion to cover Dahlgren's dash. That was the plan.

But unfortunately plans are nothing; planning is everything, and even Wilmoth's superlative ability to gather intelligence for this operation was not omniscient. An intelligence gap was now about to pour its friction into the plan. Wilmoth had provided Dahlgren with the location of every RVC in Essex and the information that they drilled on Sundays once a month, but he could not tell them if they all drilled on the same Sunday, and if so, what Sunday of the month. Dahlgren had decided that the odds would be three to one in their favor that the RCVs would not be drilling on that Sunday even if they all had the same training schedule. He was wrong on both counts. As his train sped through Hornchurch, he did not see the 15th RVC assembled on the green and shielded by the town.

THE IRISH SEA OFF DUBLIN, 3:45 P.M., SUNDAY, APRIL 3, 1864

Lisovsky did not allow the success of transporting Meagher and his men to Dublin to blind him to both the peril and opportunity that beckoned. His squadron was in the Irish Sea, the *Mare Nostrum* of the British Empire, a lair of the Royal Navy, unviolated in living memory by any enemy. That was peril, indeed, more than to cause all but the boldest to fly to safety. But what God in his mystery took away with one hand, he gave with the other. The Irish Sea teemed with shipping. The Mersey's rushing tides sent great Liverpool's endless stream of ships into that sea as did countless other smaller ports in Ireland, Scotland, England, and Wales. Liverpool had grown rich as the main British terminus for trade with the Americas and infamous as the builder of the Confederate commerce raiders that had sparked this war.

For the Russians there was no question of the choice between peril and opportunity. The Imperial Navy had much to avenge. Its last triumph had to been to sink the Turkish fleet in Sinope harbor in 1853, the very event that triggered the British and French declaration of war. Their fleets had driven the Russian fleet into its own naval bases where they were bottled up as at Kronstadt outside St. Petersburg or pounded to pieces as at Sevastopol in the Crimea.

Now they could feed on such seaborne wealth as no one since Drake and the sea rovers, who had tormented Spain's new-world treasure fleets 250 years before, encountered. Lisovksy's first catch simply sailed into his arms on course to Dublin, then another and another. White sails and columns of coal smoke speckled the sea as ships funneled into Dublin. He could simply act as a weir and the let the ships swim on their own into his trap. And that he did, netting eighteen ships in three hours until the smoke of their funeral pyres hung over the Liffey mouth like an announcement of doom that would draw every Royal Navy ship for a hundred miles. Soon he sailed directly across the sea to raid the Mersey mouth itself hoping to catch a large number of ships waiting to take the morning tide up the Mersey into Liverpool. Let the people of England's second city watch the smoke from the ships that were their commercial life's blood ascend into heaven. He could not think of a greater humiliation for Great Britain and for the Royal Navy.

Lisovsky was beyond amazement as his squadron darted out to sea again. Where was the Royal Navy? Its ships should have doubled their patrols almost immediately after the declaration of war had been delivered late yesterday. The entire operation, Meagher and Dahlgren's expeditions, had all been timed to follow immediately on the heels of Russia's declaration of war. That timing was of no importance to the Americans who were already at war, but vital for the Russians if they were to have any diplomatic standing. The Americans had acceded to their ally's necessity. Still, he thought, it could all be the natural result of the fact that most of the Royal Navy's bases were on the Channel coast best able to war with their traditional enemy, the French. Many of their ships were already on station now in North American waters. Yet, there could not be this much good luck.

The answer to his question lay in the Foreign Ministry dispatch box sitting in Lord Derby's study in his country home. He had come down late for breakfast and only opened it at noon to find its only contents a letter from the ministry duty officer and the sealed message of the Russian ambassador. He was surprised in reading the letter that de Brunnow had called so late on a Saturday. It was utterly out of character with that dignified old man and the punctilious traditions of the Russian diplomatic corps.

He leaned back in his chair to read it carefully. His face turned white, and his jaw went slack. Then he shot to his feet and shouted for his private secretary. It was not long before two carriages raced out of his graveled driveway, his secretary heading for the nearest telegraph station while Lord Derby headed directly for London with Russia's declaration of war.

OFF VICTORIA ISLAND, BRITISH COLUMBIA, 7:52 A.M., SUNDAY, APRIL 3, 1864[10]

Admiral Popov had brought his entire squadron, the three corvettes, *Bogatyr*, *Kalevala*, and *Rynda*, and the screw clippers *Gaidamak* and *Abrek*, north to Victoria Island to trail his coat down the coast of British

Columbia snaring British shipping sailing in and out of the San Juan de Fuca Strait.[11] That strait was a large body of water about ninety-five miles (153 km) long, forming the principal outlet for the Georgia Strait and Puget Sound to the Pacific and the boundary between the United States and Canada. The strait wrapped around the southern tip of Vancouver Island. Popov was hoping also to tempt out whatever British warships were at the Esquimalt Royal Navy Dockyard on the southern tip of Victoria Island, which bordered the strait on the north. The dockyard was only a secondary base of the Royal Navy in the Pacific; its primary base was at Valparaiso in Chile, a continent away from California.

It was a bold move, and Popov's instructions directed him to do as much damage as he could to British and French shipping. Those instructions had calculated that war would be declared by this date and directed him to act regardless of formal notification. For his part he calculated that the richest pickings would be found in these waters. Even more important was the opportunity to inflict a defeat on the small force the Royal Navy had based at Esquimalt, two corvettes and a handful of gunboats. Such a defeat would give His Imperial Majesty the clout to demand in any treaty negotiation the annexation of this part of Canada along the Pacific to Russian America (Alaska). If the Americans had similar aspirations, their absence would deprive them of any right to the spoils.[12] Rear Adm. Charles H. Bell, the commander of the American California Squadron, refused to take his major ships, the steam screw sloops, USS *Lancaster* and *Narragansett*, away from the defense of San Francisco. Already British ships had been raiding the coast off southern California and intercepting traffic off San Francisco itself. Popov had talked himself blue in the face trying to convince Bell to send those ships with him. The eleven 9-inch Dahlgren guns aboard the *Lancaster* and the huge 11-inch on the *Narragansett* would have been the heaviest guns in any fight with the British. If Popov had seen the tension between his missions of commerce raiding and decisive engagement, he did not seem bothered by it.

The pickings had indeed been rich, a half-dozen vessels in a single day had been taken. When the *Kalevala*'s lookout reported four British warships steaming out of Esquimalt with their guns run out, it was clear that the Royal Navy had picked up the gage regardless of the odds. Popov was happy to oblige with his seventy guns to the British forty-two.[13]

Capt. E.W. Turnour of the *Charybdis* commanded the little British squadron. As word of the appearance of the Russian ships raiding the approaches to the strait, he did not take long to weigh his options. He was clearly outnumbered and outgunned two to one, even if he used his two small gunboats that were designed for shore bombardment, not actions at sea. The prudent thing was not to risk his ships in such an unsure fight and thereby leave this British colony at the Russians' mercy. But this was a man whose boyhood hero was Lord Nelson; he had immersed himself in the life of that great fighting sailor. He had fashioned his life around the Socratic admonition to be what you admire most. So it was not surprising that Nelson's words came to mind: "Our Country will, I believe, sooner forgive an officer for attacking an enemy than for letting it alone."[14]

He had the immediate advantage of being in formation line ahead with *Charybdis* in the lead followed by *Alert* and the gunboats. Popov's ships were scattered for a dozen miles in their wide-cast net to snare enemy shipping. Turnour headed for the closest Russian ship, *Bogatyr*, with his engines wide open. Through his glass he could see that the Russian naval ensign bore a red stripe along the bottom, signaling that it was Popov's flagship. *Bogatyr*'s captain, Piotr Afansievich Chebyshev, tensely waited for Popov's decision; he was just as eager to engage, advantage or no, as Turnour. The ship's very name demanded it, for *bogatyr* meant gallant, heroic knight in Russian. Popov realized that unless he ordered the captain to sail away from the British in order to gather up the rest of the squadron, he would be the one outgunned. "You will engage the enemy, Captain." Chebyshev almost leapt forward to give the order. *Bogatyr* turned toward the British as its signal flags flew up ordering the rest of the squadron to converge on it.

The first shots were fired by the pivot bow guns of both *Charybdis* and *Bogatyr* and missed, but as the range closed *Charybdis* counted the first hit. *Bogatyr*'s mainmast splintered, groaned, and fell like the giant of the forest it was once to fall over the side. The Russian ship slowed as the mast with its sails and rigging acted like a drag on its engines. The debris also masked most of its portside guns. And it was on this side that *Charybdis* came up while *Alert* split off to rake its starboard side. Turnour brought his ship to pointblank range to let his 8-inch smoothbores disembowel the Russian, their shells exploding across the gundeck in clouds of wooden splinters and iron fragments or punching through the hull to burst inside.

Still *Bogatyr* fought, honoring its namesake. Chebyshev strode over the shattered deck through the splinters, oblivious to the danger, encouraging his men, as the surviving gun crews worked their pieces to the command of "*Ogon! Ogon, bogatyri moi! Ogon!*" ("Fire! Fire, my heroes! Fire!") The years of exacting training that Popov had imposed were paying off as the men stood to their guns, half their crews dead or dying. Chebyshev knew that between the mast dragging in the water and the damage to his ship, the Englishman would win. He would have to strike or go under. Russian captains were not allowed to strike, and he had no intention of going under.

If Turnour had his hero, so did Chebyshev — the Adm. Pavel Nakhimov, who destroyed the Turkish fleet at Sinope and then brilliantly commanded the defenses of Sevastopol. Chebyshev had served under him, and mourned his death at the siege as if he were his own father. He did not even have to ask himself what Nakhimov would do. He grabbed the naval infantry lieutenant, "Petya! Get your men together. We board the Englishman. The man's eyes grew wide, then he exclaimed, "*Xhorosho, Kapitan!*" and was off. "Boys, boys," the captain shouted to the remaining men on the deck. "Arm yourselves, my boys!" He grabbed a powder boy by the arm. "Go to the engineer and tell him he must give me all power in three minutes." The frightened boy scampered off below decks wending his way through the debris and bodies. Somehow the grapnels were found and cast over the few yards to hook onto *Charybdis* where the Russian bow and the English stern were closest.[15]

Chebyshev and the barely twenty men he could muster, naval infantry and sailors armed with pikes and cutlasses, huddled on the bow as the ship lurched forward. *Bogatyr* ran into *Charybdis*, and as the captain leapt over the small space to land on the English quarterdeck. A Royal Marine lunged for him before he could get his balance; he felt the blades slide through the skin of his ribs and out the back of his coat. He twisted away, tearing the rifle from the man's hands. The red coat disappeared in a flood of Russian naval blue as his men poured aboard. It was all he could do next to parry the sword of a British officer, then strike back himself. In that suspension of time when the mind can think as clearly as if was a detached observer while animal-like the body reacts, he realized it was the English captain.

Now *Rydna* was coming up into the fight to find the gunboats had interposed themselves. *Kalevala* was only few miles behind. Miles to the east, the Russian clippers unaware of the battle raced toward a group of sails coming their way, eager for more prizes. It would not be long before they discovered that they were twenty-three merchant ships in convoy with a Royal Navy escort.[16] Rear Adm. Sir E.T. Long aboard HMS *Hastings*, a fifty-gun ship-of-the-line, ordered his ships forward to engage. Long was that sort of fighting admiral who the Royal Navy seemed to sow like dragon's teeth. He had run down and hanged slavers off West Africa, taken his squadron of gunboats in the Crimea almost onto the shore to bombard Russian forts, and in China had led his gunboat flotilla up a river into the teeth of the Chinese defenses and been severely wounded. Now he led a strong squadron from the Royal Navy's Australian Station, escorting five infantry regiments from New Zealand and Australia. The Russian clippers turned and fled west to warn Popov.

Before long all they had to do was follow the pall of gunpowder smoke that hung over the battle. *Kalevala* was now in that same unequal fight with *Charybdis* and *Alert*. *Rydna* had sunk little *Forward* and was turning *Grappler* into firewood, when Turnour's lookout reported the appearance of the Russian clippers. He signaled *Alert* to turn about and engage. Minutes later the lookout reported a forest of sails coming behind the clippers. When the chase was done, and Long rowed over to *Charybdis* to congratulate Turnour on his splendid action, he found him kneeling amid a corpse strewn quarterdeck over a dying Russian officer. Long stood in silence as the man clutched at his sword to offer it to Turnour, blood frothing at his lips from the wound in his lung. "No, Captain, I could not accept the sword of such a gallant man."

When news eventually reached Britain of the victory of the battle of San Juan de Fuca, Britain went wild. The bells pealed from Inverness to Dover. The newspapers, which had had little good to report for a long time, christened Turnour a new Nelson and made much of the last dramatic moment on *Charybdis*'s quarterdeck as an exemplar of British chivalry. For his intrepidity Captain Turnour would return home a national hero be knighted by the queen. In his heart of hearts, though, he valued the comparison to Nelson far more than the knighthood.

9

General Grant's Army of Invasion

NUMBER 10, DOWNING STREET, SUNDAY, 4:40 P.M., APRIL 3, 1864

Disraeli's Sunday afternoon had already been turned into chaos before Derby's telegram was rushed into him. Meagher's seizure of Dublin had not prevented a number of loyal men from fleeing the city to race up and down the coast to find any craft able to put to sea. These had made for Liverpool, and their alarm had cleared all traffic from the telegraph lines. One telegram after another was sped up to the Prime Minister's residence. The authorities in Liverpool had not direct knowledge or confirmation, but the Royal Navy's ships in port were preparing to take the morning tide.

On the face of it, the stories were fantastic; the American army and Russian navy had taken Dublin by coup de main. Disraeli could believe that one rumor could be magnified, but not a half-dozen accounts from men closely questioned by the authorities in Liverpool. Derby's telegram was the thunderbolt that made it all too real. He summoned the Russian ambassador and the cabinet. He knew that most of them were at their country homes on the weekend or guests elsewhere in the country. Even their deputies would be difficult to find. He must act on his own. His secretaries now took his dictation in relays as telegram after telegram went to fleet and army to stir every naval base, ship, regiment, the yeomanry and RVC in the Kingdom into a frenzy of activity. The civil authorities throughout the island were also notified to place in effect the measures necessary to ease military movements, increase security, and prepare the local population for invasion. The railways were ordered to be at the disposal of the government for the transportation of troops. All these measures had been put in place during the war scare with France of the late 1850s that had also created the RVCs. If there was a flaw in this planning, it was that measures had been directed primarily to counter a cross-channel invasion from France and not one aimed at Ireland.

Nor from Essex. No word of Dahlgren's raid had leaked out. Cutting the telegraph wires prevented any immediate warning even if people along the line were aware of the train full of Americans heading west, which they were not. By the time Disraeli was alerting the British military establishment of the danger in Ireland, Dahlgren had already seized Romford. Leaving half his men there to hold the station, cut the telegraph lines, and destroy the tracks up and down the main line from Colchester to London, he took the remaining two hundred into the late afternoon for ten-mile dash to Waltham Abby.

Dash may not have been the right word as the afternoon light dimmed. A horse could do four miles at a walk in an hour and six miles in a trot, and twelve miles in a gallop. They could have galloped the whole way in less than an hour, but then their horses would have nothing left for the return ride. The usual method was to alternate a walk and trot and make six miles an hour.[1] Dahlgren pushed them at less walk and more trot to get to the Abbey in an hour and a half. They skirted Hainault Forrest to the south of its high ground, turned north to pick up the main road through the Roding River valley, crossed the river and passed up into Epping Forrest. Just beyond was Waltham Abby and its powder mills and beyond that less than a mile was Enfield Lock and its factory. Luckily, the area was thinly inhabited and wooded. That's where Dahlgren's famous luck started to go thin. His guides rode up ahead and disappeared into the woods to divest themselves of their American uniforms. It took Dahlgren precious minutes to realize that they were not coming back. Now the early late-afternoon rays began to lengthen over the halted column.

At Romford, things quickly began to get out of hand. The two hundred men that Dahlgren had left behind to secure the railway station and conduct mayhem up and down the tracks could not at the same time keep the town from leaking like a sieve. Riders carrying the news went in every direction, to wherever there was a local RVC, two miles south to Hornchurch and seven miles northeast to Brentwood, and to raise the alarm in every village and town. It took one rider only two miles on the way to London to find a functioning telegraph office at Brookham.

WALTHAM ABBEY, ESSEX, 5:45 P.M., SUNDAY, APRIL 3, 1864

Now it would be a race. Had Dahlgren known how the country was being raised behind him, he could not have acted with any more ruthless determination. Men were pulled at gunpoint out of the few cottages they passed and pressed into service as guides as the column galloped the last mile. Barely a half hour behind schedule, they rode through the little town with its ancient abbey. Troopers dismounted to break in doors to drag men from their dinner tables to the screams of their wives and children to press them as guides to the powder mills a short distance away. Patrols were set on the road leading out of town.

It was not every Sunday night that two hundred cavalry rode through the streets of Waltham Abbey. If that had not been enough to bring the town into the streets from their Sunday dinner, the smashing in of doors certainly did. People had milled in the streets demanding to know who these strangers were. The troopers were only too happy to tell them that they were part of General Grant's army of invasion that had already reached London and would soon have the town in flames and the queen their prisoner. It was worth the look of shock on their faces.

One man kept his presence of mind in the confusion and sought their commander. He knew a thing or two about soldiering and dismissed the troopers' stories of an invasion as so much cock and bull. But the troopers were real soldiers, easy in their saddles and in that way a man carries his equipment. They just were not British soldiers, and though they spoke English, it was American-accented English. It crossed his mind that they might be Canadians, but no soldiers in this island had dared treat civilians this way since Cromwell, and these were clearly living up to that standard.

All he had to do was look for the color bearer to find the commander. There it was, down the street, the lamplight from a window picking out its unmistakable white stars and red and white stripes. Yes, Americans. Next to him was a mounted sailor, also a color bearer. This flag he recognized instantly from its black double-headed eagle on an orange and black field. And Russians! He had seen those colors on too many Crimean battlefields. The implications were enough to stupefy an ordinary man, but Hope Grant had called him a "quick-witted fellow" who could take a situation in with a glance. Grant did not mention a man lightly in dispatches. Now he walked with a limp to those colors. As two of the townsmen were brought to the young blond officer evidently in command, the man focused on him. The officer leaned over slightly from his saddle to the clutch of prisoners. "Do you know the way to the powder mills and to the factory at Enfield Lock?" Both heads bobbed in frightened assent.

The man was shocked when two soldiers marched another man up to the young officer. "Found him at the inn just like you said we would, sir."

"Ah, Mr. Abel," the officer said, "Allow me to introduce myself — Colonel Dahlgren, United States Army. You, sir, are my prisoner. These two soldiers will be your escort."

Abel's face turned red. He was a scholarly-looking man, clean-shaven but with fine sideburns. "I must protest, sir! I am a subject of Her Majesty, and . . ." His protest was cut short as the soldiers hustled him away.

The man had heard enough. He had come to know Abel in his frequent visits to conduct research on propellants at the powder mills. Waltham Abby was a small place. He slipped away as the cavalry with its terrified guides trotted away to the powder mills. His servants had been waiting with great anxiety in the hallway for his return. He saw his groom and said, "Edward, saddle my horse immediately. And the bay for yourself."

He went to the study and took his Colt revolver from his desk drawer. The irony of using an American-made pistol on Americans was not lost on him. If it could do in a Russian, Hindu, or Musulman, an American was also game. He spun the chamber to check that it was fully loaded and stuck it in his waistband. He went out the back door to find his horse ready. "Here she is, Sir Robert," the groom said as he pressed a knuckle to his forehead. The groom offered his intertwined fingers to help where the Russian bullet had stolen the spring from his leg. He then leapt onto the bay. Wilson took him by the arm. "Ride to the Colonel at Naseing and tell him to call out the Yeomanry. Tell him that American cavalry has been here and gone to the powder mills and then will go to the factory at Enfield. He must intercept them there. Do you understand?"

The groom nodded quickly. He had been Wilson's orderly in India. No one would ride faster than this old soldier of the Queen.

It had taken barely minutes for the Americans to reach the entrance to the Royal Powder Mills. The watchmen at the gate offered no resistance. There were lights only in the main office building, another safety precaution. Leaving unattended oil lamps on buildings containing immense amounts of gunpowder was not a good idea. At least Dahlgren did not have to worry about hustling the workforce to safety. He said to his ordnance officer, "Get to work, and join us at Enfield. I expect your success to announce itself even before you report in person." The man grinned and disappeared with his team following the railway tracks that wound through the grounds from one well-spaced building to another, their chemical lanterns bobbing in the dark.

Sir Robert Wilson, VC, late captain of the 9th Lancers, took the first road out of town in the direction of Enfield. Just as he cleared the last house, he was challenged by two horsemen who loomed out of the trees. He pulled his pistol and drove his spurs into the horse's flank. The animal leapt forward straight for the Americans. Sir Robert fired first and emptied a saddle and then crashed his horse into the other trooper sending them careening into a ditch. He kept going, taking a hedge in one clean jump, shots from the other American's Spencer flying around him as he sped through the dusk.

Dahlgren had just finished giving his instructions to his ordnance officer when he heard the shots. He rode over to the guide and put his pistol in his face. "If we are not at Enfield Lock in fifteen minutes, you are a dead man."

Wilson had more than a small advantage of time; he knew the shortcuts through field and wood, especially fords through the shallows of the Lea River that ran parallel to the community of Enfield and the factory. His horse clawed its way up the bank trailing water and right onto the road to the RSAF worker's village. Wilson put spurs to the animal and galloped down the long street of Enfield Lock paralleling the river shouting, "The Americans are coming! The Americans are coming!" Doors opened and men stumbled into the street to see what was causing all the noise. Wilson rode back down the street, "Men of the 41st, to arms, to arms!" He stopped in front of a public house as a crowd gathered, and there he explained the danger to the factory and gave his orders. He was the soldier again in the crucible of crisis. The men of Enfield Lock knew him, though their own colonel was nowhere to be found, and his orders were obeyed. They rushed home to hurriedly put on their uniforms and snatch their Enfields as others ran through the community passing the order. In three minutes he had a squad, in five a platoon, and in ten two companies. That was enough. Men were still buttoning coats and uniform details. "Hang the buttons!" he shouted. "Fix bayonets!" There was rasp as the bayonets were drawn, then a wave of clicks as they were fixed over their rifle muzzles. He waved his pistol at the Royal Small Arms Factory, and bellowed, "Forward, march!"

That moment found Wilson's groom pounding on the door of Naseing. As soon as it opened he rushed through the scandalized butler and shouted, "Colonel Palmer, Colonel Palmer, call out the Yeomanry!" Palmer emerged from his study, recognized the groom, and got the story out of him. It was simply unbelievable, Americans in Essex and the powder mills and factory in danger. Yet, Wilson was a serious man who had earned the Victoria Cross. He was no fool. The Yeomanry was Palmer's pride and joy for thirty years, organized to protect those very threatened places. In ten minutes the men on his estate were galloping through the neighborhood to rouse the rest of the Yeomanry. He retained the presence of mind to send one man was off to the nearest telegraph station.

NUMBER 10, DOWNING STREET, SUNDAY, 6:40 P.M., APRIL 3, 1864
Disraeli could hear the huge crowd collecting outside the prime minister's residence demanding news. The content of the telegrams from Liverpool had leaked out and spread faster than cholera. More insistent than the crowd was the press, and Disraeli had personally given a brief but official interview to a committee of reporters. He was determined to inform the public fully. Extra editions were printing at this very moment throughout

London and humming over the wires to every newspaper in the island.

Now though he had a more immediate problem. The shadow of his cabinet sat in council; almost every head of ministry was missing, as were most of their deputies, and the government would have to report to Parliament before the day was out. Disraeli did see one comforting face, the Duke of Cambridge, one that he never thought he would. The commander-in-chief of the British Army may have been obstinate in the face of doctrinal and organizational innovation, but he knew the establishment of the British Army better than any man alive. Right now he was spreading out a map of the stations of the army in Great Britain.

"The most proximate reinforcements that can be sent to Ireland from western England and Scotland are those from Glasgow and Manchester. Unfortunately, those closest to ports on the Irish Sea consist of only one regiment of foot, one of cavalry.[2] After them, the next closest are three cavalry regiments and one regiment of foot in Birmingham, Sheffield, and York in central and eastern England. I have given orders that they entrain at once for Liverpool.[3] But it is infantry that we will need to recapture Dublin, and our infantry is concentrated at Aldershot, London, and the Channel ports, many of those regiments preparing to depart for North America."

As he was speaking a secretary entered and placed a telegram in Disraeli's hand. He waved Cambridge silent. "From Brookham in Essex," he said. "American cavalry has seized Romford. Claim to be the advance of an army of invasion under General Grant. Arrived on the London, Tilbury, Southend Line. Several hundred departed north toward Hainault Forrest."

Cambridge snorted in contempt. "Damned rumors. The news from Ireland conjures Americans under every bed."

The secretary came back with another telegram. Disraeli scanned it and said, "The telegraph office reports that all lines north of Brookham have gone dead."

In the stunned silence a rattling tremor began to creep through the building, trembling the table and the glass ceiling lamps. Pictures bounced on the walls. Disraeli watched an inkwell dance over the side of the table. Everyone was transfixed, until screams rose from the crowd outside. Then the sound of a deep roar shattered window panes as the cries of the crowd turned to a primal moan. Disraeli rushed to north window and looked out at what the crowd had seen. There far to the north, a black cloud rent with streaks of red was billowing skyward until its head gushed out to the sides, framed by the pale late-afternoon light.[4]

1. London
2. Aldershot
3. Birmingham
4. Brighton
5. Chatham
6. Colchester
7. Devonport
8. Dover
9. Edinburgh
10. Glasgow
11. Gosport
12. Jersey (not shown)
13. Kensington
14. Maidstone
15. Manchester
16. Norwich
17. Parkhurst (Isle of Wight)
18. Pembroke
19. Plymouth
20. Portsmouth
21. Preston
22. Sheffield
23. Southton (Southampton)
24. Schorncliffe
25. Sterling
26. Walmer
27. Winchester
28. Woolwich
29. York

GARRISONS OF THE
BRITISH ARMY
IN GREAT BRITAIN
1864

Karamales 2013

ROYAL SMALL ARMS FACTORY ENFIELD, 6:45 P.M., SUNDAY, APRIL 3, 1864

Dahlgren's ordnance team had successfully blown the individual buildings at the powder mills, which had caused the inkwell to dance off the cabinet room table. What they had not counted on was a sympathetic explosion of a thousand tons of gunpowder loaded on a string of barges on the Lee River adjacent to the mills. It was that explosion that had broken the windows of London twelve miles to the south, raised the hellish specter of that cloud, wiped out the ordnance team and their fifty man escort, and wrecked Waltham Abbey.

Wilson had just led the 41st over the Lea River bridge into the factory yard as Dahlgren, and his troopers rode in from the other direction. Neither man had time to order his men into action before the individual powder mills buildings began to explode one by one, each sending a shock wave through Enfield Lock. The conflict of men stood in silent awe of this terrible force of nature. The following explosion of the powder barges sent a shock wave that threw men and horses to the ground, blew out the factory's sawtooth windows and tore great gaps in the roof. In moments chucks of debris in every size and shape began to rain down, much of it smashing through the factory roof and striking men already prostrated in the yard by the shock wave. Abel's papers from his laboratory fluttered to the ground like a huge flock of seagulls.

As the explosion waned to a rumble, the yard was a seeming battlefield strewn with lifeless corpses, but in minutes the corpses began to stir as men sat up and struggled to their feet. Some just sat heads in their hands moaning. The Americans were worse off for having been thrown from their horses by the blast. Rimsky-Korsakov shook the ringing from his ears and looked around. He saw the imperial standard on the ground, Sailor Sergei's hand still clutching the staff, his head smashed from a chuck of debris. Kolya staggered over to pick it up. He heard a familiar voice. "There, boy, there; poor boy, poor boy." It was Dahlgren pinned under his stunned horse flailing its legs as it tried to get up. The Russian took the bridle and helped the animal up, pulling Dahlgren with it as he clung to the pommel of his saddle. Luckily the horse had fallen on his cork leg. Blood ran from his nose and ears, and he slumped in the saddle.

At the same time, Wilson was being helped up by a few of the volunteers. He took a deep breath, pulled himself together, and walked among the men urging them to find their weapons and get into line. He could see a fire gushing out of the broken sawtooth windows of the factory where flaming debris had ignited combustible material in the vast workshop hall. Dahlgren was getting his own command back into order, though most of the men were now on foot, many of the horses had fled or were in no shape to mount. They had been broken to the saddle at their horse farms but not trained to the discipline of a cavalry horse nor developed the affection for a particular rider that would keep them there despite the terror. Frederick Abel may have been used to a life of research, but his wits were quick enough to grab the reins of a loose horse. He slipped away in the gloom to take with him Lincoln's last hope to find a way out of the niter shortage.

With so much mayhem inflicted on man and beast, not a shot had been fired. The English and the Americans at first were too caught up in their own misery that all thought of combat had evaporated. But that was not to last for long as Dahlgren and Wilson got their men into some order. The afternoon was now fading into twilight as the last glow of the sun was giving way to the faint purple blue of the horizon. Wilson's men began to murmur about the fire in the factory stirring with unease as the flames poured from window after window in the roof.

Wilson acted first. Grabbing the color bearer of the 41st, he walked across the yard toward the Americans. Dahlgren trotted out to meet him carrying his own color. Kolya darted after him with the imperial standard. They came to a halt six feet apart.

They exchanged salutes. Wilson said, "Captain Wilson, 9th Lancers, commanding the 41st Middlesex Rifle Volunteer Corps."

"Colonel Dahlgren, United States Army." He wasted no time on formalities. He knew his plan was in shreds and could only possibly be mended by bold effrontery. "I demand the surrender of your command, sir. My regiment is on the vanguard of the army of invasion. We will be in London in two days. Your position is hopeless."

"The hell you say!" The adamantine self-confidence of the island race reared up in Wilson's entire being. "Army of invasion! When pigs fly. You can be nothing more than a raid, sir. The game is up. You have failed. It is you who will surrender."

Dahlgren took a quick glance at the burning factory and the huge black pall from the powder mill and thought to himself that he had not entirely failed. Yet he could not deny he was in a fix, and this man Wilson was no green volunteer. He knew his business. He could only spin this out in hope that some advantage would turn up or he would, indeed, have no choice but to surrender. Seated on his horse he could see men by the score joining the rifle green ranks of the volunteers. They already outnumbered his men by more than three to one.

DUBLIN CASTLE, 6:42, SUNDAY, APRIL 3, 1864

Meagher allowed himself a few minutes to take a deep breath by himself in the private apartment of the Lord Lieutenant of Ireland, the former

Lord Lieutenant, he told himself. It all seemed a dream; in less than twelve hours he seized the capital of his country, destroyed eight hundred years of British rule, and declared the Irish Republic to the delirious joy of his men and the Fenian crowds that swarmed into the castle yard. The telegraph has sent the joyous news of liberation to every corner of the island. "Rise," the wires sang, "Rise for Ireland, rise for freedom!"

After that deep breath, he took an equally deep drink of the Lord Lieutenant's fine Irish whiskey. A glorious warmth spread through him, beckoning for another such rush. He took the bottle when the door opened to admit Sergeant Major Wright. A look of consternation fell on his face but hardened to resolve as he walked over and simply took the bottle from the general's hand. Meagher let him. "Ah, Sergeant Major, you are my guardian angel." He had given Wright a veto on his habit that he allowed to no other man since that night early in the last year before Fredericksburg when Wright had saved him from falling drunk into bonfire in the camp in the dark of night.

"It is time, sir. The council and Mr. Adams are waiting."

"And so it is, Sergeant Major." He clapped him on the shoulder. "A long time since Fredericksburg." He meant more than being saved from the fire. Fredericksburg had been the last time he had led the Irish Brigade into battle, more a slaughter pen than an honest man-to-man fight. He had resigned rather than lead his men into that again and in protest to Secretary of War Stanton's refusal to let him recruit back to strength again. Six month of regret had followed until the war with Britain when in one day he recruited fifteen thousand New York Irish and earned Mr. Lincoln's gratitude and the stars of a major general. His reputation had flown to the heavens with his victories at Cold Spring and Clavarack. In this one, glorious day he had added the liberator of Ireland to his deeds.

The guards to Presentation Hall presented arms as Wright flung open the polished double doors for Meagher's grand entrance. The dozen men of the Provisional Council of the Republic of Ireland and Charles Adams came to their feet around a table of rosewood so polished that the light of the candles danced in ruddy reflection. The twelve were the secret leadership of the Fenians who had been taken as much by surprise by Meagher's coup de main as the Lord Lieutenant. Meagher had been at pains at their hurried meeting as he cemented control of Dublin to explain that it had been necessity that had kept them in the dark. No word of this enterprise of Ireland could be allowed to leak out. Any umbrage was cowed by the realization that all their dreams and conspiracies had come to life. Now it was not just daring talk, but action, commitment, life or death, and the awful clarity that they were in it to the knife. Bold talk was one thing, a daring military coup still another, but the burden of organizing a government and rallying a people to it was entirely of a new order. Revolutionaries by their very nature were long on eloquence and short on the necessary executive experience. The men in this room were no exception. Carried away by the elation of the moment Meagher perhaps as well as his cabinet did not fully understand the nature of the task ahead.

This moment, though, was symbolic, ceremonial, and political. Meagher stood before the sword-draped throne as both the head of state and head of government of the Irish Republic. The foreign minister designate introduced Mr. Charles Adams as the representative of the President of the United States. Adams bowed to Meagher, who had already been a party to these arrangements, but the formalities of diplomacy required this show. "Your Excellency, on behalf of President Lincoln, the United States of America extends its recognition of the sovereign authority of the Irish Republic and its government. Mr. Lincoln also charged me with conveying his great personal satisfaction that the United States is the first nation to extend recognition to the Irish Republic. I am also charged with proposing a treaty of alliance between the United States and the Irish Republic, for which I have full authority to negotiate." Neither Meagher nor he had mentioned that the treaty had already been written in Washington.

ROMFORD, ESSEX, 6:43 P.M., SUNDAY, APRIL 1864

The railway station burned around the Americans. Dead men in blue and rifle green were strewn about the platform and the high street leading up to it. The only thing that had kept them from being overrun were the two Gatling guns that done much slaughter among the men of Hornchurch. The alarm brought to the 15th Essex RVC while at drill put them immediately on the road the two miles north to Romford. On the outskirts of the town they had been fired on by American pickets, and the first of them had died. They met death, not the death of the old or sick in bed, but red-handed death in all its primal violence. Every man underwent that shock as they marched past the dead on the road.

Their colonel had the wit to send out a company as skirmishers down the high road as he questioned local men eager to tell them that the Americans were at the station. The sudden outbreak of rifle fire told him that his skirmishers had made contact, and he rushed the RVC forward down the high street to meet the survivors of his skirmishers falling back, some dragging wounded men with them. He put his companies column, each company deploying across the street, and ordered the advance—straight in the fire of two Gatlings. The forward company simply melted away in the bullet streams and the added fire of Spencer repeaters, the colonel at their head. The rest just panicked at the leaden hell tearing into them, turned, and fled back up the high street pursued by the Gatlings until they spilled into side streets, doorways, and safety.

Death had sorted them in those minutes in the profoundest sense. The cool men, those who could keep a clear head in the midst of man-killing chaos, rose to the moment. An officer here, a sergeant or corporal there, and often just a private man who was willing to lead. The others instinctively followed for there is a magnetism of courage that attracts the ordinary man as a magnet draws iron filings. Now they benefitted from their amateurishness. The rigidity of the regular army had not sunk to their bones. There would be no more charges up the high street. Instead, guided by local men they went by side streets to surround the railway station, found their way into upper floors of surrounding buildings and on rooftops and began to fire. The first to fall, the object of their special wrath, were the Gatling crews.

The same wave of warnings that had brought the Hornchurch men to Romford had also reached seven and a half miles up the railway line to Brentwood. In a half hour the 3rd Essex RVC was assembled and marched south. It would not be until nine that night that they filed into Romford guided by the orange-red glow from the burning station. Warned off from a direct assault on the station, their companies added to the ring of fire hemming in the Americans. Night assaults by platoons darted onto the station platform or broke into the outer buildings and warehouses held by the Americans. Then it was as much a contest of rifle butts and bayonets as of bullets. Slowly the ring tightened.

Inexperienced as they were, they were Englishmen, filled with that granite-like resolve of their warrior race that had broken the ambitions of every tyrant thrown up by the continent. In them was the same defiance of the invader of the Saxon shield wall at Hastings as their ancestors had shouted, "Out! Out!" to the Norman host as it crashed into them again and again. They did not know if there were thousands more of the enemy marching across their fair Essex. The enemy here was all they cared about.

That enemy tasted desperation. Half were dead and wounded and ammunition all but gone. Their surviving officer knew that Dahlgren's route of escape the way he had come was now slammed shut. Dahlgren was on his own. The officer now had only a responsibility to his surviving men. He pulled out his blood-stained handkerchief, stuck it on the point of his saber, and went to the bullet-splintered door.

Twenty-five miles away at Maldon, Lieutenant Colonel Adams had ridden into his own hornet's nest. It had been a quick ride to this seaport from Southend. They arrived ahead of the news of their coming, not stopping to do any damage along the way. The docks and railway station at Maldon was the objective, and as everywhere else they found the town in sleepy Sunday repose. Adams set his men to work, and the good people of Maldon found themselves shocked wide awake. The docks and warehouses were fired first, then the ships, until flames licked the harbor, sending dirty clouds of black smoke into the spring sky. The railway station and the locomotives and cars were next.

Adams was standing on the platform, arms on his hips, surveying the destruction with great satisfaction. His orderly next to him flew backward onto the platform just as Adams heard the crack of a rifle. Another bullet splintered the platform at his feet. He dived off the platform into the gravel around the tracks. The sound of Spencers now joined the distinctive crack of the Enfields. His men were returning fire. That's just what he did not need—a knock-down, drag-out fight. Suddenly a body fell off the platform right on top of him; the corpse wore green. More footsteps and English voices rushed over the platform. Now faces looked over the platform directly at him. A man in green jumped down and raised his bayonet. Adams struggled for his pistol, but his right arm was pinned under the dead man. Another voice, "Stop, man. Take him prisoner." The bayonet lowered. Then more shots and the man on the platform was hit, falling forward with a groan onto the man standing over Adams. He got up and fled down the tracks.

The 23rd Essex RVC had not been drilling this Sunday, but when Adams men flaunting the Stars and Stripes had ridden through the streets shouting of the invasion army behind them while setting fire to the town's livelihood, the men of Maldon had not waited for orders. Hand after hand threw on green coats, slung on ammunition pouches, snatched up Enfields, and flew into the streets looking for trouble. They did not know it, but ghosts were also rushing to arms, but not with rifles. These wraiths wore byrnies of scale mail, and carried swords, axes, and spears. At their head was the Earl of Essex, dead these thousand years. It was here that the men of Essex had flung themselves at Viking invaders, going down in a defeat so glorious that there was not a British boy who had not read the epic poem of their deeds and resolved to live up to their heroism. Of such memories empires are built.

And defended. Four hundred Maldon volunteers were driving fewer than a hundred thoroughly unhappy Americans through the streets when the railcars in the yard filled with coal oil began to burn with an explosive intensity. Flaming jets of oil arced into the town setting more fires. Adams was lucky that the explosion was absorbed by the dead bodies over him, but he was horrified to see the burning oil flowing through the gravel toward him. He started screaming for help. Again two faces peered over the platform, but these wore dark-blue American army caps. They leapt down, heaved off the corpse, and pulled Adams to his feet. They pulled him along, shielded by the platform and the thickening black smoke. They reached an alley where some of their horses had been left with a horse-holder for each of the four horses. Other men were running into the alley, turning to fire at their pursuers. One man crumpled in the street. Three turned, went to one knee, and sent a stream of fire from their repeaters. Another fell forward to sprawl on the cobbles.

By this time Adams was mounted, as were barely a dozen others. He pulled his pistol, drove the spurs into his horse, and charged into the street with his men shouting behind him. A man brought up the rear holding the reins of two horses for the men guarding the alley entrance. The RVC skirmishing line stopped, surprised at the sudden charge, just long enough for the Americans to ride pistoling their way through; no one had time to draw saber. The second skirmish line was not so easy. Three saddles were emptied before they reached it. Adams shot his first man in front of him, then another who raised his rifle at him. A third drove his bayonet up through his hand. The pistol flew away as the Englishman wrenched Adams from his saddle like a hooked fish. This time a trooper had drawn his saber, his pistol empty, and charged through killing the Englishman with a downward stroke between neck and shoulder. He reached down his hand for Adams, who had barely regained his feet and kicked his foot out of his facing stirrup. With his unharmed hand Adams grasped the trooper's hand, put his foot in the stirrup, and heaved himself up behind the saddle. The horse leaped forward under the trooper's spurs and carried them through a side street that quickly became a country lane. Adams looked back; there were only three men following them. Behind them Maldon burned.[5]

ROYAL SMALL ARMS FACTORY ENFIELD, 6:55 P.M., SUNDAY, APRIL 3, 1864
Wilson played for time. Every minute he spun out the parlay more men of the 41st streamed over the Lea River Bridge to join his band. He also sensed that this young American colonel was playing a bad hand. His men looked too nervous to be the spearhead of anyone's invasion. Unlike Mr. Mawcaber, something then really turned up for him.

Palmer's Essex Yeomanry had had the good fortune to be in a dip in the road bordered by dense trees when the shock wave from exploding powder mills barges swept over them. Palmer had pushed them on to Enfield and arrived by the same road that Dahlgren had used. He could see the flames licking through the factory roof and the clusters of men in the yard. He drew his saber in one clean sweep and heard more rasp from their scabbards behind him. He ordered the charge. Dahlgren's men barely heard the pounding of hooves before the Yeomanry crashed into them. He had only been able to gather fifty men before he took the road, but fifty men charging into dismounted men from the rear was a thing of terror. Dahlgren turned to see the Yeomanry hacking their way through his mostly dismounted men. They scattered trying to get away from the plunging horsemen. Dahlgren glared at Wilson for violating the truce of the parlay. "Damn you!" he spat and drew his saber. Wilson threw himself backward in the saddle lying almost flat on the horse's rump as the saber sliced through the air where his head would have been. He righted himself and fired wildly, hitting Dahlgren in the leg. The man did not even wince to Wilson's surprise. The tide of men and horses swept into them, and Dahlgren found himself racing along trading blows with a Yeomanry trooper. They rode right into the 41st as it charged across the yard. He parried the man's blade, knocked the next blow aside, and drove the point into his throat, wrenching it free as the man slid to the ground. By then the tide had rushed past him to join the slaughter of his command. Only the Gatling crew had kept together, and it evened the butcher's bill as the barrels sent a regiment's firepower into the Enfield Lock men. But only for moments. The Yeomanry fell upon the crew hacking and stabbing, but the gunners died hard emptying saddles with their pistols until the last of them went down.[6]

Dahlgren was about to ride back into the chaos to share the fate of his men when he felt a hand on his shoulder. He whipped around in the saddle to strike, but it was Kolya who had found a horse. "You can do no more, Ulrich. They must not capture us. We must fly." Kolya tore the imperial banner from the staff and wrapped it around him. He led the way down a dark road. Dahlgren followed in a mood as black as the charger he rode, the bile rising to his lips.

ROYAL HORSEGUARDS BARRACKS, LONDON, 8:22 P.M., SUNDAY, APRIL 3, 1864

The telegrams had been tumbling in screaming of a massive invasion force rampaging throughout Essex. Romford in flames, Maldon in flames, Burnham on Crouch in flames, Chelmsford in flames, even Colchester attacked. Royal Powder Mills and Royal Small Arms Factory destroyed. American cavalry raiding and destroying everywhere. Large columns of infantry marching inland toward London and Colchester. For Cambridge, the awful realization that the Americans could be in London before reinforcements from the southern garrisons had shaken him. Disraeli had cancelled his address to Parliament at Cambridge's frantic urging. The emergency was too great to consult Parliament at this time.

They had agreed that the queen must be rushed to safety. Buckingham Palace was ringed with the Grenadier Guards, bayonets fixed. Outside the palace, 1st and 2nd Life Guards waited on horseback, sabers drawn. Inside the palace the queen's carriages were being packed for her escape to her Channel estate. Panic had rippled through London, and the roads to Surrey and Kent were filling with carriages. The railways had been taken over by the government, and there was no escape by them. Instead they were devoted to bringing troops from Aldershot in Hampshire and Shorncliffe in Kent, five more regiments of foot. All RVCs within marching distance from the surrounding counties were ordered to march to London. The rest of the garrison of London and the city's RVCs were marching toward Stratford northeast of the edge of the city—Royal Horseguards, 12th Lancers , 1st and 2nd Coldstream Guards, and 1/60th Foot from the Tower—in all only a regular brigade of infantry and one of cavalry and few thousand of the RVCs, a paltry force to stop whole divisions, a dagger poised at the heart of the British Empire. More RVC men were put to work digging entrenchments under supervision of the Royal Engineers. Six companies of Royal Engineers were on their way from their camp at Chatham along with companies from the three depot battalions located there as well. All thought of reinforcing Ireland had evaporated.

Trying to sort out the mass of wild information flowing over the telegraph was Lt. Col. Charles Freemantle. Cambridge had plucked him out of his staff duties to do just this because no man in the British Army in London had a greater grasp of the Americans at war than Freemantle. In 1863 he had taken three months "shooting leave" to tour the Confederacy where he had been treated with great deference as a Coldstream Guards officer who might be able to influence his government to come to the South's aid. Shooting leave was the euphemism for an intelligence-gathering mission under the guise of a normal leave of absence.[7] He had arrived on the field of Gettysburg in time for the worst of the fighting and had been an eyewitness to Pickett's charge. Freemantle had told Cambridge right out that he did not believe the Americans could launch a major invasion without some intelligence of it leaking out; however, if by chance they had achieved this miracle, the British would have the fight of their lives on their hands. That had not done the duke's confidence any good, for he keyed on the later evaluation.

Freemantle was that rarity in the British Army, not only a skilled line officer but what passed then for a military intellectual. It was the power of objective analysis that he brought to his task. First he separated the reports by those of actual eyewitnesses and those that were unsubstantiated information. A vital pattern revealed itself in that a number of telegrams, including the most current, came from the telegrapher at Brookham. That told him that the Americans had not got that far yet. A non-telegraphic report was the explosion that had cracked windows in London. The direction of that evil cloud and the size of the explosion itself meant that it only could have come from the Royal Powder Mills at Waltham Abbey, which then led to the logical conclusion that a force of Americans of undetermined size had got as far as the western border of Essex. The close proximity of the Royal Small Arms Factory Enfield led then to the next logical conclusion that it too could be a target directed against the war-making power of Britain as much as the powder mills had been.

That analysis was confirmed with his close questioning of a few men who had arrived in person from Romford to describe the seizure of the town by a railway-riding force that unloaded horses, part of which had ridden north. North was the direction of the powder mills and the factory. Their estimate of the size of the force conflicted from five hundred to a thousand. None of these men had any military experience to properly judge the size of the force and admitted that they had not seen the entire force. So Freemantle concluded that a good deal of exaggeration was involved. The force was certainly not a thousand and probably less than five hundred. Next he ascertained that the Americans had arrived on the London, Tilbury, Southend line on a northbound train. Following the line south led to its terminus at Southend-on-Sea. "Exactly," he thought to himself. Whatever force had landed had come from ships unloading on the great pier. There were no other ports on that line. He immediately went in person to the Admiralty to report his findings.

On his return, he found a telegram that had just arrived from Brookham from the commander of the 3rd Essex RVC. It contained a clear account of the fighting in the town, definitely confirming that they were fighting American cavalry, not infantry, and that the 15th Essex from Hornchurch had already been in action. He estimated the size of the American force at a few hundred and that they were surrounded in the rail yard. Freemantle allowed himself the satisfaction of analysis confirmed. But as usual, though, that piece of the puzzle just posed more questions.

What of the rest of the reports? How did he know which were true and which were not? And how did the pieces fit into the piece he already had? Thousands of lives and the fate of great London depended on the answers to these questions.

At that moment Disraeli was desperately trying to persuade the queen to depart for the safety of her Channel estate. He had rushed over to Buckingham Palace when she sent word that she had changed her mind and was not leaving London. Victoria sat on her settee as calmly as in any normal visit by the prime minister.

Disraeli was quite clear in his mind what the political value was of his close relationship with the queen. That did not exclude his genuine devotion to Victoria as his sovereign and admiration for her as an accomplished women. When he had come to power that relationship had been discussed in his cabinet. He had argued that the queen was both able and knowledgeable to a remarkable degree on what was going on in her Kingdom and had been trained by Prince Albert and some of the most accomplished men in politics over the last twenty-five years. To the snide comment that "she was, after all, only a women," Disraeli had retorted, "Yes, to all her other accomplishments she adds feeling and intuition."

Now that formidable woman was telling him she would not leave the capital. Disraeli said, "Mum, the government must insist on your safety, which cannot be guaranteed in London at this time."

"Mr. Disraeli, would Elizabeth had left London even had Parma set foot on this island with his entire army?"

"Your Majesty, under those circumstances, I have no doubt that the loyal gentlemen around her would have carried her to safety regardless of her command."

"We are not amused, Prime Minister."

"It is not my intention to amuse or offend, Mum," Disraeli added in order to find an argument that would budge her, "but to point out that your security in London requires at least three battalions of the Guards, trained men vitally needed for the defense of the city."

"We understand the city's rifle volunteer corps have been called up and those of the surrounding counties are on their way as we speak. Take our Guards. Prime Minister, there will be Englishmen enough to guard us." In end, Disraeli did not carry Victoria away, but he took the two battalions of the Life Guards cavalry. They made a splendid sight clattering away on their big horses, their nickeled breast and back armor and Greek revival helmets nodding with the trot. Her last battalion of the Grenadier Guards she kept, the oldest regiment of the British Army and the one with the closest association with the protection of the monarch. She would have mortified them had she entrusted amateurs entirely in their place.[8]

SOUTHEND-ON-SEA, 8:35 P.M., SUNDAY, APRIL 3, 1864

Lamson paced his quarterdeck. Dahlgren was late. He had missed the rendezvous time an hour ago. Adams was late too, but two hundred of his men had filed back into Southend over the last hour. Before the sun had gone down, he had seen the smoke rising from the Essex countryside off into the distance. Then he had ridden into town to confer with the Marine major commanding the occupation of the town. Men were still trickling in. He gave the major firm order to abandon the town at 9:00 P.M. no matter what. Dahlgren knew what being late meant. Every minute he waited, he expected to see the Royal Navy in force descending on him. The fact that he had not been blown out of the water by now he could thank Meagher for. Several powerful British ships had steamed out of the Thames right past the pier. They had been dispatched to the Irish Sea, as had most of the ships in the Navy's channel bases before any news of Essex.

Now the Royal Navy would suffer from the dilemma articulated by the Prussian Chief of the General Staff, Helmuth von Moltke, "Order, counterorder, disorder."[9] Most of those ships rushing at top speed to the Irish Sea would have to be recalled to defend Mother England itself. That would take time, first to find the ships fast enough to catch up with them, and then the time to reverse course and steam back the way they had come to converge on the Essex coast. It was through this window of disorder that Lamson would have to escape, though he did not know what was happening, he could surmise the reason. Meagher must have raised holy hell in Ireland. He could also surmise that as soon as Dahlgren's raid entered the British brain, the tide would change bringing the Royal Navy howling after him.

One ship had a head start on all the rest and was beyond recall. HMS *Prince Albert* had put to sea again after its refit and before the news of Ireland. It had entered the Irish Sea as night fell and by midnight was cruising off the coast of southern Wales when the watch identified a half-dozen fires at sea. Coles immediately ordered, "Beat to Quarters." Only dying ships could illuminate the sea that way.

As *Prince Albert* strained her engines to reach the burning ships, those of HIMS *Aleksandr Nevsky* were taking her away from them. After raiding the ships waiting for the afternoon tide off the Mersey mouth to Liverpool, he had dispersed his squadron to more easily pick off individual ships in the Irish Sea, retaining only a corvette. The squadron would rendezvous off the south coast of Ireland.[10]

EPPING FOREST, 2:02 A.M., MONDAY, APRIL 4, 1864

They were five now. After escaping the carnage at Enfield, Dahlgren and Kolya had disappeared into the dusk down a country road when they heard horses behind them at a gallop. They pulled up into the shadow of the trees as the Russian sailor Feodor, and an American soldier with a prisoner came barreling by. Feodor had survived Palmer's charge and seen his officer escape with the colors; his place was with him. He had leapt onto a Yeoman, pulled him off the horse with brute strength, mounted himself, and followed Dahlgren and Rimsky-Korsakov. He soon found an American riding with him, pistol in hand, driving a frightened civilian on another horse.

Dahlgren barked an order, and Kolya followed in Russian. The two pulled up. "Private Collins, sir! A Company, with a captive." The young man's cap was gone, and there was a long wound running down his temple to chin where a saber had wickedly nicked him. The blood dripped black in the gloom. A very frightened Frederick Abel trembled on his horse.

Dahlgren pulled out a handkerchief to put against the wound, as he said, "It's going to hurt like hell, Collins, but it is not serious. These scalp wounds are worse than they seem." He kept to himself the elation that at least two of the men had come through. That Private Collins's devotion to duty had brought the chemist Abel with him was going to be problematic now.

They walked their horses down forest trails till two in the morning when they found an empty woodsman's hut. After shuttering the windows, they dared light a fire. There Feodor boiled some water to wash Collin's wound. They ate what rations they had carried in their saddlebags. Luckily there was tea and a kettle. The hot brew never tasted so good to any of them. For the Russians who were a tea-drinking culture, it was a comfort of a happy feature of life; for Americans who were mostly coffee drinkers, it had the touch of the exotic, and for Abel it was a bit of the calm normality in sudden chaos, but any way for all of them it was hot and welcome.

Dahlgren pulled from his coat a map and carefully unfolded it on the table. He studied it for a few minutes. It was a familiar route his finger traced across Essex. "Kolya, we had enough time at sea for me to think through several branches of escape should things go bad." He gave Rimsky-Korsakov a wry look, "and I think our situations qualify." Collins hung over the map as well with that familiarity of American soldiers. Feodor, who did not understand a word that was being said, hung back. Charts and maps were for officers only, things of great secrecy, best left alone. As a precaution, Abel was in a back room tied to a chair behind a thick door.

"I don't intend to surrender, and I'm sure you do not want to either." Young as he was, Rimsky-Korsakov looked upon his representation of the honor of the empire as a holy thing for which he would give his life. To let the British capture the imperial banner, which he had now entrusted to Feodor as his color bearer, was unthinkable. Nevertheless, he did not see an alternative to a glorious death, which greatly distressed the imaginative artist in him.

Dahlgren went on. He pointed to a place on the map. "I think we are here, near this little place called Debben Hall near where we crossed the river to get into this forest. If we go about two miles south, we can cross the valley where it narrows and get into Hainault Forest. Then we can go west following this ridge line till we reach River Crouch. That's about twenty-five miles as the crow flies but longer the way we will have to go to seek cover and mostly at night. The river is marshy on both sides and leads into larger marshlands until it gets to the sea. Thank God Wilmoth's report was in such detail of Essex. There's a lot of smuggling that hides in the marshes. I hope to find a boat and slip out to sea and head for the continent."

Collins turned green at the last comment. He had been sick on the *Vanderbilt* almost the whole way. That ship was as big and steady as you could find at sea, but the prospect of a little boat in the seas he had seen was terrifying. Not Dahlgren, who had been a navy brat and learned to sail small boats almost since childhood. Not so Kolya, who was a trained sailor; his naval academy training had emphasized small boats in the Baltic, which could be as rough as the North Sea. Nor Feodor either, had he know what was being said, for he was fifteen years an able-bodied sailor in the Imperial Navy. When Rimsky-Korsakov told him, Feodor brightened up. The sea was home, and these damned horses had done nothing but make his ass sore.

1 0

"Old Soldiers of the Queen"

KENNEBUNK, MAINE, 1:45 P.M., MONDAY, APRIL 4, 1964
Troops had been detraining all day on the north side of the Kennebunk River into the ruins of the town where the British had defeated VI Corps' attempt to relieve Fortress Portland the previous October. The news of Portland's fall less than a week before had been met with intense disappointment by the men of the Army of the Hudson. They had been arriving in southern Maine for days as the railroad system of the Northeast had been devoted to their transfer from Upstate New York's Canadian border.

They had been relieved in place by the IX Corps, another detail from the Army of the Potomac. Maj. Gen. Ambrose Burnside had been finally relieved of its command; his honest and repeated protestations of his inability at high command had been proven prescient too many times to risk him in a command of such importance.

Maj. Gen. Dan Sickles had recovered enough from the loss of his leg at Gettysburg to be given this independent command, the only non-West Pointer to be so rewarded. Meade had said flatly that he would resign if Sickles were returned to command his old III Corps. He had clearly identified Sickles as the author of the scathing articles on his command at Gettysburg under the pen name of Historicus.[1] Nevertheless, Grant and Lincoln concluded that they could put up with the man's flamboyance for the fact that he was a natural leader and a hard fighter.

Disappointment quickly hardened into resolve to liberate Gallant Portland for the Army of the Hudson. With VI Corps added to its order-of-battle, Sherman now had over sixty thousand men.[2] He had arrived a few days before the rest of the Army to supervise the building of a base of operations at Kennebunk and had welcomed Maj. Gen. Horatio Wright back to the command of his corps after his exchange. He had also brought his own team of commanders from the West, such as Maj. Gen. John A. Logan to command XI Corps and Maj. Gen. James McPherson to command XII Corps. Both were gifted commanders who worked well with each other.[3]

Sherman was also pleased to receive another officer to his command, though he had never met him before—Maj. Gen. Joshua Chamberlain and his Maine Division. Chamberlain and his men had been exchanged after the surrender of Portland and were national heroes for their stout defense of the city. To that shrunken band, the other Maine regiments in the army were transferred so that it formed a small division of two brigades that Sherman assigned to XI Corps to round out Logan's command to three divisions. It was thought that no men would fight harder to drive the British men than sons of their own native state.

Sherman was enormously buoyed by the song the men were singing, "The Old Soldiers of the Queen," based on a song of the Revolution.

> Since you all must having singing and won't
>   be said "Nay,"
> I cannot refuse when you beg and you pray.
> I will sing you a song (as the poet might say),
> Of Queen Vicky's old soldiers who ne'er ran away.
>
> Chorus: We're the old soldiers of the queen,
>   And the queen's own regulars
> At Cavarack we met with Yankees one day,
> We got ourselves up in our finest array.
> Our heads bid us and, and our hearts bid us stay,
> But our legs were strong-minded and took us away.
>
> Chorus: We're the old soldiers of the queen,
>   And the queen's own regulars
>
> We marched into New York with fifes and with drums,
> With muskets and cannons, with swords and with bombs,
> This great expedition cost infinite sums.
> But some underpaid Doodles, they cut us to crumbs.
>
> Chorus: We're the old soldiers of the queen,
>   And the queen's own regulars
>
> They fought so unfairly from back of the trees,
> If they'd only fought open we'd have beat them with ease.

They can fight one another that way, if they please,
But we don't have to stand for such tactics as these!

Chorus: We're the old soldiers of the queen,
     And the queen's own regulars

'Tis true that we turned, but that shouldn't disgrace us,
We did it to prove that the foe couldn't face us.
And they've nothing to boast, it's a very plain case,
Though we lost in the fight, we came first in the race.

Chorus: We're the old soldiers of the queen,
     And the queen's own regulars[4]

THE PINEY WOODS JUST NORTH OF PONCHATOULA, LOUISIANA, 12:05 P.M., MONDAY, APRIL 4, 1864

Ben Grierson had personally scouted every mile of the enemy supply route from the train station at Ponchatoula to Baton Rouge. He had not only gained a careful appreciation for the care that Bazaine had taken to defend it but of the French cavalry patrolling it, especially those Chasseurs d'Afrique in their light-blue jackets and red trousers. The Mexicans had named them the Blue Butchers; they were deadly on patrol. Having been raised from French colonists in Algeria to subdue the native Muslim population, they had become expert at small warfare. Grierson had barely escaped them more than once. What worried him most was the construction by slave crews of an extension of the railroad from Ponchatoula to Baton Rouge that if successfully built would transform a three day wagon trip to only an hour by rail.

That was why he had concentrated his raids on the blockhouses and convoys in the last third of the route leading to Baton Rouge—to draw the Blue Butchers in that as far away from Ponchatoula as possible. Three days before, though, large Confederate infantry and artillery columns had filled the road to Ponchatoula. Grierson thought at first that Bazaine had called his bluff and was going to deal decisively with his raids by crushing him, but the troops had just kept on marching to Ponchatula and entrained for New Orleans, at least two divisions worth. He kept Franklin informed in detail, especially of the stories of deserters his men had scooped up in the piney woods that Taylor was off to take Missouri back from the Yankees. No one was more surprised than Grierson when the last of the Confederates had departed.

He concluded that these events just made his job easier and was glad that he had also taken up Rear Admiral Porter on the offer of a diversion.

Grierson looked at his watch. Five minutes after twelve. He expected Porter was in action.

Indeed he was. His ironclad fleet had bolted down the river to blast away at the Franco-Confederate lines in front of Port Hudson while Franklin made ostentatious preparations to issue from his own defenses to attack the enemy to fix Bazaine's attention anywhere but Ponchatoula. One squadron steamed down river to attack the defenses of Baton Rouge and another to attack enemy shipping on the river south of there as far as New Orleans.

Now all Grierson had to worry about was the French regiment behind earthworks around Ponchatoula. He was watching from a camouflaged platform in the top of the pines a quarter mile away. One of Franklin's Corps d'Afrique brigades was concealed below him.

He was keen on the arrival of trains and departure of convoys. Two trains had arrived since yesterday and were being loaded aboard the wagons of a convoy, over a hundred wagons. There were plenty of slaves to do the unloading, which gave the French troops very little to do except chase after the few black women in the camp. Their patrolling had fallen off as well since he had carefully stopped all raids and combat patrols anywhere near the garrison. Reconnaissance patrols instead had kept a minute watch on the comings and goings of the French. They were immeasurably helped by the slaves who were periodically let out to gather wood. Grierson had a perfect understanding of the location of every tent, guard post, and ammunition box in Ponchatoula as well as the routine of the guards, their posts, the changing of the guard, and the noontime nap they took. When a few of the slave informants saw the dense ranks of the Corps d'Afrique in the woods, they could scarcely be restrained from rejoicing.

They were mystified when men of the Corps borrowed their clothes. The wagons were filled with rocks and a layer of logs. Under some of the smaller pieces of wood axes, rifles and pistols were hidden. When the plan was explained to the slave leader of the wood party, he volunteered to go along since he was on good terms with the French guards.

The wagons lumbered out of the woods, the men singing a work song that was now familiar to French ears. The wood party was a part of the regular rhythm of the garrison. The guards did not even bother to wave them through, just leaning on their rifles. When the third wagon stopped just halfway through the gate, the guards were only amused at the wagon driver's evident distress with his mules as he cursed them for their always ill-timed display of stubbornness. Any bit of entertainment out of the ordinary was always welcome, and they focused on him.

They did not pay attention to the slaves next to the wagons reaching in among their tools. The guards died in a fusillade of shots. The Corps d'Afrique men shot the mules, leaving the heavy wagon to block the gates, and killed the last of the guards. With the first shots, Grierson watched one of his cavalry regiments break from the woods and dash the quarter mile to the gate. The black regiments double-timed out of the woods right after them just as four batteries of guns hidden in the woods begin lobbing shells into the camp among the French tents.

The cavalry arrived just in time as the French had rallied to try and retake the gate, but the Corps d'Afrique men fought like devils to hold it. The first of the horsemen worked past the wagon and into the firefight at the gate. A few went down careening off the bridge, but others crowded past the wagon to trample over the bodies carpeting the entrance to the gate and fan out into the camp.

The head of the infantry column was only a hundred yards from the gate when the French gunners manned their pieces and fired into them. The solid shot and shells tore ranks away at a time, but the columns came coming stumbling over their dead or going around. They flooded through the gate, a steel-tipped wave just as a French bayonet charge was driving back the dismounted cavalrymen who had fought through the gate. It was rare for a bayonet charge to be driven home against men who were willing to receive it. Invariably the charge either petered out against an obstinate defender or the defender flew. Either way bayonet rarely crossed bayonet. But this time it did in a stabbing melee where the shouts and curses were all in French for the Corps d'Afrique spoke French as well, not necessarily the pure language of la belle France but that New Orleans gumbo heavily spiced with Congo.

The black column surged and broke through the gate. The coffee mill guns among the artillery concentrated on the French guns crews and swept them from their pieces. Inside the camp the French were driven back step by step until it was clear that they had nowhere to go except the swamp. The eight hundred survivors surrendered.

Disarmed, they were forced to watch the former slave crews of their Confederate allies joyfully loot their camp. Grierson quickly turned them to destroying the rail spur toward Baton Rouge. His cavalry taught them how to heat the ties red hot on fire and then wrap them around telegraph poles, et viola, Ponchatoula hairpins. Inside the camp were warehouses filled with supplies destined for Bazaine's army that would now sustain Grierson's command, as well as the hundred wagons and mule teams. There was also a mule stable for replacement animals for the convoys.

Franklin's orders had been to wipe the Ponchatoula railroad station off the map and destroy the tracks as deep into the woods and swamps as possible. It now occurred to Grierson that he had captured not only two locomotives but over fifty railcars. More of these fine English-made locomotives and their cars were expected according to the interrogation of the station personnel.[5]

HMS *PRINCE ALBERT*, THE IRISH SEA OFF THE COAST OF CORK, 6:45 P.M., MONDAY, APRIL 4, 1864

Captain Coles looked at the sun as it prepared to dip below the horizon. He drove a fist into his open hand out of sheer frustration. His chance to catch the Russians would disappear with the sun. Last night he had steamed to the burning ships and intercepted the lifeboats of the crews making their way by sail to Wales. Their stories were unanimous: Russians raiding in the Irish Sea! There was not a Briton who would not dare the impossible to avenge this insult. That night he had assembled his gun crews and every man that could be spared. He explained the gravity of the situation, that they were at war with the Russians, and that Her Majesty looked with special favor on this ship named for the late Prince Consort. Nothing would give the queen greater satisfaction than this ship be the means of England's revenge. They had cheered him wildly. He hoped their morale would make up in some small degree for the minimal gunnery training they had had in the first turrets in the Royal Navy. For that matter, the entire crew had only that one earlier and brief voyage together, not nearly enough to shake down into a fighting team. None of that mattered. He would find the enemy and fight.

He had grasped at the only bit of useful information he could glean from a quick questioning of the merchant crews. The course of the two Russian ships was in the direction of the coast of Cork. He had steamed through the night on that same course and had intercepted and warned a number of British ships, two fast rich steamers of which he had ordered to accompany him. The captains were at first relieved to have such an escort only to realize that they were doing the escorting. *Prince Albert* sailed inconspicuously between them almost invisible to an approaching ship.

Sure enough, by midmorning a burning ship was spotted by its smoke. Coles steamed in that direction and was quickly alerted by one of his lookouts in the shrouds towering over the steamers that two ships were approaching at high speed trailing their own smoke.[6] Coles's glass quickly confirmed that they were warships, one a frigate and the other a corvette. His marines drummed out "Beat to quarters," as he prepared his virgin ship for action.

In minutes a ball fired from the frigate splashed into the water just ahead of the larger of the two British steamers. As Coles had directed the captains, they slowed to a stop. When the Russians were only a few hundred yards away, *Prince Albert's* engines gave the ship full power, and she sprang out from between the steamers, her four turrets already turned to starboard in the direction of the Russians.

Aboard *Aleksandr Nevsky*, Lisovsky leaned over the rail as the ironclad shot out from between the two steamers, exclaiming in shock, "*Muzha Boi!*" (My God!) Before he could give the order to reverse engines, *Prince Albert's* guns fired simultaneously. Lisovsky saw the enemy ship lurch back into the water ten feet from the recoil of its four turret guns. Its shells penetrated just under his quarterdeck, exploded, and threw much of the deck and the admiral overboard and threw carnage into the gundecks.

Prince Albert steamed for the Russian ships, which had started to fight back. Half of *Aleksandr Nevsky's* original fifty-one guns had been replaced by American 9-inch Dahlgrens while in New York. The Russian gunners started to respond, but their 79-pound shot just bounced off the 10-inch armor of the turret fronts, leaving only deep gouges.

Inside the turrets the tars worked their guns with a will that was almost superhuman. Every man was eager to do his best. Coles was amazed at the rate of fire they were getting, something that he thought it would take months to achieve. Shell after shell gutted the Russian, leaving her gun deck nothing but a hell of splinters, dislodged guns, and blood. The inevitable cartridge exploded, starting a fire, and spread quickly through the stricken ship. With the admiral and the captain dead, the ship was slow to surrender. No one could be found with the authority to do so. Instead men were jumping overboard to save themselves from the fire. It spread to devour the masts and sheets and gushed out of the gunports and great gaping splintered holes in her sides.

The frigate was now nothing more than a dead pawn on the board of imperial strategy, but the smaller corvette, the eighteen-gun *Variag* was still game and had steamed around to the ironclad's port side opposite the guns firing on *Aleksandr Nevsky*. Her shot also just bounced off the turrets; her original Russian guns also failed to harm *Prince Albert's* 5-inch armored belt.

As the turrets turned to take her under fire, *Variag's* captain chose the better part of discretion and steamed away at full speed, its engines straining to put distance between them. Not enough. Coles turned the ship broadside to the fleeing Russian. Again she lurched ten feet backward from the recoil of her guns. The stern of the Russian disintegrated, snapping her rudder and jamming her propeller. She struck.

HOTEL DU VILLE, NEW ORLEANS, 11:00 A.M., MONDAY, APRIL 4, 1864

"Oh, *cher*, Bazaine has been so indiscrete in the arms of Venus. Ah, men. He tells me because I am his conduit to the *libres*. I am, of course, but not in the way he thinks. We *libres* are *Americain* though we may often say it in French. It is not Louis Napoleon who is waging war against slavery. Bazaine thinks that bags full of gold Napoleons will buy us. Perhaps, but we are good businessmen. In this market no one will stay bought for long."

Pryce Lewis did not know what to admire most about Clio Dulaine — her stunning beauty or the workings of her mind. Cleopatra could have taken lessons. Lewis suspected that Lucrezia Borgia could also have learned a thing or two. She was Sharpe's chief agent in New Orleans, and the general had made it clear that Lewis was to be guided by her. He suggested, "Perhaps bags of Her Majesty's sovereigns can complicate things for our field marshal?"

"Indeed, *cher*, General Sharpe has put you in the perfect position to throw the apple of discord among our friends, or shall I say a basket of such apples. You do not need my advice. You are doing so well and so soon too. *Tres bon*."

She was referring to the expertly forged letters of credit from British cotton mills as well as the £100,000 in gold (over $2,000,000) he had been spreading to buy up every bale of cotton at prices that crowded out the French buyers. He had shown up a week before with an impeccably forged passport that showed he had come through Mobile along with forged letters of introduction, both Confederate and British, that fooled the British counsul and ensured his cooperation. The French cotton buyers had run to their counsul, who had run to Bazaine, which resulted in more bags of gold Napoleons spread among influential hands. They were competing with gold sovereigns, most of which went into Confederate hands to buy friends for Britain. He had put it about that Her Majesty would make a much better friend to the Confederacy than the French who seemed to think that Louisiana belonged to them again. That wish was certainly the thought for Gen. Richard Taylor. Bazaine's increasing involvement in local politics, his buying of influence, and the insulting assumption of sovereign authority had made many senior Confederates question the value of the French alliance.

Since their joint victory at Vermillionville in October, there had been no other victories, only the grinding and difficult siege of Port Hudson and costly failed assaults. Jefferson Davis had put up with French effrontery because he needed Napoleon's treaty, army, and money, but it only aroused his deepest jealousy for the sovereignty of the Confederacy. The British, on the other hand, would sign no treaty, it being an impossibility to do so with a slave-holding government, but offered their military support freely and seemed to bend over backward to respect Southern sovereignty. It was a paradox of sorts — French substance that was hollow and British diffidence that was substantial in effect. The British had no interest in Southern territory. Their interest in defeating the United States simply required Southern independence. It was clear that British strategy now required multiple states in place of the Old Union. The French, on the other hand, had an interest in Southern territory that determined everything else including their hold on Mexico.

So far it had not proved possible to use the British against the French in Louisiana. The British had made it clear that their priorities were limited to defeating the United States, and they seemed to acquiesce to French primacy of interest in Louisiana. Until now. Suddenly there was a British subject in New Orleans spending gold in a stream that could only have come directly from a royal mint and suggesting British support that they were not willing even to admit privately.[7]

Davis jumped at the chance to put the French in their place. It surprised both Clio and Pryce how fast he reacted. Confederate troops from the combined army before Port Hudson had been arriving in New Orleans by train for the last several days. Clio sipped her coffee. "I tell you, *cher*, that Bazaine was livid that Taylor left only the French to carry on the siege. But that Taylor, butter wouldn't melt in his mouth. He had the effrontery to say to the *Marechal du France* himself, this Duc du Vermillionville, this representative of His Majesty, Louis Napoleon, Emperor of the French, that under his command the Confederate divisions had accomplished little; he instead would use them to reconquer Missouri for the Confederacy. *Mon Dieu, cher*, what a scene! It is something I will entertain my grandchildren with."

THE MARSHES OF RIVER CROUCH, ESSEX, 7:12 A.M., THURSDAY, APRIL 7, 1864
It was a hard thing to be the prey when the heart was that of a predator. Dahlgren had charged at the head of a regiment at Brandy Station, led raids that had made him a hero, and howled in the pursuit of Lee's army after Gettysburg, always feeding on the surprise and fear of the prey. Now with the roles reversed he saw it as a game of cat and mouse where every escape was a victory for the mouse, a snap of the fingers in the feline's face. The fact that the odds were all with the cat just made the game more exciting.

After the night in the woodsman's hut, they set out just as the dawn's first blush rose in the east from the direction of the sea. They rode hard all day on country roads counting on chaos to be their cloak, skirting Hainault Forest to the east and then following the ridge south to pass Brentwood and then picking up the high ground around Billericay. The word of invasion had spread everywhere by now so that the sight of galloping men in uniform was a cause for alarm. At dusk they hid in a small woodland with some great house jutting its turrets beyond the treetops.

Dahlgren had among his worries what to do with Abel. It was not as if the odds were likely he was going to be able to carry him off to new employment at the Dupont powder mills in Pennsylvania. That chance flew away when he missed his rendezvous with Lamson. There was also the problem that whatever escape they attempted, Abel would be an enormous liability. What to do?

It was a cold meal they all shared that night. "Mr. Abel," Dahlgren said, "Let me suggest an arrangement that will make all our lives a bit easier. If you give me your word that you will not try to escape, I will not have you tied at night or your hands to the pommel of your saddle during the day."

Sleeping on often damp leaves had been an unsettling experience for the chemist though not nearly as much as riding with hands tied. He had hardly ever ridden a horse in his life, and to be charitable, his seat was so unsteady that he lived in terror of being cast to his death. As a scientist, he could see the logic of the offer and immediately accepted.

At first light on the morning of the sixth, Feodor scrambled up a tree as if it were a mast. In ten minutes he was sliding down to land on the forest floor like a cat. He ran up to Rimsky-Korsakov to jammer away in Russian. Kolya peppered him with questions, then turned to Dahlgren. "The English are beating the fields for us, Ulrich. They have troops on line for miles with local people guiding them. They have dogs too. We must go." Collins helped Dahlgren onto his horse and strapped down his wooden leg. No one questioned that it was that leg that kept them conspicuously on horseback. Feodor had unconsciously in all innocence called him *nash molodoi geroi polkovnik* — our young hero colonel! Despite the leg, they all recognized that indefinable quality of the man who could pull them through.

Now even that ability seemed to have run its course of miraculous near-run escapes on this morning as the mist rose off the marshes. They had reached a patch of woods near the marsh edge, just in time to avoid a patrol of lancers picking their way through the soft ground, poking lances into every large clump of reeds at the waters edge. They were fine fellows under Dahlgren's critical eye, riding excellent horses, clad in dark blue with red front tunics and a red crest to their Uhlan helmets. Red and white pennons flew from their lances, which they handled with a quick second nature. An officer rode out onto a small pier to which several boats were tied. He stood up in his stirrups and gazed about.[8]

The four held their breaths as two of the lancers trotted up to the woods, but a sharp command brought them back as the group moved on down the marsh bank and disappeared as it meandered out of sight. Dahlgren spurred his black out of the woods and onto the pier. "Yes," exclaimed, clenching his fist. There was a marsh boat, just the sort of craft to wend its way through the shallow water and reeds. The others had ridden up and dismounted when Feodor shouted and pointed.

The Lancers were riding toward them at a full gallop back from the way they had come; their lances dipped as the officer drew his saber. Collins needed no order but fell to one knee with his Spencer. He drew in a breath as the officer filled the rifle's simple site and slowly squeezed the trigger. The man flew back in the saddle and fell off the horse. Again he held his breath, then fired. A lancer crumpled. The rest slowed as they got to the soft ground. Dahlgren, still mounted, fired over Collins's head with his Colt revolver and claimed another lancer. The last four were still game and spurred their mounts forward. Dahlgren then shouted and drove their three horses off the pier straight at the lancers as they approached. The animals kept the lances too far away from him as he shot another one from his saddle. The trigger then clicked on an empty chamber. It almost killed him as he dodged a lance thrust and pulled his mount back. The lance thrust again just as the black reared and buried itself in the cork leg. Dahlgren drew his own saber and severed the shaft of the lance. The lancer pulled his own saber and closed.

The last two the lancers clambered onto the pier. One of them stabbed Kolya in the leg, and the lieutenant fell with a scream. Before the lancer could wrench out the lance head, Feodor threw himself up and carried him off his horse and into the water. It was not deep but deep enough for the Russian's grip around the man's throat to keep him under water till he went limp. The other lancer leveled his lance at Collins, who jumped into the water knocking Abel down as he flew past.

The lancer was peering over the side ready to jab his lance wherever the American reappeared when Dahlgren crashed into him, throwing man and horse into the water. The animal struggled to its feet and waded ashore. The lancer popped to the surface and went down gasping. Collins waded over to him and pulled him to his feet, coughing water, his bedraggled Uhlan's helmet still strapped to his head, then helped him onto the pier where he lay gasping. He finally got a few words in between coughing. "Can't swim." He rolled over, looked at Collins and muttered, "Thanks, mate." He sat up at the noise of a nervous hoof tapping the wooden planking and saw Dahlgren towering over him on the black. His eyes widened as he saw the broken lance shaft and pennon protruding from his leg.

Dahlgren's attention was all on Kolya now. Feodor had climbed back onto the pier and was trying to stop the bleeding, but it just oozed through his fingers. "Look, mate, there's a bandage in my horse bag," the lancer offered. Collins ran to where the lancer's horse was grazing and returned with it. The lancer unrolled the lint-filled pad, pressed it to the wound. Then he fastened a tourniquet, tightening and loosening it. He looked up and smiled. "Learned this from Miss Nightingale at Scutari, I did. An angel she was, Miss Nightingale. Saved me leg, she did, and when I was on the mend she taught us these things to save soldiers' lives. God bless 'er." He looked pleased with himself, then said, "Loosen it every fifteen minutes." Kolya gasped the translation to Feodor, who nodded.

He stood up, a small, lithe man in his early thirties, looked at Collins, who had the Spencer pointed at him, and at Dahlgren on his horse. He came to attention and saluted Dahlgren. "Sir, Corporal Townsend, 12th Lancers."

Dahlgren returned the salute knowing full well that the man knew who he was. "At ease, Corporal. I thank you for the assistance you have rendered our comrade. Nevertheless, you have presented me a problem I do not need at this time." He looked long and hard at the lancer, then scanned the woodline. "Collins, go check the bodies for any written documents. Hurry." Collins took off at a run.

Dahlgren was still figuring out what to do with the lancer when Collins shouted, "I need help! This officer is wounded."

"Help him," Dahlgren gestured, and Townsend was off like a shot. Together Collins and he brought the wounded officer to the pier to lie next to Kolya. Collins's shot had put a 52-caliber bullet straight through his shoulder, a clean wound. The man tried to sit up but fell back on one arm. He looked up and around, but Dahlgren on his black took all his attention. "Lieutenant John Beauchamp, sir," he said. "I say, you must be that Dahlgren chap. Worse luck for me."

"At your service, Lieutenant."

The man had not lost his equanimity and managed a wincing laugh. "A small change in our positions, sir, and I would be a hundred thousand pounds richer."

"You have me there."

"No, sir, you have me here." He looked at Dahlgren's lack of recognition and realized. "You have no idea that the government has put a hundred-thousand-pound bounty on your head, sir? Everyone in eastern England is hoping to collect."

"They shall be disappointed."

"I dare say, so far you've given the hounds a good run all this way from Enfield. Gave the whole of England a bad scare with this invasion story. Very good there. Society fled London in its carriages. Couldn't get a train, all commandeered by the government. Hell of a time getting the regiment through that mess." He looked about and muttered about his poor lads, then went on to describe the chaos created by the invasion scare on top of the fall of Dublin. Dahlgren's hopes leapt at the news that Meagher had succeeded. He was more concerned with Beauchamp's description of how half the British Army and every RVC from half of England had converged on Essex determined to cast out the invader. There had been small battles at Romford and Maldon but only a few prisoners had been taken, mostly lost cavalrymen wandering the countryside. Dahlgren had thought that was a lot of information to be passed down anyone's chain of command so soon whereupon Beauchamp authoritatively cited the London *Times* as his source.

"As I've said, sir, you've given the hounds a damned fine race, but we've got you. The regiment will be looking why this patrol did not return; must've already heard the gunfire. Best to surrender now, no dishonor, sir, none at all. In fact, whatever happens you've made history, and besides you've got the wounded Russki officer here." Kolya glared at him. The imperial banner wrapped under his coat now had a large blood stain.

Dahlgren said, "Completely unacceptable. This fox still has a good run in him, not just the one I had in mind before you lancers arrived." He pointedly looked at the boat and sighed, turned to Rimsky-Korsakov. "Kolya, we shall have to forget the boat; I cannot risk your wound at sea." Then he looked back at Beauchamp and laughed. "This fox still has hundred Celtic bolt holes in Mother England! You will never find him."

The sudden distaste on Beauchamp's face told him he had hit a nerve. He looked over to Collins. "Round up three horses for us." Then he turned back to the lieutenant. "I have a better idea than surrender. Can you ride with that shoulder?"

"Of course, sir; I am a lancer."

"Collins, help Townsend put the lieutenant on a horse. Townsend, you will guide the lieutenant to medical attention. I release you both." He turned to Abel. "Well, sir, there is no use of your coming with us. You have been a gentleman. I release you to accompany the Lancers."

He watched Townsend walk away leading the lieutenant's horse. He knew how much Lincoln had hoped to find a gun cotton substitute for niter and that Abel could have been the key to it. That Sword of Damocles would continue to hang over the country. Dahlgren just could not do anything about it.

THE WINTER PALACE, ST. PETERSBURG, RUSSIA, 11:15 A.M., FRIDAY, APRIL 8, 1864

The great bronze bells of the imperial city rang the whole day as word brought by the *Almaz* of war with Great Britain spread through the city. On the heels of that came news that the Lisovsky's squadron was savaging the commerce of the Irish Sea after landing an American expedition that had seized Dublin and that an American landing in England had struck panic throughout the proud island. The Emperor paraded his household troops, the Guard du Corps in their white crested Greek helmets and shining breastplates, manned by the sons of Russia's nobility, and the Preobazhensky and Semenovsky Guards Regiments. The crowds filled the aquamarine sky of the far north with thundering shouts of "Uhrah! Uhrah! Uhrah!" Alexander II and his sons, all in uniform, were met with even greater shouts when they appeared on the balcony of the Winter Palace. The crowd began to chant, "Constantinople!" over and over.

The public had already heartily approved the award to Lisovsky and Meagher of the Military Order of the Holy Great-Martyr and the Triumphant George first class with its enameled white cross and superimposed gold star hanging from a stripped orange and black ribbon, the colors of Russian military glory, fire, and gunpowder. This order had been awarded only twenty times before to senior commanders against an exterior foe of Russia. It was a heady honor indeed to be included among the likes of the great Suvorov and Kutuzov, the Prussian von Blücher, and the Briton Wellington.

From another window Prince Aleksandr Gorchakov, the imperial foreign minister, and Cassius Clay, the American ambassador, were watching. "You see, Mr. Clay, the people, the army, and the emperor, they are all one." At sixty-six, Gorchakov was already one of the most respected and influential diplomats of the century. He was a great gentleman in his bearing and restraint, with delicate features.

"I am positive that the news of our joint expedition will be received in the United States with no less enthusiasm." Clay was a Kentucky abolitionist, the rarest of southern birds, and had successfully employed his famous bowie knife in a number of duels fought to defend his principles. Lincoln had rewarded him with the ambassadorship to the court of the tsar.

"The country senses when war is necessary. We have a better educated population now than we had even in the Great Patriotic War against Napoleon." He smiled delicately as if reminded of something. "Every Russian knows why this war is necessary: to humble the insufferable pride of Great Britain." Then he looked off into the distance. "And to replant the cross on the dome of the Hagia Sophia in Constantinople.

Maj. Gen. Joseph Hooker at the height of his glory before the battle of Chazy (author's collection)

Lieut. Gen. James Hope Grant, Commander of Her Majesty's Forces in North America (author's collection)

Maj. Gen. George H. Sharpe, Chief, Central Information Bureau (CIB), John C. Babcock, Lieut. Col. Michael Wilmoth, Lieut. Col. John McEntee (author's collection)

Brig. Garnet Wolseley, later in his successful career as the greatest of Victoria's generals (author's collection)

Col. George Denison, Commander, Canadian Royal Guides (author's collection)

Col. William McBean,
Commander, 78th (Highland)
Foot (author's collection)

Officers of the 60th New York Volunteer Infantry Regiment (author's
collection)

Vivian's Brigade on the opening night (18-19 March) of the battle of Chazy (author's collection)

Army of the Hudson in the night combat crossing of the Little Chazy River on the night of March 22 (author's collection)

A Scot Fusilier Guards sergeant. The Scots and Grenadier Guards closed the battle of Chazy with their counterattack, March 23 (author's collection)

Maj. Gen. Thomas Francis Meagher, liberator of Dublin (author's collection)

Adm. Stepan Lisovsky, Russian Imperial Navy, Commander of the Baltic Squadron (author's collection)

Col. Ulric Dahlgren, leader of the great raid into England (author's collection)

Lieut. Nikolai Rimsky-Korsakov, Imperial Russian Navy, musical genius and Col. Dahlgren's aide (author's collection)

Lieut. Col. Charles Francis Adams, Jr., Commander, 1st Massachusetts Cavalry (seated in rocker) (author's collection)

Co. C., 1st Massachusetts Cavalry, the men who made the Great Raid (author's collection)

The Royal Small Arms Factory Enfield, the maker of the superb Enfield Rifle for the British Army (author's collection)

Frederick Douglass, the lion of emancipation and Lincoln advisor (author's collection)

A commanding officer of a British Volunteer Rifle Corps (VRC) (author's collection)

British Yeomanry cavalry and Militia infantry (author's collection)

Maj. Gen. Joshua Lawrence Chamberlain, Hero and Avenger of Portland (author's collection)

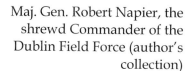

Maj. Gen. Robert Napier, the shrewd Commander of the Dublin Field Force (author's collection)

Marshall of France François Achille Bazaine, Commander, French Forces in North America and the *Armée de la Louisiane* (author's collection)

French infantry of the *Armée de la Louisiane* (author's collection)

Elizabeth Van Lew, the great Union spymistress of Richmond (author's collection)

US Colored Troops (USCT) at the Second Battle of Big Bethal (author's collection)

Capt. Cowper Coles,
Commander, HMS *Prince
Albert*, and advocate of turreted
warships for the Royal Navy
(author's collection)

HMS *Prince Albert* with its four turrets (author's collection)

The great cavalry battle at Hanover Junction, May 6, 1864 (author's collection)

"General Lee to the Rear" – at the battle of Hanover Academy, May 7, 1864, Lee's troops would not attack if Lee exposed himself (author's collection)

Rear Adm. David Farragut, commander of the U.S. First Fleet at the battle of the Chesapeake, May 7, 1864 (author's collection)

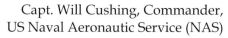

Capt. Will Cushing, Commander, US Naval Aeronautic Service (NAS)

Lieut. Gen. Ulysses S. Grant, General-in-Chief, Armies of the United States (author's collection)

Maj. Gen. Winfield Scott Hancock, commander of the Army of the Rappahannock at the decisive battles of May 7, 1864 (author's collection)

USS *New Ironsides*, Farragut's heavily gunned and armored flagship at the battle of the Chesapeake, May 7, 1864 (author's collection)

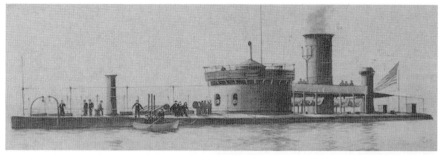

USS *Dictator*, John Ericksson's behemoth monitor, the largest and most powerful ship in the U.S. Navy (author's collection)

USS *Alligator*, the original submersible that lead to a entire new dimension of naval warfare (author's collection)

HMS *Warrior*, the first of the Royal Navy's ironclads, the largest ship in the fleet and its pride and joy (author's collection)

One of the floating batteries of the Royal Navy's Great Armament brought across the Atlantic to pound Fortress Monroe into submission (author's collection)

The 11ᵗʰ Hussars and the 9ᵗʰ Lancers, were the cream of British cavalry and the only mounted regiments in British North America (author's collection)

Maj. Gen. John Logan, commanding XI Corps at the battle of Saco against the desperate attack of the British 12ᵗʰ Brigade, May 7 (author's collection)

"Yes, yes, it is not some minor thing," he said. "Do you recall the Decembrist Revolt in the first year of the reign of His Imperial Majesty's father? A cabal of young officers became intoxicated on the ideas of the French Revolution and attempted to replace Nicholas I with his brother Constantine. The troops were told to shout, 'Constantin y Constitutsiya!' [Constitution and Constitution!] The lads duly shouted, but thought Constitutsiya was Constantine's wife. We have come a long way since then."

"Indeed, sir, your country as is mine is alive with energy and progress."

"More important at this moment is that we share the same enemy."

"Of course, Prince, of course."

THE FIELD OF TALLAGHT, SOUTHWEST OF DUBLIN, 10:25 A.M., FRIDAY, APRIL 8, 1864

Had he known of the Order of St. George, Meagher would have been immensely flattered, but if asked to choose, he would have gladly traded every such European bauble for a more hearty response to his call for volunteers. He had expected a flood and got barely a trickle.

Ireland held its breath waiting to see who would have the upper hand. The seething hatred of England in the hearts of the million and half Irish who had fled the famine had conditioned the exiles to imagine that that same hatred burned as deep and as hot still in the Old Sod. They did not consider that those most cruelly used by the famine and English indifference were either dead or fled the country. Many of those who remained were the better off, those who had something left to keep them home, and those who had survived the great dying. Too, the boldest and most desperate had gone.

Reinforcing that caution in the Irish population was uppermost in the mind of the Lord Lieutenant. The Duke of Abercorn had ridden directly to the garrison at the Curragh and ordered it to Dublin as well as the remaining regiments in the country to converge in as well. His prompt action secured the telegraph as the communications means by which the military resources at hand could best be used. He too, like Meagher, knew that the first days of the crisis would be critical. The numerous military depot battalions were ordered to assemble what troops they had, secure weapons and ammunition storage, and make themselves visibly apparent to the local population. The northern Protestant counties on their own had called out their militia, much of which was marching south to Dublin.

Abercorn was lucky to find on a visit of inspection to the troops at the Curragh, Lt. Gen. Sir James Yorke Scarlett, Adjutant General to the

Forces, who had commanded the Heavy Brigade so well in the Crimean War. As senior officer, Scarlett took command of the forces at the Curragh with dispatch and by the next morning had them on the road to Dublin.

Working for Meagher, though, was the diversion of British attention and resources to the invasion of Essex. The initial news staggered the Protestant Anglo-Irish and Scots-Irish who were the bedrock of local support for the Crown. If ever there was a time for their nerve to crack it was then. A hysteria blew through them, akin to that brought on by the terror of the Armada in the time of Elizabeth I. But it was Abercorn's strong hand that kept them in check, for the man refused to take counsel of his fears. Then that momentary panic passed on the clarifying news from London that the invasion of Essex had been nothing more than a daring raid. A few regiments began to arrive from garrisons in eastern England and Scotland, those initially ordered there by the Duke of Cambridge.

By that time, British cavalry patrols were probing the outskirts of Dublin. Meagher had not entirely wasted his time in that week; his Balloon Corps company had kept its four balloons around the periphery of the city and were able to warn him of the Scarlett's approaching force. That warning was vital, for it gave him the initiative to strike first.

His advance guard of the 69th New York made contact with the 15th Hussars, the British advance guard on the outskirts of Tallaght, only a few miles from Dublin to the southwest and immediately deployed with the 28th Massachusetts on the right and the 83rd New York on the left, with three batteries of artillery on a rise behind them. His two Republic of Ireland regiments he placed in reserve.[9] Meagher climbed the old bell tower of the rebuilt church of Tallaght and saw the scarlet lines approaching. He raced down, leapt on his horse, and seized the national color from the color bearer. He rode down the front of his little army waving the green flag, shouting, "The eyes of Ireland are upon you, my boys!" An ovation rippled along the ranks as he passed, for the Irish knew their history. Tallaght was the site of a monastery built in the eighth century by St. Mael Ruain that was to become along with the monastery at Finglas known as the "Eyes of Ireland" centers of learning in the island's golden age of memory.

Lord Scarlett had scrapped together every fit man he could lay his hands on. That meant three regiments of infantry in the Curragh Brigade, an engineer company, and the Hussars. He had no artillery at all. All the Royal Artillery companies in Ireland, those that had not already shipped to America, had been in Dublin with the 8th Artillery Brigade. Some of their Armstrongs were now manned by Meagher's Irish volunteers, a few of them former members of those very batteries. Guns or no, Ambercorn had ordered the commander to strike for Dublin immediately lest any delay in the government's reassertion of control give heart to a rising throughout the island. In the last two days he had been reinforced by the 4th and 5th Dragoon Guards from Cahir and Dundalk, giving him a small cavalry brigade. Scarlett was delighted to see the 5th Dragoon Guards, for that had been his regiment and the one he had led in the Crimea before acceding to command of the Heavy Brigade.[10]

If the British had no artillery, Meagher had no cavalry. It was an even trade of sorts. The Hussars had given Scarlett a clear picture of Meagher's force. He concluded that without guns he could not afford a pounding match. He would have to be quick and deliver a shock of cold steel with his infantry while the Dragoons swung around to strike the Irish from the rear in a grand charge. He did not think of the enemy as anything but the Irish, not the Americans. He did not like the way so many hostile faces had peered over stone field walls and through windows as they had forced marched here. Should he fail today, those faces would become more than hostile.

At six hundred yards the case shot, canisters of large lead balls, burst into the oncoming British, who did not hesitate but closed ranks over the dead and dying and kept the pace. At three hundred yards the enemy's rifle fire erupted and the front ranks began to drop men. Scarlett had expected this all as the necessary butcher's bill to cross the beaten zone, but the fire did not slacken as he assumed it would as the enemy laboriously reloaded their muzzle loaders. Unknown to Scarlett, the Irish had Mr. Spencer's and Mr. Gatling's new toys to send a continuous sheet of lead into the redcoats, more than ten times the firepower of the most well-drilled regiment in any army firing muzzle-loaders.

The British battalions were simply melting away in that blaze when 1,200 Dragoons struck Meagher's rear. The two volunteer regiments in their path were ridden down and scattered. They had been turned about to face the charge too late. They were too green, and the charge was nearly upon them. The leavening of British Army deserters in their ranks had not had time to transmit the discipline of the regulars. It was the hardest test of untrained men to face a determined cavalry charge, and few had ever passed. They got off a scattered ill-aimed volley and the broke, proving over again Homer's description of "Panic, brother to blood-stained rout" the horsemen washed over them, and one rode away waving a regimental color.[11]

The Dragoons sabered their way through the fleeing mass toward the artillery on its rise. Meagher rode in among the volunteers, desperately trying to rally them, and only drew the Dragoons toward him. Brigadier General Kelly was more effective. He ordered the reserve companies of the Irish Brigade to turn about as the Dragoons surged over the guns, just in time to receive their now disorganized ranks with sustained repeater fire. The Dragoon wave went down in a screaming tangle of dead and dying animals and their riders. Again and again they charged only to add to the carnage. In the midst of the dragoon swarm was Meagher, his color bearer, and small escort, in a ring desperately fending off the Dragoons. One by one they went down, until the 69th concentrated its fire to clear a path for them to escape into their ranks. They cheered as Meagher of the Sword rode in among them and turned again to face the enemy waving his blade in defiance.

At last the Dragoons retreated, leaving a heap of men and horses along the Irish Brigade's firing line. When Scarlet heard the Irish cheer, he knew he was beaten. He ordered a retreat. As his shrunken ranks turned about, their faces reddened as the Irish waved their fists at them shouting, "Boyne! Boyne! Boyne!"[12]

Meagher could claim the victory since he still occupied the field, but the word "Pyrrhic" seemed to describe it in reality. His two Irish volunteer regiments were effectively destroyed, the survivors would barely make only a half-dozen companies. His artillery crews had been savaged as well by the Dragoons, but many of them had hidden under the guns and caissons. Fortunately, the losses of the Irish Brigade were light. But it was a victory all the same, one that would reap great profit if properly used. The Glorious Field of Tallaght would suit his cause very well. The bells of Dublin rang again that day. He would have had less cause to rejoice had he known that every port north and south of Dublin was unloading reinforcements from Britain and even less had he bothered to pay attention to his ordnance officer's report of ammunition expenditure in this most glorious of battles.

Nor did he see a Dragoon ride up to a downcast Lord Scarlett and throw at his feet the colors of the 1st Regiment Brian Boru.

NUMBER 10 DOWNING STREET, LONDON, 2:00 P.M., SUNDAY, APRIL 10, 1864
For a seemingly frail wisp of man, the Prime Minister had shown the strength of Tantalus over the last week, or as he put it, the most interesting week of any prime minister. In a single day, he had ridden through a triple storm — the Russian declaration of war, the fall of Dublin, and the thankfully so-called invasion of England. He alone in the cabinet could put such a positive interpretation on it.

The political storm that erupted had been the least of his immediate worries, the most important being Russia, Ireland, and Essex, in that order. It had become clear by the sixth of April that there was no invasion of England by the American army of U.S. Grant. It had been, after all,

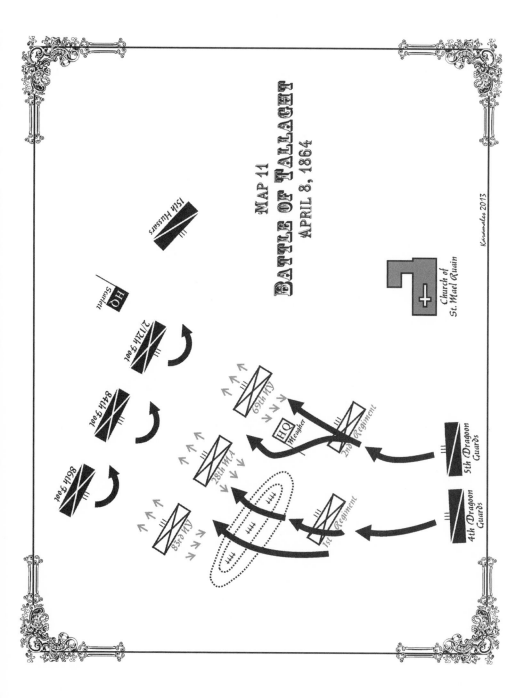

MAP 11
BATTLE OF TALLAGHT
APRIL 8, 1864

Kriminder 2013

Church of
St. Mael Ruain

15th Hussars

HO Stanton

2/72th Foot

84th Foot

86th Foot

69th HV

HO Meagher

2nd Regiment

5th Dragoon Guards

82nd FV

1st Regiment

4th Dragoon Guards

50th FV

only a raid, the most daring of raids to be sure, but only a raid. Essex had been swarming with troops to find the invaders, but a hundred thousand men (regulars, yeomanry, militia, and RVCs) instead only rounded up the survivors of the raid, men captured at Romford, Enfield, and Maldon and a few dozen roaming the countryside, barely three hundred in all. Another three hundred dead and wounded had been found. The ships they had arrived on at Southend-on-Sea had disappeared to the mortification of the Royal Navy, triply so when it was discovered that the American ships included the *Kearsarge*.

Although it had been only a raid in the strength of fewer than a thousand men, it had done real damage and not just to the Royal Powder Mills and Royal Small Arms Factory. It had forced the British to take their eyes off the Irish ball when the fall of London seemed imminent. And now this fellow Meagher had made more than good use of that distraction by beating the British Army at Tallaght, the first defeat of British arms in the isles for God knows how long, at least since Bonnie Prince Charlie tried to throw out the house of Hanover.[13]

All this was correctable. The powder mills and factory could be rebuilt, and the rising in Ireland suppressed. These would be done. As he sat in his office, Disreali could see the reverse flow of British military power to Ireland. The first good news had been of Captain Cole's victory over the Lisosvky's flagship and escort off Wales. The second was the interception and taking of the other two Russian frigates a few days later. The Irish Sea was again the British *mare nostrum*. The third was the conclusion reached by Lieutenant Colonel Freemantle that the Americans had shot their bolt; they could not repeat these forlorn hopes much less launch a real invasion of the British Isles.

So it was safe to concentrate on crushing the American expedition in Ireland. How much it would cost was another matter. The news of Tallaght had forced a lot of fence-sitters in Ireland to jump for the rebellion. News was coming across the Irish Sea of district after district, town after town, declaring for Meagher. Not only rebellion but civil war loomed over Ireland, for not only the Protestants remained loyal but a significant part of the Catholics as well. Disraeli suspected that the harsher the Crown's treatment, the more it would fan the rising. He definitely did not want to summon the ghost of Judge Jeffrys. To the Duke of Cambridge's rage, Disraeli had issued the order that the Irish were to be treated with leniency.

Cambridge was already in a constant foul mood for having been so badly humbugged by the Essex Raid and had been more than ready to make the Irish pay for it, but Disraeli had made that impossible. Instead, the focus of his ill-temper had become Dahlgren, the man who had made him into a fool. It was bad enough to be so publicly embarrassed but having been made so by a one-legged "boy" had cast him into an abyss of ridicule. He had been the one to insist that the queen be evacuated, that the London was in imminent danger and could fall at any moment, and he had very publicly pledged that he would die at the gates of London before a single American would enter. *Punch* was having a field day with it. Dahlgren embodied the whole damned mess, and he desperately wanted to parade him as a trophy. For that reason, Cambridge had kept too many troops, it was said, still in Essex to hunt the raider down. He had feared he had escaped with the American ships, but had brightened when the 12th Lancers reported a brush with him that indicated he was being hidden by Irish traitors somewhere in Essex or nearby. So he redoubled his efforts until every home great and small, every barn, every gamekeeper's lodge, every pigsty, haystack, and dunghill had been searched and searched again.

Disraeli could only imagine the site of Dahlgren being dragged through the streets of London, hopping along on one good leg behind the duke's horse. It was too ludicrous to imagine that the British government or public would be so lost to decency as to permit such a thing. That only would, of course, have made Dahlgren more of the international hero than he already was, if the reports of the foreign press were to be believed. In his ancestral Sweden he was a sensation. In Prussia he was the toast of every officer's mess as the ultimate blond Nordic hero. The French were enjoying themselves enormously at Albion's shame and referring to Dahlgren as a chevalier, the gallant knight, another Lancelot to put the English in their place. In Vienna every dollop of whipped cream (*Schlag*) into a cup of coffee was accompanied by a snigger. He did not want to think what would be the effect when the news reached India where the embers of the Great Mutiny hid here and there concealed only by the ash of British reprisals.

Then there was Russia, the true north of Disraeli's strategic compass. He had warned against taking sides in the American Civil War. But official London had done just that with its blatant sympathy for the Confederacy that had turned a blind eye to the building of commerce raiders for its navy which in turn had provoked Lincoln into threatening war. So much tinder and so many matches. It had been mocking fortune to ignore the real, inherent danger. And war did come, and Disraeli, ever the master of opportunity, had used it and the Palmerston government's bungling to ride into office with a Tory majority. He had championed the preservation of the Empire now that war with the United States threatened British North America. He had had no animosity to the United States before the war and had discerned no reason to make it a permanent enemy for the next century through a Carthaginian peace.

Nevertheless, the rage of the British was incandescent and needed an immediate focus. Disraeli assured the House that the Americans had shot their bolt in these raids and that the Royal Navy guaranteed it. He then announced to the House, with every ounce of his legendary eloquence, that the ironclads already in commission would be sent across the Atlantic to join HMS *Warrior* and *Defiance* to ensure the capture of Fortress Monroe, the destruction of the American fleet at Norfolk, the capture of the same base for the use of the Royal Navy, and the complete control of the Chesapeake Bay (Appendix D). He coined the term "the Iron Fleet," to describe the ironclad flotilla, which caught the public imagination, and ended with a rhetorical pun that "We know trust in naval hope as we have already in our military hope," playing off name of the new commander of the Royal Navy's forces in North America — Adm. Sir James Hope and Gen. James Hope Grant, commanding the British ground forces in Canada. Admiral Hope sailed with the ironclads to replace Milne and with the direct instructions of the Cabinet to bring the American navy to battle and destroy it. James Hope had been the obvious choice for Milne's successor. He was known as fighting admiral and had commanded HMS *Majestic* in the Crimean War and as commander of the East Indies and China Station had smashed through the Taku forts in the Second Opium War in 1859 and later faced down a Russian attempt to seize the island of Tshushima in 1861. He was able, experienced, and aggressive.

Disraeli also played to assuage public fears by stating that ground reinforcements from the British Isles to Canada would not be resumed until Ireland had been settled. His ulterior motive was to hold them for the inevitable clash with the Russians. He also calculated that the Royal Navy's wooden warships could more than deal with the Russian navy.

Through all of this and above all he had warned again and again of the Russian threat. Russian messianic expansionism was the true threat to the British Empire. To destroy Turkey and surge down the Levant to overrun the new Suez Canal under construction would at one stroke sever the promise of efficient communication with the richest jewels of the empire in India and beyond. Then the Russians would march down from Central Asia through Afghanistan to batter on the gates of India itself. In his mind's ear he could hear the bells ringing from one end of Russia to another and wondered by what hellish miscalculations had The British Empire embarked on a two-front war at opposite ends of the planet.

THE PETERSEN BOARDING HOUSE, WASHINGTON, DC, 11:15 A.M., SUNDAY, APRIL 10, 1864

They had all arrived by separate ways to the boarding house used mostly by actors and soldiers. They came in the back way. On the street a man paused, sure that he had recognized one of the men, but shrugged sure that it could not be Sanders. They had served together at the consulate in London more than ten years ago. The man shook his head and walked on, thinking that time had dulled his memory. Sanders and the others found his way to the first floor room just inside the front door.[14]

Anyone passing by would find the door locked. Someone loitered in the hallway outside to make sure no one came by and tried to listen in. Nevertheless, the occupants of the room all spoke in whispers as they huddled around a small table. Inside, besides George Sanders, were Richard McCullough, John Wilkes Booth, and one of Mosby's Rangers named Walter Weems Bowie, and Thomas Harney, from the Confederate War Department Torpedo Bureau known as a destructionist, an expert in explosive devices.

Bowie had until recently been providing the regular connection between the espionage organization in Washington and Lee's army. His summary of Grant's preparation and intended tactics for his spring offensive were so accurate that Lee's use of them played a large part in frustrating the Army of the Potomac when it finally advanced. As Mosby assumed more and more of the responsibility of maintaining that intelligence connection, Bowie transferred to Mosby's command, which then escorted Harney with his explosive devices through the lines to a safe house in Washington.[15]

Sanders was in charge. The original plan had been to blow up the White House with Lincoln, and hopefully his cabinet, but that had become impossible because of the tight security around the building. Sanders commented, "This General Sharpe has the place so tightened up that Lincoln himself needs a pass signed by Sharpe. Everywhere he goes, he is well-guarded now. When he travels to his cottage at the Old Soldiers Home, a company of cavalry accompany him sabers drawn.

"The problem has become not whether we can kill him with a bomb but where we are going to place the bomb. And when. That is where you come in, Booth. We have concluded that the theater is the best place. We know he frequently attends the theater and especially Ford's across the street. We can place the bomb under his box and set it to go off during the performance. The beauty of this is that we know he will come here. We plant the bomb and wait for him."

Booth added, "He is likely to be at Ford's anytime over the next few months. He is sure to come to see my brother play *Hamlet* early next month; I cannot think of a more perfect performance for our business, gentlemen. The play's the thing in which we will do far more than catch the conscience of this king. "He laughed out loud at his own joke. "*Hamlet* is one of Lincoln's favorites." Then he added, the smile falling from his face, "And Edwin his favorite performer." He was jealous of his brother even in the approbation of the man he intended to murder.[16]

"Booth, your job is to get Harlan and the bomb in the theater. That is the one thing we cannot do. It is up to you. Can you do it?"

"Of course, I can." Booth said louder than Sanders would have liked.

"Then we need someone with access to the theater to set it off when Lincoln is in his box. Harlan can't be around when it is time to set it off."

Booth just smiled, radiating the charm that had made him so irresistible. It would be the part of a lifetime.

11

"Just Pitch into Him!"

THE WHITE HOUSE, WASHINGTON, DC, 1:10 A.M., SUNDAY, APRIL 10, 1864
It was a glorious Spring day in Washington made more serene by the
calm of a Sunday. A few church bells still peeled. The dogwoods in
white and pink, wild cherries, redbud trees, and the fragrant purple-
blue wisteria were in blossom. In Dublin at the same time the wagons
with their burdens of pain from the field of Tallaght made their way
to the city's hospitals and churches. People lined the streets, their faces
stricken at the moans and screams from the wagons. Others rushed
along to give water and bread to those inside. From one wagon a shriek
of utter despair rent the air. "My God, why hast Thou forsaken me!"
From the stricken crowd a priest ran forward to climb into the wagon.
He held the young man in his arms and whispered, "Say with me Our
Father," and through shudders of agony, they did, joined by the others
who lay on the blood-slicked straw.

Of this and everything else that had s transpired in Ireland and England,
no word had yet reached North America though steamers were straining
their engines to the limit as they raced across the Atlantic with the news.
It was without that information that Lincoln and his war cabinet would
be determining the future direction of the double war faced by the Union.

Lincoln began a review of the means and resources of war with
a story. "A picket challenged a tug going up Broad River, South
Carolina, with:

"'Who goes there?'"

"'The Secretary of War and Major-General Foster,'" was the pompous
reply.

"'Aw! We've got major-generals enough up here—why don't you
bring us up some hardtack?'"[1]

Lincoln turned to Stanton and Carnegie. "So, boys, do we have
enough hardtack for the rest of this war?"

Stanton, who had learned to live with being the butt of one of Lincoln's stories, nodded to Carnegie, who picked up the thread. "Production of repeaters, ironclads, balloons, and submersibles is on schedule, and in the case of the repeaters, ahead of schedule." It had been to Carnegie's genius for organization that in such short time American industry had been put in such an effective harness as to begin to efficiently producing the new means of war. That effort would be studied for generations.

Lincoln felt the little Scotsman's pause. "But?" he asked.

"Niter, Mr. President. Dupont's best efforts with guncotton have not been successful. The eight thousand tons we on hand will last only until the end of the year. We can scrape more out of caves and dunghills, but it will severely limit our ability to carry on the war in other than a defensive way."

"So we can fight like hell until December, I guess." He looked over at Grant. This was not new ground for either of them, but it was best to have these issues out on the table for those charged with making war.

"Mr. President, if that is our limit, we must defeat the British in Canada first. Then we can finish off the rebels." The general got up and went to the map that covered most of one wall. "If we were to attempt to conquer the whole country, it would dissipate our forces and require time-consuming sieges of Montreal and Quebec. Instead, we grab them by the throat." His finger stabbed at Maine and ran up the Atlantic coast to Halifax. "We retake Maine and drive north to take Halifax. At one stroke we sever the only rail link the British have with Canada and take their major naval base in North America."

Gus Fox added, "Yes, Halifax has all the facilities of a first-class naval base, vital to sustaining a fleet on blockade. They do not have another on this side of the Atlantic. And if they try to run up the St. Lawrence in the summer, we can build forts at points where it narrows to shut it down. Canada withers on the vine."

Grant again: "Sickles's IX Corps will demonstrate against Montreal and hold British forces there, while Sherman and the Army of the Hudson strike to Halifax. By this we force the enemy to disperse while we concentrate at the decisive strategic point."

Seward's hawk-nosed face was smiling. "If you can do this, General, I can squeeze a peace out of the British."

Lincoln stood up and walked over to the map, pointing at Louisiana. "With any luck, if Franklin can take advantage of the raid on Ponchatoula, we may be able to see both of Jeff Davis's foreign friends off. Bazaine should be in a world of hurt about now."

Grant was already revealing more of his plans than he would have liked to, but the President had promised him that the timing and details would be entirely in his hands and that Grant did not even have to inform him. General Sharpe and Lafayette Baker, head of the Secret Service, had been plucking one British spy after another from employees of the federal government. The State Department clerk who had sold the Russo-American treaty to the British had already been tried by military commission and hanged. Sharpe and Baker, however, could not guarantee that there were not others.

Seward could usually see the flaws in any argument and asked, "And what of the rebels while we subdue Canada? Are we to give them the rest of the year for nothing?"

"No, our armies will move against theirs at the first opportunity. Every army will be committed so that the rebels cannot shift reinforcements from one to the other front."

What Lincoln and Grant had not wanted to discuss even in front of the war cabinet was the news from Richmond courtesy of Miss Van Lew that Longstreet was being detached from Lee to strike at Fort Monroe.[2] That news had been reinforced by the scouts and agents of the Army of the Potomac who observed the movement of the Confederate First Corps in the direction of the James Peninsula.[3] Even if the fort held out, the tenuous supply route across the peninsula and the James River to Norfolk Naval Base would be severed. Then it would be the fleet at Norfolk and the Army of the James that would wither on the vine.

NEW ORLEANS, 2:00 P.M., SUNDAY, APRIL 10, 1864

Bazaine was, indeed, in a world of hurt. He had returned to New Orleans to remonstrate with Taylor over the withdrawal of most of his troops for the expedition to Arkansas when Ponchetoula fell. The French Army before Port Hudson was cut off at one stroke, its supply line severed. He at once set out to ride the more than hundred miles along the Mississippi to rejoin his army. With every mile his heart sickened as it was driven home to him that there was no road that paralleled the river. The river itself had been the great highway of Louisiana, and the U.S Navy controlled it most of the way. The roads that did exist all fed from the great sugar and cotton plantations to the wharves along the river. Everything else was a country lane. Where there were no plantations, pine woods stretched forever.

It would take four days of hard riding on good roads for Bazaine to reach his army. Without those roads Bazaine realized that he simply would never arrive in time to save his army. The only recourse was the river, as dangerous as it was. He commandeered a fast French steamer and ordered it north. When the captain objected, saying the American

Navy prowled the river, he shouted, "Damn the Americans. I, a Marshal of France, command you."

For Maj. Gen. Félix Charles Douay, acting commander of the Armée de Louisiane, the hurt was far more immediate. The continued siege of Port Hudson was clearly untenable. The army itself was trapped. There was no hope of retaking the depot at Ponchetoula. The Americans were snapping up the blockhouses on the road, and his own cavalry could only delay the strong American cavalry force pushing toward Baton Rouge. There was no escape by the river either. The only way out was overland along the roadless riverbank. For Douay the decision was obvious, which did not make it any easier. Douay was a good soldier who had fought in the Crimea and Italy; his bravery at Magenta and Solferino had been rewarded with general's rank. He did not suffer from a want of physical or moral courage. In any case, Franklin decided for him by coming out from Port Hudson with most of his army to maneuver around his flank. Leaving part of his cavalry to delay him, Douay promptly evacuated the siege works and marched south to Baton Rouge.

Franklin rushed after to snap at his heels. He sent messenger after messenger to Grierson to press to Baton Rouge at all costs. If he could take the city before the French, they could bag the whole army. More importantly, Franklin the next day had put two infantry brigades on transports under Admiral Porter's command to seize Baton Rouge before the French arrived. The current and the transports' engines made far better time than even the most hurried pace of the French infantry.

Porter's gunboats and ironclads surged down the river escorting the Union brigades, and with them were a dozen mortar boats that had been used to lob their huge shells up and onto Vicksburg on its high bluff. The French columns were already flowing south along the road that paralleled the river. Beginning five miles north of Baton Rouge the road swerved to parallel the river on some low bluffs barely two hundred yards inland. As Porter's ships steamed past, the crews could see the columns in their blue coats and red pantaloons, the undefeated might of the French Army, marching at that quick pace perfected originally under Napoleon I. Between the regiments artillery batteries with their bronze guns drove their teams on.

At the sight of Porter's flotilla, Douay shouted "*Merde!*" and turned to order his regiments to peel away inland. Too late. Porter had signaled from his flagship the order to fire at that very moment. The big guns of the ironclads and gunboats rippled in a continuous thunder sending their balls and shells directly into the dense column. At two hundred yards they could not miss; there had not been a more one-sided slaughter since Pickett's Charge at Gettysburg. The guns were followed by the mortars dropping huge shells onto the road and beyond where the French were fleeing. That beyond was nothing but muddy cane and cotton fields. Whole gun teams were swept away on the road or trapped in the sucking mud of the fields to be cut down as their drivers desperately but uselessly whipped their horses on. From the flotilla, through the smoke, observers could see bodies and even guns and caissons hurled through the air.

Douay never got to issue his order, for his body was one of those sailing skyward to fall broken into the cane. No one knew to take command. The lead French brigades had been savaged and had fled through the fields pursued by shrieking shells and solid shot. The rest of the column that had not come in range backed up in confusion as terrified men came running back down road stampeding around the regiments still on the road.

In that hour of chaos, Porter's transports landed at Baton Rouge and poured ashore the infantry brigades against feeble resistance. The city had been the logistics base of the Franco-Confederate army and was filled with warehouses, remount corrals, hospitals, wagon parks, and all the other services and facilities that keep armies alive. There were almost no combat troops other than provost guards, and these were brushed aside. Within another hour they were fighting off the attempt of the remnants of the French cavalry being pushed upon the city by Grierson's superior force. Again and again the French turned to throw charges at the Americans. Grierson had dismounted some of his regiments to use their repeaters against which the French charges collapsed. His other regiments counterattacked, joined by the infantry coming from the docks. Surrounded, the French commander recognized reality and rode out to Grierson under a white flag to offer his sword. Only a squadron of Chasseurs d'Afrique managed to find an opening to the south of the city and cut their way through.

Grierson took command of the combined force and prepared to defend the city. More American infantry began arriving by transport until he had ten thousand men at hand. At the same time Franklin's two corps made contact with the rear of the French army, deployed into line of battle, and attacked. Clumsily the French tried to deploy out of column. At the same time, Porter's mortar boats began sending their shells in high trajectories into them. These heavy shells meant to smash fortifications were great man-killers.

Grierson's patrols told him of the unfolding battle to the north of Baton Rouge and he led his troops out of the city to attack. The French fought back; they were veterans of countless battles in Algeria, the Crimea, Italy, and Mexico, but they fought not as an army but as broken parts. No one knew who was in command. Panic spread on that same wind, as cries of *"Sauve qui peut!"* (Save yourselves!) began to signal the unraveling of the force in a mass of terrified men. Soldiers started to surrender, but still a core of tough men fought on, now pressed into a tightening circle, a deadly target for coffee mill guns and infantry repeaters. At five in the afternoon the remnant of the Armeé de Louisiane threw down its weapons.

As the French army died, the captain of the French steamer pushed his boilers beyond the danger point to take Bazaine up river. With every mile the steamer's captain marveled at the absence of American ships and rejoiced at his good fortune. He would have not been so elated had he known that they were concentrated at Baton Rouge assisting in the destruction of the French army. As for Bazaine, he was more than elated. He was convinced that his star was still strong and it would carry him to his army in time. A few miles below Baton Rouge, that run of luck ended with the sighting of that pall of smoke that signaled a battle ashore followed by an American ironclad coming downriver. Bazaine ordered the captain to put him ashore even if it meant running the steamer aground, and that was just what it took. He jumped his horse into the water and struggled ashore, put his spurs to it, and galloped north. It was not too long before he encountered the chasseurs fleeing the fall of the city. They were spent men, drained of courage. They followed him reluctantly but peeled away a few at a time till he rode alone. Still he rode on.

KENNER, LOUISIANA, 8:25 P.M., SUNDAY, APRIL 10, 1864

This small town on the New Orleans, Jackson, and Great Northern Railroad was just settling into bed when the trains came down from Ponchatoula one after another and sped south the eight miles to the Crescent City. Ponchatoula had fallen six days before, but the Confederates had had no direct word other than the broad hint that none of the trains they had sent north had returned and that the telegraph had gone dead. The railroad ran on a raised bed through thirty-five miles of swamp with lakes Pontchartrain and Maurepas on either side, a rather effective barrier to communications.[4]

It had occurred to Grierson after the capture of Ponchatoula now that he was driving the French back to Baton Rouge that the Corps d'Afrique would be unemployed. He was a firm believer that when offensive operations were underway, no one should be sitting on his hands. As a result the men of the corps filled the railcars speeding through Kenner, all five thousand of them. A half hour later they erupted from those cars into the main railroad station in New Orleans. The city fell as quickly as it had to Admiral Farragut's fleet in April 1862. New Orleans was profoundly undefensible. It had no advantages of ground and instead possessed the ruinous disadvantage being at sea level. The Confederate brigade and French regiment in garrison were caught in their barracks and camps able to offer only a brief though spirited fight.[5]

Clio Dulaine and Pryce Lewis crawled out of bed that next morning after a wild night celebrating the fall of the city to the thunder of guns. Clio threw open the French doors to the wrought-iron balcony to see the Stars and Stripes waving over city hall once again as the *libres* filled the streets in a spontaneous festival that put Mardi Gras to shame.[6]

THE DOGGER BANKS, 8:10 A.M., MONDAY, APRIL 11, 1864

A fishing smack drifted through the fog that blanketed the sea. A rich fishery of cod and herring sixty-two miles off the eastern coast of England, the Dogger Banks covered 6,800 shallow square miles and ran 161 miles north-south and fifty-nine east-west in the middle of the North Sea.[7] It was into this that Dahlgren had steered their stolen boat in order to hide in plain sight. The banks were heavily fished by large numbers of British trawlers and among them he calculated the smack would arouse no curiosity.

The smack had led a double life, a legitimate fishing boat to any inspector and a smuggler by night. Woolen sweaters and slickers found onboard gave them an unobtrusive look as they slipped eastward through the marshes and out into the North Sea on a late tide with falling darkness to hide them from the Royal Navy patrols. Luckily those patrols had thinned as the British concentrated their warships to isolate Ireland.

Although they shared no language, Dahlgren and Feodor worked wordlessly together in the language of small boats. Collins's time was devoted to whatever unskilled help Dahlgren needed but mostly to tending Rimsky-Korsakov, whose wound was getting worse. The rations they had found aboard had lasted until the day before, and the water would run out in only another day or two. Luckily the fog was so thick that it seemed to congeal on the skin and run down the face. Simply sticking out the tongue would refresh a man, but ultimately it could do little more. The fog that acted like a cloak of invisibility also meant that the wind was still. They drifted among the trawlers, only occasionally seeing a vapor-blurred lantern and then a shrouded shape loom out of the fog.

Dahlgren had hoped to slip through the British trawlers in the Banks and then dash for the entrance to the Baltic. His goal ultimate was St. Petersburg, the only allied port in Europe. From the Russian capital he could get back into the war, and Kolya could return the Imperial colors in his charge. Other ports such as Hamburg, Bremen, and Copenhagen were closer and safer but would mean he would be interned to sit out the war. But as Kolya sickened, it became clear that he would be dead before they ever reached the eastern Baltic. Already he was delirious. In any case, the rest of them would be dead of hunger and thirst shortly thereafter.

Those cheerful thoughts were cut off by the low eerie moan of a foghorn and the sound of a paddle wheel slowly churning water. Dahlgren instantly went on guard. Collins and Feodor froze. Collins leaned over and put his hand over Kolya's mouth. The fishing trawlers were all sail-powered; what was coming near was not a fisherman. The *slap-slap* of the paddle wheel grew nearer. The foghorn sounded its fugue warning, low and deep, ghostlike. The *slap-slap* drew nearer. There was nothing they could do; the air was still as the sound came on them. The ship appeared dimly through the fog, a bare glimpse, its gun ports open, its great encased paddle wheel, cascading with water, then was swallowed up by the fog again. Another low rumble of its horn told them it was steaming away.

HEADQUARTERS, HER MAJESTY'S FORCES IN NORTH AMERICA, MONTREAL, 1:11 P.M., TUESDAY, APRIL 12, 1864

Sharpe may have disrupted the British spy ring in Washington, but Wolseley's agents were thickly spread across the entire Canadian-American border. He did not have to have a transcript of the American decision to knock the British out of Canada to conclude what was coming. Detailed information of the concentration of the Army of the Hudson at Kennebunk told him all he needed to know. Hope Grant listened carefully to all of this and merely grunted, "Of course, that's what any fool would do."

He hobbled along on his cane and sat in a sunny window to gaze out at the river below. His wound still pained him, though he would not say a word. "Doyle will be lucky to delay Sherman. Damned railway." The Americans were finally using their numbers where it would count. Lt. Gen. Sir Hastings Doyle, who had finally taken Portland, had fewer than fifteen thousand men. Sherman would be coming at him with sixty thousand or more. Even that instinctive sense of British superiority blanched at those odds. They would not be facing savages armed with sharpened mangos either.

The operational problem was not just one of numbers. Unless Portland and the area immediately to the south could be defended, it would not matter if Doyle was able to delay Sherman's drive north. The loss of the railway would be fatal, and the railway ran through Portland up the Maine-Vermont border to Quebec A decisive battle would have to be fought to save the railway south of Portland. Grant just sat in the sun and thought. An occasional word or grunt was all Wolseley could hear.

HEADQUARTERS, ARMY OF THE POTOMAC, BRANDY STATION, VIRGINIA, 9:20 A.M., WEDNESDAY, APRIL 13, 1864

Ever since Babcock's scouts had begun to bring him information on the movement of Longstreet's corps, Meade rejoiced at the opening to strike Lee with one-third of the Army of Northern Virginia absent. He did more than rejoice. He ordered the Army of the Potomac to be ready to move. Lee represented not just the main army of the Rebellion and not just a great general whose reputation was enough to unnerve an enemy. For Meade, Lee was the source of his mortification. Lee had oh-so-cleverly humbugged him last year to slip past him and attack Washington. The nation's capital had come within an ace of falling to the combined British-Confederate attack. Lincoln had withstood tremendous political pressure to relieve him. He had not forgotten Gettysburg. Meade's reputation, an officer's most precious possession, now depended on vindicating Lincoln's faith in him.

That meant crushing Lee. It was one thing, however to withstand Lee's hammer blows at Gettysburg and entirely another to smash him in a battle of maneuver. If ever there was a man determined to try, it was Meade. The reequipment of half of his infantry with Spencers and the incorporation of dozens of Gatlings was an advantage he was eager to employ.

The telegram from Grant that morning was all he needed to order the army to march toward Lee, who was concentrated at Gordonsville. The grass was not yet high enough to graze the tens of thousands of horses and mules of the army. Yet he calculated that it was not high enough to feed Lee's animals either. Instead, he emptied every wagon that carried tents or personal property to fill them with fodder.

Lee for his part had had a healthy respect for Meade even before Gettysburg, and the battle had only certified it.[8] Yet, he thought he could avoid a pitched battle and delay Meade by maneuver and entrenchment long enough for Longstreet to snap the supply lines that sustained the Federals in the James Peninsula and at Norfolk. Lee was confident. For the first time in the war, his men were well-clothed, well-shod, and well-fed. There was an abundance of everything now that an army could want, and all made in England or France. That included several batteries of excellent breech-loading Whitworth rifled guns whose accuracy at long range was legend. Gone were the days when a British visitor like Wolseley would stare open-mouthed at a Confederate division marching past with the seat out of hundreds of pair of trousers. Lee had said that was no problem since the enemy never saw that part of them. The despondent war-weariness that had settled over his army after Gettysburg had been replaced with a sense of optimism that the war was now winnable with the British and French on their side.

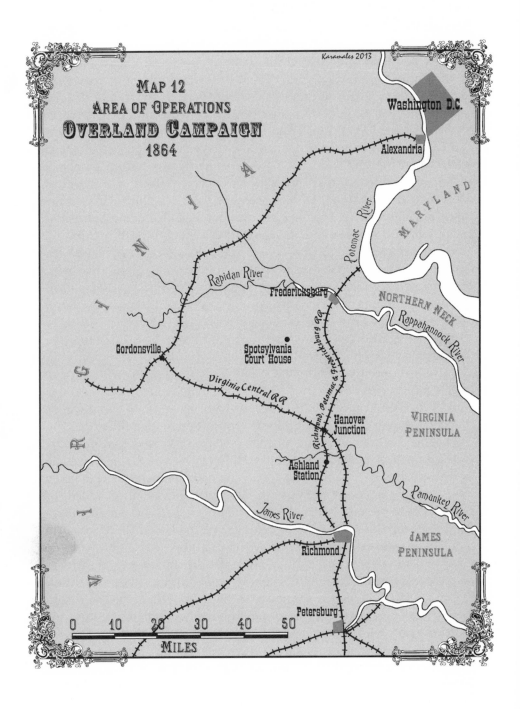

YORKTOWN, VIRGINIA, 8:20 A.M., FRIDAY, APRIL 15, 1864

The alert from Sharpe that Longstreet was on the way never reached Baldy Smith, who had only assumed command of the new Army of the James in the last few days. The 9th Virginia Cavalry, whose specialty was scouting and raiding, had cut the tenuous Union communications across the Northern Neck. Longsreet's First Corps sped by train from Gordonsville to Richmond and then force marched to Yorktown on the James Peninsula, its advance guard actually passing on the road one of Van Lew's messengers trying to get through Union lines.

Smith had been played a very bad hand. His Army of the James included the X and XVIII Corps, all very fine on paper, but the troops for them had not been able to be gathered into the planned order-of-battle because the British controlled the waterways of the bay and the rivers that would have allowed for their distribution. Most troops were in the Plymouth-Norfolk area across the James River from Fortress Monroe. Most of the regiments evacuated from enclaves on the coasts of North and South Carolina had put in there along with the North and South Atlantic Blockading Squadrons. The X Corps and most of the troops intended for XVIII Corps crowded into the area, numbering over forty thousand men.

Worse off was XVIII Corps, only recently under the command of Maj. Gen. Godfrey Weitzel. Another of the U.S. Army's superb engineers, Weitzel had been rewarded with corps command for his accomplishments as chief engineer of the Army of the James. Now it was the very defenses he had constructed that bared Longstreet's way. Those defenses consisted of the remodeled Confederate fort at Yorktown on the York River and the other fortifications that stretched across the three miles across the peninsula all manned by only one brigade. At Newport News on the James there was a brigade and some cavalry and artillery. The garrison of Fortress Monroe was barely two thousand men, mostly heavy artillery, who would be no use in the field. Outside the Fortress itself in the vicinity of the ruined town of Hamilton were the five thousand men of two brigades from the force that had been besieging Charleston when the war began.

Of all the forces evacuated with the blockading squadrons, these two brigades had been landed on the James Peninsula instead of Norfolk. One brigade was made up of four regiments of hard men from New Hampshire and Maine commanded by Col. Thomas G. Stevenson. The other could not have been more different. Commanded by Col. James Montgomery, it consisted of the 54th Massachusetts and 3rd and 34th U.S. Colored Troops (U.S.C.T.).[9] The first two regiments had been raised from free men of color in Boston and Philadelphia. The last had been recruited from liberated slaves in South Carolina. Montgomery had one of the most unsavory reputations in the army. A Kansas Jayhawker, he was described as "a sincere, if unscrupulous, antislavery zealot."[10] He had burnt undefended Southern towns, stating "that the Southerners must be made to feel that this was a real war, and that they were to be swept away by the hand of God, like the Jews of old." He had raised the 34th from escaped slaves, and discipline had never been strict, not much called for in the burning of defenseless plantations and towns and in brushes with state militia.[11]

Bivouacked near the ruins of Hamilton, Montgomery's regiments were in the midst of the more than fifteen thousand contrabands from nearby areas of Virginia, most of the adults employed as a workforce for the army. The hallelujahs rang to the heavens when they beheld so many black men smartly wearing Union blue. Montgomery's regiments marched north to join Weitzel's single brigade at Yorktown, for upon assuming command, the corps commander had ordered all three brigades forward. With them was the 1st U.S. Colored Cavalry Regiment. It had recently been formed, but had been recruited from veteran infantry and the so-called "outlaw negroes" who had roamed the swamps of eastern Virginia and North Carolina, men who had already freed themselves.[12]

Smith had no inkling of the approach of the mighty First Corps of the Army of Northern Virginia. Instead, his attention was now riveted by the renewed assault by the Royal Navy on Fortress Monroe. He watched awestruck as the heavily armored gunboats, mortar vessels, and floating batteries of the Great Armament poured shot and shell at the granite walls of the fort and lobed the huge 36-inch mortar shells, inside. turning barracks, hospitals, repair shops into a shambles.[13]

The gun crews cheered as 15-inch shot from the giant Rodman guns in the fort's casemates spat their 440-pound shot to hole a number of those same batteries. One was already sinking and another floating away on fire as its exploding ammunition threw debris high into the air. The British fire hardly slackened; there were dozens of those vessels. Behind them steamed frigates, and especially the great broadside ironclads, HMS *Warrior* and *Defiance* in case the surviving U.S. Navy's monitors dared come out and fight again and risk being "Bazelgetted" again as the expression came to be.

Smith was no longer a witness to this grand spectacle. He had collapsed inside the casemate from which he was watching the battle. His staff rushed to him as he shivered and writhed on the stone floor, a cold, clammy feel to his skin. One of them said, "It's the malaria again." They made him as comfortable as they could; to move him was to run the deadly risk of crossing the mortar-swept central yard of the fort. Nor did anyone think to inform the commander of the XVIII Corps that he, as senior officer of the Army of the James, was now in command of the army.

WARWICK COURTHOUSE, VIRGINIA, 9:20 P.M., FRIDAY, APRIL 15, 1864

Weitzel, even if he had known of his succession to the command, had enough to do for at that moment Longstreet fell on the defenses of the peninsula with two of his divisions. It was a magnificent show, but little more than that, for the Confederate field artillery was not all that effective against substantial earthworks. It was enough, though, for Longstreet's purpose — to fix the enemy's attention on his front. Just by sitting on the peninsula, he severed Union resupply of both Fortress Monroe and Norfolk.

A flotilla of barges led by Confederate gunboats came down the James and landed just below the outlet of the Warwick River near the Warwick (County) Courthouse. For the first time in almost three years, the Confederates no longer had to fear the superior U.S. Navy presence on the James. A shortage of coal kept the gunboats that normally patrolled the river moored at the Norfolk Navy Yard. Hood's old division, now commanded by Maj. Gen. Charles W. Field, poured ashore and struck east for the road that led to Fortress Monroe. A hard-fighting, able man, Fields wasted no time. It was twelve miles to Hampton, the town outside Fortress Monroe. As he rode to the head of the column, he shouted to each regiment, "March on, boys! March on!"

Colonels Montgomery and Stevens were at the same time also urging their men forward on the same road but going north. The brigade from Newport News was taking a parallel road at the same time. Eight thousand Union and Ten thousand Confederate troops were about to collide, to each other's total surprise. This was the classic meeting engagement in which the side that attacks first and aggressively would usually win by seizing the moral ascendancy. That rule was about to be modified by circumstances. The point of collision was in three-mile strip of wooded country cut by swamps and waterways with almost no room for maneuver. It was near one of the first skirmishes of the war in 1861 at Big Bethal.

It turned ugly with the first shots. The 1st Texas of the famed Texas Brigade was in the lead and marching to a fight, though they did not expect it for another six miles. The lead Union regiment was the 34th U.S.C.T. with Colonel Montgomery riding at its head, the senior officer. A quick-witted Texan's bullet punched a hole in his forehead.

The Texans responded to the sight of black troops with a burst of rage that drove their bayonet charge deep into the ranks of Montgomery's men. The 34th, both ill-disciplined and surprised, panicked and broke with the Texans pursuing them with no-quarter. Behind them the 54th formed across the road at the opening sound of gunfire. In minutes fugitives from the 34th were pushing through their ranks. The Texans' bayonets were within yards of them when the 54th fired. Stunned by the point-blank fire, the Texans hesitated. The 54th charged and drove them back upon 4th Texas, which in turn fired and stopped the Union attack. Now both sides began to try to find the enemy's flanks by extending their lines with new regiments on either side of the road in the woods as they came up. They quickly found swamps on either flank, leaving a gap of barely a quarter mile. So it became a slugging match. The 3rd U.S.C.T. held the 54th's right while Brigadier General Stevens came up to assume command of the fight and feed his own regiments to the left. A few miles to the west, the Newport News brigade ran into a Confederate brigade also trying to use that parallel road. They too were also hemmed in by the woods, waterways, and swamps and could only crowd together to pound away at each other. The Second Battle of Big Bethal in its first minutes had surpassed the butcher's bill of the 1861 skirmish. Neither side could gain an advantage as they went on killing. Luckily for the 1st Colored Cavalry, they could take no part in what was an infantry donnybrook. Stevens threw them out on his far right flank, beyond the natural obstacles, to cover a wide expanse of open fields lest the Confederates attempt to flank the Union brigades. As senior officer on the field, he also assumed control of the Newport News Brigade fighting to the east and ordered its 3rd New York Cavalry to reinforce the 1st Colored on his open flank.

At the same time farther to the north, Longstreet's assaults broke through the defenses west of Yorktown. Weiztel was barely able to save his men behind the fortifications of Yorktown as most of Longstreet's two divisions surged south. All he could do was take the enemy under fire with the guns of the fort before they disappeared into the woods. More than twenty thousand Confederates were about to show up at the Second Battle of Big Bethal within a few hours. Weitzel could only watch them in silent rage. He could see from beyond the woods the puffs of rifle fire from his lone cavalry regiment, as Col. Benjamin F. Onderdonk's 1st New York Mounted Rifles tried to delay the onrushing Confederates.

Longstreet was informed quickly of the stalemate at Big Bethal and switched his brigades to the west at Halfway House. West of the constricted area in which the battle was being fought was a six-mile stretch of open fields bisected by the Northwest Branch of the Back River arising from the swamps Black Kiln Creek. South of the river, the two Union cavalry regiments were the only Union force in Longstreet's way. They had deployed to cover the ford just below the mill a few hundred yards south of the bridge over the river. Elsewhere the banks were marshy, though occasionally they would have thirty to fifty feet of solid ground easily bridgeable with timbers.[14]

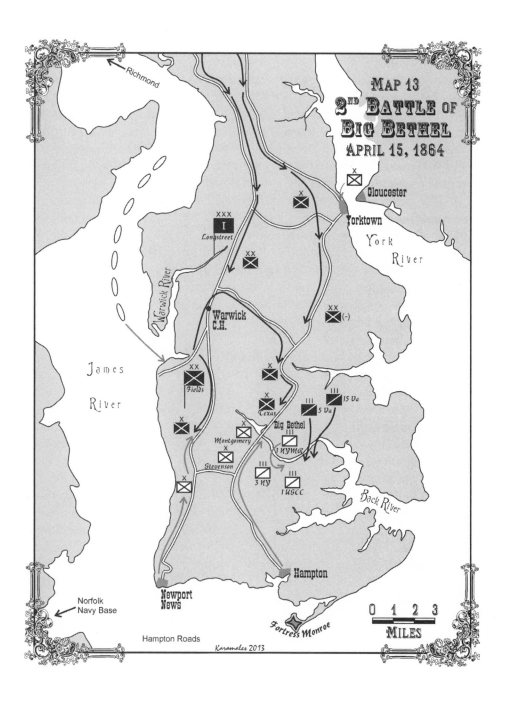

MAP 13
2ND BATTLE OF
BIG BETHEL
APRIL 15, 1864

Before long men from the 1st New York Mounted Rifles, mostly wounded, began drifting back across the ford describing how their boys were up against the two detached Virginia cavalry regiments of Lomax's Brigade. Lee had chosen them to reinforce Longstreet because some of the men from the 5th and 15th Virginia Cavalry had been recruited from the James Peninsula and nearby Northern Neck. They were invaluable now in using every well-known fold in the ground, trail, and copse to steadily push Onderdonk's men back. They needed every bit of local guile because Onderdonk's men were armed with Sharps repeaters. They had been recruited as mounted rifles, paid for their own weapons, and thereby packed a much heavier punch than other cavalry regiments armed with only the older Sharps single-shot carbine.

The New York men began filtering back now by platoons and companies, splashing across the river to take up positions behind the makeshift defenses already thrown up by the other two cavalry regiments. They could see the puffs of black gunpowder smoke not too far off showing where the last of Onderdonk's men were still fighting. Then firing stopped, and the last company came galloping down to the river and splashed across the ford. The last man was their colonel, who conspicuously turned his horse on the riverbank to fire one last round at the enemy before spurring the animal across.

As senior officer he took command of all three cavalry regiments and would gladly have stood off three enemy brigades if they tried to force the ford. The cavalry breechloaders and repeaters gave him a considerable firepower advantage. Longstreet was not about to make it that easy for him, though. The enemy cavalry departed to the west while Confederate infantry columns now appeared. Artillery batteries wheeled into place and immediately opened fire. The first rounds passed over the men crouching behind their quickly dug, shallow holes to land among the horses behind held in the rear. For every three men in the firing line, a fourth was holding their horses. Into this shell after shell exploded, killing and panicking man and beast. Then the guns shifted to the cavalrymen along the bank. Onderdonk realized that he could not hold against the guns and the heavy infantry assault that was moving toward the ford. He sent a messenger galloping to Brig. Gen. Stevens fighting in the woods and swamps.

Stevens was pleased that he had stopped the enemy cold, a strange term now that the woods were burning. It had been a dry spring, and fighting had set the pine straw and dry leaves afire. Flames raced up the pines to consume their crowns in searing explosions. The men on both sides drew back, dragging the wounded where they could. Where they couldn't shrieks keened above the roar of the fire. Nature had come to his aid, he thought, until the messenger thrust Onderdonk's dispatch into his hand. It read, "Large infantry force supported by artillery is attacking. I can no longer hold your flank. I can delay while you withdraw." Now Stevens was faced with the most difficult of all maneuvers—to break contact and retreat in the face of a determined and skillful enemy. His first action was to send the messenger on with his own order to the Newport News brigade to retreat to Hamilton.

Stevens walked down the firing line giving his orders and shouting to his boys that the Good Lord had barred the enemy's way with fire to protect their flanks as he had done to save the Israelites from the Egyptians. It was just the margin they needed as he began pulling them out. In an hour, save for the rearguard, they were crossing the bridge over Southwest Branch of the Back River and filing into the landward defenses of Fortress Monroe, a line of earthworks that stretched from the river two miles to an inlet on off the bay. Onderdonk was as good as his word and had held the ford as long as he could, which was long enough. The Confederate infantry forced the ford, but Onderdonk's cavalry delayed until Lomax's cavalry appeared from the west where they had made a makeshift bridge. Their charge in the Union right finally collapsed the cavalry's organized opposition and turned it into a rout. Longstreet's artillery caught them again as they were streaming over the bridge clogging it with dead and dying horses and men. Lomax's regiments crashed into the bunched survivors who had not been able to cross. A few men with the presence to jump off their horses and pick their way over the bridge escaped. The rest were cut down or captured. To the east the Confederate brigades cut off the retreat of the Newport New brigade. Only a few hundred men were able to make it to Hamilton. The rest surrendered. Thus ended Second Big Bethal, a shattering Union defeat that now put the landward side of Fortress Monroe under Confederate artillery fire and hung a hideous fate over the fifteen thousand contrabands trapped outside its walls. For with the Confederate forces came the slave catchers to return them to their masters.[15]

MONTREAL RAILWAY STATION, 2:45 P.M., SATURDAY, APRIL 16, 1864

If Wolseley had spies across the border so did Sharpe in reverse. It did not take long for them to begin relaying information that most of the Montreal Field Force had been given marching orders to entrain at Montreal. The Irish were very helpful in this and very well placed, not in the chambers of high council but in the laundries and stables where a keen eye and ear can learn just as much.

The news of the American raids on the British Isles, especially the seizure of Dublin and the declaration of the Irish Republic, had stunned

all of Canada. Without a shot being fired in North America, the British
population there suffered a paralytic crisis in confidence. If the Americans
could do what France, Spain, and Russia never could, then the pillars of
their world suddenly trembled. It dawned on the Anglo-Canadians that
they really could lose this war in a replay of the American Revolution
when the peace agreed to by the Crown forced their Tory or Loyalist
ancestor to abandon their homes and migrate to Canada in the first place.
This time there was nowhere else to go if the Stars and Stripes waved
from Halifax to Montreal.

For the French Canadians the prospect that their British overlords
would surrender them as readily as their French ones had in 1763 at the end
of the Seven Years War was suddenly a reality.[16] More than one decided
it was time to hedge their bets. For them adjusting to new overlords was
something they had practiced for almost a hundred years already.

None of this affected Hope Grant's decision to fight it out. If
anything, the news that Lee was dispatching Longstreet to drive the
Americans out of their redoubts at Norfolk and Fortress Monroe made it
imperative. Simultaneous operations against the Americans at opposite
ends of their country would seriously stress them. They could not be
strong everywhere. He quickly dispatched the fourteen thousand men
of his 2nd Division and the Guards Brigade to reinforce Hastings Doyle at
Portland. He also ordered a dozen more Canadian battalions to reinforce
him. All in all, it would give Hastings almost forty thousand men. He
had no doubt that his remaining division could fend off any attempt by
Sickles and his corps to threaten Montreal.

To underline his priority he sent Wolseley off to support Doyle. To his
infinite distress, his wounds bound him to his headquarters in Montreal.
As Wolseley took his leave, Grant drove the point home. "Joe, we're rolling
for the whole pot. Give them a bloody nose, and we make it through
another year. Victories, Joe. Governments like victories." He willed himself
to recover; he would not miss the coming battle for the world.

There was more than one man in Montreal who would not miss
the coming fight for all the world. Martin Hogan was one of them. He
had volunteered to be a nurse in the American prisoner hospital on the
outskirts of the city. The British fed and cared for their prisoners far better
than either the Union or the Confederacy. So it was a rare man who left a
warm, well-fed barracks to carry on among the gangrene and death, and
the British were eager for any volunteer with no questions asked.

If the barracks had been well-fed, they had also been well-guarded
and had not yielded a single crack to Hogan's guile. The hospital could
be no worse and probably a damn sight better with so much coming
and going amid the tension of death and suffering. There his guile fell

on fruitful ground. Security was not a priority for the Royal Medical Corps. "God bless 'em," said Martin under his breath. What security there was to the camp was a single Canadian sentry all of fifteen years old, a boy really without a beard and gangly like a colt who stood with a rifle almost as tall as he was by the hospital doors.

Hogan walked into an alcove where white smocks for medical personnel lined a wall on pegs. He snatched one and threw it on. As he walked out he picked up a clipboard and a pencil. The pencil he stuck behind his ear, and seemingly without a care in the world he walked out of the hospital, his eyes intent on the papers attached to the clipboard, and right past the oblivious guard.

A few blocks away into the town Hogan concluded another change of coat was prudent. The opportunity staggered past him, a Canadian volunteer with too much good cheer. Hogan clapped a friendly hand on his shoulder, suggested they stop for another drink, and guided him to an alley. A few minutes later, the scout emerged with a new scarlet coat and shako. Feeling rather pleased with himself, he walked around a corner and right into the arms of the Provost Guard. They were rounding up strays, put Hogan with a half-dozen forlorn volunteers and marched them to the train station where the reinforcements for Doyle were loading. That afternoon he was heading east coincidentally on the same train as Wolseley.

SAN FRANCISCO, CALIFORNIA, 2:22 P.M., SATURDAY, APRIL 17, 1864

Sam Clemmons had the bar captivated with his story of a jumping frog. He was in rare form, so rare, indeed, that he kept a room full of San Franciscans indoors on a gloriously clear and sunny day. He was winding the final punch line when the sound of cannon from the bay was heard. He improvised a line: "Ah, even our Russian friends appreciate the story." A certain relief went through the audience; San Francisco had been worried when the Russian squadron had left, especially since there had been no word of their whereabouts since their prize crews had brought a dozen captured British ships to the bay. Now their return would reestablish the security of the city. But the sound was different from the normal salutes fired by the Russians when passing the fort at the entrance to the bay and the return salutes. It was growing into a continuous roar. His story fell flat as every head turned to the doors of the saloon.

Minutes seemed to pass as no one moved. The spell was broken when the doors burst open and someone ran into to shout, "The British! The British are attacking the forts!" The saloon emptied in seconds as everyone rushed into the street. The roar of the cannonade was now

plain to hear. A pall of smoke could be seen rising from the Golden
Gate. People ran to rooftops and balconies to watch as the Royal Navy's
frigates sailed back and forth pounding the great masonry fort at the
narrows of the Golden Gate.

What no one could hear or see in San Francisco that day were
the hundreds of long boats pushing out from two dozen transports on the
lower seaward side of the San Francisco Peninsula. The British had
gambled on the weather, low odds indeed at this time of year when the
coast was often fogbound in the San Francisco Bay area of which Sam
Clemmons someday would write that the coldest winter he had ever
spent was one summer in San Francisco. It took a large dose of Nelson's
luck. The Royal Navy had discovered once more that acceptance of bold
risk more than anything else was the surest way to summon Nelson's
ghost. Its reward was a fine, sunny day.

It took great skill at handling boats to get them through the heavy
surf, but the British tars were up to it. Of the scores of boats only two were
capsized, spilling their crews and red coated passengers into the cold
50-degree water, some to die of hypothermia before they could be fished
out, a deadly payment for the expedition's good luck. From those that
landed first, British infantry sped up the rising beach to the high ground
and looked down beyond into dunes and scrub. San Francisco beckoned
only a few miles beyond. Over the next few hours five thousand men
from five British regiments and accompanying artillery and engineers had
been put ashore. By late afternoon they were marching on San Francisco,
whose only defenses faced the sea.[17]

HEADQUARTERS, PORTLAND FIELD FORCE, PORTLAND, MAINE, 3:49 P.M., WEDNESDAY, APRIL 20, 1864

Wolesely's single eye scanned the report to find its essence, then carefully
reread it to absorb the totality of it. He shook his head in admiration. Hope
Grant had been right. The Americans could not be strong everywhere.
The American VI Corps had quickly departed Kennebunk to return to
the Army of the Potomac. The odds had suddenly become tolerable.

It was clear that Lee had poked a very sharp stick in the American
eye. Dispatches just arrived from the army's liaison with the Royal
Navy's blockade force in the Chesapeake reported that Fortress Monroe
was tightly invested by Longstreet and under relentless attack by the
navy. Meade was trying to bring Lee to battle, but the grand master of
war had dodged and sidestepped him time and time again as the days
melted away. Wolseley could have wished for more information from
the spy ring in Washington, but it recently had gone quiet. He did not
like that. He would have to goad them into action.

SS *VASA* IN THE SKAGGERACK, 8:55 P.M., APRIL 20, 1864

Dahlgren leaned against the railing and drank in the cool Scandinavian spring. The ship was passing through the strait separating the North from the Baltic Seas, with Denmark on their right and Sweden on their left. It had been five days since his companions and he had been plucked out the water, near death from thirst, by the *Vasa*. Looking back, it seemed like a miracle. When the fog had lifted, he steered out of the banks and the protection of the British fishing fleet in a hopeless attempt to reach Denmark before they all succumbed. A squall had given them enough water to slake immediate thirst. Kolya hung on, poor boy, humming something about a bumblebee.

It had appeared as a small smoke trail to the northwest, by all odds another British warship. His sail could not match the speed of the ship's engines as the distance closed. Eventually the ship's outline became visible, and there were no gunports picked out in white paint. He put the smack on an intercept course; again, the odds were still that it was a British ship. Captivity, after all, was better than an ignominious, unknown death at sea. The ship was just over a quarter mile away when Dahlgren made out its colors—blue and yellow.

He let go the rudder, painfully rose, and began waving his arms and shouting. Feodor and Collins looked at him as if he had gone mad, but the Russian took the rudder and kept the smack on course. Dahlgren pointed to the coming ship. Feodor kept on the course. The ship came about as the smack nearly collided with it. An old man, with a rich white beard and the authority of a captain, shouted down at him in Swedish. Dahlgren had enough of his grandfather's language to invoke the first law of the sea and beg aid to the distressed. Commands bellowed in Swedish. A cradle dipped over the side, and Dahlgren and Feodor lifted Kolya into it. He then sent the other two up the rope ladder and followed. With one leg it was a painful process until Feodor's strong hand reached under his arm to haul him up.

He found a doctor working on Kolya already, the captain standing over them. Dahlgren hobbled over to him and saluted. The man saw him drag his leg. His blue eyes suddenly widened, and a torrent of Swedish burst out. Dahlgren could only shake his head and mumble in very broken Swedish that he did not understand. The captain switched to English. "You are Colonel Ulrich Dahlgren?"

"Indeed, I am, sir." Dahlgren was more than surprised at the question.

The captain took his hand in both of his and shook them vigorously. "We know about you in Sweden, hero of Gettysburg! Three times I have been stopped by the British to search my ship in the last four days. I ask them why, and they tell me they look for you. 'And why?' I ask. And they tell me what you have done. They are so angry they could spit nails."

"I am afraid I have been without news for three weeks, Captain . . . ."

"Oh, my bad manners. I am Olaf Abrahamson, captain of the *Vasa*. We are bound for Stockholm. Yes, the British tell me also that there is great rebellion in Ireland, but that is all I know. I take you to Stockholm with me."

"We cannot pay you, Captain."

"Pay? You go first class to Stockholm, young lion of Sweden!"

HEADQUARTERS, ARMY OF THE POTOMAC, SPOTSYLVANIA COURT-HOUSE, 4:00 P.M., WEDNESDAY, APRIL 20, 1864

"Just pitch into him, Meade!" Grant was visibly impatient.

General Meade did not like the way the General-in-Chief of the Armies had just addressed him. Meade was a good and loyal soldier but prickly about his due as commander of the Army of the Potomac.

"I would gladly, General, but Lee gives me no opportunity." He went on to describe how Lee would repeatedly deploy for battle and then slip away before Meade could "just pitch into him."

"If he doesn't give me the slip, then I find powerful entrenchments in my way, so powerful I would never attempt an assault. How I wish Lee had never been an engineer." That was bitter praise, for Meade himself was an engineer.

"Sharpe tells me Lee has no more than sixty thousand men now that Longstreet is in the Peninsula. You have twice that many with another twenty-five thousand men of VI Corps on the way.[18] I suggest you stop dancing to his tune. Fix him with part of your force seeming get ready to assault those entrenchments and march toward Richmond with the other. That will have him running after you for a change."

Grant had made the decision to plant his flag with Meade's army. Longstreet's descent into the Peninsula had thoroughly upset his strategic plan of Canada First. Worse yet, Lee's Old Warhorse after his victory at Second Big Bethal had trapped what was left of Weitzel's XVIII Corps in the defenses of Yorktown on the Peninsula and put Fortress Monroe under siege from the land. If Longstreet was not driven away, the dominos would begin to fall—Yorktown, Fortress Monroe, X Corps, and Norfolk Naval Base—fifty thousand army and naval personnel and most of the Union fleet. It would be a catastrophe of the first order. Raids on the British Isles, though they had sent Northern morale sky high, could never balance such a loss.

Through the night, Grant and Meade worked out the next step in the campaign.

They were not the only ones working through the night. Gus Fox prowled the secret facility at the Washington Navy Yard to push through the completion of the Alligator class of submersibles and equally haunted the dock to watch the USS *Shark* and *Barracuda* rush through their shakedowns in the East Branch river. *Stingray* and *Dolphin* would be ready to splash into the water the next day and be ready with God's help in two weeks. It had taken superhuman efforts to get them this far ahead of schedule.

The Navy Yard was more than busy. Every square foot was in active use, and not just the rebuilding efforts from the damage done by the British attack in October, but the casting of guns, repairs, and new construction of all sorts. The yard was also the home of both the army and navy's balloon corps, or as Fox kept insisting for the latter, the Naval Aeronautical Service (NAS). The fact that the yard was also constructing the new class of attack aeroships for both services made things even more tense. No man was more navy in his soul than Gus Fox, and he naturally felt that possession was trump in any argument with the Army. He wanted *all* the aeroships under construction for the U.S. Navy. That put him on a collision course with Sharpe because the Army's Balloon Corps reported to him. After it had been allowed to disband itself through command indifference after Chancellorsville, Sharpe had revived it as a reconnaissance tool for his new CIB. He assigned individual companies to support the various armies with the proviso that they worked directly for each army's intelligence staff. These were the stationary balloons that had already been in use but larger and more capable. They were not the issue. The issue was the allocation of the new attack class.

It was Fox who had seen the potential for naval warfare from the way a single balloon had sunk two British warships in the East Branch during the attack on Washington. He had the vision as well to see that the naval lieutenant who had gone up in the balloon with Thaddeus Lowe had been promoted to captain and given command of the new NAS. Already Will Cushing had had a reputation for daring intrepidity as well as immortal good luck. Fox hoped that good luck would rub off on the NAS.[19] And it had most wonderfully. Under Cushing's command, the new *Stephen Decatur* had helped sink two British blockade ships allowing the Meagher and Dahlgren expeditions to escape into the open sea. That immense cigar-shaped airship was now tethered at the Navy Yard along with the Army's *George Washington*. The brand new *John Paul Jones* and *Andrew Jackson* rested next to them undergoing the last stages of construction.

If ever there was a man eager for interservice collision it was Fox. On the other hand, if ever there was a man who could pour oil on troubled waters it was Sharpe. The Bible was full of similar words that Sharpe used to good effect on Fox, soft words to turn away the Assistant Secretary of the Navy's wrath. He had set the mood with a fine dinner, an excellent wine, and fine cigars that they were both puffing away at in the dining room at the CIB headquarters. They were the only two at the table. Fox had arrived ready to cross swords, but was now in a far better mood than when he had walked through Sharpe's door.

When the sliding doors shut, he flicked an ash. "All right, Sharpe. What do you want?"

Sharpe smiled and drew a long drag on his cigar and took his time to blow a perfect smoke ring. "What I want, Mr. Assistant Secretary, is for us to avoid forcing the President to play Solomon with the balloons. Babies and balloons both do not do well when divided by a sword. And it's tough on the mothers too."

Fox laughed. "Depends how tough the mother is, Sharpe."

"I think it depends on how smart the mother is." He got up and pulled down a map of the Chesapeake and Virginia. "Look at the situation." He could see Fox starting to get his back up at another attempt to put forward an army position. "Calm down, sir. You misunderstand me. The issue at hand is control of the Chesapeake. Control gives us a base for the fleet right on Jeff Davis's doorstep. And that base means we can easily support an army moving on Richmond. Everything pivots on control of the Chesapeake."

Fox was surprised. "I've never heard an army officer speak with such sense, General. Of course, everything pivots on control of the Chesapeake."

"Given that, sir, we are faced with limited resources. There are not enough aeroships for both the Army and the Navy to have separate fleets."

Wary again, Fox said, "I will not give up the Navy's balloons."

"I'm not asking you to. The Army will gladly put the *George Washington* and the *Andrew Jackson* under the Navy's operational control in the upcoming operations to free the Chesapeake."

"In exchange for what?"

"For nothing." He smiled. "Only, when Army needs are paramount, we expect the Navy's aeroships to support ground operations. It makes no sense for the Army's aerosphips to remain idle when the Navy has a critical need for them. It works the other way as well."

Fox was still wary. "And who decides whose needs are paramount?"

"Only you and I, Mr. Assistant Secretary, only you and I. That way any knock-down-drag-outs we have over the issue will stay in this room."

Fox stood up and extended his hand. "Done," he said.[20]

GORHAM, NEW HAMPSHIRE, 9:22 P.M., FRIDAY, APRIL 12, 1864

John Lynn, the stationmaster of Gorham, was a responsible man. When the British had come down from Canada, he agreed to continue running the station and swore an oath to take no action injurious to the Crown. Upon returning home, he had put the hand he had raised in affirmation into the fire; it had taken it months to heal. From that day, that maimed hand had slowly begun to lay like a weight upon the railroad. Schedules were missed again and again, cargoes misplaced or sent in the wrong direction, and a wave of sabotage of the line began to plague it across the state in the thirty miles from Groveton to Shelburne growing as the weather improved. That thirty miles was the responsibility of John Lynn, not as stationmaster but as new covert head of the Coos County militia. What better place than a major locomotive yard and repair facility such as Gorham to wage war against the occupier?

His activities had brought Sergeant Knight rapping on his door late one night. Jim McPhail was most interested in what mischief the men of New Hampshire could make to ease the advance of Sherman's army and had sent his chief of scouts to find out. Lynn like all upper New Englanders was not one to boast. Instead, he just said, "Come with me tonight."

That night Lynn was riding the Portland train in the locomotive as far as Shelburne to assuage British frustration of the very problems he was organizing. It was a goods train, no passengers. At the last minute, he brought along a new assistant, a tall redheaded man. Tonight's problem would serve to divert suspicion away from him. He looked at his watch; they should be in Shelburne in twenty minutes. "Well, 'should' is a subjective term," he thought. The White Mountains hung darkly on the right; there were no farms or towns to throw out a bit of light. "It should be anytime now," he thought. He wrapped his arm around an iron handhold and motioned Knight to do so as well. The engineer and firemen similarly braced themselves. The two Canadian militiamen guards with them did not notice. They were sitting smoking on the woodpile. It was here where the train had to slow down to make a difficult curve in the line. Then he felt it, the sudden jolt as the locomotive slipped off an unbolted rail in a high-pitched screech and plowed into the soft ground next to the track. The two Canadians went flying with the wood into the dark.

1 2

A Long Shot With a Limb in Between

Taking Dublin had been easy; feeding it was another matter. The greatest city in Ireland with over a hundred thousand people required a huge amount of food on a daily basis. Meagher's planning had been somewhat excessive in its optimism and equally deficient in its planning for the mundane requirement of eating regularly. The English would immediately have identified it in one snide word what they considered an Irish trait—fecklessness.

The problem of feeding the city was compounded by the season; crops were still being sown, not harvested. What stocks remained were from last year's harvest, and, of course, the Royal Navy slammed the door shut on importation with its blockade. But then there was the potato. Blight-resistant varieties had returned the potato to its central place in the Irish diet, and it stored well and for up to a year in the straw-lined pits of the country people or even in the ground. It was also difficult for a government tax collector or army requisition to snatch away, but it might be bought or even donated if the owner were sure which way the wind blew now. Meagher sent out foraging parties with British gold looted from the Lord Lieutenant's funds to encourage the surrounding countryside to bring their produce into the city.

The countryside was in a chaos spreading throughout the island. News of Tallaght had run through the island shattering Royal authority except for Ulster where the Protestant Supremacy was ensured by a hardheaded majority. The fence sitters started jumping. Unhappily for Meagher, the chief fence sitter was Paul Cullen, the Catholic Archbishop of Dublin, and he was not budging. He had condemned Fenianism as a secret society, forbidden to good Catholics, and he and the other Irish bishops had encouraged the pope to condemn it as well. It was a matter of principle from which he would not retreat. To it he added the argument that the church, as much as it wished Ireland to be free, could not condone rebellion against lawful authority that would consume the lives of countless innocent people and bring down the wrath of the English on the Catholics of Ireland and their church. Without the lead of their parish priests, many of the fence sitters would stay where they were.[1]

Still, thousands of recruits poured into Dublin in the week after Tallaght from the surrounding counties. Then they suddenly stopped coming. Gen. Scarlett may have been down, but he was not out. He threw his cavalry around Dublin to cut it off from all contact with the rest of the island. Foraging parties from the city were repeatedly attacked, until they required a whole regiment as escort. Even then every attempt was like running a bloody gauntlet in order to bring back a pitiful sustenance.

The cordon was getting thicker as British reinforcements poured into Ireland. Western England and Scotland were stripped of their regular garrisons followed by Aldershot and the channel port garrisons that had already not shipped off for North America: nine infantry and seven cavalry regiments plus fifty-four RVCs, almost sixty thousand men. Another forty RVCs were being prepared to reinforce them if necessary.[2]

The RVCs closest to the great embarkation ports came from their own or adjacent counties; the green-clad volunteers of Cheshire and Lancashire in England and Flintshire in Wales boarded ships in Liverpool on the Mersey, and those from Ayrshire, Renfrewshire, and Lanarkshire in Scotland assembled in Glasgow on the Clyde.[3]

For Capt. Henry Hay Norie, commanding 9th Company, Ayrshire RVC, soldiering had become all too real. He had left a wife and newborn in the care of his in-laws as he nervously shepherded his men to their assembly point, entrained for Glasgow, and then the shipping out for Ireland. The 9th Company was the type usually found in a rich Lowland agricultural country like Ayrshire. It was an independent company essentially since there were not enough men in any one locality to form an entire RVC. The 9th and thirteen other companies were scattered over the rich coastal potato and berry fields and in the rugged Galloway Hills.

Norie was a good sort, the gentleman farmer who volunteered to command the company when it was formed in his district a few years before during the war scare with the French. There was no thirst for military glory or peacocking around in his uniform. Rather, it was an obligation of his social position, something a gentleman would naturally lead. With that obligation was also a middle class conscientiousness to his duty that made for a solid unit. He was considered a fair man who other men took their quarrels to for an honest resolution and hands shaken afterward. His seventy-three men were of the middling social set, well-off enough to buy their own uniform, equipment, and rifle.

There were some small farmers and farm workers whose expenses had been paid by subscription that Norie had encouraged and been the first to contribute to. By and large, they were men of good Presbyterian sense, education, and seriousness. Norie had one hope—that he would bring them all back home.

These columns in scarlet and green were not just reinforcements for Scarlett's force around Dublin. The cavalry especially fanned out throughout the island, the most immediate and impressive expression of British might followed by a large number of RVCs. Disraeli had insisted that a full-blown rising be prevented at all costs, by a great show of force to remind the country of the power of the government and to bring back as many as possible to their allegiance and remind the rest that they had made the right choice by taking no action. The scarlet-clad regular infantry regiments were reserved for the capture of Dublin itself.

Disraeli was able in a widely and applauded reported speech to the House to state that "this Kingdom has not only sent a mighty expeditionary force to North America, but has sown the dragons teeth in its warlike English soil to summon a mighty host for Ireland, a host greater than was sent to the Crimea at which the world then marveled." Disraeli understood morale.[4]

HAMPTON ROADS, 2:35 A.M., SATURDAY, APRIL 24, 1864

Flashes of artillery and the fiery arcs of mortars from Longstreet's siege train pummeling Fortress Monroe from the land lit the night sky. By day the Royal Navy's Great Armament pounded it from the sea, giving the garrison no rest. This night, the view from Hampton Roads showed the fort silhouetted against the flames of burning barracks and clouds of smoke with the crack and thump of artillery racing over the water. It was an unforgettable sight for the boat's captain, Lt. Josiah Mason, as he watched from the observation hatch of the USS *Shark* as it steamed semi-submersed past the fort. He ducked back down inside the hull and said, "Sir, you must come up and see this!" Lieutenant Colonel Wilmoth climbed up the ladder to take in the fireworks. The light flickered across his awestruck face. Behind him by two hundred yards similarly transfixed was the captain of the *Barracuda*.

So it was a question of who was more surprised when *Shark* ran into a British longboat looming out of the dark. The longboat was lifted half out of the water, spilling its crew of tars and jollies into the water. One man fell right onto the hatch, knocking Wilmoth down the ladder and himself falling in after. The man was dazed from landing headfirst onto the metal deck. A sailor whacked him alongside the head with a wrench for good measure. It was a Royal Marine officer.

Mason shouted for full speed and then scrambled back up the ladder. He was just in time to give the order to put the boat hard to starboard to avoid another collision. He hoped *Barracuda* would avoid what appeared to be dozens of boats heading to the fort. The boat's engine soon distanced *Shark* from the boats, and in fifteen more minutes the darkened water battery with its great Rodman guns could be made out against the red glow from inside the fort. A sentry's shot pinged off the hull next to him as he shouted, "Don't shoot! Don't shoot! U.S. Navy!"

A bullet grazed his sleeve and another splashed in the water. He heard a cacophony of voices shouting, "Shoot it!" and "Hold your fire!" all at the same time. Cutting through the confusion a command voice bellowed, "Silence!" And there was silence. Stentor himself could not have done it better. "What the hell are you, Navy?" Mason could see an officer standing on the scarred parapet.

"The submersible USS *Shark*, by God!"

The boat came up against the water battery wall with a bump. The officer was fascinated by the strange apparition as Mason yelled, "Don't waste time looking at the damn boat. We just steamed through an enemy flotilla of longboats loaded with troops coming this way."

Stentor thundered, and the onlookers rushed back to their pieces. "I'll see you later," Mason said and dropped back into the observer's hatch. *Shark* pulled about as its engine blew sparks out of its funnel. The boat pulled away from the water battery and headed back into the dark. He slid down the ladder and was met by the expectant eyes of the crew. "We're going back out to raise hell with the English longboats, boys." He looked down at the enemy officer who was sitting with his head in his hands. A sailor stood over him with a three pound wrench while Wilmoth was trying to make him comfortable. "Here, man, take a jot," he said handing the man a small silver flask.

The Marine took it. "Damned decent of you, colonel,"[5] and took a long swallow.

Out there in the dark the loss of the lead boat with the commander of the flotilla had confused the lot of them. The second in command was slow to find out just what had happened as the boats crammed with Royal Marines crept on now essentially leaderless. Stentor had done more than just keep his men at their guns. A whump from a mortar in the fort sent a flare popping over the water, casting them in relief on the shimmering water. The water battery's Rodman fired first, sending a 352-pound shell skimming just over the surface and right through the flotilla, turning longboats into matchsticks and flying bodies before it exploded. From the fort's facing casemate galleries smaller guns dropped their shot into the mass of boats. Another whump and a new flare replaced the dying one. Inside *Shark* the crew braced as the forty-foot hull scooped up one boat after another, tipping them over into the water.

Dawn would find the bay littered with overturned boats, bodies, and debris. The British attempt to take the fort's water battery by surprise and spike the deadly Rodmans had been a disaster that had cost six hundred Royal Marines and sailors dead and prisoners. *Shark* pulled back up to the water battery before first light. This time the fortress commander was on hand to greet Mason and thank him for his timely warning. He was surprised to see a figure in a scarlet coat emerge from the hatch preceded by a very young army lieutenant colonel. "Oh, yes, General, we have a prisoner. May I present Lt. Col. Sir George Bazalgette, Royal Marines."

Before Stentor could reply, Wilmoth stepped forward. "This man is now in the custody of the Central Information Bureau. I must speak to the commander of this garrison on instructions from the President."

BLUFF MOUNTAIN, VERMONT, 10:25 A.M., SUNDAY, APRIL 25, 1864

The view from the mountain was perfect. The town of Brighton nestled below between the base of the mountain and the lake named Island Pond (for the island in its midst). What interested George Custer and Judson Knight was the roundhouse, shops, and all the other facilities of a major rail yard. Island Point Rail Yard was the midpoint on the Grand Trunk Railway between Portland and Montreal. If the Grand Trunk Railway kept Canada alive, the Island Pond Rail Yard was the railway's heart, pumping the life's blood traffic in both directions.

Knight and some Vermont militia had brought Custer to the top of the hill, but what directed Knight to that point in the first place was the intelligence from the CBI in Washington in Wilmoth's meticulous handwriting. The report all but said, "Look here if you want to find the place that will cause the most pain."

"Damn," Custer said quietly. He positively lusted after what he saw below and was already thinking how he would strike when Knight tapped him on the shoulder and pointed down the slope. A man in a red coat was trudging toward them. He stopped, looked over his shoulder, unbuttoned the coat, threw it into the bushes, and resumed his climb up. As he got closer, Knight jumped up. "I don't believe it!" He rushed down to meet the man and was waiting by a tree when the man came up by him.

"Well, talk about the luck of the Irish!" The man turned on his heel. "Martin Hogan, you could fall into the black pit of hell and come out with your arms full of sunshine!"

"Knight!"

"I must say, Martin, that red coat was becoming."

"Faith, my skin was itching at the shame of it the whole time."

"The armor that scalds with safety."

"Yes, Shakespeare must have been an Irishman to have that much wit about him."

Knight laughed and slapped him on the back, "Are you hungry, man?"

"No, Her Majesty has just fed me a hearty meal of roast beef and white bread in the yard below. Nothing is too good for a soldier of the Queen."

They bantered until they found Custer and his guards, and Knight introduced his prodigal scout. Custer congratulated Hogan on his escape, but when the young Irishman wanted to wax on about his exploit, the general cut him off. "What did you see in the town and yard?" Hogan suddenly switched from good-natured Paddy to all business as he precisely described the yard and the garrison of the town pointing out each visible facility, blockhouse, and entrenchment from the mountain top.

"About a thousand men, you say?" Custer asked to pin down the point.

"Sar, it's two whole battalions of Canadians: the 55th and 89th Sherbrooke Battalions. And green they are, raised only in the last two months. They've got a dozen British sergeants and corporals screaming at them night and day to whip them into shape. From the look of them, they will need a lot more screaming."

"And you found all this out in less than one day?"

"Sar, it helps to have one's countryman about. The Irish came to build the railway, and hundreds stayed to settle. Well, as you may not have heard, Sar, but we are a talkative people. One down there who wore the Queen's uniform in the Crimea and India scoffs at what use these Canuks would be to anyone in a fight except as targets."

Custer's eyes sparkled as the breeze picked up his long blond curls. He struck his gauntleted hand with the other fist. If ever there was a man for the main chance, it was Custer. Hit 'em, hit 'em, and keep on hitting 'em. A rain of blows was the best shield — the attack without mercy. He leapt on his horse. "Let's get going."

NORFOLK NAVAL BASE, VIRGINIA, 1:55 P.M., SUNDAY, APRIL 25, 1864
Rear Adms. John Dahlgren and Samuel Phillips Lee and Maj. Gen. Quincy Adams Gillmore were hard men to impress. Wilmoth's youthful face and lieutenant colonel's shoulder straps had taken them aback even if it was an age of boy colonels, as those dynamic men in their early twenties were called who rose on the wings of sheer talent.

Wilmoth reminded Dahlgren of his own son, Ulrich, in an unconscious transference of paternal affection. In any case, all three had heard stories of this remarkable young man who had saved Lincoln's life in the battle for Washington and had risen so high so quickly in the mysterious Central Information Bureau. Word had spread through the flag officer grapevine of the highly useful information that seemed to come out of Wilmoth's shop. He stood at the right hand of Major General Sharpe, who was now one of Lincoln's closest advisors. Youth or not, he was to be treated seriously.

Lee had commanded the North Atlantic Blockading Squadron and was now senior officer commanding all naval forces penned up in Norfolk. He was a Virginian and a cousin of Robert E. Lee, which caused more than one officer earlier in the war to question his loyalty, to which he would tartly respond, "When I find the word 'Virginia' in my commission, I will join the Confederacy."[6] He was proof that like his famous cousin, the Lee men were handsome.[7] Gillmore had been the top of his 1849 West Point class and was a master of siege warfare and had pioneered the destructive use of rifled naval guns against stone forts. He had commanded Union troops besieging Charleston, and had insisted that the negro 54th Massachusetts be treated equally with his white regiments. John Dahlgren was still recuperating from his wounds suffered at the battle of Charleston the previous October, the greatest victory of the U.S. Navy. Lee had invited him as a courtesy.

Wilmoth also as a courtesy informed the admiral of the news of his son's raid and how it had not only created the greatest panic since the armada but had crippled the British ability to make gunpowder and rifles, at least for the short run. Dahlgren was devoted to his boy and simply radiated pride. Wilmoth went on to say, "I'm sorry, Admiral, but we have had no word of where your son is now. Our latest information is that the the British are still searching for him. Mr. Lincoln asked me to tell you that he has directed that every effort be given to getting your son out of Britain."

"Now, gentlemen, I am fulfilling another presidential order to inform you of the plan for coming operations to break the British grip on the Chesapeake and of your part in that plan." In meticulous detail he described the unifying strategy of the operation, the forces allotted to it, and the timing. He then described in equal detail the British naval forces in the bay and nearby Virginia and North Carolina waters. Of particular interest was his analysis of recent additions the Royal Navy's order-of-battle. He did not tell them that this intelligence came from Van Lew's ring in Richmond. "There are indications that all the available British ironclads are making the crossing as we speak — seven ships." He did not tell them that this had been gleaned from British newspapers smuggled in from Canada.

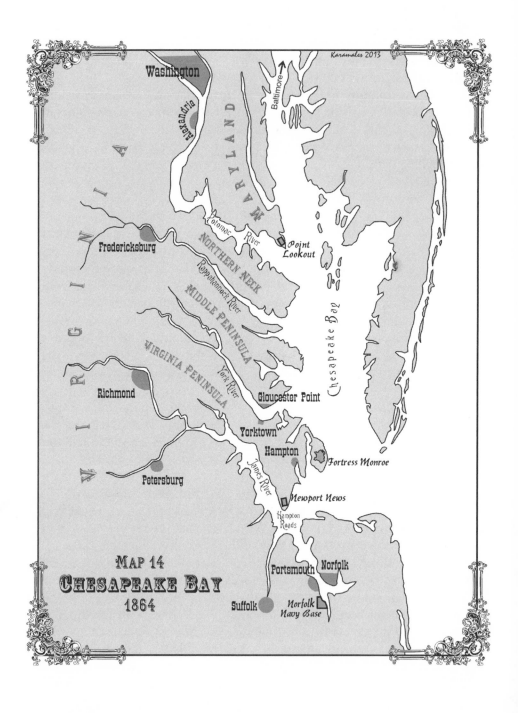

Karamales 2013

Washington

Alexandria

MARYLAND

Baltimore

Potomac River

Fredericksburg

NORTHERN NECK

Point Lookout

Rappahannock River

MIDDLE PENINSULA

VIRGINIA

Chesapeake Bay

VIRGINIA PENINSULA

York River

Richmond

Gloucester Point

Yorktown

Hampton

Fortress Monroe

James River

Petersburg

Newport News

Hampton Roads

MAP 14
CHESAPEAKE BAY
1864

Portsmouth   Norfolk

Suffolk   Norfolk Navy Base

"Admiral Lee, the plan calls for you to engage the British with all the forces at your disposal. The submersibles *Shark* and *Barracuda* will support you."

Lee was a fighting man, but he was also practical. "I must point out to you, Colonel, that this plan must succeed because I have only enough coal to power my ironclads and a few other ships for one sustained action. After that they are only so much scrap tied up to the docks here."

Wilmoth's eyes now grew hard, and his tenor voice fell several octaves. "The President also instructed me to tell you that if this operation fails, the war is lost, and the Union fails with it."

NORFOLK NAVAL BASE, VIRGINIA, 7:15 P.M., SUNDAY, APRIL 25, 1864

That night the officer's mess had several new guests. Wilmoth, of course, and Lt. Col. George Bazelgette, Royal Marines. Wilmoth had made sure Bazelgette was invited rather than dumped in the stockade for prisoners. Indeed, he was a celebrity famous on both sides of the Atlantic for his coup de main in the capture of Fort Gorgas in Portland Harbor and for his dramatic capture of two monitors right under the nose of Fortress Monroe. The Navy considered the latter to be its worst day since the CSS *Virginia* had played havoc with the fleet's wooden warships in Hampton Roads two years ago. Nevertheless, as gentlemen and naval officers, the sting of defeat did not prevent them from the courtesy due a gallant and admirable foe. Not to be outdone, Bazelgette paid a great compliment to Rear Admiral Dahlgren for his victory at Charleston.

"I must say, Admiral, after the battle of Charleston Nelson must be swimming in his barrel of brandy.[8] No other navy could have done it except one descended from the same stock as mans the Royal Navy itself."

Dahlgren bowed in return but refrained from saying his ancestors were Swedish. Their prisoner was proving to be a gracious gentleman himself, as was evident from the smiles and bonhomie around the table, and Dahlgren saw no need to quibble. He did notice that the mess steward replaced every sip from Bazalgette's wine glass. He did not know that it was on Wilmoth's instructions.

Admiral Lee, whose monitor force had been cut almost in half by Bazalgette's exploit, said, "Well, we did hone our skills in two wars with the Royal Navy, and there is no better teacher. A sailor does not know war unless he has fought the Royal Navy."

"You must forgive me, sir, but we hope to keep on teaching you."

Laughter.

"Yes, the loss of the monitors was most unexpected, but how did you think of such a tactic?"

"It occurred to me that your monitors had no means to protect themselves from boarders. It then was only a matter of getting a boarding party onto the monitors. The answer was small fast steamers. They were too fast to be taken under fire and were maneuvering to ensure that."

"Brilliant as that was, Colonel, I would say it was a tactic that would not work a second time. Fool me once, shame on you. Fool me twice, shame on me."

For the first time, Wilmoth entered the conversation. "I think there will be an opportunity for further test of tactics before too long once our monitors come out again." He paused and bowed slightly to Lee. "I only assume there will be action; as an army officer, I know less than nothing about naval warfare, only that our navy will come out after you at some point. In that case, our remaining monitors are still more than a match even for your two remaining ironclads here in the Chesapeake. What are their names?"

"HMS *Warrior* and *Defiance*."

Wilmoth responded, "I seem to remember that their sister ships were lost at Charleston by the same monitors that will sweep you out of the Chesapeake."

"But, Colonel, you should not expect the odds to remain in your favor."

"How is that?"

"You are not the only ones building ironclads."

Wilmoth gave a very good imitation of confusion. "But our newspapers say that your building program is behind schedule and that the ironclads you do have are surely being kept home for defense, especially since the Dahlgren raid and Dublin."

Bazalgette laughed and then took another deep drink. "Don't be surprised if you wake up and find more than *Warrior* and *Defense* in the bay soon."

"*Yes!* So they are coming to the Chesapeake," Wilmoth thought to himself. It was all he could do to keep a placid face. He reminded himself to give the mess steward a big tip the next morning.

DUBLIN CASTLE, 8:29 P.M., THURSDAY, APRIL 28, 1864
Sergeant Major McCarter feared he could no longer put off the steady stream of men who demanded time of Meagher. These were not officer seekers. He had turned away even Brigadier General Kelly and the cabinet ministers of the new government. Meagher that night was meeting only with an amber-filled bottle. Day by day it grew worse. McCarter had put the fear of God into everyone around the general, but still the whiskey got through.

This was the time for Meagher to be everywhere, the beating heart and brain of the war of liberation, but he had withdrawn into himself and his bottle as soon as the British had cut off Dublin. Kelly knew full well what needed to be done and just did it. Under his firm hand, the city became an armed camp as entrenchments sprouted along its edge. Outlying houses were torn down as troops and civilians heaped up the earth and cut down countless trees. And when it came to it, he was the one who treated with the British general who came in under flag of truce to demand the city's surrender.

Maj. Gen. Sir Robert Napier was a fighting man, which was why Disreaeli had plucked him out of the Indian Army shortly after the war began. He was not the only one. Indian Army officers by and large were battle-tested in hard-campaigning.[9] British Army officers, especially those who made a career of politics at Horse Guards, had, to the PM's mind, been found wanting on too many occasions. He had no hesitation in facing down the Duke of Cambridge over this matter. For Disraeli results counted; he had read enough British history to see the waste attendant on social promotions in the army. He had not forgotten the Duke of Wellington's letter written during the Napoleonic Wars:

"When I reflect on the characters and attainments of some of the general officers of this army . . . I tremble; and as Lord Chesterfield said of the generals of his day, 'I only hope that when the enemy reads the list of their names he trembles as I do.'"[10]

Such officers had been responsible for the scandals and wanton waste of life in the Crimean War. Disreali had no intention of trembling. So he went to a different barrel looking for more generals like James Hope Grant, and there he found Napier, an engineer and a man with a talent for storming fortresses from India to China. Ferocious combat service in the First and Second Sikh Wars, along the Northwest Frontier, in the Indian Mutiny, and Second Anglo-Chinese War piled up brevet promotions, mentions in dispatches, and the thanks of Parliament and the Indian Government. In the last war he had commanded the 2nd Division under Hope Grant. Victory rode with these Indian Army officers, and a clean victory is what Disraeli desperately needed as quickly as possible in Ireland with a major war in North America and the second shoe about to drop somewhere in the Balkans. His orders to Napier were direct, personal, and peremptory. "Bring peace to Ireland. I do not want some historian in the future to say that we made a desert and called it peace."[11]

Napier dashed protocol and came himself to meet with Meagher only to be told by Kelly, "The President of Ireland and commander-in-chief of her armies is indisposed." Napier had dealt with too many pretentious princes and chieftains to be put off by this. Napier eyed Kelly carefully;

his information indicated that the man standing before him was the real victor of Tallaght. His experience and instinct told him that he faced another fighting man. He came to the point. "I have come to demand the surrender of Dublin and its garrison."

Kelly laughed, "And it was your surrender I had thought you had come to offer."

Napier took the Celtic effrontery in his stride. "Your position is hopeless, General. Her Majesty's forces are flooding Ireland. What little unrest your arrival has provoked has been suppressed. You cannot receive assistance from America. You have a great city to feed. There is no dishonor in surrender under such circumstances. You have played the game and lost."

Kelly would rather bitten his tongue off than utter what he said next. "I do not admit for a moment that this is so, but for courtesy's sake, I will convey your terms to General Meagher for his amusement." Napier had ensured that these terms would find their way into Dublin on their own as well. They were both seductive and corrosive—seductive because they were lenient beyond all expectation and corrosive because they ate away the do or die courage fired by thoughts of a Carthaginian peace. The terms were simple:

1. The American regiments would be allowed to surrender with the full honors of war; officers to retain their swords and sidearms.[12]
2. All members of the American regiments would be treated as lawful prisoners of war regardless of country of birth and to be liable for exchange;
3. All civilians of Ireland who reaffirmed their loyalty to the Crown, including those who had taken up arms under the authority of the American forces, would be granted amnesty.

Grand terms they were, but they meant nothing if they were not already being made a reality by the RVCs who were marching into every corner of Ireland. Men of good sense, like Captain Norie in Donegal. For these Scots and Englishmen, Ireland was alien, almost like a distant land though their ancestors had been making their fortune there for half a millennium or more. Much of it had not recovered from the famine, its population barely more than half of its pre-famine peak of 8.5 million. Poor it was and bitter and Catholic. News of Tallaght had sent the sparks into all that bitter tinder to set a thousand smolders that here and there sparked into flame.

But Tallaght had been a false hope, more ephemeral glory than conquered and held ground. Meagher had too few men to hold anything beyond Dublin itself, and the few thousand volunteers who had flooded in right after the battle were of no use as untrained men. At best they could man the entrenchments they helped to dig around the city. So the countryside and the towns were left waiting in expectation. Those who jumped for the green flag soon found that they had no weapons and that British cavalry and RVC battalions were spreading over the island like spilled quicksilver reestablishing the Queen's Peace with a firm but restrained hand.

So it was that Captain Norie came to those villages in Donegal with his 9th Company of the Ayrshire RVC. The first men he sought out were the village priests to pay his respects, an act they did not go unnoticed. He knew the priests were the most influential men in their parishes and there was no better way to spread the news of Crown policy and of the terms offered to Meagher and those who had gone over to him. The men of Donegal were not strangers, for thousands had fled the famine to settle in Ayrshire across the Irish Sea and not a few worked on Norie's farm. His next visits were to the kin of these men to give them word of their relatives, again an act that did not go unnoticed. He then went to the parents of the few hotheads that were well known to plead with them to save their sons from folly. He also paid in good coin for the provisions and lodging of his men and for a few public works that put food on the table of the poorest. The handful of irreconcilable men he simply arrested and confined, again something that did not go unnoticed. Men like Norie were doing more damage to Meagher than ten thousand more British regulars.

THE WILDERNESS, VIRGINIA, 6:11 P.M., THURSDAY, APRIL 28, 1864

Meade had been pitching into Lee for two days, and all he had to show for it was a growing butcher's bill without having put a dent in the Confederate defenses. Every time he tried to outflank the enemy, Lee was there first and the ground spouting new entrenchments. Those entrenchments did much to counter the increased firepower of Union repeaters. The Confederates were better armed and supplied than Meade had ever seen before. Especially troubling was the amount and quality of their artillery and ammunition, thanks to British industry. The days appeared gone when the Confederate infantry threatened to kill their own artillerymen if they ever dared fire over them because the poor quality of Southern-made ammunition caused all too many rounds to drop among their own troops. Ironically ammunition was a headache for Meade now. Since so many of his men were armed with repeaters, they used them and expended unprecedented amount of ammunition.[13] This, in turn, put even greater demands on his overland supply lines. It was there that Lee's cavalry under Maj. Gen. Jeb Stuart was raising hell, so much so that he had to detail most of a division to secure them. Lee was fighting him to an obvious standstill, which made Meade's already sharp tongue as cutting as an obsidian razor. It did not help that Grant had pitched his own tent and headquarters only a few hundred yards away from his own.

Grant was not happy either. Meade had pitched into Lee just as Grant had ordered. Lee was altogether different from the Confederate generals he had bested in the West, a great captain as he had been warned. The staff he had brought from the West had boasted that they had seen nothing but the enemy's backs, only to be told by the veterans of the Army of the Potomac, "You haven't meet Bobby Lee yet." So Grant just sat there in front of his tent, puffed on his cigar, and thought.

YORKTOWN, VIRGINIA, 2:25 P.M., FRIDAY, APRIL 29, 1864

If he had known about Grant's cogitation, Godfrey Weitzel would have hoped that a good deal of it was about his own desperate situation. Somewhere in the fort the day before, the last hardtack had been eaten. Weitzel had already twice refused Longstreet's demand for his surrender. Engineers like Weitzel were obdurate and clever men, but they did have to eat. With the river closed to the U.S. Navy and friendly traffic, he could look to resupply by water. He concluded that if the food could not come to his shrunken command, his command would have to go to the food. The problem was that half of one of Longstreet's divisions lay outside like a cat in front of a mouse hole patiently flicking its tail.

The only thing that gave Weitzel any hope of escape was that Longstreet himself was not there. He was directing the siege of Fortress Monroe now that the British had supplied the heavy siege guns and mortars to pound the landward side of the fort. Wietzel's only chance now was to break out to the north and march up the bank of the York and then along the bank of its tributary, the Paumunkey River, foraging on the Rebels as they went, find a crossing, and press on toward the Union base at Fredericksburg. As his enlisted servant blurted out, "Nobody asked me, General, but that's a long shot with a limb in between."

Long shot or not, Weitzel saw no other choice but a breakout. Surrender was out of the question. The breakout was planned for two in the morning.

His decision would still have stood even if Grant had informed him of his overall decision. The general-in-chief's problem was threefold—to get Lee into the open field by threatening something he had to defend, rescue Weitzel's command at Yorktown, and relieve Fortress Monroe and the Norfolk Navy Yard. His decision was designed to solve all three problems. He detached Hancock's II and Wright's VI Corps from Meade's army and created a new force of almost sixty thousand men, the Army of the Rappahannock. Its base would be Fredericksburg, and it would advance down the Richmond, Fredericksburg, Potomac Railroad (RF&P) toward Richmond. Its immediate objective was Hanover Junction where the railroad intersected with the Virginia Central Railroad that went from Richmond west to the Shenandoah Valley. When Hancock seized that junction, he would completely sever Lee's supply lines while at the same time being in a position to fall upon Richmond or trap Longstreet in the Peninsula (or both) — three good reasons for Lee to abandon his constant entrenching. As soon as Lee began to move, Meade would follow and engage him in the field or trap him between himself and Hancock.[14] Since Hancock's army would be the decisive maneuver force, Grant decided to accompany it.

Of course, Grant was used to the Confederate generals in the West, a far more compliant lot than those in the East who had tormented the Army of the Potomac. Indeed, he had not met Bobby Lee yet.

HEADQUARTERS, PORTLAND FIELD FORCE, PORTLAND, MAINE, 3:50 P.M., FRIDAY, APRIL 29, 1864

Wolseley's train ride to Portland had convinced him that the region shielding the Grand Trunk Railway line — a series of mountains and water barriers — was a defender's dream. The closer to Portland, the better it got. From the northern tip of Long Lake to Portland was forty-two miles of lake, river, and canal. The most daunting obstacle was the twelve-mile-long Sebago Lake covering forty-five square miles. From its southern outlet was twenty miles of river and canal to Portland. In that twenty miles a small army could hold a large one for a very long time.

Unwavering confidence made it the instinctive choice. If this had been against an enemy anywhere from Egypt to China, the British would fall upon them with a torrential rain of blows. Against a European enemy, they would strategically advance and tactically defend, allowing the enemy to impale themselves on a hedge of implacable British steel. That had worked from Agincourt to Waterloo to the Alma.

Wolseley found Doyle to be of exactly that mind. Hope Grant had nothing to worry about in the man's aggressive spirit. There was more than simple British pugnacity. The siege of Portland had taken seven months, seven long, exasperating months, against a tenacious and skillful foe. The government had not been happy with the slow pace, and every dispatch ship had carried hectoring demands that Portland be taken forthwith. Worst of all, was the British victory at Kennebunk that should have been his. It was Doyle who had left a minimal force to hold Portland while he advanced to attack the relieving American VI Corps. Hope Grant had landed in time to race south and assume command of the battle, a resounding British victory. The laurels had fallen on Grant instead of himself.[15] Rubbing salt in his wounded pride, the Americans had sortied in his absence to overrun his siegeworks and camp, something for which he was awarded complete blame. He had much riding on the coming collision.

Wolseley's train ride had also alerted him to another reason for seeking a decisive encounter. The Grand Trunk Railway was fragile artery on which Canada depended for its life's blood. The long stretch from New Brunswick through Maine, New Hampshire, and Vermont to Quebec made it a magnet for American mischief. As the weather improved, train after train began to run off rails unbolted from their ties. Attacks on British repair crews invariably followed. Prisoners claimed to be from the state militias, but seldom wore anything that could be construed as a uniform. By the laws of war, they could then be shot out of hand and were. The British were not hesitant to do so or to burn any farm of hamlet within a mile of each attack. Surviving farms near the railroads screamed that the owner was a collaborator.

To their surprise, American attacks increased with the burnings. The subjugation of all of Maine had never been attempted; there were just too few troops. The largely rural inland counties hardly ever saw a red coat. For British purposes, control of the coastal towns and the railroad was essential. From that secure hinterland, the militias stirred with the spring. Raids on the railroad and attacks on British patrols had become a constant. So far, Doyle had used only Canadian militia to protect his lines of communications, and there were not enough of them.

Wolseley's solution, which he put to Doyle, was to concentrate the entire recalcitrant population of the counties along the railroad into large camps to deny the militias any support. Doyle was visibly taken aback. "Look here, Wolseley, this is not India or China. We are not among the heathen. These are white people who speak English! Good God, man, I'll hear not more it." Wolseley tucked the idea into the pocket of his mind.[16]

He would have been more forceful in his argument had he known of Sherman's interest in the same subject. At that moment Sherman was being briefed by James McPhail of the CIB's support of the rising of the militias in the occupied areas of upper New England. "General, we have opened a second front against the enemy by smuggling weapons and ammunition and trained men into the occupied areas. We have a network of informants that gives us detailed knowledge of the railroad and British efforts to protect it. They are raising holy hell along the British line of communications. Not only is the Grand Trunk wheezing, but its protection is absorbing more and more Canadian militia. Unlike trained troops, they tend to get out of hand with reprisals and looting, which in turn drives more men into the militia."

Sherman was a man of nervous energy, and the briefing was conducted as they walked up and down in front of his headquarters. "McPhail, we shall have a go at them presently. Can you raise the militia to a new level of enthusiasm to coincide with it?"

"Yes! Just give me a week's notice, and we will bring the railroad to a stop."

"More than that, McPhail. I need the militia to appear on the enemy's communications in such numbers that they cannot be swept away by few battalions. I want to bleed Doyle just when he needs every man."

"Just give me a week, General."

"The clock is ticking."

YORKTOWN, VIRGINIA, 2:00 A.M., SATURDAY, APRIL 30, 1864

Weitzel was intent on his own timepiece as the second hand clicked up toward twelve and the hour hand almost full onto two. Unseen in the dark below was the huddled 11th Connecticut, the forlorn hope of his breakout plan, bayonets fixed and no rifle loaded so as not to give away the desperate lunge until it was upon the enemy.

The night was overcast, blotting out the ambient light of the stars. Only a faint glow came from the south where Longstreet's heavy artillery was hammering away at Fortress Monroe. The only other light was from the Union garrison at Gloucester Point a quarter mile directly across the York River. So close, yet so far. British gunboats had come up as far as the fort to cut off reinforcement and resupply across the river. The fort's guns had made that a costly effort, but it did keep the fort cut off.

Weitzel had learned of the disaster at Second Big Bethal by way of Longstreet's demand for his surrender, which listed in detail the losses of the battle. He had replied that he would not add to Longstreet's surfeit of good fortune by accepting his offer. Bold words, indeed, for a commander whose men had been on short rations and now had not eaten that day at all. More likely, he thought to himself, it was a case of talk was cheap. Escape was like ten years in jail, as Lincoln was wont to say—easy to say but hard to do.

What made Yorktown so easy to defend was the same thing that would make escape close to impossible. The riverfront of the fort measured 1,200 yards, the landward trace was twice as long, and most of it to the west and north was faced by a very bad swamp. No wonder Longstreet's besiegers had not bothered to assault. Hunger would reach the garrison long before an attacker could make his way through the swamp. Yet, it was that swamp that had to be crossed for the garrison to escape. Luckily an intact bridge still ran north over the mouth of the swamp as it drained into the York River. A Confederate battery guarded the other end. That meant a sudden and silent night assault with the bayonet. The cloak of night felt heavy with dread.

He turned to give the order for the attack when he heard shouting. "Damn," he muttered, "Who the hell is that?"

Then a familiar voice rang out, "General Weitzel, stop the attack! Stop the attack!" It was his cipher clerk. Weitzel climbed down from the redoubt as a muffled lantern cast a dull glow on the face of the clerk and another man behind him dressed in shabby clothes.

"Who the devil is this?'

The man said, "Anson Carney, scout for General Grant."

"Sir, I was about to burn my cipher when the river guards brought this man up with cipher message from General Grant. He handed Weitzel the message. It read, "Stand fast and maintain your position. General Hancock is on his way to your relief with II and VI Corps. Expect him by the seventh of May. Grant."

Weitzel swore. It was an order impossible to obey. His men had already gone a day without food. Their remaining energy would be better used breaking out to meet Hancock halfway. The messenger spoke, "Sir, I just came across the river from Gloucester Point; General Grant has driven a supply column to Gloucester. Everything that can float upriver has been collected there too. If your guns can hold off the British tonight, you should be resupplied for a few more days by morning. General Grant gave me a personal message for you. He said, "Hold on. I will not leave you in the lurch. Hold on."

MARTHA'S VINEYARD, MASSACHUSETTS, 4:10 P.M., SATURDAY, APRIL 30, 1864

Capt. Enoch Greenleafe Parrott decided he had never seen anything half so satisfying in his thirty-three years of service. He walked out onto the deck of the pilot house of the ironclad USS *Canonicus* and drank in the hellish results of his handiwork. The Royal Navy's forward operating base on the island was a shattered wreck. What had not been reduced to splinters or sunk was burning including warehouses, a dozen supply ships. Explosions in the ammunition dump sent debris and unexploded shells high into the air. Two American transports had unloaded an infantry regiment to secure the harbor and ensure that the British did not return. His ship and the double-turreted ironclad *Monadnock* had sortied from Boston early that morning, easily fought their way through the few enemy wooden ships on close blockade and fell upon the British base by noon. The corvette guarding the base was sunk with two hits from *Canonicus*'s 15-inch guns.

These two ships were only part of the fruit of the ironclad program set in motion by the building of the original monitor. They and sister ships had been rushed to completion by Carnegie's reorganization of defense industries. The day after their sortie, five more ironclads had also pushed their way through the blockade from New York — USS *Dictator, Onondaga, Tecumseh, Manhattan,* and *Mahopac.* The last three as well as *Canonicus* were ships of the eponymous class. Waiting to join them on their journey south was the USS *Saugus* in Wilmington, Delaware, another *Canonicus* class monitor. The others were all the first ships of their classes. All were armed with 15-inch Dahlgren guns.[17] [18]

As the flotilla exited the Verrazano Narrows into the Lower Bay of New York, a ship flying the Bralizian flag passed them heading up the narrows. She was hailed by *Dictator* and responded that she was the *Dom Pedro I* with a cargo of rubber. The crew took it as a good omen that the British blockade was flimsy enough to encourage foreign ships to sneak through for the premium prices offered in the North. The much closer Union blockade of Southern ports had still allowed enough foreign blockade runners to slip through to sustain the Confederacy for two years. The blockade of the North by the British was a far more arduous task.

Rear Admiral David Glasgow Farragut flew his pennant from the *Dictator.* At sixty-three years of age, Farragut had spent fifty-three of them in the navy. His father was a merchant captain from the Spanish island of Minorca and fought for the Patriots in the Revolution. On his death, his good friend, the future naval hero, David Porter, adopted the seven-year-old boy. By age nine, Farragut was a midshipman, and by eleven had seen action in the War of 1812. At age twelve he commanded a prize crew. By the start of the Civil War, if any man was navy to the bone, it was Davey Farragut, whose reputation among the old salts of the fleet was second to none. He proved that by boldly fighting his way past the river forts guarding the approach to New Orleans and capturing the city in April 1862. His support of Grant in the Vicksburg campaign was essential to that victory.

Men followed him because he was fearless, innovative, and possessed an unerring good sense for the dynamism of naval combat and for getting the best out of his men. One story that made its way around the fleet had him on his quarterdeck in the attack on Port Hudson in March 1863 unbraiding Lt. Winfield Scott Schley. "Captain, you begin early in your life to disobey orders. Did you not see the signal flying for near an hour to withdraw from action? . . . I want none of this Nelson business in my squadron." In Farragut's cabin later, he said to Schley, "I have censured you, sir, on my quarterdeck, for what appeared to be a disregard of my orders. I desire now to commend you and your officers and men for doing what you believe right under the circumstances. Do it again whenever in your judgment it is necessary to carry out your conception of duty."[19]

As the lines had been cast off *Dictator* at the Brooklyn Navy Yard, a courier had rushed up to the ship and leapt on board. He delivered a telegram from the President. Fearing some reverse of plans, Farragut opened it, only to smile. It read: "Fair seas and following winds. A. Lincoln."

FORD'S THEATER, WASHINGTON, DC, 3:22 P.M., MONDAY, MAY 2, 1864

Booth knocked on the stage door. He waited and knocked again, this time rapping on the door with the silver end of his walking stick. He turned to Harney, who was dressed as a day laborer, and smiled confidently. The man began to look nervous. Booth said, "I told you not to worry. Monday is not a performance day. Everyone else's is resting from Sundays performances. We will find very few people here today."

Just then the door opened, and the old doorkeeper, John Peanut, named for the snacks he sold during performances, looked out. "Oh, Mr. Booth is it?"

"Peanut, I have a trunk for my dressing room." Peanut glanced down at the large leather-bound trunk on the ground and the workman standing by it. He would normally have offered to help, but Booth was known to have no use for little people. Even though a tip was customary, he said nothing but only held the door open.

Harney heaved the trunk to his shoulder and followed Booth inside where Booth asked the old man, "Anyone else here today, Peanut?"

"No, Mr. Booth. Mr. Ford was here earlier, but he went home." Without another word Booth walked down the hall to the dressing rooms. Peanut shuffled off to tend to his sweeping.[20]

As soon as he was gone, Booth changed direction to the backstage. He lit a lamp, lifted the ring of a trap door, and descended. Putting the lamp on the hard-packed dirt floor, he reached up as Harney slid the trunk down to him. After Harney followed, Booth led the way with the lamp to the end of the passage that curved a bit after reaching where stage right would have been. Booth pointed to the ceiling. "Up there is the presidential box where the tyrant will be sitting. Plant your device there."

Harney retrieved the trunk and took out his bomb, filled with fifty pounds of gunpowder. He placed the bomb on top of a brick wall on which oak beams for ceiling rested, fitting just between the beams. "The wall will force the explosion upward."

"Just where we want it." said Booth.

Harney dusted off his hands, took one last look at his handiwork. He connected the clockwork timer that would trigger the detonation to the bomb. "Now, don't forget to set the timer as I showed you. You should have plenty of time to get out after you set it."

"Oh, yes, indeed, man." He laughed softly. "You see, this passage leads to another trap door and runs to the Star Saloon next door. I will have time to set it and be leaning over the bar savoring good Southern bourbon when the bomb blows King Lincoln to hell."[21]

ENTRANCE TO CHESAPEAKE BAY, 3:44 P.M., TUESDAY, MAY 3, 1864

It was with just such fair seas and following winds that Adm. James Hope and his iron fleet had crossed the Atlantic and now entered America's great waterway. Hope immediately assumed command of all Royal Navy forces operating in the bay and meet with Longstreet to coordinate the reduction of Fortress Monroe. Hope offered the use of more heavy mortars, siege guns, and several companies of Royal Engineers (sappers) that had arrived in a convoy of transports. Longstreet eagerly accepted.

Since the British were in such a giving mood, he was not shy in suggesting other ways they could be of assistance. Two days later, a large British naval force and transports steamed up the bay past the mouth of the Rappahannock and turned into the Potomac River. Washington panicked as the word spread that the Royal Navy was again attacking the capital. A steady stream of carriages and packed trains went north past large areas of the city that were still mounds of rubble and ashes.

Lincoln sauntered over to the telegraph office at the CIB right across Lafayette Circle from the White House. The War Department's telegraph office would be haunted by Stanton, whose tendency to alarm was unsettling. Lincoln found Sharpe's offices to be island of calm and information. "Well, boys," he said as he eased himself into the stuffed chair that Sharpe had reserved for him, "What have Jeffy D. and Bobby Lee put Her Majesty's navy up to this time?"[22]

Sharpe was scanning the latest telegram. He looked puzzled. "It seems that they are not coming up the river; they have stopped at its mouth opposite Point Lookout." Then he just said, "Damn!"

It was Lincoln's turn to look puzzled.

Point Lookout was the southern tip of Maryland's St. Mary's County. It was also the location of Camp Hoffman, the largest POW camp in the Union. Established after Gettysburg to confine the more than five thousand unwounded Confederate prisoners taken in that battle, it covered thirty acres barely five feet above sea level. By this time, the number of prisoners had swollen to more than ten thousand.[23] These men were a resource more precious than gold to the Confederacy. The flood of British equipment and supplies that had reoutfitted the Confederate forces could only go so far. What the South needed was men. She had scrapped the bottom of the manpower barrel already, and British arms and uniforms were no use if there were no men to use them. There were indeed men, many tens of thousands, but they were POWs in the North. Since U.S. Grant had suspended the cartel that exchanged prisoners, the steady return of released men to the armies had come to a stop.

The Royal Navy was doing something about that. Its guns had leveled the small forts around the POW camp and the camp for the Union guard regiments. Their ships boldly sailed up to the docks to threaten further mayhem as transports unloaded Confederate infantry. The stockades were ringing with the rebel yell, and even before their rescuers could free them, the men inside burst out through the gates and tore the plank walls apart with their bare hands. Their guards had fled.

Capt. Cowper Coles was given the honor of taking HMS *Prince Albert* a few miles up the river to trail the Royal Navy's coat in front of Washington. He went a little further and lobbed a few shells at Fort Washington a few miles south of Alexandria on the Maryland side of the river. Then with a triumphant shriek of the ship's steam whistle, she turned her backside to the American capital.[24]

1 3

Running the Roads

Meagher passed not too steadily along the parapet of the great redoubt named for the American president. He was trying to encourage his boys as the British artillery flared through the early morning darkness with an endless rain of shells. Behind him trailed Brigadier General Kelly and Sergeant Major Wright. Kelly could tell that it was not the impact of the shells that made Meagher sway so. He turned to Wright and grabbed him by the arm, "For God's sake, Sergeant Major, get him back to the castle."

Meagher had grandly rejected the seductively generous terms of surrender and declared he would fight on for a free Ireland. Napier had promptly put Dublin under close siege. "Not so much as a mouse shall get in or out of Dublin," he had said. Briefly that had worked for Meagher and his Fenian council, who in the absence of contradictory information, were able to speak boldly of how the entire island had risen and an army of volunteers was massing to break the siege. But Disraeli's policy of pacification was strangling the rebellion. It was not long before the emptiness of those words began to seep into the mind of every man.

Kelly had not even that long to come to the awful conclusion that the game was up. After Tallaght his spirits had soared like everyone else, but when the volunteers stopped coming, and the British threw down heavy siege, he recognized the inevitable. That same hopelessness had not been lost on Meagher, who found solace in the bottle, and on the Fenian council, which fed its doubt with endless sterile argument as if words alone had magic. For all that Kelly had been the soul of the defense. A man of a valiant but practical nature who had the love of his "brave byes," he prowled the defenses, buoying morale and seeing with that unseen eye the weak and vulnerable points. He also seemed to have the knack of being on the spot to commit his reserve whenever the British attempted an assault.

For their part, the British were unable to smash their way into the city. There had been great reluctance to damage the architectural gem that was Dublin. Disreali had been quite clear in his instructions to Napier: "We cannot be put in the position of saving Dublin by destroying it." Such savagery would undermine the pacification policy and damage British prestige in Europe, something that had already suffered immensely by the Dahlgren Raid and the fall of Dublin. Disraeli had made it quite clear that a negotiated surrender was the result the government wanted. So Napier's gunners were constrained to target only the makeshift earthen defenses of the city. Within that constraint, though, they were accurate and deadly. Hunger was also working for them. Rations had been cut and cut again for the men, and the civilian population was getting desperate.

Napier did more than passively let hunger do its work but actively used it to affect the enemy's morale by proclaiming that any civilian in Dublin would be escorted through the lines and fed. Meagher had clutched at the opportunity to rid himself of hungry mouths, and the streets were filled with people fleeing the city. Napier ensured that field kitchens lavishly fed the refugees in sight of the defenders.

THE WHITE HOUSE, WASHINGTON, DC, 9:22 A.M., THURSDAY, MAY 5, 1864
As soon as Lincoln left the White House he tipped his hat to the squad of Sharpe's 20th New York that served as his escort whenever he walked nearby to either the War Department or CIB. If he was going any distance by carriage a platoon of Sharpe's 3rd Indiana Cavalry rode with him sabers drawn. Sharpe and the entire cabinet had insisted after the assassination attempt during the battle of Washington last October. Normally, he would have had a joke or story to tell the boys, but today he was clearly preoccupied. "Let's go see Mr. Stanton, boys," was all he said.

Today it would all be coming together. The armies and the fleet were all on the move from Maine to Virginia. Only yesterday morning had the awful news of the fall of San Francisco to the British arrived. The stock market had crashed because of the loss of the enormous gold reserves of California. Overnight the Treasury could not sell a single bond. To prove the old wives' tale that disasters came in threes, Sharpe had just informed him that newspapers smuggled out of Canada were confirming with undisguised glee the dispatch of Britain's entire ironclad fleet to the Chesapeake. That would be the one thing that could wreck the joint effort to regain control of the bay. Then events would just drift the country into defeat. National morale was an exhaustible quality, as was the stockpile of niter. He did not think it could survive another severe setback.

His shoulders sagged with the weight of the world. It was not just this crisis, but the relentless tide of them in his presidency and its accumulated weariness that bore down on him so. The war had laid more than the burden of responsibility on him. It had taken his darling boy Willy of typhoid two years ago. He had found in Sharpe an open heart and had said to him, "Do you ever find yourself talking with the dead? Since Willie's death, I catch myself every day involuntarily talking with him as if he were with me."[1] This glimpse into the dark place in Lincoln's soul where ghosts flitted about had taken Sharpe aback. Had all the storms of the last few years seriously weakened the roots of this oak of a man? If he gave way, the nation would topple with him. He had discussed this with Lincoln's devoted secretaries, John Hay and John Nickolay, both of whom had similar worries.

In an exercise of will, Lincoln forced himself to think of what lay on the credit side of the ledger of war without which this new crisis would have swamped the country already. Chief among them was the creation of a national intelligence service and the appointment of George Sharpe to lead it. The man and his organization proved to be what future generations would call a combat multiplier, doubling the strength of the armed forces by providing the intelligence that allowed for their most efficient use. Efficiency and innovation were the pillars of the reorganization of defense production under the guidance of the War Production Board and its chief, that little Scotch devil, Andrew Carnegie. Because of these reforms, repeating weapons in great numbers were reaching the armies and production of submersibles, aerosphips, and ironclads were bearing fruit. The Army had delivered two victories in the field—driving back the British attack in Upstate New York and destroying the French army in Louisiana. The latter had bonus effects of seriously weakening the prestige of the Louis Napoleon and French arms and calling into question the strength of his regime itself. Defeat was a great sower of doubt.

Across the Atlantic, Disraeli was thinking through a similar calculation. He had ridden to power on a drumbeat of defeats unparalleled in British history of the last three hundred years. He did not bear the blame for them, but he thereby assumed the responsibility to set things right. Instead, more blows had fallen on the British Empire in the last month. The defeats in October had been on the distant battlefields of empire. Those of this April had struck at the center of British power. He had to admit that the raid into Essex was brilliant by spreading panic that an American army of invasion was about to descend on London. That and the Russian squadron savaging commerce in the Irish Sea had struck at British prestige and that unique English sense of invulnerability. The

fall of Dublin had been more dangerously concrete and followed by
the disaster at Tallaght, the first defeat of British arms in Ireland since
Cromwell's time. For a few terrible weeks, it seemed the whole island
would burst into flames. Then had come the news he was dreading
most — the Russian declaration of war.

Although the British had the wealth of empire to finance the war, it did
not mean that the cost would be borne easily. American commerce raiders
had seriously panicked British shipping all the way from the Indian Ocean
to the South China Seas. Insurance rates by Lloyds had skyrocketed,
especially after the Russian commerce raiding in the Irish Sea and the ease
with which the Americans had made two serious landings in the British
Isles. The loss of the enormous American market was compounded by
the new loss of the Russian market as well. These two countries were
also the major suppliers of grain to both Britain and most of the rest of
Europe.[2] The wheat supply from Canada was now tenuous at best. The
loss of access to foreign grain had been a major cause of the huge death toll
in Ireland during the famine. Bad harvests in Russia were compounded
by the Europeans buying up the American surplus first, leaving none for
London when it realized the extent of the catastrophe.

Now with Russia's entry into the war, Britain was caught between
two stools. The conflict in North America was such that it could not be
fought on the cheap. It was all or nothing. Canada hung in the balance.
With Russia opening a theater almost half the planet away, India now
would also hang in the balance. Canada had three million loyal British
subjects, blood of British blood, and bone of British bone. To abandon
them would make Britain's reputation stink for hundreds of years and
place it on a par with Bourbon France that had abandoned the Quebecois
in 1763. India, on the other hand, was the treasure chest of the empire.
Lose Canada, and the Empire would survive; lose India, and it would
collapse. It made Solomon's judgment sound easy.

Disraeli found himself paying special attention to the growing
voices demanding an end to the war. They were resonating off the deep
animosity to slavery in the British public. Despite Disraeli's private
urging of Jefferson Davis to begin to do away with the South's peculiar
institution, the Confederate president was resistant. He thought he
could have it both ways. It was said that he could teach a mule about
obstinacy. Other voices spoke of the millions of kin that had emigrated
to the United States, making this war one of fratricide. John Bright
repeatedly gave voice to these sentiments in the House, ending every
speech with "Make peace, you fools!"

In the ledger's positive column, Disraeli could point to the collapse
of the rebellion in Ireland and the inevitable recapture of Dublin. In

New York the British Army had administered a drubbing to the Americans at Chazy, ironically the same battle Lincoln counted as a victory. California, where Midas has left his golden touch, had been snatched from the Americans. The Iron Fleet had been dispatched to secure the control of the Chesapeake, secure the naval base at Norfolk. The permanent loss of the bay would cripple American attempts in the eastern theater to defeat the Confederacy. In fact, British rearmament of the Confederate armies made them more dangerous to the Americans, taking pressure off Canada. British greatest advantage was her status as the foremost industrialized country in the world many times the size of the United States and Russia combined. The shipyards, steel mills, cotton mills, and thousands of other enterprises pouring out a stream of the weapons of war unparalleled in history, not least of which were the scores of ironclads on the ways. Finally, there was something positive in the French defeat in Louisiana. Britain had no interest in France reestablishing itself in North America, which had plainly been Louis Napoleon's aim. An independent Confederacy would find its sole patron in London and not in Paris.[3]

HANOVER JUNCTION, VIRGINIA, 9:30 A.M., THURSDAY, MAY 5, 1864

Little Phil Sheridan sat on his magnificent black warhorse, Rienzi, watching the destruction of the Virginia Central Railroad west of Hanover Junction.[4] The new commander of the Cavalry Corps of the Army of the Potomac had been one of Grant's successful generals in his western campaigns and had come east with the new general-in-chief. This son of an Irish immigrant was one of the black Irish with dark hair and fierce, penetrating black eyes. He stood barely five foot three inches tall, but he was the biggest cavalryman this army had ever seen. An aggressive talent for the kill was what set him apart. One of his subordinates described his influence as "like an electric shock. He was the only commander I ever saw whose personal appearance in the field was an immediate and positive stimulus to battle." Another summed him up when he said that he was "a little mountain of combative force."[5]

His corps was in fine shape, on well-fed horses, his men experienced, well-trained, and well-armed with the new Spencers. His two divisions were commanded by talented officers, Brig. Gens. David M. Gregg and James H. Wilson, and his reserve brigade of mostly regular regiments by one of the army's bright young talents, Brig. Gen. Wesley Merritt.

It was Wilson's 2nd Brigade that was so busy in wrecking the railroad. This was the twenty-seven-year-old brevet brigadier general's first combat command as a cavalry officer. He was commissioned as an engineer in the West Point class of 1860 and had so impressed Grant that he was the only member of his staff that he had appointed to a combat command. David McMurtie Gregg had taken the 1ˢᵗ Brigade further down the line to wreck another section of the line. Unlike Wilson, he had been commissioned in the cavalry, and ironically at West Point had been the best of friends with both Stuart and Sheridan. He was a bold and aggressive officer who had rubbed Stuart's nose raw at Brandy Station and repulsed him at Gettysburg on the third day. Sheridan would come to rely upon this quiet Pennsylvanian in the days to come.

Sheridan had taken the corps and dashed the twenty-five miles from south of Fredericksburg to Hanover Junction in a day of hard riding. Hancock's Army of the Rappahannock was following. Now the railroad ties were making bonfires. The soft iron rails thrown on them were glowing red when a half-dozen gloved men grasped each end and wrapped them around telegraph poles, something he had learned from Sherman. The smoke from the fires could be seen even beyond the trees. Sheridan was determined to wreck the railroad severely enough that the enemy could not repair it in time to affect the operations underway.

As talented as Sheridan was, he was playing on the board of war with a grand master. Sheridan's departure from around Spotsylvania had not gone unnoticed by his counterpart. Maj. Gen. J.E.B. Stuart notified Lee immediately, who ordered him to follow Sheridan with his own cavalry. Six hours after Sheridan reached the junction, two miles south of the North Anna River, Stuart's scouts were briefing him on the disposition of the Union cavalry. They had slipped through Sheridan's pickets without detection. It did not take long for Stuart to realize that this was the opportunity to pay back the Union cavalry for its surprise attack on his camp at Brandy Station the previous June. The humiliation still stung. Attempting to redeem himself in the Gettysburg Campaign by taking the time to trail his coat past Washington, he failed Lee at the great battle. That only doubled down on the shame.

No one could say, though, that Stuart did not learn from his mistakes. More than his own honor was at stake. Sheridan's cavalry had put its boot on the throat of the Army of Northern Virginia. If Stuart could not drive them away, the army was doomed — cut off from resupply with Meade in close pursuit and Sheridan across his route of retreat. He counted himself lucky that the enemy cavalry corps had only two divisions since its first division had been sent north to the Army of the Hudson last fall. The first thing he did was send couriers racing to Lee and Longstreet to inform them of the dire threat to the army's communications and to Richmond. The second was to attack.

HAMPTON ROADS, 11:35 A.M., THURSDAY, MAY 5, 1864

Just as Stuart's couriers put spurs to their mounts, Admiral Hope's iron fleet of six ironclads steamed Chesapeake Bay — *Royal Oak, Hector, Prince Consort, Royal Sovereign, Prince Albert,* and *Wivern* — bearing 106 guns and manned by 2,400 men (Appendix D). The rumble of heavy guns rolled across the bay from Hampton Roads, where the ongoing attack on Fortress Monroe thundered on. A cloud of black powder smoke guided them across the bay.

Upon joining the squadron already in the bay, Hope transferred his flag to HMS *Warrior,* the largest ship in the Royal Navy and the first of its ironclads. *Warrior* with the smaller HSM *Resistance,* was part of the originally part of the force that had descended on the bay after the outbreak of war. Their sister ships, HMS *Black Prince* and *Defence,* had been sunk at Charleston in October. He immediately took a steam launch to do a personal reconnaissance of Hampton Roads and observe the attack on Fortress Monroe and then called a meeting of his captains the next day.

It was at this meeting that he was informed that Lieutenant General Longstreet was approaching in a launch to pay his respects. The ship's crew sprang to action to prepare a fitting welcome. The gun salute for a lieutenant general began firing as the launch approached. Longstreet climbed aboard as the boatswain's whistle pierced the air and a platoon of Royal Marines presented arms with a snap. The first thing Hope noticed about his visitor was that he was a big, powerful man who carried himself with a menace of a predator. He was known as a great warrior among the British, and Hope's captains were eager to meet him. Military protocol required the introductions to the several dozen captains, and Longstreet had not got halfway through when the noise of another launch engine approached and a man started shouting, "General Longstreet, General Longstreet!" A Confederate officer scrambled up the ship's ladder, strode across the deck, and saluted. It was Maj. Moxley Sorrel. Longstreet dreaded what had brought his young and very capable chief of staff to him in this manner.

Sorrel bowed to the British officers and said, "General, a dispatch from General Stuart of the utmost importance." He handed the message to him, unaware that he had captured the complete attention of the cream of the Royal Navy with the drama of his arrival. Longstreet read it quickly and then asked for a private word with Admiral Hope. "I must depart at once. The enemy has placed General Lee's army in great danger. Major Sorely has already ordered the corps on the road in my name. I must ride to catch up."[6]

BRIGHTON, VERMONT, 11:49 P.M., THURSDAY, MAY 5, 1864

The Canadian patrols around Brighton had had the predictable pattern of inexperience, and that was their undoing. One by one they fell prey to Custer's 1st Vermont Cavalry Regiment.[7] The Vermont men especially were rougher than required. Some of the men were from Brighton and the surrounding counties. To say that they were eager to fall upon the railroad center was an understatement. None was more eager than the Vermonter's commander, Col. William Wells, of whom Custer had said, "He is my ideal of a cavalry officer." He had commanded a battalion of the regiment and repulsed Stuart himself at Hanover just before Gettysburg and at the battle itself rode in the suicide charge that killed his brigade commander. His gallantry in that campaign won him the Medal of Honor.[8]

It was Wells's mission to capture and wreck the railroad yards at Brighton as the opening move in Sherman's campaign to retake Maine. The 1st Vermont was reinforced by the 2nd Massachusetts Infantry, detached from the Army of the Hudson's provost guard brigade. These fifteen hundred would be faced by two Canadian militia battalions of about a thousand men. Wells, however, would have experience and surprise on his side, not to mention a thousand Vermont state militia that would attack from the north side of the town first to distract the defenders from his own attack from the south. Wells expected nothing more of the militia than that distraction.

He looked at his watch; there was a half hour before the attack was to begin. A whistle in the distance made him glance in that direction. First smoke above the trees then a locomotive and endless cars appeared from the north. The train came to a halt in the station. "Good," he thought, "another fat prize." The car doors opened, a stream of men in red filled the platform and smartly formed ranks. Through his glasses, Wells could tell that these were not militia. He did not realize that it was the Guards Brigade itself that had stopped for a hot midday meal. Suddenly the sound of firing came echoing over the lake next to Brighton. He looked at his watch again. The militia had attacked early.

The Guards Brigade commander immediately assumed command of the post of Brighton from the Canadian militia officer there and promptly moved his battalions to the sound of the guns. Col. E.R. Wetherall had come out to Canada in late 1860 as chief of staff to the previous commander of British forces in North America. Grant gave him command of the Guards, which he ably led at Chazy, and had praised him in dispatches for breaking the jaws of the American encirclement.

By the sound of the gunfire outside of town, this promised to be a good fight. He put the Grenadiers and Scots Fusiliers on line abreast and led them forward as Canadian pickets came rushing back through their ranks. He ordered one of the Canadian garrison battalions to form a reserve in his rear. It did not take long for his skirmishers to make contact with the militia clumsily making its way forward. The thin British line stopped the Vermont men in their tracks with one crushing volley. The brigade's battery now opened fire dropping shells into the militia. Wetherall ordered a bayonet charge, and with a shout the Guards rushed forward. The militia got off a ragged volley and fled into the woods. They ran so fast through the briars and the brambles that the British could not catch a single one.

At the north end of town, Wells's cavalry came crashing in, riding down the Canadian pickets. The 2nd Massachusetts followed with the bayonet. In ten minutes the rail yards had fallen, and the destruction of the rail facilities had begun. That very moment futher down the rail line the New Hampshire militia under the leadership of John Lynn, reinforced by the 1st West Virginia Cavalry guided by Sergeant Knight, were swarming into Gorham also to the complete surprises of the Canadian. Almost simultaneously, the two most important rail yards on the American leg of the Grand Trunk Railway had been captured.

Hearing the crash of gunfire from the town, Colonel Wetherall halted the pursuit of the militia. A frantic Canadian officer rode up to blurt out that American cavalry and infantry were in the town. Leaving the Canadian battalion to guard against a sudden rebirth of the militia's courage, he turned the Guards battalions back. They ran into the dismounted Vermont cavalry behind some of those ubiquitous Vermont stone walls. The slaughter of Tallaght appeared to be set again in bloody motion for the British as their front ranks dropped in the fire stream that struck them. If ever the Guards were to waver, it was now, especially now, as an American battery unlimbered to throw case shot into them. But it was not now. Wetherall ordered the drummers to beat the charge and rode to the front. With a shout the Guards rushed forward straight into the fire of the Spencers. They fell by the scores but pressed on over the fallen. The Scots Fusiliers were the first to reach the wall. The fury of their rush made the Vermonters flinch as they closed. The bayonet has an incredible affect on the mind of the man about to meet its sharp end, especially if his own rifle is not equipped with one. The cavalry broke and rushed back to where their mounts were being held and fell back into the town.

Wells had to pull the Massachusetts men away from wrecking the yards and into line of battle, but Wetherall was not giving him the time as he pushed into the town. The Guards overwhelmed each company as it came up and before they could mass their firepower. The fighting broke up into multiple combats in the streets and gardens of Brighton, and in this man-to-man fighting, the big men of the Guards had an advantage. Still they paid as groups of men in dark blue and scarlet fought from house to house, leaving trails of bodies. Before long the inevitable fires started turning buildings into torches. The commander of the Canadian battalion watching the militia disobeyed his orders as the crescendo of battle reached him. Leaving two companies to deal with the militia, he rushed his remaining men back into the town to join the fight. They came just in time; the Guards needed a moment to catch their breath, something the Canadian attack would not allow the Americans to do.

Until then Wells believed that he could hold off the British but not now as the fresh Canadians entered the fight. He looked about him; many of the facilities of the rail yard were burning and soon would be of no use to the enemy. He had accomplished half of his mission, the more important half — to wreck the yards. If they were useless to the enemy, it would not matter if he did not hold the ruins. So, he ordered a retreat and extricated his men as fast as he could. They retreated down the line to the south. Eventually, when he had broken contact, he stopped to begin tearing up the tracks.

HANOVER JUNCTION, VIRGINIA, 3:30 P.M., THURSDAY, MAY 5, 1864

The dismounted Union cavalrymen guarding the Chesterfield Bridge thought the approaching cavalry shrouded in a cloud of dust to be the advance guard of Hancock's army. The bridge crossed the North Anna a half mile west of the railroad bridge of the RF&P Railroad. When it was too late to matter to the guards, the 35th Virginia Battalion broke into a gallop, screeched out the rebel yell, and rode them down in a flurry of sabers and pistols. After them came the powerful cavalry division of Maj. Gen. Wade Hampton. This forty-five-year-old general was a superb horseman and a bold and audacious cavalry commander. The wealthiest planter and largest owner of slaves in the South had no military experience at all when the war started. He was found to be a natural cavalry commander, every bit as good as Stuart but without the showmanship.

At the same time that Hampton's men were streaming over Chesterfield Bridge, the smaller division of Maj. Gen. Fitzhugh Lee splashed across the unguarded Ox Ford on the North Anna a few miles to the west and in one mile reached Anderson Junction on the Virginia Central Railroad. Fitzhugh Lee was Robert E. Lee's nephew and had served with his uncle in the 2nd Cavalry in Texas before the war, distinguishing himself in actions against the Comanche Indians. Wilson's 2nd Brigade, in its frenzy of destruction of the railroad, was separated into many small dismounted parties. Lee's brigades rolled them up north and south of the station, taking many prisoners.[9]

Sheridan had little time to help Wilson. Hampton's brigades were converging on Hanover Junction where Sheridan's other division and his reserve brigade was concentrated. He had only been alerted to the approaching enemy by a surviving cavalryman from the bridge guard who had left bloody gouges in his horse's flanks from his spurs to give the warning. Sheridan ordered up Gregg's division and Merritt's brigade.

Halfway between them was a small stream of fateful name — Bull Run. Ironically, it was not *the* Bull Run of the battles of 1861 and 1862 in Manassas County to the north. Only the name of this Hanover County stream was the same. Stuart waved his black-plumed hat as he crossed saying to his boys that the name alone brought luck to Southern arms. Sheridan also noticed the name and muttered that it was time to change the enemy's luck.

The ground between them was largely open farmland with small woodlots.[10] Stuart and Sheridan could not have picked a more classic cavalry battlefield if they had searched all of Virginia. It was as the Greek general Epaminondas had described the battlefields of his native Beoetia — "the dancing floor of war" — so could once fair Virginia in this terrible war succeed to that honor.[11]

ENTRANCE TO CHESAPEAKE BAY, 3:48 P.M., THURSDAY, MAY 5, 1864

Farragut's squadron entered the great bay guided also by the smoke of the ongoing battle for Fortress Monroe barely twelve miles distant. A British picket boat fled ahead of them to give warning. Behind the ironclads came a line of supply ships loaded with coal and ammunition for the ships trapped at Norfolk. One ship, the most closely guarded of all, carried the special gas generator wagons and aeroship ground crews. Guarding them was a half-dozen sloops and the powerful wooden frigate USS *Brooklyn*, armed with twenty Dalhgren 9-inch guns.

From the telegraph station on the tip of the Virginia Peninsula a message instantly flew across the wires to Washington that Farragut had arrived. The Washington Navy Yard suddenly flew into action with the suddenness of a release of great tension. The last preparations were made before the new submersibles USS *Dophin* and *Stingray* steamed down the Potomac. The gas generators began pumping hydrogen into the cigar frames of the *George Washington*, *Stephen Decatur*, *Andrew Jackson*, and *John Paul Jones*. Gus Fox rushed to the Navy Yard to witness their departure. Lincoln and Sharpe arrived soon thereafter to cheer them on.

From Farragut's flagship, USS *Dictator* the signal flags flew up to order the squadron to prepare for action. The line of ironclads broke into two parallel divisions three hundred yards apart with *Dictator* halfway between and parallel with the lead ships. Into the space between the divisions, the supply ships and their escorts entered. It was a defensive formation meant to fight its way through the Royal Navy's blockade of Norfolk.

Surprise would do half the work. The picket boat gave Hope barely a half hour's warning.[12] The signal flags shot up with the order to prepare for fleet action. Beat to quarters sounded on dozens of ships. Unfortunately, Hope's discussions with his captains did not include instructions on a fleet action with a large monitor force entering the bay. They had concentrated on the continuing blockade of Norfolk and attack on Fortress Monroe. The only offensive instructions were those in case the U.S. Navy issued from Norfolk.

Farragut's force arrived in the midst of Hope's efforts to form a battle line just to the east of the fort in the bay. The Americans gun crews had their orders to aim for the enemy masts when they could. His object was to force his way past the British ships. To slug it out ship to ship would trap him in a knock-down-drag-out fight when his objective was to get into Norfolk. A demasted ship's movement was hindered if not paralyzed by the mass of shattered mast, spars, and sails dragging over the side.

The British ships began to fire as soon as their guns could bear. Some of their rifled guns had the range on the American smoothbores, but they chose to concentrate their fire on the monitors rather than the wooden warships and supply ships in the center of the American formation. HMS *Royal Oak* found herself at the apex of the American formation. Her broadside of six 7-inch Armstrong breech loaders and twelve 68-pounders concentrated on Farragut's flagship, but *Dictator*'s low freeboard and single turret were very small targets. Those hits it did get on the turret merely left dents in its 15-inch armor. But when *Dictator*'s own twin 15-inch Dahlgrens spoke, *Royal Oak* shuddered under impact of two 400-pound shells tearing through her armor and detonating inside. *Onandaga* and *Monandnock*'s twin Dahlgrens also spoke. The mainmast snapped and fell over the side. Fires were breaking out when the American formation passed on either side, each ship firing into her. *Royal Oak*'s hull was wooden; originally laid down as a ship-of-the-line, she had been cut down to a single gun deck and remodeled as an ironclad. Her wooden structure had made it impossible to build any watertight compartments or fit transverse armored bulkheads as had the all-iron *Warrior* and *Resistance* classes. She now paid the price for this shortcut. With great sections of her ironclad wooden hull smashed open, she began to flood.

Capt. Cowper Coles' *Prince Albert* on detached duty had been cruising the bay and instantly turned about when the American ships had been sighted. She came up on the starboard of the Americans and immediately engaged the closest monitor, the USS *Mahopac*, the last in line. *Prince Albert*'s four 9-inch smoothbores were the most powerful guns the Royal Navy possessed, and Coles was determined to use them at the closest range his guns could be depressed for *Prince Albert* rode higher in the water than the American ship. As he closed the range, *Mahopac*'s guns fired with one shot a clear miss and the other striking across his deck to miss the mainmast but sweeping away the funnel. The men in *Mahopac*'s turrets were knocked to their feet and stunned in the midst of reloading by the double impact of British 9-inch shot. Coles's second and third turrets fired down at *Mahopac*'s deck with shells that easily tore through the deck armor and exploded inside. The American ship slowed and fell out of line, a huge plume of smoke gushed from the hole in its deck. She began to settle; no one emerged from the ship as the water lapped over the deck and poured through the holes in the deck. She went down quickly.

Farragut broke through with all of his transports despite the loss of *Mahopac*. In what would become known as the battle of Running the Roads, both sides had drawn blood. It would not be the last.[13]

BIDDEFORD, MAINE, 3:55 P.M., THURSDAY, MAY 5, 1864

Biddeford's fame had long been hidden under a bushel. Massachusetts had so long and loudly claimed to have the first English settlement in New England at Plymouth, that almost no one knew that Biddeford had been settled in the winter of 1616–17, about four years earlier than Plymouth. Its next claim to fame would definitely be better remembered. Both the British and American armies in Maine were marching to that very spot.

Biddeford was a logical place to fight, with rolling fields and pastures offering good maneuver room for both sides to the south, especially since both sides were determined to attack. The town was almost equidistant from Portland and Kennebunk, about fifteen miles. The Saco River ran just north of the town, and a twin town, also named Saco, lay just across a bridge on the north bank of the river. The Saco divided into two falls that dropped forty feet (twelve meters). There was only one problem with the rolling countryside south of Biddeford as a battlefield for the British. They would have the Saco River at their back. On the other hand, the town with all its substantial factory buildings could become a fortress that could cover a British retreat across the Saco River bridge.

Doyle's small cavalry brigade (9th Lancers and 11th Hussars) trotted across the bridge in the middle of the afternoon and rode south to find the Americans that the army's scouts reported were advancing north on the main road. They did not have long to look. Custer's lead brigade met them about a mile and half south of the town. At the same time the leading patrols of both sides clattered onto opposite ends of a covered bridge over a small stream. The Hussar officer in the lead drew his saber in one fluid motion, spurred his horse forward, and screamed, "Charge!" The horse hooves on the wooden bridge planks echoed and magnified in the covered bridge. He crashed into the American officer who was still drawing his pistol and cut him out of the saddle. His men flew past to hack and stab and the enemy now halted on the bridge. The impact knocked men off their horses to be trampled on the plank floor. It was almost impossible to turn a horse around or fire a pistol through the screaming, heaving mass of horses and men. The Americans at the rear got out finally and galloped back the way they came with the Hussars in pursuit.

It was then that the Hussars found out how their less than efficient carbine was outclassed by the American colt revolvers and Spencer repeaters. The fight on the bridge alerted Custer's 1st Michigan coming up the road with their general at its head. They were ready when the survivors of the first patrol came hurtling past them with Hussars in pursuit only to run into the repeater and revolver fire from the charging Michiganders.

Custer's men chased the Hussars back across the bridge just as the British cavalry brigade came into view down the road. Custer's horse artillery and Gatling batteries were just bringing up the rear when both sides began to deploy. He had had the good judgment to send an aide racing back to Sherman to announce that contact had been made. The British cavalry commander had done the same thing when he realized that Custer was streaming across the bridge, but his message arrived a half hour after Custer's. Sherman put that thirty minutes to good use. The pace of the infantry was increased on the parallel routes being taken by his two corps. Like Napoleon, Sherman was a great believer in marching separately and uniting to fight together. Two corps marching on the same road one behind the other would mean that the second formation would take much longer to get into battle than the first, just when mass was vital. By marching on a parallel route, both corps would bet able to get into the fight at the same time.

A second courier announced that the British cavalry had been sighted and were with infantry marching up behind. With luck, Sherman thought, he could trap the smaller British force between his two corps if Custer was successful in getting the enemy to deploy. He had done just that. General Doyle immediately ordered his two divisions to spread out from column to an advancing line. Wolseley argued forcefully against such an early deployment without greater knowledge of the enemy's position and action, but Doyle informed him that the army commander had made a decision, not invited debate.

HANOVER JUNCTION, VIRGINIA, 4:10 P.M., THURSDAY, MAY 5, 1864

Stuart had also made a decision. He had to break the Union cavalry with one brutal shock. He could not budge them with a series of small unit actions. In response Wade Hampton's large division spread out in regimental columns and advanced toward Gregg's division. His trumpeter signaled the advance, which was echoed by regiments and companies all along the dusty advancing front. Sabers flew out to glitter in the clear May sun. Stuart rode along their front his famous flack plume whipping behind his gray hat.

Sheridan realized that Stuart had gone for broke and rode along the front of Gregg's division waving his hat. "Break 'em, boys! Break 'em!" Each regiment cheered as he passed, the men caught up in the intoxicating excitement of the moment. Gregg ordered them forward, and thousands more sabers rasped from their scabbards.

Sheridan was not about to get completely lost in the glories of the *arm blanche*.[14] His field artillery batteries had already been positioned on the few small rises and began to fire. Shell's burst among the Confederate cavalry, emptying saddles and sending animals crashing in sprays of blood. As they got closer, the guns switched to case shot, which swept away whole sections, but still they closed up.

The columns met in a wide stretch of wheat fields with the young grain just fresh and green. Horses went down in the impact, throwing their riders into the mass of hacking and shouting mounted men. Here and there the more practical had sheathed their sabers and were firing with their pistols, but it was a still a fight of steel on steel. Men would say this was the most savage cavalry fight of the war—men from Massachusetts, New York, New Jersey, and Pennsylvania and men from Virginia, Georgia, South Carolina, and Mississippi.

Both Stuart and Sheridan bided their time until the moment when they each would fulfill the primary role of the senior commander in battle, the commitment of the reserve. For Stuart it was Young's Brigade of the 7th and 20th Georgia Cavalry and Cobb's Legion (9th Georgia). In the 7th Georgia, the four Zipperer boys had come through the entire war unscathed. They had always taken care of each other. Their mother, unlike so many in Effingham County, had received no bad news. Each day she would walk to the post office and ask if she had mail. On the days that she didn't, the kindly old postman with his droopy mustache would say, "Don't worry, no news is good news." Now that burden of taking care of his younger brothers, Jeremiah, Telbert, and Phemuel, was especially heavy on Lt. Christian Edward Zipperer; he could feel in his gut that everything rode on this fight. Other men in the reserve had their burden as wells. Maj. Ashley Wilkes in Cobb's Legion had one of a different sort. He had two women to go home to in Clayton County, and only one was his wife. But it was the sort of problem a man kept to himself. The men trusted him because he was a gentleman — fair, brave, and careful of their lives, though a bit wistful at times.

For Sheridan the reserve was Merritt's brigade of regulars. Yet it was Sheridan who had the greater dilemma. Fitzhugh Lee's scattering of Wilson's 2nd Brigade put the Confederate division on Gregg's flank whenever he finished chasing Wilson's men. From the survivors of the attack, he thought Wilson's entire division had been wrecked and was mystified that a commanding officer of such caliber as Wilson could let that happen. Sheridan realized he had one reserve and two contingencies. Merritt's Reserve Brigade could not be in two places at once. To the rear they sat their horses nervously waiting for the call to action.

Right there on the wheat fields of Hanover Junction in the struggling mass of men and horses was the fulcrum of the American civil war. The men sensed it and did not hold back. Those not in the fight strained to be in it. Only the occasional wounded man staggered away on foot or leaned, bleeding over his mount. Riderless horses darted from the fight. Regiments pulled out of the melee, collected themselves, and attacked again. A dull roar hung over the trampled wheat punctuated by the clash of metal on metal or the retort of pistol shots. A Confederate participant would write there "was a great and imposing spectacle of squadrons charging in every portion of the field — men falling, cut out the saddle with the saber, artillery roaring, carbines cracking — a perfect hurly-burly of combat." A Union officer echoed him. "The fighting was hand-to-hand and of the most desperate kind."[15]

Stuart waited for the moment to commit his Georgians. He was wondering what the hell had happened to Fitzhugh Lee. He did not have long to wait. Lee had chased Wilson's men just far enough to get them off the battlefield. He had several hundred prisoners as well, mostly men who had been tearing up the tracks when his men came hooping and hollering down upon them. Surprise more than anything had shattered this veteran brigade. Now Lee had gathered his command and turned east where the sound of the guns called. It was then that Stuart's messengers found him to be able to guide him to Sheridan's rear. Lee was not the only one marching to the sound of the guns. The routed men of the 8th New York Cavalry had found the tail of Wilson's other brigade and alerted him to the disaster. Now Wilson was also on the move east to pick up the pieces and get in his own licks.

Elsewhere, more men were on the move also sensing that the climax was approaching. Shortly after he had dispatched Stuart to Hanover Junction, General Lee stole away from the Army of the Potomac.

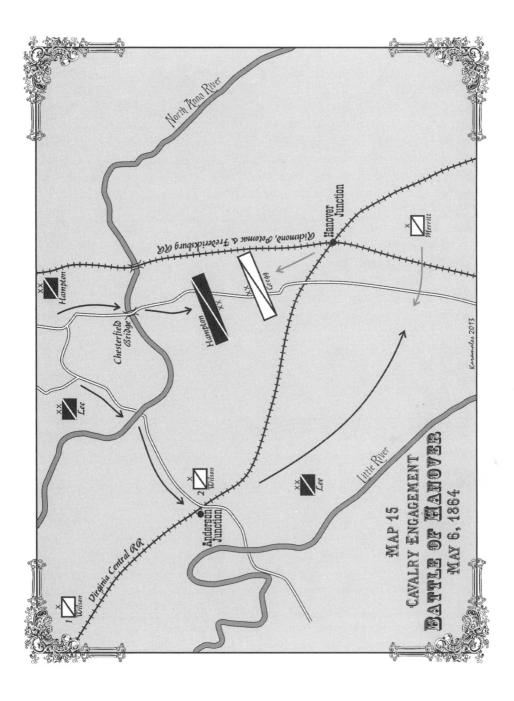

MAP 15
CAVALRY ENGAGEMENT
BATTLE OF HANOVER
MAY 6, 1864

Meade would only discover that the next day, but Hancock's Army of the Rappahannock was already on the move to the junction, only two days behind Sheridan. From the James Peninsula Longstreet's corps was marching rapidly to the junction as well.

ONE THOUSAND FEET ABOVE THE POTOMAC, 7:25 P.M., THURSDAY, MAY 5, 1864

Capt. Will Cushing wished he could will *Stephen Decatur* to go faster than her seven knots, but was thankful that the glistening Potomac below shone like a silvery highway in the deepening shadows of early evening. Nicknamed *The Barbary Pirate* by her crew, the *Decatur* was Cushing's flagship.[16] He had been with her when she had sunk the HMS *Nile*. She was now the flagship of the aeroship squadron that Cushing commanded. *Decatur* and *John Paul Jones* formed the Navy Division and *George Washington* and *Andrew Jackson* the Army Division, the fruit of, some would say, unnatural interservice cooperation fathered by Fox and Sharpe. It would be the first time that aerosphips went into battle as a formation.

As he paced the small deck, Cushing looked out at the other three great aeroships. His thoughts then went to the Navy's submersibles steaming down the same river. He had to smile to himself about something the ship's namesake had once said after seeing one of Robert Fulton's early steamboats. "It is the end of our business; hereafter any man who can boil a tea-kettle will be as good as the best of us."[17] Yes, indeed, the Navy had changed from the day of wood, wind, and sail. Now it was all steam and iron. It was a young man's navy, too, in so many ways. The young grasped the new technologies that seemed to disquiet the older senior officers. For Cushing, this was not enough, for steam and iron were only tools of action. They earned reputation, promotion, and glory — the unchangeable rewards of the man of war.

Soon the stars had come out to reflect on the river, which soon gave way to the great bay, and eventually the gun flashes of the relentless siege of Fortress Monroe confirmed Cushing's navigation. The running lights of the other aeroships showed that the formation was intact. Cushing hoped that the British crews kept their eyes off the skies. Running lights were needed to keep the squadron together on its way to Norfolk. Of course, if the transport with the hydrogen generator wagons and ground crews had not made it with Farragut to Norfolk, this flight would amount to only a one-way training voyage.

Below him off Hampton Roads, the Royal Navy's fighting ships swayed gently at anchor. Admiral Hope had kept the men busy for the big fight that was so near men could taste it. Busy eventually meant tired, and most men gladly fell into their hammocks when they could.

The watches, though, were time for men to gaze not just across the water but upward at the majesty of the heavens to refresh the soul. Not a few men, then, noticed the four sets of moving lights in the night sky in the direction of Norfolk. The news was taken directly to Admiral Hope who instantly thought of the fate of the blockaders off New York last March. He thought to himself that the Americans would not have it all their way the next time.

HANOVER JUNCTION, 11:10 P.M., THURSDAY, MAY 5, 1864

The three younger Zipperer brothers searched over the day's carnage hoping against hope that they would not find their big brother's body on the field, rather that he was a prisoner. Lieutenant Zipperer had been conspicuous in the breakthrough of the 7th Georgia, and somewhere in the regiment's death ride he had disappeared.

Stuart had seized the moment when the 8th Pennsylvania had been fallen back under a charge by the "Comanches" of the 35th Virginia Battalion. A gap had opened, and Stuart waved the reserve straight into it, riding at their head, shouting, "Give them the saber, boys!" The three regiments headed straight for Sheridan's guns and trains. The 6th New York Independent Battery had an advanced position right in the path of the charging Georgians. "The gallant fellows of the battery hurled a perfect storm of grape" into them, a survivor would write. Still, they rode right through it, leaping downed horses and men, and into the battery, hacking and shouting at the gunners who fought back with pistols and sponge staffs. No quarter was asked or given, and almost every man of the battery was dead or wounded when the Georgians resumed their advance.

To the west Fitzhugh Lee's men attacked as well. His four Virginia regiments and the 1st Maryland Cavalry Battalion made a grand sight as they advanced, too grand for Sheridan. He had been about to commit Merritt's Reserve Brigade to save his guns when the Virginians appeared on his flank. The guns would have to take care of themselves as Merritt threw his regulars at Lee's men.

The breakthrough of the Georgians had done more than endanger the guns and trains. It had shattered the Union line, which frayed, snapped, and then began to fall back. Like a thrown spearhead, the Georgians flew forward to the next two batteries to the right, the 20th and 21st New York Light Batteries—Gatlings.[18]

This was the last time the Zipperer brothers saw their older brother. He disappeared in the sheet of lead that brought the entire front of all three Georgian regiments crashing into the ground in a bloody tangle of dead and screaming horses, fallen and wounded men crushed by their mounts or slashed by their flailing hooves. There were no intervals between blasts that men could advance through as with the artillery. The bundles of six steel barrels on each Gatling just kept spinning and whirring as they fired, stopping only briefly to slide a new magazine into the gun. It was leaden storm that piled up the Georgians in a wall of equine and human flesh. Finally, they could stand no more and fled—fled, not retreated.

Gregg's men rallied by the guns and counterattacked. Merciful night fell to pull the exhausted regiments apart. By then it was doubtful if there was a single horse on either side that was in condition enough to charge. Merritt's regulars had stopped the Virginians in a smaller version of the big fight to the north of the Junction. Fitzhugh Lee withdrew his men to join Stuart just in time to miss the return of a much chagrined Wilson and what was left of his brigade. Sheridan personally commended the crews of the Gatlings that night. It had been a close run thing, and he owed much to those crews. He had done what he had set out to do — cut off the communications of the Army of Northern Virginia. He wondered what options Stuart was contemplating until Stuart's hat was brought to him, its black plume bent and smeared with blood.

The Zipperer brothers finally found Christian Edward. His legs had been pinned under his dead mount. The whole field was dotted with lanterns as stretcher bearer parties sought out the wounded. A party of Yankees had found him first and were prying him out from under the horse when he cried out, "Have a care of my legs, boys. They're both broke." His brothers recognized that voice and rushed toward the lantern light. The stretcher bearers in blue took no fright when the Confederates appeared out of the night. Angels of the battlefield, they and their counterparts in gray were called, and it was unthinkable to harm one. They gathered around their brother as a Yankee held a lantern over him. Phemuel said, "Thank you kindly." Telbert added, "We'll take him, friends." Christian Edward groaned as they tried to lift him. One of the Yankees said, "Leave him on the stretcher. You can have it. We'll get another."

A few yards away lay the body of Major Wilkes, a bullet through his noble forehead. That bullet had spared him of years of dithering over which woman he really loved.

HMS *WARRIOR*, 11:44 P.M., THURSDAY, MAY 5, 1864

Admiral Hope sat up through the night pondering the results of the afternoon's events. He had been shocked with how easily the American monitor force and its transports had broken through his ships and inflicted a good deal of damage. The loss of the *Royal Oak* had at least been avenged by *Prince Albert*'s sinking of a monitor.

Captain Cowles had come over to personally report on the engagement. He was a striking figure with his slim figure and long, luxuriant blond beard. He also had the ear of both Disraeli and the Queen, a consideration not to be dismissed and instead put to advantage. Certainly Her Majesty would be more than pleased that the ironclad named for her dead husband had added an American monitor to the two Russian ships she had sunk. Hope was coming to realize that there was a basis for the confidence Prime Minister and Queen both had in this man, dispelling the cloud of ill-feeling an iconoclast invariably attracted.

"The low freeboard of the American monitors has been a great advantage in presenting the narrowest of targets, but it has its own inherent weaknesses, Admiral. Bazalgette showed us one of them by his daring in March. Another one is that the low freeboard exposes the deck to plunging fire, and there decks have only one inch of armor. Our own ships have been criticized for their great height compared to the American ships, but that greater height allows our guns to fire down at a proper angle to strike right through their decks, especially *Prince Albert* with only seven feet of freeboard.

"You should have seen the strike of my guns smashing open the enemy's deck. One can only imagine the carnage in the small ships engineering spaces. She went down like a stone without a single survivor."

Hope flickered in Hope's eyes. "Yes," he said to himself, "turn the enemy's advantage against himself."

MONTREAL RAILWAY STATION, 1:30 A.M., FRIDAY, MAY 6, 1864

The special train with steam up sat next to the platform awaiting its single passenger. Hope Grant limped across the platform with a cane followed by a few aides. It felt so good to get out of that drafty headquarters and be doing something. His wounds still ached, but he felt his strength returning. Wolseley's telegrams had stopped coming, and then word came of the attack on Brighton. He must get to Portland before the battle that he knew was coming.

14

"We've Got 'em Nicked"

The Confederate capital had held its breath all through yesterday as the great cavalry battle raged at Hanover Junction barely thirty miles to the north. Elizabeth Van Lew and her fellow Unionists were also full of expectations, though ones their Confederate neighbors would not have appreciated. Van Lew had had a huge American flag smuggled into her house to display on the day Union troops marched into this nest of traitors.

She had something far more urgent, though, than getting to spread the flag over her roof. She was flitting through night to the home of Samuel Ruth, the superintendent of the RF&P Railroad, one of the most ardent Unionists in the city. Single handedly he had been waging a very effective second front against the Army of Northern Virginia. The RF&P was the main supply route of Lee's army, and Ruth made sure it operated at a depressingly low level of efficiency. He diverted attention from his dead hand on the switch by being one of the most vocal supporters of the Confederacy.[1]

He opened the door with a candle in his hand, saw who was there, pulled her in, looked about, and closed the door. "Miss Van Lew, what a chance you have taken by coming here! For both of us."

"Great risks must be taken now, Mr. Ruth. Longstreet will arrive in the city by noon and be rushed to Hanover Junction on your railroad." She did not tell him that a clerk, one of her sources in the War Department, had brought her that information only an hour before. He already knew her sources were impeccable."You must do what you can to slow him down."[2]

WILLIAMSBURG, VIRGINIA, 3:03 A.M., FRIDAY, MAY 6, 1864
Weitzel had come to that same conclusion as he had watched from Yorktown's parapet Longstreet's Corps marching at a hard pace out of the

Peninsula. The early evening was still bright enough to see the columns as they passed and hear the jingle of equipment and the shouts of officers. Something was up. Longstreet was clearly needed elsewhere and needed in a hurry. The last of the besiegers of his position had barely disappeared at the tail of the Confederate column when Weitzel put his garrison in full marching order to pursue and wound them if he could. The men were eager; they had been cooped up far too long and felt the grudge. No sooner was the lead regiment out the gates, when Union cavalry came up the same road the enemy had come by. They were the remnants of the three cavalry regiments that had been driven into the defenses of Fortress Monroe after Big Bethal. The commander at Fortress Monroe had sent them out to tail Longstreet. They also had a score to settle.

He sent the cavalry forward while at the same time sending couriers to Fortress Monroe ordering the surviving troops there north. The cavalry caught the last brigade in Longstreet's column eleven miles up the road at Williamsburg at midnight. The gray infantry had been plodding along in that dreamy half-asleep, half-awake marching stride when the cavalry appeared out of the dark. The men in blue rode in among them firing pistols and slashing with sabers to bring them wide awake.

NORFOLK NAVY YARD, VIRGINIA, 7:45 A.M., FRIDAY, MAY 6, 1864

After bringing his flotilla into Norfolk, Farragut promptly transferred his flag to the broadside ironclad USS *New Ironsides*, the Navy's only broadside ironclad. *New Ironsides* had been built in parallel with the USS *Monitor* to confront the Confederate ironclad CSS *Virginia* two years before and had proved her worth as Adm. John Dahlgren's flagship at Charleston. At 4,120 tons she was the biggest ship in the Navy, after USS *Dictator*, although less than half the size of HMS *Warrior*. But she packed more than twice that ship's firepower with her fourteen 11-inch Dahlgren smoothbore guns that had battered *Warrior*'s sister ship, *Black Prince*, to death at Charleston. Her high freeboard made her the most effective platform from which to observe the battle and command the fleet. She differed from the British broadside ironclads in that her rolled armored hull slanted out downward at 17 degrees, the first ship to have such armor intended to make enemy shot ricochet.

Farragut had assembled his captains and unfurled from his flagship an entirely new flag. "Gentlemen, this is the flag of the 1st Fleet of the United States Navy, the first such numbered or named fleet in our history. It was presented to me by Mr. Lincoln himself at the presidential mansion. As I left, he said to me, "Admiral, I pray that every day this flag flies it will be a fine Navy day." There was a happy murmur of approval at the commander-in-chief's use of such a fond naval term.

They all remembered Lincoln's handsome praise of the Navy last year when he said, "Nor must Uncle Sam's web-feet be forgotten. At all the watery margins they have been present. Not only on the deep sea, the broad bay, and the rapid river, but also up the narrow muddy bayou, and wherever the ground was a little damp, they have been, and made their tracks."[3] Lincoln's words had been much appreciated by the fleet, but his veto of a bill abolishing the grog ration cemented their devotion, especially below decks.

More important than a flag was the round of inspections Farragut made of every major ship in the fleet. He counted the seven new ironclads he had brought and the surviving four Passaic class monitors that had also fought so well at Charleston and a fifth of the class, USS *Sangamon*, that had already been at Norfolk, each armed with an 11-inch and 15-inch Dahlgren in a single turret.

With the *New Ironsides* that made twelve ironclads. There were also four prewar frigates, three sloops, and nine gunboats, giving him twenty-seven ships of all types. Gunboats usually mounted one to two guns and were used primarily in attacking coastal positions, but they had been used in the fleet action at Charleston where their large guns were particularly effective. There were also dozens of other smaller ships lightly armed, fit enough for blockade but suicide in a fleet action. These he stripped of crews to ensure full compliments aboard his other ships.

As absorbed as Farragut was in readying the fleet, he was never too busy to take to take the enemy into account. When he asked Admiral Lee what he had learned of the enemy, he was surprised when Lee said, "I think you need to speak to that young army officer from Sharpe's organization. He's a walking encyclopedia. And Captain Cushing as well."

It took all of Farragut's open mind to accept that an army officer could tell the Navy about an enemy afloat, but there was a calm seriousness about the young man that compelled attention. Wilmoth was at pains to explain how the CIB served both the armed forces. Then he laid out the enemy's order-of-battle, listing every ship in the bay. Though the British had only seven ironclads to the American twelve, all but two of them dwarfed his turreted ships.[4] In addition they boasted 124 guns to the 41 on the American ironclads. Wilmoth made the point of noting that all but two of the American guns were far more powerful than any of the British guns.[5]

The wooden heavy hitters of the fleet were the heavy frigates *Minnesota* and *Wabash* and lighter frigate *Powhatan* bristling with ninety-five 8-, 9-, 10-, and 11-inch Dahlgrens, more firepower than all the British ironclads put together. The sloops and gunboats were armed with another twenty-three guns, of which nine were the hull-busting 11-inchers. The sloop USS *Brooklyn* that had escorted the supply ships was almost as heavily armed as the frigates with twenty-one guns.[6]

Then Cushing laid out a diagram of their most recent deployment obtained by a personal reconnaissance flight he had taken the day before. Admiral Hope had drawn his ships back from Hampton Roads and into the widest part of the bay just inside its mouth, an area almost thirteen miles square where there would be ample room to fight a fleet action. Apparently he had placed his armored floating batteries as a barrier through which the Americans would have to fight. Behind them were the seven ironclads, one ship-of-the-line, seven frigates, six corvettes, and eight sloops — twenty-nine ships in addition to twenty-five gunboats and thirty-two floating batteries.

Farragut had been thinking for some time of the inherent weakness of the American ironclads that needed to be masked. The first was low freeboard and vulnerability to the tactics of being rammed. The second was their speed of at most seven knots against the average of eleven for enemy ships. That extra speed would allow the British to maneuver with a flexibility and concentration he could not match with his own ironclads. Only his wooden ships matched the speed of the enemy. What to do?

At sixty-three Farragut had the vigor of a man twenty years his junior. His white hair covered a mind that was active and innovative. Like Nelson he understood in his bones the laying of one ship against another to fight it out to the end. His mind was rapidly digesting the information these two young men had laid before him. He realized that tomorrow would be far more than the greatest naval battle in American history, greater than Charleston, and the greatest of all battles on the sea since Trafalgar. He was not afraid of the fight. Indeed, he looked forward to it; like Robert E. Lee, he was a naturally combative man who rather enjoyed the whole thing.

What awed him was the forces being brought together for the first time. It was not only the unprecedented concentration of ironclads that made all the wooden ships on both sides nothing more than auxiliaries. He had drunk up every bit of information on the employment of ironclads and questioned everyone he could with firsthand experience. His command of the flotilla coming down the East Coast had also given him firsthand feel for their operation.

What truly impressed his imagination were the aeroships and submersibles. He had met with Cushing after his successful attack on the enemy blockading ships with his aeroship and thoroughly picked his brains. They had spoken long into the night about the possibilities of such a new weapon, and next day Cushing eagerly took him aloft. Fox had given him a tour of the submersible factory at the Navy Yard, and again he squeezed everything of value of the manufacturer, inventor, and captain of the *Shark*. He insisted on going on a training mission on the boat as well in the Eastern Branch and down the Potomac. It crossed his mind that Nelson himself would have given his other arm to play with such toys.

BIDDEFORD, MAINE, 8:23 A.M., FRIDAY, MAY 6, 1864

The courier whipped his lathering mount on as he crossed the bridge over the Saco River into Biddeford and continued south. He rode into the rear of the army clearly deploying for a big fight. He found the command group, reported, and handed his dispatch to Doyle.

"Bloody hell," he muttered as he read the dispatch. He straightened himself in the saddle and said, "Well, gentlemen, it seems the Guards have been detained a Brighton." He passed it to Wosleley, who immediately understood the import. The railway had been cut. Brighton had been saved but Gorham lost. Militia were swarming the railway, cutting it everywhere and isolating the rail station garrisons. Even if the Guards marched to rendezvous with the Portland Field Force, it would take a week. By then the issue would be decided, if Doyle chose the fight in front of him.

He turned to Doyle, "Sir Hastings, the loss of the railway changes the entire basis of the campaign. Even a victory on this field will serve no purpose in the defense of Upper and Lower Canada."

Doyle replied, "The enemy is before us, sir. We will strike them."

"Sir Hastings, let us fall back across the Saco and defend the river line until we can reestablish control of the railway."

Doyle was getting annoyed, firstly at Wolseley's effrontery to suggest that a British army would withdraw from an enemy in the field and secondly that he throw away the opportunity to gain a victory. "General Wolseley, notice that the enemy is advancing. We should never be able to show our faces at home should we turn tail, even if Sherman would let me."

Wolseley desperately wished that Hope Grant were here now.

So did Sherman. He wanted to beat the best the British had. That would settle matters in a dramatic way, but he would fight whoever was in front of him. Lieutenant Colonel McEntee had told him that at most the British would have thirty thousand men on this field. He was bringing over fifty thousand in the Army of the Hudson, but was ostentatiously deploying only the men of the XI Corps. The XII Corps he had directed to the east to be able to come up on the British flank.

The XI Corps deployed and then halted; its regiments began seeking the folds in the earth in this rolling countryside. Coffee mill guns heretofore deployed in six-gun batteries now scattered themselves in pairs with the infantry. Sherman had sifted the experience of the battle of the Chazy where British artillery focused on the neatly lined up batteries and took them out. Now if only Doyle would attack first. Sherman was sure he would, especially since he had come out from behind several excellent river lines he could hang a solid defense upon.

Wolseley saw the issue as clearly as Sherman and pleaded once again with Doyle to retire. "Sir Hastings, I must point out that the Americans are employing the same tactics the Iron Duke employed against the French with such success. He hides behind good ground and entices us to attack against his concentrated firepower." If only he could sway Doyle and postpone the battle.

At that moment the seeming answer to his prayers had arrived in Brighton on a lathered and wheezing horse that foundered as soon as he dismounted. At the first break in the line, Hope Grant had unloaded his horse and ridden it hard to Brighton. He now ordered the Guards to march to Gorham. Somewhere along the line they would find trains to speed them to Portland.

HEADQUARTERS, CIB, LAFAYETTE SQUARE, WASHINGTON, DC, 9:01 A.M., FRIDAY, MAY 6, 1864

Sharpe looked up from his desk at the rap on his office door. One of his junior officers entered. Sharpe had a policy of rap, pause, then enter for his staff. It was Lt. John Aimes, the officer who sorted out visitors. "Sir, there's someone I think you should speak to, a Mr. William Ludlow." Aimes gave him a summary, and Sharpe agreed to see him.

Twenty minutes later Sharpe walked in on Lafayette Baker, head of the Secret Service, with Ludlow in tow. Sharpe and Baker cordially disliked each other. Sharpe did not approve of Baker's shameful abuse of his spy-catching wit to shake down merchants and others. Baker saw in Sharpe a rival who had taken over presidential security from the Secret Service. No wonder. Baker still smarted from the fact that one of his bodyguards assigned to protect the president had tried to kill him. It had been a huge black eye.

"Mr. Baker, allow me to introduce Mr. Ludlow of the State Department." Even Baker was surprised at his story. Ludlow had mulled over in his mind the identity of the man he had seen go into the alley next to the Petersen Boarding House until he was convinced that it, indeed, was George Sanders. "Sanders and I served in the London consulate in 1852; I was only his secretary at the time. I had heard later he had gone south when the war started."

Baker had become instantly interested as soon as Sanders name was mentioned. He knew that the man had been working with the

Confederate Secret Service and had been advocating a number of extravagant schemes. Ludlow went on to say, "There was one thing you never forgot about after being associated with Sanders. He was almost rabid in his hatred of tyrants and repeatedly called for their assassination." He reached into his coat and handed Baker a card de visit. "Here is a picture of the man."

By that evening both Baker and Sharpe's organization had spilled every possible agent into the streets of Washington with copies of that photo. Some of the copies were still damp so quickly had they been snatched from the development liquid of Sharpe's photography office.

CHESTERFIELD BRIDGE, VIRGINIA, 2:15 P.M., FRIDAY, MAY 6, 1864

Stuart's cavalry had disappeared from Sheridan's front as the advance guard of Hancock's Army of the Rappahannock reached the North Anna River and began to cross. Sheridan saw what could only be the approaching command group rode up to meet Hancock himself. He found Grant riding with him. Still mounted, they reached across to shake hands, then rode off under the shade of some trees to talk.

Sheridan briefed them on the success of the cavalry battle; Grant was well-pleased. Hancock then said, "As far as I know, Lee is still sitting around Spottsylvania keeping Meade company. We are on his rear." Then he rose in his stirrups, a big man on a big horse, and slammed a gloved fist into an open palm. "We've got 'em nicked, Sheridan! We've got 'em nicked!"[7]

Grant was not the demonstrative sort, but he added, his cigar clenched at the side of his mouth, "Seems like that."

Sheridan knew Grant well by then and realized a definitive statement when he heard it. Hancock, on the other hand, was a new acquaintance. He was not easily impressed by other men, but Hancock was an exception. The man oozed command. It was said of him that if he were to show up on a battlefield dressed like a civilian and gave orders, they would have been instantly obeyed such was his commanding presence. He was as a hard and gifted a fighter as any man who went to war. Three times at Gettysburg he had held the fate of the Union in his hands, and three times he had done exactly the right thing to forestall the enemy.[8] Sheridan did notice, however, how pale he looked. His wound in the thigh suffered at Gettysburg had not entirely healed.

The sudden sound of cannon fire to the north turned their heads. It was Lee's turn to forestall Hancock. He had arrived faster than anyone had expected. Without another word, Hancock turned his horse and galloped back over the bridge. He rode into chaos. His II Corps' 2nd Division had been struck in column by a howling Confederate attack.

He heard the ululating Rebel yell in thousands of voices. Rifle fire exploded from regiment after regiment as they tried to stem the flood. He sent couriers north to hurry Wright's VI Corps into the fight. At one point Grant's newly set up headquarters seemed to be right in the path of a Confederate attack. An aide came running up shouting that they had to get the hell out of there. Grant just leaned back in his camp chair and suggested that some artillery be brought up instead. In moments a reserve battery unlimbered right in front of him and blew canister into the face of the attack.

At that moment most of Longstreet's Corps—almost twenty-five thousand men—were entraining at the Richmond station of the RF&P at 8th and Broad Street for the thirty-mile ride to Hanover Junction. Longstreet had marched them relentlessly from the James Peninsula to get there so fast. The trap that had been set for Lee—caught between two forces—was now being laid for Hancock.

BIDDEFIELD, MAINE, 3:20 P.M., FRIDAY, MAY 6, 1864

Sherman was in a rage for being humbugged by the British. They had given every impression of readying an attack. Instead they had begun to withdraw in such a manner that he was fooled until the very end. He had spat out his cigar and threw his hat on the ground. Then he had unleashed Custer.

His cavalry ate up the ground until they found their way barred by the British cavalry brigade. The 9th Lancers and 11th Hussars stood there like a wall spreading out on either side of the road, one thousand of the finest cavalry in the world.[9] The Wolverines of Custer's 1st Brigade of Michigan regiments, his old command, had a similar opinion of themselves.[10] Custer threw his regiments out along either side of the road as well. He did not have time to use his repeaters to blast his way through. It would have to be the old-fashioned way—the saber. Across the field he heard bugles and pulled up his mount to see the British advancing toward him.

He gave the command. Fifteen hundred sabers rasped from their scabbards. The American bugles answered the British, and the Wolverines' horses stepped off. Both sides trotted forward, keeping their formations until at two hundred yards the trumpets sounded the charge. Sabers went down to point forward as lances dipped at the level, their pennants streaming behind their lance heads. They meet with a crash that sent men and horses to the ground as both sides streamed into each other, turning the fight into hundreds of individual combats. The 9th Lancers introduced the Americans to their special weapon for the first time, cutting right through the 5th Michigan only to be hit by the 1st Michigan, Custer's reserve. The Americans drew their pistols and introduced the Lancers to Mr. Colt's invention.

American numbers and repeater firepower began to tell, but still the British would not leave the field. The commander of Custer's second brigade saw the immediate opportunity and fell upon the British rear. The Hussars and Lancers were trapped and outnumbered by more than three to one, and still they kept fighting as long as arms had strength to swing a saber or thrust a lance. Now numbers and repeaters told. Sherman rode up with his staff to find Custer gloating over his victory with both captured standards in his fist. He ostentatiously threw them at the feet of Sherman's horse. Sherman rode next to him, leaned over, and said between clenched teeth, "The enemy has escaped, sir."

Doyle had changed his mind after all. Wolseley's arguments had sunk in. He had no choice but sacrifice his cavalry to cover his withdrawal.

NORFOLK NAVY YARD, VIRGINIA, 4:11 P.M., FRIDAY, MAY 6, 1864

The four great aeroships hugged the earth, tied down by their great tethers. Their ground crews brought by Farragut's transports were busy pumping new hydrogen into them. The ordnance teams stood by ready to begin loading the special aerial bombs that had been developed for them. The navy yard seethed with activity as ammunition and coal also brought by Farragut were transferred by an endless stream of contrabands to the ironclads and other warships that had been trapped there. Across the roads alongside the water battery at nearby Fortress Monroe the four submersibles were tied up, their crews also making final preparations.

Out in the bay, Admiral Hope's ships were equally busy preparing for the battle they knew was coming. Every captain studied the admiral's orders detailing Captain Cowles suggestions. The attack on Fortress Monroe had been suspended as the floating armored batteries of the Great Armament were strung out in the path of the enemy three deep. Behind them the British ironclads and other warships also positioned themselves. It would be a long night.

The longest night of all was Admiral Hope's. He had the ghost of the battle of Charleston to haunt whatever sleep he could get. He had read the reports of the battle with a creeping sense of horror at what the big American guns could do. Those damned Dahlgrens. Even their carriages were more efficient. The Royal Navy had tried to buy the guns before the war, but the Americans had refused to sell, no fools they. Every attempt to obtain their dimensions had failed.[11] Still, the Royal Navy was not bereft of advantage. Cowles's tactic was one, and, of course, Bazalgette's. Then again he could always rely on the tars, those hearts of oak, whose relentless ferocity and efficiency in battle were legendary. He could also rely on the high gunnery skills of the fleet. No navy in the world could so reliably hit their targets under the most demanding conditions. Then there was the sheer weight of metal his ships would be able to throw at the Americans tomorrow–almost 750 guns aboard his fleet. If all else failed, they could simply try to pound the Americans to pieces.

THE LINCOLN REDOUBT, DUBLIN, 11:15 P.M., FRIDAY, MAY 6, 1864

The sentries peering into the night at the British positions felt it first as a tremor, then the earth heaved under them sending them into the eternal night. The mine driven under the Lincoln Redoubt by the sappers of the Royal Engineers lifted a fifty-foot section of the earthen wall a hundred feet into the air along with men and Gatlings. It all fell to earth with a shuddering thud. Then only dust hung in the dark. Rockets now shot into the sky to hang flares as the assault parties rushed forward.

Those men in the redoubt not killed or wounded in the blast were too stunned to react quickly before the storming party of the 86th Foot was among them stabbing with the bayonet. The 86th had suffered terribly from the American repeater fire at Tallaght and asked to be allowed to get even by leading the storming of the redoubt. Raised in Protestant County Down in Ulster it had over the years recruited many Catholic recruits. If ever there was regiment that was an amalgam of the green and orange, it was the 86th, and it had remained steadfastly loyal, priding itself that not a single man deserted. The dead and wounded of Tallaght had sealed the regiment's loyalty with their blood.

Maj. Henry Stewart Jerome raced over the rubble as the first man into the redoubt, followed by Sgt. James, who caught up with him. They paused only long enough to exchange grins. Both had won the VC in the Indian Mutiny, and much was expected of them. The night, lit only by fires of burning buildings, was their ally, for it shortened the distance between men, ideal for the bayonet. And the bayonet took precious few prisoners that night. The regiment lived up to its nickname of the Stickies.

As they broke out of the redoubt and into the city, they halted to let the big men of the 2nd Coldstream Guards rush by. Byrne muttered in his brogue, "It's about time those pretty boys got into a fight."

The explosion had caught Meagher glass in hand in his rooms at Dublin Castle. He darted from his chair so suddenly that he knocked over the table, sending he bottle to shatter on the floor. He shouted, "Sergeant Major!" strapped on his sword and rushed none too steady down the broad stairs. In the castle's vast courtyard all was confusion. No one knew what had happened except now every British gun was pounding the defenses. Meagher looked to the glow in the west where the redoubt was. His head had cleared instantly. He gathered what men he could and headed for the redoubt.

BEFORE BIDDEFORD, MAINE, 5:00 P.M., FRIDAY, MAY 6, 1864

Sherman was still so mad he could have bit right through a ten penny nail. Doyle had got his army back across the Saco and immediately deployed his troops north and south along the river to prevent a crossing. They had been just in time to drive XI Corps advance guard back to the south bank in a sharp fight. Custer was smart enough to keep his distance from Sherman. He ostentatiously wore his left arm in a sling, the gift of a lancer. He had the way to his tent lined with captured lances to drive home the point of his destruction of a superb regiment, but Sherman's reproof stung his pride of a man who had so completely "sought the bubble of reputation in the cannon's mouth."

Despite Sherman's displeasure, he invited Custer to his mess that evening for a dinner hosting surviving captured enemy officers. Custer arrived, his yellow locks brushed to luster that only fine blond hair could achieve and dressed in a fresh uniform. Sherman made a point of noting how badly outnumbered the British cavalry had been and that their self-sacrifice in ensuring the successful escape of their army was worthy of Lord Tennyson's most sublime efforts. One of the officers tactfully commented that their army had not escaped, merely had withdrawn to advantage. Sherman laughed because he realized the joke was on him. His smile fell off his face when he glanced at Custer.

Custer did not brood. His mind was elsewhere. That elsewhere was with his scouts along the Saco River searching for a ford. He would redeem himself if he died doing it.

He was luckier than he knew. His scouts were led by the country people to a half-dozen hidden fords known only locally and not apparent to a visitor or an occupier. They were back by midnight, and a half hour later Custer brazenly woke Sherman up to tell him of his plan.

THE RP&F RAILROAD STATION, RICHMOND, VIRGINIA, 7:15 P.M., FRIDAY, MAY 6, 1864

All the way down in Virginia James Longstreet was also spitting nails. Chaos at the railroad station and nearby yards had brought the movement of his corps to the pace of a snail with consumption. He had driven his corps to the utmost of the men's endurance to get them to the Richmond station on time only to find that the trains that should have been waiting had been sent off in every direction early that morning. The manager of the RF&P claimed to have only heard about the requirement shortly before Longstreet's men had begun to arrive, and truth to tell, the War Department had been grievously tardy in formally notifying him.

That cut no ice with Longstreet, who paced the platform in greater distress than Sorrel had ever seen him in before. Compounding his disquiet was the loss of two brigades on the march to Richmond by pursuers from the Peninsula. One brigade had been shattered; the other was holding the road. Every once in a while one big gauntleted fist pounded into the open palm of the other hand. His thick long beard shook with anger as he watched his men in their thousands, already tired, simply waiting in ranks for the trains that should have been there — waiting, waiting, waiting when they should already have ridden the thirty miles to south of Hanover Junction and gone into battle. Instead, hundreds were asleep on the dirt of the streets or on the plank sidewalks.

Lee was up there on the line somewhere, Longstreet knew, with the enemy before and behind him. It would not be the first time that it was Longstreet who was the only one able to come to Lee's rescue. The way he had fallen on the Yankee flank at Second Manassas two years ago when the army was on the point of being overwhelmed had shattered the enemy and sent him flying. And at Wilderness, his corps double-timed onto the field just as Lee's flank was about to collapse, staggered Hancock's advancing corps, and threw it back in defeat.

At last a single train crept into the station. Then it just stood there. No one moved forward to water the iron beast's boilers and fill its cab with coal and wood. Neither did the stevedores move to unload whatever was in the cars. The wagons just stood there, still. Longstreet watched in disbelief as nothing happened. Sorrel was already giving orders, and two regiments hustled up from the street to tear open the car doors. The cars were filled with firewood, barrels of tar, and scrap iron picked up in Danville on the Virginia-North Carolina border. It took another hour to unload them before the 5th and 15th Virginia Cavalry could begin to board. The train finally chugged, or rather wheezed, its way north out of the station. Its engine was one of the worn-out original Confederate machines. The new British engine had been changed in Danville and was now nearing the South Carolina border. The old engine gave out barely ten miles north of Richmond. The cavalry detrained and took to the road. Such were the efforts of Samuel Ruth and Crazy Bet Van Lew.

THE CHESTERFIELD BRIDGE, VIRGINIA, 10:01 P.M., FRIDAY, MAY 6, 1864

Lee's attack on Hancock had melted away in the storm of fire from the Yankees' repeaters. Even men who had transformed the phrase "Southern Valor" into a given on every battlefield could not withstand a ten-to-one firepower disadvantage. Lee's losses had been horrific. Only the onset of night saved what was left.

Couriers from the nearest telegraph stations told him that Longstreet's corps had arrived in Richmond in the early afternoon. He had expected the vanguard of First Corps to arrive on the field to fall upon Hancock's rear by late afternoon, but nothing happened. Meade could not stay fooled for long and must even now be forced to march after him. No soldier in North America was more resourceful than Lee and more optimistic that no situation was truly hopeless, but now darkness had fallen on a battlefield where he had been stopped cold by an obdurate enemy to his front while a relentless enemy closed upon his rear. The difficulties seemed insurmountable. Everything hung on Longstreet's arrival.

He was right about Meade. The Army of the Potomac had moved within three hours of Lee's departure, alerted by the scouts of the BMI. Ninety thousand men in blue filled the roads southeast of Spotsylvania determined to be in on the kill.

While Lee weighed his odds, Grant paced the Chesterfield Bridge to the consternation of the sentries. He too was weighing the odds. Lee had hit Hancock like a sledgehammer that afternoon, but the new Army of the Rappahannock was veteran to the core and had held. His solitude was interrupted by the hooves of Sheridan's horse as it clattered onto the bridge right up to him. The little Irishman bounced off his horse and handed the reins to an aide who led the animal away. The two were alone in the shadows at the center of the bridge. "Longstreet's coming up from Richmond. We had a message from the Van Lew woman."

"When?"

"Thirty minutes ago, one of her colored men came into the lines. His horse fell dead from the ride."

"How do we know it's from her?"

Sheridan turned and shouted, "Cline!" Sharpe's chief of scouts walked over from Sheridan's escort, and Sheridan raised Grant's concern. "Yes, he's for real, General. I saw him at Van Lew's truck farm."

The glow from the tip of Grant's cigar brightened in the dark as he took a good drag. "Well, Phil. It's up to you to keep him out of this fight tomorrow. Can you do it?"

"Damned right."

SACO RIVER, TEN MILES ABOVE BIDDEFORD, MAINE, 4:20 A.M., SATURDAY, MAY 7, 1864

Custer's cavalry brigades splashed across three hidden fords of the Saco less than an hour before dawn. Custer, his arm no longer in a sling, was the first man across after his advance guard. On the other bank, his scouts were waiting for him. A few words were all he needed, and he headed north as a courier sped back across the river to hurry the XI Corps, which filled the country lanes leading to the fords, their way lit only by the starry night.

Eight hundred miles to the south in Virginia Stuart's cavalry was also crossing a river, the North Anna again, at Jericho Mill, three miles east of the Chesterfield Bridge while a third of a million men—Americans and Britons—were stirring in the predawn darkness to light fires for their coffee and bacon or filing through their ship messes for tea and an early breakfast. Longstreet's Corps at last was arriving five miles south of Hanover Junction. It was as if in that predawn moment, pregnant with the day, an entire continent held its breath.

In Washington, Lincoln had walked through the sleeping White House, unable to rest. With his guards he went for a walk and arrived at Sharpe's headquarters to find the Chief of the CIB also awake. He was so grateful for the fresh hot coffee that Sharpe pressed into his hand. The warmth of the cup was the first comfort he had had in a tortured night. The President of the United States and his chief of intelligence just sat there sipping their coffee, waiting for the telegraph to come alive with news, any news. Until then, they could only wait. What was going to happen was now completely out of their hands.

THE SURRATT BOARDING HOUSE, 604 H STREET, NW, WASHINGTON, DC, 5:00, SATURDAY, MAY 7, 1864

That morning's heavy rain kept the boarding house's occupants inside, those who were awake. So no one was likely to see how the street at both ends had been quietly closed off by soldiers of Sharpe's 120th New York Volunteer Infantry.[12] Both Sharpe and Baker were watching the boarding house from the building across the street as assault teams from both organizations slipped up to it, Baker's men to the front door and Sharpe's soldiers to the rear through the backyard.

Mary Surratt had been up early to start breakfast for her family and boarders and was the first to see the soldiers as they rushed through the back garden. She was running to the stairs to warn the boarders when both doors were smashed open and hard, shouting men filled the house. She was seized on the stairs as the men rushed up to break open doors. Gunfire! More shouting. Men crying out in pain. Then down the stairs she saw the men drag George Sanders and Thomas Harlan. More men came through the door, one of them a general. A man reported on the shooting. "We had to kill one of them. He fired at us and wounded one of my men." The body was dragged down the stairs. It was Richard McCulloch.

The deal that Sharpe worked out with Baker was that he would conduct the interrogations. He sat there across a small table from Harney in a bleak cell of the Capitol Prison. The room stank. It was early May, but the room was cold and damp. Harney looked at Sharpe and saw a man who was completely at his ease. A soldier brought in two cups of steaming coffee.

"I can't abide a morning without my coffee, and I'm afraid I have missed mine all because of you, Mr. . . . ? Do join me. We have a lot to talk about." Harney clutched at the coffee as if were a line thrown to a drowning man and felt its warmth.

"Such as your hanging," Sharpe said. Harney jerked up, spilling some of the coffee. "I'm afraid we have no choice in the matter. Spies are hanged. After all, it was your government that began the practice, and I'm afraid we must insist."[13]

Sharpe observed the man coming apart. "Of course, if you were be of assistance, that would be taken into account. You could simply go home after the war. I doubt if we would want to hold onto spies then."

It took another hour of gently coaxing before Harney coughed up the plot and told him about the bomb. He ratted out Sanders and McCulloch. One was already caught and the other dead, so it did not matter much. Of Booth, he said nothing, but that would hardly satisfy Sharpe, who wanted to know how he had got into Ford's Theater to plant the bomb. He named an actor who Booth had told him had just left to trod the boards in growing obscurity in the Midwest, Edwin Forrest.

An hour later Sharpe was under the stage at Ford's with a detachment of Army ordnance men. They found the bomb. The sergeant who lifted the bomb down staggered under its weight. They examined it outside. "Fifty pounds of powder at least. It would have caused this whole part of the building to collapse, General."

A thoroughly mortified Tom Ford was completely cooperative. He faced not only possible arrest as an accomplice, but even if he escaped that, professional ruin. He called in his entire staff for Sharpe and Baker to question. The only one who was not there was John Peanut, who had had death in the family somewhere in Pennsylvania, and no one knew exactly where. The timing was suspicious.

Baker said, "Pennsylvania's a big state. It will take time to find him. Sharpe would leave that to Baker, whose organization was more suited to that. What bothered him was the accusation that Edwin Forrest had been the one who had helped Harney into the theater to plant the bomb. Forrest had been one of the greats of the American stage, though now fallen on hard times. Ford confirmed that Forrest had gone off to the Midwest to play the small towns that no leading actor would bother with.[14]

Ford was incredulous when told Harney had named Forrest as the one who had assisted him to place the bomb. "He's a Northern man, born in Pennsylvania. I have never heard him utter a single positive word about the Rebellion. I can't believe it." Immediately John Wilkes Booth came to mind, but he said nothing. Edwin was a lifelong friend, and he shrank from dragging his family into this thing.

JERICHO MILLS, VIRGINIA, 5:30 A.M., SATURDAY, MAY 7, 1864

Robert E. Lee stood his horse by the ford below Jericho Mills as his infantry crossed in the first light. The men were tired from hard marching and hard fighting, but they had a capacity for endurance that never ceased to awe their commander. Yesterday's fighting convinced him that Hancock was too hard a nut to crack before Meade fell upon his rear. So he was stealing a march and breaking contact to sidestep Hancock and head for the RF&P below Hanover Junction where he would meet Longstreet and resupply his army, at the same time keeping between the enemy and Richmond. With any luck, Longstreet would be moving as well to meet him.

Stuart's cavalry ran into the Union pickets of Wilson's Division strung out south of the river. Ten miles to the south, Sheridan had placed Gregg's five thousand cavalry squarely across Longstreet's path thanks to Van Lew's warning. His only reserve was Merritt's Brigade. Longstreet's cavalry screen (5th and 15th Virginia) quickly found the Yankees, and the eruption of their firing line alerted Longstreet who was riding at the head of his first brigades. He galloped ahead to see for himself.

THREE MILES SOUTHWEST OF WILLIAMSBURG, VIRGINIA, 6:15 A.M., SATURDAY, MAY 7, 1864

Weitzel had been up before dawn after only an hour's sleep. His brigade roused itself, made coffee, fried bacon, gnawed on hardtack, and waited to resume the fight. They had marched into chaos the night before. Knots of rebs blundering about in the dark after the cavalry had run through them still had fight in them; they had found a lot more when they came upon Longstreet's other brigade drawn up in line of battle across the Richmond road. The only light they had was the flashes from their rifles and a barn on fire. The firing eventually died down as each commander pulled back a bit to get control of their brigades, now dangerously scattered. Then they all lay down and immediately fell asleep save for nodding sentries.

Before dawn his scouts were out to see if the enemy were still there. Gunfire told him they were. He was taking a report from a scout when a horseman on lathered animal galloped up from the southeast. Someone pointed Weitzel out to him, and he rushed over. He gave only the most cursory salute and blurted out, "Colonel Stevenson is on the way with the two brigades from Fortress Monroe. He is an hour behind me, sir."

"Lieutenant, my orders could not have reached them in time to get here so fast."

"Don't know about your orders, but Col. Stevenson, as soon as the cavalry left, he said, 'I can smell a fight.' We marched all day and night."

DUBLIN CASTLE, 12:35 A.M., SATURDAY, MAY 7, 1864

Meagher had been too late with the reserve 69th New York to save the Lincoln redoubt. Instead he had led them waving his sword to counterattack the Coldstream guardsmen as they rushed out of the shattered work. It had been a savage encounter, bayonet to bayonet, in the dark streets with only the flickering light of burning buildings. It was as if Meagher was trying to throw his life away, but emerged from each swirl of death unscathed, his sword red to the hilt. Sergeant Major Wright would write later that he was like a warrior king of ancient Ireland of whom the glorious bards wrote. Yet glory was not enough to tip the scales now that the redoubt had fallen and the enemy was streaming into the city.

Street by street the Irish were pushed back, their repeaters, if they had any ammunition left, of less use in the dark streets than a good bayonet or pistol. By late morning all that were left had fallen back upon Dublin Castle. For the first time in hundreds of years, the complex was going to revert to its original purpose of castle, a walled place of defense and refuge. Barricades were thrown together to block its gates and other entrances. Men scattered through the great buildings to fire from the windows at the lines of men in red who pushed down the streets. A surviving Gatling gun at the main gate made a slaughter pen of the British troops attacking down Parliament Street from the river until the survivors scrambled into houses or feigned death. Elsewhere the red columns flowed through the streets, cutting off every escape from the castle.

Napier had come through the redoubt himself shortly after it had fallen to bring what order he could to the most chaotic of all combats, city fighting. Dublin would be luckier than Dehli though, the last major city to fall to the British by storm and to be brutally sacked.[15] He followed closely behind the attacking troops, but by the time they had cornered the last of the Irish in Dublin Castle, he pulled his men back and sent out a flag of truce.

Meagher and he met in before the Gates of Fortitude and Justice flanking the Bedford Tower with all the military pomp that both sides could muster. Honor guards, drummers, and color guards marched behind the two generals. The Union flag of the United Kingdom and the Green Flag of Ireland and Stars and Stripes snapped in the wind as Napier and Meagher approached each other and saluted. They spent the barest moment seeking to find some clue in the body language and the eyes. They found in each other the proud Celt and obdurate Saxon, a meeting repeated down the centuries of Irish history.

As befitting the one who sought the parley, Napier spoke first. "Sir, I have come to entreat you to stop any further unnecessary effusion of blood and the surrender of your command."

"British demands are no longer currency in the Republic of Ireland, sir."

Napier had steeled himself for this dance around the subject. "It is plain, sir, that your position is hopeless. Any further loss of life will not alter that fact."

Meagher knew full well the truth of that, but still this was high drama, and he was looking at the future when this moment was history. "I will not treat on any terms but those that recognize the Republic of Ireland by Her Majesty's government."

Napier would have rolled his eyes had he not been a man of great self-control. His better instincts won out. He reached out as one man to another and placed his hand on Meagher's arm. "General Meagher, you have played the game and lost. Words will not alter that. There was never a chance you would succeed. But history will acknowledge another fact — the boldness and valor of you and your men. You have covered your defeat in honor."

Meagher knew these words would resound down the years, but the dance was not yet over. "Whatever the facts, General, I cannot throw my men upon the mercy of Judge Jeffreys. They have conducted themselves as soldiers and soldiers of the United States of America."

Napier knew that a chip had been thrown on the table. He now threw out one of his own. He was under intense political pressure to end this business as quickly as possible and at the least cost in blood and destruction. Disraeli had had the good sense to ensure the widest possible discretion was allowed Napier. "General Meagher, the terms I offered earlier are still good. For God's sake, sir, let us spare spilling of the blood of good men and the destruction of your own country's capital."

"My own country's capital, sir? You have no idea of the bitter irony of your words."[16]

"I Would Rather Die a Thousand Deaths"

NORFOLK NAVAL BASE, VIRGINIA, 7:20 A.M., SATURDAY, MAY 7, 1864
The British picket ship waiting outside the American naval base turned about and fled as Farragut led the battle fleet into the Roads. Hope's signal flags alerted the fleet, and within seconds of their reading, the drums rolled, "Beat to Quarters," on every ship.

With a precision that was the envy of every navy, the British ships assumed their final position. Hope placed his floating batteries and gunboats directly in the path of the oncoming Americans, almost sixty vessels in a deep hedge meant to disrupt their formation and do as much damage as possible with its mass of guns. The gunboats were towing the floating batteries. A half dozen of the gunboats had been designated the mission of ramming and boarding the monitors a lá the late lamented Bazalgette (the British did not know he was a prisoner). Behind them and in parallel he placed his heavy hitters in three divisions. The center formation was made up of the seven ironclads and the fleet's single ship-of-the-line, HMS *Edgar*, because of its heavy and more up-to-date ordnance. It would have to take the place of the lost *Royal Oak*.[1] Fore and aft of the ironclads were two composite divisions of frigates, corvettes, and sloops.

Hope's intention was to be able to concentrate his firepower against the American ships that passed through the floating batteries and gunboats. The line ahead formation also gave him considerable flexibility to adapt to whatever contingency arose. He steamed slowly east to give his fleet as much open water as possible for the coming fight. He did not want his ships to come within reach of Fortress Monroe's 15-inch Rodman guns.[2]

FIVE MILES NORTH OF SACO, MAINE, 7:30 A.M., SATURDAY, MAY 7, 1864
Custer arrived on the Portland road at the head of his division, and it was a moment for him as sweet as meat off the bone. He had his

horse put on a show of dancing, which amused the men immensely. They had accomplished the ultimate feat of which every cavalryman dreamed — to sever the enemy's line of communications. He sent a brigade dashing north to see what damage they could do on the way to Portland and almost immediately overran a fifty-wagon train of supplies headed to Doyle.

It would be hours before Doyle realized what had happened. He had other things to worry about. Sherman's XI Corps following Custer had crossed the Saco to the west of Doyle and attacked down the north side of the Saco River overrunning one of his brigades and driving back the next one. Doyle spurred off with his reserve brigade, leaving Wosleley to watch Sherman, who was directly across the river, or so he thought. Wolseley realized to his dismay that the army's scouts, Denison's Royal Guides, were not able to tell him anything. Those scouts who had slipped south of the Saco simply never returned. They had more to fear from the local militia swarming the area than Sherman's security. Wolseley gave the order to the remaining division to be prepared to march at once. These were the men who had done so well at Chazy.

At that moment the advance guards of Sherman's XII Corps was crossing at three hidden fords to the east of Biddeford-Saco, fords discovered by Sergeant Knight and his scouts. As soon as the first regiment was across, Knight and his scouts went north to look for Custer.

Lieutenant Colonel McEntee himself was at that moment reading the message just received from telegrapher in the observation balloon directly south of Biddeford. They had caught the movement of the enemy division to engage the XI Corps and identified the other division still encamped around Saco and perhaps even more importantly had spotted the movement of a large cavalry force several miles north on the Portland Road. The easternmost balloon also reported no enemy activity whatsoever in that direction, only the XII Corps columns marching west north of the river. He found Sherman in front of his headquarters, which was being broken down in preparation to move. The general was nervously pacing back and forth, running his fingers through his scraggly red beard. As soon as he saw McEntee approaching, he focused his whole being on him. McEntee summarized the reporting and his conclusions that the enemy's attention was to the west of Saco, the force in Saco itself had not moved, that there was no opposition to the east of Saco, and that Custer had cut the Portland Road.

Sherman's eyes glittered. He spun on his heel, mounted, and dashed off after XII Corps.[3]

FIVE MILES SOUTH OF HANOVER JUNCTION, VIRGINIA, 7:35 A.M., SATURDAY, MAY 7, 1864

Stuart's men had been up at dawn pushing Wilson's men back in a continuous skirmish. Lee had also had the army up and marching at first light. There was no breakfast but what cold rations they could munch from their haversacks on the march. The men barely had time to pee before they were off. Time was everything. It occurred to Lee that both Wellington and Napoleon had things to say apropos to this moment. The Iron Duke, when questioned by a feather merchant on what was the essence of strategy, simply replied, "Pee when you can." Napoleon, always the more dramatic, had said to a courier, "Go, sir, gallop, and don't forget that the world was made in six days. You can ask me for anything you like, except time."[4]

Time, time, time. How long would it take Meade and Hancock to figure out what he had done and react? Every minute they tried to make sense of what was going on was that much further out of harm's way. It could not be long now since Stuart had made contact with their cavalry late yesterday, but would they think it was a feint or a raid by Stuart, or more, he wondered. His chief of staff, Colonel Charles Marshall, put words to that same thought. Lee could only say, "It is always proper to assume that the enemy will do what he should do."[5]

It was prudent that he should bear that in mind, for Grant had been well-served by John Babcock and his BMI.[6] Babcock's scouts had found the tail of Lee's withdrawing army, followed it south as some rushed forward to find Grant and Hancock and others to the rear to inform Meade. Putting this information together with Wilson's reports of Stuart's movement, Grant gave Hancock the order to prepare to intercept Lee. At first light as Lee's men woke on the hard ground, Hancock's balloons began to ascend. His own men had already been on the road in the last dark hours of the morning. By the time the sun rose, the head of the long blue column was already past Hanover Junction.

Longstreet had also wasted no time, and with the dawn had sent his brigades forward against Sheridan's dismounted cavalry. Only then did an exhausted courier from Lee find him. The possibility of crushing Hancock between them was gone, and it was now Longstreet's mission to hold open the door by which the Army of Northern Virginia would escape. He immediately dispatched his two cavalry regiments to make contact with Stuart, and then turned his attention back to smashing Sheridan.

That was not going well. The usual trickle of wounded that staggered rearward in any fight was a freshet then a flood. He could hear the high volume of fire from the enemy and the new machine-like buzz of the

Gatlings. But push Sheridan back he did. His artillery laced the lines of the dismounted cavalry and savaged the Union horse artillery. Slowly Sheridan gave ground.

CHESAPEAKE BAY, 9:45 A.M., SATURDAY, MAY 7, 1864

The submersible squadron left Fortress Monroe at midnight and ran on the surface into the bay. What sparks had come from their small funnels were swallowed by the night. And no one saw them to bobbing to the rear of the British fleet, as all eyes were forward in the direction of Farragut's main battle fleet. If that were not enough to rivet their attention, the sudden appearance from the direction of Norfolk of the four aeroships certainly did. Admiral Hope commented to his flag lieutenant, "Now we shall see what these new balloon guns can do."

His own attention switched to the approach of Farragut's ships in four parallel divisions each steaming line ahead. In the easternmost division were seven frigates and sloops. The other three divisions were all ironclads. To either side of each of the ironclad divisions were gunboats and sloops.

The British batteries and gunboats opened fire immediately as the American ships came in range. With his glass Hope watched the hail of projectiles converging with great accuracy on the leading monitors. They seemed to steam on as if they were nothing but clouds of gnats flying them. When the monitors fired in return, their huge projectiles disintegrated every floating battery they hit in a spray of shattered armor plate, bodies, and guns. They could not miss for the British batteries and boats were in a deep formation, and those shot were bound to hit something.

As the lead monitors broke into the British formation, the Bazalgetters sprang forward. HMS *Speedwell* and *Dart*, 570-ton Philomel-class screw gunboats closed in on USS *Dictator* from either side, on their decks the boarding parties of armed sailors and Marines. The only slightly larger USS *Penobscot* rushed ahead to intercept *Dart* on *Dictator*'s larboard side. At one hundred yards its 11-inch 172-pound shell blew through the *Dart*'s hull to explode in the engine spaces. On *Dictator*'s starborad side, her escorting gunboat had itself been intercepted by several British gunboats. *Speedwell* churned by to ram the huge monitor and ride up on its deck. The tactic had worked well on the smaller Passaic-class monitors, only one quarter *Dictator*'s size, causing them to list dangerously. *Dictator*, though, at over 4,300 tons showed hardly any list with the small gunboat beached half on its deck and half in the water. The boarding party was jumping down when the turret swung forward and literally blew *Speedwell* off the deck with the blast of both its 15-inch Dahlgrens. Dictator plowed on trailing the gunboat's debris.

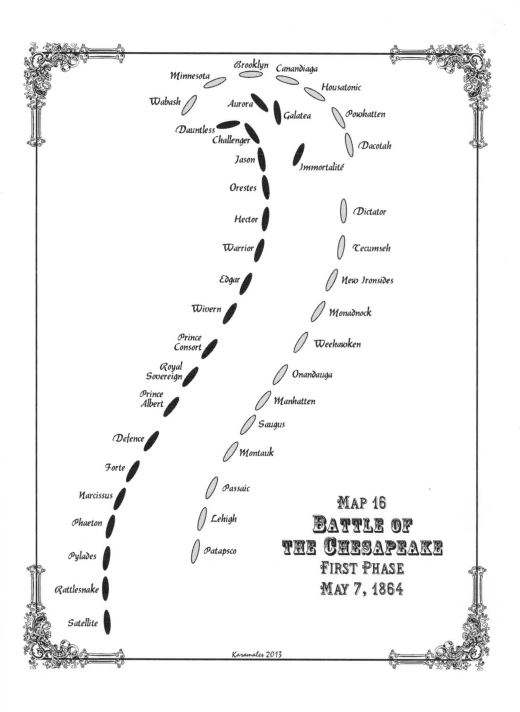

Minnesota
Brooklyn
Canandiaga
Housatonic
Wabash
Aurora
Galatea
Powhatten
Dauntless
Dacotah
Challenger
Jason
Immortalité
Orestes
Hector
Dictator
Warrior
Tecumseh
Edgar
New Ironsides
Wivern
Monadnock
Prince Consort
Weehawken
Royal Sovereign
Onandauga
Prince Albert
Manhatten
Saugus
Defence
Montauk
Forte
Passaic
Narcissus
Lehigh
Phaeton
Patapsco
Pylades
Rattlesnake
Satellite

MAP 16
BATTLE OF
THE CHESAPEAKE
FIRST PHASE
MAY 7, 1864

Karamales 2013

At the tail of the left column HMS *Lee* and *Landrail* converged on the small Passaic-class monitor, USS *Sangamon*. The U.S. gunboat *Monticello* was already drifting on fire, knocked to pieces by the gun batteries it had passed. *Sangamon*'s turret was desperately shifting to bring its guns to bear on *Lee* when *Landrail* struck it, riding up on its aft deck, depressing the guns as the ship was pressed down on its port side. Marines and armed tars leapt over the side and onto the deck. Its hatches flew open and men scrambled out pistols and cutlasses in hand to defend the ship. It was hand to hand on the deck when *Lee* rode up on the forward deck. The two gunboats equalized the pressure on the deck righting it as water swept over the deck. Its guns now were stabilized on a level plain. They swung slowly to *Lee* and fired. The gunboat was blown back into the water, sending its boarding party flying through the air. HMS *Snipe* now came alongside as the turret crew hurriedly tried to reload. *Snipe* fired its 7-inch Armstrong gun directly into the 15-inch gun aperture just as the crew was lifting the powder charge. The 110-pound shell exploded just inside the turret as it struck the gun muzzle. The powder bags ignited, and blast shot out of the twin apertures in two orange jets, burning the turret crew alive. *Sangamon* was dead.

No one noticed far to the rear of the fighting the small smokestacks of the submersibles being retracted as the boats prepared to slip under the water.

SACO, MAINE, 10:30 A.M., SATURDAY, MAY 7, 1864

However much Wolseley had wished that Hope Grant was on the spot, he now put that aside. A courier had come rushing from the fighting west along the river to report that Doyle was dead and that the enemy was pressing them hard. The mantle of command fell easily on his shoulders. He assessed what he knew — the enemy in strength was driving back the army's 2nd Division toward Saco. This was the division that had conducted the siege of Portland and won the battle of Kennebunk last October. A majority of its men were Canadians whose nine months of hard service had turned into more than adequate soldiers. The Americans appeared to still be occupying Biddesford and were keeping up a heavy sniping and artillery fire. Their damn balloons hung in the air south of Biddeford and for several miles east and west of it. To the east, there was no information, and that was what was troubling. If there was nothing going on there, then Denison's scouts should have reported just that. Instead, they simply disappeared.

Wolseley turned to Denison. "George, take your remaining Guides and find out what is going on to the east of us. For God's sake, hurry, man. I have to act within an hour or two at most, and I await your report." The sound of battle to the west was getting louder.

A few miles east of Saco, a half–dozen nondescript men hid in some woods. "Well, I'll be damned," Hogan muttered as he peered through the branches behind which Knight and he watched the road. Then he grinned and said, "Isn't it grand!" more a delighted statement of fact than a question. Knight watched as a four Royal Guides in their nickel-plated Greek revival helmets (which by this time they had learned to hide with a burlap cover) trotted toward them. Hogan knew that Knight would have been perfectly happy to let them ride by. He was not a believer in bushwacking the other side's scouts. In this case, Hogan thought, he will be glad to make an exception. He leaned over. "That's my former host, the one that promised to hang me. It is himself, Colonel George Denison, commander of the Royal Guides. Imagine, a representative of Her Majesty's government wanting to hang an Irishman!"

He was right about the bushwacking. Knight was eager to make an exception for the man who was the counterpart of both McEntee and himself. He drew his pistol and looked at his companions. "Prisoners, boys, especially the colonel." They burst out of the woods within yards of the Guides, whooping and hollering and firing. The lead Guide pitched out of his saddle and another lurched forward, clutching his shoulder. By the time Denison drew his pistol, Hogan was on him and smashed him across the face with his own revolver. The man swayed in the saddle as Hogan brought the pistol down on his face again, again, and again until he slid to the ground. Hogan looked down and said, "Well, saar, forgive me the lack of a rope, for I would dearly love to return your hospitality, but Colonel McEntee would like a little talk with you."[7]

TAYLORSVILLE, VIRGINIA, 10:35 A.M., SATURDAY, MAY 7, 1864

It was not just five thousand exhausted dismounted cavalrymen who held off Longstreet's First Corps for three long hours that morning grudgingly giving ground. It was Sheridan and five thousand cavalrymen. He rode up and down the firing lines oblivious to the fire as the bullets and shells thinned his staff until he was carrying his own general's flag and waving it over his head, doubling the fighting spirit of each unit as he passed. Of course, the Spencers and Gatlings helped too, but his men had taken fearful losses from Longstreet's artillery battalion ably commanded by Col. E.P. Alexander, and the fact that the Confederates outnumbered him five to one, which tended to equalize the firepower advantage of the repeaters, as did Alexander's fine new English guns. Still, Longstreet's mighty First Corps, called even by its enemies the most powerful offensive formation in American history, had only been able to push Sheridan back a mile, just outside small town of Taylorsville, four miles south of Hanover Junction.

Longstreet himself was fighting off a living nightmare. The firepower of the enemy cavalry reminded him of every one of those blood-soaked days when men were thrown at the massed firepower of the enemy — first there was Malvern Hill, then Fredericksburg, and that most evil of all days, July 3, at Gettysburg when he had begged Lee not to march into the jaws of that fire trap. Worst of all in its own way was the spinning barrels whirring and glowing in the night of those infernal Gatlings as he led his corps on the flank attack at Chattanooga.[8]

Sheridan was so intent on the battle that he did not see the big man on a big horse ride up behind him with an army commander's flag whipping in the breeze. Hancock watched him for a moment and took in the field with that single quick glance, the gift of the great commander. In another moment U.S. Grant joined him and then Maj. General Wright commanding VI Corps. It was only then that an aide tugged on Sheridan's sleeve to point to the grove of commander's flags that had sprouted. Sheridan turned Rienzi and trotted over to them. "Stopped him cold, the great Longstreet, we did

Grant reached out to shake Sheridan's hand, as did the others. Wright then rode off quickly to see to the deployment of his corps. Hancock laughed. "Sheridan, you've given Longstreet a very bad morning. Now let Wright have a turn, and we shall ruin his whole day." They watched for a moment as Wright's lead brigades double-timed onto the field, their rifles over their shoulders in a undulating hedge of bayonets, peeling left and right and moving up behind Sheridan's men who were only too glad to fall back through them.

Information now seemed to fly at this group of generals — couriers from Wilson telling of his desperate fight with his small division to hold Stuart from getting past Hanover Academy and reach Ashland Station five miles to the southeast on the RF&P Railroad. Hancock's chief of his BMI reported what the analysis of interrogations and scout reports as well as his company of balloons. "Lee is definitely behind Stuart. If Stuart gets past Wilson, he will take Ashland Station and then reestablish his supply lines on the railroad and be able to withdraw into the defenses of Richmond." He then pointed to the west and said, "Hanover Academy is over there about two miles.[9] If Lee passes it, he can also come right up on Longstreet's flank and fight with a unified army again. He can execute either or both of these options, General."

Grant said, "The last thing we want is for Lee to get his army into the defenses of Richmond. We must avoid a siege at all costs. Where the hell is Meade?"

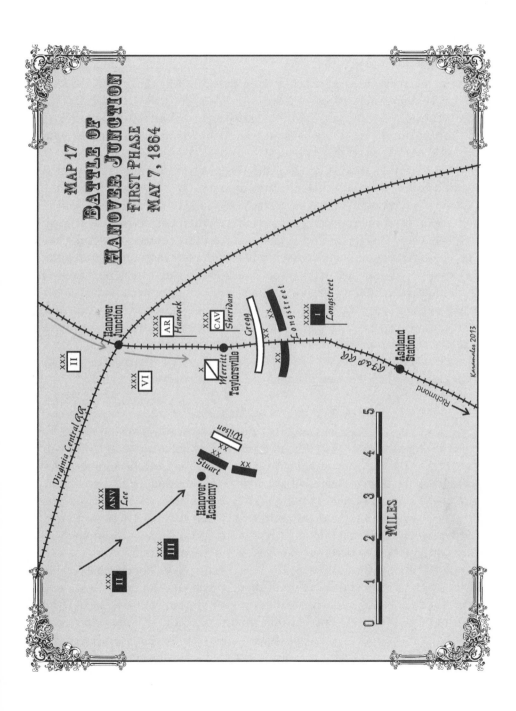

MAP 17
BATTLE OF
HANOVER JUNCTION
FIRST PHASE
MAY 7, 1864

The officer replied that some of Meade's scouts had come into his lines with the news that Meade was now half a day behind Lee. Grant turned to Hancock. "I think II Corps would be of real use to Wilson about now."

Hancock said, "It will take him hours to get there in strength. His corps is behind Wright's."

Sheridan seemed to crackle with energy. "My Reserve Brigade is fresh. I can get there before II Corps."

"Do it," Grant said without hesitation. Sheridan was already galloping away. "Hancock, I think you should send the next division to back him up until II Corps arrives."

At that moment just north of the Hanover Academy Lee rode up to Stuart, who was intently watching the fighting. "General Stuart, what is the delay?" Stuart had not heard that sharpness in his voice since that painful afternoon on the second day at Gettysburg when he had ridden up with his exhausted cavalry behind him only to be coldly reproved for being late to the field. For a man who loved Lee like a father it was wounding beyond all measure. For a man who loved Stuart like a son, it was no easier. "I will have them on the run shortly, General. They have been uncommonly resolved to fight it out today." Just then a solid shot struck the tree they were under, showering them with leaves, branches, and splinters. Lee calmly picked a six–inch splinter from the back of his hand. With that same hand he patted the neck of his splendid gray-white mount, Traveler, as blood soaked his gauntlet. "Thank God, old friend, you were spared."

CHESAPEAKE BAY, 10:30 A.M., SATURDAY, MAY 7, 1864

The roar and thunder of two great fleets in action dulled the senses to everything else. Even had it been a peaceful watch on a calm sea, it was not likely that the attachment of mines by the divers of the submersibles would have been detected. Large magnets jumped from the divers' hands to the iron hulls, the slight ring lost in the noise of battle. The torpedo was than affixed to the magnet. That is how it was supposed to work. The submersibles had had a far more difficult time keeping up with the British battle line even though it was moving at only a few knots. The divers had had even greater trouble in floating across the space between a moving hull and their own boat, hoping against hope that their air hoses did snap. But in the end all four found a target. Two of the torpedoes were successfully mounted and their long wires back to the boat and their ignition batteries let out. To the surprise of the other two divers, instead of iron hulls they found the copper sheathing of wooden hulls. The torpedoes could not be mounted. They had been unlucky enough to find HMS *Prince Consort* and *Royal Sovereign*, both built originally as wooden ships-of-the-line and then cut down and converted to ironclads, their hulls sheathed in copper.[10]

Farragut's plan had been for each division as it penetrated the floating battery and gunboat screen to turn to starboard and form a single line ahead paralleling the enemy's. He had driven home to his captains the necessity of keeping this formation, and they pulled it off, though with some gaps. As they broke through the enemy's small vessels, the heavy fire from Hope's ironclads and wooden ships converged on the lead ship of each division. British gunnery was excellent, but even at that close range, the monitors were small targets. Still, the turrets rang with hit after hit, sending vibrating shock waves through the metal armor. A lucky hit from HMS *Royal Sovereign* on the gun aperture of USS *Saugus* struck the muzzle of one of its 15-inch guns, breaking off a good six inches and throwing fragments through the turret, wounding a half–dozen men. The surviving gun fired, and its shell exploded on the enemy ship's deck, bringing down its mainmast. Farragut's captains were following his orders to initially demast the British ships so that the broken masts and sails would fail over the sides and act as a slowing drag on them and mask their guns.

Barely five hundred yards separated the ironclad battle lines, thick black clouds of powder smoke hanging in the space between punctuated by the darting red tongues of discharging guns. The two battle lines were steaming slowly parallel. The bay was too narrow a field of fight for high–speed maneuvers. It was now two boxers in a small ring pounding away at each other as they slowly steamed east to the wider part of the bay. Hope was pulling the battle into more open water where his speed advantage could come into play. Two more British ironclads saw their masts come crashing down in the first ten minutes of the fighting. Even if Hope wanted to increase speed as he reached more open water, he could not unless he wanted his formation to break up as the demasted ships fell behind.

Hope took heart from good effect of Captain Cowles's tactics of plunging fire that had already smashed through the deck of USS *Montauk* and left it dead in the water, smoke pouring out of its torn open deck. Another of the smaller *Passaic*-class monitors, the *Weehawken*, was also put out of action. Deadly accurate British gunnery from HMS *Wivern*'s four 9-inch rifled guns had found a flaw and cracked her turret armor, and another round had penetrated, killing everyone inside. The powder bags inside exploded, bursting the turret.

Farragut broke his own battle line to bring *New Ironsides* up against HMS *Warrior*, Hope's flagship and the first and largest of the British ironclads at 9,200 tons. *New Ironsides*'s crew took enormous pride in having sunk *Warrior*'s sister ship, *Black Prince*, at Charleston the previous October and was now determined to inflict the same fate on the pride of the Royal Navy. *New Ironsides* seriously outgunned her opponent, her 11-inch Dahlgrens against the 7-inch Armstrongs and smaller old 68-pounders. Although the breech–loading Armstrongs were accurate and quick firing, their 110-pound shot simply bounced off the angled, rolled steel armor of *New Ironsides*. *Warrior's* own armor was quickly torn open along its entire length, as the 172-pound American shells exploded inside the gun compartments. Only its innovation of interior armored bulkheads prevented the exploding shells from causing even more mayhem.

Farragut's wooden division at the head of his battle line suddenly increased speed to pass around the head of the British lead division, pounding its lead frigate, HMS *Aurora*, to pieces with the converging fire of almost all its seven ships. *Aurora* fell out of line exposing the next ship HMS *Galetea* to the same converging fire with much the same result.

With the lead two frigates smashed and blocking his way and his orders to maintain line ahead now manifestly irrelevant, Captain George Hancock, C.B., of the next frigate, HMS *Immortalité*, sought out the nearest American ship, the frigate *Powhatan*, steamed right through her fire to come right up to her at ten yards.[11] *Immortalité* was a big, new, and well-armed screw steam frigate with a heavier broadside than the older sidewheel steamer *Powhatan*, whose ten Dahlgrens could still knock Hancock's own ship into matchsticks.[12] Hancock had in the year prior to the war, been detailed by the commander of the Royal Navy's North American and West Indies Station to coordinate repairs for the British ships at American navy yards where he had gleaned every bit of information he could on the Dahlgren guns for which he gained a most healthy respect. He knew that if he was to have a chance against the *Powhaten's* guns, he had to get in close and inflict a crippling shot right off.

Powhatan's larboard sidewheel disintegrated, its great arms flapping broken on the water while the starboard wheel kept churning turning the ship in a circle. Hancock just rammed her rather than follow as his gunners kept up the relentless gutting of the American ship. He was the first man to board *Powhatan* and led the fight up to the quarterdeck where he found the American captain dead besides the shattered wheel and its fallen helmsman.

The rest of the British division led by HMS *Dauntless* made a hard turn to larboard to bring itself parallel with the American ships and bring their guns to bear. It was then that wrenching shudders ran through HMS *Wyvern* and *Hector*. The torpedoes attached to their iron hulls detonated, and the sea gushed inside.

Only the balloon gun crews, their eyes skyward, noticed then the line of aeroships coming in from the west.

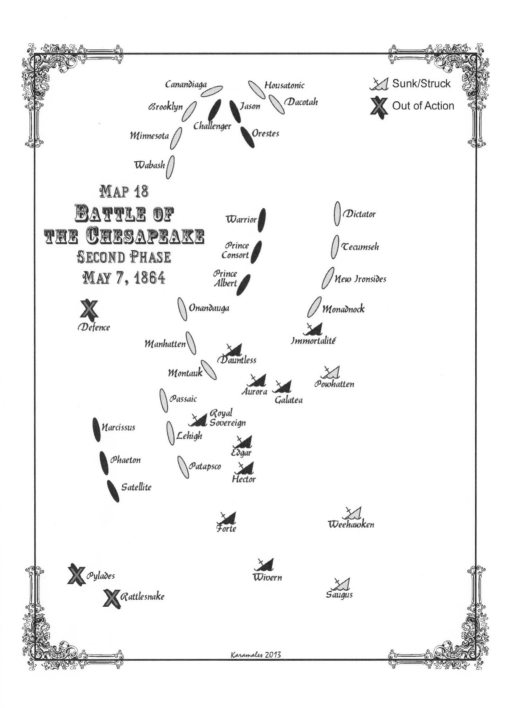

Sunk/Struck

Out of Action

Canandiaga

Housatonic

Brooklyn

Jason

Dacotah

Challenger

Minnesota

Orestes

Wabash

MAP 18
BATTLE OF
THE CHESAPEAKE
SECOND PHASE
MAY 7, 1864

Warrior

Dictator

Prince
Consort

Tecumseh

Prince
Albert

New Ironsides

Onandauga

Monadnock

Defence

Immortalité

Manhatten

Dauntless

Montauk

Powhatten

Aurora

Galatea

Passaic

Royal
Sovereign

Narcissus

Lehigh

Phaeton

Edgar

Patapsco

Satellite

Hector

Forte

Weehawken

Pylades

Wivern

Rattlesnake

Saugus

Karamales 2013

SACO, MAINE, 12:30 P.M., SATURDAY, MAY 7, 1864

Wosleley looked at his pocket watch on the picket line to the east of Saco. As it read 12:30, he snapped it shut, turned on his heel, mounted, and rode back into town. Colonel Denison had not come back. He must now act without whatever information he could have brought.

His orders were quick and decisive. Within minutes the 1st Division was set in motion to prepare to march west. He reviewed what he knew. A strong enemy force believed to be Sherman's XI Corps was pushing the 2nd Division back onto Saco and the XII Corps remained south of Biddefield observing his own force that was now getting in marching order. He then reviewed what he did not know and that was what was going on to his east. If XII Corps was still just across the river, then what had swallowed up all his scouts? There had been reports of militia swarming the area. That could explain the missing scouts. He was not completely satisfied with that answer, but since Doyle had seen fit to throw away his cavalry brigade as a rear guard, he had no speedy way to find out. Yes, speed was the answer. He must strike the enemy pressing in from the west with such speed shock that if their XII Corps should somehow cross the river and threaten his rear, he would be able to turn on it and defeat it as well. In any case, British soldiers were fighting and dying, and his place was with them.

The order of march had the 12th Brigade in the lead. Grant had promoted McBean of the 78th (Highland) Foot to command the brigade, and now he rode with him as the troops marched out of Saco. "McBean, strike them hard again and again. We don't have a whole day to pound each other like Wellington at Waterloo."

"Aye, General, me bonny boys will give them the cold steel." He turned as the Highlanders strode by, their kilts flowing around their knees. They were glad to have the kilts back as the warm spring weather had sent their trews back into storage. The pipers were playing the cocky "The Drunken Piper." McPeak laughed out loud and said to himself, "Aye, there's me brave laddies."

In a half hour they were passing through a growing crowd of wounded men making their way back to the field hospitals. Dead men and wounded who could go no further were scattered on the side of the road. Most of these were Canadians, but there was a sprinkling of men from three British regiments.[13] The sound of fighting flared quickly coming their way, then a flood of fleeing men blocked the road. A Canadian field officer raced up to McPeak and screamed that the 2nd Sherbrooke Brigade had collapsed and that they must retreat. McPeak waved him off, saying, "Tsk, tsk, man, we just got here!" He threw the 78th and 73rd Foot on either side of the road into the fields that bordered thick woods with the 26th Foot and the Canadian 17th Levis Battalion behind them and gave the command to fix bayonets. The sound of twenty-five hundred bayonets fitting into their muzzle slots made a brief rattle and suddenly stopped. McPeak rode up to the 78th's pipe major. "McLeod! Play me 'Scotland the Brave,' man." The pipes skirled the bold air, and when the pipers paused as it reached that special crescendo, the battalion filled it with a resounding shout of "Hoy!" the challenge of one host to another across the havoc of war. On the other side of the field, more than one man born to the heather felt the tears running down his face.

"The Brigade will advance!"

ANDERSON STATION, VIRGINIA, 12:35 P.M., SATURDAY, MAY 7, 1864

The Old Snapping Turtle they called him, Maj. Gen. George G. Meade. It was not a term of endearment. He had the sharpest tongue in the army and did not care who felt its edge.[14] Today he was snapping at everyone within range, particularly his commanders, demanding to know why they could not quicken the pace. Particularly lacerated at this moment was his V Corps commander, Maj. Gen. Gouverneur Warren. Warren was a military engineer, a profession for careful men with a good eye for detail. It was this good eye that grasped on the first day of Gettysburg that the critical Little Round Top was undefended. It was his warning that saved the hill and some say the battle.

As a corps commander he was too careful, always making sure that everything was in order and every danger prepared for before he moved. He had not the alacrity of a killer's instinct. His corps was slow. The Army of the Potomac had made good hard-marching time to catch up with Lee with I Corps in the lead the day before. This morning V Corps took the lead and the pace of advance slowed perceptibly. Unpleasant as he was to those around him, Meade was an excellent soldier who knew how to move with alacrity. An engineer himself, he had been able to avoid the temptation to become obsessed with time-consuming precision when speed was required.[15]

Now he was talking to Warren in a voice that carried down the marching column that was passing. "I've seen glue run up a tree in January faster than this corps is moving, General!" Warren did not appreciate the audience that was grinning as it marched by; his pride was the touchy sort, but he was smart enough not to argue with Meade when he was in this state. The troops enjoyed it immensely, though.

Meade did not leave it at that. He rode down the column giving each brigade and division commander a piece of his mind. Not surprisingly, the column picked up its pace.

CHESAPEAKE BAY, 12:39 P.M., SATURDAY, MAY 7, 1864

Cushing lead the bombing run on board the aeroship *Stephen Decatur* with *John Paul Jones, George Washington,* and *Andrew Jackson* in line behind. He thought it a splendid sight, the scores of warships wreathed in smoke, some on fire, others sinking, but most still fighting it out. He watched as a heavily listing British ironclad suddenly went over onto its side then began to settle by the stern. Men were swarming the water around it or in boats trying to get as far away as possible before the undertow sucked them down with it. He would learn later that it was HMS *Hector* whose wound had been inflicted by the submersible *Dolphin*. HMS *Wivern* was also settling, its hull torn open by *Shark*'s mine. USS *Powhatan* was a funeral pyre, and monitor *Passaic* was dead in the water, another kill scored by Captain Cowles and the *Prince Albert*. HMS *Defence* was afloat but all her starboard guns had been silenced by *Lehigh* and *Patapsco*. She fell out of line unable to bring any guns to bear and fighting fires raging through her wrecked gundecks as ammunition exploded.

The battle had moved on out several miles closer to the entrance to the bay. The British ironclad force had been reduced to *Warrior*, the useless *Defence, Prince Consort,* heavily listing *Royal Sovereign,* and *Prince Albert,* with ship-of-the line *Edgar,* and supported by the second division of three frigates and three corvettes. The first division, except for that fighting devil *Immortalité,* had been wrecked by the overwhelming firepower of the big American frigates.

All semblance of maintaining line ahead was gone, as ships were now locked in individual duels. Slugging it out with these twelve British ships were the ironclads *New Ironsides, Dictator, Tecumseh, Onondaga, Manhattan, Monadnock, Patapsco,* and *Leghigh*. The British ships had suffered far more damage. Their exposed masts and rigging and the greater vulnerability of their armor belts and turrets against the crushing 440-pound shot and 400-pound shells of the American 15-inch Dahlgren guns had begun to tell. The forward turret of *Prince Consort* had been smashed open, and she had been holed repeatedly, putting great strain on her wooden frame. *Prince Albert* had not gone untouched either. One of its four turrets had been holed and jammed shut. She was taking water from a hit at the water line. The heavier USS *Dictator,* pride of John Ericsson, closed in to finish her off, but one of her boilers burst driving the men out of the engine compartments. She slowly fell out of line. *Warrior* was being beaten to death by *New Ironsides* and *Monadnock*. That monitor's turrets were almost solid masses of dents, testimony to the accuracy of British gunnery, yet they were still fighting, the men almost deaf from the constant clanging impact of shot and shell, testimony to the inferior striking power of

British guns. HMS *Edgar* edged in to take some of the pressure off Admiral Hope's flagship and steamed right into the guns of *Monadnock*. Her double turrets fired four huge shells to explode inside the multiple decks of the great ship.

The British frigates and corvettes were engaging the last three ironclads getting the worst of it. None of their guns could do more than dent the turrets, and the Americans were keeping too close to let them fire downward at their vulnerable decks. Already frigate *Pylades* and corvette *Rattlesnake* had fallen out of line so badly damaged by the American 11- and 15-inch guns. *Narcissus* kept up a steady but ineffective fire despite her wounds as the blood ran down the scuppers and flames licked through the splintered holes in her gun decks.

Most of the anti-balloon guns on the British ships had already been smashed or their exposed crews swept away when Cushing led his aeroships in for their strike. Their priority targets were the ironclads, and so they flew over the frigates and corvettes at the tail of the column. Cushing came down to three hundred feet in the "Barbary Pirate" and released his rack of explosive bronze shell bombs[16] mixed with incendiaries onto *Prince Consort*. Half fell into the sea behind her, but the others fell perfectly down the deck in a ripple of explosions and billowing flame.

John Paul Jones's target was HMS *Royal Sovereign*, and its aim was even better than Cushing's. Soon that ship's upper deck was a mass of wreckage and fire. *George Washington* entirely missed *Warrior*, her bombs all falling to the larboard of the ship. *Andrew Jackson* followed, released too soon onto *Defence* only to see half the bombs fall into the sea and the other half hit *Forte*'s bow, disintegrating it and the foredeck and sending incendiaries spilling fire down its wooden decks. Aboard corvette *Pylades* a midshipman Pulver ran up to the abandoned 20-pounder Armstrong balloon gun, shoved off the dead gunner draped over it and swiveled it on its mount directly in the path of oncoming *Andrew Jackson*. He jumped back and pulled the lanyard. Its incendiary shell punched through the sky and right into the aeroship's hydrogen-filled balloon. For a split second nothing happened, then a jet of blue-orange flame spurted from the rent fabric of the balloon, which spasmed in a pulse of incandescent fire and collapsed slowly onto itself. The compartment beneath plummeted downward trailing the burning balloon until the entire mass crashed into the sea in loud hiss.

ONE MILE NORTH OF THE HANOVER ACADEMY, 1:15 P.M., SATURDAY, MAY 7, 1864

All it took was one last charge by the 6th Virginia Cavalry, and what was left of Wilson's cavalry division gave way. Private James Faulkner found himself alone as he rode up pistol in hand to take the surrender of three dismounted enemy who held their rifles butt end up. A dozen other Yankees had run for the woods twenty yards away. Out of nowhere Stuart himself rode up waving his black-plumed hat and his blue eyes flashing. He had outrun his staff to be at victory's spear tip and reached over to shake Faulkner's hand. Faulkner was awed not only by Stuart the man but in the sense of triumph that radiated from him as he said, "We've got the damned Yankees on the run again!" He knew Lee was watching. He had done it, broken through. Already the 6th Virginia was mopping the last of the Yankees that had not hightailed it away, and his couriers were galloping to find Longstreet.

He stood up in the saddle to get a better look just as one of the fleeing Yankees reached the woods, turned, and fired. Stuart flew back in the saddle, leaned over, his plumed hat falling into the dust, said, "I am shot," and fell to the ground. Faulkner flew from his horse to rush to Stuart's side, but the general was already dead as he fell into Faulkner's arms. The three prisoners did not need to think. They bolted for the woods.

Stuart's death at the critical moment would cost precious time that Lee did not have. Suddenly, the reins of Lee's cavalry arm went slack. His staff caught up with him, and at the sight of him on the ground cried out in anguish. The most conspicuous was Captain Heros von Borke, known as the Giant in Gray, for his six feet four inches and huge sword. He was a Prussian officer who had left the 2nd Brandenburg Dragoons to come and fight for the Confederacy and had been commissioned and assigned to Stuart's staff where he became a good friend and confident of the cavalier cavalryman. Now, his Prussian stoicism was undone. He would be the one to inform Lee. It was minutes before anyone thought to tell Hampton that the command had devolved on him or Lee that the man whom he loved as a son had fallen. Time seemed to freeze for the Army of Northern Virginia at that very moment that the army needed to ride on its flowing back to safety.

Into this suspended animation rode Sheridan with Merritt's Reserve Brigade. Sheridan had come across a steady stream of wounded on the road, then more and more hale men, and finally someone who could tell him that Wilson's Division had been fought out and scattered. He arrived to drive off the scattered 6th Virginia and dismount his regiments to take up positions from which their repeaters could do the most damage.

Lee was enormously relieved when Stuart's courier arrived to announce that the enemy cavalry had been broken. He could see himself from his observation post in the small steeple of Hanover Academy how Wilson's troopers seemed to melt away. He ordered his corps commanders to hurry their troops forward with all speed. His first brigade would be coming up to go into battle to support Longstreet shortly. Ever since he had dispatched his favorite corps commander to the James Peninsula, he had said that without the First Corps was like going into a fight with only one boot on. He had hardly sent those orders when he saw through his glass a large force of Union cavalry sweeping forward and scattering Stuart's disorganized regiments. Horse artillery dashed up, unlimbered, and began firing quickly.

It was then that the giant Prussian climbed up onto the viewing platform under the steeple to bring the news of his friend's death.[17] Lee had that great balance of character and will to let him plough through those moments that would stun other men, but even he was shaken. He turned pale, and for long moments he could not speak, and when he did he could only say, "I can scarcely think of him without weeping."[18]

So lost was he in grief in that steeple platform that for a few moments he did not notice the brigades of Maj. Gen. A.P. Hill's Third Corps flowing on either side of the Hanover Academy.

THREE MILES WEST OF SACO, MAINE, 1:25 P.M., SATURDAY, MAY 7, 1864
The Highlanders passed scattered bands of the 1/39th Foot falling back dragging many wounded with them, a look of desperation in all their grimed faces. Then they came upon the dead of the 39th where they had fallen marking where the firing line of the regiment had been. Most of the 39th lay there still. Now Highlanders began to fall, first a few then dozens with each step, not here and there, but whole squads. Seeing the carnage, McPeak stood up in his stirrups and shouted, "Seventy-Eighth! Take them at a run! Charge!" The men roared "Cuidich 'n Rhi!" in response and bounded forward. The 73rd Foot on their flank also shouted and raced forward not to be outdone by the Scotties as did the 26th Foot and the Canadian battalion behind them.

Two hundred yards away a mass of blue infantry stood firing; between the regiments sections of coffee mill guns chattered, and over them all shells flew at the oncoming Highlanders. It was the 2nd Division of XI Corps, regiments from Massachusetts, New Jersey, New York, Ohio, and Pennsylvania, many of whose men had fought and beat the British at Claverack the year before. Doyle's brigades had melted away in the face of their firepower already today. Now they shook their fists as they fired, shouting for the enemy to come on. Their Spencers fired and fired, their sound a symphonic counterpoint to the *click-bang* machine hammer of the coffee mill guns. Maj. Gen. John A. Logan rode behind the first rank of regiments waving his hat. "Come on, you Limey bastards, you want another taste!" He had already driven back Doyle's brigades, and the smell of victory was heady.

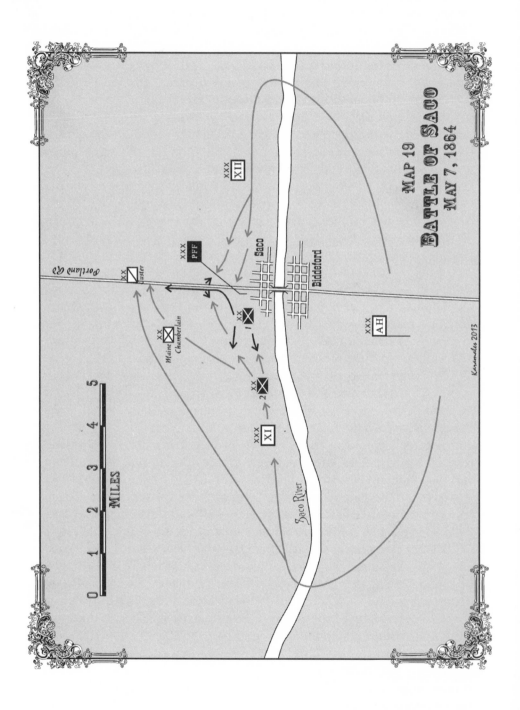

MAP 19
BATTLE OF SACO
MAY 7, 1864

The 78th and 73rd raced into a storm of lead no men had ever faced before, but the last of them just kept coming with the 26th Foot and the 17th Levis Battalion. Somehow McPeak had come through unhurt; he had scrambled from his dying horse to join the 26th charging past him and joined them. The Americans had just kept firing. In a charge, one side or the other would lose its nerve before the two closed upon each other. Either the charging men would lose their will to continue in the face of a steady fore, or the defender could lose his nerve in the face of a determined attacker. The only times when two groups pitched into each other with the bayonet was when one side could not get out of the way.

Today was an exception.

NORFOLK NAVY YARD, VIRGINIA, 2:30 P.M., SATURDAY, MAY 7, 1864

The *John Paul Jones* slowly settled on its landing ground in the navy yard. Its ground crew ran over to tie her down as hydrogen wagons lumbered over to refuel her. Only when they were finished and removed would the ordnance wagons come out to replenish her bombs and incendiaries. *Stephen Decatur* and *George Washington* came down beside her. Cushing stepped down to supervise the work to find that Wilmoth had rushed over to meet him.

Wilmoth had become a byword in the CBI for his unflappable nature and coolness in a crisis, but now he was almost jumping up and down to learn how the battle had gone. He could tell without a word as soon as he saw Cushing's huge grin.

"God, Mike! It was glorious. To see a great naval battle from the air. Then to be part of it. The world will never be the same."

"Details, man! I want details." He handed Cushing a brandy flask.

"Bless you, Mike," he said as he took a good swig.

"We're winning, by God! Our attack did them in, I am sure. We hit three ships. The incendiaries are more dangerous than the bombs. As we left we could see all three ships on fire from our attack. Masts, sails, rigging—all make for a great fire. I tell you, Mike, no one in his right mind will ever take a masted ship into a battle again."

"Did you see anything of the submersibles?"

"Not a thing. But there were a number of ships that were listing or settling."

Cushing took the brandy flask back for another long swig. "I tell you, Mike, the world will never be the same again."

Nothing could have been more true for Admiral Hope. He knew he had lost and ordered the captain of *Warrior* to break off action and head for the open sea. He would have communicated that order to his surviving ships by signal flag, but *Warrior*'s masts and rigging were masses of splintered wood and cordage spilling over the deck and into the sea. All that was left was a midshipman to gallantly wave his flags from the shattered stub of the mainmast. *Defence* and the surviving frigates and corvettes nearby read the signals and broke off action. Their greater speed meant that they could outdistance the enemy ironclads quickly, though their guns could follow for well over a mile. Captain Cowles aboard *Prince Albert* realized what was happening when he saw *Warrior* and the others break off action and head east to the entrance of the bay. His second turret had just been knocked out of action. The *Dictator*'s guns struck the hull below the turret. The two shells burst inside, killing or wounding all eighteen men pushing the capstan that revolved the turret. The sea coming through the waterline holes in her hull was slowing the ship down as she turned to trail *Warrior* and the others.

A dozen sloops and gunboats had also broken away and were making for the bay entrance. They had taken aboard as many of the crews of the floating batteries as possible. American sloops hung on their rear hoping to snap up any that fell behind. The only fighting still going on was *Immortalelité*'s death struggle with the big American frigates *Wabash* and *Minnesota*. Captain Hancock realized that these two ships were the only ones capable enough to pursue and inflict serious harm on the retreating ships. He attacked them both to fix their attention on his own ship. He fought her until she was kindling and the survivors of the fleet had escaped. Then and only then did he strike.[19]

ONE MILE NORTH OF THE HANOVER ACADEMY, 2:30 P.M., SATURDAY, MAY 7, 1864

"Little Powell's got on his battle shirt!" The word went through the ranks of the Third Corps as it deployed north of the Hanover Academy. They knew they were in for a fight. Lt. Gen. A.P. (Ambrose Powell) Hill was riding through them wearing his red calico hunting shirt, something he always donned before a good fight. The most brilliant of Lee's division commanders, the thirty-five-year-old Hill had been given the new Third Corps before the Gettysburg Campaign but had fallen ill during the battle and played no real part. He had also fallen sick in the fighting around Spotsylvania. Described by a historian as "always emotional . . . so high strung before battle that he had an increasing tendency to become unwell when the fighting was about to commence." Others would say the illnesses were stress induced from the gonorrhea he had contracted as cadet while on furlough from West Point.[20] Today he seemed his old swaggering, aggressive self. That was nothing less than a miracle after the terrible wound he had suffered at the battle of Washington the previous October. Reports that he had been cut in two by a jagged shell splinter had been only slightly exaggerated. Yet, to the astonishment of his doctors, he had healed enough, barely enough, to climb back into his saddle.

Lee's orders had been preemptory. Break through to Longstreet at all costs. Now all that stood before him was a single cavalry brigade. His men would scatter them with the first advance. He was wound up as tight as a top at just then; he knew how desperate the situation was. Hill had barely sidestepped a trap at Hanover Junction the day before where his own corps had taken heavy, heavy losses. It all depended on him to link up with Longstreet. Richard S. Ewell's Second Corps was behind him and could offer no assistance. It all depended on him. As he worried, masses of blue infantry streamed onto the field where only a cavalry brigade had been only moments before. It all depended on him. The weight of it pressed down on him until his joints began to ache, and his half-healed wounds screamed and throbbed, and his heart seem to race out of control, as it seemed to want to burst from his chest.[21]

He looked over to his aide. His face pale with sweat beading on his forehead, he said in a low voice, "Captain, ride to General [Richard H.] Anderson, and tell him that he must assume command, as I am indisposed."

By the time Anderson was able to assume command, Lee had ridden up to the forward brigade demanding to know why the attack had not begun. Hill had been a favorite of his, but at this moment his face turned to stone when he heard that Hill had fallen out again. He then said with all the force of his being, "General Anderson, you will break those people so that the army may pass." Unfortunately, by this time the enemy's II Corps was also marching onto the field to reinforce the VI Corps division that had already arrived.

A scout rode up to the group, his horse wet with lather and half dead. "General Lee, Meade is barely two miles to our rear and coming up fast." Everyone around Lee was stunned; Meade had been expected to be at least a half day behind them. Lee turned to Anderson without the least expression of distress. "You have one hour, General."

TWO MILES WEST OF SACO, MAINE, 2:55 P.M., SATURDAY, MAY 7, 1864
The last of the Highlanders had fought over McPeak's body like the warriors at Troy to keep the body of their chieftain from the Jonathans, but even they finally went down. All that was left of the 78th were the wounded scattered along the path of their charge. The colors of the 78th and 73rd were now waving overhead by men in Union blue. The division now advanced over the littered field toward Saco.

A mile to the north Logan's 3rd Division had broken the attack of the 3rd Hamilton Brigade with the same concentrated firepower. Only the remnant of the 47th Foot fought a stubborn rearguard at terrible cost along with a single battery of the Royal Artillery. Only the rapid fire and accuracy of their breech loading Armstrong guns kept the Americans at bay.

Wolseley had been stunned by the smashing of the two brigades; survivors and the walking wounded rushed past him, beyond all caring, and here and there a single gun or caisson, all that remained of an entire battery. His last two brigades were most certainly going to suffer the same fate. This battle was lost; his only duty now was to get the men out that he could by way of the Portland road to the seaport where they could find refuge within the defenses under the guns of the Royal Navy.

Logan was not going to give him much time. His two divisions were attacking. Through the initial fighting his reserve had been the Maine Division. The men were not happy about sitting this fight out, and only Chamberlain's calm presence as he rode down the ranks telling them to be patient kept the grumbling under control. That patience was rewarded when Chamberlain received Logan's order to strike northeast toward the Portland road. As the Maine men stepped off with a long stride, the lead division of XII Corps entered Saco and pushed west. Sherman was determined to catch the British between his two corps.

Wolseley was everywhere in the chaos, putting life back into the scattered groups of broken units, rounding up the mob of fugitive Britons and Canadians, and putting them on the road north along with his trains. He ordered everything but the ammunition wagons and ambulances abandoned. Next on the road was the still uncommitted Dublin Brigade. His rearguard was the 1/Rifles of the Montreal Brigade. He knew that if any regiment could hold off a determined enemy it was the Rifles. Their deadly marksmanship would counter to some degree the American firepower. The rest of their brigade had hardly marched off when the Rifles went into action. Wolseley heard the crash of musketry behind him as he hurried the tail of the column on.

They had hardly gone a mile when American infantry appeared on the right of the Montreal Brigade's three Canadian battalions. The XII Corps had arrived. Sherman was determined that McPherson's corps would clamp its jaws shut on this part of the enemy. These three Canadian battalions were the first three to be raised and had performed with distinction in every battle. Wolseley rode up to the brigade commander and pointed at the deploying blue lines. "You must throw them back." The Canadians wheeled into line and attacked with a precision and confidence that no imperial battalion would be ashamed of. "Forward the Prince of Wales!" shouted the commander of Canada's premier battalion, the 1st Battalion, the Prince of Wales Regiment, as he lead it forward as he had done at the battle of Claverack. The sudden charge caught the arriving Americans off balance, and the Canadians drove them back picking up two colors. Wolseley had watched from the road and shouted, "Well done, Canada!" It had been the only bright spot of the day.[22]

ONE MILE NORTH OF THE HANOVER ACADEMY, VIRGINIA, 3:30 P.M., SATURDAY, MAY 7, 1864

Grant and Hancock had arrived on the field just as Anderson launched the entire Third Corps into the attack to break through the thickening Union lines. "Just like Gettysburg on the third day, General," Hancock observed as the gray brigades surged forward, the Union artillery tearing great gaps in their ranks even before they got within rifle range of the blue infantry. A rider galloped up to them and handed Hancock's chief of the BMI a note. The man scanned it and burst into a huge smile. "General," he said looking at both of them, "Our balloons report a huge dust cloud coming down from the north directly behind the enemy. It is Meade, and they estimate he will be here in an hour."

Hancock had been right. It was just like Gettysburg. His old II Corps was repeating their repulse of the massed Confederate attack, but this time their lethality was multiplied by their repeating weapons and Gatling batteries. And again, just as at Gettysburg, Lee rode among the shattered regiments as they staggered back from the attack, dragging their wounded with them. This time it would not be like Gettysburg because Hancock was attacking on the heels of the enemy's repulse.

Lee had only one reserve, the division of Maj. Gen. John B. Gordon, of Ewell's Second Corps. The rest of Ewell's corps had turned to face Meade. If anyone could save the day, it was the dapper little Georgian who had heroically led his lead brigade over Long Bridge in the battle of Washington and been severely wounded when the attack had collapsed in the converging fire of a dozen coffee mill guns. He had survived the abattoir of Long Bridge and was nursed to health in a Union hospital and exchanged in February. He had had no military experience before the war had found in him a natural and gifted commander. One of his men said of him that he was "the prettiest thing you ever did see on a field of fight. It'ud put fight into a whipped chicken just to look at him." [23]

Gordon's brigades formed on line with the precision of a field parade despite the artillery that was beginning to find them. He raced down the line on his jet black charger so that every man could see that their commander would lead the attack. He stopped before the center brigade and gave the command to advance. His brigades stepped off briskly the square stars and bars battle flags whipping the breeze. He was surprised when Lee appeared on Traveler to ride with him. He was shocked when Lee drew his sword. "My God," thought Gordon, "he means to go in with us." He turned his horse in front of Traveler and grabbed its reins.

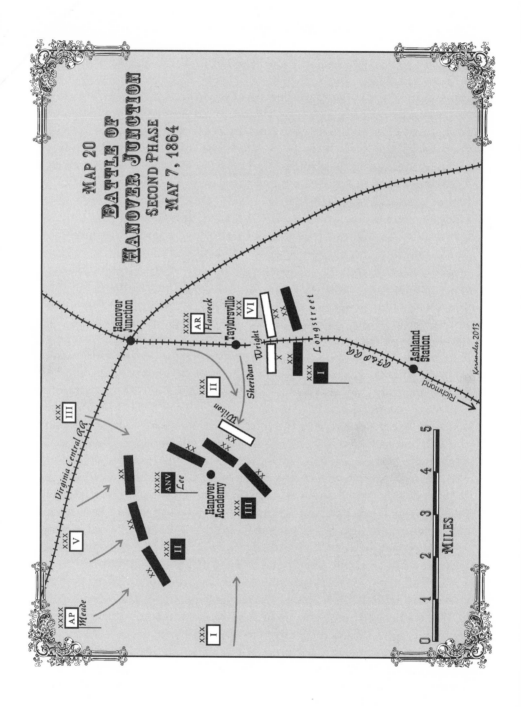

MAP 20
BATTLE OF
HANOVER JUNCTION
SECOND PHASE
MAY 7, 1864

"General Lee, this is no place for you! Do go to the rear, sir. These are Virginians and Georgians, sir—men who have never failed—and they will not fail now." He turned to the men who had been watching this scene intently. "Will you fail, boys? Is it necessary for General Lee to lead this charge?"

There were loud cries of "No! no! General Lee to the rear! General Lee to the rear!"[24]

Men came from the ranks to grab Traveler's bridle and pull him to the rear. "It seems, General Lee, that the men will see you out of harm's way if they have to pass both you and Traveler over their heads." Those men did lead him back through the moving ranks of the division who waved their hats and cheered Lee. "God bless you, Marse Robert!" He saluted them with his sword as the tide of Southern manhood surged past him.

Their attack was irresistible, and for the last time the Rebel battle flags streamed on to victory, driving back Hancock's leading division commanded by Brig. Gen. John Gibbon. At a terrible cost they broke them, pushing back the very men who had broken the high tide of the Confederacy at Gettysburg on that bloody third day. Hancock spurred away from Grant without a word, rode up to the next division commanded by Brig. Gen. Francis Barlow. "Go in, Barlow! Drive them back! Your objective is that building," he said pointing to the Hanover Academy." He then raced off to his third division and the one from VI Corps and sent them in as well. The gray brigades were struck in front and on their flanks by a mass of men in blue that all but overwhelmed them. Gordon's men did all that men can do that afternoon. Those Virginians and Georgians did not quit the field easily, falling back step by step making the enemy pay for each yard.

Lee's heart had raced as Gordon's men smashed through that Yankee division. From that height of hope it then sank to despair as masses of the enemy first stopped them and then come on in an inexorable tide. Behind him to the north the sound of battle now erupted. His staff all turned their faces in that direction. At the Hanover Academy Lee said calmly, "That must be General Meade. He has finally caught up with us."

RICHMOND, VIRGINIA, 5:12 P.M., SATURDAY, MAY 7, 1864

An officer came dashing up to the mansion but did not even have time to dismount before Davis called down to him asking what news.

"Yankees! Yankees and niggers! They came right through the defenses on the Williamsburg Road; there was no one guarding them."

Davis's first thought was to find troops somewhere, but then as the gunfire grew closer, it was his family that he ran to find. Sticking a pistol into his waistband, he ordered the servants to hitch the team to his coach as his wife looked at him, fear barely under control but under control as was to be expected of a great lady. "The enemy has someone entered the city. I must get you and the children out immediately."

Then the doors shuddered and splintered until the leaves flew apart. Black men in Union blue rushed into the marble foyer with carbines leveled. Davis and his wife could hear the servants screaming as heavy boots bounded up the stairs. They could hear a voice shouting, "Find him, boys! Alive!"

Davis drew the pistol and chambered a round. "Be brave, my love."

FIVE MILES NORTH OF SACO, MAINE, 5:30 P.M., SATURDAY, MAY 7, 1864
The sound of fighting lessened as Wolseley hurried his shrunken command north on the Portland road. The Rifles and the Canadians had held the Americans long enough to give the rest of them a good marching head start. Then rifle and artillery fire burst out from up the road. He rode ahead to see wagons and ambulances rushing back down the road and the 29th Foot deploying. He found the brigade commander who was getting his other battalions into line as well. The man pointed ahead. "As far as I can tell, the enemy is on the road, but in what strength I don't know."

"Let's find out," Wolseley said and dashed up the road to where it crossed a rise. A deployed American division was barring his way, and on the flanks he could see masses of cavalry. The commander of the 15th Dublin Brigade rode up beside him. "Your orders, sir."

The 3,800 men of this big brigade was the only organized force he had left, and the enemy in front of them outnumbered them by at least three to one. The British Army had come to expect odds like that in its conquest of empire. Wolseley did not hesitate. "You will bring up your brigade and break them in the center and hold the road open long enough for the rest of the army to get through. I will put all our remaining artillery in your support." Then he grasped the man by the arm and said, "You must do this quickly or it is not done at all. Our rearguard can't last much longer."

Three batteries of Armstrongs lashed their way across the fields to that rise in the road, unlimbered their guns, and went right into action. The Dublin Brigade went forward with 1/10th, 29th, and 45th Foot on line heading straight for the center of the American division. The Canadian 5th Royal Light Infantry of Montreal and the 6th Hochlega Light Infantry followed on the flanks to protect the brigade from the enemy cavalry.

This was just what the Maine men had been waiting for, a straight knock-down-drag-out fight with the invaders of their home state. They stood their ranks as the Royal Artillery blew holes through them only to close up. Their own artillery opened up concentrating at first on the enemy artillery then switching to case shot for the British infantry and then to canister at four hundred yards. At the same time the infantry opened up with rifle fire in such a concentrated volume that the lead British ranks seemed to disintegrate.

Custer lead his old Michigan Brigade into a charge on the Canadian 5th only to see them stand fast and deliver a volley that sent the front rank of his cavalry crashing into the ground. He immediately dismounted his men to use their repeaters that quickly began to thin the Canadian ranks. On the other flank Davis's Brigade had come in behind the 6th Canadian and caught it unprepared. The battalion came apart as it was struck by 1,200 cavalry.

Seeing the enemy flanks coming apart, Chamberlain rode along the division front through the shell and rifle fire shouting, "Bayonets!" Behind him the long blued blades came out of their scabbards and snapped onto their rifle muzzles. "Charge!"

HANOVER ACADEMY, VIRGINIA, 9:15 A.M., SUNDAY, MAY 8, 1864

The academy building had not been improved by the fighting that had swirled around it the day before and had ended up in Union hands. Early that morning soldiers hurriedly cleaned it up as much as possible. Grant and Hancock were waiting in the master's large book-lined study.

The man who rode up with a single aide and a color bearer wished with all his heart that he had fallen yesterday. Robert E. Lee could not avoid the inevitable, though every atom of his warrior spirit rebelled against. But even a blind man could see the game was over. He had fewer than thirty thousand men left and was surrounded by almost five times that number. Hancock had barred his way to Richmond while Meade had fallen upon his rear and overrun his trains. There was no hope. He had told his staff that night when he had accepted Grant's invitation to discuss terms of surrender, "There is nothing left me, and I would rather die a thousand deaths."[25]

EPILOGUE

FORD'S THEATER, WASHINGTON, DC, THURSDAY, JUNE 1, 1864

Edwin Booth had played for Lincoln before, but this night was special. The country had gone wild when Richmond had fallen so soon on the heels of the victories of the Glorious 7th of May, and *Hamlet* had been a command performance for the president. All the talk was of the sudden collapse of the Confederacy — Lee's surrender, the fall of Richmond, and Davis's capture all in one calamitous day had stunned the South and taken the heart out of the rebellion. Longstreet had fallen back on Richmond only to see the Stars and Stripes raised by Weitzel over the Davis's presidential mansion. Caught between Union-controlled Richmond and the armies of Meade and Hancock, Longstreet, ever the realist, briefly weighed his options, realized the game was up, and surrendered. General Joseph Johnston surrendered his Army of Tennessee to Maj. Gen. Thomas outside of Atlanta as soon as he heard of Longstreet's surrender and Davis's capture.

After a sharp battle, Sickles had taken Montreal on May 12. Quebec, to which Hope Grant had retreated with the Guards Brigade, was expected to capitulate any day now, and Sherman had just put Halifax under siege. Washington was almost giddy with excitement as events unfolded with amazing speed.

Miss Van Lew did get to spread her giant American flag over her roof as Richmond fell. When her neighbors threatened to burn her house, she defied them from the porch pointing them out by name and threatening retribution from the Union troops when they arrived. The crowd then thought better of it. Grant's first order to reach Weitzel was to put a guard on her house. Grant himself called on her on his return from the Hanover Academy. He would appoint her as postmistress of Richmond for both his terms as president (1869–1877).[1] He then went to see Davis, who had been confined to the mansion to inform him of the President's order to send him to Washington.[2] Grant then took the first steamer back to the capital

333

and was now in the box with the Lincolns. The President had insisted. His only other guest was Sharpe.

Despite all the celebrations, Edwin Booth was not happy. He had agreed to give the part of Hamlet to his younger brother against his better judgment. John had threatened a family row if Edwin had not given in. Edwin was the greatest tragedian of the age, and Hamlet was his part. No one could play it better, and he was jealous of his hold on it. The play was a charity event for the Sanitary Commission, and at least, Edwin thought, his difficult younger brother would get no box office from it. The rehearsals had not gone well. John was flamboyant and physical, but had not the slightest clue how to plumb the depths of the Danish prince. It was the greatest part in the English language, and John simply had no respect for it. Edwin had cringed but carefully coached John, who seemed to miss the whole point; he had carried himself on the family name and his famous good looks. Such people did not easily take advice.

The play had stumbled through to Scene IV, and George Sharpe had excused himself from the President's box to get a glass of champagne at the lobby bar. He had rarely scene Hamlet played so clumsily. "Poor Edwin," he thought, "must be cringing." As he proffered the glass for a refill, Tom Ford came up to him. "Enjoying the play, General?"

Sharpe arched one eyebrow, and Ford looked a bit crestfallen. "You don't have to say anything." He got a glass himself. "You remember when you came through looking for the bomb and asked to see everyone who worked here?"

Sharpe gave him his complete attention.

"Old John Peanut was not here. Well, he just arrived and is working here tonight." He pointed to the man at the small concession stand. "Oh, John, come over here."

Peanut came over, a look of confusion on his face. "The general here has a question for you."

"What do you know about the bomb that was planted under the stage?"

"Oh, sir, nothing at all. "I left here on May the fourth to go see my ailing sister in Fairfield, sir, I did."

As Sharpe talked with Peanut, Edwin was watching from stage left as his brother, now alone on the stage, began one of the most famous soliloquies in the play in Act IV.

> How all occasions do inform against me,
> And spur my dull revenge! What is a man,
> If his chief good and market of his time
> Be but to sleep and feed? a beast, no more.

Lincoln bent over the railing of his box to hear it all. He had been disappointed in the hash John was making of the lead. He would much rather have seen Edwin play *MacBeth*, but Mrs. Lincoln had insisted. Young John Wilkes made the ladies swoon. Lincoln thought to himself as Booth butchered those immortal lines, "What do I not do to indulge this woman?"

In the lobby, Sharpe asked Peanut if shortly before he left Washington had Edwin Forrest escorted into the theater someone he did not know carrying anything bulky. "No, sir, I did not see much of Mr. Forrest. He had not been well."

> Sure, he that made us with such large discourse,
> Looking before and after, gave us not
> That capability and god-like reason
> To fust in us unused. Now, whether it be
> Bestial oblivion, or some craven scruple
> Of thinking too precisely on the event,
> A thought which, quarter'd, hath but one part wisdom

Grant was not enjoying himself much either. The play did not appeal to him. He could not abide a ditherer. Mrs. Grant had pleaded a sick headache. She did not like Mrs. Lincoln, but he could not refuse the presidential invitation. So he just squirmed and looked about the audience to see if there were any officers he knew.

Sharpe was about to thank Peanut for his help, when the old man said, "No, sir, Mr. Forrest was seldom about. But Mr. Booth came in one afternoon with a man carrying a leather trunk. It looked heavy. Mr. Booth said it was for his dressing room." The champagne glass fell from Sharpe's hand as he dashed for the stairs. [3]

> And ever three parts coward, I do not know
> Why yet I live to say 'This thing's to do;'
> Sith I have cause and will and strength and means
> To do't. Examples gross as earth exhort me:
> Witness this army of such mass and charge
> Led by a delicate and tender prince,
> Whose spirit with divine ambition puff'd
> Makes mouths at the invisible event,
> Exposing what is mortal and unsure
> To all that fortune, death and danger dare,
> Even for an egg-shell. Rightly to be great
> Is not to stir without great argument,

But greatly to find quarrel in a straw
When honour's at the stake.

Lincoln was surprised at the venomous looks that Booth was throwing up at him. He brazenly made eye contact over and over again. The audience had begun to sense it too, and faces followed those looks up to Lincoln to see his reaction. Edwin was appalled. He could only think that John's Southern sympathies had got the better of him.

How stand I then,
That have a father kill'd, a mother stain'd,
Excitements of my reason and my blood,
And let all sleep? while, to my shame, I see
The imminent death of twenty thousand men,
That, for a fantasy and trick of fame,
Go to their graves like beds, fight for a plot
Whereon the numbers cannot try the cause,
Which is not tomb enough and continent
To hide the slain?

Sharpe ran down the hallway leading to the president's box. The two guards from his 120th NY leveled their bayonets until they recognized him. "Open the damn door!" he shouted at the very moment Booth stopped, swept his eyes across the audience, and almost shouted the last lines.

O, from this time forth,
My thoughts be bloody, or be nothing worth!

With that he strode across the stage to stand almost under Lincoln's box, reached into his doublet, pulled out a small revolver. Pointing it straight at Lincoln, he screamed, "*Sic semper tyrannis!*" and fired.

As he shouted, the door to the box flew open. Sharpe saw Booth pointing a pistol up from the stage. He grabbed the back of Lincoln's rocker and pulled it back just as Booth fired. Lincoln disappeared from view. He fired again at Grant, who had twisted around to grab Lincoln. The railing splintered. Mrs. Lincoln screamed and broke the tension of disbelief; the audience bolted to its feet, women screaming, men shouting. Booth turned to run backstage, but Edwin had run out onto the stage and grabbed him. John was much the stronger man and struck his brother over the head with the revolver, but still Edwin would not let go. Before John Wilkes could escape he was overwhelmed by men from the audience who had flooded onto the stage. It was all

Grant could do to keep him from being beaten to death as he shouted commands down to the stage.[4]

In the box Lincoln looked up from the floor to see Sharpe peering at him. His wife's shrill, unending scream had brought him back. He felt a great pain in his shoulder. "Mother, for the love of God, be still! I am all right." He winked at Sharpe. "I tell you, General, I have been shot more often in this war more than most soldiers. I should apply for a pension."[5]

Booth's capture and interrogation led to the unraveling of the entire Confederate Secret Service plot to assassinate the President, although Jefferson Davis could not be directly tied to it. Lincoln was much-criticized for the personal interview he gave Davis in the White House before his declaration of a general amnesty, but for the President, the gesture at the reconciliation of the nation was paramount. His statement, "Let us have peace," was long remembered. He was disappointed at Davis's unbroken intransigence. The rest of the world simply marveled that he had not been hanged.[6] The Confederacy that Davis continued to insist was a reality, however, had disappeared completely by Independence Day. By Christmas Day, the Stars and Stripes once more flew over the entire length and breadth of the Old Union.

By Christmas the Stars and Stripes also flew throughout British North America from the Great Lakes to the Atlantic, except for Quebec City, which held out until the armistice. Halifax had fallen to Sherman after a siege of six months. The country was in no mood to give any of it back.

The shock wave of disaster had stunned the British. Disraeli's government barely withstood a no-confidence vote in which a hundred of its own backbenchers voted against it. He was forced to form the first modern British war cabinet by sharing power with the Liberals in a coalition government. That it brought William Gladstone into the cabinet was gall and wormwood to Disraeli, but it did mean that the country would be politically united. It also removed the corrosive embrace with the now expiring Confederacy and the cousins war that had so disquieted millions of households. English-speaking people would no longer be killing each other. A united Britain could now face the other and far more important threat.

The Russians were finding willing allies in Europe. Prussia signed a secret treaty almost immediately. In St. Petersburg, a final ball was thrown for the officers of the army soon to march on Constantinople and place anew the Cross on the dome of the Hagia Sophia. Czar Alexander II used the occasion to present Colonel Dahlgren with the Cross of St. George and approve his participation on the campaign. He also ordered a Cossack escort for the young officer.[7]

So it was an opportune time for Lincoln to suggest that representatives of the United States and Great Britain meet to discuss ending the war. Disraeli eagerly accepted though it galled the British beyond all measure. He had to remind the country from the House that the war with Russia continued and was far more dangerous to the well-being and safety of the Empire. He made the argument that the war had not gone entirely the American's way. They had lost their gold mine of California and that the Royal Navy still stopped American trade. The Americans could not mint coin from battlefield victories. Lincoln realized this as well as the fact that the country's niter supply was reaching its end. The United States would quickly arrive at a point where it had nothing to shoot and nothing to pay for it if it did.

The sticking point, though, was Canada. The British would spend themselves into ruin rather than give up any part of the Empire, especially one where three million of their own race lived. The war would continue until the Union flag flew there again. Secretary Seward and the new British foreign secretary, George Villers, Lord Clarendon, met in Havana under the good offices of the Spanish government to hammer out a solution. In the end it was a simple return to the status quo ante, with the centerpiece of a trade of California for Canada. The Seward-Villers Treaty, or the Treaty of Havana, as it was more commonly called, was signed on July 24, 1865.

It was amazing how many parties were so upset by the peace. The Russians were livid for Lincoln had shamelessly violated their treaty by making a separate peace. His response was that the country needed peace, but he sweetened their disappointment by agreeing to sell them repeating weapons in any quantity they wanted.[8] The Irish seethed that Canada was not traded for Irish independence. That would have killed the treaty in its cradle for the British would no more cede Ireland than Wales or Scotland. They also had the ultimate argument—they held it, and the Irish Republic was a political corpse. That hardly satisfied the more die-hard and fantasy-prone element for whom political reality was not a strong suit. They were to find a welcome home in the Democratic Party.[9] Finally, Lincoln also had to withstand the public's outrage that considered Canada just spoils of war, especially since the United States had been trying so long to take it. The campaign to oppose the treaty ran under the motto of "Three Times is Lucky!"[10]

Still Lincoln would not budge on the treaty he had so publicly signed and submitted to the Senate. "California for Canada is a good deal. California's got gold and Canada's got ice. It doesn't take a lawyer to figure that out."[11] He knew, though, that he had to provoke the

American people's respect for the core principle of the consent of the governed and so had insisted in the treaty that the return of Canada be contingent upon a plebiscite among Canadian voters on whether they wanted incorporation into the Union or return to British sovereignty. The resulting vote was a resounding acclamation of loyalty to the Empire and their sovereign. The American public was both disappointed and chagrined that anyone would pass up a chance to become an American, but the treaty in the end passed by one vote. Needless to say, Lincoln had the two votes of California's senators.[12]

Seward also extracted a treaty from the French. It had something to do with the threat of "Get out Mexico or we will drive you out," and the down payment on that threat was made by a hundred thousand man army assembling in Texas under Sheridan's command.

As it was, public attention soon turned to the pressing issues of reintegrating its own wayward states into the Union and the fate of millions of former slaves. It was to be an unending series of vexations for Lincoln, who consoled himself that if the war had continued for another year untold more lives would be lost and ruin inflicted on the country. As peace settled over North America, Russia marched into the Balkans, sparking off a chain reaction that set the rest of the world on fire — but that would be another story.

APPENDIX A

Order-of-Battle at the Battles of Chazy
18–23 March 1864

British Army
Montreal Field Force (Maj. Gen. James Hope Grant) (30,100)
Headquarters Staff (100)
The Royal Guides or the Governor General's Bodyguard (150)
9th (The Queen's Royal) Lancers (650)
1/16th Foot (750)
12th Battalion Volunteer Infantry (Canadian)
21st Battalion Volunteer Infantry (Canadian)

1st Division (13,950)
    1st Montreal Brigade (2,750)
        1st Battalion, The Rifles
        1st Battalion The Prince of Wales Regiment (Canadian)
        2nd Battalion The Queens Own Rifles (Canadian)
        3rd Battalion Victoria Volunteers Rifles of Montreal (Canadian)
        G Battery, 4th Artillery Brigade (Field)
    3rd Hamilton Brigade (2,000)
        1/47th Foot
        11th Battalion Volunteer Infantry (Canadian)
        13th Battalion Volunteer Infantry (Canadian)
        8th Battery, 10th Artillery Brigade (Garrison)
    12th Brigade (4,600)
        78th (Highland) Foot
        26th Foot
        73rd (Perthshire) Foot
        17th Levis Battalion Volunteer Infantry (Canadian)
        A Battery, 5th Artillery Brigade

15th Dublin Brigade (3,800)
    1st Battalion, 10th Foot
    29th Foot
    45th Foot
    5th Battalion Royal Light Infantry of Montreal (Canadian)
    6th Battalion Hochlega Light Infantry (Canadian)
    D Battery, 5th Artillery Brigade
Artillery Brigade (1,250)
Division trains (800)

2nd Division (13,500)
    11th Hussars (600)
    Guards Brigade (2,200)
        2/Grenadier Guards
        2/Scots Fusilier Guards
        2nd Battery, 10th Brigade
    Portsmouth Brigade (3,500)
        53rd Foot
        55th Foot
        58th Foot
        20th Battalion Volunteer Infantry (Canadian)
        H Battery, 8th Artillery Brigade
    1st Kingston Brigade (2,800)
        1/6th Foot
        1/15th Foot
        14th Battalion Volunteer Infantry (Canadian)
        15th Battalion Volunteer Infantry (Canadian)
        F Battery, 4th Artillery Brigade (Field)
    2nd St. Johns Brigade (2,900)
        1/30th Foot
        86th Foot
        15th Battalion Volunteer Infantry (Canadian)
        16th Battalion Volunteer Infantry (Canadian)
        D Battery, 4th Artillery Brigade (Field)
    Artillery Brigade (1,300)
    Division Trains (800)

United States Army
    Army of the Hudson (Maj. Gen. Joseph Hooker, Maj. Gen. George
    H. Sharpe, Maj. Gen. William T. Sherman) (54,310)
        Staff: 200
        Scouts: 50

Army Provost Marshal Brigade (2,600)
    27th Indiana
    2nd Massachusetts
    3rd Wisconsin
Army Trains: 3500

XI Army Corps (Maj. Gen. Adolph von Steinwehr) (17,410)
    2nd Division (Brig. Gen. Orlando Ward) (8,250)
        1st Brigade (2,500)
            33rd New Jersey
            134th New York
            154th New York
        2nd Brigade (2,900)
            33rd Massachusetts
            55th Ohio
            73rd Ohio
        3rd Brigade* (2,850)
            27th Pennsylvania
            73rd Pennylvania
            136th New York
    3rd Division (Maj. Gen. Carl Schurz) (8,450)
        1st Brigade (3,100)
            45th New York
            143rd New York
            101st Illinois
        2nd Brigade (Col. Wladimir Krzysanowski) (2,600)
            58th New York
            119th New York
            141st New York
        3rd Brigade (Col. Frederick Hecker) (2,750)
            68th New York
            80th Illinois
            82nd Illinois
    Corps Artillery (710)
    1st New York Light, Battery I
    New York Light, 13th Battery
    1st Ohio Light, Battery I
    1st Ohio Light, Battery K
    4th United States, Battery G

XII Army Corps (Maj. Gen. Alpheus Williams — not present) (24,900)
    1st Division (Brig. Gen. Thomas H. Ruger) (8,550)

      1st Brigade (2,950)
          123rd New York
          145th New York
          46th Pennsylvania
      2nd Brigade (2,700)
          13th New Jersey
          107th New York
          150th New York
      3rd Brigade (2,900)*
          5th Connecticut
          10th Connecticut
          3rd Maryland
          1 Artillery Battery (attached)
2nd Division (Brig. Gen. John W. Geary) (8,050)
      1st Brigade (Col. Charles Candy) (2,500)
          5th Ohio
          7th Ohio
          29th Ohio
      2nd Brigade (Col. George A. Cobham, Jr.) (2,650)
          29th Pennsylvania
          109th Pennsylvania
          111th Pennsylvania
      3rd Brigade (Col. David Ireland, Col. Paul Vivian) (2,900)
          60th New York
          78th New York
          102nd New York
          3 Artillery Batteries
3rd Division (7,700)*
      1st Brigade (2,800)
          66th Ohio
          28th Pennsylvania
          147th Pennsylvania
      2nd Brigade (2,200)
          61st Ohio
          82nd Ohio
          75th Pennsylvania
      3rd Brigade (2,700)
          26th Wisconsin
          137th New York
          149th New York

Corps Artillery (Maj. John A. Reynolds) (600)
     1st New York Light, Battery M
     Pennsylvania Light, Battery E
     4th United States, Battery F
     5th United States, Battery K

3rd Cavalry Division (Maj. Gen. George A. Custer) (5,650)
     1st Cavalry Brigade (1,800)
       2nd New York
       5th New York
       18th Pennsylvania
       2nd United States, Battery M (120)
     2nd Cavalry Brigade (2,500)
       1st Michigan
       5th Michigan
       6th Michigan
       7th Michigan
       New York Light, 6th Battery (130)
     3rd Cavalry Brigade (1,100)
       1st Vermont
       1st West Virginia

Total number of troops committed: 38,950

*Formations formed from the reorganization of the Army of the Hudson following the influx of veterans, volunteers, and drafted men following the beginning of the war with the British.

APPENDIX B

Stations of the British Army

(Corrected to 27th August, 1863, inclusive)[1]

Great Britain

London

    1st Life Gds (Regent's Park)

    2nd Life Gds (Hyde Park)

    Royal Horse Gds (Windsor)

    12th Lancers (Hounslow)

    3/Grenadier Gds (St. Georges Brks)

    1st Coldstream Gds (Portman St)

    2nd Coldstream Gds (Windsor)

    1/Scots Fus Gds (Wellington Brks)

    1/60th Foot (Tower)

Aberdeen

    33rd Depot Bn

Aldershot

    6th Dragoon Gds

    13th Hussars

    3/Grenadier Gds

    1/3rd Foot

    1/6th Foot

    1/24th Foot

    37th Foot

    59th Foot

    2/60th Aldershot

    64th Foot

    *73rd Foot

    76th Foot

    87th Foot

    4th Arty Bde

    A Troop Royal Engr Train

10th Co, RE
24th Co, Re
26th Co, RE
Military Train (2nd Bn)
Military Train (5th Bn)
Birmingham
1st Dragoons
2nd Dragoons
Brighton
*9th Lancers
Chatham
1st Depot Bn
2nd Depot Bn
3rd Depot Bn
7th Co, RE
20th Co, RE
22nd Co, RE
35th Co, RE
36th Co, RE
37th Co, RE
38th Co, RE
39th Co, RE
40th Co, RE
Colchester
4th Depot Bn
8th Depot Bn
9th Depot Bn
Devenport
1st Co, RE
Dover
*78th Foot
85th Foot
2nd Arty Bde
Edinburgh
3rd Hussars (Piersbill)
4th Hussars (Newbridge)
10th Hussars (Newbridge)
92nd Foot
Glasgow
41st Foot
19th Co, RE (Survey)
Gosport
*26th Foot

Jersey
    61st Foot
Kensington
    2nd Co, RE
Maldstone
    Cavalry Depot
Manchester
    14th Hussars
    49th Foot
Norwich
    18th Hussars
Parkhurst
    5th Depot Bn
Pembroke
    8th Depot Bn
Plymouth
    1/2nd Foot
    75th Foot
    5th Arty Bde
Portsmouth
    2/1st Foot
    *53rd Foot
    *55th Foot
    6th Arty Bde
Preston
    11th Depot Bn
Scheffield
    1/8th Foot
Schorncliffe
    1/5th Foot
    83rd Foot
    9th Arty Bde
    23rd Co, RE
Southton
    16th Co, RE (Survey)
Walmer
    6th Depot Bn
Wincester
    7th Depot Bn
Woolwich
    1st Hvy Arty Bde
    13th Arty Bde
    8th Co, RE

Military Train (1st Bn)
York
    16th Lancers
Sterling
    22nd Depot Bn

Ireland
Dublin
    1/10th Foot
    1/11th Foot
    2/19th Foot
    *58th Foot
    8th Arty Bde
    13th Co, RE (Survey)
    14th Co, RE (Survey)
Athlone
    12th Depot Bn
Birr
    13th Depot Bn
Buttevant
    15th Depot Bn
Belfast
    14h Depot Bn
Curragh[2]
    *11th Hussars
    15th Hussars
    2/12th Foot
    29th Foot
    32nd Foot
    45th Foot
    84th Foot
    86th Foot
    17th Engr Co
    Military Train (6th Bn)
Cahir
    5th Dragoon Gds
Dundalk
    4th Dragoon Gds
Limerick
    17th Depot Bn
Cork
    20th Depot Bn

Templemore
    16th Depot Bn
Fermoy
    18th Depot Bn
    19th Depot Bn

Mediterranean
Cephelonia
    1/9th Foot
Corfu
    2/2nd Foot
    2/4th Foot
    2/6th Foot
    2/9th Foot
    3rd Arty Bde
    29th Co, RE
    30th Co, RE
Gibraltar
    2/9th Foot
    2/8th Foot
    100th Foot
    1st Hvy Arty Bde
    3rd Co, RE
    27th Co, RE
    33rd Co, RE
Malta
    2/15th Foot
    1/22nd Foot
    2/22nd Foot
    1/25th Foot
    4/1st Rifle Bde
    Royal Malta Fencible Arty
    3rd Arty Bde
    28th Co, RE
    31st Co, RE

British North America
Canada
    1/Grenadier Gds
    2/Scots Fusilier Gds
    1/16th Foot
    1/17th Foot

30th Foot
47th Foot
4/60th Foot
62nd Foot
63rd Foot
1/Rifle Bde
Royal Canadian Rifle Regt
7th Arty Bde (Montreal)
10th Arty Bde
15th Co, RE
18th Co, RE
Military Train (3rd Bn)
New Brunswick
1/15th Foot
Nova Scotia
2/16th Foot
2/17th Foot
15th Arty Bde (Halifax)
Bermuda
39th Foot
5th Co, RE
34th Co, RE

West Indies
Bahamas
2/West India Regt
Barbados
1/21st Foot
Jamaica
1/14th Foot
4/West India Regt
5/West India Regt
Nassau
1/West Indian Regt

India and Ceylon
Agra
25th Arty Bde
Bangalore
3rd Hvy Arty Bde
Bengal
2nd Dragoon Gds
7th Dragoon Gds

5th Lancers
7th Hussars
8th Hussars
19th Hussars
20th Hussars
21st Hussars
1/7th Foot
1/13th Foot
1/19th Foot
1/20th Foot
1/23rd Foot
27th Foot
34th Foot
35th Foot
36th Foot
38th Foot
42nd Foot
43rd Foot
46th Foot
48th Foot
51st Foot
52nd Foot
54th Foot
71st Foot
77th Foot
79th Foot
80th Foot
81st Foot
82nd Foot
88th Foot
89th Foot
90th Foot
93rd Foot
94th Foot
97th Foot
98th Foot
101st Foot
104th Foot
107th Foot
2/Rifle Bde
3/Rifle Bde
11th Arty Bde
14th Arty Bde

Bombay
  3rd Dragoon Gds
  6th Dragoons
  1/4th Foot
  28th Foot
  33rd Foot
  44th Foot
  56th Foot
  72nd Foot
  95th Foot
  103rd Foot
  106th Foot
  109th Foot
Calcutta
  2/20th Foot
Dehli
  16th Arty Bde
Jullundar
  22nd Arty Bde
Kamptee
  20th Arty Bde
Kirkee
  4th Hvy Arty Bde
  18th Arty Bde
Madras
  1st Dragoon Gds
  17th Lancers
  1/1st Foot
  1/18th Foot
  2/21st Foot
  3/60th Foot
  66th Foot
  68th Foot
  69th Foot
  74th Madras
  91st Foot
  102nd Foot
  105th Foot
  108th Foot
  17th Arty Bde
Mean Meer
  24th Arty Bde

Meerut
    2nd Hvy Arty Bde
Mhow
    21st Arty Bde
Peshawar
    19th Arty Bde
Secundarbad
    23rd Arty Bde
Umballah
    5th Hvy Arty Bde
Ceylon
    2/25th Foot
    50th Foot
    Ceylon Rifle Regt

Australia and New Zealand
Australia
    1/12th Foot (NS Wales)
New Zealand
    2/14th Foot
    2/18th Foot
    40th Foot
    57th Foot
    65th Foot
    70th Foot
    6th Co, RE

Africa
Cape of Good Hope
    2/10th Foot
    2/11th Foot
    96th Foot
    Cape Mounted Rifles
    12th Co, RE
    25th Co, RE
Natal
    2/5th Foot
West Coast of Africa
    3/West India Regiment

Miscellaneous
Mauritius

2/13th Foot
2/24th Foot
12th Arty Bde
11th Co, RE
21st Co, RE
China
31st Foot
67th Foot
99th Foot
8th Co, RE
St. Helena
32nd Co, RE

APPENDIX C

National Intelligence Assessment 12: British Ironclads
as of 15 March 1864

The following list identifies British ironclads in service and those building in British shipyards with estimated dates of completion.

Table 1. British Ironclads in Service

SHIP	CLASS	IN SVC	TYPE	LOCATION/ STATUS
Warrior	Warrior	Oct 1861	Broadside	North American waters
Defence	Defence	Dec 1861	Broadside	North American waters
Royal Oak	Royal Oak	Apr 1863	Broadside	Mediterranean
Hector	Hector	Feb 1864	Broadside	Unknown
Prince Consort	Prince Consort	Mar 1864	Broadside	Channel Fleet
Royal Sovereign	Royal Sovereign	Feb 1864	Turret	Channel Fleet
Prince Albert	Prince Albert	May 1864	Turret	Channel Fleet
Wivern	North Carolina	Feb 1864	Turret	Unknown

Table 2. Characteristics of British Ironclads in Service

SHIP	TYPE	TONS	SPEED	CREW	GUNS
Warrior	Broadside	9,210	13.0	705	40
Defence	Broadside	6,150	10.5	460	24
Royal Oak	Broadside	6,366	12.5	585	35

>>

>> SHIP	TYPE	TONS	SPEED	CREW	GUNS
Hector	Broadside	6,710	12.6	530	27
Prince Consort	Broadside	6,832	12.5	605	31
Royal Sovereign	Turret	5,080	11.0	295	5
Prince Albert	Turret	3,746	11.3	250	4
Wivern	Turret	2,751	10.5	153	4

Table 3. British Ironclads under Construction*

SHIP	CLASS	LA	DOCKYARD	ORIG. EST. COMM.	NEW EST. COMM.
Caledonia	"	1862	Woolwich Dockyard	Jul 1865	Dec 1864
Ocean	"	1862	Devonport Dockyard	Jul 1866	Dec 1864
Valiant	Hector	1863	Thames Ironworks	Sep 1868	Jun 1865
Achilles	Achilles	1863	Chatham Dockyard	Nov 1864	Mar 1864
Minotaur	Minotaur	1863	Thames Ironworks	Dec 1868	July 1864
Agincourt	Minotaur	1863	Laird	Jun 1867	Sep 1864
Northumberland	Minotaur	No	Millwall Ironworks	Oct 1868	Jan 1865
Lord Clyde	Lord Clyde	No	Pembroke Dockyard	Jun 1866	Jan 1865
Lord Warden	Lord Warden	No	Chatham Dockyard	Mar 1865	Jun 1864
Zealous	Bulwark	1864	Plymouth	Oct 1866	Jan 1865
Repulse	Bulwark	No	unk	Apr 1868	Jun 1865
Royal Alfred	Bulwark	No	Portsmouth	Mar 1867	Mar 1865
Bellerophon	Bellerophon	No	Chatham	Apr 1866	Mar 1865
Prince Albert	Prince Albert	No	Samuda Brothers	Feb 1866	Mar 1865
Wivern	N/A	1863	Laird	Oct 1865	Nov 186

Table 3. Characteristics of British Ironclads under Construction

SHIP	TYPE	TONS	SPEED	CREW	GUNS
Caledonia	Broadside	6,832	11.5	605	30
Ocean	"	6,832	11.5	605	48
Valiant	"	6,710	12.0	530	18
Achilles	"	9,829	14.3	709	20
Minotaur	"	10,690	14.3	800	36
Agincourt	"	10,800	14.8	800	28
Northumberland	"	10,784	14.1	800	58
Lord Clyde	"	7,750	13.5	605	24
Lord Warden	"	7,842	13.4	605	20
Zealous	Cent btry	6,096	11.7	510	20
Repulse	"	6,190	10.7	510	12
Royal Alfred	"	6,707	12.7	605	18
Bellerophon	"	7,551	14.2	650	15

*Does not include the twenty turreted monitor-type ships of the Revenge Class recently laid down.

APPENDIX D

Report of the War Production Board
Ironclad Production
March 15, 1864

The following ironclads of the U.S. Navy are in various states of completion with estimated dates of commissioning at which time the ship is considered ready for assignment to the fleet.

Table 2. Ironclad State of Construction

SHIP	CLASS	LAUNCH	ORIG. COMM.	NEW COMM	SHIPYARD
Camanche	Passaic		May 1865	Jun 1864	Wilmington
Canonicus	Canonicus		Apr 1864	Mar 1864	Boston
Saugus	Canonicus		Apr 1864	Mar 1864	Philadelphia
Tecumseh	Canonicus		Apr 1864	Mar 1864	Jersey City
Manhattan	Canonicus		Apr 1864	Mar 1864	Jersey City
Mahopac	Canonicus		Sep 1864	Jul 1864	New York
Catawba	Canonicus	Apr 1864	Sep 1864	Jul 1864	Cincinnati
Manay-nuck	Canonicus	Apr 1864	Sep 1864	Jul 1864	Pittsburgh
Oneota	Canonicus	May 1864	Oct 1864	Aug 1864	Cincinnati
Tippicanoe	Canonicus	Dec 1864	Mar 1865	Dec 1864	Cincinnati
Dictator	Dictator	Jul 1864	Dec 1864	Sep 1864	New York
Puritan	Puritan	Jul 1864	Dec 1864	Sep 1864	Greenpoint, NY
Onondaga	Onondaga		Mar 1864	Same	New York
Monad-nock	Miantono-moh		Oct 1864	Aug 1864	Boston

>>

SHIP	CLASS	LAUNCH	ORIG. COMM.	NEW COMM	SHIPYARD
Agamenticus	Miantonomoh		May 1865	Dec 1864	Portsmouth
Tonowanda	Miantonomoh	May 1864	Aug 1864	Jun 1864	New York
Milwaukee	Milwaukee		Aug 1864	Jul 1864	Carondelet, MO
Winnebago	Milwaukee		Apr 1864	Same	Carondelet
Kickappo	Milwaukee		Jul 1864	Same	Carondelet
Chickasaw	Milwaukee		May 1864	Apr 1864	Carondelet

Table 2. Characteristics of Ironclads Building

CLASS	TONS	CREW	SPEED	ARMAMENT	TURRETS
Passaic	1,335	67–88	7 knots	1 x 15 in. + 1 x 11 in. sb	1
Canonicus	2,100	85	8 knots	2 x 15 in. sb	1
Dictator	4,438	174	9 knots	2 x 15 in. sb	1
Puritan	4,912	211	11 knots	2 x 20 in. sb.	1
Onondaga	2,592	130	7 knots	2 x 8 in. rifles / 2 x 15 in. sb	forward / after
Miantonomoh	3,295	188	9 knots	2 x 15 in sb / 2 x 15 in. sb	forward / after
Milwaukee	1,300	138	9 knots	2 x 11 in. sb / 2 x 11 in. sb	forward / after

Table 3. Ships to Be Available to the Fleet by Date

Onondaga	Mar 1864	New York
Canonicus	Mar 1864	Boston
Saugus	Mar 1864	Philadelphia
Tecumseh	Mar 1864	Jersey City
Manhattan	Mar 1864	Jersey City
Winnebago	Apr 1864	Carondelet
Chickasaw	Apr 1864	Carondelet
Camanche	Jun 1864	Wilmington
Tonowanda	Jun 1864	New York

Kickappo	Jul 1864	Carondelet
Milwaukee	Jul 1864	Carondelet
Mahopac	Jul 1864	New York
Catawba	Jul 1864	Cincinnati
Manaynuck	Jul 1864	Pittsburgh
Oneota	Aug 1864	Cincinnati
Monadnock	Aug 1864	Boston
Dictator	Sep 1864	New York
Puritan	Sep 1864	New York
Tippicanoe	Dec 1864	Cincinnati
Agamenticus	Dec 1864	Portsmouth

Table 3. Monitors on Active Service with the Fleet

New Ironsides
Roanoke
Passaic
Montauk
Lehigh
Patapsco
Weehawken
Sangamon
Catskill
Nantucket

APPENDIX E

Order-of-Battle of the Cavalry Action at Hanover Junction

Cavalry Corps of the Army of the Potomac
Maj. Gen. Phillip H. Sheridan Commanding
Strength: App. 8,500

2nd Division, Brig. Gen. David M. Gregg Commanding
First Brigade
    1st Massachusetts Cavalry
    1st New Jersey Cavalry
10th New York Cavalry
    6th Ohio Cavalry
    1st Pennsylvania Cavalry
Second Brigade
    2nd Pennsylvania Cavalry
    4th Pennsylvania Cavalry
    8th Pennsylvania Cavalry
    13th Pennsylvania Calvary
    16th Pennsylvania Cavalry

3rd Division, Brig. Gen. James H. Wilson Commanding[1]
    First Brigade
        1st Connecticut Cavalry
        2nd New York Cavalry
        5th New York Cavalry
    Second Brigade
        8th Illinois Cavalry
        8th New York Cavalry
        18th Pennsylvania Cavalry

Reserve Brigade, Brig. Gen. Wesley Merritt Commanding
    19th New York Cavalry
    6th Pennsylvania Cavalry
    1st US Cavalry
    2nd US Cavalry
    4th US Cavalry

Robertson's Horse Artillery Brigade
    1st US Artillery, Batteries H and I
    2nd US Artillery, Batteries B, L, D, and M

Cavalry of the Army of Northern Virginia
Maj. Gen. J.E.B. Stuart Commanding
Strength: App. 6,300

Major General Wade Hampton's Division
    Young's Brigade
        7th Georgia Cavalry
        20th Georgia Cavalry
        Cobb's (Georgia) Legion (9th Georgia Cavalry)
        Phillips (Georgia) Legion
        Jeff Davis (Mississippi) Legion
    Rosser's Brigade
        7th Virginia Cavalry
        11th Virginia Cavalry
        12th Virginia Cavalry
        35th Battalion Virginia
    Butler's Brigade
        4th South Carolina Cavalry
        5th South Carolina Cavalry
        6th South Carolina Cavalry

Major General Fitzhugh Lee's Division
    Wickham's Brigade
        1st Virginia Cavalry
        2nd Virginia Cavalry
        3rd Virginia Cavalry
        4th Virginia Cavalry
    Lomax's Brigade
        6th Virginia Cavalry
        9th Virginia Cavalry
        1st Maryland Cavalry Battalion

Artillery
  Baltimore Light Artillery
  Breathed's Horse Artillery Battalion
  Washington Artillery of South Carolina
  Ashby Virginia Artillery
  Lynchburg Beauregards
  1st Stuart Horse Artillery of Virginia

NOTES

CHAPTER ONE: "I'VE BEEN TURNED INTO A COMPLETE AMERICAN NOW"

1. USS *Catskill*, Passaic class monitor, 200x46x11ft 6in, 1x15-in., 1x11-in. smoothbore Dahlgrens, 1,335 tons, commissioned 2-63. Angus Konstam, *Duel of the Ironclads* (London: Osprey Publishing, 2003), p. 93.

2. HMS *Buzzard*, Wood paddle sloop, 185x34ft, 6 guns, 980 bm, built Pembroke Dockyard 24.3.1849. J.J. Colledge, *Ships of the Royal Navy* (London: Greenhill Books, 2003), p. 63.

3. Originally named Gosport Naval Yard, this huge naval base was located at the city of Norfolk, Virginia. Early in the war it was renamed Norfolk Naval Yard.

4. During the Ice Age when the sea level was 150-200 feet lower, what is now the Chesapeake Bay was the river valley of the Susquehanna River.

5. Originally named the Gosport Navy Yard, it was renamed the Norfolk Navy Yard as the Civil War progressed.

6. During the Age of Sail, corvettes were smaller than frigates and larger than sloops-of-war, usually with a single gun deck and having more than twenty guns, usually in the case of the Royal Navy at this time twenty to twenty-two guns. A British sloop-of-war at this time with a single gun deck that carried up to eighteen guns. Gunboats usually carried one to five guns.

7. The issue of who actually started the war became something of a cottage industry in both countries after the war. The issue was definitely discussed in Peter G. Tsouras, *Britannia's Fist: From Civil War Became World War* (Washington, DC: Potomac Books, 2008).

8. *Gilbert A. Allen, *Slavery and the Confederacy* (New York: The Century Co., 1899), pp. 199–203. With secession the Confederacy considered it no longer bound by the constitutional provision that ended the importation of slaves and eagerly opened its ports to slave ships now easily slipping through the denuded Royal Navy force that had suppressed it. The resumption of the importation of slaves by the Confederacy was an enormous embarrassment to the Disraeli government, which made it clear to Jefferson Davis that continuance of the practice could and would

endanger military and economic cooperation. Davis was not impressed with the threat. The British needed the Confederacy as a co-belligerent.

9. *Edmund St. Clair, *John Bright and the Slavery Question in the Great War* (London: Mayfair Publishers, 1922), p. 233.

10. The USS *Wyoming* was a screw sloop launched in 1859, 1,480 tons, crew of 198, and mounting two 11-inch Dahlgren guns. She had been assigned to the U.S. Navy's Pacific Squadron just before the Civil War began. Until the war with Britain began, she had fought a battle against a local Japanese warlord at Shimonoseki in May 1863 and then cruised the Far East in search of the Confederate commerce raider, CSS *Alabama*, once passing barely twenty-five miles from her. *She got news of the war while in the Dutch East Indies. Ironically, her new mission was to raid British commerce, and the pickings were rich from India to Hong Kong.

11. Gavin Mortimer, Double Death: *The Truce Story of Pryce Lewis, the Civil War's Most Daring Spy* (New York: Walker & Company, 2010), p. 216.

12. Holzer, p. 235.

13. Eleanor Rugles, *The Prince of Players: Edwin Booth* (New York: W.W. Norton & Company, 1953), p. 171.

14. William A. Tidwell, *Confederate Covert Actions in the American Civil War* (Kent, OH: Kent State University Press, 1995), pp. 118–23.

CHAPTER TWO: "I CAN HANG YOU"

1. *Judson Knight, "Scouting for Hooker," *National Tribune*, June 17, 1888.

2. *Arthur Freemantle, "The Prisoner of War Cartel in North America During the Great War," Monograph, Royal Staff College Camberley, June 2, 1882. After the battles of Charleston and Claverack, the British and Americans established a cartel for the exchange of prisoners. Colonel Denison was the first senior officer they requested to be exchanged; such was the political pressure applied by the Canadian government.

3. *Major Anthony C. Torcelli, *Scouts of the Bureau of Military Intelligence*, monograph, U.S. Army Command & General Staff College, 17 February 1972.

4. *Field Marshall Viscount Wolseley, *The Great War in North America* (London: Longmans, Green, 1890), pp. 122–25.

5. Irving A. Buck, *Cleburne and His Command* (Wilmington, NC: Broadfoot Publishing Co., 1995), pp. 188–90. Cleburne was Anglo-Irish and had served four years in the British Army, reaching the rank of corporal; he emigrated to the United States after the famine, settled in Arkansas, and became a U.S. citizen. He was elected captain and quickly rose because of his natural talent for command and his very rare military experience to become possibly the finest division commander on either side.

6. *Frederick Williamson, "British and French Aide to the Confederacy in the War," *Annals of the Confederacy*, Vol. XVIII, July 24, 1884. The Confederacy imported during the period November 1863 to May 1864, 273 locomotives and 120,000 rails in addition to several hundred thousand miles of telegraph

wire. The British and French supplied enough uniforms to give every Confederate soldier a new set of clothing.

7. *James Longstreet, *From Chickamauga to Appomattox*, Vol. 2, *A Memoir of the War* (New Orleans: St. Louis Press, 1886), p. 167.

8. Paul Wagner, "The First Engagement of the New Airfleet," *Great War History Magazine*, July 24, 1987, p. 27. The *Washington* barely made it to its landing field in a park in Portland, it had lost so much gas. However, in earlier flights by the older balloons, the parts of a hydrogen gas generator were sent and assembled to ensure that there would be enough gas for return flights. Chamberlain ransacked the ruins of Portland for anything that might help patch the Washington's balloon. The *Washington* was able to limp away a few nights later and safely made it back to Boston.

9. Ulysses S. Grant, *Personal Memoirs of U.S. Grant, Selected Letters 1839–1865* (New York: The Library of America, 1990), pp. 470, 770.

10. *Michael D. Wilmoth, *The Life of George H. Sharpe* (Philadelphia: D. Appleton Publishers, 1890), p. 238. Wilmoth's biography was an honest account of Sharpe's contribution to the war effort, but it was also a work of devotion to someone he obviously admired.

11. *Colburns United Service Magazine and Naval & Military Journal, 1866, Part III* (London: Hurst Blackett Publishers), p. 421. Apparently, although the militia strength was 120,000 (80,000 for England, 10,000 for Scotland, and 30,000 for Ireland), at most 60,000 would be forthcoming in an emergency.

12. http://en.wikipedia.org/wiki/Volunteer_Force_(Great_Britain), accessed 11 Mar 11. In 1862, a royal commission chaired by Viscount Eversley was appointed "to inquire into the condition of the volunteer force in Great Britain and into the probability of its continuance at its existing strength." According to the report, as of 1 April 1862, the Volunteer Force had a strength of 162,681 consisting of:
    *   662 light horse
    *   24,363 artillery
    *   2,904 engineers
    *   656 mounted rifles
    *   134,096 rifle volunteers, of whom 48,796 were in 86 consolidated battalions and 75,535 in 134 administrative battalions.

13. Peter G. Tsouras, "Major General George H. Sharpe," *Armchair General*, July 2008. pp. 26–28; "Gettysburg Intelligence Coup," *Armchair General*, January 2009, pp. 26–27.

14. Tsouras, "Gettysburg Intelligence Coup," *Armchair General*, January 2009, pp. 26–27.

15. Edwin G. Fishel, *The Secret War for the Union: The Untold Story of Military Intelligence in the Civil War* (Boston: Houghton-Mifflin Co., 1996), pp. 293–94.

16. *The War in North America*, Vol. V (London: Her Majesty's Printing Office, 1910), pp. 272–75. Hope Grant organized the 12th and 15th Brigades to

concentrate the hitting power of his new Imperial battalions. Each brigade had three imperial and two experienced Canadian battalions and numbered about four thousand men each. The 1st Montreal Brigade, with its one Imperial and three Canadian battalions, he left intact because of its record at the battle of Clavarack and the fighting retreat back to Canada.

17. Chazy was settled around 1763 by Jean Laframboise, who is also credited with introducing apple growing to the area. Chazy is named after a French Lieutenant de Chézy, who was killed by the Iroquois.

18. Fully ten thousand of the replacements for the Army of the Hudson came from the fifteen thousand Irishmen recruited by Thomas Francis Meagher the day after the Royal Navy's surprise attack on New York City.

19. *Edmund Winslow, *British Military Intelligence in the American War* (London: Her Majesty's Printing Office, 1912), pp. 104–06.

20. *Robert M. McArthur, *Defeat and Victory: Chancellorsville to Chazy, the Life of Joseph Hooker* (Boston: Pilgrim Press, 1937), pp. 312–14.

21. *William Reese, "Send in the Tartan, Man!" The Leadership of Lt. Col. William McBean at the Battle of Chazy, *Journal of the Highland Regiments*, 12 May, 1966, p. 89.

22. *Alexander McKenzie, *A History of the 78th Foot* (Edinburgh: John Masters Publisher, 1889), p. 216.

23. *Wilson Franklin, "The Opening Round of the Battle of Chazy," *Journal of American Military Historians*, 7 January 1999, pp 37–39.

CHAPTER THREE: "PRESS ON, MCBEAN, PRESS ON!"

1. The Russian Baltic squadron consisted of the steam screw frigates *Aleksandr Nevsky* (50), *Peresvet* (51) *Osliablia* (45), steam screw corvettes *Variag* (18) and *Vitiaz* (18), and steam screw clipper *Almaz* (7). The U.S. Navy had replaced half of *Aleksandr Nevsky's* older guns with Dahlgren 9-inch smoothbores.

2. Peter Tsouras, *Britannia's Fist: Civil War to World War* (Washington, DC: Potomac Books, 2008), pp. 49–50. USS *Gettysburg* originally was a fast British mail packet captured by Lamson as it tried to run the blockade. It was refitted as a warship with Dahlgren guns and commissioned as the USS *Gettysburg*.

3. Tsouras, *Britannia's Fist*, Chapters 8 and 9.

4. Sister ship to HMS *Black Prince* was HMS *Warrior*, the first ironclad built by the Royal Navy, begun in 1859 and launched in 1861. She represented a number of innovations, such as armored bulkheads and the first all-steel breech-loading guns (Armstrong 110-pounders or 7-inch), but retained the traditional broadside configuration which resulted in her size of 9,200 tons, making it the largest warship in the world. However, the Armstrong guns for all their speed and accuracy were hugely outclassed in destructive power of the 11- and 15-inch Dahlgren guns of the new American monitors.

5. David Power Conyngham, *The Irish Brigade and its Campaigns* (New York: Fordham University Press, 2002), p. 75.

6. Thomas T. Ellis, *Leaves from the Diary of an Army Surgeon* (New York: John Bradburn, 1863), p. 54.

7. Today Meagher might be diagnosed with post-traumatic stress syndrome (PTSD).

8. Maj. Gen. Alpheus Williams, advanced to (XII) corps command after the battle of Clavarack, had been absent on leave at this time. Ruger had succeeded to the position of First Division commander. Geary as senior division commander was actually acting corps commander, which was why he had been at Fort Montgomery on his corps forward position.

9. *Vivian's great grandson, named after his ancestor, distinguished himself in the Normandy Campaign as a junior officer in the 120th Infantry Regiment. Peter G. Tsouras, *Disaster at D-Day: The Germans Defeat the Allies, June 1944* (London: Greenhill Books, 1994), ff. p. 223.

10. The Dublin Brigade consisting of regiments from the garrison of Ireland: 1/10th, 29th, and 45th Regiments of Foot.

11. *Paul H. Vivian, *The Chazy Boys: Ireland's Brigade at the Battle of Chazy* (Schenectady, NY: Union College Press, 1879), p. 82.

12. *Vivian, *The Chazy Boys*, p. 87.

13. *Joseph M. Kelly, *The Battle of Chazy* (New York: D. Appleton, 1878), pp. 110–14. Keely's work was one of the of books in the popular Appleton series Battles of the Great War.

14. *Sharpe's commission as a brigadier general was dated August 3, 1863; Ruger was promoted to brigadier after the battle of Clavarack in December 1863.

CHAPTER FOUR: AN ARITHMETIC PROBLEM

1. Peter G. Tsouras, *A Rainbow of Blood: The Union in Peril* (Washington, DC: Potomac Books, 2010), pp. 195–98.

2. *William R. Mathis, *Andrew Carnegie: The Organizer of Victory* (New York: Charles L. Webster & Company, 1889), p. 14. This work describes in detail the work of the War Industries Board and the increases in production by category.

3. Brian Moynahan, *Looking Back at Britain: Peace and Prosperity 1860s* (London: Reader's Digest, 2009), p. 28.

4. "The Demographics of France," Wikipedia, http://en.wikipedia.org/wiki/Demographics_of_France. Retrieved 4 Sep 2010.

5. "The Social and Economic Structure of Tsarist Russia," Wikipedia, http://www.blacksacademy.net/content/3750.html. Retrieved 4 Sep 2010.

6. *Richard Pittman, "The War Production Board in the Great War," *American Historical Journal*, Vol. XXV, 10 November 1916, p. 38.

7. Fox to Dupont, 3 June 1862, *Confidential Correspondence of Gustavus Vasa Fox*, I:126–28.

8. B.R. Mitchell, *British Historical Statistics* (Cambridge: Press Syndicate of Cambridge University, 1988).

9. *Harper's New Monthly Magazine*, vol. 50, December 1874–May 1975 (Harper's Magazine Making of America Project), p. 718.

10. A.J. Youngston Brown, *The American Economy 1860–1940* (New York: The Library Press, 1951), p. 42.

11. Robert V. Bruce, *Lincoln and the Tools of War* (Indianapolis: The Bobbs-Merrill Company, Inc., 1956), pp. 145–47, 211–14.

12. Hudson was the river port in upstate New York for the storage and transshipment of whale oil for most of the Northern states. It had been burned during the Clavarack campaign.

13. Psalms 91, *The Holy Bible* (King James version).

14. Pslams 18:32–40, *The Holy Bible* (King James version).

15. Pslams 19:2, *The Holy Bible* (King James version).

16. "Conservative Government 1866–1868;" http://en.wikipedia.org/wiki/Conservative_Government_1866%E2%80%931868; accessed September 18, 2010.

17. John Stauffer, *Giants: The Parallel Lives of Frederick Douglass and Abraham Lincoln* (New York: Twelve, 2008), p. 248.

18. David Herbert Donald, *Charles Sumner*, vol. II (New York: Da Capo Press, 1996), pp . 88, 129.

19. Peter G. Tsouras, *Britannia's Fist: From Civil War to World War* (Washington, DC: Potomac Books, 2008), pp. 124–28.

20. Frederick Douglass, *The Life and Times of Frederick Douglass* (Boston: De Wolfe & Fisk, 1892), p. 408.

21. Ephraim Douglas Adams, *Great Britain and the American Civil War,* vol. I (New York: Longman Green & Co., 1925), p. 79.

22. Isaac N. Arnold, *Abraham Lincoln: A Paper Read Before the Royal Historical Society* (Chicago: Fergis, 1881), p. 190.

23. A.J.P. Taylor, *The Struggle for Mastery of Europe* (Oxford: Clarendon Press, 1954), p. 233.

24. A.N. Wilson, *The Victorians* (W.W. Norton & Company, New York), p. 395.

25. Christopher Hibbert, *Disraeli: The Victorian Dandy Who Became Prime Minister* (New York: Palgrave, 2006), p. 362.

26. Gabor S. Boritt, "War Opponent and War President," in *Lincoln: The War President: The Gettysburg Lectures* (New York: Oxford University press, 1992), pp. 190–192.

27. * John Hay, *American Diplomacy in the Great War* (Boston: Beacon Hill Publishers, 1895), p. 188. The plans for Passaic class monitors had been sent to Russia the previous year in thanks for their successful efforts to forestall the creation of a coalition to force mediation on the Union and Confederacy, which would have, in effect, guaranteed the independence of the latter.

28. Alexander William Kinglake, *The Invasion of the Crimea*, vol. 1 (London: 1863), p. 43.

29. Even to this day many Greeks will not conduct serious business on Tuesdays, so unlucky is the day considered.

30. At this time Greece was not even half its present size, and a majority of the Greeks still lived under Muslim rule either in the parts of present

Greece still under Ottoman control or in Anatolia. The South Slav subjects of the Turks in the Balkans included the Serbians, Montenegrans, and the Bulgarians.

CHAPTER FIVE: BREAKING OUT

1. Rear Admiral Dahlgren, *Memoirs of Ulrich Dahlgren* (Philadelphia: J.B. Lipponcott & Co., 1872), p. 159–76.

2. Peter G. Tsouras, *Britannia's Fist: Civil War to World War* (Washington, D.C.: Potomac Books, 2008), p. 50. In July 1863, Lamson had brought a prize he had captured off Wilmington running the blockade to the Navy Yard. Gus Fox had suggested it be reconfigured as a warship and sent off to intercept the Laird Rams should they try to escape from Liverpool as had the infamous Confederate commerce raider, the CSS *Alabama*. Lincoln had come down to see how the work was progressing and wondered what new name the ship should bear. George Sharpe had been with him and suggested Gettysburg. Lincoln had instantly approved.

3. Of course, the great Dutch admiral Michael DeRuyter sailed up the Thames as far as Gravesend to administer a drubbing to the Royal Navy at the battle of the Medway in June 1667 by attacking their major naval base at Chatham. The Dutch burnt thee capital ships and ten others, and carried away two capital ships to include, HMS *Royal Charles*, the flagship of the Royal Navy. It was the greatest defeat in the history of the Royal Navy.

4. Charles Francis Adams, Jr., was the son of Charles Francis Adams, who had been U.S. ambassador to the Court of St. James until the outbreak of war and was the older brother of Henry Adams. Before the war, he had been William Sewards's campaign manager for the 1860 presidential nomination. He proved an able and bold cavalry commander after joining the 15th Mass. Vol. Regt. and served with great distinction at Antietam and Gettysburg.

5. T.J. Stiles, *The First Tycoon: The Epic Life of Cornelius Vanderbilt* (New York: Alfred A. Knopf, 2009), pp. 277, 288.

6. George Jeffries, first Baron Jeffreys (1644–1689). He is known as Hanging Judge Jeffreys because of the punishment he handed out at the trials of the supporters of the Duke of Monmouth in 1685. James II sent Judge Jeffreys (and a couple of others) to try the defeated rebels; the resulting "Bloody Assizes," especially as written up by Macaulay would make Jeffreys's reputation odious in history.

7. HMS *Nile*, commanded by Capt. E.K. Barnard, was laid down in 1839 and converted to steam in 1854; she was 2,598bm, measured 205x54 ft, and carried 10-8in, and 68-32pdr. HMS *Jason* was a wood screw corvette, commanded by Capt. E.P.B. von Donop, was launched in 1859; she was 1,711bm or 2.431 tons, measured 225X41 ft, and carried 16-8in, 1-7in, and 4-40pdr. J.J. College, *Ships of the Royal Navy: The Complete Record of All Fighting Ships of the Royal Navy from the Fifteenth Century to the Present* (London: Greenhill Books, 2003), pp. 173, 228. *Colburn's United Service*

Magazine and Military and Naval Journal, 1863, Part III (London: Hurst & Blackett Publishers), p. 606. College and the *United Service Magazine* disagree on the number of guns on HMS *Nile*; therefore, the number given by the contemporary latter source is used.

8. *Alfred Thayer Mahan, *Gustavus Fox, William Cushing, and the Founding of the Naval Aeronautical Service* (Boston: Graham & Sons, 1912), p.153.

9. *The USS *Dictator* had been rushed to completion in the frenzied acceleration of construction that immediately followed the outbreak of war. That completion was only made possible by the efforts of the War Production Board (WPB) to rationalize and prioritize war production. John P. Ayers, *The War Production Board in the Great War* (New York: Abbot & Sons, Publisher, 1899), pp. 87–92.

10. In addition to the USS *Catskill* taken by Major Bazelgette, the USS *Nipsic* was also captured in the same manner.

11. A culminating point is when you have inflicted maximum damage on the enemy with minimal loss to your own force. To go beyond the culminating point risks increasing losses for decreasing gain. A spoiling attack is meant to disrupt enemy preparations and buy you time.

12. *Alexander C. Rutledge, *Spymaster of the Union: The Life of George H. Sharpe* (New York: Excelsior Press, 1934), p. 352. Sharpe was a brigadier general when he assumed temporary command as the senior officer on the spot of the forces concentrating at Chazy. Lincoln immediately confirmed him in command and promoted him to major general.

13. Adolph von Steinwehr was a German immigrant who had served in the Brunswick Army. He rose to command of the 1st Division of XI Corps and unfortunately commanded it when Stonewall Jackson fell on it like a thunderbolt at Chancellorsville. The fault was not his but that of his corps commander, Maj. Gen. O.O. Howard who failed to refuse or fortify his flank despite repeated orders from the army commander. A fellow division commander described von Steinwehr as a "remarkably intelligent and agreeable person." His command of the 1st Division at Clavarack restored the corps' honor and earned him its command.

CHAPTER SIX: "WE CANNOT LOSE A FLEET"

1. Sherman had been known as Uncle Billy until he suppressed the Copperhead revolt in Chicago where he earned his new epithet for summarily hanging hundreds of Copperheads captured bearing arms in civilian clothes.

2. *Wars of the Rebellion and Foreign Intervention*, Vol. XXX, Chap. 37 (Washington, DC: U.S. Government Printing Office, 1888), pp. 398, 610–616. The prisoners mentioned by Sherman were mostly from the British 1st Hamilton Brigade, which had strung out on the flank west from Chazy to Sciota. Wolseley's couriers carrying the order to withdraw never arrived. The brigade's right anchor had been overrun by Custer, and the rest had remained in its positions until forced to

surrender after the battle, yielding 1,410 prisoners to add to the 207 prisoners taken at Sciota. Another 823 prisoners were taken, mostly wounded or stragglers who wandered away from their units looking for a warm house or campfire. In contrast, the British reported taking 1,888 American prisoners, mostly from Cobham's Brigade destroyed at Prospect Hill and Candy's Brigade driven into Fort Montgomery. Sherman reported 723 killed, 2,209 wounded, and 2,300 missing. The British reported 632 killed, 1,940 wounded, and 3,112 missing; however, many of the missing were killed or wounded left behind. Total U.S. losses were 5,222; total British losses were 5,144. The severest U.S. losses had been in Ruger's Brigade (321 killed and wounded) as it attempted to storm the Chazy bridge and in Hecker's Brigade (422 killed and wounded). The British reported severe losses in the Brigade of Guards as they cleared Champlain, 511 killed and wounded or 24 percent. As a percentage of forces committed U.S. losses were 9.6 percent; British losses were 16.2 percent.

3. Peter G. Tsouras, *A Rainbow of Blood: The Union in Peril* (Washington, DC: Potomac Books, Inc., 2010), pp. 111–13.

4. "HMS Prince Albert (1864)," en.wikipedia.org/wiki/HMS_Prince-Albert_(1864), accessed March 30, 2011. HMS Prince Albert measured 240 ft in length by 48 ft in the beam and was powered by a one shaft Humphreys Tennant Horizontal 2130 hp engine. She was protected by a 4.5 in. armored belt with 3.4 in. armor at the ends and the deck .75 to 1.2 in. She had four turrets, two each fore and aft of the smokestack with 10 in. of armor in the front and 5 in. on the side and rear. Unlike the American monitors, it had a much greater freeboard at 7 feet. Designed for coastal defense in shallow waters she had a deep draught of 20.5 ft.

5. London *Times*, March 20, 1863.

6. Discovery DVD Classics: *Hunt for the USS Alligator: Navy's First Sub* (Discovery Communications LLC, 2007) De Villeroi walked off the job as chief engineer during the construction of the Alligator over severe disagreements with the Navy. *However, because of his unique engineering and scientific skills the Navy hired him to be the senior engineering advisor for the *Shark* class submarine. The immediate offer of American citizenship soothed his bruised feelings enough to accept the offer. *Adolphus Meninger, The Life of Brutus de Villeroi: Creative Genius of the Submarine* (New York: D. Appleton, 189), pp. 122–25.

7. Mark K. Ragan, *Union and Confederate Submarine Warfare in the Civil War* (New York: Da Capo Press, 1999), pp. 135, 176.

8. *Hunt for the USS Alligator*. The boat was originally fitted out with paddles lining the side of the hull, but this eventually proved unsatisfactory because of the difficulty of going in reverse. The Navy redesigned the propulsion system by installing a propeller powered by the men on their cranks.

9. Experiment had proved to de Villeroi that the air was purified by pumping it through lime water, but it was only later learned that the lime water served to scrub the carbon dioxide out of the air.

10. *Alfred Thayer Mahan, *The Rise of the U.S. Navy's Submarine Fleet* (Boston: Ripley & Sons, Publishers, 1912), p. 211. The names of the rest of the Shark class as delivered, remarkably close to Fox's estimate, were the *Dolphin, Whale, Barracuda,* and *Sea Monster.*

11. Peter G. Tsouras, *A Rainbow of Blood: The Union in Peril* (Washington, DC: Potomac Books, 2010), pp. 145–46.

12. The New York press had been greatly surprised when the Russian Baltic squadron visited New York to learn that almost every Russian naval officer was fluent in English. That skill had its roots in the eighteenth century when large numbers of Royal Navy officers who had been on the beach at half pay had taken service with the Russian Imperial Navy. Their presence as teachers had been so powerful as to leave the King's English as a second language in the wardrooms of the Russian fleet. A large number of those Royal Navy officers had been Scots.

CHAPTER SEVEN: PHILOSOPHER GENERALS

1. *Horace Porter, *Grant in the Great War* (Philadelphia: Acheson Publishers, 1883), p. 119. The medical orderly who had treated Grant immediately after his head wound was right in that it looked worse than it really was. Nevertheless, excruciating headaches had prevented Grant from intervening in the subsequent fighting at Chazy. He had only arrived back in Washington the day before.

2. Lamon, Ward Hill, edited by Bob O'Connor, *The Life of Abraham Lincoln as President: A Personal Account by Lincoln's Bodyguard* (Conshohocken, PA: Mount Claire Press, 2010), p.455.

3. Peter G. Tsouras, *A Rainbow of Blood: The Union in Peril* (Washington, DC: Potomac Books, 2010), Chapter 2.

4. *A Rainbow of Blood.* X Corps was evacuated from the siege of Charleston after the defeat of the Royal Navy's attack with the South Atlantic Blockading Squadron and was disembarked in Norfolk where it came under the command of the Army of the James commanded by Maj. Gen. Benjamin Butler.

5. Wikipedia accessed 5 April 2011.

6. "The Wild Geese Today—Erin's Far Flung Exiles;" http://webcache. googleusercontent.com/search?q=cache:iK3AFg9kya4J:www.thewildgeese.com/pages/kelly.html+%22Colonel+Patrick+Kelly%22&cd=2&hl=en&ct=clnk&gl=us&source=www.google.com, accessed 6 May 2011.

7. Phoenix Park, http://en.wikipedia.org/wiki/Phoenix_Park, accessed 17 July 2011.

8. James Hamilton, 1st Duke of Abercorn (1811–1875), was noted by the *Times* to be the only peer to hold peerages in England, Scotland, and Ireland. He was a Conservative politician with experience in Ireland as the Lord

Lieutenant of Donegal and the natural pick for that office by both Lord Derby and Disreali.

9. Phoenix Park.

10. T.J. Stiles, *The First Tycoon: The Epic Life of Cornelius Vanderbilt* (New York: Alfred A. Knopf, 2009), pp. 277, 288.

11. Stiles, pp. 246–48.

12. http://www.starbacks.ca/Pentagon/1503/70sigsqn.html, and http://www.essex-yeomanry.org.uk/in-the-news/69-military-units-of-essex-4.html., accessed 11 Mar 2011. "In 1830 the West Essex Yeomanry Cavalry was raised to help the civil powers cope with the widespread agitation in Essex caused by the proposed Reform Bill," and specifically to protect the gunpowder mills at Waltham Abbey and the ordnance factory at Enfield Lock. "In the 1850's this Regiment expanded to comprise three cavalry and two artillery troops and a band."

13. David Pam, *The Royal Small Arms Factory Enfield & Its Workers* (Published by author, 1993), p. 61.

14. *Sir Robert Wilson, *Soldiering for the Queen: The Crimea, The Mutiny, and the American War* (London: Blackthorne & Son, Ltd, 1872), p. 311. Wilson had won a rare commission on merit in an infantry regiment, the 100th Foot, at a time when commissions were purchased. He won his Victoria Cross (VC) at Inkerman in the Crimea and transferred to the 9th Lancers in India just in time for the Great Mutiny; his wounds forced his retirement. In his autobiography Wilson alludes to these rumors of loot from the sack of Dehli as pure invention, though fails to account for his sudden ample means after his retirement, made all the more curious by his lower middle class origins.

15. Pam, pp. 50–56.

16. Pam, pp. 60–65.

17. J. Tuff, *Notices of Enfield* (J.H. Meyrs, Publishers, 1858), pp. 204–06.

18. Pam, p. 45.

19. The body of King Harold Godwinson, the last Saxon king of England slain by an arrow in the eye at the battle of Hastings in 1066, is buried outside Waltham Abby.

20. Royal Gunpowder Mills Waltham Abby; http://www.royalgunpowdermills.com/about.htm; accessed 7 March 2011.

21. Frederick Abel, http://en.wikipedia.org/wiki/Frederick_Abel, accessed 17 July 2011.

22. Sherman's hairpins was the name given by the troops to the twisting of rails heated red hot over a fire of ties around a telegraph pole. This rendered the rail useless; it could not be straightened but had to be melted down again, a process the South simply did not have the resources before British intervention.

23. Edmond Dédé's parents had emigrated from Haiti like so many mulattos who had supported the French. His father served as the militia bandmaster. Edmond was a violin prodigy and studied under gifted teachers, white and black. Hostility forced him to study in

Mexico and after a short return to the city, emigrated to France where he successfully auditioned at the Paris Conservatoire in 1857 where he studied. He led the orchestra at the Theatre l'Alacazar for twenty-seven years.

24. John W. Blassingame, *Black New Orleans, 1860–1880* (Chicago, 1973), p. 10.

25. Harold Holzer, ed., *Lincoln As I Knew Him: Gossip, Tributes & Revelations from His Best Friends and Worst Enemies* (Algonquin Books of Chapel Hill, 1999), pp. 117–18.

26. Hozler, pp. 120–21. Dr. Thomas Arnold was a legendary British headmaster.

CHAPTER EIGHT: *VAE VICTIS*

1. St. Andrew was crucified on an X-shaped cross in Patras in Achaea (Greece) Rimsky. The name Andrew in Greek means manly. After the collapse of the Soviet Union, the former Soviet Navy, now the navy of the Russian Federation, readopted the St. Andrew's cross ensign of the old Imperial Russian Navy in 1992. The last review of the Soviet naval ensign was witnessed by this author on Navy Davy with the Black Sea Fleet in July 1992. The St. Andrew's Cross flag is also the national flag of Scotland adopted in the sixteenth century, although the cross is in white on a blue saltire, the reverse of the Russian Andreyevsky ensign.

2. Stiles, pp. 202, 257. Both *Northern Star* and *Ariel* were ships belonging to Cornelius Vanderbilt, and like the SS *Vanderbilt* herself were considered some of the fastest and soundest ships afloat.

3. Traditionally the Russians have referred to their soldiers afloat as naval infantry instead of marines as in most other navies.

4. Edwin Fishel, *The Secret War for the Union: The Untold Story of Military Intelligence in the Civil War* (Boston: Houghton Mifflin Company, 1996), pp. 527–28.

5. Rose Greenhow was a famous Confederate spy operating in Washington during the early part of the war.

6. Fishel, *The Secret War for the Union*, pp. 306–10, 531.

7. Peter F. Stevens, *The Voyage of the Catalpa: A Perilous Journey and Six Irish Rebels' Escape to Freedom* (New York: Carroll & Graff, Publishers, 2002), p. 5.

8. Brennus was the leader of the Senones, a Celtic people who had conquered northern Itlay and went on to defeat the Romans at the battle of Allia in 387 BC and saked Rome itself, except for the Capitoline Hill, which held out. The Romans attempted to pay off Brennus for one thousand pounds of gold. According to Livy, the Romans disputed the weights the Celts used to weigh the gold whereupon during a Brennus threw his sword onto the scales and uttered the famous words "*Vae victis!*"

9. A cavalry regiment at this time was organized into ten companies of eighty men (at full strength). Any multicompany detachment was termed a battalion. The terms company and battalion would in later years be replaced by troop and squadron in U.S. Army terminology.

10. C.D. Yonge, *History of the British Navy from the Earliest Time to the Present Day*, Vol. III (London: Richard Bently, 1866), pp. 206, 206, 472.

11. http://www.enotes.com/topic/List_of_Russian_steam_frigates, accessed 29 April 2011; Russian ships and guns: *Bogatyr* 18 (2,200 tons), *Kalevala* 19 (1,800 tons), *Rynda* 11 (8,00 tons), Gaidamak 7 (1,050 tons), and Abrek 5 (1,070 tons).

12. *Edward Lyon Haythornthwaite, *British Operations in California in the Great War, Vol. I, Clearing the Seas* (London: Bidwell & Sons, 1877), p. 172. British ships at Esquimalt at this time included HMS *Alert* 17 (sloop, 1045 tons), HMS *Charybidis* 21 (corvette, 2,267 tons), and Albacore class gunboats (284 tons) HMS *Forward* 2 and *Grappler* 2. The only British regiment in the area was the 99th Foot hurriedly transferred from China at the outbreak of the war.

13. The tonnage of the Russian squadron was 6,920 tons, the British squadron 3,877.

14. Peter G. Tsouras, *The Book of Military Quotations* (London: Greenhill Books, 2005), p. 27. Nelson, 3 May 1797, letter during the battle of Bastian.

15. Russian Naval Infantry were the equivalent of U.S. and Royal Marines. They wore a distinctive white-and-blue-stripped undershirt under their blouses.

16. *John C. Wilton, *The Battle of San Juan de Fuca* (London: William Slaughter, Publisher, 1910), pp. 211–12. Besides HMS *Hastings* 50, the squadron consisted of HMS *Curacoa* 23 (frigate), HMS *Esk* 21 (Corvette), and HMS *Miranda* 15 (sloop). All five Russian ships were taken with only the loss of gunboat *Forward*.

CHAPTER NINE: GENERAL GRANT'S ARMY OF INVASION

1. William A. Tidwell, April '65: *Confederate Covert Action in the American Civil War* (Kent, OH: Kent State University Press, 1995), p.65.

2. Glasgow (41st Foot), Manchester (14th Hussars).

3. Birmingham (1st and 2nd Dragoons), Sheffield (1/8th Foot), York (16th Lancers).

4. The Royal Powder Mills at Waltham Abbey were only twelve miles north of London at this time.

5. *Everett P. Norton, *The Life and Extraordinary Adventures of Ulrich Dahlgren* (Philadelphia: J.B. Lippencott & Co., 1910), pp. 229–35.

6. *Nigel Simonton, "The Battle for Enfield Lock," *British Historical Review*, vol. XI, p. 89, September 1979.

7. "Shooting leave" was the British military euphemism for going on an intelligence collection mission in the guise of a private hunting trip.

8. *William Frederick Johnson, RM (ret), *The Rifle Volunteer Corps in the American War* (London: Southwick & Stimson, Publishers, 1987), p. 122. Five RVCs totaling 1,807 men eventually took up positions to guard Buckingham Palace: 1st, 7th, and 20th London RVCs, 23rd Middlesex, and remarkably the 1st Nottingham, or Robin Hood RVCs.

In appreciation for their service, each unit was allowed to add "Royal" to its name, for example, the 1st Royal Robin Hood RVC. It was an honor the mention of which would get you expelled from any mess in the Brigade of Guards.

9. Peter G. Tsouras, *The Greenhill Dictionary of Military Quotations* (London: Greenhill Books, 2001), p. 314.

10. *John William Greenhouse, *The Russian Raid: Terror in the Irish Sea*, 1864 (New York: Dodd, Mead, & Co., 1927), p. 197.

CHAPTER TEN: "OLD SOLDIERS OF THE QUEEN"

1. Richard A. Sauers, *Gettysburg: The Meade-Sickles Controversty* (Washington, DC: Brassey's, 2003), p. 57.

2. On April 1, 1864, the major armies and independent corps of the United States were: Army of the Hudson (VI, XI, XII Corps) (Maj. Gen. William Tecumseh Sherman); Army of the Potomac (I, II, III, V Corps) (Maj. Gen. George Gordon Meade); Army of the Cumberland (IV, XVII, XX, XXI Corps) (Maj. Gen. George Thomas); Army of the James (X, XVIII Corps) (Maj. Gen. Baldy Smith); Army of the Mississippi (XIX Corps, XXIII, Corps d'Afrique) (William B. Franklin); IX Corps (Maj. Gen. Daniel Sickles).

3. Wright had been captured riding too far ahead of his corps' first division after it had crossed the Kennebunk River and was captured at the onset of the battle by Hope Grant's cavalry. The ensuing battle of Kennebunk saw Wright's First Division cut off by the destruction of the river bridge, and most of it was captured, killed, or wounded in the subsequent fighting. Most of the prisoners had been exchanged for the like number of British and Canadian prisoners taken at the battle of Clavarck. Wright's capture in leading from the front not only did not take away from his reputation as an aggressive and skilled commander but instead reinforced it

4. Robert M. Grosvenor, ed., "The Old Soldiers of the King," *Songs of Rebels and Redcoats* (Washington, DC: National Geographic Society, 1972) lyrics on record sleeve. This song was originally composed during the American Revolution and was adapted in the Great War; references to the king were changed to the queen, from Lexington to Clavarack, and from Princeton to New York.

5. * Edward Dupree, *Decision at Ponchatoula* (New Orleans: St. Louis Press, 1989), p. 201.

6. At this time, the steam engines of ships were not efficient enough to gain enough sustained power to sail exclusively on the coal they could carry. The wind was used whenever possible to spare the coal. So the traditional sails were still a vital part of the steamship's power of locomotion.

7. *Pryce Lewis, *A Spy in Babylon* (New York: St. Edmund Press, 1895), pp. 232–35. Lewis reveals that Sharpe depleted the U.S. Treasury's store of gold sovereigns for this operation under the direct authorization of President Lincoln.

8. These were the 12th Lancers from Hounslow in the London area, nicknamed the "Supple Twelfth."

9. The 63rd New York and 116th Pennsylvania Regiments were left to garrison Dublin. The three regiments on the field also left a few companies in the garrison. On that day, Meagher had about 4,300 men on the field.

10. The Curragh Brigade consisted of the 2/12th, 84th, and 86th Foot, and the attached 17th Royal Engineer Company; the ad hoc cavalry brigade numbered the 15th Hussars and 4th and 5th Dragoon Guards. The British force numbered slightly over five thousand men.

11. *The charge of the Royal Dragoon Guards at Tallaght was immortalized in a sensational painting by Lady Butler, who would paint a similar painting of the charge of the Scots Grays at Waterloo.

12. At the Battle of the Boyne just outside the town of Drogheda on Ireland's east coast on July 12, 1690, the Protestant King William defeated the Catholic King James II, whom he had deposed in 1688. The two armies faced each other across the Boyne River; William's professional army crushed James's army of mostly raw recruits. The battle helped ensure the continuation of Protestant supremacy in Ireland.

13. The last serious defeat on the British Army in the British Isles had been at the battle of Prestonpans, outside of Edinburgh, on September 21, 1745, by the Highland forces of the Stuart pretender, Charles. The government army was led by General John Cope, and their disastrous defense against the Jacobites is immortalized in the song "Johnnie Cope."

14. *Edward G. Rittenhouse, *The Plot to Assassinate Abraham Lincoln: In the Words of the Eyewitnesses* (Chicago: Clarke & Company, 1866), p. 111.

15. William A. Tidwell, *April '65: Confederate Covert Action in the American Civil War* (Kent, OH: Kent State University Press, 1995), pp. 68–69, 183–84.

16. Eleanor Ruggles, *Prince of Players: Edwin Booth* (New York: W.W. Norton & Company, 1953), p. 157.

CHAPTER ELEVEN: JUST PITCH INTO HIM

1. Anthony Gross, ed., *The Wit and Wisdom of Abraham* Lincoln (New York, Barnes & Noble, 1994), p. 166.

2. *Michael D. Wilmoth, *Spy Mistress of the Union: The Life of Elizabeth Van Lew, Patriot* (Washington, DC: Arlington House Press, 178), p. 310. In addition to succeeding eventually to the directorship of the Central Information Bureau, Wilmoth became a prominent historian of the intelligence history of the war. He asserts that Van Lew obtained this information on Longstreet's movement from her sources, clerks in the Confederate War Department. Since Van Lew never wrote her own memoirs and destroyed most of her correspondence, historians have had to rely on other sources such as Wilmoth's to authenticate her considerable activities.

3. *John C. Babcock, *The Bureau of Military Information in the Army of the Potomac* (New York: Charles L. Webster & Company, 1882), p. 264.

4. *William F. Grierson, *From Ponchetoula to Baton Rouge: The Destruction of a French Army* (New York: Longman Greens & Company, 1954), p. 269. For five days the Confederates continued to send trains to Ponchatoula, each one of them captured upon arrival, their railcars stuffed with supplies and a steady stream of French personnel.

5. *The absence of General Taylor's Confederate army in the campaign to recapture northern Arkansas and Missouri would be seen as the consequence of Sharpe's divide and conquer strategy.

6. *Etienne Clery, *Clio Dulaine: Heroine of New Orleans* (Baton Rouge: Louisiana State University Press, 1966), pp. 320–24. Pryce Lewis married Clio Delaine and founded the *libre* dynasty of the Pryce-Dulaines, great powerbrokers for generations in New Orleans. Their great granddaughter, Clio Pryce-Dulaine, became U.S. senator in 2004.

7. The Dogger banks are believed to be the remains of a glacial moraine and varies in depth from 49 to 118 feet (15 to 36 m), averaging twenty meters shallower than the surrounding seas. In the Pleistocene, it was dry land now called Doggerland.

8. Edwin B. Coddington, *The Gettysburg Campaign: A Study in Command* (New York: Charles Scribner's Sons, 1968), p. 196. Lee said upon hearing of Meade's appointment to command the Army of the Potomac, "General Meade will commit no blunder in my front, and if I make one he will make haste to take advantage of it."

9. *The War of the Rebellion: A Compilation of the Official Records of the Union and Confederate Armies, Series 1: Volume 28 (Part II)* (Washington, DC: US Government Printing Office, 1890), p. 137. The brigade consisted of the 9th and 11th Maine and the 3rd and 4th New Hampshire Volunteer Infantry Regiments.

10. "Kansas Jayhawking Raids into Western Missouri in 1861," *Missouri Historical Review*, Vol. 54 No. 1, October 1959.

11. Originally raised as the 2nd South Carolina, the regiment was redesignated the 34th U.S.C.T. in early 1864.

12. In his first assignment commanding Union forces at Fortress Monroe, Maj. Gen. Benjamin Butler cleverly refused to return escaped slaves to Virginia slave owners, stating that since the South considered them property, they fell under the category of contraband of war, property liable to confiscation because it provided material support to the enemy's war effort.

13. Andrew D. Lambert, *British Grand Strategy, 1853–1856* (Manchester: Manchester University Press, 1991), pp. 309–27.

14. Major George B. Davis, et al., *The Official Military Atlas of the Civil War* (New York: Barnes & Noble Books, 2003), p. 76. This is a reprint of the atlas produced by the U.S. Army, U.S. Government Printing Office, 1891–1995.

15. *Jeremiah Philemon, *Casualties of the Civil War* (New York: Century Publishing Co., 1892), pp. 122–23.

16. In the United States, that part of the Seven Years War fought in North America has always been called the French and Indian War. At that conclusion of that war, the defeated French were essentially given a choice of losing either their sugar islands in the Caribbean or Canada. They chose to give up Canada and the seventy thousand French settlers there, an act that did nothing to encourage any lingering loyalty to the Bourbons or France itself.

17. *Edward Lyon Haythornthwaite, *British Operations in California in the Great War, Vol. II, The Seizure of San Francisco* (London: Bidwell & Sons, 1877), pp. 114–16. The British landing force consisted of a battalion of Royal Marines, and the 1/12 Foot from Australia and from New Zealand, the 2/14th, 40th, 65th, and 70th Foot in addition to 6th Co., RE.

18. *The large number of men in Union corps at this time was due to the return to the colors of so many discharged men who originally had enlisted for two years as well as recovered invalids and the flood of volunteers triggered by the British attack and Copperhead rising.

19. Peter G. Tsouras, *A Rainbow of Blood: The Union in Peril, An Alternate History* (Washington, DC: Potomac Books, 2010), pp. 268–69.

20. *Enoch Williamson, "Army-Navy Cooperation in the Civil War and the Great War," *American Military Historical Review*, Vol. XXI, 1890, pp. 37–42.

CHAPTER TWELVE: A LONG SHOT WITH A LIMB IN BETWEEN

1. Oliver Raferty, "Fenianism in North America in the 1860s: The Problems for Church and State," *History: The Journal of the Historical Association*, Vol. 84, Issue 274, pp. 257–77, April 1999.

2. Western England, Scotland, and Wales: From Glasgow came the 41st Foot; from Edinburgh the 3rd, 4th, and 10th Hussars, and 92nd Foot; from Manchester the 14th Hussars; from Birmingham 1st and 2nd Dragoons. These were accompanied by twenty-three RVCs and totaled 27,800 men including artillery and engineers. The Channel ports and nearby: Jersey 61st Foot; Aldershot, 1/3rd Foot, 1/24th Foot, 2/60th Foot, 76th Foot, 4th Artillery Brigade, Military Trains (2nd and 5th Battalions); Brighton 9th Lancers; Schorncliffe 1/5th Foot; Dover 85th Foot. Another 30 RVCs accompanied this force for a total of 30,300 men.

3. The first wave of forces sent to Ireland included the following Volunteer Corps: (Scotland) Ayrshire Arty VC, Ayrshire RVC, 3rd, 5th, and 18th Renfrewshire RVCs, 1st Lanarkshire Arty VC, 1st Lanarkshire Engr VC, 3rd, 4th, 19th, 38th, 86th, and 88th Lanarkshire RVCs and from England 10th, 13th, and 21st Lancashire Arty VCs, 11th, 5th, 6th, 28th, 51st, 56th RVCs, and 1st (Birkenhead), 2nd, 4th, 6th, 13th, and 56th Cheshire RVCs, and (Wales) 1st, 2nd, and 6th Flintshire RVCs. This is a total of 24 RVCs, 5 arty VCs, and 1 Engr VC.

4. "*The Times* of London, May 20th, 1864.

5. Lieutenant colonels in the English-speaking armies are addressed simply as colonel.

6. Adolph A. Hoehling, *Thunder at Hampton Roads* (New York: Da Capo Press, 1993). p. 6.

7. Field Marshal Viscount Wolseley, *The American Civil War: The Ritings of Field Marshal Viscount Wosleley* (Mechanicsburg, PA: Stackpole Books, 2004), p. 61. As a younger man Robert E. Lee had often been referred to as the handsomest man in North America. Wolseley in his writings repeatedly refers to him as handsome.

8. After his death at the battle of Trafalgar in 1805 the body of Adm. Horatio Nelson was transported back to England for burial in a barrel of brandy to preserve it.

9. At this time the Indian Army collectively referred to the three standing armies the British maintained in India: the Bengal Army, the Madras Army, and the Bombay Army. Each had its own establishment separate from the British Army.

10. Peter G. Tsouras, ed., *The Book of Military Quotations* (London: Greenhill Books, 2005), p. 223.

11. *Major General John Frederick Maurice, *General Robert Napier and the Irish Campaign* (London: Blackwoods Publishers, 1910), p. 327.

12. The honors of war allowed a surrendered garrison of a fortress to march out under arms and with colors flying to be saluted by the victor. It was a mark of great honor by the victor to the valor of the vanquished.

13. *Elijah W. Watkins, *Fire Kills: The Role of Repeating Weapons in the World War* (Philadelphia: The Neale Publishing Co., 1889), p. 299. The use of repeating weapons against the well dug-in Confederates was not as overpowering as hoped. Already protected by deep trenches and earthworks, the Confederate infantry was able to return sufficient, protected fire through the firing slots between timbers to beat back any Union attack.

14. The detachment of II and VI Corps and a cavalry division left Meade's Army of the Potomac with I, III, and V Corps and a two division cavalry corps, altogether about one hundred thousand men now that the Army had been reinforced with so many veterans returned to the colors and volunteers.

15. It was for this victory that Grant was made 1st Viscount Grant of Kennebunk.

16. The germ of this idea was to grow into the concentration camp system used in the Boer War of 1899–1902 in which large numbers of Boer women and children died of poor treatment.

17. Angus Konstam, *Duel of the Ironclads: USS Monitor & CSS Virginia at Hampton Roads 1862* (Botely, Oxord: Osprey Publishing, 2003), pp. 93–94. *Dictator*: 4,438 tons, 312 x 50 x 20.5 ft, 9 knots, 2 x 15 in. Dahlgrens in a single turret, crew 174. Monadnock: 3,295 tons, 250 ft. x 53 ft 8 in. x 12 ft. 3 in., 9 knots, 4 x 15 in. Dahlgrens in two turrets, crew 130. *Onondaga*: 2,592 tons, 226 x 49 ft. 3 in. x 12 ft. 10 in., 7 knots, 2 x 8 in. rifles in forward

turret, 2 x 15 in. Dahlgrens in after turret, crew 130. *Canonicus*: 2,100 tons, 223 ft. x 43 ft. 4 in. x 13 ft. 6 in., 8 knots, 2 x 15 in. Dahlgrens in a single turret, crew 85.

18. * Julian Corbett, *The Carnegie Reforms and Their Effect on the Naval War* (London: Nelson Press, 1901), pp. 312–15. Three of the Canonicus class were scheduled for commissioning in April 1864 even before the war with Great Britain. *Onondaga* had already been commissioned in March. *Dictator, Monadnock, Manhattan,* and *Mohapac* were completed well ahead of schedule due to the Carnegie reforms.

19. Peter G. Tsouras, ed., *The Book of Military Quotations* (London: Greenhill Books, 2005), pp. 313–14.

20. *Edward G. Rittenhouse, *The Plot to Assassinate Abraham Lincoln: In the Words of the Eyewitnesses* (Chicago: Clarke & Company, 1866), pp. 266–68. John Peanut's testimony was a key element of the prosecution of the plotters.

21. James L. Swinton, *Manhunt: The 12-day Chase for Lincoln's Killer* (New York: Harper Perennial, 2006), pp. 36–37.

22. David Homer Bates, *Lincoln in the Telegraph Office: Recollections of the United States Military Telegraph Corps During the Civil War* (New York: The Century Co., 1907), p. 205.

23. Lonnie R. Speer, *Portals to Hell: Military Prisons in the Civil War* (Mechanicsburg, PA: Stackpole Books, 1997), pp. 151–53.

24. *James T. Faulkner, *Liberation! The Rescue of the Confederate Prisoners at Point Lookout* (Richmond: Hollywood Press, 1936), pp. 277–82.

CHAPTER THIRTEEN: RUNNING THE ROADS

1. David Homer Bates, *Lincoln in the Telegraph Office: Recollections of the United States Military Telegraph Corps During the Civil War* (New York: The Century Co., 1907), p. 210.

2. At this time there was a saying that was equivalent to "Selling coals to Newcastle": "Selling grain to Russia." Tragically, the insanities of Marxist economics as practiced later in the Soviet Union, meant that eventually the region that once produced huge surpluses could not even feed itself and had to buy American grain.

3. Field Marshal Viscount Wolslely, *The American Civil War: The Writings of Field Marshal Viscount Wolseley, An English View* (Mechanicsburg, PA: Stackpole Books, 2002), p. 42. Wolseley in his "shooting leave" visit to the Army of Northern Virginia made just the same point.

4. On some period maps, Hanover Junction is referred to as Sexton Junction.

5. Thomas A. Lewis and the Editors of Time-Life Books, *The Shenandoah in Flames: The Valley Campaign of 1864* (Alexandria, VA: Time-Life Books, 1987), pp. 103–104.

6. http://en.wikipedia.org/wiki/Moxley_Sorre, accessed 31 July 2011. In Moxley Sorrel, Longstreet was blessed with the man considered to be the finest staff officer in the Confederacy.

7. *The 3rd Brigade of the Cavalry Division consisted of the 1st Vermont
    and 1st West Virginia Cavalry Regiments. Only the 1st Vermont was
    present at Brighton. The 1st Vermont had been transferred to the Army
    of the Hudson because part of Vermont was occupied by the British, an
    incentive if ever there was one to fight hard.

8. http://en.wikipedia.org/wiki/William_Wells_(general), accessed 21
    July 2011. "Wells received more promotions than any other Vermont
    officer during the war (from Private to General in less than three and a
    half years)."

9. *Fitzhugh Lee's Division consisted of two brigades, Wickham's and
    Lomax's. Wickham's Brigade consisted of 1st, 2nd, 3rd, and 4th Virginia
    Cavalry. Lomax had sent two of its regiments (5th and 15th Virginia) with
    Longstreet to the James Peninsula. The remaining two formations, the
    6th Virginia and 1st Maryland Cavalry Battalion were reinforced by
    the heretofore independent 9th Virginia Cavalry. The 1st Maryland
    Battalion was composed of six companies, rather than the normal ten
    for a cavalry regiment. At that time, the term battalion was used to de-
    scribe an organization that did not have the complete organization of a
    regiment or part of a regiment detached for a special purpose.

10. During the Civil War far more of the eastern United States had been
    deforested and put under the plow than today. Large areas that today
    have reverted to forest were once rolling farmland. Woodlots and
    remaining woods were usually well-managed for their resources of
    wood. The undergrowth was kept cleared to allow cattle and hogs to
    browse.

11. Victor Davis Hansen, *The Soul of Battle: From Ancient Days to the Present*
    (New York: The Free Press, 1999), p. 20.

12. Farragut's squadron was traveling at seven knots and hour, which
    would take it one hour and twenty-six minutes to go the ten miles to
    British squadron. The picket ship was traveling at a fast twelve knots
    and hour, which would take fifty minutes to reach the British squadron.
    Thus at most, Admiral Hope had a thirty-six-minute warning.

13. *Edwin Swinton, *Running the Roads: Prelude to Decision* (New York:
    The Century Company, 1888), p. 182. *Mahopac* went down with her
    full crew of 80 officers and men. *Royal Oak's* losses were 187 killed or
    missing, and 42 wounded.

14. The term *arm blanche* means the "white arm," referring to the heraldic
    color of the French cavalry before the Revolution and by inference the
    cavalry itself.

15. Eric J. Wittenberg, *The Union Cavalry Comes of Age: Hartwood Church to
    Brandy Station, 1863* (Washington, DC: Brassey's Inc., 2003), pp. 284–85.

16. *Alonzo W. Cushing, *The Barbary Pirate: The Feats of the Aeroship USS
    Stephen Decatur in the Great War* (Philadelphia: D. Appleton, Publishers,
    1901), p. 31. This book was written by Cushing's son whom he
    named after his brother who fell at the head of his battery at the stone
    during Pickett's Charge at Gettysburg. The name Barbary Pirate was

unofficially chosen by the crew to commemorate Stephen Decatur's feats during the wars against the Muslim pirates of the Barbary States in North Africa.

17. Peter G. Tsouras, *The Book of Military Quotations* (London: Greenhill Books, 22005), p. 238.

18. *Henry Glasdale, *The Repeater War: The Effects of Repeating Weapons in the War* (New York: The Neale Publishing Co., 1904), pp. 311–12. The Gatlings and coffee mill guns were organized into new batteries under the artillery. This was a logical development but one that employed them as artillery rather than direct infantry support weapons, one reason that British artillery, in particular, was often able to neutralize the coffee mill guns in the Army of the Hudson so well.

CHAPTER FOURTEEN: "WE'VE GOT 'EM NICKED!"

1. Elizabeth R. Varon, *Southern Lady, Yankee Spy: The True Story of Elizabeth Van Lew, A Union Agent in the Heart of the Confederacy* (Oxford: Oxford University Press, 2003), pp. 96–97.

2. *Michael D. Wilmoth, ed., *Intelligence Operations in the Hanover Campaign*, Vol. 8 in The Intelligence War series (Washington, U.S. Government Printing Office, 1888), p. 39.

3. Abraham Lincoln, letter to James C. Conkling, Aug. 26, 1863, *Collected Works of Abraham Lincoln*, vol. 6 (Rutgers University Press, 1953, 1990), p. 409.

4. The two smallest British ironclads were *Prince Albert* at 3,746 tons and *Wivern* at 2,751. The two largest American turreted ironclads were *Dictator* at 4,438 tons and *Monadnock* at 3,295.

5. The American ironclads' guns included: 23x 15-inch Dahlgrens, 14 x 11-inch Dahgrens, 2 x 8-inch guns, and 2 x 150-pdr Rodman rifles, for a total of. The British ironclads had 5 x 10.5-inch, 18 x 9-inch, 2 x 8-inch, 41 x 7-inch (110 pdr), 49 x 68 pdr, 8 x 100 pdr, and 4 x 40 pdr guns, for total of 124 guns.

6. USS *Brooklyn* was the same size (2,400 tons) and even more heavily (twenty-one guns) armed than the frigate *Powhatan* with eleven guns.

7. "To nick" meant at that time "to catch at the right point or time."

8. The first instance was when he arrived on the field of Gettysburg in the late afternoon of July 1 just as the defeated Union troops were streaming up to Cemetery Hill and Ridge. He instantly saw the critical importance of Culp's Hill and immediately sent troops to defend it; they arrived just before the Confederates. On July 2 he plugged the gap left in the Union line by Sickles defeat and threw back the Confederate force that was about to plunge over Cemetery Ridge. On July 3 his II Corps threw back Lee's great attack.

9. These two regiments had been sent to North America at almost full strength; Canada had been far healthier than the Crimea where losses to disease had reduced the entire Light Brigade of five regiments to barely six hundred men.

10. The wolverine is the state animal of Michigan, a stocky and muscular carnivore that has a reputation for ferocity and strength out of proportion to its size, with the documented ability to kill prey many times its size.

11. Robert J. Schneller, Jr., *A Quest for Glory: A Biography of Rear Admiral John A. Dahlgren* (Anapolis: Naval Institute Press, 1996), pp. 156–57.

12. The 120th NY had been raised by Sharpe at the request of the governor of New York in September 1862. He had commanded it until he had been made chief of the new BMI by Maj. Gen. Joseph Hooker in February 1863. He continued in nominal command because that was source of his commission, though the regiment's lieutenant colonel had operational command. With Sharpe's assignment to the new CIB, he persuaded Lincoln to assign the regiment to the garrison of Washington where he employed it for security operations and presidential protection. He also acquired control of the 3rd Indiana Cavalry, which had a history of special operations. Sharpe employed these regiments in the battle of Washington to stop the Confederate attack over Long Bridge.

13. Gavin Mortimer, Double Death: *The True Story of Pryce Lewis, The Civil War's Most Daring Spy* (New York: Walker & Company, 2010), pp. 183–90. Timothy Webster, Jr., was executed on April 29, 1862, as a spy by the Confederates in Richmond. Heretofore, both sides had refrained from executing spies.

14. Edwin Forrest, 1806–1872, was one of the great tragedians of the American stage in the first half of the nineteenth century. At this time his health was failing and his draw as an actor fading.

15. The British, under Hope Grant's command, sacked the splendid Chinese imperial summer palace in the Third China War of 1860. Grant declined his share of the loot and had it shared out among his men.

16. *James Joyce, *My Own Country's Capital* (London: Sylvia Beach, 1925), pp. 322–23. Since the Irish War of Independence was almost exclusively fought in and around Dublin, it was of particular fascination to a novelist like Joyce, who wrote, "For myself, I always write about Dublin, because if I can get to the heart of Dublin I can get to the heart of all the cities of the world. In the particular is contained the universal."

CHAPTER FIFTEEN: "I WOULD RATHER DIE A THOUSAND DEATHS"

1. J.J. Colledge, *Ships of the Royal Navy: The Complete Record of All fighting Ships of the Royal Navy from the Fifteenth Century to the Present* (London: Greenhill Books, 2003) p. 110. HMS *Edgar* was one of the few ships-of-the-line at this time to be equipped with heavy ordnance, forty-four 8-and 10-inch guns.

2. *Julian Corbett, *Admiral James Hope and the Ironclad Controversy* (London: The Library of Imperial History, 1905), p. 92.

3. *Michael D. Wilmoth, ed., *Intelligence Operations in the Saco Campaign*, Vol. 9 in The Intelligence War series (Washington, U.S. Government Printing Office, 1890), p. 39.

4. Napoleon, 11 March 1805, to a courier to the czar, quoted in R.M. Johnston, *The Corsican*, 1910 and Peter G. Tsouras, ed., *The Book of Military Quotations* (London: Greenhill Books, 2005), p. 442.

5. Robert E. Lee, letter to Jefferson Davis quoted in *Douglas Southall Freeman on Leadership*, 1993, and in Tsouras, pp. 149–50.

6. *Babock on Sharpe's instructions had supervised the setting up of a new BMI office for Hancock's Army of the Rappahannock, staffing it with two of his experienced officers and several of his better scouts. To this core, Sharpe had sent down the rest of the team to include cipher clerks and a company of the Balloon Corps.

7. *Peter G. Tsouras, ed., *The Memoirs of Sergeant Judson Knight, Chief of Scouts of the Army of the Hudson* (Alexandria, VA: Xenophon Press, 2009), pp. 331–32.

8. Peter G. Tsouras, *A Rainbow of Blood: The Union in Peril* (Washington, DC: Potomac Books, 2010), pp. 259–60.

9. http://www.hanoveracademy.org/about.htm, accessed 7 July 2011. "Hanover Academy was one of the first classical schools founded in America. The first Hanover Academy was established in 1859 by Colonel Louis Minor Coleman as a preparatory school for boys, closely affiliated with the University of Virginia. The hardships of the Civil War and the reconstruction which followed, forced the Academy to cease operation in 1889," not to reopen until the centenary of its founding.

10. *Alfred Thayer Mahan, *The Submersible Squadron at the Battle of the Chesapeake* (Boston: Beacon Hill Press, 1899), p. 132.

11. Peter G. Tsouras, *Britannia's Fist: From Civil War to World War* (Washington, DC: Potomac Books, 2008), pp. 51–57, 63–65, 73–74. Captain Hancock immediately prior to the war served as an unofficial naval assistant to the British ambassador, Lord Lyons, and as an observer for the Admiralty.

12. HMS *Immortalité* was the fourth British ship with this French name. The first ship of that name had been captured from the French in 1798, and the second and third ship were also French captures renamed for the original French capture. It was customary in the age of sail to retain the name of a captured ship.

13. Each of the three brigades in the British 2nd Division was composed of an Imperial (British) battalion and three smaller Canadian militia battalions.

14. *Ulysses S. Grant, *Personal Memoirs of U.S. Grant, Selected Letters 1839–1865* (New York: The Library of America, 1990) pp. 770–71.

15. Grant, pp. 701–702.

16. *John F. Feldman, *Ordnance Development in the Naval Aeronautical Service During the Great War* (Naval Academy Press, 1927), pp. 222–25. Bronze was used in aerial bombs because iron ordnance was always at risk of striking a spark, lethal on a hydrogen aeroship.

17. Von Borke returned to the Prussian Army after the Civil War and fought with great gallantry in the Six Weeks War against Austria in

1866. Upon inheriting his father's castle, he proudly flew the Confederate flag from its battlements.

18. NPS, "The Battle of Yellow Tavern," http://www.nps.gov/frsp/plan-yourvisit/yell-tav.htm, accessed 7 July 2011.

19. *William Clyde, *Hero of the Chesapeake: The Life of Admiral George Hancock* (London: Greencastle Press, 1935), p. 230. Hancock was awarded the VC and a knighthood for his gallantry in shielding the remnant of the fleet at the end of the battle of the Chesapeake. He would later command the first of the *Revenge* class ironclads and ultimately was promoted to admiral and commanded the Pacific Station, where he died in 1876.

20. Larry Tagg, The Generals of Gettysburg (Campbell, CA: Savas Publishing, 1998) p. 301.

21. http://en.wikipedia.org/wiki/Gonorrhea, accessed 8 July 2011; aching joints and heart valves are debilitating effects of gonorrhea.

22. *Edward R. McKenzie, *Well Done, Canada: The 1st Battalion, The Prince of Wales Regiment in the American War* (Toronto: The Prince of Wales Regiment Society, 1888), pp. 311–12.

23. Thomas A. Lewis and the Editors of Time-Life Books, *The Shenandoah in Flames: The Valley Campaign of 1864* (Alexandria, VA: Time-Life Books, 1987), p. 68.

24. J. William Jones, "General Lee to the Rear," *Southern Historical Society Papers*, Volume VIII   Jan-1880 No.1 pages 32–35

25. Robert E. Lee, *The Memoirs of Robert E. Lee* (Philadelphia: D. Appleton & Company, 1866), p. 534.

EPILOGUE

1. David D. Ryan, ed., *A Yankee Spy in Richmond: The Civil War Diary of "Crazy Bet" Van Lew* (Mechanicsburg, PA: Stackpole Books, 1996), pp. 18–19.

2. *John G. Chambers, *How I Captured Jefferson Davis* (Philadelphia: D. Appleton Publishers, 1866), p. 177. Chambers was a white major in the 1st USCC and attributed Davis's survival to the fact that it was he who burst through the bedroom door to confront the Confederate President. Had it been some of his colored troopers, undoubtedly Davis would have immediately fired and been killed himself. He seemed relieved to be captured by a white man. Weitzel, however, gave the honor of guarding him to the 54th Massachusetts whose men were models of military bearing and courtesy. The 1st USCC were a little too wild for him. Davis would compliment the conduct of the Massachusetts men and referred to the time when he had armed his own slaves to hunt down white bandits.

3. *Edward G. Rittenhouse, *The Plot to Assassinate Abraham Lincoln: In the Words of the Eyewitnesses* (Chicago: Clarke & Company, 1866), p. 302.

4. *George Allen Townsend, *The Trial and Execution of John Wilkes Booth* (New York: Dick & Fitzgerald, 1865), pp. 292–95.

5. Peter G. Tsouras, *A Rainbow of Blood: The Union in Peril* (Washington, DC: Potomac Books, 2010), pp. 195–98. Lincoln had been shot in

October 1864 during the battle of Washington by his traitorous body-guard, Big Jim Smoke. The shot had grazed his head. Mrs. Lincoln's reaction was similarly hysterical on that occasion as well.

6. *Edwin Marsden, *Let US Have Peace* (New York: Webster Publishers, 1895), pp. 199–203. A lithograph in *Harper's Magazine* of Lincoln and Davis sitting together became the iconic symbol of national reconciliation.

7. *William Henry Wilson, *The Life and Extraordinary Adventures of Brig. Gen. Ulrich Dahlgren* (Washington, DC: The Cavalry Press, 1934), p. 288. At this ball, Dahlgren would meet his future bride, a Russian princess, daughter of one of the czar's cousins.

8. *Vladimir A. Osipov, *Russia and the American Alliance: A Lesson in Perfidy* (Moscow: Imperial House Publishers, 1932), pp. 301–11.

9. *Thomas Francis Meagher, *The Great Betrayal* (London: Trafalgar Square Publishers, 1877), pp. 311–12. Ironically, Disrael's mild hand in suppressing the Irish revolt and Gladstone's subsequent goal of providing home rule to Ireland actually accelerated the achievement of Irish independence with no further violence within the Common-wealth that emerged in the twentieth century. To this day the Queen's portrait still hangs in Dublin.

10. The United States attempted to conquer Canada during the American Revolution and the War of 1812, bungling both attempts, hence the apropos slogan.

11. *John Bancroft, *California for Canada: The Grand Bargainthat Sealed a Peace* (Boston: Beacon Hill Press, 1902), pp. 411–413.

12. *Frederick William Seward, *William H. Seward and the Treaty that Ended the War* (New York: Newbury Publishers, 1886), pp. 299–301. Seward privately explained Lincoln's reasoning for the plebecite to his British counterpart during negotiations in Havana as laying the groundwork for the treaty's acceptance by Northern opinion.

APPENDIX B: STATIONS OF THE BRITISH ARMY

1. *Colburn's United Service Magazine and Naval and Military Journal*, 1863, Part III (London: Hurst & Blackett, Publishers, 1863), pp. 451–456.

2. *Colburn's*, p. 451. The Curragh Plain was the great summer months training ground of the British Army in Ireland. Three battal-ions(2/12th, 32nd, 86th) training there in August would be back in Dublin by October.

APPENDIX E: ORDER-OF-BATTLE OF THE CAVALRY ACTION AT HANOVER JUNCTION

1. *Jonathan Bobbs, *The Cavalry in the New England Campaign* (Monpelier, VT: Monpelier Press, 1988), pp. 11, 78. The transfer of Second Brigade's 1st Maine and 1st Vermont to operations in upper New England required the transfer of the 18th Pennsylvania to the First Brigade.

ABOUT THE AUTHOR

Peter G. Tsouras is a retired Army officer and intelligence analyst, a military historian, and the author or editor of twenty-seven works of military history and alternate history that range the broad sweep of military history from Alexander the Great to Mesoamerica to the Gulf war. His alternate history works *Gettysburg: An Alternate History*; *Dixie Victorious: An Alternate History of the Civil War*; *Disaster at D-Day: The Germans Defeat the Allies, June 1944*; His military quotation books are the most comprehensive in the English language and include *Military Quotations form the Civil War: In the Words of the Commanders* and *The Book of Military Quotations*. His history titles include *Alexander: Invincible King of Macedonia*, *Warlords of the Ancient Americas*, *Montezuma: Warlord of the Aztecs*, and *The Great Patriotic War*. He has also edited a number of alternate history anthologies as well as memoirs of German generals of World War II. Many of them have been primary selections in the History Book Club and Military Book Club. A regular guest on the History Channel and similar venues in Britain and Canada, Mr. Tsouras retired from the Defense Intelligence Agency in 2010 and lives in Alexandria, Virginia, with his wife, Patricia, where he is devoting himself to writing, his garden, and, above all, his granddaughters, Eleni Mae and Althea Rose.